WELCOME TO UTOPIA

Book One of the UTOPIAN DREAMS Series

Alan M. Atkinson

Cover by Nevena Jevtić

IngramSpark™ Edition

First Printing

2020

<u>Disclaimer</u>:
While this story is entirely a work of fiction, it is also a work of alternate history, referencing recent real-world events. Every effort has been made to show all due respect to any person or persons, living or dead, who may be peripherally or overtly referenced regarding the real-world or associated fictional events within this book. No such person will be directly named* within this book or any sequels. No named character in this story is taken from real life. Any resemblance of a named character to any person or persons living or dead is accidental and unintentional. Any resemblance of a commercial trade name to a real-world trademark is likewise accidental and is in no way intended to portray any link to the company holding that trademark. The author, their agents and publishers cannot be held responsible for any claim otherwise and take no responsibility for any such coincidence.

* Referenced by birth name, as opposed to a superheroic pseudonym or other nickname.

This book written in Palatino Linotype, using Office 365™.

Title: Welcome to Utopia
Author: Alan M. Atkinson (1970—)
Subjects: Superheroes, Science Fiction, Alternate History, Non-Binary Characters, Social
      Issues, Crime, Romance.

First Printing: 2020

Printed and distributed by IngramSpark™ (www.ingramspark.com)

ISBN: 978-0-6487296-0-0

Alan M. Atkinson
Words on Paper (Ink)
Townsville, QLD 4810
words.on.paper.ink@gmail.com

Cover design and layout by Nevena Jevtić at https://www.deviantart.com/u-svetu-maste
Cover image © Nevena Jevtić and Alan M. Atkinson
Police tape image: 'Crime Scene PNG HD Images' at http://pluspng.com/crime-scene-png-hd-8222.html
MagCard image created using Trimble® SketchUp™
Author image created using Sketch Camera™

Dedication

To my brother Reay, 1968-1989.

I wish you could've seen this.

You probably would've laughed your head off once you found out what the book was about and rubbished it all the way through. But you would've bought a copy anyway and made a sincere effort to read it. And that's good enough for me.

Also, a big shout-out to Tessa and Jade (my niece and my almost-niece, respectively), each of whom got married while I was in the process of writing this book.

Preface

I could write a whole separate novel about how this book came to be. Inspired by the writings of others and the nagging feeling that I could maybe do this myself, it's been fun and frustrating by turns. Far more has gone into it than I originally envisaged, but all of it has shaped the story into its current form.

This is not your usual 'punch out the bad guy and throw him in jail' type superhero story. Not everything is cut and dried; both the heroes and the villains sport shades of gray. The definition of 'good guy' vs 'bad guy' can change with circumstances.

Neither does it start with an origin story. The main character, Jericho Hansen, is an established hero by the time the book starts. But he has obstacles to overcome all the same, and he is very clearly just one person trying to make his way in a big world.

That said, there are a few things I want to make clear:

While I am neither gay nor a citizen of the United States, Jericho is both. As such, I have done as much research as I could in order to portray him (and those around him) as even-handedly as possible. Also, in order to remain true to the setting, I've done my best to make proper use of American idioms and spelling throughout.

Any lapses in the execution of this are all mine.

But why a gay main character? Some may be excused for wondering if I had an agenda for this particular choice. And in response, I say, "Why, yes; I did have an agenda. I wanted this book to make sense."

You see, in order for certain scenes to work, I needed either a straight woman or a gay man to be in the top spot. And as the author of this book (and a guy), I made the executive decision that I'd be better at writing a gay male character than a straight female protagonist.

In short; the plot demanded it.

Anyway, I hope you enjoy the book.

Alan M. Atkinson
December 2019

Contents

Prologue One: Discovery 8
Prologue Two: Runaway Superhero 13
Prologue Three: Passport to Opportunity 22
Prologue Four: Appeal from the Heart 23

Part One: Maglev
1 – Jericho 26
2 – Stephen 30
3 – Luke 35
4 – Madness 42
5 – Platform 48
6 – Challenger 55
7 – Minotaur 62
8 – Origin 72
9 – Revelation 79
10 – Reaction 86
11 – Bobbi 90
12 – Politics 95
13 – Powers 101
14 – Utopia 106

Part Two: Future Shock
15 – New Arrivals 114
16 – Friendly Face 119
17 – Air Taxi 124
18 – Police Stop 132
19 – Checking In 135
20 – Home Comforts 140
21 – Personal Issues 147
22 – Rooftop Encounter 155
23 – Night Patrol 162
24 – Learning Experience 168
25 – Survival Mode 174
26 – Changing Plans 182
27 – South Side 186
28 – Post Mortem 192
29 – Worst Case 196

Part Three: Murder, Most Foul
30 – Presumption of Innocence 202
31 – Clearing the Air 206
32 – Coming to Grips 216
33 – The Ugly Truth 221
34 – From the Shadows 225
35 – Making the Calls 232
36 – Sharing a Cab 236

37 – Sense of Wonder 244
38 – Within the Spire 251
39 – Interviewing, Superhero Style...270
40 – Passing the Torch..281
41 – Best Laid Plans 287
42 – Leroy in Utopia 301
43 – Reclamation and Identification 304
44 – Test of Wills 311
45 – One Small Step 317
46 – An Unintended Consequence 325

Part Four: Justice for the Fallen
47 – To Remember the Departed 336
48 – Where the Heart Is..342
49 – Of Mice and Men 347
50 – This, Too, Shall Pass 359
51 – Holding Back the Tide..373
52 – Drama in the Park...379
53 – Gone, But Not Forgotten..384
54 – Enforcing Law and Order..391
55 – Running Away, Running Toward 400
56 – A Hard-Earned Perspective...409
57 – Exercising Shock and Awe 420
58 – Out of the Blue 431
59 – Putting the Pieces Together...437
60 – A Most Unexpected Development 445
61 – "If You Love Something …"...450
62 – Welcome to Force Majeure 457

Epilogue One: Homecoming 464
Epilogue Two: The Villains 476
Epilogue Three: Manhattan Justice Recruiting 478
Epilogue Four: A New Question Revealed...........................483

Glossary..493
Dramatis Personae..498
Timeline of Events..503
Enabled Teams and Others...508

Acknowledgments..511
Author's Recommendations 512
About the Author...514
About *Welcome to Utopia* 515

PROLOGUES

Prologue One
Discovery

Manhattan Reclamation Project, Kansas
Grid Reference FC/97A
Tuesday, November 2, 1999
8:32 AM Central Daylight Time

As the Jeep rattled and jolted over the roughly graded road, Graham Bakersfield wondered how he'd ever become accustomed to the idea that a nuclear bomb had gone off in the very heartland of America, just six weeks previously. Every time he really dwelt on the idea, he got cold shivers. Worse, his duties as a foreman overseeing the rebuilding efforts covered a patch less than five miles from ground zero. Normally, this would've been far too close in both distance and time for his personal comfort. And yet, somehow, he no longer really thought about it anymore. It just *was*.

On the other hand, he mused, it was all too easy to believe that *some* catastrophe had overcome the terrain through which he was driving. All was dirt and rock and dust. There were neither trees to sway in the breeze, nor birds to perch in them; no plants or animals of any sort, in fact. Apart from the Jeep, the only movement and sound came from the enormous remote-controlled and semi-autonomous vehicles that trundled over the blasted terrain all around, carrying out the basic landscaping that would be needed before the rebuilding could begin in earnest. In between them, here and there, were the personally controlled machines doing the detail work. The construction site was bigger than any he'd ever worked on before. In fact, as far as he knew, it was the most ambitious venture of its type that had ever been attempted, stretching at least twenty miles in every direction.

All of this was overshadowed by the fact that he'd been tapped to escort a VIP into the interior of the Reclamation Project. He'd never heard of her before this day, and he wasn't quite sure who she was or what she did, but Samantha Colburn was apparently as Very Important as VIPs got; short of hosting the President himself or an actual member of Force Majeure. From what he could tell under the hairstyling and makeup, she wasn't much over forty (as he himself was) but she wore it with considerably more aplomb. Even the hard-hat and high-visibility vest required by OSHA regulations looked more like fashion accessories on her than items of personal protection.

The Jeep topped a rise and headed down toward the construction trailer that he'd been assigned as his mobile base of operations. A substantial antenna array on the roof allowed him to relay orders from company headquarters out to the semi-autonomous vehicles under his control, and to communicate with operators in the field. There was also a satellite dish allowing him to maintain contact with the outside world, given that no cell signal would penetrate this deep into the disaster area.

Beside the trailer was parked the bus that had transported his men to the site, surrounded by the dozens of sets of wheel tracks and tread marks made by the construction vehicles. Around the back, a large overhead tank supplied water to both an ablution block and to the trailer itself. On any other site of this type, there would've also been a diesel bowser to keep the work vehicles running, but somehow the ones they'd been supplied didn't need it. The water tank on the ablution block rarely needed refilling either, which meant there was a serious filtration system at work there. Force Majeure had supplied the equipment, so he figured it was a superhero thing.

With a screech of dusty brakes, he pulled the Jeep to a halt outside the trailer. Shutting off the motor, he worked his jaw a couple of times to dispel the illusion that he'd suddenly gone deaf. "Okay," he said, his voice oddly muffled in his own ears after the roar of the Jeep's engine. "We're here. Ninety-seven Alpha. What exactly did you need to see, again?"

"Your work orders for the last twelve hours." Her voice was crisp and no-nonsense. "The locator beacons for several of your earthmovers place them at a significant distance from where they should be, and certain tasks have not been carried out." She pointed. "There should be a hill just over there. I need to find out why it has not yet been constructed."

"Hey, I entered those orders myself," he said defensively. "If there's problems, you need to talk to the person who drafted them."

She looked him in the eye. "*I* drafted them, via a directive from Relentless. He okayed them, and I sent them out." She climbed out of the Jeep. "Which is why I need to see where the hiccup is."

"Wait, did you want a filter mask?" Graham reached into the back seat and retrieved one from the box he kept there. "The radiation …"

The Colburn woman gestured at the detector mounted in the center of the Jeep's dashboard. Another one was attached to the side of the trailer. Each was linked to a siren that, coupled with a flashing light, would warn anyone within several hundred yards that there was a radiation hazard present. Every installation and piece of machinery on site had one of these attached. "Those haven't gone off for two weeks, correct? The Technologist assured me that there was nothing more to be concerned about. I believe him."

"Yes, ma'am." But as Graham got out of the Jeep, he hung the mask around his own neck. If Ms. Colburn was on speaking terms with the man whose scientific innovations had underpinned the entire decontamination and rebuilding effort to date, it meant she was definitely highly connected. But he was still a careful man. It had saved his life on more than one occasion.

Ms. Colburn reached the trailer and took hold of the door handle. A corner of Graham's mouth lifted in a grin as he reached into his pocket for the key. She'd get nowhere fast, doing that. But to Graham's surprise, the door opened easily for her. She turned to face him; one immaculate eyebrow raised. "You leave it unlocked?"

"I most certainly do not," he retorted, taking the key out. "And this is the only key on site. Let me have a look at that."

With a silent gesture—*all yours*—she stepped back out of the way. He leaned in close to examine the door, which indeed seemed to be unlocked. Inserting the key in the lock, he turned it, locking the door. Turning it the other way unlocked it once more.

"Someone's got a spare key," he muttered, restraining his natural urge for profanity. "Stay out here. I need to see what's missing." It was clear to him now; whoever had unlocked the door was the one who'd messed with the work orders on the semi-autonomous earthmovers. There really were no other suspects. Where they'd gotten the key from, he had no idea. He could guarantee it hadn't come from *him*, though.

Ms. Colburn did not dispute his right to go in first. "Clearly, we're going to have to upgrade the security on these trailers."

"Yeah, no crap." He pulled the door open and peered in, ducking back quickly in case the intruder was still inside. Unlikely, given that his own men were already on site, but not impossible. However, as it turned out, the trailer was empty of people. There wasn't even anyone hiding in the tiny bathroom, proven by the fact that the door into the cramped cubicle was wide open. He climbed up the two steps and entered, still wary.

The place hadn't been trashed, which was a source of both relief and confusion. In his experience, people protesting a construction site had a tendency toward wrecking anything that could be damaged and spray-painting everything else. Destroying paperwork to slow down the work was also a favorite tactic. But everything was as he'd left it, and that included the electronic tablet he'd been issued when he first signed on as foreman of FC-97A. They hadn't stolen it, or even smashed it. Almost smugly, it sat on his desk in pride of place. Staring at it, he pushed his hard-hat back and scratched his head. "Okay, I don't get it."

"What is it that you do not get? Saboteurs are an uncomplicated bunch, Mr. Bakersfield." Ms. Colburn climbed into the trailer behind him. "Destroying things and wrecking construction efforts are what they live for." As she came up alongside him, her eyes widened at the sight of his desk. "My goodness, they certainly made a mess."

He grimaced, feeling insulted. "They didn't touch a thing. This is how I work."

"Ah." She shot him a sideways glance. As if to cover her gaffe, she took up the tablet, handling it with easy familiarity. "Hmm. It seems that the only work orders that were altered are the last ones you entered. They're still on the screen. Just a few numbers were added. If this was sabotage, it's the most ineffectual and ham-handed way it could've been done. We should be able to fix the damage in a matter of hours." As she spoke, she tapped away at the tablet.

"Yeah, that's what I don't get." He shook his head. "It's gonna take longer to change the lock on the trailer than to deal with the actual problems they caused. What was the point of all this?" As he spoke, he gestured at the trailer in general. "I mean, what were they doing? Leaving a message? 'We can do a lot worse than this'?"

That was when he saw the folded note pinned to the corkboard. More importantly, he saw the name written on it in clumsy block letters: **RELENTLESS**.

"Hey, what's this?"

"What's what?" Ms. Colburn looked up as he reached for the note. "Stop! Do *not* touch that!"

Graham would forever after credit his innate caution for his immediate reaction. At her first word, he jerked his hand back as if the paper were electrified. Only after he'd completed his instinctive withdrawal did he turn his attention fully to her. "What? Why? What do you see?" Whatever she'd spotted, he was damned if he could see it, but there had to be *something* there to cause her violent response.

"That note is addressed to Relentless," she explained patiently, as if to a child. "All of this? Designed to bring the note to his attention. Whatever's on it is meant for his eyes, and his eyes only. It's more than your job is worth to read it before he gets his hands on it. More than *my* job is worth, for that matter."

"So, what do we do?" he asked, gesturing at the offending scrap of paper. "It's not like we can lock up the trailer or shut down the sector for any length of time."

For an answer, she picked up the phone, an old push-button model that shared the desk with stacks of paper. An immaculately manicured nail stabbed out a phone number, too fast for him to keep track of the digits.

"Hello, yes," she said briskly. "Samantha Colburn here. Get me Relentless." A pause ensued. "*Yes*, it's important. Give the phone to him right now." Graham got the strong impression she was trying to avoid rolling her eyes.

A moment later, she began speaking again. "Yes, sir, it's me. I'm doing that check at Ninety-Seven Alpha. It wasn't operator error, as we initially thought. It was all a ploy to get our attention. There's a note here, addressed to you. No, I haven't looked at it. Yes, sir, we can wait."

She hung the phone up, then released a ladylike sigh. "Well, that's that. Relentless will be here in a few minutes, and then it'll be out of our hands."

Graham stared at her incredulously. "And you're not in the least bit curious about who left the note and why, or what it says?"

This time, she did roll her eyes. "Of *course* I'm curious, but unless you have a special insight as to who may have gotten into the trailer, our best clue is in that note. Which we are *not* going to read."

It was clear she wasn't going to budge on the subject. With a shake of his head, he went outside and studied the ground. Unfortunately, the morning's startup activity had thoroughly overlaid all evidence of anyone approaching the trailer. Before he and Samantha had turned up, of course.

When he turned around, she was standing in the doorway to the trailer, effectively blocking him from going back in. He looked down the road, shading his eyes and wondering what Relentless would be driving, to get him there in just a few minutes.

"Don't bother," she told him. "He won't be coming by road. He's a few miles away, but all he has to do is get in contact with Tourbillon. After that, they'll be here in seconds." Descending the steps, she closed the door behind her.

Graham still couldn't get over the way she was casually namedropping the members of a *superhero team*. "So, what's it like?" he asked. "Being Force Majeure's secretary, I mean."

"Please," she said with genteel emphasis. "I am employed by Relentless as his personal assistant."

"What's the difference?"

"A 'secretary' is someone who takes dictation and types up documents," she said. "I organize his schedule for the most effective and efficient use of his time. And when he has too many things to do at once, he delegates some of those tasks to me. Such as this one." She seemed primly proud of that fact.

Graham nodded slowly. "Gotcha. So, what's it like, being a superhero's personal assistant? 'Specially one like Relentless?" A boss with a temper was bad enough; one who could also crush a house brick in his bare hand would bring matters to a whole new level.

To her credit, Ms. Colburn took a moment to think about her answer, rather than reciting a meaningless platitude. "Fulfilling," she decided at last. "I've worked for many people who made empty promises they never intended to honor. When Relentless says he'll do something, I know it'll get done. Nobody stands in his way."

He snorted. "Because, you know, he's Relentless."

She smiled slightly, though he suspected she'd probably heard variations on the same joke a thousand times already. "Precisely."

As if summoned by her voice, a vertical circular swirl of darkness began to form, several yards away. It quickly grew until it was about eight feet across, then Relentless stepped out of it. Accompanying the leader of Force Majeure was a slim figure in a charcoal-hued hooded cloak; Graham recognized this one as the aforementioned Tourbillon. The black swirl vanished as quickly as it had appeared, almost seeming to soak into the teleporter's garment.

Relentless was *huge*. Graham Bakersfield was not a small man, but the superhero had to be almost seven feet tall, with enough muscle mass to make him look almost stocky. He wore a helmet, which doubled as a mask, painted black with silver trim. His breastplate bore the same color scheme. Hanging from his hip was a heavy-looking sledgehammer with a specifically technological theme to it; Graham fancied he could hear it humming with power.

"Ms. Colburn." The superhero's voice possessed the same sort of deep, rumbling power as an earthmover downshifting to deal with a problematic obstacle. "I understand you've found something interesting."

Samantha Colburn nodded. "Sir. This is Graham Bakersfield. He found the note and called it to my attention."

Relentless nodded once, briefly. "Good. Where is it?"

She pointed at the door of the trailer. "Still on the corkboard. We didn't touch it."

Fully aware that she could have easily thrown him to the wolves by describing the sequence of events in even a slightly different way, Graham opted to stay quiet.

"Excellent," rumbled Relentless. "Stay here." Opening the trailer door, he climbed inside, bending forward slightly to fit under the frame. Graham could hear the structure creaking, and it actually sagged a little on its suspension. *Christ, how much does the man weigh?*

A moment later, Relentless exited the trailer with the note in his hand. It was unfolded, though Graham could not see whatever writing was on it. The big man glowered at Samantha and Graham for a few seconds, then glanced down at the note. "Neither one of you has read this?"

"No, sir," said Samantha promptly. Mutely, Graham shook his head in agreement.

"And you don't know who could have put it there?" This time, his eyes were fixed on Graham.

"Uh, no, sir," Graham stammered. "Whoever it is must have a duplicate key, but nobody's supposed to have one of those." He held up his own key. "This has never been out of my—"

"Not a duplicate key." The observation from Relentless was as sudden as it was definitive. He pointed at the door, which had swung shut behind him. "The lock was picked." Then he turned and focused his attention on Graham. "The official story will be that the system suffered a glitch. You tell nobody about the note. Is that understood?"

"A—absolutely." It was all Graham could think to say.

"Good. Ms. Colburn, we're done here."

"Yes, sir." As she moved to Relentless' side, Samantha Colburn met Graham's eyes briefly. He read a message in the glance. *You've got a second chance. Don't screw it up.*

Tourbillon raised a hand and the black swirl emerged from nowhere, spinning up to the right size. Relentless stepped through first, followed by Samantha. Last was the hooded figure, then the swirl vanished.

Standing alone next to the trailer, Graham decided that he really didn't want to know what was in the note that badly after all. *Hero or not, getting that guy pissed at me is the last thing I want.*

- End of Prologue One -

Prologue Two
Runaway Superhero

22nd District Police Station
Chicago, Illinois
Saturday, December 17, 2011
9:28 PM Central Daylight Time

Vanessa Power shifted her legs uncomfortably. While there should've been room to spare inside the power armor—it had recently been upgraded to take her next growth spurt into account—she was wearing heavy winter clothing under it instead of the usual light bodysuit. This was cramping her movements, making it hard to bend her arms and legs with any sort of ease. Fortunately for her ability to control the armor, the neural-induction receptors placed throughout the suit needed little in the way of skin contact—her uncovered head and neck, within her helmet, were perfectly adequate for this—to function properly.

She tried to focus on that, so she didn't have to think about anything else. About *everything* else. About the fact that her entire *universe* had just exploded around her, and nothing would ever be good or nice again.

A mental impulse activated the suit's neuro-induction display for the dozenth time, projecting information on to her mind's eye.

Primary Suit Systems: nominal.
Secondary Suit Systems: nominal.
Power Reserves: 97%
Operational Duration in Standby Mode: 103 hours.

She realized that the female police sergeant sitting with her (the woman's nametag read FOSTER) had said something. With an effort, she assumed a polite expression for the woman's sake. "I'm sorry, I missed that."

Sergeant Foster had faded blonde hair and a careworn expression. She was clearly trying to be motherly, but her attempts were falling woefully short. It was quite apparent that even if she'd been taught how to handle distraught sixteen-year-old girls, the fact that Vanessa was wearing power armor potentially capable of leveling the building was a complication she hadn't been trained to deal with. Still, Vanessa had to give her props for the effort.

"I said, would you like a cup of tea?" Foster spread her hands and gestured toward the kitchenette counter. "We have cookies. Or I could fetch you another soda from the machine."

"What I *want* is to talk to someone in charge who can put me through to the Mayor's office so I can tell him exactly *why* he should have my father arrested," Vanessa said forcefully. "What's taking so much time?"

"I'm not entirely certain, but I'm sure they're working on it," Sergeant Foster said soothingly. "Now, these are very serious allegations you've made—"

"They're *not* allegations!" snapped Vanessa. "I was *there!* It *happened!*" She clenched her fists. A message popped up in her NID.

Haptic Trigger detected. Deploy Micro-Missiles? Y/<u>N</u>

Hastily, she declined. Fortunately, the system was weighted toward not deploying, so if she got a cramp at the wrong moment, she wouldn't accidentally blow a hole in the wall. With elaborate care, she relaxed her hands.

"Miss Power, I'm afraid they *are* allegations until independent proof is gathered." Sergeant Foster was blissfully unaware of the weapons going back into standby mode, encased in the metal surrounding Vanessa's forearms.

Vanessa had had enough. She activated another system via the NID.

Sensory Systems deployed.
Directional Audio Gathering System: Active.
Audio Filtering: Active.
Speech to Text or Live Audio? S/<u>L</u>
Display Pseudo-Sonar Imagery of Targets? <u>Y</u>/N

Green crosshairs overlaid themselves onto her vision and she settled down to see what she could find out.. As she turned her head, doing her best to appear to be looking idly around the room, humanoid shapes moved back and forth in her field of view. She placed the targeting sights onto one shape after another, bringing forth snatches of conversation.

"—randa rights do not include the right to order a pizza—"

"—uck's sake, did you just shit yoursel—"

"—orry honey, we're balls to the wall here—"

"—tuation with Vanessa Power? I've just had—"

She stopped and brought the crosshairs back to the person who had just been speaking.

"—er mother, who pinned my ears back hard. She's told me that until she has her kid back in her care, she's holding everyone in the building personally responsible for her welfare."

There was a mumble from the phone the guy was holding. Vanessa couldn't focus the audio gathering closely enough to decipher it.

"Yeah," said the police officer. "She said she's coming right over and she'll clear this whole thing up. Team Power saved my life one time. Do I think the old man really molested his kid? Hell if *I* know. The sooner the Mayor's office takes this mess ov—"

Vanessa had heard enough. She'd told them that she wanted to talk to the Mayor. But they'd contacted her parents instead. *They're coming here. To take me home again.* The fear that clenched in her gut then boiled into anger. *I'm never going back.*

Abruptly, she stood up. A mental command flipped her visor down and locked it into place. Sergeant Foster rose as well, startled but clearly trying not to show it. "Miss Power, what's the matter?"

"The *matter*," said Vanessa bitterly, "is that someone called my parents. I *trusted* you guys not to go behind my back."

"Even if they come in, you don't have to go with them if you don't want to." Sergeant Foster spoke soothingly. "We can protect you."

Vanessa laughed harshly in her face. "*They* are Adam and Tesseract Power. You couldn't stop them from doing *shit* if they weren't inclined to let you." Accessing the neuro-induction display, she gave the order for the micro-missile launcher to briefly deploy. Metal folded away and the sleek little projectiles emerged from hiding. "See that? That's *nothing* to what my father has on his suit."

Letting the launcher stow itself again and ignoring the stunned look on Foster's face, she swung her head toward the front of the building. The quasi-sonar image showed blurry movements, and she centered the crosshairs on two images that were moving in her general direction.

"—ere is she? I want to see her. I want to make sure she's okay."

Vanessa froze. That was her mother's voice.

She's here. In the building. If she wants to make me go back with her, there's nothing I can do, even in this suit, to stop her. The fact that she was in the middle of a fully staffed police station didn't even cross her mind as a factor, except as potential collateral damage.

Her course of action was now clear. There was a fire evacuation map on the wall, showing the quickest way out of the building. She headed for the door to the break room and pulled it open. Behind her, Foster said something, but Vanessa had long since ceased paying attention to her.

"Vanessa?"

Slowly, she turned. Her mother stood there, at the other end of the corridor. Tesseract Power, like Vanessa, was a redhead; she displayed the Team Power uniform, composed of vibrant blues and golds, with pride. Under the uniform, Vanessa knew, her mother wore an advanced PowerTech exoskeleton.

PowerTech Industries, her father's company, sold a lightweight mobility frame on the civilian market. These incorporated an extremely basic version of the neural-induction system within her own suit, allowing many who would normally be dependent on wheelchairs or walkers to stand, walk, run and even play sport with the assistance of synthetic proprioception. The one her mother wore was as far beyond those as the newest generation space shuttle (in which her father had also had a hand) was ahead of a World War One biplane. Even without it, sparring with her was an exercise in 'name that bruise'. With the speed and strength it gave her, any serious fight was over before it began.

Vanessa straightened her arm toward her mother, palm forward. "Stay back, Mom," she warned. This activated a different haptic trigger, which she acknowledged; a rising whine filled the air between them as the under-mounted laser charged. The crosshairs flared bright in her NID; changing hue to an angry, pulsing red to warn her that she was going weapons-live. She had no illusions about her ability (or her resolve) to actually *hit* her mother, but the threat was there.

"It's going to be all right, Vanessa." Tesseract had stopped, at least. "We can talk about what you believe happened—"

"I know what happened!" shouted Vanessa. "He was on top of me! He tried to pull my clothes off! I don't even want to think about it! *But it happened!*"

"I know you believe that *something* happened ..." Tesseract took a step forward as she tried again.

"Stay back!" Jerking her arm downward, Vanessa fired the laser at low power. The carpet just in front of her mother's foot blackened and smoked. Tesseract's forward movement stopped.

"It's more than what I believe." Vanessa breathed deeply, trying to maintain control of both herself and the situation. "Look at the security footage. You're good at investigating. *Investigate.* The day I see in the news you've had him arrested and charged is the day I come back. And one more thing."

"I'm listening." Tesseract Power's eyes were measuring the distance between them. Vanessa knew she was calculating the odds of closing the range fast enough to knock Vanessa's arm aside before the laser could fire again. *She could probably do it, too.*

"Don't leave Buddy alone with him." Vanessa stared at her mother, willing the older woman to understand. "Don't let that *monster* hurt my brother." There was no way Vanessa could get back to the house and spirit Buddy away without her parents intervening—even if she could convince him to come along—so this was the only other option she could see to keep her nine-year-old brother safe.

Tesseract's eyes went flinty. "Nobody is going to hurt your brother."

That, at least, Vanessa could believe. Her mother did 'momma bear' better than anyone she knew. The trouble was, she had a massive blind spot where it came to her husband; Vanessa's father.

Vanessa had heard the story a thousand times. Before her parents had married, before the Challenger Act was even finalized, Tesseract had been faced with one of the worst threats a superhero could encounter; an adversary who knew her secret identity and was willing to expose it. But then Adam Power had stepped up and neutralized the threat in one bold, unprecedented move. The sacrifice of his secret identity had led to the establishment of Team Power and was the reason why Tesseract Power would never believe such a thing of her husband. And before this day, Vanessa would never have believed it either.

But she'd come out of the bathroom in her flannel pajamas after brushing her teeth, to see her father just turning away from the armor stored on its rack in the corner of her bedroom. Suspecting nothing, she had sat down on her bed and picked up her brush from the dresser to run through her shower-damp hair. She'd managed exactly one brush-stroke before he was on top of her, groping her through her pajamas and trying to kiss her.

She'd fought him off and he'd fled her room. It had happened. She didn't *care* what her mother said. She wasn't safe in the same house as him.

I'm never going back.

Accessing her NID, she pulled up yet another menu.

Flight Systems activated.
Warning: Obstacles in close quarters.
Activate Collision Avoidance Systems? <u>Y</u>/N

Her suit thrusters flared to life, and she launched herself down the corridor away from her mother. An office door was directly ahead; she clenched her fist in her right gauntlet once, twice, three times. That was the signal for "I don't have time to mess around with menu commands". The launcher deployed itself again and a micro-missile scorched off the rails before she had time to second-guess herself.

She'd put the crosshairs on the door handle; one-tenth of a second later, the missile blew it clean out of the door. Her suit hit the wooden barrier, smashing it half off its hinges, then she continued across the office and out through the window. Glass shattered, and then she was into the open air.

It was cold out, she knew, but her suit could handle it. What it *couldn't* handle was the imposing suit of power armor standing on a rooftop across the way. She knew that suit almost as well as she knew her own. *That's Dad's armor.* Even thinking his name made the bile rise in her throat.

She kicked her suit into high gear, pulling up and over the police station in a climbing turn. Behind her, she heard his thrusters roar into action. Her suit was lighter and more agile; she could keep ahead of him in the short term. But he could outlast her, or disable her suit with an EMP strike, or blow her out of the sky if he wanted to. She didn't *think* he'd shoot her down, but she hadn't thought he'd sexually assault her, either. If she was going to get away, she had to do something *now*.

Her supply of flares and chaff was limited but she needed to drop out of sight, so she blew through them all in seconds. Then she played her trump card.

Activating Stealth Mode.
Warning: Prolonged use of Stealth Mode will result in higher than normal drain on power reserves. Do you understand this warning? Y/N
Do you wish to leave a frequency window open for radio use? Y/N
Do you wish to leave a frequency window open for tracking beacon use? Y/N
Operational Duration using Stealth Mode during flight: 12 hours 14 minutes.

A skin-level force field mapped over every part of her armor, then flickered as it went into active camouflage mode. Her heat emissions were similarly disrupted; she wasn't *invisible*, but it was the closest she was going to get. At the same time, the sound of her thrusters went from a dull roar to a faint whisper. This had the downside of a somewhat higher power draw, but not even the best PowerTech sensory systems could pick her out from the background noise now. Or so she hoped.

As she straightened into level flight, her father burst through the cloud of fluttering foil and burning magnesium, then came to a hover. "Vanessa?" he called out. "Vanessa? Come back, baby!"

Gritting her teeth, she rounded a building, so she didn't have to hear his voice anymore. Then another, and another. Slowly, she made her way west. Out of the city.

I'm never going back.

Flying just fast enough to use the suit as a lifting body, she flew onward, following the maglev rail. Three times, she was nearly picked up on radar by PowerTech drones flying a search pattern. The third time, she realized what she was doing wrong; the gleaming rail made a nice bright landmark, for both searcher and refugee. Angling northward, she flew until it was out of sight, then turned west again.

Extending the suit's stub-wings made for slower going, but it let her stretch the power reserves. Normally, she could've flown across the country and back more than once on a full charge, but she didn't dare drop out of stealth mode. As a result, the suit was chewing power like a frat party consumed beer and pizza. It didn't help that she kept feeling the impulse to turn south again and she couldn't understand why. It wasn't as though she'd be any safer from her father, and right now she needed to stay away from the maglev rail.

As the darkened landscape rolled by beneath her, she couldn't help going back over what had happened in a vain attempt to make sense of events. She hadn't been asleep or dreaming; every detail was razor-sharp in her mind. There was no doubt that the man who had attempted to force himself on her was her father, Adam Power. Worse, her mother had not immediately jumped to her defense, but had instead questioned her version of events. Now, she had no idea who she could trust. *I am never, ever going back.*

Two hours into the flight, her power reserves were still in the high seventies. Her original goal had been Seattle, but now she was reconsidering. If she started a gentle curve around to the south, at her current rate of power consumption she should be able to make Los Angeles easily.

Her internal debate over the matter was rudely interrupted when every icon available to her neuro-induction display activated at once, flashing more danger signals within the virtual image-space than a five-alarm fire. Audible warning buzzers within the helmet blared in counterpoint to the urgent messages popping up in her NID.

Warning: Stealth Mode offline.
Warning: Fuel Cells venting. Power Reserves compromised.
Warning: Secondary Suit Systems offline.

What the hell? What's going on here? She triggered menus as fast as she could, trying to force a suit restart and get past whatever glitch the operating system had encountered.

Warning: Suit Restart failed.
Warning: Power Reserves at 59%.
Warning: Primary Suit Systems failing.

Around her, the suit jolted, the thrusters surging and then stuttering in and out. She flicked through the few remaining menus, cutting non-essential systems out of the loop and trying to reverse whatever the hell was causing her fuel cells to vent their contents to the night air. Fortunately, the suit also incorporated high-density batteries; while these didn't have anywhere near the storage capacity of the fuel cells, they couldn't be accidentally discharged either.

Warning: Power Reserves at 37%.
Warning: Flight Systems offline.

Crap, crap, crap. Adrenaline flooded through her as the thrusters died for good. She pulled up a specific menu and activated the emergency auto-landing option, cursing herself for not doing this earlier. The auto-landing function was hard-wired into the suit's capabilities and involved air brakes, a landing chute, and the ability to draw on all power reserves, no matter how limited. This was where the batteries would come into their own.

Warning: Power Reserves at 13%.
Warning: Battery Pack ejected.
Warning: Emergency Auto-Landing Sequence disabled.

The air brakes, which had begun to extend, retracted again. With a bang of explosive bolts, the landing chute detached from its niche behind her shoulders without ever deploying properly. And with it went the battery pack, and her last chance for a simple, safe landing.

What the hell? That shouldn't even be possible. None of this should be possible.

Warning: Emergency Tracking Beacon disabled.
Warning: Power Reser&*#@:;…

As the power died, the warning buzzers cut out, along with the NID itself, leaving a profound sense of emptiness in her head. Gone was the running analysis on the suit's failing (now failed) systems. Also gone, the neuro-induced synthetic proprioception that had allowed her to operate the suit as an extension of her own body and experience the airflow over the suit's exterior. All that was left was her, the silent suit, and the whistling wind audible through the helmet's insulation.

Of that, the only things keeping her airborne and alive right then were the suit's stub-wings. Had they been retracted, as they normally were, she would've had about ten seconds before the power armor smashed into the rock-hard midwinter soil at several hundred miles per hour. The suit's padding was augmented by her winter clothing, but no amount of cushioning was going to protect her from being pulped against the inside of the armor under that kind of impact.

The stub-wings weren't so sophisticated as to contain dedicated control surfaces; their function was more to reduce energy expenditure by improving the overall aerodynamics of the suit. Fortunately, the suit had one last built-in fail-safe, in that the joints and articulation remained flexible in the event of power loss. This was a common precaution for anyone using 'fully invested' power armor, where the user's limbs extended into the suit's arms and legs. The alternative was to risk being locked into place like a store dummy in the event of a power failure.

This meant that in a pinch it was possible to use the suit's posture to change the angle of the stub-wings and thus the direction of travel. As the suit's trajectory began to curve downward into a dive, she arched her body. This angled the stub-wings upward and pulled her descent back into level flight for the moment, with the inevitable trade-off that she lost airspeed. It wasn't a perfect solution, but it would keep her alive for another minute, so she took it.

Up ahead, starlight shimmered off the frozen ground; stub-wings or no, she would die when she hit it. She was just traveling too damn fast, and the suit's air brakes were out of commission, so the inevitable crash-landing would require a miracle to survive. But then she saw the white-edged black ribbon and she knew she'd found her miracle. An ice-covered river running from north to south, it offered a single, sole chance of landing safely. It would take everything she had to pull it off, but she was all out of better options.

Tilting downward, she concentrated on flying the dead suit as precisely as she could. Pulling a deliberate descent raised the airspeed perilously high, but she couldn't help that. She stretched her arms wide, doing her best to replace the non-functioning air brakes. This was still going to hurt.

The river loomed closer as she skimmed over the frozen terrain. She lost as much height as she dared, her heart in her mouth. With the suit systems down, the collision-avoidance radar was nothing but ballast; one power line in the wrong place and she would be toast, in more ways than one.

In level flight with no thrusters, her arms held out with all her strength against the freezing slipstream, she felt herself losing airspeed. Up ahead, beyond the river, she saw headlights travelling from south to north. A remote, analytical part of her mind noted that the vehicle was traveling at a reasonable clip, which meant it was on a sealed road of some kind.

The riverbank whipped beneath her and she put all extraneous thoughts aside, bringing the second stage of her plan into action. Twisting her body as hard as she could, she put everything she had into banking the suit hard left to line up roughly along the river. As wide as it was—maybe a thousand feet, at this point—it was still far too narrow for her needs if traveling across it. *Along* it, however …

At this point, her lack of precise control bit her in the ass. As she dragged the right-hand stub-wing into the air, the suit stalled out and lost lift altogether. Out of control, she tumbled, flailing. *I should've started turning sooner.*

On the knife-edge of panic, she stilled her mind and followed the procedure that had been drummed into her. Tucking into a ball, she snapped out of it with her body aligned along the direction of travel. Immediately, she felt the lift once more as air flowed over the stub-wings. She was gliding again, but the mishap had cost precious altitude, and she was halfway across the river already.

More carefully, she angled around; by the time she was flying straight once more, there was less than five feet of separation between herself and the dark ice beneath. And her airspeed was still higher than she was strictly comfortable with.

She didn't want to hit the ice any faster than absolutely necessary. Punching through and into the freezing water beneath would be as much of a death sentence as impacting the ground on either side of the river. Even if she made it out of the water, hypothermia would kill her before she got half a mile. Which was why she was coming in at the shallowest angle she could manage.

And then there was no more time. Even with the stub-wings, the suit's glide ratio was for crap. The suit hit the ice, leaving great cracks everywhere, and bounced. Inside the suit, Vanessa felt as though she'd just slammed into Mount Rushmore. She hit again, then skidded face-down across the ice. From the uneasy feeling, however, the ice wasn't all that thick. She could *feel* the crunching, crackling sensation of it subsiding as the heavy suit scored its path diagonally along the river.

And then the cracks spread ahead of the suit, and she saw water spraying up around the faceplate, freezing onto it in the night air. By her internal calculations, she was getting close to the other side of the river. This was a good thing, because the suit's forward momentum was almost spent; it was about to break through the ice for good and sink to the bottom.

There was a very specific posture that her father had trained her in, then told her never to assume unless she absolutely had to. Now, at the last moment, she assumed it; arms held *so*, legs held *so*, fists clenched, and index fingers making a trigger-squeezing motion. This activated the manual switches distributed throughout the suit, connecting internal storage batteries into a single circuit. Half a second later, explosive bolts blew the entire back of the suit off. Using a slightly different mechanism, the gloves and boots—and helmet—also came away from the suit. A giant punched her in the gut as an airbag inflated beneath her, blowing her clear of the sinking wreckage to spin crazily through the air.

She'd been trained in gymnastics from almost before she could walk, allowing her to get her bearings before she landed. Twisting in mid-flight, she got her feet underneath her, but it was still a rough landing. There was no way she was going to keep her footing, so she let herself go down, absorbing as much of the impact as she could. Hitting the ground with bone-jarring force, she rolled over and over, curled into a ball to protect her vital organs. When she finally came to a stop, she sat up and looked around. She was bruised and battered, and the helmet faceplate was cracked all the way across, but she was safely on dry ground; for a given definition of 'safe'.

Her heart still thundering in her chest, she scrambled to her feet and pulled her helmet off just in time to watch as the patch of dark water where her suit had vanished began to freeze over once more. *That could've been me, if I hadn't hit the ice just right. Or if Dad had timed the sabotage a little earlier or later, I'd be wrapped around a hill or a tree right now. And nobody would ever know why.* It was a sobering thought, in a night full of them.

It was cold, but that was only part of the reason she was shivering as she removed the dead boots and gauntlets and pulled the hood up over her head. The adrenaline still in her system was another part of it; the stark realization that she'd just survived a determined attempt to murder her with her own suit was the third part. Moving automatically, she stashed the remnants of the suit in the hollow of a dead tree. The fewer traces she left of her passing, the better.

Gotta keep moving. Shoving her hands deep into the pockets of her fleece-lined jacket, she turned and started trudging up the bank, her eventual destination the road she'd glimpsed earlier. The first order of business was to distance herself from where she had crash-landed on the ice. The second, to be carried out at some later date, was to return with some method of salvaging her suit before anyone (including her father) found it.

She still had trouble wrapping her head around the idea that her father had deliberately sabotaged her suit. Had it been his way of ensuring that she'd never tell of what he'd tried to do to her? She had no doubt he was the one who'd rigged her suit to fail; after all, he'd been fiddling with it just before she came out of the bathroom. The most chilling realization, biting deeper than the wind swirling around her, was that he'd done it *before* he knew how she would react to his advances.

He'd already decided that I needed to die, no matter what happened.

I don't want to believe it. But it happened, so I have to believe it.

I can't let this beat me. I can't let him win. I have to keep moving.

Reaching the road was easier than she'd expected. The wind was still bitterly cold, but she found she could handle it. Her breath blew away in long streamers as she turned, getting her bearings. To the south, the lights of a small city or large town glowed in the distance. Setting her hood more firmly on her head, she started out with a determined stride. This felt like the right way to go. There would be a bus terminal. Farther south would be a bigger city. Places like that always held opportunities for someone who was strong, smart and determined.

All her life, she'd been taught that she was someone special. That there was nothing she couldn't achieve, given the right tools. Which was a good thing because as of right then, she was on her own. There was absolutely nobody else in the world she could depend on.

I'm Vanessa Power. I got this.

- End of Prologue Two -

Prologue Three
Passport to Opportunity

Monday, September 16, 2013

re: Application to join Force Majeure

The Force Majeure Team <admin@fmmail.utopia.org>
to me

FORCE MAJEURE™
Proudly Protecting America Against All Foes, Foreign & Domestic

Dear G-Man,

We have reviewed your application to join Force Majeure, and we believe it has merit.
You are hereby invited to attend an interview to try out for the position.

Time: 9:00 AM, October 7, 2013
Place: The Spire, Utopia City

Best wishes,
Samantha Colburn

Executive Assistant to Relentless

- End of Prologue Three -

Prologue Four
Appeal from the Heart

Dear Stephen,

There has to be a better way of doing this, but I don't know what it is. By the time you find this letter, I'll be on the way to Utopia. I hope you can forgive me for the deception.

I want to make this absolutely clear:

I am not leaving you.

I would never leave you. You mean too much to me. No matter what happens, I love you. Whether I get accepted or not, I will always love you.

Being a superhero makes me who & what I am, you know that. And you encourage & support me in it, which I appreciate more than I can ever express. But I want to be more than a small-town hero in a backwater city for the rest of my life. I want to go _professional._ Now I've got that chance & I want to see if I can do it. This is something I have to do.

It'll just be three days. 72 hours & I'll be home again. One day for the interview with Force Majeure & 2 more for any follow-ups. Home by Wed lunch time. It'll be like I never left.

Hey, if I get in, you'll be dating a member of FM! Should raise your readership (I know, bad time for jokes).

Home in three days. Promise. Forever yours,

Jericho

PS, love you!

PART ONE

MAGLEV

Capes? Cowls? Cogs? Who even *thought* of these names?
- Jericho Hansen

1
Jericho

Savannah, Georgia
Sunday, October 6, 2013
4:02 PM Eastern Daylight Time

Jericho Hansen sat on the edge of the bed, holding the letter in one hand and an envelope in the other. He'd read and re-read the single page more than a dozen times since writing it, and he was sure of two things. The first was that he would never be able to express himself more clearly than he'd already done. The second; Stephen would still insist on not understanding. *But I'll cross that bridge when I come to it.*

There was a creak from the living room, and he froze. After a few seconds without hearing any more sounds, he allowed himself to relax long enough to slide the letter into its envelope. Leaning over slightly, he folded back the pastel-pink comforter—Stephen's idea, not his, though he had to admit it kept them warm on cold winter nights—and placed the envelope on his boyfriend's pillow.

When he'd first gotten powers and gone out as a costumed hero, Jericho had assumed he'd find social acceptance and maybe even companionship among his like-minded peers. That was, after all, the basic theme of every second superhero sitcom. As it turned out, Savannah held slim pickings for either one. The city's only other costumed protector was a brash, loud, crude redneck who went by the name of Pickup and piloted a highly modified 4×4 which could become a bipedal robot with the Confederate flag emblazoned across its chest (otherwise, the hood of the truck). He didn't like Jericho, and the feeling was mutual. Even though both were technically heroes, their political and social viewpoints made them polar opposites; they'd clashed on more than one occasion. Boyfriend material, he was not.

But then there was Stephen; at thirty-one, he was eight years older than Jericho. Stephen was involved in the Enabled (otherwise known as super-powered) scene as well, but from an entirely different angle to both Jericho and Pickup. Specifically, he was the owner, editor, photographer and sole employee of a moderately successful web-magazine called *Gay!Power*, which showcased 'alternately oriented' heroes. They'd met when he contacted Jericho's costumed identity of G-Man (the 'G' stood for 'gravity') via social media to set up an interview and a photo shoot. Jericho had accepted a subsequent offer of dinner, and things eventually progressed from there.

While it hadn't been love at first sight, they'd eased into a relationship that managed to outlast the first clumsy attempts at intimacy and become something deeper and more meaningful. It hadn't been all smooth going; Stephen had had to ask Jericho to move in with him several times before he accepted. It was only on their first anniversary, when Stephen posed the offer yet again, that Jericho's underlying trust issues had finally allowed him to say yes. And that was ... *Jeez, has it been six months already?*

Their one and only spat had come about a month after Jericho completed the move, when Stephen advanced the idea of a much more *private* photo shoot, one with less in the way of costume and more in the way of suggestive poses. Jericho had nothing against the concept of skin shots as such, but as a respected superhero, that wasn't the sort of exposure he wanted; so to speak. Despite Stephen's assurances that the pictures would never reach the public eye, he'd turned the idea down flat. After sulking for a few days, his boyfriend had dropped the subject and it never came up again.

On occasion, he'd heard of low-tier Enabled going the other direction; committing flashy but relatively harmless crimes, surrendering to the police for a reduced sentence, then using the notoriety as a springboard into the skin trade. *Their bodies, their choice*. It was his choice not to, and he'd never regretted it.

That was the closest they'd come to having a serious disagreement … until now. Their happy streak had been broken when Jericho got the email confirmation for his tryout interview to join Force Majeure.

He wasn't sure if Force Majeure was *the* most powerful superhero team in the world—the metric for determining this varied from observer to observer—but it was definitely up there in the top five. Counting only those within the continental United States, it rated as the most prominent by far. While the core membership was based in Utopia City, they had satellite teams of secondary members in cities all over the country. Jericho knew he had no chance of becoming a part of the inner circle, but even being accepted into one of the auxiliary teams would fulfill his long-held goal of becoming a professional superhero. Of course, to do that, he would first have to get to Utopia City.

He'd originally asked Stephen to accompany him when he got the email. Stephen, after all, had been taking regular trips long before the maglev came to Savannah. Given how Enabled were spread all over the country, it followed that gay and lesbian heroes were extremely thin on the ground. It was almost always inconvenient for them to come to Savannah (not to mention the fact there wasn't much incentive for them to travel to one corner of America to be featured in a niche publication such as *Gay!Power*). So, when it came down to it, Stephen had to go to them rather than vice versa.

It used to be that whenever he had a prospect, Stephen would fall out of bed at an ungodly hour and take the bus to wherever he needed to go. Now that it was possible to take the maglev directly from Savannah, he could rise at a much more civilized hour and still get where he was going in good time.

Jericho had figured this travel experience would be invaluable for his first trip out of state, right up until he ran into the brick wall of Stephen's refusal. Which didn't make a great deal of sense, considering how Stephen himself traveled so regularly to gather material for the magazine. But there it was. No matter how much he loved Stephen and respected his views, Jericho wasn't about to let his own dreams die by the wayside. He was sorry, but Stephen was going to have to learn to accept that.

However, there was one tiny snag with his resolve: the interview was tomorrow, and Stephen was still adamantly opposed to his going. They'd spent the last month arguing the issue back and forth, and so it had come to this. Sneaking out behind the back of the man he loved. *I hate myself.*

Straightening up, he caught his reflection in the dressing-table mirror. Hazel eyes stared back at him from features that might have been described as delicate but for his firm jawline. His build matched his face; tall and slender, wiry rather than bulky. Reaching up, he pushed his shoulder-length brown hair back from his face, bunching it at the nape of his neck. A hair-tie lay on the dressing-table; it was the work of a moment to pull his ponytail through it. The mundane act helped him to clear his thoughts and push past the illogical certainty that the guilt he felt was written all over his face.

His overnight bag was already packed. Going to the bedroom window, he slid it up on its runners, taking care to ensure that it didn't make any noise. When it was open wide enough for him to climb out with ease, he picked up the bag from where it rested beside the bed. Leaning out the window, he grimaced at what he saw. While the window was set into a niche in the wall which would give him cover from potential witnesses, directly below him was a thick hedge. He was entirely capable of jumping farther out to avoid it—due to his powers, the two-story drop would be no obstacle at all—but that would take him out of the niche and make his exit a lot more public than he wanted. It would be a case of either fall into the hedge or risk endangering his superhero identity.

In sitcoms, of course, this sort of dilemma cropped up all the time. But this wasn't a sitcom, where any problems would be solved before the credits rolled. Whatever mistakes he made now, he'd have to wear the consequences. There was nothing for it; he'd have to take the third option.

Closing the bedroom window with as much care as he'd taken in opening it, Jericho slung the bag over his shoulder and moved to the bedroom door. It was Sunday afternoon and the latest issue of *Gay!Power* was due to be posted at midnight, so Stephen *should* be neck-deep in his editorial fugue. He claimed that he did his best work under pressure; Jericho personally believed he was a procrastinator of the highest order. However, whichever way it was, there was always the chance that Stephen would be paying enough attention to catch Jericho as he snuck out of the apartment. He grimaced, knowing that it was a risk he'd have to take.

Easing the bedroom door open, he breathed a sigh of silent relief as he recognized Stephen's trademark staccato typing emanating from the spare room his boyfriend had sequestered for the production of the webzine. He didn't bother closing the bedroom door, not wanting to risk making any more noise than necessary. Holding the strap of the bag so tightly he could feel the weave of the strap impressing itself on to his palm, he went straight to the front door. At any second, he expected to hear the typing stop and for Stephen's querulous voice to ask him where he was going.

Opening the apartment door as quietly as he could, he stepped outside then carefully closed it behind him. The *tac-tac-tactac-tac* of Stephen's typing was cut off as the heavy wooden door clicked shut. Letting out a breath he hadn't been aware he was holding, he stepped backward away from the door, then violently jumped as a car horn sounded on the street outside.

"Shit," he muttered, realizing the cab he'd called had arrived while he was concentrating on getting out of the apartment without alerting Stephen. *If he keeps honking, Stephen's gonna look to see what's going on. Screw that.* The stairwell leading down to ground level was down the corridor, but he was still two floors up. Time, as the saying went, was of the essence.

Breaking into a run, he got to the stairwell in seconds. With a quick glance over the railing (both up *and* down, because he wasn't an idiot) he took a deep breath … and vaulted into empty space. It was a fall of ten feet to the next landing, but his powers allowed him to reduce the effect of gravity on his body, letting him drift downward like a leaf on the breeze. Before his feet quite reached the surface of the landing below, he grabbed the rail and swung himself out over open air once more. Ten seconds after first jumping over the rail, he stood at the bottom of the stairs, not having touched a single step.

The cab was waiting at the curb as Jericho jogged from the apartment building, holding the bag in his arms. He didn't want to draw attention to himself by running, but the longer he delayed, the greater the chance that Stephen would notice his absence. Opening the car door, he slung his bag inside, expecting every moment to hear Stephen call out from behind him. As he climbed into the back seat, the driver raised an eyebrow but didn't offer any comment. The man had probably seen this sort of thing a dozen times before. In the last week, even. "Where to, buddy?" he asked in a bored tone.

"Train station," Jericho replied breathlessly. There was no way he'd normally be winded from such minor exercise, but the tension was squeezing his diaphragm hard.

The driver pressed the button to start the meter, put the car in gear, then paused with his foot on the brake. "Regular or maglev?"

It was a no-brainer; he wanted to get to Utopia City *today*, and there was no faster way to get across the country at short notice. And of course, none of the country's remaining domestic airlines serviced Utopia City. "Maglev." Even saying the word felt weird.

"Utopia Maglev Lines, comin' right up." The cabbie angled the car to the left, then hit the indicator to merge with traffic. "We should be there in ten."

"That'll be ideal," Jericho assured him. Pangs of guilt still assaulting him, he looked out the back window at the receding apartment block.

Stephen, I hope you can forgive me for this.

2

Stephen

Only three months had passed since the establishment of the maglev in Savannah, but already the polished cylindrical metal 'rails' were a feature of the skyline. Ten feet in diameter and supported sixty feet above the ground by impossibly slender pylons, they tracked into the city from the north, west and south. Following roadways for the most part, all three rails converged on the transit station, where a complicated cloverleaf arrangement allowed trains to arrive and depart on a regular basis while somehow not interfering with one another.

Jericho had no idea how that was done; in all the time he'd been out and about, during night and day, he'd never actually seen the maglev in action. He'd heard the train was fast, but *how* fast he still had no idea.

As the cab rolled up to the drop-off section of the stand outside the station, there was one such rail that ran directly overhead and vanished into the distance, while another descended in a wide looping arc that disappeared behind a security fence. Several taxis were already waiting to pick up; as Jericho watched, two people got into the cab at the head of the line. More were walking up to the row of taxis; he figured they'd gotten off the train.

The driver pulled the cab to a halt and stopped the meter. "That'll be twelve fifty, buddy."

"Uh, no problem." Jericho dug his wallet out of his pocket and extracted one of his credit cards. "You take Amex, right?"

"Sure thing." The driver took the card and swiped it through the hand-held device before handing it back. Leaning forward between the seats, Jericho tapped his PIN into the machine.

A few moments later, as the tiny printer was chattering out his receipt, there was a flash of movement from outside the windshield. Startled, Jericho looked up. "What was that?"

"Train," the cabbie responded laconically. "Want your receipt?"

"No, thanks." Jericho stared distractedly out through the windshield. The pristine rail gleamed in the afternoon sun. "I don't *see* a train."

The driver chuckled. "That's 'cause they go like a bat outta hell. It's already outta sight. You have yourself a good trip."

"Right, thanks." *Bat out of hell. Okay, then. This should be a fun ride.* Grabbing his bag, Jericho opened the door and climbed out of the cab. As soon as the door shut behind him, the cab moved forward to join the line of taxis which were even now picking up more passengers from the station.

Shading his eyes against the afternoon sun, he squinted up at the transit station. It didn't look like much from the outside. He'd heard somewhere that the building had originally housed a bus depot, back in the eighties. If true, the intervening years had not been kind to it. While the frontage had been repaired and repainted, the half-dozen steps that led up from street level were still cracked, chipped and a little slumped. In addition to that, a wheelchair ramp had been installed to bring the building up to spec. This had required the removal of one of the steel-and-brass handrails that flanked the stairs, making them look oddly lopsided.

Still, he wasn't there on account of the building's aesthetic appeal. Taking a deep breath, he jogged up the steps. Despite his carefully held resolve, his nerve failed him as he got to the front doors. As he wavered on the threshold, the doors hissed open to let desiccated, chilly conditioned air wash out over him, flavored with air-freshener. The blue-white glare of the fluorescent lighting within simultaneously beckoned and repelled him. *Do I want to do this?* he asked himself, not for the first time. *I mean, do I really want to do it?*

He could always go back to the apartment. When Stephen was working on the latest issue of the webzine, he tended to ignore everything around him. However, the chance of his noticing Jericho's absence grew stronger with every passing minute. In any case, even if Jericho went straight home, Stephen would immediately recognize the overnight bag full of clothing—and other things—slung over his shoulder and realize exactly what he'd been about to do. There was no way he could ditch it, because included in the 'other things' was his costume. It wasn't the best costume in the world, nor the slickest, but it was *his* costume. It was what separated him from every other superhero out there. Well, that and his powers.

Walk in or walk away, he told himself. It should've been a simple choice, but his desire to make something more of himself was balanced by the certain knowledge that recriminations and teary phone calls would be coming his way once Stephen found out he'd gone. He hated himself for letting the mere thought of his boyfriend's emotional reaction pull this sort of blackmail on him, but he couldn't help being the way he was. For long seconds he wavered, unable to come to a decision.

"Hey, dumbass. You gonna stand there all day?" The voice came from a woman pushing a stroller with one hand and dragging a wheeled suitcase with the other, waiting to enter the transit center. She squinted at him aggressively, or perhaps that was the effect of the sun in her eyes. Her blonde hair, he noted abstractly, had dark roots to it. The infant strapped into the stroller—the blue romper suit suggested that it was a boy—waved its arms and blew bubbles. He almost envied the child its carefree existence. *Have your fun while you can, kid.*

Behind the woman was a scrawny guy wearing a threadbare coat over faded denim overalls, with an unshaven chin and a mustache which was doing its level best to droop down far enough to cover that feature. He glowered at Jericho as irritably as the woman had but added nothing to the conversation. Jericho didn't know the guy by face or name, but he knew his type: good ol' boy. Also known as 'redneck'. There'd be no benefit in arguing with either person, especially considering he *was* currently blocking the door.

"Sorry, folks," he said automatically, and stepped aside. The woman entered first, clicking her tongue in a disapproving *tch* as she did so. Her male companion followed on, not even affording Jericho that much recognition. He watched as the doors closed again, feeling his motivation wither and fade along with the dying gust of conditioned air from within the building.

Come on, he told himself. *It can't be that hard to walk in and buy a goddamn ticket. Millions of people do it every day.* He wasn't sure if he was being accurate there, but it sounded good inside his head. Unfortunately, it didn't sound good *enough*. The entry to the transit station was unknown territory, while the taxicab stand was right there. Stephen was probably still working on the webzine, and he could—

His phone rang, and he froze. *Please let it be Cousin Luke, or even Mama.* But deep down, he knew who it was. Grimacing in anticipation, he pulled it from his pocket and looked at the screen. His intuition was dead on the money; Stephen's number stared back at him.

When Jericho was a lot younger, his daddy had once told him that the best way to avoid losing an argument was to never get into one. That was all well and good, if it could be managed. Unfortunately, it looked like the argument had come to him. If he refused the call, Stephen would call back. Worse, if he turned the phone off now, the conversation they'd have once Stephen *did* contact him would make what was coming positively enjoyable by comparison. Swiping to answer the call, he put the phone to his ear. "Hello, Stephen."

"Is this how you've decided to leave me, Jericho?" Stephen had the 'more in sorrow than in anger' tone down pat, even though his voice was slightly tinny in Jericho's ear. "Pack your bag and sneak out? Was I going to get a phone call in a day or so?"

"What? No! I *left* you a letter! On your pillow, in the bedroom!" Taken aback, Jericho moved a few steps away from the transit center doors to give himself a modicum of privacy from anyone who came out. While he didn't think that someone would deliberately eavesdrop on the conversation, there was no sense in taking chances.

"Oh, that?" Stephen didn't sound in the least bit mollified. "I already found it. Should I be impressed that you actually took the time to write a pen-and-paper 'Dear John' letter?"

Jericho grimaced. He'd spent a long time trying to get Stephen to accept what he needed to do, then almost as long figuring out exactly how to word the letter so that Stephen wouldn't freak out. *Doesn't help if he doesn't read it.* "It's not a 'Dear John'. You wouldn't listen to me when I tried to explain, so I put it all in the letter. *Read* it. I'll be back by Wednesday at the latest. Three days. Seventy-two hours. That's *it*."

"Yes, that's what they all say." Stephen's voice had a catch in it now; Jericho couldn't tell if it was real or affected. "And then it's another few days, then a week, then they never come back."

Still holding the phone to his ear, Jericho dropped the overnight bag at his feet and leaned in against the wall. "Stephen," he pleaded as he pressed his forehead to the sun-warmed bricks. "Please don't say that. I'm not *leaving* you. I never *would* leave you. I *need* to do this thing. I need to know if I *can* do it. This isn't about you and me. Why can't you understand that?"

"Because I *don't* understand," Stephen insisted. "Why do you have to go away to be a superhero? Why can't you be happy being one right here?" Though he didn't say it, Jericho heard *with me* loud and clear.

It was like Stephen wasn't listening to a single word Jericho said. *If he even read the letter, he didn't pay attention to anything except what he wanted to see.* Closing his eyes, Jericho barely managed to avoid heaving a sigh of exasperation. Stephen would recognize it in a heartbeat, which wouldn't help the situation in the slightest. "It's not *about* being a superhero somewhere else. It's about joining Force Majeure. I applied for an interview back in *August*. You were there when I *did* it!"

"I know," Stephen said, his voice rising. "And I know I didn't say anything *then*, because I never thought they'd *answer* you. You're not meant to be a superhero out there. You're meant to be here, in Savannah. With me." *And there we go.* "You're *my* hero. I'm your Vicki Vale, remember?"

Jericho felt a catch in his throat at the corny line. The first time Stephen had used it, he'd thought it was the most romantic thing he'd ever heard. Even now, it was an integral part of their relationship. Merely hearing Stephen say it evoked so many fond memories that a pang of loneliness went through his chest.

Which only made what he had to say all the harder. "I know. And you always will be. But if you had such a problem with it, you should've said something *before* they sent me the confirmation email." He clenched his eyes shut. "I'm sorry if you don't like it, but I've gotta do this. The interview's tomorrow, so I'm going. I'm sorry, but that's the way it is."

"So that's it." Normally, Stephen was a delight to be around, but when the older man got his bitch on, nothing and nobody was sacred. "You just want to go off to Utopia City and hang out with your fellow Masks. Maybe meet some cute guy in a tight costume and forget all about me."

Jericho did his best to refrain from gritting his teeth, but he doubted that he'd been totally successful. *Now you're deliberately pissing me off.* The words almost came out of his mouth, but a last-second intuition warned him that this was exactly what Stephen wanted. *If I start cussing him out, he'll turn it right back on me. He's always been able to guilt-trip me.*

Neither did he bother correcting Stephen about the 'Mask' label; his boyfriend knew all about the official terms. Given his work with *Gay!Power*, Stephen was actually quite savvy about Enabled culture. It was obvious in this situation that he was ignoring everything he knew so he could have yet another dig at Jericho.

Eighteen months ago, Jericho had looked up to Stephen as a cosmopolitan man of the world. Now, he was starting to see the cracks in the pedestal he'd once placed his boyfriend on. Taking a deep breath, he pushed his mind back on track and lowered his voice from sheer habit. "I'm doing this because I want to turn professional. You know, get *paid* to be a superhero?"

Not only would it be amazing to get a salary to do what he loved, but one thing every professional superhero had was an action figure. To the uninformed, such things might seem more of a vanity item than anything else, but popular figures were money in the bank.

"I thought you did it because you liked to do it, not because you wanted to get *money* for it." This was stage two of Stephen's bitchy mode, where his voice started to get whiny and he used whatever means he had to guilt Jericho into changing his mind. Jericho loved Stephen dearly, but he hated that stage. He much preferred it when Stephen got firm with him; that approach had a far better chance of changing Jericho's mind. The problem was, Stephen had trouble doing 'firm' in a convincing fashion.

It occurred to Jericho that even though it was ultimately his decision and his alone to go to Utopia City, he probably wouldn't have had the confidence to take this step if Stephen hadn't spent the last year and a half telling him what a great hero he was. *Jeez. If I told him* that, *his head would probably explode.*

"Hello? Are you even listening to me?" Stephen's demand dragged Jericho's attention back to the here and now.

"I just got distracted for a second," Jericho said hastily. "I'm listening to everything you say."

"I wish you wouldn't go." Stephen sniffled audibly, going straight to stage three. *Oh, no, not the tears.* Jericho loathed the tears. "I don't feel safe without you around anymore."

As much as Jericho didn't want to admit it, Stephen had a point. About five weeks previously, before the email from Force Majeure had come through, his boyfriend had been attacked while driving home from the store one night. He'd stopped at a red light, whereupon several men burst from the shadows and surrounded the car. One of them had shattered the driver's side window with a tire iron, then Stephen was dragged from the car and thoroughly beaten. They'd taken his wallet and phone—and, oddly enough, the groceries—but left the car, probably because it was a dilapidated piece of shit. After they were gone, Stephen had managed to crawl back into the car and drive himself back home, as he couldn't afford a stay in the hospital.

To his everlasting guilt, Jericho had been out in costume as G-Man on that specific evening, on the other side of town. He'd only found out about the assault when Stephen rang him from home. Since then, the bruising had gone down and the cuts were healing, but Stephen's face was still puffy in places and he was missing two teeth. Emotionally, he'd fallen apart, leaving Jericho—who was scarcely less shattered by the experience—to help him pull himself back together. Since then, he'd refused to go out alone at night, only venturing forth if Jericho was with him. For his part, Jericho had kept an eye out for the gang of muggers, but they seemed to have vanished back under whatever rock they came from.

Jericho drew a deep breath. "Listen, Stephen, it's only gonna be three days. Seventy-two hours. That's *it*." As he'd explained in the letter, it was one day for the interview and two more in case he had a call-back. Three at the most, until he found out if he was in Force Majeure or not.

Stephen's voice was petulant. "It doesn't matter what I say, does it? You're just going to go anyway. Why do I even bother talking, if you're not going to listen?"

Oh, jeez. Jericho searched his brain for the words to calm his boyfriend down, but he had no idea what to say. "Uh—"

That was when the phone was plucked from his grasp. A voice said in his ear, "For *fuck's* sake, J, stop bein' such a chickenshit."

3
Luke

Turning fast, Jericho dropped into a combat stance as his adrenaline surged. He was shaping up for a palm strike before he recognized the grinning dark-skinned man who'd snuck up on him. "Luke, what the *hell* do you think you're doing, taking my phone?"

"Gotcha, cuz," chuckled Luke. "Shoulda seen your face. Friggin' *priceless*."

His pulse still pounding in his ears, Jericho shook his head. "Don't *do* that. I nearly cleaned your goddamn clock."

Luke's grin turned into a smirk. "Oo, does 'oo think 'oo can fight?" Playfully, he raised his fists and feinted a punch at Jericho.

It would've been easy to step in past the lazy blow and lock up Luke's arm, but his cousin didn't deserve that, so Jericho chose to roll his eyes instead. "Asshat," he said, but without heat. The adrenaline was still singing through his veins; he breathed deeply, willing himself to relax. "Did Stephen send you?"

On second thought, this didn't seem even remotely plausible. As Jericho's cousin, Luke may have gotten along (mostly) with Stephen, but he and Jericho were kin. More to the point, they'd been best friends for years, and as such tended to side with each other. Thirdly, Jericho was at that moment on the phone with Stephen, and he'd said nothing at all about Luke.

"Hell, no," Luke said cheerfully. He held the phone to his ear. "Steve? It's me. He'll call you back." Ignoring Stephen's tinny expostulations, he hit the icon to shut the call down. "He still fixin' ta stop you from goin'?"

Jericho rolled his eyes. "You know it." Then he eyed his cousin suspiciously. "Wait a sec. *How* do you know? And what *are* you doing here?" It struck him as considerably more than a coincidence to have his cousin turn up at the exact right time to intercept him at the transit station.

Luke chuckled again. "I ain't never been to Utopia City. When I heard you was fixin' ta go, I reckoned I'd tag along an' see the sights. An' whenever y'all is fightin', you scrunch up your shoulders like ya wanna be anywhere but there. Or to put it another way, I had me a hunch." From the amusement in his tone, he thought he was being hugely funny.

Jericho tried not to wince at the pun. "Oh, ha ha. But seriously, how'd you know I was even gonna be here? Did you have someone watching the apartment? Or have you been staking this place out for the last few days?" He didn't like the idea of being surveilled at the best of times, even if it was Luke doing it.

"Nope." Luke was clearly enjoying his cousin's confusion. "See, I knowed ya wouldn't let Steve stop you from goin', an' I knowed things was gettin' close, so I jes' kept an eye on my phone an' had Livy drive me over when I saw you start headin' for th' station." He pulled the cellphone from his pocket; while not the latest model, it was still pretty good. "Or did ya forget we got locator apps for each other's phones a while back?"

To his embarrassment, Jericho had honestly forgotten that little detail. He stared at Luke, not sure whether to be impressed or even more irritated. "And how long have you been using *my own damn phone* as a goddamn tracking beacon?"

Luke shrugged. "Long enough. Ain't gonna let my favorite cuz go off ta Utopia City all by hisself, am I? Ya might git yourself lost on th' way, an' then where'd we be?" His grin was wide and ingenuous; Jericho distrusted it immediately. Due to their great-grandfather's prejudices, Luke had grown up on the wrong side of the tracks, and still had more than a few friends in low places. He was up to something; Jericho was certain of it.

He'd known Luke long enough that he trusted his cousin not to pull anything shady on him personally, but he could virtually guarantee that Luke had his own reasons for going to Utopia City. The fact that he'd basically bugged Jericho so he could 'coincidentally' show up at the same time just meant that he didn't care if Jericho knew he was going there as well.

When it came down to it, all that Luke and Jericho really had in common were one set of shared grandparents—Papaw Joe, who'd been killed in Vietnam, and Mamaw Penny, who'd died in a car accident when Jericho was five—and the fact that they both topped six feet. Jericho was twenty-three, slim and wiry with straight hair and fair skin. Luke, five years his senior, was heavier set—all muscle—and about an inch shorter, with the tightly kinked hair and dark-coffee skin that denoted mixed ancestry. And of course, Jericho was gay while Luke was straight as a ruler.

Despite their outward differences, they got along well; Luke had been the first person Jericho had come out to, once with his orientation and again with his powers. Jericho had no siblings, but Luke was a good substitute for an older brother. Luke's sister Serena, also older than Jericho (albeit by six months), was good company as well. Since Jericho had come out of the closet, he'd consulted them both on relationship tips more than once.

As for the color issue, for Jericho it simply didn't exist. Or rather; he was *aware* of its existence, but he wanted no truck with it. If some asshat had a mind to cause problems with folk just because their skin was a different color, he was altogether ready to kick their asses for them.

Some might've considered this to be an uncommon state of mind for a homegrown Georgia boy but again, it was all down to family. Specifically, his mother. A no-nonsense New Yorker, Dahlia Hansen not only came from money of her own but now also had her own law practice in Atlanta. She'd raised him with very different views from the local norm, aided and abetted by his father. He had vague memories of tirades delivered by a terrifying elderly man—Great-Granddaddy Frank—in his infancy, but the old man had died when he was four. It was no coincidence that he'd also known Luke since he was four. As far as he was concerned, having an aunt and cousins with much darker skin color was a fact of life, and he *would* take issue with anyone who felt differently. While he was aware that not everyone in Savannah (or even his own family) thought that way, his attitude could be summed up as: *Screw 'em. Kin's kin, and nothing's gonna change that.*

He'd once asked his cousin why he insisted on maintaining the back-streets accent, when he was anything but poor or stupid. Luke's father Leroy had grown up in the same relatively affluent surroundings that Jericho himself had, but after he was kicked out of home and found himself surrounded by a lower stratum of society, he'd let his own speech patterns slip and merge so as to fit in. He could still converse in the upper-middle-class accents of his youth, but among family and friends he relaxed into a more laid-back turn of phrase.

Luke, on the other hand, had been brought up almost on the streets, and spoke the argot as easily as he breathed. Leroy had made sure his education included a grounding in more affluent ways of speaking, but Luke preferred his way. Besides, as he put it, the 'buckra' hated nothing more than a smart black guy. If he talked like a 'know-nothin' jig', it was a lot easier to do business with them. When it was just the two of them, Luke tended to lapse into what he was used to, but whenever he felt the need to make a good impression, he could up his game.

Jericho's diction, by contrast, was a little more precise than the norm. This was partly because he'd grown up with his mother's New York accent, and partly because he'd spent a couple of years attending the same college where his parents had met; the combination of which had blunted his Southern accent a mite.

"Yeah, right," he scoffed, good humor overtaking his irritation. Even though he could tell Luke was trying to blatantly bullshit him (just because Luke wouldn't take Jericho's money didn't mean he wouldn't lie to his cousin's face), Jericho never could stay mad at Luke for long. "Gimme my phone." He held out his hand expectantly, and Luke dropped the handset into it. "You do know Stephen hates being called Steve, right?"

"Well, duh. I wouldn't call him that, otherwise."

That, Jericho could believe. His cousin was a natural at finding people's buttons and mashing them as hard as he could. Stephen's fussiness and inability to take a joke merely meant that Luke enjoyed messing with his head quite a bit more. It was telling to note that Luke had never bothered trying to make a good impression on Stephen, especially in the last few weeks.

Just as Jericho was about to put the phone away, it rang in his hand. He didn't even have to look to know it was Stephen. Automatically, he went to answer it, but paused when he caught Luke's disapproving stare. "What?"

Luke's answer was as flat and uncompromising as the tone of his voice. "Cuz, you answer that an' I'm gonna hafta take away your man card."

The phone rang again, insistently.

"My what?" Jericho wasn't sure he'd heard correctly. "You do know I'm gay, right?"

Luke spread his hands. "An' that makes a lick o' difference how? Hang up the goddamn phone."

Meekly accepting that Luke was right, Jericho swiped left to decline the call. "Okay, now what? You know he's just gonna keep calling back, yeah?"

"Well, *duh.*" Luke gestured at the phone. "So, turn the fuckin' thing off. Or put it on airplane mode. One of the two."

There was nothing else for it. Feeling like a novice acrobat stepping out onto the highwire for the first time, Jericho flicked the screen to bring up the option for airplane mode. A few seconds later, it was done. Now, Stephen couldn't reach him even if Jericho *wanted* him to.

"Good," Luke said approvingly. "So, you're still fixin' ta head to Utopia City, yeah?" When Jericho didn't answer immediately, he frowned. "Did ya wanna go or not? Simple question, cuz."

Jericho grimaced, feeling the conflict sharply. Of *course* he wanted to go, but Stephen was going to be seriously pissed at him for not picking up when he rang back. It was going to take a *month* of chick-flick nights to get him out of the doghouse, and that would be if he went home straight away. "Yeah, but Stephen ..."

"Steve'll still be there when you git back," Luke said briskly. "That your bag there?"

"Yeah, it's mine." Jericho watched as Luke leaned down and grabbed the overnight bag by one strap. Somewhere deep inside, he wondered why he was letting Luke get away with pushing him around like this.

"Here." Luke shoved the bag into Jericho's arms. "Now let's git movin'. Them tickets ain't gonna buy themselves."

Surrendering himself to the inevitable, Jericho allowed Luke to shove him in the direction of the sliding doors. They opened before him and he stepped inside. The chilly air washed over his face and raised goosebumps on his forearms, and the mid-afternoon sunlight was replaced by the sterile fluorescent glare.

You know something? he told himself. *I'm gonna do this, and screw the consequences.* Stepping forward, he lost contact with Luke's hand, and heard his cousin's grunt of approval. As his eyes cleared from the outside glare, he found himself in a kind of anteroom with a waiting room beyond. *No more pussyfooting around. The cat's out of the bag, so I might as well make the most of it.* The accidental pun made him smile.

Even if Stephen read the letter and took the time to think about it, Jericho knew his phone would basically explode with calls as soon as he turned it back on. It was the way his boyfriend operated; Stephen didn't believe in 'subtle'. That knowledge was enough to take the incipient grin off his face.

Once he got to Utopia City, he decided, he'd turn his phone on and take whatever Stephen had to dish out. He'd be far enough away by then that he couldn't simply choose to turn around and come back, especially not with Luke at his side. The epiphany was as sudden as it was startling: *I know why I didn't push back when Luke was telling me what to do. Because I know deep down that this is what I need to do.* And maybe, with time to cool down, Stephen might come around. At least Jericho could hope so, anyway. *Better to ask for forgiveness, et cetera …*

Putting aside his worries for the moment, Jericho looked around for a ticket window. To his initial confusion, there were none to be seen. Instead, people seemed to be using the upright electronic kiosks that were lined up on each side of the room. Approaching the first free one, he looked it over. It was tall and blocky, not unlike a seventies-era arcade game console. The large square touchscreen made the similarity almost painfully obvious, while an oval card-reader at the bottom right corner of the screen bore the interlocked letters UML. Stepping up alongside him, Luke began to look the adjacent kiosk over with every indication of interest.

The UML logo popped up at the top of Jericho's screen as he studied the thing. Beneath the logo, the words 'PURCHASE TICKET' appeared as white text inside a deep green rectangle. *Okay, that sounds about right.* Reaching out, he tapped the rectangle. It vanished, making room for more text to scroll chattily across the screen.

WELCOME TO UTOPIA MAGLEV LINES.
WHERE WOULD YOU LIKE TO GO TODAY?

"Hey, cuz, should I go with 'List' or 'Type In'?" asked Luke from the next one over, as the same two options popped up on Jericho's screen.

"Dunno. Let's try 'Type In'." Jericho's choice was rewarded with a keyboard overlay on the screen, from which he selected 'U'. The keyboard disappeared, and a list of cities starting with that initial scrolled up from the bottom of the screen. Jericho wasn't overly surprised to see 'UTOPIA CITY' at the top of the list, superseding several other names that would normally have preceded it in the alphabet.

He tapped it, and more text scrolled up to inform him of the travel time to Utopia City (two and a half hours) and how long before the train departed (twenty-eight minutes). There were five stops on the way there; or rather, five cities that the maglev passed through. The list began with Atlanta and ended with Kansas City. After Kansas City, of course, would be Utopia City. He tried to mentally calculate the distance but couldn't get any more precise than 'around a thousand miles'.

"This cain't be right." That was Luke, beside him. Jericho glanced over, to see him staring at the displayed fare. "Eighty-eight bucks? That's way too cheap."

It *did* seem a little light, but that was what the machine was saying. An addendum caught his eye. "If we want to use our phones, it's only ninety-nine."

"No phones," Luke said firmly. "We'll pay the eighty-eight flat rate." He ran his hand up his face and back over his head. "Though I'm *fucked* if I know how they can afford to charge that low."

Jericho shrugged. "Me too, but that's what they're doing." He tapped the appropriate icon.

YOU HAVE SELECTED A NO-COVERAGE FARE OF $88.00.
PLEASE SWIPE YOUR MAGCARD TO VERIFY, OR PRESS <u>BACK</u> TO RETRY.

"Swipe my what again now?" muttered Jericho out loud, realizing that he'd very possibly skipped an important part of the preparation for this trip. If UML only accepted payment via a 'magcard', whatever that was, then he'd be stuck taking the bus or regular train. In fact, he had no idea how to acquire such a card, given that this was the first he'd heard of them. *Shit. I'm gonna miss my interview, aren't I?*

"Uh, cuz, what's a 'magcard'?" asked Luke at the same time. "It's askin' me for one … wait, somethin's happenin'."

"Me too." Jericho eyed the new line of text that had just appeared on the screen before him.

DO YOU WISH TO PURCHASE A MAGCARD?

He frowned. "Did yours just ask if you wanted to buy one?"

"What the hell is this shit?" Luke didn't sound pleased. "Did this thing just understand what I was sayin'? 'Cause that's some next-level creepy shit, right there."

"Uh, I think mine did too," Jericho said. Hesitantly, he reached out and tapped the 'YES' button on offer beneath the text. Another line of text appeared.

PLEASE PLACE YOUR HANDS ON THE SCREEN.

As he read the text, it scrolled up to make way for a pair of hand-shaped outlines on the touchscreen. "Okay, this is new."

"Screw 'new'. This shit's gettin' weirder an' weirder," muttered Luke. He leaned over to watch what Jericho was doing. "You gonna do what it says?"

"Looks like the only way to get a ticket, so yeah." Jericho didn't feel nearly as confident as he tried to sound. But despite his misgivings, he put his overnight bag on the floor between his feet and did as he was told, pressing his hands onto the outlines. The screen flashed twice, then the outlines disappeared.

YOUR ACCOUNT HAS BEEN CREATED.
PLEASE SWIPE THE DEBIT OR CREDIT CARD OF YOUR CHOICE ON THE
    READER TO DETERMINE YOUR SOURCE OF FUNDS.

This was also news to Jericho. "It can *do* that?"

"Fucked if I know, cuz." Luke dug in his pocket for his wallet. "But I'm about ta find out."

Following his cousin's lead, Jericho pulled out his own wallet. Selecting his least-used debit card, he swiped it across the glowing sensor panel, expecting nothing to happen. After all, the card wasn't chipped, and he'd never heard of a sensor panel that could read non-chipped cards.

THANK YOU, JERICHO HANSEN.
PLEASE INPUT PIN FOR THIS CARD TO COMPLETE LINKUP.

Below the text, a numeric keypad appeared.

"Well, crap. Looks like it *can* read that. Damn." Taking a deep breath, Jericho tapped in the requisite PIN code. It was his emergency-money account, and he only ever kept about fifteen hundred in it. While losing that cash would sting a little (not that he *expected* Utopia Maglev Lines to rip him off) he could handle it, if it happened.

"I'm still tryin' ta figure out how it can tell my name from my card," Luke said. "Is it time ta start worryin' yet?"

"Dunno. I'll let you know." Jericho watched as more text scrolled upward onto the screen.

CARD LINKUP COMPLETE.
YOUR MAGCARD IS READY FOR USE.

The keypad vanished and there was a grinding noise inside the kiosk, then a small panel in the front of the machine dropped open. Within lay a shiny new card bearing the UML logo, with the word 'MagCard' tastefully printed in the bottom-right corner. His interest piqued, he took it out and examined it. Turning it over revealed the same logo and card title on the other side.

"Well, dang." Luke took an identical card from his own kiosk. "Looks like they forgot ta put our names on 'em. We better not lose 'em, or git 'em mixed up."

"I think that's the general idea," Jericho agreed dryly, though he considered Luke's concern to be valid. The machine had known his name; what was stopping it from individualizing the cards? "Seems they can't do everything."

The screen cleared of all text. When it filled again, the text was bright red and slightly larger than normal, surrounded by a flashing red and yellow border.

MANDATORY WARNING:

UTOPIA MAGLEV LINES DOES NOT PERMIT THE CARRIAGE OF FIREARMS, AMMUNITION, EXPLOSIVES OR ILLICIT DRUGS.

ANY SUCH ITEMS MAY BE STORED IN LOCKERS PROVIDED WITHIN THE TRANSIT STATION, WITHOUT PENALTY.

ATTEMPTING TO COMMIT AN ILLEGAL ACT VIA UTOPIA MAGLEV LINES WILL RESULT IN REVOCATION OF TICKET, FORFEITURE OF TICKET PRICE AND ARREST BY LOCAL AUTHORITIES.

ATTEMPTING TO DAMAGE THIS TRANSIT STATION OR DISRUPT UML OPERATIONS BY WAY OF FIREARMS OR EXPLOSIVES WILL RESULT IN EXTREME REPERCUSSIONS FROM FORCE MAJEURE.

DO YOU UNDERSTAND THIS WARNING?

More than a little disconcerted by the forceful wording, he tapped the button that read 'YES'. He half-expected Luke to make some sort of smartass comment, but no such thing happened. *Wonders will never cease.*

THANK YOU.
PLEASE SWIPE MAGCARD TO CONFIRM TRANSACTION.

"Oh, yeah," he muttered. "I need to do that." Carefully, he swiped his brand-new card across the glowing sensor panel, which beeped agreeably at him. More text scrolled over the screen, verifying that the MagCard link had been verified and the transaction confirmed. He'd also been charged five dollars for the card, and ten for the boarding fee. This would apparently be folded into the total fare when he got to the other end, once he used the MagCard to swipe his way off the train. By the time he had his wallet put away, the screen had gone blank once more.

"Well, that was easier than I thought," he observed as he picked up his bag once more. As daunting as this had seemed when he first walked in, he figured a lot of that had been his ongoing distraction with Stephen. With the ticket bought, if not specifically in hand, all he had to do now was get on the train.

"Uh, ya know they never give us no PIN numbers for these cards," Luke pointed out. "How are we s'posed ta keep 'em secure?"

That was ... a good point. "Not sure. Maybe it's all biometrically coded." Jericho snapped his fingers at the recollection. "When we put our hands on the screens? I bet they were gathering data then." He shook his head. "A built-in PIN. Now I really *have* seen everything."

Luke blinked. "Sum*bitch*. That right there's some tricky shit. Though I dunno how they're gonna stop folks that are fixin' ta bring guns an' shit on board from actually doin' it."

"Or drugs." For his part, Jericho wondered how they were going to prevent someone from just walking on board with a backpack full of weed, unless they went with the low-tech expedient of searching all luggage before boarding. While he had no proof, he was reasonably certain Luke had done just that on occasion with the regular train. But guns were a bigger problem. A small enough pistol could be concealed virtually anywhere under a bulky garment; detecting one with an eyeball search would be well-nigh impossible. As he understood things, Georgia's concealed-carry laws didn't necessarily forbid people from carrying firearms into areas where 'no weapons' signs had been posted, so they couldn't rely on being able to have transgressors arrested.

While Jericho had never owned a gun himself, he didn't have a problem with those who did, or even with the concept of concealed carry. In his experience, most people were sensible about such matters. A gun, after all, was both a tool and a potentially dangerous object. It made sense to treat them with caution, and to accept legislated limitations on their ownership and use.

This being the deep South, however, not everyone shared his views. There were those (Pickup, among others) who implicitly believed that the right to bear arms had been handed down from on high along with the Ten Commandments, and acted accordingly. Such people, when encountering a prohibition against carrying firearms into any given place, had been known to move heaven and earth to get that prohibition lifted.

If I see something illegal happening, I'll do something about it. But otherwise it's UML's problem, not mine. Slinging his bag over his shoulder, he followed Luke through the automatic doors into the waiting room.

4
Madness

Spacious and comfortable with vending machines off to one side, the waiting room had chairs, ceiling-mounted TV sets and digital signs apparently doing a countdown. It also held the answer to the question of how UML was going to stop people from simply walking onto the train with guns: instead of the more usual turnstile gates, entry to the platform was regulated by four separate installations that looked exactly like airlocks. Each one appeared to be about six feet wide by twelve deep and came complete with sliding glass doors blocking off each end, as well as a UML card-swipe beside the entry door.

Above the entry doors was a sign that stretched across all four airlocks in six-inch-high lettering.

WARNING: PER UML REGULATIONS, ACCESS TO PLATFORM REQUIRES SCANNING FOR CONTRABAND ITEMS. MAXIMUM OF FOUR PERSONS PER SCAN CYCLE.

Below the main sign, a series of easily deciphered symbols reiterated what could not be transported on the train. As far as Jericho could tell, these translated out to 'no guns, bullets, explosives or illicit drugs'.

"Well," he observed quietly to Luke. "I guess they *can* stop people from getting on with guns." He was perfectly fine with that. While the maglev system was the overwhelming choice for mass public transport within the United States, it wasn't popular with *everyone*, mainly because it was closely associated with Force Majeure. Some resented them for their powers, some for their prestige, and some because they had strong government affiliations. It would only take a few shooting incidents on the maglev to reduce its overall popularity; fortunately, this had not yet been managed.

In any case, he didn't have any 'contraband items' in his bag, and he didn't feel like waiting out on the platform for a half an hour when he could relax in comfortable surroundings instead. And if Luke was carrying anything to worry about, Jericho was pretty sure his cousin would've made an excuse to go and discreetly dispose of it by now. While Luke wasn't the most law-abiding person Jericho knew—or even in the top ten—he wasn't *stupid* about it.

An Amber Alert poster on the wall caught Jericho's eye; it displayed the face of Vanessa Power, age sixteen. Vanessa, a strong-jawed redhead, was the daughter of the superheroes Adam and Tesseract Power, and as such a member of the public superhero group Team Power. However, she'd been missing since December of 2011.

The disappearance had made the news in a big way at the time but was just a part of the background noise by now. With events closer to home taking up his attention, Jericho hadn't been following the case, so he had no idea if there'd been any recent developments. The poster wasn't much help, as it looked like an old one.

He turned his attention to the rest of the room, where Luke was already heading toward a row of seats. The overhead TVs added their noise to the muted bustle in the room, while the three digital signs he'd noticed earlier displayed city names. The timers by the names were counting down.

JACKSONVILLE 11:13
ATLANTA 26:13
COLUMBIA 41:13

He knew that their route led through Atlanta, so they had a little time to wait. At the very least, putting his phone on airplane mode meant he wouldn't have to worry about dealing with calls from Stephen until they got to Utopia City. He'd once asked Luke how straight guys dealt with this sort of drama from their other halves. Luke had laughed out loud at the notion that straight guys handled it any better than gay guys did. "Flowers, chocolate, an' lotsa grovellin'," had been his cousin's advice; a little to his surprise, he found that it worked. To a point, anyway.

Picking a seat beside Luke's, he dropped into it and arranged the overnight bag in his lap. The chair was surprisingly comfortable; as Jericho was adjusting his posture for maximum relaxation, Luke pointed at the nearest screen. "Hey, check it," his cousin said. "What are th' odds they'd have an ad runnin' for the place jes' when we're sittin' down?"

Leaning back in the chair, Jericho found that he had a good view of the TV in question, which (as Luke had noted) happened to be playing a commercial for Utopia City. "Not totally surprising," he decided. "We *are* in a UML transit station, and I hear Force Majeure buys a lot of airtime."

"Yeah, good point." Luke settled back to watch the ad.

In a very real way, Utopia City had been the making of Force Majeure. And vice versa, of course.

Over the course of the 1990s, several particularly vicious supervillains had risen (or fallen) to heretofore unprecedented levels of infamy. Some began their careers during 1988 and '89, but it wasn't until 1990 and later that the general public truly became aware of them. These were people who danced to their own tune, and that tune was mass murder. One and all, they fell away again before the decade was over, but while they were in the public eye, they rewrote the book when it came to the sadistic and twisted use of super-powers. As far as Jericho knew, only a few of them had associated with one another in any meaningful way—the body count would have been much higher, otherwise—but by the end of the decade they were being collectively referred to as the 'terror villains of the nineties'.

The inevitable backlash began in early 1997 but failed to gain much in the way of traction until mid-1998, when a newcomer superhero team called Force Majeure began to make the news. Specializing in brutal, no-mercy takedowns, they prioritized terror villains over the less extreme types of supervillain. Over the next thirteen months, they managed to far outperform the efforts of both mundane law enforcement and other heroes, hunting down and killing no fewer than seven of the out-of-control Enabled villains with no losses to their own side.

On September the fifteenth of 1999, the apocalypse-themed terror villain Doc Iridium announced on national TV that he was going to 'blow up Manhattan' in one week if the federal government did not move to summarily declare Force Majeure outlaws, and issue a warrant for their immediate arrest and execution. Almost as an afterthought, he also demanded one billion dollars for his trouble.

It wasn't hard to understand his animus toward the team. With their extremely public (and fatal) takedown of Raider one month earlier, Force Majeure had all but completed a clean sweep of the nation's terror villains. Understandably concerned that they were setting their sights on him next, he was going all-in on a pre-emptive strike.

Five days in, something went wrong during a live televised repetition of his threats, and he went off the air in mid-rant. The superheroes and first responders who'd been combing the island of Manhattan brick by brick were all greatly relieved to find it was all a hoax. That is, until the news broke about the destruction of the *other* Manhattan; a sleepy little college city in the middle of Kansas.

New York City was safe but ninety thousand people were dead, and more than a thousand square miles of farmland lay devastated and irradiated under a mushroom cloud. Given that Doc Iridium was the last of his unlamented breed, it somehow seemed fitting for him to be hoist with his own petard in such a dramatic fashion. The death toll, however, meant that nobody was celebrating. The phrase 'nine-twenty' would be forever burned into the American consciousness.

Force Majeure, in the meantime, had voluntarily surrendered themselves to the nearest FBI office, who had no idea what to do with them. When the team was notified of the catastrophe, they offered to assist in undoing the devastation. With no better options available, the US government signed an open-ended contract for them to reclaim the city and the radioactive farmland surrounding it.

Once the green light was given, it took less than a day for Force Majeure to deal with the raging wildfires and safely precipitate the fallout cloud. One week later, they'd expunged the radiation from the land and (somehow) decontaminated the water table while they were at it. Then they *really* went to work, applying their considerable technical expertise toward constructing a community of the future. Somehow, along the way, they never moved out.

Fourteen years on, Utopia City was indisputably *the* most technologically advanced metropolis in the world, a proof of concept which had made Force Majeure into a household name. It also held the highest per-capita population of superheroes in the United States.

The commercial made heavy use of panning shots that showed futuristic buildings—including the iconic Spire, the figurative and literal hub of the city—and distant flying objects. Jericho wasn't sure if these were people or vehicles; he'd once heard something about Utopia City having flying cars, but details eluded him. In the background, a voice-over extolled the opportunities to be found by people who were willing to work hard to get ahead.

"Dang," muttered Luke. "Whoever they got doin' the voice actin' is *good*. If I didn't already have me a ticket, I'd be about ready ta buy one anyways."

Jericho grinned but just as he was about to make a comment, the TV cut away to a breaking news announcement. Scrolling across the bottom of the screen, the banner informed everyone in the room that the news was coming in live from Tallahassee, Florida. The first shot was of the WCTV studio, where the news anchor was still straightening his tie. Noticing that he was on the air, he smoothly picked up a sheet of paper and began to address the camera.

"Good afternoon. I'm Mike Weatherby, for WCTV News. We've just now received word that the Madness is attacking the State Capitol building. Tomahawk and Wavefront are en route but aren't expected to get there for a few minutes yet. Fortunately, Relentless and Independence of Force Majeure were in town for an unrelated event and are reportedly on the way as well. We don't have anyone on site, but there's apparently someone live-streaming the event online. Viewer discretion is advised."

The picture cut to a blurry image of four people, the footage shot from between trees or bushes from what Jericho could tell. A man and a woman were standing in front of what appeared to be an ornamental fountain with dolphin sculptures in it. A second man, solid and blocky, stood in the fountain itself while the fourth person, a woman, hovered about ten feet above the other three. Behind them loomed a tall, imposing building, which Jericho assumed was the aforementioned capitol. As the image sharpened, it was easy to see that all four were ragged and disheveled; hair was tangled, and the faces of the men were unshaven. Jericho had never encountered the Madness personally, but these people definitely fit the profile.

"Holy shit, dude, are you getting this?" As far as Jericho could tell without being able to see the speaker, the guy sounded male and in his teens. "This is fuckin' insane!" To his horror, the words ended in a giggle.

"Oh, shit," muttered Luke, mirroring his own thoughts. "They're high."

Jericho shook his head, but in horrified disbelief rather than disagreement. Teenagers, baked out of their minds, in the middle of a supervillain attack. There may have been a situation more likely to create casualties, but he wasn't sure what it was.

A sharp popping sound caused him to duck his head slightly in reflex. He'd only ever been shot at once, but the experience had left a lasting impression. Fortunately, nobody in the room seemed to notice or care. On the screen, the view swung crazily until the camera was focused on a police car parked at the foot of a set of stairs. Both officers were out of the car; one was firing his service weapon at the four superhumans. The other was yelling and gesticulating at whoever held the camera phone, clearly trying to get them to vacate the area. There was another stoned giggle, and a hand came into view, giving a friendly wave in return. Then the camera turned back toward the Enabled on the forecourt.

Now that he was paying closer attention, Jericho could see that there were bodies strewn around the fountain, as well as a serious-looking scorch mark across the frontage of the capitol building. He wondered what had caused that, then winced as the flying woman jerked her arm back. Blood dripped from it, visible even on the shaky image as she raised her other hand. A blue glow built around it, discharging then a moment later. Luke visibly cringed and Jericho gritted his teeth as a sound like a thousand fingernails on just as many blackboards shrilled through the room. A brilliant violet-blue beam with an actinic white-hot core struck the car dead center, enveloping it in a tremendous ball of fire.

Jericho went cold all over as he concluded that both officers were almost certainly dead. As the hood of the luckless car flipped skyward, Jericho heard another stoned giggle. "Holy shit, dude! That was brutal! I'm so tweeting this shit. Hashtag masks two, cops zero." He wanted to reach through the screen, grab them each by the scruff of the neck, and bang their heads together. *And you're about to join them, you insensitive asshats!*

"Fuck you, assholes," Luke muttered. "Those guys were righteous. You goddamn mouth-breathers." The comment was very … *Luke*. His cousin had strong opinions on several issues, and one of them was that if a body got himself into a bad situation, he shouldn't bitch about being in trouble. As far as Luke was concerned, standing there and pointing a camera at rampaging Enabled was not only a good way to get killed, it was also an ideal solution for cleaning the shit out of the shallow end of the gene pool. At the same time, his praise of the cops showed the strength of his feelings on the subject, given his usual distaste for law-enforcement personnel. Jericho silently agreed with both sentiments.

"Joey, man, maybe we should move away a bit?" The new voice was a lot closer to the camera, if the occasional fuzziness was any indication. "They don't look really friendly."

That was, by definition, an understatement. Even though the teenagers seemed to be about thirty or forty yards away from the Madness, they were still close enough to be in dire peril, and stoned enough to have no idea of the danger they were in. He grimaced, fully aware that he and Luke were about to witness a second double murder, and that they were unable to do a damn thing about it. On the screen—the idiot was still pointing the phone at the Madness—he saw the blue glow begin to build up around the woman's hand, this time aimed directly at the camera.

At the same time, in the background, there was a distinct metallic report as the blocky figure tore one of the ornamental dolphin sculptures free. With no apparent effort, the guy threw the sculpture at the two teens, its metallic form tumbling over and over in the air. Along with Luke, Jericho jolted backward in his seat as the ad hoc projectile loomed large on the screen. Barring a miracle, it was definitely going to hit the one with the camera. Right up until a silvery streak slashed out of nowhere and drove the oncoming metal mass sideways with a tremendous *clang*, making them both jump.

"The hell?" Luke blurted out loud. "What happened?"

"No idea," Jericho said, leaning forward in his chair in an unconscious effort to get a better view of what was happening. *What the hell was that?* He searched the screen for a clue, but all he saw was a battered and bent dolphin statue lying at the bottom of the steps, next to the still-burning police car. Also, the flying woman's hand was glowing ever brighter. Considering what the previous blast had done to the vehicle, a couple of reckless teenagers were going to pose no challenge at all for its destructive power. Whatever had knocked the dolphin sculpture aside wasn't going to save them now.

Abruptly, the image blurred into darkness, accompanied by a deep THOOM that made Jericho jump yet again. Again he heard the screech, but it cut out after just a moment. A few seconds after that, the darkness in front of the camera shifted and resolved into individual sections of armor plate; very *distinctive* armor plate, black with silver trim. Jericho caught his breath as he realized that he was looking at the broad, armored chest of none other than Relentless himself.

As the leader of Force Majeure stepped away from the teenager, he came properly into view for the first time. Jericho watched as he raised one heavily gloved hand as if to wave at someone. With a clash of metal on metal, the haft of an ornately studded mace smashed into his palm. His fingers closed over it as if welcoming it home. *Sonovabitch. He used his mace to knock the dolphin aside, then tanked the goddamn beam to save the kids.*

"Well, fuck me sideways," Luke said softly, apparently having come to the same conclusion. "That there is major goddamn badass."

Jericho couldn't help but agree. He'd read a lot about Relentless and knew that he stood between six and a half and seven feet tall, but the camera angle made the veteran hero look far taller and more imposing. More to the point, even though Relentless was wearing a helmet that covered his face from the cheekbones up, it was easy to tell that he was extremely irritated. With a glower that would've caused a charging rhino to rethink its priorities, the iconic hero pointed his free hand at the camera. **"What do you think you're doing, you idiots?"** he boomed, the sub-bass registers in his voice almost overloading the TV speakers. **"Are you *trying* to get yourselves killed?"** Imperiously, he gestured down the street. **"Get back out of the way. NOW!"**

Jericho smiled grimly to himself. *Called it.* From the looks of it, the teens didn't even think to argue. They just hurried back, with any luck sobered by the close call. As the image swung about in a motion-sickness inducing fashion, Jericho caught a glimpse of the spot where Relentless had landed. The hero's boot-prints were impressed half an inch into the sidewalk, with cracks radiating outward in all directions.

"Holy shit, dude, Relentless is fuckin' hardcore," giggled the first teen. "I nearly pissed myself when he yelled at us." As he spoke, he began to slow his pace.

"Joey, you did piss yourself," his friend said. "I think—" The unmistakable report of a rifle shot interrupted his words.

Both teens stopped and turned around. Jericho gathered that they were standing in the middle of an intersection, but they were still far too close to the action.

"What was that?" asked one of them. "Relentless didn't have a gun." The camera tilted upward, toward the top of the capitol building. "Hey, dude. Look up there. Someone on the roof."

"Lemme see." There was the sound of a scuffle, and the image swung crazily. "Don't be a douche! Lemme see!"

"Fuck you. Let me zoom in." The image centered on the capitol building once more and enlarged steadily. It was a good phone, Jericho had to admit. His own phone didn't have a zoom capability like that. "Hey, is that Independence?"

"Dunno, can you see her ass?"

"Dude, she catches you looking at her ass, she'll shoot *your* ass!"

"Hey, that's my future wife you're talking about!"

Jericho tuned the voices out as he leaned forward to study the image. The focus wasn't perfect, but he could see the muted red and blue tones of the costume, the platinum-blonde ponytail flying in the breeze, the claymore hilt protruding up over her shoulder ... and the assault rifle she was holding as she leaned over the edge of the roof. A flash from the muzzle coincided with another sharp *crack*.

"Well, that's definitely Independence," Jericho said quietly. She was widely known to be a past master with the rifle and the sword, and probably any other weapon she chose to pick up. Between her and Relentless, this fight was going to be extremely brief and extremely brutal.

"Good," agreed Luke, then apparently addressed the idiots with the phone. "Now get the hell out of there afore y'all get anyone *else* killed, you stupid goddamn asswipes."

As if in answer to the comment, a roaring sound overrode the noise of the battle. The camera turned to show a suit of red and white power armor coming in for a landing. The suit looked as though it had been cobbled together from surplus military missiles, right down to the markings painted on the legs and arms. However, as the wearer stepped forward, it became obvious that this was more a theme than a reality; the movements were far more fluid than would be possible from such a patchwork effort.

"What the hell are you two morons doing here?" Tomahawk—Jericho recognized the suit now—shook his helmeted head. "You've gotta be kidding me. C'mere." A red and white articulated gauntlet loomed large on the screen, and suddenly the phone was tumbling to the ground. It landed face down, the camera pointing skyward. For the first time, Jericho got to see the people behind the voices. Even allowing for the foreshortening, he wasn't particularly impressed. They were scrawny and unkempt. From the angle the camera was looking from, it was easy to see that one of them had indeed wet himself.

"Hey!" yelled the guy who'd had bladder issues, trying to pull his arm free of Tomahawk's implacable grip. "Lemme go! I got rights!"

"My phone!" complained the other. "That's a good phone!"

"I don't give two shits about your phone," Tomahawk told him deliberately. "I'm getting you two to safety so I can help Relentless clean up the mess." It was impossible to tell if the action was purposeful or not but with his next step, a large metallic boot descended on the phone. After a horrendous *crunch,* the signal was no more.

5
Platform

As the image switched back to the TV studio, Jericho got up and slung his bag over his shoulder. Luke looked up at him. "Where ya goin', cuz?"

"Out to the platform." Jericho inclined his head toward the scanning airlocks. "We're not gonna see any more of the fight, and it was just about over anyway. I dunno how good Tomahawk is, but Relentless and Independence are gonna *wreck* those murdering asshats' whole day. All we're gonna see now is folks who think they know what they're talking about, doing a post-mortem on the fight. It'll be boring and they'll get most of the facts wrong, so I'm not gonna bother." There was nothing more frustrating, he'd long since decided, than listening to a so-called 'expert' get the entire thing wrong when it was perfectly clear what had really happened.

Luke's eyebrows rose but to Jericho's relief, he got to his feet without making any of the smartass comments that he was capable of. Slinging his backpack over his left shoulder, he followed Jericho toward the nearest 'airlock'. The trouble was, it seemed that other people were looking to get on the train, so lines had already formed before each set of sliding doors. On the upside, each scan cycle only took a few seconds, so there was no danger of missing the train.

As Jericho shuffled forward with the line, he came within earshot of a low-voiced argument between the woman with the stroller and the man who'd arrived with her. This was basically inevitable, given that the couple were standing right in front of two of the entry doors, currently blocking others from using them.

"I can carry what I want when I want!" declared the man in a fierce whisper. "It's my constitutional, God-given right!" He slapped the left side of his coat, then gestured at the sliding doors beside him. "And ain't no machine's gonna tell me different."

Crap. Jericho could tell the signs. The man with the overly bushy mustache had just been upgraded from 'redneck' to 'redneck with a gun'. *There's always one.* If this guy's views on giving up his firearm (even to comply with a legal requirement) didn't include the phrase 'cold dead hands', Jericho was willing to eat his entire costume. Without salt.

"Don't be a dumbass!" the woman snapped back, then glared over her shoulder to where Jericho was watching them. "What the hell are *you* looking at, asshole?"

"Not a thing," Jericho replied mildly. "But you think maybe you can take the argument elsewhere? You're blocking the way there." Behind him, he was aware of Luke standing silently by. No matter what happened, he knew his cousin would be there to back him up.

"Fuck you!" The woman turned away from him and swiped her card angrily across the reader beside her. "Franklin, you go put that thing in a goddamn locker. I'll be on the goddamn platform." The doors swished open, and she towed the suitcase and stroller into the scanning airlock. Jericho watched as the doors hissed shut behind her. Even as they locked into place—he heard the click from where he was—the far doors were opening to let her onto the platform beyond.

Muttering to himself, Franklin did the precise opposite of what the woman had told him. Specifically, he swiped his own MagCard across the reader of the next scan-lock over. The doors opened and he stepped inside. Immediately, he moved to the far end, no doubt anticipating a quick scan cycle.

For a long moment, nothing at all happened. Then, as Jericho and Luke moved forward another space, the near doors opened wide and a red light started flashing within the scan-lock. Over the speakers came a voice that had to be computer-generated, from its utter lack of emotion. **"Attention. Scanning has detected a loaded firearm. Firearms and ammunition are not permitted on Utopia Maglev Lines. Please remove them from the premises at once."**

"What? No!" Franklin kicked one of the glass doors. It refused to budge. Then he tried to lever them open with his bare hands. This didn't prove any more effective. "I got my rights, you stupid machine! Constitution says so!"

The sliding doors apparently didn't care about Franklin's rights, constitutional or otherwise. Even when he threw his entire weight against the doors, they didn't budge. From the dull thud and the hiss of pain that resulted, Jericho surmised that the door was made of something tougher than normal glass.

"Attention. Attempting to damage this facility is a crime. Your actions have been recorded. The authorities are being notified."

This was rapidly developing into a situation. Tensing, Jericho activated one of his powers. Down by his left side, partially concealed in his cupped hand, he began to form a tightly packed gravitational anomaly about the size of a tennis ball. This was what he called a 'G-tag'; more specifically, a glue-tag. If Franklin looked like pulling the gun out and using it, the 'tag would be ideal for jamming the mechanism, but he didn't want anyone else to see him doing it.

"Cover me," he murmured to Luke; without looking, he felt his burly cousin step into place to block the view of everyone watching. God *damn*, it was nice to have good backup.

In the next moment, Franklin came storming out of the scan-lock. "You don't get it, do you?" he demanded of the crowd. "This is the first step! They'll come for your guns! Then they'll come for *you!*" Amid catcalls and requests that he shut the hell up, he began pushing his way toward the exit. "You'll see! You'll all see! They're taking away our rights! *They're conspiring against America!*" The automatic doors closed behind him, cutting off his voice. Along with several other people within earshot, Jericho let out a tiny sigh of relief.

"Thank fuck for that," muttered Luke. "For a second there, I figgered he was gonna try shootin' the place up. That coulda gone real bad."

Jericho silently agreed as he relaxed his power and let the G-tag dissipate. With innocent civilians in the line of fire, there would've been a need to act decisively even after the gun was disabled. Whether or not his power use was noticed, this would get the attention of the news services, and he *really* didn't want that sort of scrutiny. *Especially not now.*

Fortunately, the crisis had been averted. In front of him, the scan-lock beeped to indicate its availability, so he swiped his MagCard and stepped inside as the doors swept open. Luke swiped as well, keeping the doors open, and stepped in after him.

Sliding shut behind them, the doors locked with the same click he'd heard before. For a long moment, nothing happened, not even a wave of laser light passing over them. *Maybe UML should put something like that in, just for show.* Even as he started to wonder if Luke had packed something the scanners didn't like by accident (or on purpose), the scan-lock beeped and the doors in front of him opened.

Emerging from the scan-lock, he went a few yards out onto the platform. Luke followed along with his backpack still on his shoulder, craning his neck to look around. Jericho couldn't blame him, because there was a lot to look at. Perhaps a hundred and fifty feet from end to end, the platform was so new that there was still a lingering trace of fresh paint smell. It featured white-tiled walls, an ornate digital clock overhead, a vast rendition of the UML logo worked into the concrete underfoot, and of course the train waiting at the platform's edge.

Magnetic levitation was a concept that had been around since the dawn of the twentieth century, but with the advent of Force Majeure and the engineering prowess of Transit and the Technologist, it had taken a quantum leap forward. The 'train' at this point consisted of a single passenger car, but *what* a passenger car. Twenty feet high and maybe a hundred feet long—though the exact length was hard to gauge due to the raked-back aerodynamic shape—the gleaming-white marvel of technology hovered on a cushion of magnetic force. If he hadn't seen footage of this sort of thing on the news, it would've been all too easy to dismiss it as something out of science fiction. Beneath it was the broad cylindrical polished metallic rail that he'd seen before; here, it was half-buried in the rough gravel.

"Before I forget, thanks for backing me up in there," he said quietly. "Coulda gotten nasty."

"Eh, weren't nothin'," Luke said with a grin. "Always wanted ta be a sidekick, anyways." He indicated the people streaming across the platform and boarding the passenger car. "Shouldn't we be gittin' on board with everyone else? Train's right there."

Jericho shook his head. "Not our train. That one's heading for Jacksonville." He pointed at the overhead clock. One readout indicated that the current time was 4:42 PM, the next that the current train at the station was indeed due for Jacksonville, and the last one was showing '02:19' and counting down.

"Right." Luke glanced at Jericho. "I heard tell Independence likes women. That right?"

"I'm the last person to ask if it's true or not, but I heard it too." Jericho shrugged. "I also heard she and Relentless are a thing. Tabloids'll tell whatever story's gonna sell. Wouldn't put too much stock in it." The rumor mill had a habit of labeling powerful independent women as lesbians, no matter how true it was (or wasn't). As far as he was concerned, how Independence conducted herself and who she conducted herself with was her concern and nobody else's.

The one other person on the platform who seemed to be waiting for the next train happened to be the woman with the stroller and the suitcase. She was standing off a little way, talking animatedly on her cellphone. Seeing Jericho and Luke looking in her direction, she shot them a hostile glare then ostentatiously moved off a little way. From what he could tell, she never stopped talking the whole way, expertly cradling her phone between shoulder and ear as she pushed the stroller with one hand and dragged the suitcase with the other.

"Well, *that* was right neighborly," Luke observed. "Wonder if it's 'cause you asked 'em to move aside, or if she jes' don't like black folks?" His tone was light, but his gaze was serious. Jericho didn't have to wonder why; like his cousin, he'd seen this shit happen far too often.

"Not sure." Though he could hazard a guess. While there *were* people out there who thought that overturning *Roe v. Wade* and repealing the Thirteenth, Fourteenth, Fifteenth and Nineteenth Amendments would be a great way to start fresh with a brand-new United States, he seriously doubted that was the case here. At worst, she probably thought Luke was 'the wrong sort of people' to be around. Which was bad enough in its own way—racists and bigots made for uncomfortable neighbors—but unlikely to pose an immediate problem to Luke or himself. "I figure she's a garden-variety redneck asshat, to be honest. But she could just be having a bad day."

"Yeah, well." Luke snorted, then changed the subject. "So, them Madness assholes. Reckon G-Man coulda taken 'em?" It was a favorite tactic of his; to refer to Jericho's costumed identity as if his superhero persona were a third party, so they could discuss the matter in public with nobody the wiser.

"Hm." Jericho rubbed his chin in thought. While the four Enabled whom Relentless and Independence had engaged were typical of the Madness, the villains in question weren't a coherent group as far as anyone could tell. The Madness had been appearing for about the last five years, popping up in crowded areas and attacking indiscriminately with powers that were as varied as they were unexpected. There were only three to five perpetrators at a time, and nobody ever saw them arrive. Neither costumes nor tactics were employed, which made it a little easier to fight them. When captured or killed, they always turned out to be people who had gone missing for no known reason; one theory had it that the trauma of gaining powers had sent them insane.

Which raised another puzzle: the Madness always lost their powers within twenty-four hours, making it all the more bizarre, as everyone *else* with powers got to keep them. Unfortunately, even after the powers were gone, the psychotic mindset endured, which made it hard to find out any information at all from them. As far as anyone knew, they didn't even call themselves the Madness; that was a name given to them by an internet hoaxer who'd tried to claim credit for the attacks. However, after he was arrested and debunked, the name stuck.

One of the more popular theories was that someone was experimenting with a way to grant powers and getting rid of the failures in a cruel and dramatic fashion. Despite intensive investigation by the FBI, NSA, Force Majeure and others, no evidence had emerged to narrow down the identity of the hypothetical villain or villains behind the Madness.

"That's a tough one," Jericho decided at last. "He wouldn't have been able to block that hit like Relentless did. But he could've at least helped, by getting bystanders out of the way, and by not getting in the way himself." *And afterward, maybe get Relentless' autograph. Those two idiots were seriously lucky that him and Independence were in town.*

"That's fair," Luke allowed. He started wandering away from the scan-locks, but instead of moving toward the train, he headed along the platform. His movements might have appeared random to anyone else, but Jericho knew better.

A moment later, Luke's intent became clear. Although he was nowhere near the woman yet, she looked up from her phone call and shot him a poisonous glare. Then she stomped off toward the far end of the platform, dragging the stroller and still talking nineteen to the dozen on her phone. *Well, that answers that question.*

"You do love triggering bigots, don't you?" asked Jericho as he came up alongside Luke.

Luke's innocent expression needed a lot of work. "I got no idea what you're talkin' about, cuz. Jes' takin' a stroll while I'm waitin' on th' next train."

Jericho rolled his eyes. "Pfft, yeah, right. Do me a favor. Don't sit next to her on the maglev. She'd probably call the cops on you for 'riding the train while black'. That, or have a stroke from pure outrage." He didn't *think* Luke would go that far, but his cousin had surprised him before.

Luke opened his mouth, probably to come out with a smartass comment, but he was interrupted by a musical tone coming from the public-address speakers. **"Please stand away from the edge of the platform,"** announced a synthesized female voice. **"The train is now leaving. The next train is due to arrive in thirty seconds."**

"Thirty *seconds?*" repeated Luke. "How the hell are they gonna git another train in here so … well, fuck *me*." He paused with a look of astonishment on his face at the same time as Jericho heard a long growing *whoosh* from behind him. Wondering what the hell was going on *now*, Jericho turned an instant before the tail end of the passenger car vanished out of sight of the platform. He gaped, barely able to believe what he'd just seen. In just a few seconds, the entire thing had just … *gone*.

It didn't escape him that the frankly incredible level of acceleration achieved by the hundred-ton-plus bulk of the maglev car indicated a level of raw power which was utterly, hilariously, far in advance of anything made with by pre-Artificer engineering. The fact that it took place in near-complete silence merely underlined the fact that the maglev was *the* future of transport in America.

"Please stand away from the edge of the platform. The next train is due to arrive in fifteen seconds."

Jericho was about to tell Luke about the cabbie's 'bat out of hell' remark when he was interrupted by a startled curse from Luke. Dropping the backpack, his cousin took off like a sprinter from the starting blocks. Jericho spun around, seeking the reason for Luke's action. When he saw it, his blood froze in his veins.

At the far end of the platform, the woman waved her free hand as she spoke on her phone. Unfortunately, her attention was more on the phone than the stroller. She'd also failed to see that the slipstream from the departing maglev had caught the stroller, which was now rolling quietly toward the edge of the platform. Worse: if the announcements were to be believed, the next one was literally due at any second.

It wouldn't matter if he called out and alerted the lady. In the three to five seconds it would take her to realize what was going on and react accordingly, her child would be over the side. Luke had clearly figured that out and was doing his level best to avert a tragedy, but even the most optimistic view of the situation still made one thing blatantly obvious. Barring a miracle, the stroller was going to reach the edge and flip over, subjecting the baby to a six-foot face-first drop onto rough gravel, before Luke ever got close enough to stop it. The kid would be lucky to survive the experience, and that wasn't factoring in the upcoming arrival of the new passenger car.

Fortunately for the infant, Jericho didn't have to depend on miracles. His control over gravity wasn't limited to falling slowly, or making other things fall slowly. That specific ability was contact-only, but he did have ranged options to call on; specifically, his G-tags.

Dropping his bag, he brought his right hand up and around in a throwing motion. With an effort of will—harsher than before because he had the merest razor-shaved margin of time to work with—he formed another tennis-ball-sized G-tag in his cupped palm. As part of the same motion, he flicked his wrist and sent the gravitational anomaly on its way. Outwardly identical to the glue-tag he'd made inside the station, this was the other type of G-tag he could create, called a push-tag. A second 'tag formed in his left hand, but he let it build power instead of throwing it immediately. The one he'd just thrown, visible only due to the refraction of flickering rainbow-light through it, crossed the intervening distance in far less time than the corresponding tennis ball would have.

This was fortunate for all concerned, as the stroller was far too close to the edge of the platform when the G-tag whipped past Luke and struck it, dissolving into its structure and imparting a backward push. Lacking the power it would've possessed had he put more time into forming it, the 'tag didn't manage to slow the stroller down by much. It was better than nothing, but this alone would not save the baby.

The front wheels of the errant stroller went over the edge when Luke was still several yards away. Jericho knew that once the back wheels followed suit, it would be all over. Luke must have thought the same thing, because he kicked off and launched himself through the air, hands reaching for the stroller.

Jericho made a split-second decision and switched targets for his second 'tag from the stroller to Luke himself; launching the gravitational anomaly, he hit Luke with it while he was still in midair. Because he'd held this one a little longer, the G-tag had more punch behind it. It hit Luke in the small of the back and dissolved, permeating his body with a proportionately stronger directional impulse than its predecessor had with the stroller. Not stronger overall, as Luke was several times heavier than the stroller and baby together, but enough to give him a solid shove forward. Without pausing, Jericho formed and flung two more 'tags on the heels of the first two.

Luke landed heavily, his outstretched hands still four feet short of the runaway conveyance. Under normal circumstances, his rescue attempt would've ended there, but the extra momentum from the push-tag (and the fact that his body was now treating the platform as a slight downward slope) overcame the friction of his jacket against the cold concrete. He slid forward just far enough that his hand closed on the back wheel of the stroller as it went off the platform. Strong fingers locked tight around a worn, ragged plastic wheel. The stroller came to a halt, three wheels off the edge, suspended between salvation and disaster.

For a long, frozen moment Luke strained, his free hand crossed over in front of his body, straining downward against the concrete platform. He wasn't dropping the stroller, but he couldn't pull it back up either … until Jericho's last two 'tags arrived. The first hit the stroller, permeating it with the vague notion that 'down' was now a little bit *up*, thus lightening the load somewhat. The second 'tag hit Luke in the middle of the back, defining *his* 'down' as being to his left; giving him and the baby a weak but significant boost away from the imminent peril.

It was all Luke needed; with a massive effort, he hauled the stroller up and over his body, rolling away from the edge. Just as the stroller cleared the danger zone—by so tight a margin that it was pushed aside by the inrush of wind—the new maglev car arrived and braked to an impossibly rapid halt. The stroller landed on the platform and fell over backward, while the baby (still safely strapped in) began to squall mightily. Luke let the wheel go and collapsed onto his back. For his part, Jericho let out a breath that he hadn't been aware he was holding. *That was far too close.*

Jericho dispelled the ongoing effects of his G-tags, as they were no longer needed. Then he leaned down and scooped up his bag with one hand and Luke's backpack with the other. Trying to quell the reaction quivering in his stomach, he headed in his cousin's direction.

A few seconds later, the woman registered her baby's crying and went to reach out to the stroller, then turned around when her groping hand found nothing. "Richie!" Her shriek echoed the length of the platform. Dropping her phone, she lunged toward the wayward stroller. Jericho watched as she fell to her knees beside her baby. It took her three tries to disconnect her child from the safety straps, then she snatched up the kid and hugged him like she was never going to let him go.

"You okay there, Luke?" Jericho asked as he approached. "Hey, lady, you know my cousin just saved your kid's life, right?" He knew he really shouldn't rub it in, but it was rare that he was able to savor moments of true karma.

Still holding Richie tightly to her, the woman stared blankly up at Jericho. As the meaning of his words sank in, her gaze traveled slowly down to where Luke still lay prone on the platform. Propping himself up on one elbow, Luke gave her a brief wave. Jericho figured he was too winded to speak yet.

"Oh, uh … thank you," she said roughly, then picked up the stroller. Still holding her child close (he suspected it would be more than a little while before she felt secure in letting the kid out of arm's reach) she started to move away.

"Hey." Jericho was about to say more, but Luke sat up and shook his head.

"Don't bother, cuz," he wheezed. "They'll change or they won't. Cain't force it nohow."

This was Jericho's experience too, but he held a more optimistic view of people than Luke did and thus was more easily disappointed when they failed to live up to normal human expectations. Dropping the backpack, he offered his hand to Luke. "You okay?" he asked again. "Looked like you hit the ground pretty hard there."

"I'll live." Luke took hold of the proffered hand; Jericho set his weight and heaved. Luke came to his feet without more than a minimum of effort. "Thanks for the helpin' hand."

Jericho was reasonably sure that Luke was talking about more than being assisted to his feet, but he couldn't say anything about it right then. "No problem," he said, still feeling a little shaky.

That had *definitely* been far too close.

6
Challenger

Fortunately, there'd been nobody else on the platform to see what Jericho had done. The only potential witness had manifestly failed to see a single thing. With any luck, the momentary distortion of the light through the G-tags wouldn't even show up on the security cameras, and anyone viewing the footage anyway would presumably be more interested in the way Luke had rescued the kid than in what Jericho was doing, twenty yards away. G-tags didn't leave fingerprints, after all.

Luke picked up his pack and slung it over one shoulder once more, then indicated where the passengers from the newly arrived maglev were streaming across the platform and moving through the scan-locks. "Looks like we're gonna git first dibs on any seats. Got any preferences?"

Jericho shrugged, feeling growing excitement within his chest. Not only was he *going* to Utopia City, but Luke was coming with. Or rather, *Luke* was going to Utopia City and dragging Jericho along for his own good. He wasn't quite sure why he'd never asked Luke to come along in Stephen's stead. *Maybe I was too traumatized by Stephen being a dick that I assumed nobody else would want to come along?*

However, he didn't want to think about that right now. Slinging his overnight bag more securely over his shoulder, he followed Luke toward the open train doors. Even now, the sight of the technological artifact before him took his breath away. Part of his mind had trouble accepting that something so big could be supported on mere magnetic fields. But then, as he entered the doors, his ability to sense anomalies in the local G-field detected gravity generators augmenting the lifting force from below.

He relaxed a little; he was comfortable with gravity. Although his G-sense came paired with what he called his G-shake—the ability to rapidly remodulate the local gravity field around him—he didn't have any way to aim the latter. And even if he was powerful enough to pull it off (which he doubted) disrupting one of the forces maintaining the train's stability while it was traveling at full speed would almost certainly end in catastrophe, so he ruled that to be a solid pass on even trying.

The last few people stepped off, giving Luke and Jericho room to board. Looking around as he followed Luke onto the train, Jericho could see that the aesthetic was all about passenger comfort. There was a wide aisle, with two rows of seats down each side, each as luxurious as he imagined accommodations to be in the average super-first airliner. At one end, on either side of the doors that would presumably connect with the next passenger car along (once there was one) were the restrooms. The other end held vending machines for food and drink. Directly opposite the entry doors, almost recessed into the far wall, was a stylish spiral staircase that allowed access to the upper deck.

The incoming passengers were only just starting to cross the platform; while there weren't all that many, Jericho didn't want to be stuck in the company of a lot of other people right then. "Let's go up," he suggested, nodding toward the staircase.

"Sho'nuff." Luke led the way up the stairs, with Jericho following. The passenger car had another set of entry doors on the upper level, but Savannah's maglev station was still in the first stage of completion. This meant everyone had to come in through the lower doors, and not many were going to come up top when there were free seats downstairs. Or at least, Jericho hoped so.

The upper level also had restrooms and vending machines, but the seating was arranged a little differently. Instead of having them all facing in the same direction, each pair of bench seats was set on either side of a small table, as per the 'dining car' setup in regular trains. Even more interestingly, there was a discreet switch built into each table. Jericho was pretty sure he knew what the switches did, but he decided to wait until he sat down to test one out.

There were doors at each end of the upper level as well; Jericho guessed that just like the ones on the lower level, they would be securely locked. Over each set of doors was a digital sign with the word 'DEPARTURE' on it, with minutes and seconds counting down the time until the train left the station. This information was repeated on three similar signs set at intervals into the ceiling. As of that moment, they had about thirteen and a half minutes to change their minds and get off the train. *Yeah, like that's going to happen.*

Jericho was still feeling a little shaken over what had happened on the platform, over and above the fight he'd had with Stephen, so he moved toward what he assumed was the back end of the maglev car. Reaching up, he stuffed his overnight bag into the overhead luggage bin, then flopped into the seat and leaned up against the corner. Luke took off his backpack and put it in the bin as well before closing the lid, then sat down heavily beside him. "Well, holy shit. Is this the friggin' lap of luxury, or what?"

Luke wasn't far wrong—the seats were redolent with the classic new-car smell— but Jericho didn't care right at that moment. Leaning his head against the window, he did his best to ignore Luke while trying to think calming thoughts. Everything would be all right; by the time they got to Utopia City, Stephen would've calmed down. Jericho would call him, and everything would be good. Savannah didn't even have a branch office for Force Majeure but maybe, if Jericho was accepted onto the team, he could get posted back here as the leader of a new satellite team. *Yeah, that's gonna hap-*

"So, how'd it feel to be th' sidekick this time round?" asked Luke, keeping his voice low but sporting a wide grin. He jabbed Jericho in the ribs with his elbow. "I totally *rocked* out there."

Normally, Jericho would've disputed the 'sidekick' title, but Luke had definitely earned his kudos. "You sure as hell did. That kid absolutely owes you his life." Not for the first time, he reflected that Luke would've made a far more effective hero than he'd ever be, if a lot darker and grittier. *I'd pay money to see that.*

Luke jabbed him again, this time with his finger. "So tell me, cuz," he said, his voice a lot more serious. "Why didn't ya jes' stick that thing to the platform soon as ya saw it movin'?"

Luke, of course, knew about the glue-tags. When they struck a target, they created a gravitational field around the point of impact that made everything within a certain radius adhere to each other and pull in toward that point. However, this wasn't the whole story.

"Okay, for starters, the stickiness falls off pretty fast," he said by way of explanation. "Secondly, it depends on surface area that's touching. Stroller wheels have a total surface contact of about half a square inch. To make that work, I would've had to generate a pretty strong 'tag, which meant letting it get a lot closer to the edge, *or* nail one of the wheels directly to get as strong a field as possible sticking it to the concrete. I *can* hit a moving target that small—I've done it before—but I wasn't gonna bet a kid's life on it. And then there's the other thing."

Luke's expression showed enlightenment and curiosity by turns. "Other thing?" he asked. "What other thing?"

Just as Jericho opened his mouth to reply, a couple of people came up the stairwell and looked around before picking a table some distance away from them. Still, Jericho didn't want to risk the newcomers overhearing even a meaningless fragment of the conversation. Leaning forward, he flipped the switch on the table. A light came on beside the switch; immediately, all ambient noise cut right out. *Huh, so it works both ways. Good to know.*

"And what the hell's *that?*" Luke eyed the switch warily.

"Privacy bubble," Jericho explained, trying not to sound smug. "I read about it online. It raises a field around the table that stops sound coming in or out." He leaned past Luke and stuck his hand outside the field, then snapped his fingers. No sound came back to them. "See?" According to the UML website, it was a Force Majeure patent, reportedly used by high-level businessmen and national leaders the world over.

Experimentally, Luke flipped the switch back and forth a few times, like a kid playing with a new toy. The outside ambient noise popped on and off, as though someone were fiddling with a TV remote. "Huh," he grunted finally, leaving it in the 'on' position. "Friggin' modern technology." He turned back to Jericho. "So, what's that there 'other thing' you was talkin' about?"

Jericho snorted. "You. I didn't have a clear shot because your big ass was in the goddamn way. And there's no way in *hell* I was gonna throw a glue-tag that might just hit you and cause you to trip because your foot got stuck to the floor at the wrong moment."

"What, really?" For the first time, Luke looked taken aback. "Cuz, are you sayin' I got in th' way?"

Jericho shook his head. "No. Well, yes and no. If you hadn't been there, I could maybe have tried a Hail Mary glue-tag, or a series of push-tags, or one big 'tag of either type just before it went over the edge. I would've had to time it exactly goddamn right, and there's no guarantee it would've worked. Or if I could get closer, a G-shake. But that's not a certainty, either. And doing a G-shake with you there would've definitely put you on your ass."

"Yeah, no shit," Luke said sourly. While the G-shake could be useful in stabilizing or destabilizing an area of several yards across, Jericho mainly utilized it to unsettle opponents by attacking their inner ear equilibrium. Luke had once asked Jericho to demonstrate it on him, then vowed never again, once he stopped throwing up. "So ya reckon you coulda saved th' kid in time?"

Jericho waggled his hand from side to side. "Fifty-fifty chance. Maybe forty-sixty. I would've *tried*, but there's a good chance I would've failed, and probably done something to give myself away."

"Well, that ain't good." Luke didn't look overly thrilled. "So what happens if someone got a picture of you throwin' a G-tag an' decided ta out ya?"

"Well, they *won't.*" Jericho wasn't quite sure if Luke understood the implications of the question. "They're legally not allowed to."

"Legally, my ass." Luke snorted. "Folks wanna take a pic like that an' sell it to th' papers, they'll do it. Money's money."

"But the papers won't *print* it," Jericho tried to explain. At Luke's skeptical expression, he paused for thought. *Now, how do I explain this?*

As a delaying tactic to get his thoughts in order, he pulled the hair-tie out and ran his fingers through his hair. Slowly, he put the tie back in place. "The papers aren't allowed to print anything that might out me, or any other publicly known hero for that matter. The Challenger Act says they can't. Most everyone knows it's a really bad idea to do it." At least, he hoped that was true. There were asshats everywhere.

Luke tilted his head. "Challenger Act? Ain't that jes' there so big-time government-type heroes can get reporters chucked in jail for diggin' into their secret identities and stuff?" He gave Jericho a semi-apologetic look. "Sorry, cuz, but you ain't exactly big-time. Or government."

Closing his eyes, Jericho rubbed his thumb and forefinger over the bridge of his nose. "Government-affiliated heroes aren't the only ones it covers. I'm protected, too." But when he opened his eyes again, Luke's expression still held a distinctly skeptical air. "Well, I *am*."

"Okay, smartass," Luke retorted. "How come you're protected too?"

"Fine. Let's start from the top." Jericho looked directly at his cousin. "What do you know about Challenger himself?"

The question caused Luke to roll his eyes, which wasn't surprising. This had been referenced in every TV quiz show since the early 1990s. "The space shuttle that blew up in the eighties, duh. Nobody knows who the guy was, but he got powers jes' in time to save everyone on board. First superhero ever. Died about nine, ten years ago after bein' in a coma for a few years. Did I miss anythin'?"

Jericho shrugged. "Nothing much. Except, well, everything important. Such as the fact that as soon as word got out about his powers, every news outlet and foreign government started digging *hard* to find out who he really was. Or she, even. We still don't know if it was a guy or a girl behind those force fields. There *were* two women on board, after all." The force fields in question had been an opaque red and gold in color and could be shaped in a great many ways, including as a knightly suit of armor. What they were *really* good at was concealing Challenger's identity.

"So how come nobody figured it out straight away?" asked Luke. "I mean, if I was the bad guys, I'd'a counted the folks left behind in the crew an' worked out who it was from that."

It was a smart question, but Jericho had never thought Luke to be an idiot. Smartass, yes; idiot, no. "The guy in charge on the day was on the ball. He told base security to get everyone involved into his office before anyone could start counting heads and was on the line to the FBI in another thirty seconds. All the spectators got kicked off site and Canaveral was locked down *hard*. It didn't get unlocked until they had everyone up to and including the National Guard on watch outside the place. In the meantime, the feds were rounding up the families and putting them in protective custody." Jericho wondered briefly what the families of the crew must have thought, given that the federal agents wouldn't have had much time to explain matters—even if they knew what was going on. "By the time word did get out, it was too late for anyone on the outside to do anything about it. Of course, that was only a stopgap. Within the day, the newspapers were publicly offering serious money to anyone who could give up Challenger's real identity. I mean, it was the scoop of the century. Nobody cracked, but I bet some of them were pretty tempted."

"An' that's when they come up with the Challenger Act, yeah?" Luke leaned back with a self-satisfied air. "Told the reporters to go git fucked." His attitude suggested that he'd gladly do *that* all day long.

"It wasn't *quite* as simple as that." Jericho had read up on it from sheer personal interest. "They had to hold an emergency sitting of Congress, but it helped that there were already laws in place that they could base it on. Title eighteen US Code, uh, section seven nine something or other. Basically, it's the bit about keeping defense information out of the hands of foreign governments."

Luke frowned. "Okay, I git that you don't want every asshole out there knowin' who you are under the mask, but how'd they make it about national defense? Ain't that a bit of a stretch?"

"You're forgetting one important fact." Jericho held up a finger. "Challenger was the *only* Enabled on Earth right then. The whole idea was so new, they weren't even *using* the term 'Enabled' until later. They didn't know how it'd happened, and they didn't know if it was going to happen again. So Challenger—let's call him 'him' for the moment—was about the most important guy in America. They declared him a national asset whose function would be impaired if his identity was ever revealed. This made even *trying* to find out who he was, or trying to tell someone else if you already knew, into flat-out treason—which meant jail time, at the least. Even *failing* would put you in the shit. But if you succeeded, and if he died because of it, that was the death penalty, right there." He grinned at Luke's slightly stunned expression. "And yeah, that made the newspapers back *right* the hell off."

"No goddamn surprise, there." Luke paused. "Still, there's gotta be more to it than that." He looked searchingly at Jericho. "'Cause that still don't explain why *you're* covered."

"True," Jericho conceded. "That wasn't the end of it. Turns out there were a lot of people with a vested interest in finding out who Challenger really was, so they went to the Supreme Court and tried to have the Act overturned."

"Wait, what the hell?" Luke sounded almost offended. This was almost amusing, given his nonchalant attitude toward the law. Especially where it came to minor things such as speed limits and the dealing of mild narcotics. "They can *do* that? I always thought once a law was set, you hadda follow it, no matter what."

"Not exactly." Jericho shrugged. "I mean, you've gotta follow it, but you can always challenge it if you think it's unconstitutional. The papers were basically claiming that the Act went against the First Amendment. But about the same time as they started getting into their stride, the news broke that there were other Enabled out there. Challenger wasn't the only one anymore. More importantly, he *was* the only one currently covered by the Act, so the others were basically fair game. The news organizations that had been backing the court case pulled their money out, and it fizzled. There were some folks who wanted to keep it going but without the big guns backing them, they were shit out of luck."

"But that still leaves you out in the cold, right?" protested Luke. "You independent guys was right back where y'all started."

"That's the way it was for a while, yeah," agreed Jericho. "For the most part, it was okay. People really only had to make sure they didn't drop any hints about their private lives to a reporter. But it turned out that some of the folks who were involved in the first case hadn't given up. They didn't give a shit about the First Amendment; they just didn't like that there were people out there who were different from them that they couldn't beat up or push around."

"Ah, right." A look of enlightenment spread over Luke's features. "*That* sorta people."

"Yup." Jericho nodded. "That sort of people. And they really didn't like it when the Enabled had powers and they didn't, 'specially when the Enabled could hide who they were to protect themselves while they were off the clock. So, a whole bunch of people formed an activist group called Unmask, trying to pressure heroes into revealing their identities and to smear the names of the ones that didn't play along. A few Enabled got mobbed and beaten up. Others were framed for crimes, or worse. Like what happened to Surgeon One." He looked at Luke expectantly.

Luke's return expression wasn't promising. "Sorry, cuz. Never heard of him. They kill him?"

"Not … as such, no. And he was a she." Jericho tried again. "You've heard of Mutilator and Devastator, right?" He was certain those names would get a hit.

There'd only been two terror villains who had consistently teamed up with one another, after all.

"Uh, yeah." Now Luke's tone said *duh* in all but actuality. "Did *they* kill her?"

Jericho shook his head. "No. See, Surgeon One was a hero who did surgery on a level no other doctor could match. She was arrogant as hell, but she could pull off operations that were impossible by any normal standard, so they tolerated her. The story goes that she wanted to call herself 'Surgeon General' but the government pulled the plug on that, so she ended up going with 'Surgeon One'. The trouble was, she got way too cocky. Her skills made her a millionaire before she turned twenty, but she couldn't be bothered trying to conceal who she was to her friends. Probably because she thought her fame and money would get her out of anything."

From the look on his face, Luke could see where this was going. "I'm guessin' it didn't."

"Nope. Some fringe elements of Unmask got hold of her family and blackmailed her into committing atrocities with her skills. Nobody's sure if she just decided she liked it, or if she snapped. Either way, she did what they told her, then added her own flourishes. Her family got out of it okay, but when the footage of her willingly rebuilding people into monstrosities got out into the public—because of course Unmask videotaped the whole thing—she ended up as a social pariah. She was investigated for the crimes she'd been 'forced' to commit, her accounts were frozen, and all her surgical work dried up. She lost everything. If she hadn't snapped before, she did then. When she went villain and became Mutilator, Unmask was over the moon. She'd 'proven' their point in a big way."

"With a gun to her head," Luke pointed out. "Surely they took that into account."

Jericho shrugged lightly. "The footage of her doing the surgery is … disturbing. It really looks like she's enjoying herself way too much. Anyway, she ended up as a cautionary tale for everyone else. Unmask stopped being a joke, and everyone started taking them real serious. They started sharing tips on who was harassing them, who was likely to get pictures or try to follow them home, and things like that."

Luke shook his head. "Sum*bitch*. I thought Grandmama's stories about the sixties were bad."

"They *were* bad," Jericho corrected him. "You guys had it worse than we ever did. All we had were a few edge cases like that. And they were over and done before I ever got powers. It just got very … *intense* .. for a while." He paused, trying to remember where he was up to. "Anyway, after Mutilator stopped being news, Unmask must've figured they were losing ground, so they got their patsies to start another court case to try to force unaffiliated heroes to show their faces. It was supposed to be all about accountability and transparency. Of course, it was obvious to anyone with half a brain that what it was *really* about was control. Some people just don't like *not* holding all the aces."

Luke snorted in derision. "Meanwhile, villains got to keep their masks, yeah? *That's* goddamn fair."

Which only paralleled Jericho's thoughts on the matter. "Yeah, but they didn't want to push the issue with *actual* villains, who might push back with lethal force. Anyway, as far as they were concerned, everyone with a mask was a potential criminal. If it'd gone through, I'd be breaking the law every time I mask up." Jericho shook his head. "In the end, the Supreme Court found in favor of maintaining secret identities. To make it harder for anyone to duplicate what happened with Surgeon One, they even amended the Challenger Act to include independent Enabled like me. You know, folks who were just trying to do the right thing without any government backing." His expression soured. "Of course, that wasn't the end of it *either*."

"It wasn't?" Luke was starting to look a little shell-shocked. "How much *more* of this shit did y'all have to go through? And how come I never heard nothin' about it afore now?"

"This all happened back in the eighties and nineties, remember?" Jericho spread his hands. "We were *kids*. I only know about it because I went looking. I can recommend a couple of books on the subject, if you want. Anyway, the *third* court case wasn't about the newspapers or the activists. This time it was big business, trying to walk back the amendment. They dressed it up in a lot of legalese, but they were basically trying to get privileged access to the secret identities of non-government heroes so they could cash in on us. Or so they said. Personally, I'm pretty sure it was worse than that."

Luke shook his head. "Every time I reckon you're about done surprisin' me, you say somethin' like that. What the hell's worse than *that?*"

Pensively, Jericho rolled his head on his neck. "I got no proof for any of this, but some of those businessmen were rumored to have a lot of money sunk into foreign interests. China, Russia, places like that. Or maybe the foreign interests had a lot of money sunk into *them*. Suppose these foreign interests were bankrolling the guys behind the court case?"

It didn't take Luke any time at all to get the gist of what Jericho was saying. "Holy shit, cuz," he breathed. "You're talkin' about actual motherfuckin' *spies* fixin' ta git access to *our* superheroes' secret identities."

If the matter hadn't been so potentially serious, the injured national pride in Luke's voice would've made Jericho smile. "Well, like I said, I got no proof, but it pretty well lines up with all the facts. Sometimes I wonder just what they had on these guys. Was it only money involved, or were there favors being done under the table? What does it take to convince someone to betray their superheroes—their *country*—like that?" He'd heard it said that every man had his price but to him, trust was sacred. If a body didn't have that, he had nothing.

"Cock*suckers*," growled Luke, his fists clenching on the table before him. "I hope they got their asses kicked for tryin'." Unsurprisingly, he held a dim view of big business. Especially when it came to the bigger corporations where (as Jericho had once heard him put it) old white guys did their best to screw everyone else over for shits and giggles. Throwing foreign spies into the deal merely made it worse.

"Pretty much." Jericho didn't feel the satisfaction he normally would have, because he knew what was coming next. "That case lasted through to 'ninety-seven, right up until all that shit came down, and the Minotaur destroyed Inspire."

7
Minotaur

He didn't have to explain the reference. It had made international news, back in the day. Formed in 1988 by the heroes Arfogwyr and Challenger, Inspire had been the world's first official superhero team, though they'd only really come into their own when they later recruited Castellan.

The trio of artificer, dynamic and prodigy, working in concert, had been the first to demonstrate how the three powersets could become far more than the sum of their individual capabilities. From their example had come the term 'Inspire team', informing the creation of virtually every other superhero team in the world.

The Minotaur … was something else altogether. Despite the villain being dead and gone for sixteen years and counting, that name still had the capacity to inspire revulsion. Even Doc Iridium, infamous in his own right, had only managed to eclipse his fellow terror villain's reputation when he accidentally perpetrated the Manhattan catastrophe.

Standing a good eight feet tall in the bronze-colored power armor built to resemble his namesake, the Minotaur had specialized in a particularly horrific method of serial killing. Kidnapping his victims almost at random, he would drop them into a pre-constructed maze replete with death-traps, then televise their gruesome deaths live to the world. These victims had ranged from children snatched off the street to celebrities and government officials. Friends and loved ones of the victims could phone in and pledge ransoms to save their lives. Sometimes the Minotaur accepted the ransoms, and sometimes he didn't. Occasionally, he even spared a life. Most times, he just took the money. Anyone making it to the exit of the maze had to get past him. None ever had.

His first truly high-profile target was the family of the US Attorney General, along with the families of several of the AG's subordinates within the Criminal Division of the Department of Justice. The victims were taken in late 1990, in retaliation for the capture and ongoing trial of the terror villain known as Charnel. Even while all possible legal avenues were being explored to get them back, the inhuman Charnel was broken out of maximum-security holding by its fellow terror villains; in retrospect, it became clear that the hostage situation had never been anything more than a distraction. Once the breakout was accomplished, the Minotaur blew up the maze and killed all his hostages, simply because he could.

No significant action was taken by the government in response to this, which Jericho considered to be an unconscionable betrayal of men and women who had merely been trying to do their jobs. Apparently, the families of career civil servants weren't seen as all that important in the grand scheme of things. There was a rash of resignations and replacements, and life went on. But in a very real way, this episode had been a ranging shot, and the true attack was yet to come.

The government's hands-off attitude changed dramatically in January 1997. During the previous year, while on the campaign trail, the man who would become Vice-President had made comments about terror villains. The Minotaur attacked his motorcade on the twenty-fifth, not long after the inauguration. Jericho didn't know how many Secret Service agents died trying to protect the VP from the terror villain, but it hadn't been enough. Three days later, the Vice President showed up in the Minotaur's latest murder maze.

The response was immediate; ignoring an undercurrent of calls to 'never negotiate with terrorists', the White House pledged a staggering amount of money to have him returned safe and well. The money vanished, but the VP's horrific death was broadcast live from coast to coast, mere hours later. This precipitated the instigation of meticulously laid-out action plans intended to deal with terror villains in general and the Minotaur in particular. The overall consensus was that it was about damn time.

The 'War on Terror Villains' went into high gear when the terror villain Carnifex surfaced in Texas in late February. While there was no evidence that the feral mass-murderer shared any responsibility for the Vice President's death, he still had a triple-digit body count and was thus deemed an acceptable target. The ensuing manhunt went on for ten days and covered half the state, culminating in a hail of gunfire in a Dallas shopping mall on March the seventh. Twenty-three bystanders and law enforcement officers died along with Carnifex, either caught in the crossfire or shredded by the terror villain's final berserk rage. The nation mourned the death toll, but at the same time celebrated the event as a win for the forces of law and order.

It was perhaps a case of hindsight being twenty-twenty, but Jericho wasn't the least bit surprised that the terror villains had retaliated in kind. The Minotaur waited, as patiently as a cat at a mousehole, for precisely one week before he crashed a briefing of the President's chiefs of staff being held in the White House Situation Room. Nobody knew how he got inside the secure building, and pursuit proved suicidally dangerous, but he left behind seven corpses; one of these was the President.

The newly minted Vice President barely had time to realize he'd been promoted in the most brutal way possible before the surviving Secret Service agents activated their worst-case contingency plan and whisked him away. As the order went out to spool up the engines of Air Force One, he was sequestered in the ultra-secure Presidential bunker deep beneath the White House, surrounded by his personal security detail. As soon as the plane was ready for takeoff, Marine One plus four decoy choppers would make the flight from the White House roof to the airfield. This was to be treated as no less an emergency than an imminent nuclear attack. In the meantime, the next in line to be Vice President was flown to Camp David to be sworn in. While the brand-new President-to-be waited, he had himself sworn in by remote video link and dictated a statement to be aired immediately: "The United States does not bow to terrorism, foreign or domestic. We will stand firm."

But when the agents went to collect the President and his personal detail, they found one agent missing and everyone else shot to death from close range. A bloodstained note pinned to the President's chest with a large knife read, 'We can do this all day,' and was signed 'False Flag'. The shape-changing terror villain had clearly infiltrated the security detail days before, coordinating his actions with the Minotaur's to engender the absolute maximum chaos from the situation.

The Vice President (now President, via a last-minute amendment to the swearing-in ceremony) barely hesitated once he was briefed-in on the situation. Within twelve hours, at a hastily convened press conference, he rescinded the Executive Order implementing the War on Terror Villains. Some called him cowardly, but these were in the minority. Most decided that it was the only smart move. A tense twenty-four hours followed, but no more attacks took place over that time. The man who would've been next in line to become Vice President quietly resigned, while his deputy stepped up and took his place, and made history as the first woman to hold that office.

The nation, its psyche bruised and battered by the hits, took a breath and tried to pretend that survival equaled victory in this case. This willful self-delusion lasted for another four months, until the destruction of Inspire gave them one hell of a wake-up call.

"Yeah, I heard *something* about that," Luke confirmed. "I'm guessin' you know more details than me, though."

"It isn't pretty," Jericho warned him. "I dunno if the underworld decided that him killing two Presidents and a Vice President was going too far, or if Castellan had been developing his informant network all this time, but around then people started dropping hints about where his murder mazes could be found. Inspire kicked its efforts into high gear, crashing them and saving as many people as they could. When they hit the first one, they got half the people out; with the second one, they saved all but a few. For the third one, they disabled the booby-traps and rescued everyone with time to spare, and only missed capturing the Minotaur by a matter of minutes. Everyone thought they had him on the run, and I guess they did. But then he found out who Arfogwyr was."

"Wait, wait," Luke protested. "Ar-vog-who?"

"Arfogwyr," Jericho repeated, carefully ignoring the fact that it had taken him a while to get the pronunciation right himself. "It's apparently Welsh for 'armor'. She was Inspire's artificer. Anyway, the Minotaur found out her real identity—"

"Artificer?" Luke frowned. "That's like a 'cog', right? Them's the ones that build the super high-tech shit? Force field belts and jetpacks?"

"Will you goddamn quit *interrupting?*" Jericho shook his head. "I swear, you're worse than Stephen. And *yes*, an artificer is *exactly* the same as a cog. Except 'cog' is a stupid shorthand name made up by the papers. 'Artificer' is the *official* term."

With a sinking feeling, Jericho watched a very familiar shit-eating grin spread across Luke's face. "Well, it might be to you, cuz, but there's a lot more of us than you, an' we all call 'em cogs."

Jericho's G-sense nudged him, but he didn't let his expression change. "It doesn't matter. I'm Enabled, and I say it's 'artificer'."

Luke snorted. "Yeah, like that gives you th' right ta tell us what ta call things."

"Well, true." Jericho shrugged elaborately, then leaned forward and glanced out the window to draw Luke's attention in that direction. "Oh, and just by the way? We're moving." *Payback in three, two, one ...*

As Luke stared past Jericho at the scenery which was now blurring past the window, his face paled slightly. "Jesus shit, how fast are we *goin'*?"

His reaction was understandable. There'd been exactly zero sensation of acceleration, at least to normal human senses, though Jericho's powers had filled him in the moment they started moving. He'd given the train car a few seconds to build up to a reasonable level of speed before alerting Luke to the fact, for the sheer satisfaction of seeing the look on his cousin's face.

In those few seconds, the car's velocity had already passed a hundred miles per hour, with no sign of reduction in its rate of acceleration. As Jericho leaned back against the seat, there were still no G-forces to be felt. However, unlike Luke, he knew why, if not exactly how. "Right now, we're pulling two gees. Increasing our speed by forty miles per hour, every second."

"An' why the *hell* are we not squashed flat against these friggin' seats?" Luke demanded, still looking slightly unsettled.

Jericho made a careless gesture. "This thing's got gravity generators that redirect felt acceleration. All the forces that should be throwing us around are adjusted so it's just one gee, straight down."

"How do you know that?" Luke frowned at him suspiciously. "An' how the hell does that even *work?*"

Jericho grinned back at him, enjoying the feeling of being out in front of his cousin for once. "Gravity powers, remember? The tech they're using plays right into that. I'm not even going to try to interfere with it, but I can see what it's doing. I can also feel our acceleration and our speed. As for the mechanics, damned if I know."

So smooth was the maglev ride, he doubted a cup of water would even show a ripple. Deeper within, he could feel the artificial gravity field affecting the train; or rather, *fields.* Two of them, separate but complementary. As he'd told Luke, he was unwilling to attempt influencing them in any way, but he could certainly sense them shifting and working to carry out their respective functions.

The first was generated from within the train and seemed to be aimed at ensuring the comfort of the passengers, adjusting all outward forces to (as he'd put it) one gee, straight down. The other was apparently generated by the rail itself and augmented the magnetic lifting force to keep the train on track, as it were.

Leaning back against the window, he looked out at the streets flashing by, twenty-something yards below the maglev car. Already, they were getting close to the city limits. "But I *can* tell you that right now we're clocking about four hundred forty miles per hour." The last of the buildings whipped by and they were in the clear. Deciding to yank Luke's chain a little, Jericho casually pointed out the window. "And so's the train we're joining up with."

Luke's head whipped around so fast that Jericho worried for his neck. "Fuck me sideways. That thing's movin' pretty damn fast too. Are we gonna hit it? It looks like we're gonna hit it."

At first glance, he did have a certain amount of reason for concern. The three-car train Jericho had indicated was traveling toward them on a converging course along a broad cylindrical rail that shone in the sun, identical to the one their own passenger car was riding on. He took a moment to admire the design. As he'd already noted, the front end of each car was aerodynamically curved while the rear was concave, with the upper deck noticeably displaced backward. This, it now became clear, allowed the maglev cars to join together with a minimum of fuss to form a single interconnected entity. He couldn't read the speed by eye, and his powers didn't reach that far, so it was only an educated guess that it was matching them in speed.

However, UML had an unprecedented safety record; since the company's inception, not one of their trains had ever suffered an accident. There *had* been two cases of domestic terrorism where explosives were used to damage a section of rail, but in both situations the safety mechanisms had activated, preventing any casualties. Force Majeure had deployed in force, so to speak, on each occasion, bringing down the attempted saboteurs with extreme prejudice. Not much had been left for the cops to do, or even arrest.

Jericho pointed at the other train. "See how the rail curves? I figure our rail's gonna meet up with it. We'll just get out in front and slot into place."

He felt comfortable in saying this; while a little light on detail, the UML webpage had provided quite a bit of information about how the maglev system operated. Each maglev car was semi-autonomous in operation, attaching to the front of a train when leaving a station and dropping off the back end when splitting off to join another train or stopping at their destination. 'Train', in this instance, simply meant 'bunch of passenger cars all going in the same direction'. In a very real way, it was like an enormous, intricate, never-ending game of musical chairs being played out all over America, giving every passenger an express ride to his or her destination.

Luke didn't look overly comforted. "But what if—" A slight jolt, accompanied by a solid *clunk,* interrupted him. "What the shit?" Leaning over, he stared out the window. "What the hell was *that?*"

Looking up toward the nearest digital sign, Jericho saw that it now showed 'ATLANTA', with the timer reading '29:30' and a large '1' in a square box. As he watched, the seconds began counting down. He nodded toward the sign. "That was us connecting on to the front of the train, like I said." He let a snarky note come into his voice. "Try to keep up, will you?"

Almost on cue, the connecting doors next to Luke opened and half a dozen people wandered through, looking for places to sit. About the same number of people already in the passenger car got up and headed through the connecting door, toward the back of the train. *They must be getting off in Atlanta.*

Wearing a rather dubious expression, Luke leaned into the aisle and looked between the connecting doors before they closed, as if to verify there really was a train back there. Not that there was anywhere else the people could have come from. "Right, now we got that settled," he muttered as he sat down again, his face just a little pale. "Not exactly what I friggin' expected."

"You didn't really have to come along, you know," Jericho told him, feeling somewhat amused. "Wait'll I tell Livy how the great Luke Hansen is scared of a little speed." It was made all the funnier by the fact that Luke had spent a great deal of his teenage years competing in illegal drag races.

At the mention of his wife's nickname, Luke gave Jericho an extremely filthy look; it seemed that he was recovering fast. "Low friggin' blow, cuz. She won as many races as I did. She wouldn't *never* let me forget it."

"Yeah, but it'd be funny as all hell," Jericho countered. His grin widened as he envisaged the expression on Olivia's face. She had a lively sense of humor, skin a couple shades darker than Luke's, and long gorgeous hair. "Figure she'd let it go around Christmas. Year after next."

"Funny man." Luke turned his head to watch as two more people entered their car and found places to sit. "So, I got me a question. Every stop we go by, we lose a car an' gain a car, yeah?"

Jericho slid around in his seat until his head was resting against the window, then hooked his left ankle over his right knee. "There's a little more to it than that, but that's basically the situation, yeah. Why?"

Luke made a motion as if he were counting on his fingers. "So, happen ya git on the train in Miami, by the time ya git off in Seattle, there ain't no cars left from the train that ya started with. Which means all the way through the trip, you're movin' from car to car jes' so's you can stay on the damn train. Any way a body could git around that?"

Jericho shook his head, amused. "Nope. There's this one comedian, Jerry or Gary someone, who does a routine about it. He calls it 'Walking from New York to LA'. It's pretty good." He'd seen the guy's show a few times, though he couldn't remember his name. Now that he was actually *on* the maglev, the skit seemed even funnier. "It's just the way the system works."

"Goddamn hilarious." Luke's tone was sour. "So what were we talkin' about, anyway?"

Jericho frowned, trying to remember. There'd been so many new experiences in the last ten minutes that he wasn't quite sure anymore. "Okay, the train started off and freaked you out ... okay, before that, we were talking about powers ... oh, yeah. Artificers. Arfogwyr, in particular."

"I still say more of us call 'em cogs." Luke's smirk was back in full force.

Jericho ground his teeth and let out an aggravated sigh. "Whatever floats your boat. *Anyway,* she built the base that Inspire used. I saw a picture of it, over in Seattle. It was like a castle, all in silver and white. They called it Caerwyn, which apparently means 'white castle' in Welsh or something. She also outfitted Castellan with his power armor and sword when he joined." The armor hadn't been anything special so far as that sort of thing went; all it did was afford Castellan a certain amount of protection and strength. But then, that was all the veteran hero had ever needed.

"Castellan … that sword of his could cut through anythin', right?" Luke squinted in recollection. "I 'member seein' a TV spot on him, from back in the day. He cut clear through an I-beam with it. The edges were *glowing,* after. Scary shit, right there." He scratched his head. "Did he even *have* powers?"

"Well, *yes.*" Jericho wondered why he even had to explain this. Didn't everyone know this sort of thing? "Castellan was a prodigy. That *was* his power."

"Prodigy?" Luke looked slightly lost for a second, then his face cleared. "Wait a minute. Is that what folks call—"

"Being a prodigy tunes you up to the absolute peak of human capability and a little bit beyond," Jericho interjected hurriedly. "You know, the Olympic-level, brooding-on-rooftops, hyper-competent, midnight avenger type? That's what they call a prodigy." He snorted derisively. "Took 'em 'til about 'ninety, 'ninety-one to figure out that it was a friggin' powerset in its own right." *With any luck, Luke'll leave the subject alone now.* But even as the thought crossed his mind, he knew it wasn't going to happen.

"Yeah, I *thought* so," Luke said triumphantly. "'Prodigy' is just a prettified name for what us normal folks call a 'cowl', right?" He glanced speculatively at Jericho. "You've got that, don't ya? There was that one time you went a week straight on about four hours of sleep."

Startled, Jericho stared back at him. "Have you been stalking me?" He remembered the episode. He'd had more sleep than Luke seemed to think, and afterward he'd slept for a solid day, but staying awake had been *easy* for him. While his Prodigy rating wasn't huge, it was useful as hell on stakeouts.

"Keepin' an eye on you, cuz. There's a difference." The grin on Luke's face widened. "So, what's that one we'uns call 'capes'?" In an irritating tone that was pure *Luke,* he added, "You know, the ones who can fly an' shoot lasers from their nostrils an' stuff? Your name for it starts with 'dy' and ends in 'namic', yeah?"

Jericho already had his mouth open to enlighten his cousin when the penny dropped. *You sonovabitch. You've been playing me all along.* "How much *do* you know about this stuff?"

Luke gave him an elaborate shrug. "When my favorite cuz decided to become Enabled, I figgered it was my job ta find out as much as I could."

"So what the hell was this whole conversation about, if you already knew what I was talking about?" demanded Jericho, ignoring the reference to 'deciding to become Enabled'. That bit was so wrong he didn't even know where to begin. "Have you just been wasting my time on purpose?"

"Well, sho'nuff." Luke didn't even try to deny it. "You're still all twisted up inside about Steve, so I figgered ta distract ya. It worked, didn't it?"

"Yeah, well," grumbled Jericho. "Even though some of us would *still* like to see those terms die in a fire." He knew he was being a purist but dammit, the simplistic nicknames demeaned the entire rating system and made people think less of Enabled. Quite apart from being unnecessarily alliterative.

"Yeah, yeah." Luke was definitely having fun now. This was, as far as Jericho could tell, what he lived for. "I can see that. Why use a short word when a long one'll make it sound a shitload classier?" Luke's grin widened to the point where it was blatantly obvious he was doing his best to wind Jericho up. "So, do capes really wear capes? And what about spandex? Some of them costumes I seen on TV … well, they don't leave much to the friggin' imagination, is all I'm sayin'."

Jericho rolled his eyes, relieved to be on stable footing once more. "Spandex is for losers, posers and fetishists. And don't get me started on capes. If you're gonna wear a costume, wear something that's not gonna get in the way in a fight." Spandex and capes were both topics rife with the possibility of inciting flamewars on various online boards and had done exactly that many times over. He had no doubt that this trend would continue for as long as there were Enabled—and people who thought they knew more about Enabled than the Enabled did—on message boards.

"Y'know, Relentless wears a cape." Luke's smirk was in full shit-stirring mode now. "So do Lady Quantum an' the Technologist, an' Tourbillon's robes are prob'ly worse'n wearin' a cape. Fact bein', th' only ones who don't wear anythin' like a cape are Independence, Silent Knight an' Transit. Less than half th' team. Ya gonna tell *them* that it ain't a good idea while they're interviewin' you?"

"Screw you," Jericho retorted without heat. "They're *Force Majeure*. If they want to wear capes, they've earned it. It's the idiots who wear 'em to look cool that I'm talking about."

"Yeah, well." Luke, mercifully, seemed willing to leave that subject alone. "Anyway, ya said somethin' about how the Minotaur figgered out who Ar … Arvog … fuck it, who she really was. Their *artificer*," he corrected himself, apparently just to be contrary.

"Wait, you know about the other stuff, but you don't know about this?" Jericho looked askance at his cousin. "I thought you'd been looking this sort of thing up?"

"I looked up the stuff about what *you're* goin' through, cuz," Luke corrected him. "Not about the rest of it. An' I'm kinda curious. So what happened? He kill her?"

Jericho sighed. "By all accounts, she put up a fight, but she was out of costume and he didn't care about collateral damage. So yeah, he killed her, just like that." Raising his hand, he snapped his fingers. "And when he left, he took her head and her hand."

"Why'd he … oh, right." Luke winced. "To git past security, right?" The idea seemed to make him as queasy as Jericho himself felt about it. The most direct way of defeating a biometrically coded system was also the messiest. The card in his wallet didn't seem quite so cool now.

"Got it in one." This story didn't really have a happy ending, but Jericho forged on anyway. "He went straight to Caerwyn and used Arfogwyr's hand and eye to get in. Challenger was there, but the Minotaur didn't go after him immediately. He snuck around for a bit first, planting explosives." Jericho paused, suddenly pensive. "You know, I can't help wondering if he had some sort of knack for architecture. He built mazes and death-traps out of basically nothing and made them work, and he managed to bring down Caerwyn with only a few demolition charges."

"Well, it don't matter now, 'cause the asshole's dead," Luke pointed out pragmatically. "What happened then?"

"About what you'd expect," Jericho said unhappily. "The Minotaur had the element of surprise on his side. He went on the attack and got in one good hit before Challenger managed to raise his force field. After that, he couldn't hurt Challenger, but Challenger couldn't score a good hit on him either. And Challenger would've been bleeding pretty badly, so all the Minotaur had to do was wait him out."

"Bleeding?" This got a frown from Luke. "What the hell'd Minotaur hit him with?"

Jericho looked questioningly at him. "You ever hear about the Blood Rose? No?"

He was less surprised than he should've been when Luke shook his head. It seemed most people were more interested in today's heroes than yesterday's villains.

"Not so's you'd notice," Luke admitted. "I'm guessin' it ain't jes' some kinda flower. Some kinda Artificer weapon, like Castellan's sword?"

"That's pretty much exactly what it was," Jericho confirmed. "From what I've read and the pictures I've seen, it was a stabbing spear with a short handle and a thick blade. The blade was made of some kind of deep red metal, but that wasn't the scary thing. The scary thing was that what looked like the blade was in reality hundreds of smaller blades, all packed together in the shape of a larger blade. When he slashed someone with it, the blades opened up and delivered dozens of cuts, all as deep and nasty as the original one would've been. And when he stabbed someone, they flared out like flower petals and *spun*."

"Jesus wept," Luke said after a moment of horrified silence. "That's goddamn ... who even *makes* somethin' like that?"

"Maybe the Minotaur, maybe someone else?" Jericho shrugged. "I have no idea. But he only slashed Challenger with it, which was a small mercy. If he'd stabbed him instead, Challenger would've died then and there. There's rumors about people who survived being stabbed with the Blood Rose but if that's true, I dunno who they are. Anyway, Challenger couldn't bring the Minotaur down, but he did manage to send out a distress signal. I'm not totally sure about the timeline after that, but Castellan's on record as having arrived on site just after the explosives went off. The Minotaur had already left, and Caerwyn was reduced to rubble, but Challenger was still barely alive. He had the slash from the Blood Rose and injuries from the roof falling in on him, so he was in a pretty bad way."

"Which is what put him in the coma in the first place," guessed Luke, accurately. "He never woke up, did he?"

"No, he did not." Jericho took a deep breath. "There's not much to it after that. Castellan got Challenger to the hospital, then headed out after the Minotaur. Now, Castellan's a high-end prodigy, so he's about the best there is when it comes to kicking ass one-on-one. The Minotaur no doubt knew this, so he went and hid in the middle of his latest goddamn murder maze. The place was lousy with death-traps, but Castellan carved his way through them like they were nothing."

"Okay, that's a bit hard to believe," Luke said. "I mean, I heard he's good, but he's jes' one man, y'know? That sounds like somethin' out of a movie. All it'd take is one wrong move an' he's dead, an' there ain't no retakes."

"That's what separates prodigies from everyone else," Jericho said patiently. "Every prodigy has a bone-deep certainty that they—we—should be doing things a certain way, aiming for a certain result. Our powersets and specialties are optimized to make life easier for us when we're following that. This gives us what some people on the boards call 'focus' and others call the 'sweet spot'. We might not always know we have it, but it's there. If we're doing what our focus makes us good at, if it hits the sweet spot of our powerset, we take a whole lot of stopping. If we try to go against it, we're even worse off than an average guy without powers. And if someone else does something bad that goes directly against our focus, we take it really personally."

"Yeah?" Luke eyed him curiously. "What's yours?"

"Trust," Jericho's voice was blunt. "Trust and loyalty. Once my word's given, I stick to it. My powers literally enforce it."

"Well, duh." Luke shook his head. "You always been a straight arrow, cuz." He grinned slyly. "So ta speak."

Jericho rolled his eyes at the terrible joke. "Asshat."

"Yeah, well." Luke didn't deny it. "What happens if folks you trust screw ya over? You lose your powers or somethin'?"

"Nothing as drastic as that," Jericho assured him. "It just hurts a lot. And when I say 'a lot', I mean a *lot*." He thumped his fist against his chest. "In here."

"Shit." Luke looked stricken. "So, all of them times I bullshitted about stuff to ya …"

"Didn't do a goddamn thing." Jericho chuckled at the look on his cousin's face. "You forget, I *know* you. You've been shading the truth since you were in short pants. I don't care about you making shit up. I just trust you not to lie about anything that might hurt me."

Luke seemed to consider that. "Right. Fair'nuff. So, what-all happened with Castellan goin' after th' Minotaur?"

Jericho nodded. "Well, like I said, he made it through the maze. I'm not saying he didn't take a hit or three on the way, but he got through to the Minotaur more or less in one piece."

"An' kicked his ass?" asked Luke, who'd apparently seen the way this was going.

"Pretty much," agreed Jericho. "One on one, fresh off the mark, he would've wiped the floor with the Minotaur any day of the week. This was why the asshat put all those death-traps between them. He was scared shitless of Castellan. Which, you know, just about anyone would be. Anyway, Castellan was injured and his armor was damaged, but he still put the hurt on the Minotaur."

Luke frowned. "You're talkin' like it wasn't all cut and dry."

"Well, no. He handed the Minotaur a beating, but the Minotaur got a lucky shot on Castellan's right arm with the Blood Rose. Castellan dropped his sword and the Minotaur stomped on it. Broke the hilt."

"Shit, what'd he do then?" Luke was leaning forward, waiting to hear what happened next.

Jericho chuckled. "What he did then was stone-cold pure badass. He lured the Minotaur in, then—with his off hand, mind you—disarmed him. Took the Blood Rose away from him like taking a toy away from a kid. Then he went straight through the Minotaur's guard and stabbed *him* with it. Gave him a taste of his own medicine."

"Ouch." Luke winced in sympathy. "That musta hurt, in more ways than one." A moment later, he frowned. "Wait a minute. How do ya know that's exactly what Castellan done? I mean, the guy prob'ly told a good story an' all, but how do we know that's how it went down?"

Jericho leaned back in his seat. "The Minotaur was the kind of asshat who always used to put cameras in his mazes, so folks would have to watch their loved ones die. He must've expected to beat Castellan, too. Didn't quite turn out the way he expected. His suit had a full-coverage mask so you can't see his face on the footage, but I bet his expression was priceless."

Luke snorted. "Sucked to be him, then. Asshole."

"Yup." Jericho nodded. "The footage stops about then though, because the *other* thing the Minotaur always put in his mazes was demolition charges. Him getting stabbed must've tripped a failsafe, because the maze started to fall in. Castellan's armor was in pieces, his sword was busted, and he was more dead than alive from the injuries he'd taken from the death-traps and the fight. But he got out of there, because prodigies just don't goddamn give up. About five minutes after he got outside, the whole thing collapsed into the ocean. Castellan survived, but … well, Inspire was done. He retired a few weeks later, once he was healed up enough to check himself out of the hospital. Challenger went into long-term care, with everyone around him sworn to secrecy about who he really was. He died a few years later. There's a gravestone in Arlington with his name on it, but I'm pretty sure nobody's buried there. Who he actually *was* is still a national secret."

Luke shook his head in confusion. "Wait a sec. Ya jes' said Castellan was more dead than alive, but a few weeks later he walked outta th' hospital? Who *does* that?"

"Prodigies," Jericho explained succinctly. "We pick up skills fast, we can push ourselves way past normal human limits, and we pretty well get over anything that doesn't kill us straight off the bat. It's basically the opposite of flashy, but you don't *ever* underestimate a prodigy."

"Right." Luke's expression was pensive. "So, they ever recover th' Minotaur's body?"

"I know what you're thinking," Jericho told him. "If you don't have a body, he's not really dead, right?" He waited for Luke to nod, then went on. "Wrong. That's Saturday morning cartoon thinking. Yeah, I know, a few heroes have come back from the dead, and so've a few villains. But they're almost exclusively prodigies, or dynamics with powers that let them fake their deaths. Castellan was asked about that, and he said he'd be worried if it was just the Blood Rose and the fight, or just the maze collapsing into the ocean and the fight … well, yeah. Any two of those factors would've given the Minotaur some wiggle room. With the fight *and* the Blood Rose *and* the fall into the ocean with a million tons of rock on top of him, even Castellan figured it simply wasn't survivable. And that's if the Minotaur *had* a Prodigy rating. If he didn't, not a hope in hell." He shrugged. "He was the sort of media whore who craved public attention. If he hasn't shown up in sixteen years, I'm guessing Castellan knew what he was talking about."

"Okay, gotcha." Luke nodded. "So that ended the court case?"

"Sure as hell," confirmed Jericho. "If someone hadn't sold Arfogwyr's real identity to the Minotaur, the whole thing never would've happened. So, they nailed the whole thing down. Government-affiliated heroes, like Force Majeure, are protected like nuclear launch codes. The rest of us, if anyone tries to out us, it's treated like domestic terrorism."

"An' what happened to th' guys pushin' th' case?" Luke had a certain glint in his eye. "Don't tell me they jes' got ta walk away."

Jericho shook his head. "Nope. Turned out the FBI had been investigating some of them for years over allegations of money-laundering and stuff for their foreign partners. When the Inspire thing happened and the case ended, they got pulled in for serious questioning. Some of them ended up doing time. There were even a couple of shady-ass property developers who had their assets seized under civil forfeiture and *then* did time."

He chuckled darkly and leaned back in his seat. "By the time the dust settled, the Challenger Act was bulletproof. *Nobody* wanted to poke that particular bear again."

8
Origin

"Okay, so you're covered." Luke accepted the history lesson and conceded the point but didn't give up the main thrust of his argument. "But supposin' you *was* outed. What do ya think your folks'd say then?"

Jericho shrugged. "Dunno. I mean, shit, I'm pretty sure they don't even know."

Luke stared at him. "Any particular reason ya haven't friggin' told 'em? Hidin' something that big from kinfolk ain't good. Why the hell didn't you tell 'em afore ya told *me?*" It wasn't anger Jericho could hear in his voice; not quite, anyway. Still, he wasn't happy. "Where the hell's your *head* at?"

Jericho took a deep breath. "I tried." Luke's expression showed disbelief. "I *did*. About a week after … yeah, after that." *After I got my powers.* Closing his eyes for a second, Jericho was back in the moment. He could feel the terror again as the wall flashed past him, the pavement coming up fast. Above him, the faces peered over the edge of the roof, their expressions half-triumphant and half-terrified. Again, he could smell the alcohol and hear the harsh voices. *Hey, fairy. Hey, can you fly? Fairies can fly, can't they?* The feeling of the hands as they grabbed him, the shocked look on Troy's face as Jericho reached desperately out toward him. The momentary sensation of weightlessness, then the sure knowledge that he was falling. Falling to his death.

But he hadn't died. Instead, he was reborn. Halfway down, when his blood was thundering in his ears so hard he thought he was going to have a heart attack before he ever hit the ground, Jericho had … slowed. Drifting gently to the ground like a leaf. Not sure what was happening, terrified out of his wits, he twisted around to land on his feet, and ran. Ran and ran and ran.

He'd been on summer break, after celebrating his twenty-first birthday at college in New York and trading his virginity off with that of a bi-curious roommate, both on the same night. Alcohol had been involved. Back in Savannah, still not having come out to his parents, he spent a week building up the courage to visit a local gay bar. His confidence deserted him just after he got in the door, and he dithered until a cute guy who'd been standing at the bar came over and introduced himself.

Troy was smart, funny and interesting, and Jericho was immediately smitten. What he *didn't* know was that there were people who went to places like that with the aim of picking up young hopefuls and luring them somewhere quiet. Once alone, the victim would be ambushed by a bunch of thugs who would then proceed to kick his ribs in or do even worse. Troy was one of the people who did the luring.

From the look on Troy's face, he hadn't known of their plans to throw Jericho off the roof once Troy talked him into going up there. Either way, Jericho wanted nothing more to do with him. He just hoped that the other man had learned an important lesson. In any case, when Jericho next encountered the group (this time in the precursor to his eventual G-Man costume), Troy wasn't with them, so maybe he had. Jericho could only hope so, anyway.

After that fateful night, it had taken him two full days to get up the nerve to test his powers. To ensure privacy, he'd told his parents he wasn't feeling well and locked himself in his room. After several hours of experimentation, he decided that he had some kind of control over gravity. While he couldn't make himself fly—which he *still* considered to be unfair in the extreme—he'd ended up with some useful abilities from his Dynamic rating.

His slow-falling ability was instinctive by nature and was on all the time unless he wanted it off. It could also be imparted to anything he touched, up to about a ton in weight. He could also make things *heavier*, but he had yet to find a good reason to apply this effect to himself.

The next aspect of his power was expressed in the G-tags. These could be stacked to become stronger, but each subsequent 'tag (of either type) had a steadily reduced effect. To his irritation, push-tags didn't work on anything that was also under the effect of his slow-fall ability, even himself.

His G-shake could end a fight before it began or alter the stability of objects in an area, but he couldn't concentrate the effect to determine the roll of a die. Objects already on a precarious balance could be made to fall or prevented from doing so. As a side effect, the G-shake also disoriented and nauseated everyone in his immediate vicinity; very useful in a fight against multiple opponents, less so for any allies.

As a crude approximation of radar, his G-sense could be applied to detect dense objects in his immediate vicinity, the larger the better. More usefully; it gifted him with an absolute sense of balance, an awareness of exactly which way was up at any given time as well as his current speed and acceleration, and a precise understanding of the mass of anything he was holding.

None of which took away from the remembered trauma of the moment. It definitely *helped*, especially after he took the step of dropping out of college. His intent right then had been to track down the people who'd nearly killed him before they could hurt anyone else; the decision to become a superhero was secondary. While his parents hadn't understood, they'd accepted his decision and his father had given him a job at the company in the same week.

He'd located and dealt with the people who'd thrown him off the roof, then spent a further two months refining his costume and starting on his martial-arts training before taking on the superhero identity of G-Man. Still, some wounds were too deep to easily heal. Every time he recalled the way Troy had turned on him after making him feel he was among friends, he felt a deep and abiding pain. What this said about his need to achieve membership with Force Majeure, he wasn't quite sure he wanted to know.

He opened his eyes, only to find himself face to face with Luke's intense brown gaze. Suddenly he felt like a kid again, with his cousin cast in the role of a disapproving adult. "I went to them a week after," he said again. "I tried to talk to them over breakfast. But I was so damn nervous that I totally screwed it up. Started and stopped a dozen times. Finally, Pa took pity on me and told me that they knew. So I left it at that."

"Okay, good, so they *do* know." Although he sounded confident with that sentence, Luke gave him a questioning look. "Why'd ya say they didn't?"

Jericho shook his head. "No. I *thought* they knew. But as I was walking out, Mama said that they'd known for years, and they supported my choices."

Slowly, Luke's head thumped back against the headrest. "They thought you was comin' out to 'em as gay," he realized. "Fuck. Did ya set 'em straight?" He glanced sideways at Jericho. "No pun intended."

Jericho sighed and shook his head again. "I just can't do it. I can't look them in the eye and tell them that I go out and fight crime at night." He had no idea how they'd take it, and was scared to find out.

"You're gonna hafta tell 'em *someday*, ya know that, right?" Luke's tone was serious. "Ain't fair on 'em to hold out like this." He tilted his head. "Wait a sec.

What'd ya tell 'em you was goin' ta Utopia City for?"

"That I was applying for a job there. Lots of unpowered folk live and work there too." Jericho was reasonably sure of that. The ratio of normals to Enabled, at last estimate, was about sixty-three thousand to one, which made the entire Enabled population of the United States equivalent to that of a small town. Utopia City, going by what he'd read, was anything but a small town.

"But you already work *for* your daddy's company," Luke pointed out. "How's your folks takin' that?"

Jericho snorted. "I'm basically a paid intern, entry level position. All it is, is make-work until I get another job somewhere or go back to college. It's not like I've got any desire to run the company someday. They asked me and I said no." He shrugged. "It's just not my thing. Anyway, once Serena gets her business admin degree, they've got a position for her, and the top spot in another twenty years or so." And God help anyone who tried to use her gender or skin color as an excuse to push back on her. Serena was as tough-minded as they came.

Luke nodded. "Yeah, I heard somethin' about that." He sounded pleased for his little sister. "Okay, so if they think you're goin' there for work, what about you an' Steve? They think he's goin' there too?"

That caused Jericho to wince. "They ... don't know about me and Stephen." He grimaced at Luke's expression. "It's not *like* that. Pa ... I'm pretty sure he's doing his best to tolerate the fact that I'm gay, but he doesn't want to know any details. And I don't think Mama would like me being in a relationship with an older man. So ... I haven't told them." And then of course, there was Stephen's stance on interracial relationships. He of course knew of Luke's parentage, but had apparently chosen to either accept or ignore it. If he visited Jericho's parents and saw one of the photos of Uncle Leroy with Aunt Ellie without knowing who they were, and made a comment about it, Jericho would *never* hear the end of it.

Luke rolled his eyes. "For a superhero, you're *such* a friggin' pussy. An' given that, what the *hell* makes ya think you—no, scratch that. What makes ya think *G-Man* can make it as a big-city superhero, you chickenshit?"

Taken aback by the use of his Enabled codename, Jericho stared at his cousin. Normally, Luke was much more respectful about it. "What do you mean? I *am* making it as a superhero. I mean, I *am* a superhero." He decided to stop talking before he confused himself.

"You're a superhero in *Savannah*," Luke retorted, then blew a raspberry. "That bar's pretty friggin' low. There's what, three Masks for the whole damn city?"

"Two," Jericho muttered, not bothering to correct his use of the slang term. Lots of normals used it, along with not a few Enabled, but Jericho found it irritatingly non-specific. Anyone could wear a mask, after all. "Me and Pickup. Thinkster died last year. Overdose." He'd never been quite sure about Thinkster's credentials. The man had claimed to be able to read minds, but as he shunned company, his credibility was a little doubtful. Also, the drinking didn't help. The drug use hadn't been too much of a surprise, considering that the man had been a known alcoholic for years.

"Goddamn *exactly*," Luke said. "You sho' you even up to it? It's pretty friggin' quiet in Savannah compared to, well, *anyplace* else."

Jericho rolled his eyes. "*Yes*, I'm up to it. I've stopped lots of crime." He conveniently didn't mention the long nights of patrols where he'd neither seen nor heard anything for hours.

"You've stopped *muggers*," Luke corrected him. "Oh, an' ya dealt with them gay bar bashers. Big fat hairy deal. You ain't never stopped no bank robberies or solved any murders. I bet the cops don't even Gordon you."

The term was from popular culture, indicating the act of a police officer unofficially sharing information about an ongoing case with a superhero. Some police departments tacitly condoned the practice, while others comprehensively banned it.

"Shows what you know, smart guy," Jericho countered. "Detective Villanova's asked for my opinion on several cases, thank you very goddamn much." He hadn't *solved* the cases, but he liked to think that he'd given the detective valuable input on them.

"Villanova?" Luke snorted derisively. "*Raul* Villanova? He ain't talkin' to you on account of you bein' a superhero. He's doin' it 'cause he saw the photo-shoot that Steve did of you. Probably fixin' ta ask you on a date sometime."

Jericho stared at Luke. His cousin had a grin on his face, but it wasn't the know-it-all smirk he wore when he was pulling a joke. "Villanova's *gay*? Really?" It was something that Jericho had never considered. Though when he thought back over the cases he'd been called in on, especially the ones that had little to no bearing on his capabilities, he had to wonder if Luke wasn't onto something there. *Sonovabitch. Villanova was* Trevoring *me, not Gordoning.* Unlike 'Gordoning', he wasn't quite sure of the origins of 'Trevoring'; he just knew it was shorthand for helping out a superhero in the hope of getting into their pants.

Luke rolled his eyes. "Cuz, your gaydar's for shit. 'Course he's gay. I know the guy—not well, but I know him. Hides it well, but there's tells. An' no offense, but if he's Gordoning you, it ain't 'cause of your street rep. I mean, shit, ain't nobody's hardly ever heard of you. You ain't even a celebrity in *Savannah*." That hurt more than Jericho was ready to admit. "What makes ya think you can hit the big time an' go pro?"

"That's *it*. I'm outta here." Pissed off beyond all forbearance, Jericho stood up and went to scramble over the table. He didn't care where he sat, but he was going somewhere else before he ended up punching Luke over this.

Before he could get his foot up on the seat, Luke grabbed his arm and hauled him bodily back down again. "Siddown."

It was lucky that Jericho didn't have eye-beam powers, or the glare he gave his cousin may just have caused serious bodily harm. "I'm not in the mood for your shit right now. I'm going to another car." He went to stand up again, only to be forced into his seat for a second time.

Luke gave him a determined stare. "I c'n do this all day long. You ain't goin' noplace 'til you answer the goddamn question."

Settling back into the seat and closing his eyes, Jericho breathed deeply for a few seconds, pushing the anger down and away. *Luke's not Stephen. He really does want to know.* When he felt in control again, he opened his eyes and nodded. "Fine. You know my powers, right?"

Luke nodded. "That thing with gravity. Weird blobby shit that makes light turn all rainbowy. An' you can make things heavier or lighter, an' shake shit up."

"Right. My G-tags and the other stuff." Jericho took a deep breath. *One step at a time.* "That's my Dynamic rating. But then there's my Prodigy rating."

"Yeah, I already knew about that." Luke raised his eyebrow slightly. "But doesn't that jes' help you stay awake?"

Jericho grinned back at him, pleased that he could finally turn the tables on his irritating cousin. "I might've fudged over that a bit. It's low, but it's not *that* low."

Now he had Luke's interest. "Fudged over by how much?" He eyed Jericho cautiously.

Jericho shrugged. "Well, for one thing, I'm a black belt equivalent in Krav Maga." He grinned at the look on Luke's face. Graduate Level in Krav Maga wasn't *exactly* the same as a black belt, but it was a comparison that his cousin would immediately grasp.

"Krav Maga?" Luke's tone was incredulous. "You have *got* to be shitting me. So you really *can* kick ass." It wasn't a question.

Jericho's grin widened. "So, you still think you can keep me in this corner?" He could think of four ways to get out of his seat, none of which Luke would enjoy.

Luke carefully cleared his throat. "So, they, uh, git many people with, uh, two ratings?"

So now *we change the subject.* Jericho decided to cut his cousin some slack. "Dual power ratings aren't uncommon. It happens enough that folks shorten it to DPR, or 'dipper', which before you ask, *doesn't* stand for 'double dipper'. Anyway, you get about as many DPRs as you do straight ratings."

"Huh." Luke seemed to think about that. "What about triple power ratings? They git many of those? And whadda folks call them ones? 'Trippers'?"

Jericho shrugged. "Well, I guess it's *technically* possible to have a triple power rating, but I've never heard of one being reported. Figuring out ratings is hard enough at the best of times."

Luke nodded. A moment later, Jericho saw his face clear. "*Wait* jes' a friggin' second. *That's* how they pulled off that acceleration bullshit." With both hands, he gestured around at the train car. "Cogs made all this, didn't they?"

"Yeah, the whole maglev system's Artificer-built," Jericho agreed, choosing to ignore the word Luke had used, in the interests of not starting that shit up again. *Cogs, my ass.* "But it's not standard Artificer tech, if there's such a thing. You know Transit? She's beyond super-genius when it comes to designing and building transport of any kind. And once any technology's been built, the Technologist can take it and make it *better.* It's one of his tricks. They worked together on this project. It's a once-off. You're not gonna see anything bigger or better than it anywhere in the world."

He didn't have to explain any further; nearly everyone in America knew the names of the seven founding members of Force Majeure, as Luke had proven a few moments ago. "I'm pretty sure that the Technologist has a straight Artificer rating, but Transit's almost certainly a DPR with some sort of Dynamic mechanokinesis power. I've seen footage of her redesigning and rebuilding an aircraft quite literally on the fly. It's hella impressive."

"*And* she's got a great ass," Luke said pragmatically. When Jericho stared at him, he shrugged. "What? I watch the news too."

Jericho glared at him. "Transit is a widely renowned hero who helped transform the nation," he said sternly. "Artificers across America, across the *world*, would give their eyeteeth to work alongside her. She is *not* a pin-up model. Her work's an inspiration to us all."

"And so's her ass," Luke said reasonably. "Hey. I'm probably never gonna meet her. Her work ain't never gonna inspire me to greatness. But I knows a world-class ass when I sees one. Jes' sayin'." He shot Jericho a sly glance. "Or are ya telling me you ain't gonna be checkin' out the Technologist or Silent Knight when ya meet 'em? Or ... *Relentless?*" He gave the name full court press.

Jericho wasn't buying it. "Luke, be serious. I am *never* gonna meet those guys in a social setting. It's just not gonna happen." Belatedly, he added, "Besides, I've got Stephen." Though now that the suggestion had been made, his mind could not help drifting to Relentless. The live footage he'd seen of Force Majeure's leader was still stark in his mind. As Luke had pointed out, Relentless did wear a cape, which was unusual among non-flying Enabled; with his build, he carried it off well. Tall men with broad shoulders were a hot button for Jericho, as was a brusque and unapproachable attitude. He wasn't certain what that said about him, but he was pretty sure that Relentless also had the latter in spades. *Argh, no. Wrong line of thought.* "Stop infecting my mind," he said irritably.

"Hey, all I did was say the names." Luke smirked at him. "You're the one who's thinkin' of a foursome right now."

"I am *not* thinking of a foursome!" But of course, once the idea was implanted, he was. Closing his eyes, he scrubbed at his temples with the heels of his hands. "No. Just … no. Don't even *insinuate* something like that. The last thing I want is to start thinking about that sort of thing while I'm being interviewed by them. I've *got* a boyfriend, dammit!"

Luke may have been a dick at times, but he was also Jericho's friend. "Okay, sorry, cuz. Didn't mean ta push." He gave Jericho a few seconds to answer. When he didn't, Luke forged on. "You okay there?"

Opening his eyes, Jericho nodded. "Yeah. Just not feeling the greatest. Stephen kinda accused me of going off to Utopia City to hook up with cute guys, and then you said the same thing. I mean, does he really think I'm such a goddamn man-slut? Do *you?*" He hated the feeling of not being trusted. It *hurt.*

"Not really, no." To give him his due, Luke gave the question proper consideration. "I was jes' yankin' your chain. But ya gotta understand that Steve's pretty friggin' insecure where it comes to y'all. Shit, he thought *I* mighta been makin' time with ya when ya first introduced us."

"What, really?" Jericho stared at him. "That's stupid."

Luke nodded. "Yeah, but look at it from his side. I know what gets your motor runnin'. I seen ya lookin' at folks." He jabbed his thumb into his chest. "Ya like big guys like me. Steve knows that too. Might could be he thought I was a rival, I reckon? An' ya *know* how he feels about black on white."

"But … you weren't. You aren't." Jericho floundered, searching for words. "I've never even *thought* about you like that."

"Yeah, I know." Luke chuckled. "Believe me, I know. I ain't never caught ya checkin' me out even once."

"Well, of *course* not," Jericho protested. "You're my *cousin.* And my best friend. I've known you since forever. I mean, *eww.*" Jericho shuddered theatrically, but he was serious. He'd known Luke since he was four and Luke was nine, and they'd done *everything* together. Luke had always been his cool older cousin; no matter what he was doing, he had time for Jericho. He was *kin.*

Anyway, that wasn't important right now. This was the first Jericho had heard about Stephen feeling insecure. He'd managed to hide it pretty well, though … "Ah, *shit.* So *that's* why he was being a douche about the goddamn trip. All that passive-aggressive shit and the whining, without actually flat-out telling me not to go." It all made sense now. For a weird definition of 'sense'.

"Yeah." Luke nodded sagely. "He's scared if he puts his foot down, you'd go anyways an' not come back. An' then there's …" He paused, as if he'd lost his train of thought. "… I mean, you're younger an' better lookin' than him, right? To him, it'd kinda make sense that you'd be able to find someone else. If you was interested. Which you ain't. Right?"

"Wait," Jericho said. Something was bugging him about how Luke had just said that. "Back up a little. And then there's what?"

"What?" Now Luke looked a little uncomfortable. "Nothin'. I was thinkin' about somethin' else."

Jericho shook his head. For someone who could bullshit so fluently on the spur of the moment, Luke was sure as hell doing a crap job of it. "I lied better than that the time your mama caught me feeding the dog under the table. Whatever you were gonna say, spill it."

Luke grimaced. "Shitfire, cuz. I don't wanna keep secrets from ya, but I dunno if it'd hurt ya more ta know or not know." There was genuine pain in his eyes.

A chill crept down Jericho's spine. "You're saying if I *don't* find out, it's gonna hurt me?"

"Might hurt more if I tell ya right now." Luke pinched the bridge of his nose. "Sum*bitch*, this is hard."

"I'll take the hurt I know is coming." Jericho's eyes bored into Luke's. "Stop screwing around and tell me already."

"Fine." Luke sighed. A muscle in his jaw twitched. "Ya remember when Steve got beat up?"

He didn't need to say any more; Jericho recalled it vividly. "Jeez, yeah," he said. "That was really scary." Looking over at Luke, he frowned. "I know you aren't gonna implicate yourself in anything, but you've got a few fingers in a few pies around the place. You know something about this you haven't been telling me?" *Because if you do, when I get back, I'm gonna be kicking some heads.*

Absently, Luke rubbed his knuckles. Jericho caught sight of pink scarring, vivid against the rich chocolate of Luke's skin. *Fresh* scarring, where the skin had split and only healed recently. "Might could say that," his cousin admitted warily. He tensed, glancing sideways at Jericho. "It was me an' a couple of the guys that done it."

9
Revelation

The feeling of betrayal slammed into Jericho, turning his world upside down. For a long moment, his brain refused to make sense of Luke's words. *Luke was the one who beat on Stephen?* "The … *hell?*" he choked out. "Luke … *why?* Why would you *do* such a thing?" And why hadn't *Stephen* told him who'd done it? They'd had days of privacy as Stephen slowly mended, where nobody could possibly listen in on them. *Why didn't he tell me?*

Luke's face was set in grim lines. "Me an' the boys was jes' outside o' town. Li'l place on the bayou where we go for private business. Saw headlights comin' in, thought it might be cops or whatever, so we got ready to haul ass. When I saw it was Steve's car, I reckoned it was him an' you, comin' out for a bit of fun in the woods. So me bein' me, I snuck up to scare the hell outta y'all. But when I shone the flashlight in the window, it wasn't you with him. He was suckin' face with some sumbitch I ain't never seen before."

"Wait." Jericho barely recognized his own voice. "Stephen … he'd just gotten back in town a couple days before. He'd gone to Augusta, to do an interview. He brought the guy *back* with him?" *What was his name? Fly Guy? Something like that?* Blood roared in his ears. He felt dizzy, blackness wavering at the edges of his sight.

Luke shrugged awkwardly. "Looks like, yeah. So anyway, I—"

"Shut up. I don't want to hear it." Everything was hitting Jericho with a rush. Even though they'd only been together eighteen months, Stephen had become one of the constants in his life. Sure, he checked out other guys from time to time—who didn't?—but he'd never stepped out on his boyfriend. And after all that drama, *Stephen* had been cheating on *him!*

Every time he went out of town to do an 'interview', was he sleeping around? Unpleasant truth shattered Jericho's view of reality and rearranged it into a new picture, like a sinister jigsaw puzzle. Stephen's out-of-town interviews had always taken three days, no matter where he went. It was a matter of record that the maglev could get someone anywhere in the United States in eight hours or less. *Has he been cheating on me all this time? Is this why he was so sure I'd be cheating on him?*

The list of people Jericho trusted implicitly wasn't all that long. There were his parents, of course, and Luke and Serena and Uncle Leroy and Aunt Ellie. Once he'd gotten to know Olivia, she'd made it onto the list. So, of course, had Stephen.

But only one of them had betrayed him like this. Only one of them had taken his trust, had *earned* his trust, and then stabbed him in the back. The knowledge penetrated straight to the core of his focus, devastating him like nothing else could. Physical pain was something he could deal with; this level of emotional anguish was something else altogether. Nausea welled up in his throat and he only avoided tossing his cookies by the narrowest of margins.

Clenching his eyes shut, he drew deep, shuddering breaths. *In, out. In, out.* The influx of oxygen into his lungs served to steady him, helping bring his heart rate down and alleviate the lightness in his head. Just as he felt himself coming back to some semblance of an even keel, a sudden twisting sensation in his gut threatened to overcome his hard-won equilibrium. The world felt as though it was falling away sideways, but in a totally different way to his previous physical distress.

"What the hell?" He opened his eyes, to see that the windows were polarized to a dead black, lights illuminating the interior of the passenger car. A moment later, with another gut-wrenching jerk, the world returned to normal, leaving the taste of bile at the back of his throat. The windows cleared up once more, to show the countryside flashing by outside, unchanged. He found his both his stomach and his brain calming down again; presenting him with a problem based on his powers helped to center him in more ways than one.

"Okay, that was friggin' weird," Luke observed. He eyed Jericho carefully, as if wanting to make sure that his cousin wasn't about to break down altogether. "You got any idea what it was about? Why'd they darken th' windows on us?" He seemed entirely unfazed by the sideways twist; a moment later, Jericho realized that Luke hadn't even felt it. It had only been detectable with his powers.

"I got a good idea." Jericho figured he could've broken it more smoothly, but he decided he owed Luke a little bit of a hard time for holding out about Stephen. "We just passed another train."

Luke's eyes went gratifyingly large. "The *hell?*" He gestured out the window, at the singular lack of another rail in view. "How ...?"

"We're sitting on top of the rail, but it's a big-ass cylinder," Jericho said flatly. "You might've noticed that the cars don't even wrap halfway around it. We swing around until we're hanging off the side. The other train does the same thing, on the other side. We pass each other, then swing back on top. Simple." The gravity within the car had stayed 'down' the whole time but he'd felt the twisting sensation, as well as the extra output from the gravity generators in the rail to keep the car from tumbling to the ground below.

"Jesus *wept* ..." Luke shook his head. "Cogs an' their *friggin'* technology." He ran his hand over his face. "An' the blackout was so's we wouldn't shit ourselves when everythin' went ass-up an' sideways?"

"Got it in one," Jericho said bluntly. He took a deep breath. "So tell me what happened."

Luke frowned. "Thought ya didn't wanna hear about it." Jericho could see the concern in his face.

"Just shut up and tell me." He didn't care if he wasn't making sense anymore. If Luke was talking, then Jericho didn't have to.

"Fine, option B it is." Luke sat down again.

Jericho stared at him. "What option B? I told you to shu—oh." He closed his mouth again.

Luke nodded. "Soon's I knowed what the hell was goin' on, I jes' seen red. Busted the window with my flashlight an' dragged Stevie-boy outta the friggin' car. Told the guys they'd git a twenty percent discount if they gave the other asshole a proper workin' over. *Then* I beat the ever-lovin' hell outta your motherfuckin' cheatin'-ass boyfriend." He told the story as if he were recounting a night on the town. *Yeah, we went and had drinks at the bar. It was a quiet night.*

"The other guy ... did he live?" If Luke had blood on his hands ... Jericho didn't *want* to know. But he had to ask the question anyway.

"Reckon he did. Told the boys to dump him someplace he'd be found." Luke's voice and expression both denoted his extreme lack of care factor. "You're kinfolk. *Nobody* screws with kinfolk. If this guy was makin' time with Steve, he was screwin' with you. Steve was screwin' with you too, but I reckon you woulda been pissed if I broke his friggin' kneecaps an' dumped him in the bayou for the 'gators, so I jes' tuned him up a bit. Told him to straighten up an' friggin' fly right, or I'd git back to him. Then I drove him home myself."

So, Stephen even lied about that. Jericho could understand Luke beating up on Stephen for stepping out on him, but he couldn't believe that Luke hadn't *told* him until now. His jaw muscles began to ache from the way he was clenching his teeth together. "Luke ... why didn't you ...?"

"Tell you?" Luke shook his head. "It's about bein' fair. I catch the asshole cheatin' on you, I can beat the livin' hell outta him or I can tell ya. Cain't do both. Reckoned I'd give him one chance ta make it right."

"Oh." Jericho closed his eyes, feeling the hot tears in his eyes that he refused to shed, thinking about Stephen. *Can I go back to him? Can I even look him in the face after this?* His voice was hardly there when he spoke next. "So why are you telling me now?"

Luke shrugged. "You asked. If you ask, I ain't gonna lie. I don't owe Steve *shit*."

Jericho turned away to the window, staring with tear-blurred eyes out at the passing scenery. With every second that went by, he was getting farther and farther away from his cheating boyfriend. Luke had beaten Stephen up to make sure he didn't cheat any more, but that didn't erase what he'd *done*. There'd be no trusting the man again. Every time his boyfriend met with someone, Jericho knew that he'd be wondering, *will he do it again?* He pulled out his handkerchief and used it to wipe his eyes and blow his nose.

"Cuz ...?" Luke's voice was hesitant.

"Shut up." Jericho tried not to sound too harsh. It wasn't Luke's fault, no matter how much Jericho wanted to lash out at everyone around him. Luke was his friend. *Luke* had stood firm by him. "Gotta think. Work this out."

The flip-side to having focus was the need to maintain it. Popular culture made much of the tendency of prodigies to brood on rooftops. Brooding was quite a common way to center oneself, but it also depended on the type of focus. Other prodigies filled in war diaries, maintained their weapons or went into a meditative state. The technique didn't really matter; the results did.

Of course, it also required the prodigy to be alone for it to work properly. Being in company, even if Luke was being quiet and the rest of the passengers were on the outside of the privacy bubble, made it hard to reach the proper mental state where he could go over his issues in the quiet of his own mind. He needed a proper rooftop, and the train was going too fast to consider climbing on top, even if he *could* figure out a way to get outside.

Just as he thought he was getting there anyway, yellow lights began to flash on and off in the compartment. Jericho didn't turn his head, but he didn't have to; they reflected off the inside of the window into his eyes. At the same time, the noise of the compartment burst in on them. There wasn't much of it but after the silence of the privacy bubble, it was still a mild shock to the system. Foremost in this was the PA system as it began an announcement in the same emotionless voice that he'd heard back in the station.

"Attention, all passengers. Attention, all passengers. This train will be passing through Atlanta in six minutes. All passengers stopping in Atlanta, please move to Cars Four through Five. All passengers for the Atlanta to Montgomery train, please move to Car Six. All passengers for the Atlanta to Charlotte train, please move to Car Seven. All passengers for the Atlanta to Chattanooga train, please remain in this car. Do not forget your luggage. Utopia Maglev Lines takes no responsibility for luggage left on the train or passengers failing to make their stop. We hope you have enjoyed your trip. This train will be passing through Atlanta in five minutes. All passengers stopping in Atlanta ..."

As the message began to repeat, he heard the connecting doors hiss open as people moved back toward the rear car. He couldn't do much about the lights, but the recorded message was getting a little annoying. Flipping the switch for the privacy bubble did nothing. *Must be shut off for the announcement.*

With a sigh, he looked out the window once more. Suburbia was giving way to the outskirts of Atlanta, with tall buildings in the distance; visible only because of the maglev's height above ground. Turning his head, he glanced at the nearest digital sign. The display was now showing 'CHATTANOOGA', with nearly twenty minutes to go. He couldn't bring himself to care. Pillowing his chin on his crossed arms, he stared morosely out the window.

After what might have been five minutes, the flashing lights cut off, and blessed silence fell. "Rear cars musta gone," Luke observed, in the tones of someone who considers themselves an expert on the situation.

"Work that out for yourself, did you?" Jericho tried not to sound too sarcastic, but it was hard. Luke hadn't deliberately set out to hurt him with the bombshell about Stephen, but he sure as hell hadn't helped. Jericho found himself resenting Luke for telling him, while simultaneously being pissed at him for not spilling the beans earlier. He knew it wasn't fair on his cousin, but unfortunately, knowing and caring were two different things at that moment. His irritation at the failed brooding attempt didn't help either.

As they blasted through the middle of Atlanta, the windows blacked out again. Once more, the gut-wrenching twist happened, then the train straightened out again. When the view cleared, the cityscape outside was still blurring by at ... *huh. That's odd.* The train had slowed by about thirty miles an hour, but he wasn't sure why. At that moment, he couldn't bring himself to care all that much.

All too soon, the city gave way to suburbia once more, with barely a chance to see any landmarks. He watched the incoming cars swooping around to join with the front of the train; shortly after they went out of sight, there was a familiar-sounding *clunk.* Following that was the faint hiss as the connecting doors at the front of the car opened to let passengers through. Jericho ignored all of that; as far as he was concerned, the rest of the world could go take a long walk off a short pier.

After a moment, he heard Luke get up. *Good. He's gone to sit somewhere else.* He was perfectly happy to ride the rest of the way to Utopia City on his own. Reaching out without looking, he flipped the switch for the privacy bubble. The minor noises from elsewhere in the train car disappeared, allowing him to wallow in self-pity without any distractions. No, not self-*pity*, Jericho decided. What he felt was self-*righteousness*; while he'd done exactly nothing to hurt Stephen, the asshat had chosen to repay him like this. He couldn't believe that he hadn't seen it before. *Some goddamn superhero I am. I didn't even see this coming.*

"Cuz." It was Luke's voice, followed by sound of him settling into his seat. Jericho turned his head away, not even willing to acknowledge him. Then he heard paper being unwrapped. The smell of cookies came to his nose, followed by a faint crunch. "Hey, this is pretty good. Want one?" A faint sliding sound heralded a second cookie, still in its wrapper, as it came to rest against his hand.

"No, I don't want a goddamn cookie," Jericho mumbled. "I don't want anything. Just shut up and leave me alone." Despite his words, he'd changed his mind. Now he hoped that Luke wouldn't go away; as Jericho's oldest friend, Luke was a comforting presence. Well, so long as he didn't actually *talk*, anyway.

"I dunno how to do this, cuz," Luke said after about half a minute. *So, of course he's gotta run his goddamn mouth.* "I dunno how to deal with this shit." Jericho felt a hand rest on his shoulder for a moment; a squeeze, and then it was gone again. It provided more comfort than he was willing to admit.

If Jericho didn't look around, Luke was going to keep talking at him. The only way it could get more awkward was if Luke tried to hug him or something. As far as Jericho knew, Luke was okay with him hugging people, but Luke himself didn't hug guys. It simply wasn't his thing. Jericho didn't want to inflict that horror on him, so he turned around. "What the *hell* are you trying to do?" he demanded. Irritably, he snatched up the cookie, ripped off the wrapper, and took a bite. It was quite good, but he refused to let himself enjoy it. He was hungry, that was all. The next bite was equally delicious.

"Cheer you up," Luke said simply. "Ya know, you're a real asshole when you're pissed off?"

Jericho tried not to gape at him, while he gazed guilelessly back. "What the hell are you *talking* about?" Jericho asked disbelievingly. "*I'm* the one who got cheated on, here! You never told me, you just near on put his ass in the emergency room. And then you sprang it on me with *zero* goddamn warning. And you're calling *me* the asshole here?" He finished off the cookie, not caring about the crumbs he scattered as he ranted.

"Well, sorry for wanting to be on your friggin' side!" Luke snapped back. "I'm not the one who cheated on you, remember? I'm the one that found out about it an' kicked his ass for you so's he wouldn't do it again!" He glared at Jericho, then shook his head irritably. "Are you even gonna tell the fuckwit that ya know, or jes' never talk to his sorry ass again?"

Jericho's lip curled. "You know, I hadn't decided. You seem to be determined to interfere in every goddamn aspect of my life. Why don't *you* choose for me?" Despite his monumental level of pissiness right then, he wondered if he'd gone too far. He'd argued with Luke before, but never quite on this level.

"I beat hell out of him so's he'd keep it in his pants!" Luke snapped back. He wasn't quite yelling, but it was close. "I know how friggin' happy y'all was together. Even if he *did* end up bein' an enormous douche about you comin' to Utopia City. Mistakes friggin' happen. Jesus *shit*, this ain't the end of the world." The windows blacked out halfway through his speech but he never faltered; by the time he finished, they were transparent again.

"Losing twenty bucks is a *mistake*," Jericho countered. "Getting a speeding ticket is a *mistake*. Screwing the guys he's interviewing for articles in the magazine is the act of a total goddamn shitheel. Getting *caught* is a catastrophic fuckup of the highest degree." He paused; normally, he never used the 'f' word. It just wasn't part of his vocabulary. But on this one occasion, it seemed to fit. Absolutely nothing that Stephen had done deserved forgiveness, in his eyes. Trust that had once been rock-solid was now washing away like a sandcastle at high tide.

"I seem to recall that's how y'all got together in the first place," Luke said. "He was interviewin' you, an' he asked you to dinner, or somethin'?" He took a couple of deep breaths, apparently to help himself cool down.

Jericho rolled his eyes. "Yeah, that and a photo shoot. But it was different with me. For one thing, he wasn't already seeing someone else." Which, in his view, changed everything. If Stephen had been with someone at the time, there was no way Jericho would've even *considered* going out with him.

"That ya know of," Luke pointed out bluntly.

On the verge of protesting that he would've known if something like that was going on, Jericho paused. *Shit. I really wouldn't have.* "Yeah," he admitted. He *hoped* he hadn't accidentally pushed someone else out from Stephen's favor, but in the absence of a jilted lover contacting him, how would he even know?

"Which reminds me. How come y'all's goin' out together anyways?" asked Luke. "I mean, I know your type, an' he ain't it. Now *that* guy, on th' other hand ..." He pointed surreptitiously across the aisle at a man in a business suit sitting at one of the tables.

While no movie hunk, the guy was both tall and wide across the shoulders. He was seated at an otherwise unoccupied table diagonally across from where Jericho and Luke sat, with a laptop open on the table. From what Jericho could see, he was intent on his work, ignoring everything around him. As the man typed on the flat keyboard, Jericho could see he wasn't wearing a wedding ring. His heart rate sped up a little; *tall, broad and standoffish. Just what the doctor—no!* Exerting firm self-control, he brought that train of thought to a screeching halt. *Even if Stephen's cheating on me, it's not over 'til it's over.*

He pulled his attention away from the man across the aisle and focused once more on Luke, who was wearing an irritating half-grin. "Yeah, that's more your style," his cousin noted smugly. "So why ain't you with someone like that?"

"Because as much as it may surprise you to know, Savannah isn't exactly a wide-open city where everyone can show off their preferences and get away with it," Jericho snarked. "I kind of owe it to Stephen that I even took the chance of dating him. After that gay bar fiasco, I was really skittish for a while. Took me and Stephen quite a few dates before we slept together. And I might've let our relationship get serious because I was lonely, but I wasn't about to walk out on him just because I'd met someone who appealed to me more. That's a dick move, and I don't play that game."

"Even if he cheats on you?" Luke spread his hands slightly. "Ya know, once Steve started steppin' out on you, you didn't owe him a goddamn thing."

Jericho shook his head. "That's not the way it works. There's a mutual trust thing going on, and until he looks me in the eye and says that he's not willing to go the distance and fix the shit that he's pulled on me, then I'm not gonna assume we're done. I owe him that much, at least." He gave Luke a dirty look. "Anyway, didn't you beat the shit out of him so he *would* stay faithful to me?"

"Sho'nuff I did, yeah," Luke agreed. "But now *you* know, you git th' chance ta decide whether or not you want his cheatin' ass in your life or not."

This was all true. Jericho couldn't dispute that. But he couldn't simply walk away from Stephen without at least giving him the chance to defend himself. Even if that defense was a sincere apology and a promise never to do it again. At the very least, he'd maybe learn to trust Stephen again in about five or ten years.

It wasn't an ideal solution, but there *were* no ideal solutions. Jericho settled back in his seat to fume about the sheer unfairness of the world. An unfairness that was compounded a few minutes later, when the yellow lights began to flash again.

"Attention, all passengers. Attention, all passengers. This train will be passing through Chattanooga in six minutes. All passengers stopping in Chattanooga, please remain in this car. All passengers for the Chattanooga to Huntsville train, please move to Car Six. All passengers for the Chattanooga to Knoxville train, please move to Car Seven. All passengers for the Chattanooga to Nashville train, please move to Cars One through Four ..."

The digital sign clearly stated that the passenger car was the fifth one in line. Sullenly, Jericho got up and collected his bag from the overhead bin. As they moved forward, Luke tried to make a joke about 'walking from Savannah to Utopia', but Jericho ignored him. The connecting doors opened before them, revealing a short passage through to the next car. On either side of the passage were the rubber-covered edges of the heavy exterior doors that would close off the nose and tail of each maglev car when they were separated. These were canted at a ridiculous degree to conform with the aerodynamic slope of the nose. The next set of connecting doors hissed open automatically, admitting them into the passenger car beyond. Several tables were empty, so Jericho took the nearest one, shoving the bag in the overhead bin once again.

Luke sat down next to him and leaned back, looking more than a little smug, so Jericho turned back to the window. His upset emotions regarding Stephen were no less strong, but as Luke had noted, he was more angry than grieving. It all seemed so vastly *wrong*; how could a relationship of eighteen months, everything he'd put into it, just vanish like that? How could Stephen *do* what he'd done? How could Jericho have trusted him so completely?

Unaccountably, the train sped up again as it blew through Chattanooga, topping out at a shade over four hundred fifty miles per hour. Neither of them commented on the five-second blackout in the middle of the city. Uncaring, Jericho watched the incoming car loop around on its track so it could attach itself to the front of the procession. The jolt of connection was almost unnoticeable, but that was probably because there were other cars in the way. He went back to watching the buildings blur by like a sped-up film, until they gave way to the suburbs again.

In a way, traveling like this was kind of restful; with no stops, no rush of people getting on and off, he could be properly pissed-off at the world. He sat and stared out the window. While his eyes saw what passed before them, his brain totally failed to take it in.

10
Reaction

It seemed like no time at all had passed before the yellow lights were flashing once more. He didn't recognize the landscape that was blurring past the window—four hundred miles per hour was not conducive to spotting landmarks—but the automated announcement informed him that the train was approaching Nashville. He tried to ignore it, but then Luke nudged him. "Cuz."

"What?" he asked irritably.

"We gotta move, unless you wanna go to Louisville." Luke was already on his feet.

"What?" Jericho roused himself to listen to the announcement.

"… five minutes. All passengers stopping in Nashville, please move to Car Five. All passengers for the Nashville to Memphis train, please move to Car Six. All passengers for the Nashville to Louisville train, please remain in this car. All passengers for the Nashville to St Louis train, please move to Car One through Four. Do not …"

To back this up, the digital sign was now showing 'LOUISVILLE 34:31'.

"*Jeez.*" Jericho thumped his head back against the headrest in extreme irritation. He still hadn't dealt with this shit about Stephen, and now he had to move *again?*

"Cuz?" Luke had the overhead bins open and was holding his bag out to him.

"Yeah, coming." Jericho heaved himself to his feet. Taking the bag, he slung it over his shoulder. All of a sudden, that comedian's skit didn't seem quite so funny anymore. Stalking past Luke, he made his way forward along the train. Three cars on, he found an unattended table, shoved his bag in the overhead bin, and sat down again. By this time, he was even more pissed off than before. It didn't help his mood that as the train passed through Nashville, its speed dropped away by more than a hundred miles an hour, to just under three-forty. *I want to get there sooner, not later. What the hell's going on here?*

Flipping on the privacy bubble, he turned fully away from Luke. He kicked his sneakers off and brought his legs up onto the seat, unseeing eyes staring out the window. Deep down, he knew he was being unfair to Luke, but he couldn't bring himself to care. It was easy to be angry at him. It was even easier to be angry at *everything.*

Between the quiet of the privacy bubble and the ease of the ride, Jericho felt his eyelids beginning to drift shut. He didn't want to sleep. With the fires of resentment still burning hot, he wanted to keep stewing about Stephen, and how the man had betrayed him. It was something beyond his experience; up until that point, nobody he knew had ever pulled that sort of shit on him. It hurt more than he was willing to admit. Stephen had been his first serious lover, and while Luke was correct in that the older man was far from Jericho's perfect ten—a little shorter, somewhat pudgy, and entirely too vain about his carefully styled ginger beard—Jericho had grown to love him entirely on the merits of his personality, not his looks.

Still can't believe he did that to me … Jericho's eyes closed, and he slipped into a doze. It wasn't a deep sleep, but neither was he entirely awake. He roused briefly when the gravity went weird for a few seconds. Opening his eyes, he was just in time to see the polarization fading from the windows. The view was now nothing more than fields, trees and the occasional road.

Though more awake than asleep, he was unwilling to move or think deeply about what was going on. His drifting thoughts rolled on, until they were once more interrupted by the flashing of the yellow lights. This, and the renewed noise from the rest of the passenger car, brought him fully awake. Sitting up, he straightened his legs and stretched almost guiltily. He half-expected to feel the vertebrae in his back popping, but it didn't happen. His Prodigy rating let his body bounce back from virtually any sort of abuse; since he had gotten his powers, he found it easy to sleep almost anywhere with few side-effects. Cramps, muscle strains and other artifacts of poor sleep were a thing of the past. Even the microfractures and cumulative damage from long nights of roof-running and punching muggers tended to heal up almost overnight.

Luke was up again, he belatedly realized, holding their bags and waiting for him. He hadn't even registered the PA message this time. "Ah jeez, how far forward this time?" he groaned.

"Half the friggin' train," grunted Luke. It seemed that his own nerves were starting to show. Jericho still didn't care. "Nashville left us at the back end, an' we gotta git to number four afore we hit St Louis."

Jericho looked at the digital sign. Sure enough, it read 'SPRINGFIELD MO 34:55'. The car number was 8. "Jeez," he muttered as he slid his feet into his shoes and took his bag from Luke. "I really need to go on that asshat's show."

"What asshat?" asked Luke as they started forward.

"That comedian, Gary or Jerry or whatever. The one who does that thing about walking from New York to LA. I need to punch him right in the goddamn nose. It's funny, right up until you gotta do it about ten times per goddamn trip." Despite his tone, he strode forward without hesitation. Even though he'd only been asleep for twenty minutes at most, he felt refreshed and full of energy. *Gotta love having powers.*

It only took them about one minute to cover the distance to the fourth car; when they got there, the digital signs were reassuringly showing 'KANSAS CITY 48:15'. Looking over the car, he saw several empty tables. *Screw it.* He kept on walking.

"Hey, cuz, where you goin'?" He stopped and turned; Luke had dropped his backpack onto the first empty table. "This'n's good enough, right?"

"Nah." Jericho shook his head. "Let's keep going. We're gonna be walking forward again anyway. Might as well shorten the trip."

For a moment, it looked as though Luke wanted to argue the point, but he retrieved his backpack instead. "Sho'nuff, let's go."

They passed through two more passenger cars. About one minute before the train was due to reach St Louis, Jericho found a seat in Car 1, but refrained from stowing his bag. Luke looked at him curiously but followed suit. Jericho didn't bother explaining, but the way he figured it, the closer the train got to Utopia City, the more crowded the cars were going to get. Moving forward as soon as possible gave them the best chance of getting a good seat.

As soon as he heard the *clunk* of connection from the front of the maglev car—by now he was tuning out the announcement altogether—he was on his feet again. "Let's go." Without a word, Luke followed, slinging his backpack over one shoulder.

The connecting doors hissed open in front of him, and he strode forward like an explorer venturing into unknown territory. By now he was irritated enough to see this as a challenge to be overcome. He *was* going to get to Utopia City. He *was* going to join Force Majeure. And screw Stephen, screw Luke, and screw every other asshat who wanted to get in his way.

Train car after train car passed by as he pushed his pace. Behind him, he could hear Luke panting slightly to keep up; while the big guy was fit enough, he wasn't at the same level as a pissed-off prodigy. Thinking about it, Jericho did slow down a little. It wasn't Luke's fault, and he'd stood by Jericho when it counted.

When they reached what had now become the first car, there was only one table free. Without hesitation, Jericho put his bag into the overhead bin and slid into the window seat once more. Even as Luke caught up, he flipped on the privacy bubble and turned toward the window. St Louis was bigger than Nashville and Chattanooga, but the train was already out of the city, passing over forested back roads. What he didn't know was why the speed of the train had just jumped again, to over four hundred seventy miles an hour. *You know what? I don't even care anymore.*

With the walk over, he was free to reflect again uninterrupted. He was beginning to go over the time that he'd met Fly Guy, to see if he could recall any hints Stephen might have dropped about his infidelity, when Luke cleared his throat. "So, uh, cuz, I jes' wanted ta say …?"

"What?" He really hadn't meant to sound so snappy, but nor did he feel particularly regretful over it.

Luke didn't quite recoil, but he looked a little offended at Jericho's tone. "If ya wanted ta talk, we c'n talk," he said. "Sometimes things like this is easier when ya got someone ta vent to. Or listen to. 'Cause for my money, I figger Steve ain't worth—"

Jericho knew that the surge of anger he felt toward his cousin was unwarranted. Luke was only trying to help, but the trouble was that it wasn't *working*. Not wanting to yell at the man he'd long considered to be his best friend, he broke eye contact and looked away from Luke, across the aisle. All the tables were occupied, but there was no eye-candy of the type that he liked.

His gaze lingered on one woman who was working with a tablet, but only because of an odd detail; as well as long sleeves, she wore light cotton gloves. As a matter of fact, she was showing no visible skin below the neck. In her late twenties with blonde hair and glasses, she wasn't exactly Jericho's type—being a woman, for one thing—so he turned his attention toward Luke once more.

"I'm still pissed at you," he said bluntly. "You should've either kicked the shit out of Stephen and not let me know, or *not* beat him up *and* let me know about him. Not *both*."

"Well, what the hell do ya think I been *doin'* for the last month?" retorted Luke, stung into snapping back. "I never *asked* ya to push me ta tell ya! I even told ya that it was like ta hurt ya! Well, now ya know! Merry fuckin' Christmas, cuz!"

"Yeah, but now you've dumped the whole goddamn problem in *my* lap!" If Luke had kept it in-house, rather than letting the cat out of the bag, Jericho would've been … if not *happier*, then a good deal less pissed off than he was right now.

"Well, he's *your* goddamn cheatin'-ass boyfriend!" Jericho could hear the rising anger in Luke's tone. Part of him welcomed it; he wanted the release of yelling at *someone*, though intellectually he knew that Luke wasn't the author of his troubles.

"That! Doesn't! Help!" It occurred to Jericho that he'd never argued with Luke so intensely before this trip; then again, he'd never been cheated on before. It put a lot of things into perspective.

Over Luke's shoulder, Jericho saw the woman with the tablet stand up from her seat. For a moment, he thought she was going to another car, but then it became clear she was coming over to their table. His Southern chivalry put the argument temporarily on hold and he elbowed Luke in the side. "Heads up," he said, raising his chin slightly.

Luke blinked at his change in tone, then turned his head to see what he was talking about. In the next moment, the woman had reached their table, sliding into the seat opposite Luke.

"Excuse me?" Her voice was quite pleasant. Looking at her more closely, Jericho upgraded her age to late twenties or early thirties. She had an upturned nose upon which her round-lensed glasses were perched, and her blonde hair was pulled back tightly into a bun. Her gloved hands held the tablet before her like a shield.

Jericho couldn't think of a single, solitary thing to say. Fortunately, Luke was more eloquent. "Uh, hi, ma'am. Can we help you?"

11
Bobbi

Roberta Reynolds—Bobbi, to her friends and family—was thirty-two years old. She had many regrets in her life—the ill-advised tramp stamp she'd gotten at nineteen, the asshole boyfriend she'd had before Jack, the last fight with Jack himself, and having to leave her sister Melody behind on this trip, just to name four—but going to Utopia City wasn't one of them. She was determined to right the wrong she *knew* had taken place, and if it took traveling halfway across the country while rubbing shoulders with a trainload of total strangers, then that was what she was going to do.

Travel was even less fun for her than it was for most people. Most people only had their eyes and ears and noses to notice things with. And while she wasn't exactly crushed up against anyone, she was still in close enough proximity to make things unpleasant for her. All around her, dingy non-colors surged and changed. Unfortunately, it only got worse when she closed her eyes. Each nexus of emotion was shaped like a person, with swirls of muddy hues washing back and forth within. These were not the colors that she'd learned about in school; though she could see them with her mind's eye, she couldn't put them down on paper. Any attempt had the effect of bleeding them together into a grungy mess.

It was worse when she got closer to people, both emotionally and physically. Even being in the same room as a person meant that she saw them, listened to them, became more accustomed to their presence. In time, their emotional turmoil became more vivid to her, sometimes to the extent of making her nauseous or giving her a headache. If they saw *her*, it became worse. And if that wasn't bad enough, when she had skin to skin contact, their emotions threatened to overwhelm hers, to replace hers with theirs; a uniquely terrifying experience.

On the upside, she had two useful abilities. The first radiated a calming effect which ameliorated the worst of the emotions around her, but it didn't automatically calm people all the way down. The second made people ignore her very presence; she could become effectively invisible to everyone around her just for a few seconds, or to one person for as long as she concentrated on them.

Unfortunately, this didn't help with her current problem, which was why she was going to Utopia City in the first place. If anyone could help her learn to control her powers, she figured Force Majeure would know who. At the same time, she could become an established member, which would allow her to do what needed to be done.

Yellow lights began to flash throughout the car, and she looked up.

"Attention, all passengers. Attention, all passengers. This train will be passing through St Louis in six minutes. All passengers stopping in St Louis, please move to Cars Six through Seven. All passengers for the St Louis to Louisville train, please move to Car Eight. All passengers for the St Louis to Nashville train, please move to Car Nine. All passengers for the St Louis to the Kansas City train, please

move to Cars Ten through Eleven. All passengers for the St Louis to Springfield Missouri train, please remain in this car. Do not forget your luggage. Utopia Maglev Lines takes no responsibility for luggage left on the train or passengers failing to make their stop. We hope you have enjoyed your trip. This train will be passing through St Louis in five minutes ..."

The nearest digital sign now read 'SPRINGFIELD MO 34:58', with the number '1' indicating that she was in the first car. Bobbi didn't want to go to Springfield (Missouri or otherwise), so she stood up from her seat. Reclaiming her drag-bag from the overhead locker, she started on her trek back through the train. Once she trudged on through the connecting doors, she felt the burden lift from her shoulders as the emotions connected to the people behind her dwindled to nothing. Ahead of her, there was the promise of more, but she didn't know these people. She'd spent no time in this car so far, so she could stand to stay a while before it became untenable. Unfortunately, she needed the tenth passenger car back, so she moved on once more.

There was some asshole comedian—Gary Brock was his name, she thought— whose show incorporated a routine about maglev travel called 'Walking from New York to LA'. At the time she'd watched it, she'd wondered why people thought it was funny. It was even less so now, especially considering how long the damn cars were—a hundred feet or more, when the passages between them were factored in. By the time she made it back to Car Nine, the digital sign read 'KANSAS CITY 31:03'. *Oh, good. This should be fine for the moment.*

There were two tables free. With a sigh of relief, she collapsed into a seat at the closer one. While she wasn't particularly unfit, she figured that she'd just power-walked the equivalent of four city blocks in as many minutes. With the drag-bag firmly between her calves, she leaned back in the seat. *I've got to admit, they don't skimp on the comforts.*

Once, when she was about ten, she'd traveled with her mother and sister on the normal train to visit Grandpop and Grandmam in Chicago. It had taken hours each way, she recalled, and had rattled and been uncomfortable. It had also smelled funny. The maglev had taken her only half an hour to get from Indianapolis to Chicago and another three-quarters of an hour from Chicago to St Louis, and there'd been a singular lack of rattles and discomfort, or even odd smells, on either trip.

The digital timer was down to thirty seconds, with the last passengers hurrying through, when a tone began to sound. The connecting doors on the other end of the passage slid shut, followed by the matching doors on Bobbi's end. A moment later, she heard the muffled 'thoom*thoom*' as the exterior doors also sealed off. There was a jolt as the maglev car separated from the one in front. While she couldn't feel it, she knew that the car was peeling off onto a secondary rail, aiming to meet up with the westbound train.

When the timer read '29:30', she felt the less pronounced *clunk* that signaled the linkup with the new train. As if triggered by the bump, the yellow flashing lights shut themselves off and slid back into their recesses. The digital sign showed that she was now sitting in Car One. *Great, now to wait for the influx.* She took the time to pull up the cuffs of the light cotton gloves she was wearing and tuck them into her sleeves. There were more people in this train car than in the one she'd come from, and she only expected the crush to get worse as they got closer to Utopia City. Fortunately, she had anticipated something like this before even setting off on the trip, and thus had taken precautions. Skin to skin contact was something that she wanted to avoid. Once the last table was taken up, she knew that others would be taking up the spare seats at her table, but she wanted to have a little time to herself so that she could get her head together. Unzipping a compartment on her drag-bag, she pulled out her tablet. A nice soothing game of *CogWars* should fit the bill, she decided.

She was still in the opening stages of the game, establishing the defensive capabilities of her fortress and getting her offensive units started, when a fluctuation in the general emotional level around her caught her attention. *Don't look up,* she told herself. *Don't look up.* She looked up.

Two guys were had just sat down at the last free table, diagonally across the aisle from her. Both were tall; while one was a heavy-set good-looking black guy, his companion was skinnier with long dark brown hair, bound back with a hair tie. The wiry guy had a lot of ugly emotions washing through his makeup, while his big friend was nursing some irritation, as far as she could see. *Don't get involved. Ignore them. They don't exist.* Lowering her eyes, she tried to go back to her game.

Unfortunately, seeing them had opened her power to them. The skinnier guy had some sort of confused anger about him, jabbing at her brain like broken glass. She could handle it … just. Right up until it pushed into the forefront of her attention. She knew what had happened; he'd looked at her and maybe thought about her for a moment. That was all it took. He didn't need to even have an opinion of her, but the fact that he'd noticed her meant that his emotions were pushing harder at her barriers.

With a wince, she looked up again. Now the two were arguing back and forth. While the silence showed that they were inside an active privacy bubble—*so* handy for someone with her problems—their expressions made it clear that this wasn't some mild disagreement. And the more attention she paid to them, the more their emotions affected her.

This made for a problem. Utopia City wasn't far past Kansas City, but at her best estimate, she had three-quarters of an hour before the train got there. Forty-five minutes of this kind of mental jabbing and she'd have a migraine the size of Mount Rushmore, or she'd be puking in the restroom. Or both; it was hard to predict.

Her options were limited. One was that she could look downstairs to see if there were any spare seats. On balance, she was reasonably sure that there would not be. Alternatively, she could go into the second car and ride it the rest of the way to Utopia City. However, that led to the risk of getting too close to some of the passengers there, who might also be traveling her way.

There *was* a third option, which she was reluctant to go with. Unfortunately, it seemed like the best of a bad series of choices. Taking a deep breath, she took hold of her drag-bag and stood up. The long-haired guy saw her coming and said something to his friend, who also turned to look at her. *Well, in for a penny …*

Their emotions, which had been spiking almost out of control, were even now calming down, as if they'd only needed an excuse to stop arguing. The skinnier guy's emotional makeup had anger and sadness and loss—*oh, shit. He's lost someone. No … he's been dumped*—roiling through his body. Underlying all that was a solid core of loyalty and camaraderie with the muscular black guy, but there was a thread of anger toward him as well … *what the hell's going on here?*

The big guy wasn't as angry as his wiry friend, but he did have a level of irritation and frustration overlaying the same bone-deep loyalty that he shared with the white guy. *Okay, they're not about to kill each other. Good.*

"Excuse me?" she said tentatively, exerting the calming aspect of her power. If she hadn't been on the verge of a killer headache, it would have almost been funny. As if by magic, their anger began to drain away even faster than she'd expected. The relief was palpable, but she kept the soothing power going anyway.

She held her tablet in front of her as a symbolic fence. *Here's the boundary between you and me. Please respect it.*

The muscular African American spoke first, while his companion's emotions continued to whirl in confusion. "Uh, hi, ma'am. Can we help you?" He had a nice deep voice to go with his solid build and good looks. The drawl put his origins at someplace south of the Mason–Dixon line, but the polite tone was matched with a steady gaze and a level of ingrained caution.

"I hope so," she said with a smile. The calming effect kept going, washing over the two guys and dealing with the last of their anger. For a mercy, her headache was also receding. "I'm traveling to Utopia City. Are you going there too?"

It wasn't much of a guess—unless she was way off the mark, the car they were in was one of those destined to stop in Utopia City—but she read flashes of surprise from each of them anyway. "Uh, yeah," said the wiry guy. Caution began to swirl through his emotional makeup as well. "We are. Why?" The question came out perhaps a little harsher than she suspected he'd intended, but the twinge of pain that resulted was gone in a moment.

Showing a temporary resurgence of irritation, the big guy jabbed his long-haired friend in the ribs with his elbow, not gently. "Please ignore him, ma'am. He's just now found out his boyfriend's been seein' other people." He offered a surprisingly charming smile. "I'm sorry; where are my manners? I'm Luke. This rather insensitive jerk is my cousin Jericho. I'm very pleased to meet you." He held out his hand.

Bobbi shook it, equally glad for the glove and for the calming effect that she was still maintaining. "Hi, Luke. You can call me Bobbi. And I'm sorry to hear about that, Jericho. I had an absolute dirtbag of a boyfriend who cheated on me with my best friend, not so long ago." The corner of her mouth quirked upward. "*Ex*-best friend, I should say."

At her comment, an upwelling of curiosity flooded into Jericho's makeup, replacing the caution almost completely. "What did you do?"

She shrugged, pretending nonchalance. "Kicked his sorry ass to the curb. Went through some self-destructive behavior until I got it out of my system." *Did something really stupid, got powers.* "Went back to work. Found a new boyfriend." *And maybe lost him again. Go, me.*

"At *work?*" Luke stared at her, curiosity coloring his emotions as well. Caution was still there, more so than in Jericho's. "Whereabouts do you work? I mean, if you don't mind me asking, ma'am?"

She smiled. "I have to say, I like a guy with manners. I work in the office at Re-Cycle, the best motorbike repair shop in Indianapolis."

Interest flared in Luke's color scheme as if she'd flipped a switch. "Bike repair, huh? Is it just office work, or do you ever get your hands dirty?" He put his own hands on the table, where she could see the calluses and the oil ingrained under the nails.

"Not in the shop, but I do own a bike of my own," she admitted with just a little pride. "I do all the maintenance work on her myself." Her own hands were clean under the gloves, as were her nails, but only because she worked at keeping them that way.

"Really?" asked Luke, almost challengingly. "So what do you ride, then?"

"Harley softail," she shot back. "You?"

Amusement washed through his emotional mix along with an increase in the interest, clearing away nearly all the caution. "You sound pretty certain that I ride."

She made a rude noise with her lips. "You say you don't, I'm calling bullshit."

Jericho chuckled, his amusement matching Luke's. "She's got you there." Tilting his head toward Luke, he added, "He's got a road bike and sometimes he rides motocross too. Wouldn't catch me doing that. Too goddamn dangerous."

"That's because you're a wuss, cuz." Luke rolled his eyes. "One of these days you'll learn to live a little." Belying his tone, his emotional palette showed a level of deep-seated affection toward Jericho.

"Oh, ho," Jericho retorted, his eyes lighting up as he grinned at Bobbi. "Should've seen his face earlier, when we were pulling out of Savannah. Figure there's still fingernail marks in the armrests in whatever car we were on."

"Now that's just a low blow, J." Luke's elbow was lazier this time, and Jericho blocked it with his arm. Bobbi could see from their attitudes and their emotional washes that they were beginning to relax. Part of this was probably due to the influence of her power, but most of it came from their rock-solid friendship and affection toward each other.

"So, I'm guessing you work with bikes yourself, or is it cars?" she hazarded, nodding toward Luke's oil-stained hands.

"Cars," he confirmed. "I work in a garage. We get the occasional bike in, though. There was a Gold Wing a while ago. The rider managed to wrap it around a tree. You've never seen such a god-almighty mess."

"The hell?" Bobbi frowned in confusion. "Gold Wing's a road bike. How'd it even get close to a tree?"

Luke shrugged. "It was a wet road and he lost control. Shit happens."

Bobbi nodded, agreeing with the age-old mantra of bike riders everywhere. *No matter how careful you are* ... "Shit happens," she echoed.

She allowed herself to feel a sliver of hope. Now they'd calmed down, Luke and Jericho seemed to be nice enough guys. If they kept the conversation light, she figured she could handle the rest of the trip to Utopia City easily enough. *This might not be as bad as I thought.*

It was something to hope for, anyway.

12
Politics

Jericho stood up from his seat and went to slide past Luke. His cousin looked up from the intense technical discussion he was having with Bobbi—something about suspensions and crossovers, which went way over Jericho's head—and raised his eyebrows. "Is everything all right, cuz? We're not boring you, are we?"

"Nope. It's fine." Somewhat to his surprise, he meant it. "Just hitting the restroom then the vending machines. See what they've got." He looked from one to the other. "Want anything?"

Luke nodded. "Actually, yeah. Get me a sandwich, if you don't mind." He glanced over at Bobbi. "The sandwiches are seriously good, here. So are the cookies."

"Ooh. Food. I forgot to eat before I got back on the train." Bobbi smiled up at Jericho. For a girl, he thought, she had a nice smile. "Can I get one of each, please?"

"Sure." Jericho got out past Luke. Once he'd finished in the restroom, he ducked through the connecting doors into the next passenger car and had a look at the selection in the vending machines. Paying for it was simple; there was a swipe sensor for his MagCard, which he presumed added the cost of the snacks to his overall fare. *It's how I'd do it.* Picking out three sandwiches and a cookie, he swiped to pay for them and collected them as they were dispensed. As an afterthought, he turned to the drink dispenser across the aisle and got three bottles of water the same way. There were other drinks available, including iced coffee and carbonated sodas, but water was the cheapest, and he didn't need a shot of caffeine right then.

He'd seen Luke pull his speech upgrade trick before, occasionally. It was like his cousin could change gears in his brain; on the street, he talked street. In polite company, he worded things more discreetly.

When Jericho collected the water-bottles, he found that they were made of glass instead of plastic, which was a little unusual, but not overly so. *Probably a UML thing.*

Carrying the lot without dropping anything was a little difficult, but he cheated by surreptitiously sticking the bottles together with a glue-tag. While this had the effect of causing the surface of the water in each bottle to curve oddly as the liquid clustered toward the glue-tag, he didn't think anyone would notice. With a sense of accomplishment, he made it back through the connecting doors and dumped his bounty on the table, dissolving the 'tag as he did so.

"Ooh, thank you," Bobbi enthused as she grabbed one of the sandwiches. "I'm *starved.*" She grinned up at him as she pulled the packet open. "You'll make some lucky guy a good husband someday."

Jericho returned the grin as he slid past Luke. Somewhat to his surprise, he was rather enjoying Bobbi's company. She'd barely blinked when Luke told her about him being gay, which was when he would've expected her to make her excuses and leave. But she hadn't. In fact, she'd come straight out with the revelation that she'd been cheated on, too. It gave Jericho a weird feeling of kinship with her, although he was just a little jealous that she'd found another boyfriend so fast. *Straight girls have all the luck.* Though there was a vibe there that he wasn't a hundred percent sure about. It seemed to him that she was unhappier than someone with a steady boyfriend should be, though she hadn't given Luke the eye yet. *And why's she traveling alone? Did he pull a Stephen on her?*

"Hey, Jericho," she said as he broke open his own sandwich packet. "Can I ask a personal question?"

"Um, I guess," he ventured. "Don't promise to answer it, though." He grinned to show he wasn't totally serious.

"That's fair." She smiled understandingly. "So, um, how'd you find out about your boyfriend?"

Whoof, he decided. *She doesn't ask the easy ones.* "Uh, I only found out because *he* told me." He hooked his thumb at Luke without looking at him, then rolled his eyes. "Not that we've even officially broken up yet. Stephen doesn't know I know."

"Really?" Bobbi's smile widened to a grin, one with lots of teeth in it. "So, you can come back and he'll be all *hey, let's take up where we left off,* and you can be *no, bitch, we're done.* And then you share pics of his face all over the internet."

"Maybe, I guess." While Jericho liked to think he could pull off a line like that with Stephen, in his experience daydreams rarely matched up to reality. "He might cry. I hate it when he cries." Though he'd always liked it when Stephen comforted him when *he* cried. Their relationship was weird like that.

"Okay, right, so this is what you do." Bobbi's eyes were alight with interest. "When you go back, you start moving your stuff out—you *are* living with him, right?"

Jericho nodded. "Six months now." A wave of pain washed through him. *Six months. How long has he been lying to me?*

She nodded understandingly, and the pain faded away again.

God damn, *it's nice to talk to someone who understands.*

"Right," she continued briskly. "So, you start moving your stuff out. You don't tell him. A little bit at a time. This way, when you do break up with the cheating asshole, there's no big packing scene, because that's so awkward. You're trying to put clothes into the suitcase, he's trying to pull them out ..."

"I know, right?" Jericho rolled his eyes. "He didn't even want me to take this trip without him. I had to repack my bag three times, because he kept finding it and unpacking it. And I wasn't even breaking up with him then."

"Wow, harsh." She reached across the table. "I think you're better off. I really do."

Jericho took her hand for a moment. Her grip was stronger than he'd expected, but then, she did maintenance on her own motorbike. "You're probably right." He thought about that for a moment. *Wait one cotton-pickin' second.* Luke hadn't told him outright, but he'd lied about it in the clumsiest way possible, which was why Jericho had thought to ask. He turned to his cousin, suspicion building in his mind. "You *wanted* to tell me. Didn't you?"

If Jericho hadn't known his cousin as well as he did, the guileless gaze Luke gave him would have fooled him for sure. As it was, it just confirmed Jericho's suspicions. And, from the grin on Bobbi's face, hers too. For his part, Luke shrugged carelessly. "'Course I wanted ta tell ya, cuz. We're *kin.* Doesn't mean I was gonna, 'til ya asked."

"Right." Jericho thumped him lightly on the shoulder with his fist. "Asshat." He could have thanked Luke sincerely, but that would have only made his cousin intensely uncomfortable, so Jericho resorted to Bro Code 101; Shoulder Punches Are Always Appropriate. This was a system that worked for the both of them.

"So, talking about awkward subjects," Bobbi ventured after a moment. "Have you heard the latest about Team Power?" She sounded a lot more serious now.

Jericho looked at her, frowning. "I saw one of those Amber Alert posters for Vanessa in the train station, but it was an old one, and I haven't had the time to pay attention to the news over the last few days. Been kinda busy."

Luke's brow wrinkled. "I've heard about them, but not much more than that. They're a family team, right? Out of Chicago? They don't wear masks?"

"That's right." Jericho nodded. "Adam Power's an independent, an artificer. Powersuit user. Him and Tesseract have been working out of Chicago for … jeez, it must be more than twenty years now."

"Since nineteen-ninety, so yeah, twenty-three years," Bobbi clarified. "They first teamed up to capture Charnel, and they just kept working together after that. They unmasked and got married in 'ninety-four, and officially announced the name change to Team Power right after." She sighed. "I remember watching the TV spot as a kid. The Ghast crashed the wedding and tried to kidnap Tess for some stupid hostage scheme, but she threw her bouquet in his face and lit into him. Adam had to pull her off him. They said later on that she broke his jaw in two places and busted three of his ribs. I *so* wanted to be her, right then."

"Damn," muttered Luke. "Tough girl."

Jericho tilted his head, not denying the point. He also imagined, but didn't say, that getting married to Adam Power might have *also* figured into the daydreams of a girl of that age. "Well, she *is* a prodigy. Mind you, it's also pretty impressive that she's had two kids since then and it hasn't slowed her down any." He counted on his fingers. "Vanessa in 'ninety-five and Buddy in … 'oh-three?"

"'Oh-two," Bobbi said firmly. "He's eleven."

"Okay, this is something I don't get." Luke looked from Jericho to Bobbi. "How does it work with them not having secret identities? Anywhere they go, folks know them. They wouldn't have any privacy."

"Well, this is true," admitted Jericho. "They haven't had secret identities since just before the wedding. But it wasn't exactly their idea. Remember how I told you about Unmask? They faked a mugging to decoy Tesseract in, then the 'victim' ripped her mask off and they got photos of her face. Tried to blackmail her and Adam with them. This was just after their coup with Surgeon One. They must've thought they were untouchable."

Luke scowled. "Not cool."

"No argument," agreed Bobbi. "But Adam and Tess doubled down. They changed their legal names to their superhero names by deed poll in secret then unmasked in public, just before they announced their plans to get married."

"Ballsy." Luke looked from Bobbi to Jericho. "What'd Unmask do about that? From what you told me; I can't see them taking that sort of thing lying down."

Jericho nodded. "You're right, but they didn't get the chance to do anything at all. See, they were banking on the blackmail keeping the heroes honest. What they *didn't* count on was how well Adam and Tesseract worked together as a team. Between Adam's tech and Tesseract's skills, they tracked down every one of the idiots trying to blackmail them and gathered enough evidence of the actual blackmail demands that the day after they unmasked, they were able to sweep all of them up and hand them over to the cops. The evidence made it a slam-dunk case. Go straight to jail, do not pass Go, do not collect two hundred dollars. And given that Unmask had been trying to do to Tesseract what their buddies had already done to Surgeon One, they got *hammered*. Maximum sentence, forget about parole."

Bobbi grinned and took up the tale. "So, when the dead-man switch triggered and Tess's face got sent to every news outlet in the city, it was a nothing story. People already knew what they looked like. And they had enough goodwill banked by that time that people just shrugged and let them be. By the time the kids came along, Team Power having public identities was a fact of life. Vanessa started coming out with her parents when she was ten, and Buddy made his debut last month, I think."

"Wait, did the kids get powers from their folks?" Luke was looking even more confused now. "I didn't even know that was a thing."

Jericho shrugged. "It's not, as far as I know. But Adam made power armor—no pun intended—for both kids. By all reports, it's pretty kickass." He looked over at Bobbi. "So, what's happened with Vanessa since then? Any new developments?"

Bobbi grimaced. "According to leaked police reports just now making the rounds, Vanessa dropped into a precinct station on the night she disappeared, wearing her armor. She claimed that her dad molested her, and that her mom tried to cover it up. But when they called her parents, she bolted. Literally busted out through someone's office and flew out of there. Vanished into thin air, if you can believe it."

Jericho's eyes widened. "You're *shitting* me." He recalled the images and footage he'd seen of Team Power, portraying the charismatic Adam Power as a true American hero and family man. "That can't be right. Can it?" He wanted to believe it wasn't true. But there'd been other incidences in the news of well-known 'family men' who'd done that and worse. He'd even encountered a case or two in and around Savannah. *If they could do it …*

"Hey, it's just something I saw on the late news last week. I mean, I know it's bullshit. It's gotta be. Adam and Tess are *heroes*, for God's sake. They've risked their lives to save more people than I've had hot dinners. Adam nearly *died* fighting Kraken back in the nineties. There's no way in *hell* he would've hurt Vanessa." Her gloved hands, on the table, clenched into fists. "But the way they keep harping on it, like he's already been tried and convicted, flat-out burns me."

Luke frowned as he unconsciously echoed Jericho's words. "That can't be right. They love covering heroes in the news. I've seen it myself, a hundred times. They can't get enough of them."

"Depends on the hero, and depends on the news outlet," Bobbi said flatly. "Even the most reputable outlets have their biases, and the people going after Adam Power are pretty sleazy. They love controversy, the more the better, and they're willing to bend the truth pretty hard to get it."

"Biases?" Jericho blinked, confused. "What do you mean, biases?" He hadn't known Bobbi for long, but he respected her for her views and outlook. It was obvious that she didn't believe the molestation story for a moment, which was her right. The trouble was, *he* didn't know Adam Power at all, so if the news outlets were painting him as a monster, perhaps there was some truth in there? The news was the news, wasn't it?

"What, you really don't know?" Bobbi looked at him, then shook her head. "Christ, I thought everyone knew. It's all about politics. Conservative news outlets prefer government-sponsored heroes over independents, and they'll cover teams over single players. If you're neither, you've got to bend over backward to give them good copy or you get relegated to page ten, if you make any column inches at all. And that's if they don't just start making up dirt about you."

"What the hell?" Jericho stared at Luke, whose expression of surprise likely mirrored his own. "That is not something I knew about."

"Yeah, well." Bobbi's distaste was obvious from her tone of voice. "Unfortunately, it's the way things work. Everyone pretends it doesn't, but if anyone tries to change it, they run into a brick wall. It's the price of doing business."

"Huh. Anyway." Jericho shook his head, trying to get back on track. "So, what you're saying is that the conservative gutter press is taking pot-shots at Adam Power, but he can't prove he didn't do anything? That sucks." If that was the actual case, of course. He wasn't *sold* on the idea of Adam Power being a child molester, and he certainly didn't want it to be true, but his upbringing had predisposed him toward not jumping to a specific conclusion just because he didn't like the alternative.

"Especially if Vanessa never shows up again," Luke agreed. "Even if he never did anything to her, he's going to have a hell of a time proving it if she's in the wind." Behind his tone was a certainty rooted in the circumstances from which he'd been born. Jericho had never heard all the stories of his cousin's childhood, and he wasn't sure he wanted to.

Bobbi looked a little upset at Luke's words, and Jericho took the time to elbow his cousin surreptitiously in the ribs. *Nice going, asshat.*

"But what if there *was* a way to prove it?" she asked. "Prove that the police report's bullshit, I mean?"

Jericho shook his head regretfully. "Well, nobody's going to prove *that*. The cops would've only taken down what she told them. Proving what she *said* was bullshit? Can't be done outside of a court of law. Sucks, but that's the way it is." And of course, to fight allegations like that, charges would have to be laid and then disproven in court, which would require both sides to be confident enough in their respective versions of the story to be willing to show up in the first place. Without Vanessa there to give her side of things, that wasn't going to happen. And without a clear acquittal, the negative publicity would probably sink Team Power once and for all, even if Adam Power was innocent of all charges. *The court of public goddamn opinion strikes again.*

"No, but what if someone with powers looked into his head and said for a certainty that he didn't do it?" Bobbi's expression held a certain intensity. Jericho couldn't tell where she was going with this.

"What, like Thinkster?" Luke shook his head. "Sorry, that dog won't hunt. Poor sumbitch OD'd last year."

Jericho raised his eyebrows slightly at that. *I told you that myself, about an hour ago. Smartass.*

"Uh, no." Bobbi looked just a little confused. "I've never even heard of Thinkster. I'm talking about what if someone could read, you know, emotions. Look at someone while they're talking and say, 'he's telling the truth'. Look deeper and be able to say, 'this guy would never do that'. That sort of thing."

When Stephen was thinking deeply, he had a habit of stroking his beard. Jericho found himself emulating that action and stopped in irritation. "Okay …" He took the time to think his next few words through. "Assuming there's someone like that out there, which isn't a given … I mean, how many Enabled out there can hear peoples' thoughts, anyway? Only one I ever heard of was Thinkster."

"There *was* Mindscrew," offered Bobbi. "He was one of the bad ones, back in the nineties."

"Oh, right, yeah," Jericho said. "Forgot about him."

"With a name like that, I'm thinking either villain, or a hero who really didn't give a shit about being liked," Luke said with a chuckle, spraying sandwich crumbs on the table.

"Villain," Bobbi confirmed. "One of the real assholes. He started slow, hit a few casinos and cleaned out the blackjack tables until they got wise. Once his powers got known, he put on a mask and went into full-on crime. Blackmail, grand larceny, political manipulation and so on. Any inconvenient witnesses turned up dead. By the time he dropped out of sight in 'ninety-seven, he was right up there on the terror villain list."

"And he called himself 'Mindscrew' and got away with it?" Luke shook his head. "Goddamn Enabled. I swear."

Bobbi smirked. "Well, originally he tried to get them to call him Mind-Fucker, but the news organizations couldn't run that without bleeping it, so they called him Mindscrew instead. In the end, it stuck."

Jericho nodded. "Anyway, getting back to the point. Let's assume there's someone like that, but not a villain, and not strung out on drugs. I guess it wouldn't be too hard to prove they had the power to look into peoples' heads … but how do they prove that what they're saying is true? I mean, nobody else can see what they can see, yeah?" *Like what happens to me, every time this goddamn train does its sideways-flip thing.* He could get used to it, but he knew he'd never really enjoy it.

Bobbi raised her finger triumphantly. "Ah, but what if that person was a member of Force Majeure? They work with the government, right? That gives them kinda law-enforcement status, right? They could do it, and the judge would have to listen."

"They'd still have to get around what the girl said about him," Luke put in. "I mean, that's seriously damaging, right there."

"So, I'll just have to find out where she's gone and talk to her, too," Bobbi said promptly. "Find out why she's …" She trailed to a halt, looking stricken. "Uhhh …"

13
Powers

There was a long silence, during which Jericho and Luke both slowly sat up and looked at her. At first, she shrank away, but then she drew strength from somewhere and met their gazes firmly.

"Well, *dang*," remarked Luke, in what Jericho decided had to be the most eloquent understatement his cousin had ever uttered. "I'd say *you're shittin' me* but I'm pretty sure you're not."

Bobbi cleared her throat. "Please don't tell anyone," she said quietly, articulating each word with care. "I mean, I'm reasonably certain that you won't, but I thought it needed saying."

"Not a word," Jericho assured her. He peered at her. "So … all this time, you've been reading our minds?" *How much do you know about us already?*

"Not minds, not minds," Bobbi said, her voice hasty. "*Emotions.* I don't know what you're thinking. I can only see what you're *feeling.* And it's no fun at all, let me tell you. Every time someone gets upset or excited or angry around me, it feels like I've just been punched in the face. Especially if they're pissed *at* me. Headache central."

"So, why'd you sit down with us?" asked Luke practically, beating Jericho by about two seconds.

"Self-preservation," she explained succinctly. "I thought if I sat down and talked to you, maybe helped you get over your argument, you'd calm down. The only other option was leaving the car altogether, and I didn't know if things would be any better elsewhere."

"Huh. So, you sitting down with us was the equivalent of knocking on the neighbor's door at two AM and asking him to turn his stereo down." Jericho rubbed his chin, then dropped his hand to the table again. "Uh, sorry about making you feel uncomfortable."

"Oh, trust me, it could've been a lot worse." Bobbi's voice was definite. "You calmed right down, and neither one of you has tried to hit on me."

"If I can ask a question, ma'am?" ventured Luke.

She huffed a sigh. "Sure, ask away. But for God's sake, stop calling me 'ma'am'. You're making me feel old. Call me Bobbi."

"It's a respect thing, m—uh, Miz Bobbi." Luke raised his gaze to her face. "Those gloves. Are they about your power too?"

"Yes." She raised her left hand and wiggled the fingers. "Skin contact makes it a whole lot worse. Ordinary emotions are bad enough, but if someone's feeling strong emotions, it's like being caught in a flood where I don't know what's mine and what's theirs, or if I'll still be *me* once it's over."

Jericho winced. "That sounds like it kind of sucks. A lot."

"Yeah, no shit." Her voice was dry, almost hiding the underlying pain. "It's why I'm going to Utopia City. Because I *know* he's innocent, but I can't do a damn thing about it, right now."

"You *know* he's innocent?" Jericho sat forward. "You're certain about that?" While he'd been willing to keep an open mind, the surety in her voice called to him.

"One hundred percent." Bobbi took a deep breath. "See, Melody gave me the idea. She's my younger sister, and we share everything about everything. She suggested that we go to Chicago and talk to Adam Power face to face, so I could work out for myself whether he's lying or not. But she's just started in her new job, and the earliest she could arrange time off was next week. When I heard that he was holding a press conference, I jumped the gun and took the train to Chicago this morning. Melody wanted to come too, but I told her not to endanger her job, that she could come join me when she got the time off."

"What happened?" asked Luke. "When you got to Chicago, I mean. Did you get to talk to him?"

Bobbi shook her head. "No, I didn't, but I did get to see him speak. He was absolutely adamant that he hadn't touched or hurt Vanessa in any way ... and my power says he was being totally truthful." Reaching up, she rubbed her forehead. "Trouble was, there were a lot of people in that crowd and emotions were running high. I had to leave, or I would've ended up in the hospital with a three-day migraine. From there, I decided to go straight to Utopia City and see if I could speak to *someone* about jumping the queue. I mean, I applied last week but I haven't heard back yet. Can't hurt to ask, right? If anyone's got access to people who can help me learn to get a handle on my powers, it'll be Force Majeure. And once I'm in, I can get in contact with Team Power and let them know I can help clear this up once and for all." She paused, her eyes narrowing. "And right now, you're not showing nearly enough surprise at finding out that I'm Enabled. What's going on here? Did you already know?"

Jericho shared a glance with Luke. "What do you think? Tell her or not?" There were risks involved, he knew. There were *always* risks involved with sharing a secret this big. The fact that she'd already inadvertently outed herself to them was a point in favor of sharing, but there was more to consider than that. After all, they could keep her secret without ever revealing Jericho's. *On the other hand, she already knows that something's up.*

Luke frowned, apparently considering options. "I'm thinking ..."

"Wait a minute." Bobbi looked at Jericho, then at Luke. "Are you ... one of you has got powers too. Am I right?" She blinked rapidly a couple of times. "Shit, I'm right. Which of you is it?" After another glance at Jericho, she focused on Luke. "You. It's you, isn't it? What powers do you have?"

Pressing his hand over his mouth, Luke bent over and burst into snorting laughter. Jericho would have done the same, but he was too surprised to do so, not to mention just a little hurt. *What, don't I look heroic enough?*

This must have communicated itself to Bobbi somehow, because her eyes widened as she looked at Jericho again. "Oh, shit. It's not Luke. It's *you*, isn't it?"

Taking refuge in sarcasm, Jericho leaned nonchalantly back in his seat. "Well, you're not exactly spoiled for choice right now, are you?"

"Asshole." But she was grinning as she said it, in the same way that Serena or Olivia would have smiled when they said, *'Bless your heart'*. "You've really got powers?"

Jericho sat forward and picked up his water-bottle, which was still about half full. Swiping his other hand under it, he deposited a glue-tag on the bottom. Then he leaned across the table and placed the bottle in front of her. "Pick that up," he invited.

"Why?" Her expression was justifiably wary. "What'd you do to it? It's not going to explode or something, is it?"

He shook his head. "Nothing harmful. Go ahead, pick it up." A side-glance showed that Luke had gotten over his hilarity, though if he smirked any harder, he might do himself an injury. Given that Jericho had pulled exactly the same trick on him back when he came out with his powers to his cousin, this wasn't really a surprise.

Bobbi reached out and carefully took hold of the bottle, then went to lift it. It didn't move. With a frown, she tried harder. Jericho heard her grunt under her breath as she exerted more force, but it was only when she used both hands and a lot of effort that she was able to unstick the bottle from the table. She put it back on the table—where it promptly stuck itself down again—and stared at him. "What did you do? Are you one of those guys who can move things with their minds?"

"Telekinetic, and no," he assured her. "I've got gravity powers. I just gave the bottom of that bottle its own personal gravity field. Like a tiny black hole." Dismissing the effect, he nodded toward the bottle. "Try it again."

This time, she lifted it easily. Turning it over in her hand, she examined it minutely. "I can't see any difference."

"You won't," he said. "My power doesn't make any actual changes that I can see."

"Huh. Well, shit," she mused, passing the water bottle from one hand to the other, hefting it up and down as though she were testing the weight. "That must come in handy. What do you call yourself?"

He smiled and bowed slightly in his seat. "G-Man, at your service, ma'am."

"What, like the Bureau?" she asked, looking a little startled. "I didn't know they had any Enabled working for them."

"Hah, nope." He chuckled. "It stands for 'gravity', but you probably had that figured out. I haven't got any formal connection to regular law enforcement." He couldn't stop his lip from curling slightly as he said that.

A smile lifted the corner of Bobbi's mouth. "You're not a fan?"

"Not particularly," Jericho admitted. "If you hadn't noticed, the justice system isn't known for being tolerant of anyone outside the cis-het norm. Folks like me've been screwed over way too many times for ..." He trailed off and stopped as he experienced a flashbulb moment. "*Wait* a minute. What you said earlier about politics, and the way they're going after Adam Power. Is *that* why I've never made it into the big papers?"

Bobbi shrugged. "You're from Savannah, right? Georgia, no disrespect intended, is about as conservative as it gets. You're non-government, you're an independent player and you're gay. That's three strikes out of three, right there. The only way you could be worse off is if you had the same color skin as Luke. Are there any other heroes in Savannah, and do they show up as liberal or conservative?"

Jericho snorted. "Only one, now. Pickup. He drives, and I shit you not, a pickup truck that turns into a big-ass mech, with a goddamn Confederate flag painted on the hood. And he makes the front page every other week." Everything made so much sense to him, now. There was one paper in Savannah that carried articles about him, but that was a weekly and sometimes it seemed all Pickup had to do to get headlines in the dailies was rumble down the street. "I never knew. I always thought it was just me."

"Yeah, well, it turns out it was, but not the way you thought." Luke shook his head. "Sorry, cuz."

Jericho took a deep breath, then let it out again. "Right. Once I join Force Majeure, they can all kiss my ass. I'll be part of the biggest goddamn government-affiliated team out there. Let's see 'em ignore me then." Pausing, he shot Bobbi an apologetic glance. "Sorry. I meant 'us'."

She nodded in acknowledgment, a small smile curving her lips. "Works for me. I knew I was going to be meeting superheroes when I went to Utopia City, but I sure as hell didn't think it was going to be on the *train*."

Luke chuckled. "Miz Bobbi, would you be surprised to learn that Jericho and you aren't the only powered folks on this train? Because I know for a fact you're not."

Jericho's head came up as he realized the likelihood of what Luke was saying. "How do you know that? I'm not saying you're wrong. Jeez, I wonder how many other Enabled are on here?"

Bobbi shrugged. "I wouldn't worry about it. I'd say they're all doing exactly what we're doing. Keeping their heads down and not making a song and dance about it." She looked curiously at Luke. "You know something we've missed, don't you?"

"Maybe." Luke nodded toward the far end of the passenger car. "There's a couple of them that's been sitting at the other end of the car for the last ten minutes. They just got up." Despite the privacy bubble, he lowered his voice a little.

Curious, Jericho sat up in his seat, craning his neck to look over the heads of the other passengers. At the same time, Bobbi twisted around in her seat. Jericho saw the flash of color moving down the aisle a moment before she gasped in surprise. "Huh," she said. "They're in costume."

"It sure looks like it," Luke confirmed. "J, you're the superhero here. You got any idea who they are?"

As much as he would've liked to say 'yes', Jericho had to shake his head. "No." He hesitated briefly. "But the one in front looks kinda familiar."

The 'one in front' was a thirty-something African American woman wearing subdued colors, with some sort of bird in silhouette on her chest logo and a visor that looked like an eagle's beak. She also looked fit as hell, though she was favoring her right leg very slightly. A discreetly contoured knee brace explained why; leg injuries were an occupational hazard among Enabled, especially the ones who were into roof-running. Fortunately, it looked as though she was a prodigy, which meant the injury would be healed up in a matter of days. That was one of the perks of that particular powerset.

Her companion was in his early twenties, sporting an almost garish costume of bright primary colors. As he moved down the aisle with nearly every person watching, he summoned glowing balls out of nowhere and began to juggle them; as far as Jericho could tell, they weren't following the laws of physics.

While Jericho had never seen either Enabled before, he couldn't help but notice the Force Majeure patch on their costumes. The woman's patch included color-coded dots which he'd read indicated rank within the organization, though he didn't know enough to interpret them.

When they got closer, Jericho noted that the woman was pulling a wheeled suitcase and the young man had a backpack on. Before he could comment on this, Luke reached across and switched off the privacy bubble. "Hey, 'scuse me," he said to the costumed woman as the pair reached their table. "Y'all guardin' th' train, or is there somethin' else goin' on?"

The woman stopped and turned toward him. When she spoke, her voice was clipped and precise, a whole world away from Luke's down-home accent. "Sir, there's no problem. We're just taking the train, the same as you." Evidently done with the conversation, she hit the button to open the doors into the next car.

However, her juggling teammate opted to put his oar in. "Yeah, we're transferring to the Seattle office. The maglev's free for Force Majeure members so hey, it's a no-brainer." He somehow made two of the balls disappear but continued to juggle the other two with his left hand as he reached out with his right. "Hi, pleased to meet you. I'm Stage Act, and my boss here's Nighthawk. How you doing, sir?"

"I'm doin' right fine." Luke shook his hand. "Ya know, you're th' first real superhero I ever got ta shake th' hand of. It's an honor." Jericho privately decided that at some point he'd get Luke but good. *First real superhero, my ass.*

"That's cool," Stage Act said cheerfully. "It's good to meet the public. You get a chance to go on my web page, gimme a like, okay? Have a nice day, sir." With a friendly nod to Jericho and Bobbi, he moved on, following the scowling Nighthawk through to the next passenger car.

14
Utopia

Luke fell back into his seat with an outrush of breath that turned into a chuckle. "Well, that right there was pretty damn cool. Though I had a notion for a second there that Nighthawk was fixing to haul off and whup my ass but good when I started talking to them."

Bobbi flicked the switch for the privacy bubble. "The whole thing was an act." She sounded quite pleased with herself.

Jericho and Luke both stared at her. "Say that again?" Jericho asked, not sure if he'd heard right.

She grinned at them. "She was putting it on. I'd say she's keeping up her image. Pretending to be hard-bitten, rough, tough. Stage Act was amused as hell at playing the naïve youngster, too. I'd say it's a routine they have, to make people underestimate them."

Luke's eyebrows tracked up toward his hairline. "Well, butter my butt an' call me a biscuit. They totally took me in."

Bobbi nodded. "That's almost certainly deliberate. They've probably been teaming up for a while now, if they're getting transferred together. I'm guessing it's a regular routine with them." She gave Luke a perceptive stare. "Mind you, it's not unlike the act you've been putting on for me. Or were you putting on an act for *them?*"

Jericho chuckled at the chagrined expression on Luke's face. "She's got you there. You want to tell her about it, or should I?"

Luke waved him off. "I'll do it. See, Miz Bobbi, I growed up talkin' like this 'cause that's how folks around me talked. But—" He stopped as she held up her gloved hand.

"But talking like that doesn't get you into a well-paying job," she filled in. "So you learned to speak more correctly, and you talk like that when the situation requires it. Style switching isn't exactly an uncommon thing." She gave him an encouraging smile. "The only thing I'm wondering about is why you switched back to talk to the heroes."

Style switching. Huh. Jericho hadn't even known that sort of thing had a name.

"Oh, that's easy," Luke said with an answering grin. "I did that because I wanted them to see me as someone to forget as soon as they walked away. Folks like me don't draw attention from the authorities if we can possibly help it."

"I see." Bobbi's mouth quirked. "I was ready to be upset at you, but I see the logic in what you were doing. It's nice that you went to that much effort to make a good impression on me, but it's fine. Impression's been made. Feel free to talk whichever way you're most comfortable doing." She rubbed her lips thoughtfully. "But on another topic altogether, that just gave me an idea."

"Is this a bad idea or a good idea?" asked Jericho pragmatically. "Or is it one of those ideas that everyone knows is a bad move, but we go ahead with it anyway?"

"Good idea, I think," Bobbi said. "I've read up on Utopia City. Apparently there's cheap accommodation there, aimed mainly at visiting Enabled. I was going to be renting a place on my own, but why don't we share a place and split the cost instead?"

"Y'know, that there ain't such a bad idea." Luke gave Bobbi an approving nod. "Me an' Jericho was prob'ly gonna go halves in whatever we found, but goin' thirds is even better."

"Sounds legit to me," Jericho agreed. "Thirds it is." He retrieved his water bottle from Bobbi and unscrewed the cap to take a drink.

Bobbi leaned back in her seat; the most relaxed Jericho had seen her yet. "Awesome. So how long you guys going to be staying in town, anyway?"

Jericho was about to answer when the yellow lights started flashing again. He glanced at the privacy bubble switch; sure enough, the light had gone out. At the same time, the PA system cut in again.

"Attention, all passengers. Attention, all passengers. This train will be passing through Kansas City in six minutes. All passengers stopping in Kansas City, please move to Cars Five through Six. All passengers for the Kansas City to Wichita train, please move to Cars Seven through Eight. All passengers for the Kansas City to Omaha train, please move to Cars Nine through Ten. All passengers for the Kansas City to Utopia City train, please remain in this car. Do not forget your luggage ..."

"Thank *fuck*," muttered Luke, flopping back against his seat. "We been gettin' up an' walkin' jes' to stay on the damn train the whole friggin' trip."

"Don't I just know it," Bobbi said, sounding unamused. "I've been doing a lot of walking too."

"From New York to LA, huh?" Jericho said with a wry grin.

"Oh, you've seen that asshole too?" Bobbi rolled her eyes. "I don't even know why people think it's funny. I swear, I could keep fit just by riding the maglev every day."

"Sounds like they're missin' a trick," Luke suggested. "Offer low-price rides through high-traffic areas so's folks gotta walk a lot more or git left behind."

"Hmm," Bobbi mused. "That could actually work."

Jericho looked up at the digital sign. It now read 'UTOPIA CITY 19:56'. After a moment of thought, he frowned. *Wait a minute. If it's twenty minutes to Utopia City, then ...* Taking out his phone, he nudged the power button to wake it up long enough to check the time. A few seconds later, he nodded as he found his suspicion confirmed. Allowing for differences between his phone and the station clock, they'd be pulling into Utopia City precisely two and a half hours following their departure from Savannah, as noted by the kiosk back in the transit station. He was pretty sure the time zone change gave them back an hour, so they'd be hitting Utopia City at almost exactly half after six. *I wonder how they manage to time the stations so precisely. It's not like the cities are a set distance apart ... wait.*

A moment later, he had it, and he facepalmed hard enough to get both Luke and Bobbi looking at him. "Goddamn it, I'm a dumbass," he groaned.

Luke grinned at him. "Not that I'm arguin', cuz, but what exactly are you referrin' to in this specific instance?"

"The speed of the train." Jericho kept his voice down. Not that anyone could overhear him past the ongoing announcement, but there was no sense in not being careful. "I just figured out why we kept speeding up and slowing down between stations."

"We were?" Bobbi looked at him blankly. "I hadn't really noticed."

"I reckoned we mighta been goin' faster some times than others, but it weren't somethin' that I was thinkin' that hard about," Luke said. "So why *were* we changin' speeds?"

"So we'd hit the next station dead on time," Jericho said. "I'm guessing they mark it by the quarter hour. The stations are at least a hundred miles apart, so on average we're doing four hundred. Sometimes a bit more, sometimes a little less. They can probably go a lot faster than they've showed so far, but because the trains never lose time stopping, four hundred's fast enough. Anyway, the way they're timing it, we're always gonna hit the next station on the hour, quarter hour or half hour. This means that with the right computer system overseeing the whole network, working out the connections for every city would be a piece of cake."

"Well, dang." Luke looked at him admiringly. "I take back the 'dumbass' thing. That there's a mighty slick bit of figurin'."

Jericho shrugged. "It was really bothering me, that's all. I knew it was happening, but it took me 'til just now to work out *why*."

He leaned against the window as the train blazed on through Kansas City. In fifteen minutes, when he got off the maglev, he was going to be faced with some crucial choices. The first was a big one: when Stephen inevitably called him, what was he going to say? There were several options, which boiled down to: pretending he didn't know about his boyfriend's infidelity, letting him know but keeping him on, or dumping him over the phone. He liked to think he wasn't the sort of asshat who would pull the latter stunt, but neither of the other two appealed either.

The trouble was, giving Stephen a pass on his infidelity would almost certainly lead to more of the same. Once Stephen came to the conclusion that Luke hadn't told Jericho, he'd probably decide he had a clear run to keep cheating. But even that knowledge didn't—couldn't—sway Jericho from his path. Going back to Savannah *might* get Stephen back onto the straight and narrow, but it *would* invalidate the entire reason that he'd come to Utopia City in the first place. And that had to take priority.

Of course, as soon as he identified his goal, doubts began to spring up once more. *Do I really have the chops to be a member of something this big?* They'd accepted his application for an interview, but that didn't mean he'd be taken on. *How many people show up, only to go away disappointed?* Doubts began to worm their way through his certainty. The closer he came to Utopia City, the harder it became for him to believe that he really was prepared for the interview.

Bobbi cleared her throat. "Hey, Jericho."

He turned to face her. "What's up?" Part of him was glad that he'd been distracted from his self-doubts, but another part wanted to keep digging deeper.

"You'll make it." Her voice conveyed nothing but sincerity. "I promise you. You'll be great. They'll love you."

How'd she—oh. Right. He wanted to believe her, but there was also the knowledge that she could tell how he was feeling and wanted to cheer him up for her own reasons. *Self-preservation, huh?* Still, her encouraging words had an effect. Even as he wondered about her motives, he still felt better about things. "Thanks. I mean it. You know, you're about the only one who's bothered to say something nice about this?"

The mock glare she sent Luke was almost worth the aggravation. "Luke, seriously? Your own cousin, and you can't support him in something like this? I'm disappointed in you."

Jericho had to chuckle at the look on Luke's face. His cousin clearly wanted to defend himself, but at the same time he didn't want to argue with Bobbi.

The chuckle didn't help matters any. Luke gave him a betrayed look before turning back to their traveling companion. "Bobbi, ma'am, I never said he cain't git in. I jes' asked if he was certain-sho' he could pull it off once he's one of 'em."

Bobbi shook her head in exasperation. "Come *on*, Luke. You realize he was probably asking himself the same question? Then you, his friend, his *cousin*, turn around and make him think *you're* doubting him? How do you think that made him feel?"

"Ah. Shee-it. Sorry, cuz. Didn't mean to do that to you." Luke's face reflected the dismay in his voice. "I reckon you'll show 'em all once ya git there."

There was a reasonable chance, Jericho decided, that his cousin was only saying it to make him feel good. He chose to accept it at face value anyway. "Thanks, Luke. I appreciate it."

"See? Much better." Bobbi beamed at them both. "So how long are you guys staying in Utopia City, anyway?"

Jericho winced, remembering she'd asked that question just before the announcement went through. "I, uh, get my interview tomorrow morning. We'll be heading back to Savannah once I find out one way or the other. I figure Wednesday at the latest. What about you?"

Bobbi shrugged. "Well, like I said, I sent in an application, but I haven't heard back yet. My powers need to be brought into line before I can get anything else done. I just hope that someone is willing to listen to me about Adam Power." Her tone was optimistic, but Jericho saw the beginnings of a deeper worry in her eyes. Traveling to Utopia City like this was plainly a tremendous leap of faith for her.

He spread his hands. "Look, tell you what. While I'm talking to them, I'll put in a good word for you. Tell 'em what you're fixing to do. They can't have many emotion readers in Force Majeure. Maybe you really can jump the queue, after all."

Bobbi's face cleared and her eyes sparkled with delight. "If you could do *that*, I think I might give you a big wet kiss."

Jericho spread his fingers on his chest and fluttered his eyelids like a stereotypical Southern belle. "Heavens to Betsy," he drawled, overlaying his best effort at a falsetto with an exaggerated Georgia accent. "I'll have y'all know I'm jes' not that kind of girl."

Luke had been there and seen exactly this sort of behavior, so Jericho wasn't surprised when he burst into laughter, pounding the table with his fist. Bobbi was more restrained, but she giggled nonetheless. Jericho leaned back in his seat, feeling pleased with himself. *Yeah, I've still got it.*

"Attention, all passengers. Attention, all passengers. This train will be passing through Utopia City in six minutes. All passengers stopping in Utopia City, please remain in this car. All passengers for the Utopia City to Denver train, please move to Cars One through Seven. Do not forget your luggage ..."

Bobbi stifled her giggles as the announcement came through and the privacy bubble cut out. "One through seven?" She tilted her head to look up at the nearest digital display. "Oh, right. We're number eight."

"Denver?" asked Luke. "What about th' others? They usually say other names."

"Only four ways out of Utopia City," Jericho said. "Omaha, Wichita, Kansas City, Denver." He ticked them off on his fingers. "Omaha's to the north, Wichita's to the south and we just went through Kansas City. Colorado's a ways west of here. The cars going to Wichita or Omaha separated off at the last stop. Means that the only traffic in Utopia City is either stopping or going straight through."

Bobbi nodded. "That should cut down on congestion a bit," she agreed.

"Mighty slick thinkin'," Luke added, his voice admiring.

"Well, the system *was* designed by Force Majeure." Jericho was impressed all the same. The maglev network was fast, cheap, silent, efficient, non-polluting and reliable, and moved a staggering number of people around the country at near-airline speeds every day. It went right against the preconception that Enabled were only good for saving cats from trees or tossing cars around. *We really can make a difference.*

Something in the distance caught his eye, and he squinted to try to make it out.

While he couldn't see Utopia City itself, the city being directly ahead of the train, he was able to see the nearby freeway. Over the top of the multi-lane interstate highway was a large sign that he only barely managed to read before the train was past it and the highway angled under the train toward the south. "Huh. God damn. We really are here."

"What-all ya mean by that, cuz?" Luke looked at him curiously.

Jericho hooked his thumb over his shoulder. "Just saw a sign over the interstate. It said welcome to Utopia, and something about flight lanes."

"Well, that's definitely different." Bobbi's intrigued look matched her tone.

A moment later, Jericho chuckled.

"What?" asked Luke.

Trying not to smirk too widely, Jericho shook his head. "This'd be the perfect moment to say we're not in Kansas anymore."

"But ... we *are*." Bobbi didn't seem to get it.

"Yeah," Jericho said. "That's the joke."

Ignoring Luke's bark of laughter, Bobbi rolled her eyes. "Children," she sighed. "I'm traveling with children."

- End of Part One -

WELCOME
TO
UTOPIA
PLEASE OBEY ALL POSTED FLIGHT LANES

PART TWO

FUTURE SHOCK

Welcome to Utopia, home of Force Majeure …
- Utopia City advertising slogan

… you have been warned.
- a shadowy guy on a rooftop

15
New Arrivals

"**A**ttention, all passengers. Attention, all passengers. This train has now arrived in Utopia City. Please leave the car. Do not forget your luggage. Utopia Maglev Lines takes no responsibility for luggage left on the train. We hope you have enjoyed your trip. Attention, all passengers ..."

Jericho barely heard the announcement as he stared out the window, trying to take in the differences between the central hub of the maglev system and the Savannah station. In a phrase, there was no comparison. Whereas Savannah had only a single-level platform, here he was looking out at a secondary platform which would allow them to walk directly out of the upper level without needing to take the stairs. He'd previously thought the Savannah station to be impressive, with its logo-embossed concrete platform and automatic MagCard ticketing, but this blew all that out of the metaphorical water. Arched ceilings, more kiosks with touch-screen access, and what appeared to be automated luggage carts trundling across the gorgeously tiled floor under their own power; all competed for his attention. Absently, he noted that the latter were following people who were waiting to get on the train, but that aspect barely even registered with him.

"Hey, cuz." Luke's voice caught his attention, and he looked around. The yellow lights were flashing again, and all the digital signs read 'ARRIVAL'; in addition, the announcement was repeating for the third time. "We're gittin' off here, if ya forgot." The last of the other passengers were just filing out through the doors, while Luke and Bobbi got their luggage down from the overhead bins. "Or was you fixin' to stay on the train an' head on back to Savannah?"

"Oh, right. Yeah." Jericho grinned sheepishly at Bobbi. "Coming in, I felt like a hick from the sticks, looking up at all them big ol' buildings." In his defense, some of the buildings had been *seriously* tall. He stood up and worked his way out into the aisle. "Savannah just plain doesn't have anything like this."

She chuckled, dropping her suitcase to the floor and expertly extending the handle. "Trust me, we've had the maglev for a few years in Indianapolis, but our station still isn't nearly as big as this one." She looked around at the otherwise empty carriage. "I think we're it. Maybe we should get off before they decide to charge us for the return trip."

"Yeah, let's do that thing," said Luke; with his backpack still in his hand, he moved past the other two and led the way out through the exit doors onto the platform. Bobbi followed along, towing her wheeled suitcase, while Jericho slung his overnight bag over his shoulder and brought up the rear.

Once they were off the train, he could see that the station was even more impressive than he'd previously thought, with huge skylights letting diffuse sunlight through to light up the concourse. This set off the brilliantly colored tiled mosaic beneath their feet, making him feel as though he was standing in the middle of an art display.

About thirty feet in front of them, past the crowd of people waiting to get on the train and on the other side of a wrought-metal barrier, there was another passenger car, also presumably letting off passengers. Beyond that one, Jericho thought he could see yet another.

"Please stand away from the edge of the platform." By now, Jericho was certain they used the same synthesized voice for all their announcements. **"This passenger car is being taken out of service for maintenance purposes. The next passenger car is due to arrive in thirty seconds."**

Somewhat familiar with this dance by now, Jericho turned to look at the maglev car, noting that the doors were now firmly shut. It began to move, though not with the startling rapidity the one back in Savannah had exhibited. Sliding soundlessly along the track, it vanished into another part of the station.

"Maintenance?" asked Luke. "Didn't hardly look used, even."

"I think it's more a matter of making sure nothing gets close to failing," Jericho said. "I looked it up. Every time a car with a certain number of hours comes through a major hub like this one, it goes through maintenance. And if the computer I suspect they got running the show is powerful enough, they'd be able to ensure that every single one gets routed through a main hub before its hours are up."

"Makes sense," Bobbi agreed. "Luke and I do the same with our bikes. Still, that's a lot of maintenance work. I hope whoever's in charge of it doesn't slack off." She knelt beside her bag and unzipped the main compartment, then pulled out a small handbag. Slinging the strap over her shoulder, she closed her suitcase again and stood up.

"Please stand away from the edge of the platform. The next passenger car is due to arrive in fifteen seconds."

UML, Jericho decided, had all their ducks in a row. When it was possible to predict the arrival of a carriage down to the *second*, that showed a serious amount of organization and forethought. Even as he formed the thought, a new maglev car slid equally soundlessly into view. *Bingo.*

As the doors opened and people started crowding on board, Bobbi turned away from the train. "This way, I think." She pointed off to the left at a row of the same airlock-style scanners that he'd seen in Savannah, through which the last of the passengers from their carriage were moving. Like the previous ones, each had a UML card-reader next to it. *Swipe on in Savannah, swipe off here.* Unlike the Savannah station, this platform sported eight scan-locks, each with a digital sign above it. Half of these signs read 'DEPARTURES' and the other half 'ARRIVALS'; he guessed that his MagCard would only work on the 'Arrivals' side of things.

Bobbi pulled her MagCard from her handbag and stepped forward, heading for one of the 'Arrivals' scan-locks. "Let's get down to ground level. We should be able to hail a cab from there." That sounded almost disappointingly mundane, but Jericho firmly reminded himself that not *everything* about Utopia City was going to be weirdly futuristic. Pulling out his own MagCard, he swiped it over the sensor on the scan-lock he'd chosen, which opened for him with an agreeable beep and a swish of rubber on aluminum. Luke followed him in, while Bobbi took the next one over. The far doors opened the instant the near ones had closed behind him, which made sense; they were getting *off* the train, after all, not *on*. As they left the scan-lock, Luke shrugged his backpack into place.

Beyond the scan-locks, there were more kiosks as well as an almost bewildering array of stairs, escalators, and even an elevator. Jericho was interested to note that the stairs and escalators led upward as well as down, as he'd thought the skylight indicated that they were on the top level of the building. This puzzle was resolved with a quick glance at the signage, which indicated that they were indeed on Level Three. Going down would get them to Level Two or Level One, while going up would take them to what was marked as a monorail station.

"Wait, they've got a monorail?" That was Luke, apparently reading along with him.

Jericho rolled his eyes and pointed back at the maglev. "We literally just came in on the biggest monorail in the country. Pretty sure whatever they've got here isn't going to stack up to that." He turned to Bobbi. "*Are* we taking the monorail?"

"Nah," she said. "Probably won't let us off exactly where we need to go. Like I said, we'll get down to ground level, work out where we're going, then decide on how to hail a cab to get there." She headed for the escalators and Jericho followed her lead, while Luke picked the stairs. The overall drop to Level Two was only about nine or ten feet, less than he'd expected. If he'd been in costume, he would've considered using his slow-fall to glide down without touching a step. As it was, he leaned against the rail and looked around with interest.

"The hell's this?" Luke, jogging down the steps, had caught up with them. "Cuz, you too good for stairs now?"

Jericho flipped him off, then looked around at Level Two as they descended into it. There were more people here. Some, trailed by the automated carts, were moving toward the second stage of down-escalators and stairs, separated from the first stage by about thirty feet. Others were taking stairs and escalators upward, presumably bound for the monorail station. Off to the left, through the glass sliding doors of another row of scan-locks, he could see the replacement maglev car, and the passengers who were even now boarding it. Flanking the scan-locks were the ubiquitous ticket kiosks.

Softly lit ceiling panels here and there glowed with brilliant colors, arranged into oddly familiar patterns. He puzzled over it for a moment, then figured out that some of the tiled areas from above were acting as secondary skylights to illuminate this level as well. Looking around, he realized that Bobbi and Luke were moving on toward the next set of escalators, so he hurried to catch up. More specifically, Bobbi had chosen the escalators while Luke headed once more for the stairs. Jericho stuck close to Bobbi, stepping on behind her. This one dropped much farther than the previous one, going down at least thirty feet.

"Friggin' escalators again," jibed Luke as he jogged downward to keep pace with Jericho and Bobbi. "Never knew you was this lazy, cuz."

"Hey, if it's here, I'll make use of it," Jericho shot back defensively. "Just because *you* were nine before you ever saw an escalator ..."

Luke rolled his eyes. "Weren't my fault. That was all up to Great-grandpappy Frank gittin' pissy with my daddy for gittin' hitched with Mama, way back when."

"Whoa, wait a second." Bobbi half-turned toward them and made a 'time-out' gesture. "If you're going to talk family history, I'm going to need the Cliff notes."

Jericho cleared his throat. "Okay, stop me if this gets boring. Just after the Second World War, our great-granddaddy Frank started a news distribution service. He did pretty good at it." He shrugged. "Our family's pretty well-off, for the most part. He only died about twenty years ago, but up until then he basically had total control of the company. When my daddy and Uncle Leroy—Luke's daddy—turned twenty-one, they were gonna get shares in the company. Not enough to control anything, but enough to get dividends from."

"Wait a minute." With a frown, Bobbi tilted her head. "Where are your grandparents in all this? Your father's folks, I mean."

"Yeah, that's part of it," Jericho acknowledged. "They've both passed. Papaw Joe got Mamaw Penny pregnant with twins just before he got killed in Vietnam. Great-granddaddy Frank and Great-gran'maw Kate took her in and helped raise 'em. Mamaw Penny and Great-gran'maw Kate died in a car accident back in the nineties. But anyway, my daddy got born two minutes before Uncle Leroy, so he was the oldest and got all the attention. So, Uncle Leroy kinda acted out a bit. Got expelled from the private school great-granddaddy sent him to, so he ended up in public schooling. Found a girl he liked and fooled around with her a bit too much, and got her pregnant during spring break. So, they took a bus trip across to Vegas and got married in one of those instant wedding chapels." He shrugged. "Guess it seemed like a good idea at the time."

"But why go all the way to Vegas?" Bobbi frowned, looking confused. "Why not just hit up a civil registry in Savannah, or wherever?"

"Because not a one of 'em woulda let a white boy git hitched to a black girl," Luke stated bluntly. "They woulda flat-out refused, an' the ones in Savannah woulda been on th' phone ta great-grandpappy in about thirty seconds. Followed up by Mama bein' arrested on whatever charges he could make up. Pa was right smart about that, anyways. He made sure Mama weren't anywhere great-grandpappy could find her an' remove th' problem. When Pa told him Mama was knocked up and he wasn't gonna walk away from her, great-grandpappy had him beat up an' kicked out. Cut 'em off cold. They hadda move halfway across th' state just so's Pa could git hisself a job without bein' fired th' day after as a favor to great-grandpappy."

"But that's not *fair!*" protested Bobbi. "You don't cut people off in that situation. You help them out." She looked from Luke to Jericho and back again in silent appeal.

Luke gave her a level stare in return. "You know that, an' I know that. But that right there was Georgia back then for ya. Great-grandpappy, jes' like every other rich white asshole, didn't want his grandkid marryin' no black girl. Lot of folks still think that way, even now."

From the look on Bobbi's face, Jericho suspected that Bobbi was starting to realize how he'd felt when she filled him and Luke in on how the newspapers shaped the narrative according to their political views. "My God," she said, shaking her head. "And here I thought the year was twenty thirteen, not nineteen thirteen. Or eighteen thirteen."

That got her a derisive snort from Luke. "Racist assholes never go away. They jes' learn ta hide better. So anyway, he tol' everyone else not to he'p us out. My li'l sis Serena come along when I was about four. We done it tough for a few years after that 'til Uncle Beau, that's Jericho's daddy, inherited the business. He'd grown up with great-grandpappy pourin' shit in his ears, but then he went off ta learn business stuff at some fancy college in New York."

"That's where he met Mama," Jericho supplied. "She was studying law. He always told me that meeting her was about the best thing that ever happened to him. Between her and the friends he made there, he got his eyes opened. Over the next few years, he slipped money under the table to Uncle Leroy and his family whenever he could. The moment the controlling interest in the company was signed over to him, he invited them to move back to Savannah. That's when Luke and I met for the first time."

"Gave us the chance ta git back on our feet, sho'nuff." Luke gestured with his hands in lieu of shrugging. "I mean, we ain't *rich,* but we're doin' jes' fine anyways."

Bobbi shook her head again. "I thought I'd heard everything. That's just crazy."

"Not arguing," Jericho said. "But that's the way it was."

"He was a different kinda man from a different kinda time," Luke supplied.

Jericho snorted. "What Luke's trying to be polite about is that Great-granddaddy Frank was a goddamn racist and a bigot and a few other words I'm not about to say in front of a lady. Anyway, that's the lowdown on our family history." He stepped off the escalator behind Bobbi and looked around.

The ground floor of the station was even more impressive than the upper levels. While it lacked the elaborate skylights, there were even more kiosks, as well as shops and cafés scattered here and there. The entire building looked remarkably open plan, with no sign of any way to close it for the night. *Then again, does it even close?*

"So, uh, is it just me, or does this whole place seem totally automated?" said Bobbi in what Jericho suspected was an attempt to change the subject to something less awkward. "I mean, have you guys even *seen* someone wearing UML colors yet? Because I haven't."

"Huh," Luke said, looking around. "Now that ya mention it, it *is* kinda spooky."

"Yeah," Jericho agreed. "Even the folks running the shops have their own work uniforms. I guess they really are that good, here."

"Which raises the problem of where we'd get information from." Bobbi looked around, her forehead creasing in a frown.

The voice came from behind them. "Need a hand?"

16
Friendly Face

Along with the others, Jericho turned to see a guy in his late teens or early twenties leaning casually against a pillar, hands in his jacket pockets. Maybe as tall as Luke, the guy had bulk that wasn't just due to the light jacket he was wearing. "Sorry, I couldn't help overhearing. New in town? You look lost."

"Mebbe." Luke was automatically suspicious. Jericho didn't blame him. If this scenario happened to his cousin back in Savannah, there was usually a vicious beating waiting around the corner. "Lemme guess. You got somethin' ta sell us, an' we won't get us a better price anyplace else. Fuck off. We ain't interested."

The stranger straightened up from the pillar, revealing himself to be just a little taller than Luke, though not quite as broad in the shoulders. Now that Jericho was looking more closely, he registered that the guy had attractively tousled black hair and steady brown eyes. His features were strong and regular, with a firm jaw. "I'm not looking to sell you anything," he said in a tone that indicated his utter lack of care factor as to whether they believed him or not. "But do I know my way around the city and I can give you a hand to figure out where you need to go, and how to get there."

"Really." Bobbi eyed him cynically. "And what's in it for you, exactly?" Her gaze was nowhere near as hostile as Luke's, but she wasn't taking the guy at face value either. Jericho wondered what her power was reading. Was he trying to scam them somehow?

The guy shrugged. "Spot me a meal?" He spread his hands, palm up, in the universal 'I bear no weapons' sign. "Just trying to do my good deed for the day." One corner of his mouth quirked up in a half-grin which Jericho found oddly appealing. "We do things slightly differently here in Utopia, and it takes newcomers a little time to get up to speed. I can give you a head start, if you want."

Personally, Jericho wanted to trust the guy, though he wasn't sure if this was because he actually thought he was trustworthy, or because he found him attractive. *Goddamn it, Stephen! If you hadn't screwed around on me, I wouldn't even be* noticing *all these good-looking guys!* Bobbi wasn't chasing the guy away, so maybe he *wasn't* planning to rip them off at the first opportunity? He decided to keep quiet and let Bobbi take the lead for the moment, as she seemed to know what she was doing.

"Probably not a bad idea, at that," she admitted. "I've done some reading about Utopia City, but there's a lot they don't mention." She tilted her head in thought, then indicated the cafés within view. All had customers—Jericho couldn't tell if they were incoming or outgoing passengers—but some were more densely populated than others. "Pick your poison. But no seven-course meals."

The grin he flashed at her made Jericho like him even more, though paradoxically it served to still the flutter in his chest when he looked at the guy. Pouring on the charm as he was didn't turn Jericho off him, but it made him more approachable and less standoffish, and thus less of a magnet for Jericho's libido. "Thanks. I'm Thomas, by the way. Where are you in from?" Turning, he started toward a nearby fast-food stand.

"Bobbi. That's Jericho and Luke." For all that he had longer legs, she matched him stride for stride, leaving Luke and Jericho to catch up in their wake. "I'm from

Indiana. They're from Georgia."

"Huh." If Thomas was offended at being fobbed off with a generalization, he didn't show it. "That's cool. Folks come into Utopia from all over. Some of them find out they can't cut it and move on. Most of us stay." There seemed to be an edge of bitterness to his tone. "Here for work or tourism?"

"A bit of both," Jericho said. Thomas wasn't from the South, that was for sure. The way he was clipping his syllables, Jericho figured him to be from someplace in the northeast. "So, not to be rude or anything, but what's your deal? You hang around in the maglev station and talk to strangers for shits and giggles, or is this how you eat?"

"Pfft, hardly." Thomas sounded very sure of himself. Arriving at the counter, he quickly ordered two wraps and a bottle of orange juice. The resulting price made Jericho's eyebrows raise slightly; not from how expensive it was, but how cheap. Given that this was a concession stand, he would've expected slightly higher prices than normal, but the numbers he was looking at were about two-thirds what they should be. "I like to people-watch. Meet folks from all over. And if I can get the occasional freebie from someone I help, all the better."

On impulse, Jericho got out his wallet. "I'll pay for half of that," he told the guy behind the counter. "What do you take? I got Amex, debit card, cash ..."

"Just MagCard, buddy." The attendant gestured to where a reader with the UML logo was set into the countertop. "Swipe your cards and we're done."

"That's convenient," Bobbi observed as she swiped her card across the reader. "Does everything use the MagCard in Utopia City?"

"Pretty much," said the attendant. "It's backed by Force Majeure, so it's as secure as it gets."

"Huh. I guess that's pretty secure," Jericho noted with a grin. He swiped his card as well. "That's it?"

"That's it." The attendant put the purchase, contained in a paper bag, up on the counter. Bobbi took it.

"Uh, wait," Jericho said belatedly. "I forgot to add a tip." He held up his card, preparatory to swiping it a second time. "How much is good here?"

"Oh, we don't tip here in Utopia," Thomas said. "It's not really a thing." His voice was casual despite the oddity of what he was saying, as if he were talking about what the weather was going to be like, but confidently predicting a rain of frogs.

"Wait, *what?*" Luke stared at him disbelievingly. "How's that even work?"

"We don't need it," the attendant confirmed. "Minimum wage here in Utopia's a flat twenty bucks an hour, and that's before overtime, holiday pay and so on. We're required to take a certain number of paid vacations a year, and we've even got automatic health coverage. Takes a *lot* of the stress out of life, let me tell you." He gave Jericho a nod and a smile. "Thanks for offering, though. Have a nice day."

"You too," Jericho replied automatically as they moved away from the food stand. Most of the attendant's explanation had gone over his head; the part that had stuck with him, and he had the most trouble with, was the concept of not tipping people for service. *Thomas said things were different here. He's not wrong.*

Bobbi handed the bag over to Thomas. "Here's your food, and it's totally not a tip," she told him with a grin. "So, where do we go from here?"

"Just a minute," Luke interjected. "If folks do everythin' with th' MagCard hereabouts, what happens if some poor asshole gits to Utopia City an' don't got no money *in* the account the damn MagCard feeds off've?"

"He walks to a terminal and transfers some over from another account," Thomas explained. He pointed out a few of the electronic kiosks, spaced around the perimeter of the station. "Only takes a minute."

"But those are ticket vending machines," Jericho objected. "I used one back in Savannah. It didn't give me any banking options."

Thomas chuckled for a moment. "Sorry. Not laughing at you. It's just that this is a common misconception. They really should put out better literature on the subject. Come on, I'll show you." He led the way to the nearest kiosk. "See, these are multi-function, but the ones in other cities are locked into selling MagCards and dispensing tickets." Reaching out, he tapped the screen. Immediately, it came to life, showing a list of options. The first was familiar; the rest, less so.

PURCHASE TICKET
MAPS
MONEY TRANSFER
LUGGAGE CARTS
OTHER

"We don't want 'other'," he said. "That's for things like complaining about the maglev service, contacting Force Majeure, calling the cops, stuff like that." He glanced at Luke. "Did you need to transfer money, or were you just asking?"

"I was jes' askin'," Luke said hurriedly. "So, these things act like teller machines an' all?"

"Well, they *are* computers and this *is* the twenty-first century, so yes," Thomas confirmed. "So, I'm guessing you're still figuring out where you're going from here?"

Bobbi gave him a penetrating look. "Yeah. We're looking for short-stay accommodation. What's good? And by that, I mean cheap rooms and good service." Good service that got by without tips. This was something Jericho would have to see to believe.

"Oh, that's easy." Thomas gave her one of those grins he was so good at, then tapped MAPS. The screen shifted and changed … and Jericho caught his breath. Beside him, he heard Luke mutter something under his breath that sounded like "Fuck *me*."

Luke's exclamation was unsurprising, given that the image on the screen had gone from flat monochrome to three-dimensional full color in the blink of an eye. Jericho had seen footage of active holograms before, but this was the first time he'd experienced one. From what he could see, this specific hologram was a map of Utopia City; or rather, a very small part of it. Buildings, standing out in relief, skated in circles as Thomas adjusted the alignment, apparently by moving his fingers over the screen itself. The young man tapped his fingernail on—through—a complex of interlocked white blocks. "This is the Oaklands. From what I hear, it's pretty good."

"Where-all's that from here?" asked Luke practically. "Can we walk, or ain't that a good idea?"

"Not really," Thomas said, using a pinching motion on the screen to zoom out. "We're not far from the Spire. This is the station, there's the Spire. East-west maglev line runs right past it, in fact."

Jericho figured that the fine silver thread that had just moved into the picture was the maglev rail. Backtracking it to where the other three lines ran into the station wasn't difficult. The cloverleaf pattern formed by the rails around the station was a little harder to pick out, but it was visible if he squinted. His eyes moved over to the huge round building that dominated the image, extending upward as far as the screen resolution allowed. He didn't know much about Utopia City, but *everyone* had seen pictures of the Spire.

While the entire Utopia City skyline looked like something that might've been imagined in the 1950s as typical for 2013, the Spire was a step beyond. Just over a mile and a half tall, the almost alien proportions made it look like something from a hundred years hence. More than that, the Spire was the geographical and political center of Utopia City. Not only was it where the business of running the city took place, but it was also where Force Majeure made their headquarters within the city. *That's where I'll be going for my interview.*

He looked for the complex that Thomas had indicated before, and couldn't find it. "So, where are we going to, again?" he asked. *Utopia City,* he decided, *is way too goddamn big. Bigger than Savannah, that's for sure.*

"Here." Thomas double-tapped the screen, and it zoomed in. The buildings showed up again, and Jericho noted that the guy had been right. If Jericho's idea of the scale was anywhere near correct, it would be much too far to walk in a hurry.

A blue squiggle between nearby buildings caught his eye. "What's that?" he asked, pointing at it.

"Oh, that's one of the canals," Thomas said. "There's a network of them around the city to take care of water runoff, and to handle the Kansas River flow-through as well. This being Utopia, they keep it nice and decorative, because why not."

"Yeah, yeah, right." Luke nodded. "So, how the hell do we hail a cab, anyways? I don't see no phone around here, an' I dunno what th' number is."

"Come on. I got this." From Thomas' grin, Jericho got the distinct impression that he enjoyed being the guy in the know. Stepping around the kiosk and the pillar it was backed up to, the younger man led the way out through the archway into the open air beyond.

"Well, come on," Bobbi said, taking a fresh grip on her drag-bag. "He's a smartass, but it doesn't feel like he's going to try and rip us off." She moved off, following in Thomas' wake. Jericho and Luke shared a glance, shrugged, and followed along. Rather than a downrush of air as they stepped beneath the archway, Jericho instead felt an illusory popping sensation. The air temperature rose by a few degrees while the scents changed as well, from air fresheners to ozone, dust and hot metal.

"What the hell?" Luke stopped short. "That jes' happen?" He looked back into the maglev station, as if considering turning around and going back to Savannah right then and there.

"It happened," Jericho assured him. "Figure it's a weak force field to keep the cool air inside. Nice trick if you can pull it off." He was quite impressed. Most of the force fields he'd seen on TV caused a certain degree of visual distortion, but this one hadn't shown any sign of its presence at all.

"Friggin' cogs." Luke shook his head. "They build this whole damn city?" He looked across the fifty feet or so of open pavement that lay between the station and the street, with a gesture that was apparently supposed to take in the rest of the city. On a second look, it wasn't totally open. There was a row of yellow posts at about twenty-foot intervals, and beyond that a low brick wall edged the street.

Jericho nodded, not even bothering to correct his word use this time. "That's what I heard." The buildings across the street certainly bore this out with their tall and graceful lines, as far from the stodgy steel and glass office buildings of popular culture as a modern house was from a mud hut. In the sky above he could see the same sort of moving dots as he'd seen on the commercial, though he still wasn't exactly sure whether they were human or mechanical in nature. Aware that he was wasting time, he moved to join Bobbi and Thomas, with Luke close behind.

They were standing next to one of the yellow posts. Close up, it looked about the same size and shape as a parking meter, albeit with a speaker on the side and a large green button placed prominently on top. As far as he could see, the posts were spaced at intervals along the front of the maglev station. Between each post and the street was a yellow rectangle painted on the concrete pavers, maybe ten feet wide and twenty long. Oddly enough, the entirety of the inside of the 'parking space' was covered over by a metal grille instead of concrete.

"That s'posed to be a taxi stand?" asked Luke, gesturing at the yellow rectangle. His gesture and tone conveyed a certain amount of doubt, which Jericho could understand. If the cab was supposed to pull up on the yellow rectangle—and that didn't exactly explain the presence of the grille—how was it intended to get past the wall? *I'm missing something here …*

"Yup." Thomas reached out to the post and held the button down.

A feminine voice emanated from the speaker. **"Please state number of passengers, how many pieces of luggage, and destination."**

"Four passengers." Thomas's reply was crisp. "Three pieces of luggage. Destination is the Oaklands temporary accommodation complex."

"Thank you. A taxi has been dispatched. Your taxi will be arriving in forty-three seconds. Please stay clear of the marked area."

"Thank you." Thomas released the button.

As if to underscore the warning they'd been given, the yellow-painted rectangle pulsed oddly then faded to a deep red. Ignoring Luke's startled exclamation, Jericho shaded his eyes and looked up and down the street. He couldn't see anything that resembled a taxi; in fact, the only vehicles on the road looked like buses and heavy transport. And even those didn't look like what he was used to. Or smell that way, for that matter. It came to him that he hadn't smelled exhaust fumes since he'd gotten on the maglev, back in Savannah. Even now, his nose couldn't pick any out, for all that he was in the middle of a bustling city.

"Wait, *four* passengers?" Luke gave Thomas a hard look. "What makes ya think you're ridin' in our cab?"

"Hey, I'll pay my way." Thomas flourished his own MagCard. "I don't live all that far from the Oaklands and it's cheaper sharing a cab with you guys. If you don't mind, that is."

Jericho suppressed his initial reaction, waiting to see Bobbi's view on the subject. While sharing the price of a cab was good for all concerned, it didn't mean there wasn't a deeper plan going on.

"If you c'n afford a cab, why'd we just buy ya dinner?" Luke asked, ignoring the fact that he hadn't actually contributed.

"Because this way, I don't have to pay for my food *or* the full price of a taxi ride home," Thomas pointed out cheerfully. "I just saved you a bunch of aggravation figuring out where to go and how to get there, and all it's costing you is the price of a meal, less one-fourth of a cab fare." He spread his hands again. "Guys. I'm *not* ripping you off. Being totally legit here."

Bobbi nodded. "Luke, chill. He's on the level." She opened her mouth to say more but didn't get the chance. With no more warning than a sudden down-blast of air, a large yellow *thing* dropped down out of the sky and landed neatly on the outlined rectangle. Jericho stared at the apparition; one second it hadn't been there, and the next it was. He'd had his suspicions about what was flying around up there, but he hadn't expected *this*.

17
Air Taxi

It was vaguely car-shaped, but larger again by half in all dimensions. At the front, two large ducted fans spun in side-by-side mounts that let them swivel in any direction, taking up most of the space where the hood should have been. This made Jericho wonder in turn where the engine was. It couldn't be at the back of the vehicle, given that from where he was standing, he could see at least one more ducted fan in the space where the trunk should be. The windshield was chevron-shaped, angling back from the centerline to merge into the sides of the vehicle. Short stabilizer fins protruded from the fuselage of the craft. In fact, the whole thing was thoroughly streamlined, not to mention futuristic as *hell*.

"Well, shitfire an' honey biscuits. They've actually got *flyin' cars*." Luke managed to sound incredulous and reverent at the same time.

"Didn't they have a documentary about flying cars in Utopia City, a couple-three years ago?" Jericho was sure he remembered seeing it on TV, but it had to have been at least five or six years ago, and a lot had happened in the meantime.

"Yeah, they did," Luke replied, not taking his eyes off the air taxi. "But I never reckoned they'd be anythin' like *this*."

Thomas moved forward while Jericho and the others were still staring. He pulled at a remarkably mundane handle on the side of the vehicle, and a door hinged upward. *Because, of course it does.* Leaning nonchalantly against the side of the vehicle with an almost insufferably smug look on his face, he beckoned to them. "Well, come on," he said. "It's not going to *bite*."

Bobbi was the first to snap out of the spell. Moving forward with her drag-bag, she stopped and examined the interior of the flying car. Apparently satisfied by what she saw, she collapsed the handle of her luggage, hefted it, and climbed in.

Deciding to trust that the vehicle did indeed have a working engine (after all, it had just landed), Jericho moved forward and climbed in after her. The interior wasn't hugely spacious, but there were four comfortable looking seats at the back and another one in front of each of the two doors, facing inward. Each seat had armrests featuring MagCard readers as well as five-point restraint harnesses. In the middle of the cab, between the seats, was a cargo-netted area; Bobbi had already deposited her drag-bag into it. At the front of the passenger compartment was a solid partition, separating the driver's seat from the rest of the cab. This was mainly taken up with a large flat-screen monitor, currently dark. Large windows had been installed in the roof, as well as each side and the rear of the cab.

He picked the inward-facing seat on the right side of the cab and lowered himself into it. A small sticker on the partition caught his eye as he got himself settled. It portrayed a camera inside a red circle crossed by a line, with the text **UTOPIA CITY CABS ARE CHALLENGER ACT COMPLIANT.** Although he was conversant with the Challenger Act, he wasn't certain how it applied to flying taxicabs, but it definitely sounded interesting.

Luke clambered in after Jericho and dropped his backpack into the cargo net with the rest of the luggage. "Holy crap," he said, taking the seat opposite Jericho's. "This has gotta be a friggin' limo. Thought we just called a cab?"

A masculine voice crackled out of an intercom speaker right next to his ear, making him jump. **"Sorry, buddy. Just a regular cab."**

"Well, it *could* be a limo," argued Luke as Thomas climbed in, still clutching the paper bag. "It's big enough. Turn these seats so's they face backward an' you could fit another one in here."

"Hah, nope," said the cab-driver's disembodied voice. **"They trialed that. Didn't go well. Nearly everyone who rode that way got airsick. Something about traveling backward. So, the actual limos are just a bit longer with extra seats on the sides. Besides, we need to keep the screen clear."**

"Oh, right." Luke looked thoughtful as he inspected the screen. "Suppose that's a point too."

"Yup," agreed the driver. **"Okay, folks, you're heading for the Oaklands, right? That'll be … eleven bucks. Who's paying?"** The screen between Jericho and Luke came to life, displaying the price in large red digits.

Bobbi cleared her throat and gave Thomas a significant look. "We're sharing. Four ways. Right, guys?"

"Sure thing," Thomas agreed readily enough. He'd seated himself at the far end of the back seat to Bobbi, diagonally across from Jericho. Producing his MagCard as if it were a conjuring trick, he swiped it across the reader on his armrest. There was a beep from the screen, and a second line appeared under the displayed price: '$2.75 PAID'. "That's me," he announced.

"Gimme a second," Luke muttered. "I'm sittin' on my goddamn wallet." Squirming around in his seat, he managed to extract the recalcitrant item. Jericho and Bobbi had it easier, as they'd used their cards just before. One by one, they swiped their cards, each one eliciting a beep and an update in the amount paid. When Luke swiped, the running update vanished and the original price turned from red digits to green. As they did so, the door swung down and clicked into place.

"Okay, is that it?" asked Jericho.

"Not quite. Now you gotta belt up. Legal requirement." The monitor screen changed to an animated cartoon graphic that showed how to fasten the five-point restraints. **"FAA'd have my ass, otherwise."**

"Ah, right." Jericho fumbled with the belts, then figured it out and clicked them into place with the help of the screen graphic. Thomas already had his done up, while Bobbi had come in a close second. Luke sorted his out moments later. "Okay, I think we're ready."

"Good. Let's go." At Jericho's right elbow, a screen lit up, showing what appeared to be a view out through the windshield. Across the cab, another screen had activated for Luke. A bone-deep thrumming sound came from outside the cab, and Jericho felt G-forces trying to press him downward into the seat cushions. His first instinct was to use his powers to override the effect on himself, but he kept them in check as the total vertical acceleration was only around half a gee. The ground dropped away; within moments, he could turn his head to look down at the roof of the maglev station. A second or so later, the vertical acceleration eased up and the cab transitioned into forward flight, building to a total speed of fifty miles per hour. And then, as they moved out of the shadow of one of the skyscrapers, honey-gold sunlight filled the interior of the cab.

He'd been aware of the gradual onset of twilight, but it came as a surprise to find himself in the sunlight once more. Leaning forward against his restraints, he looked out the back window toward where he thought the Spire was. Just for a moment, he was rewarded with an image of the towering edifice outlined by the westering sun. In the foreground, the maglev rail reflected the light into his eyes, describing a burning path into the heart of the sunset. And then it was gone again, as the cab went into the shadow of another building.

Reluctantly, he looked back to the screen at his elbow as more buildings whipped by on either side of them. While he knew the cab wasn't going as fast as the maglev had, he was uncomfortably aware that they weren't riding any kind of rail now, and those buildings were much closer. But then his attention was taken up by the odd fluorescent horizontal stripes on the buildings themselves, colored in day-glow orange. From what he could see, the stripes were at the same level on all the buildings, maybe once every ten or fifteen stories. Fascinated, he forgot his disquiet at how low and fast they were flying. "Excuse me, but what are those stripes?"

"Flight lanes," the driver responded at once. **"Higher you are, the faster you can go."** The monitor flipped to an image that seemed to be looking out through the windshield; the same as on the screen beside him, but showing much more detail. Overlaid on it was a display showing imaginary curves and planes drawn through the air before the cab. It almost looked as though they were driving on a highway curving through the air. **"Trust me, we got just as many rules and regulations as anyone on asphalt."**

Ah-ha, thought Jericho. The sign he'd seen on the approach to the city made much more sense now.

"How about if someone can fly on their own?" Bobbi leaned forward in her seat as far as her restraints would allow, to stare at the screen. "They can't see all those notifications, can they?"

"Nope. But once they pass their flight cert, they can rent or buy heads-up goggles. Otherwise, they gotta stay low and slow." The view tilted as the cab banked to go around a building. **"Too much chance of an accident, otherwise."**

"Right." Luke seemed to be thinking something over. "Uh, hey, driver? What's them there props run on? 'Cause I ain't hearin' no engine nohow." Now that they were in level flight, Jericho belatedly realized, the thrumming sound from outside was almost non-existent.

"Batteries." Thomas, who'd been silent up until then, spoke up. He quirked a grin at Jericho's expression. "Really high-density ones."

"Batteries?" Jericho had to ask. "Really?"

"Yup." The driver's voice was casual. **"Big-ass bank of 'em, right under you. Once I finish my shift, I bring the cab into the barn and they charge up overnight."**

Jericho wasn't certain he liked the idea of trusting his life to batteries, but it was a little too late to worry about that. In any case, the cab was flying steadily, and he'd heard of stranger things. *I just traveled from Savannah to here held up by magnetic forces and gravity generators, after all.* "Do you, uh, ever have problems with them? The batteries, I mean?"

"Nope. Only time I've ever heard of them running out was when some idiots jacked a cab and tried to make a run for it. Word is, the driver had been getting close to the end of his shift, and they put it onto max overdrive to get away from the hexes. They got about five miles outside the city limits, then nose-dived into the dirt." Jericho heard a note of grim satisfaction in the driver's voice.

"Uh … hexes?" Bobbi looked dubious. "What's that?"

"Police drones," the cab driver explained. **"You won't miss 'em when you see 'em. Big blocky mothers, fan in the middle."** He paused. **"And speakin' of the devil, there's one now. One o'clock high."**

Jericho took a moment to work out which way one o'clock was, then looked up and to the right through the roof-mounted window just as the 'hex' came into view. Suiting its nickname, the ruggedly built drone was hexagonal in shape, about six feet across and one foot thick, with a circular opening in the middle that was filled with the blurring of ducted-fan propeller blades. Looking not unlike an extremely law-abiding UFO, it had a paint job reminiscent of a police car, even down to the familiar red and blue lights on each corner. The driver had been right; it really was impossible to mistake for anything else. While it was a good fifty feet above them and heading in the opposite direction, he could still tell that it was going a lot faster than the cab. Seconds later, it was out of sight.

"So ... *can* a cab on max overdrive go faster'n a hex?" The tone of Luke's question was almost ludicrously casual; Jericho didn't believe it for an instant. From the sharp glance Bobbi shot his cousin, she didn't either.

The driver chuckled. **"Not nearly, buddy. But it'll drain your power like a mofo. Only an idiot even tries."**

"Right." Jericho could have sworn that Luke sighed, just a little. The reason wasn't hard to discern, given Luke's interest in the local street racing scene back home. Quite often, these events broke up on the arrival of the police, turning them into an every-man-for-himself scramble. His cousin was quite proud at never having been caught by the forces of law and order; it probably galled him that the local 'police' had an unfair advantage in speed.

"Cheer up," he told Luke with a grin. "It's not like they're gonna pull you over for a missing tail-light." *How would they even issue tickets?*

"Hey, can a guy *buy* one of these fancy air-car things an' take it outta town?" Luke asked. With a sinking feeling, Jericho divined the direction of his thoughts. Luke had never been able to look at a car without planning how to soup it up. *God, if he got his hands on one of these things ...*

"Sorry, buddy." The cabby's voice was matter-of-fact. **"Some out-of-town VIPs get to use air-limos, but only on license from Force Majeure, and they don't get to take them out of Utopia. Even the maintenance is all done in-house. Aircars don't ever leave Utopia."**

"But why *not*?" Bobbi sounded curious. "It shouldn't be too hard to set up an operation like this in New York or LA. Taking the cabs off the street and into the air would deal with a lot of traffic congestion, not to mention air pollution. And if private owners could fly as well, gridlock would be a thing of the past."

The driver snorted a laugh. **"Yeah, and it'd take exactly one mid-air pileup before some moron decided to sue Force Majeure for supplying the technology in the first place. Plus, I've seen the way New Yorkers drive. Here, we all know the rules. It's better this way, trust me."**

Jericho cleared his throat. "Talking about rules, you've got a sticker here about being Challenger Act compliant. What's that mean, exactly?"

"Wait, what again now?" Luke swung his head in Jericho's direction, followed closely by Bobbi. Predictably, Thomas didn't react at all. He undoubtedly knew about both the existence of the stickers and the reasoning behind them.

"Well, I'm guessing you know what the Challenger Act is, yeah?" The cabbie gave them a few seconds to respond, then continued. **"Okay, then. Normally you're recorded on both audio and video as soon as you get in. If someone gets in and invokes the Challenger Act, the recording continues but it's put under Force Majeure computer seal. All we get is an audio feed. Likewise, if someone leaves something behind in a cab that looks like superhero gear, we turn it straight over to the cops and they let a Designated Liaison handle it."**

Luke's expression was intrigued. "So, if a hero hadda git someplace fast, could he call hisself a cab an' change on th' way? What if someone in another cab sees him?"

"I was more wondering what a Designated Liaison was," Bobbi put in. "But yeah, that's a good question too."

The driver's chuckle was audible over the intercom system. **"To answer the first question; yes, and we can polarize the windows on request. Like so."** In the next moment, the passenger compartment went dead black, except for the glow of the small screens on either side. Tiny lights flared to life, illuminating the interior of the passenger compartment and showing that the windows had been polarized to a mirror sheen. Dozens of reflections of the four of them came back from every angle, making it feel as though they were trapped in a bizarre carnival ride. The effect faded a second or so later, allowing the late-afternoon light to flood in once more.

"And the Designated Liaison thing?" Jericho prompted.

"That's something the cops do," the driver explained. **"Say there's a hero who's suspected of committing a crime in one of his identities, but unmasking would prove he wasn't there. Designated Liaisons are authorized to deal with that sort of situation. They've gotta sign about a million NDAs and they get paid five times as much as normal. And they've gotta have an Enabled bodyguard on hand twenty-four-seven."**

"That's fascinating," Bobbi said. "How do you know all this? And how come we've never heard of this before?"

"I've got a cousin who's on the force. He's also a DL. Makes more money than God, but he can't go out drinking with the boys, and there's a crapload of stuff he's just not cleared to talk about." The driver's tone sounded like he was glad it wasn't him. **"He says they tried it once in a couple of the other big cities, but the program collapsed after a few of the DLs went away to federal prison for accepting bribes. Apparently, they didn't want to pay 'em what they were worth. Idiots, if you ask me."** He didn't specify who the idiots were; the implication was that all parties involved could share the description.

"Wait jes' one moment." Luke sat forward in his seat. "About this-here whole Challenger Act compliance thing. What happens, say, if some Mask gits in a cab in his civvies an' then hasta do th' whole change thing halfway through? If th' driver's been talkin' to him, he mighta seen his face. Then the driver goes out drinkin' later that night an' it's all 'guess what so-an'-so looks like under his mask'. Jes' sayin', some folks love ta talk, 'specially if they knows somethin' nobody else does. An' sometimes it's real hard ta figger out where a rumor started from."

Jericho could see where Luke was coming from. As a hero, he liked to think people wouldn't do that. As someone who had a vested interest in not spreading his secret identity around, he knew he had to stay wary about that sort of thing.

"Yeah, they had to keep all that in mind from the start," the cabbie agreed readily enough. **"No matter what rules and regulations you've got in place, people will talk. So, they came up with a solution. You saw the heads-up display earlier? Everything I see while I'm on duty is image-processed by the onboard computer before it's projected on the display to overlay what's really there. People walking on the street or sitting in the cab, all I see is low-resolution contoured outlines. You could be wearing body paint or a parka, and I'd never know. But if someone identifies themselves as an Enabled, I'm happy to orbit a building while they change into or out of their costume. They get to go where they want, and I still get paid just the same."**

Another question was nagging at Jericho's mind. He tried to ignore it, but it kept on coming back. "So, uh, not to change the subject, but what about if one of those fans eats a bird or something?"

"It's not a problem." The cabbie's voice exuded confidence. **"These things are damn tough, but if push came to shove, they can fly on three lifters. It's a bit rough, and regs say you gotta set down as soon as reasonably possible, but it can be done. If we lose two, then that's an in-flight emergency and you put down as fast as you can. Flying sideways is no fun, but if you gotta do it, you gotta do it."**

"An' if you lose three?" Luke was the one who asked the question, though Jericho had been thinking it. Bobbi gave him a dirty look, to which he returned a *what?* gesture with spread hands.

"Then you call an emergency and use max overdrive on the last fan to slow yourself down before you hit the ground. It's a one-way trip, and the cab's gonna get a bit bent, but you'll probably survive."

"I once saw a two-lifter landing," offered Thomas. "Freak accident. A cab clipped a building and took out both left-hand lifters. The driver was injured, but he got it down to ground level without quite crashing."

Still listening with half an ear, Jericho peered out the window. The buildings were lower on average now, though some were still impressively tall. He could tell that there was still quite a ways to go before they reached the city limits. Below the cab, he saw a flash of sky on water, meandering off between the buildings. They were past before he got a good look, but he presumed it was the canal Thomas had mentioned.

The nose of the cab tilted upward and the thrumming from outside rose to an audible crescendo. Jericho felt himself being pressed downward into his seat by about half a gee of deceleration, then the cab began to drop out of the sky. Luke went a little green and clutched at the armrests, but Bobbi never lost her composure and Thomas didn't even seem to notice. In any case, the stomach-dropping sensation was over quickly. His power told him that they were descending at about fifteen feet per second. **"Anyway, you're here. Oaklands, right?"**

Bobbi looked out the window. "Oh, wow. We're here already? That was fast." Even as she spoke, the complex of white buildings that Jericho had seen on the map became visible through the rear window. Before he had time to feel alarm about how fast they were dropping, the fans thrummed again.

There was a brief period of extra weight—again, just half a gee—then he felt the solid *clunk* as the cab came to rest on the ground. With a click, the doors on both sides unlocked and hinged upward. **"All part of the service, ma'am. You folks have a nice day, now."**

"Yeah, thanks. You too." Jericho unfastened his restraints and climbed to his feet, then retrieved his overnight bag. While he was there, he handed Bobbi her drag-bag and tossed Luke his backpack. Stepping out of the cab, he took a few steps to get clear of the vehicle.

Thomas climbed out behind him and stretched. "Thanks," he said. "I really appreciate you letting me share the cab."

"No big deal," Jericho said. "Thanks for showing us how to use the map and all." He glanced up and down the street. "You live around here?"

"Near the market," Thomas said, gesturing toward what Jericho assumed was the west, given that it was the direction from which the last of the sunlight was streaming overhead. When he looked back, he made eye contact for a long moment before he spoke. "Well, it's been nice meeting you. Maybe catch up some time?"

Is he hitting on me? Jericho couldn't figure it out, one way or the other. He knew what he liked, but he could never tell when other guys liked him. As Luke had already noted, his gaydar was for shit. "Uh, sure," he said, defaulting to politeness.

After all, Thomas seemed nice enough. Trying to get over the awkwardness of the moment, he looked around.

All the buildings he could see were four or five stories tall, save for one just down the block which was twice that high. The architecture was aesthetically pleasing, while the streets were wide and lined with trees. Everything looked … clean. Not 'this-was-built-five-minutes-ago' clean, but neat and well-cared for. No litter, no graffiti. Overhead, streetlights were beginning to come on, combating the encroaching dusk.

As with the maglev station, the air-cab stand was a few yards off the street, with a low wall blocking it from the street and about five yards of clearance in all directions. It even looked the same as the one back at the station, right down to the bright yellow call post and the rectangular space outlined in color-changing paint, which was even now fading back from red to yellow. As Luke and Bobbi joined them, the cab doors swung down and locked into place. A moment later, the vehicle took off with a thrum of fans and a rush of wind. As it gained altitude, the struts it had landed on folded up under the fuselage. Jericho shaded his eyes against the lingering brightness in the sky, watching until it disappeared behind the nearest buildings.

"Well, dang." Luke, looking a little ruffled, was also shading his eyes. "Flyin' cars. Friggin' *flying cars*."

"Goddamn flying cars," agreed Jericho. There didn't seem to be much else to say.

"What *I* want to know is what that's about." Bobbi pointed at the grille in the middle of the landing area. "Is it something that's really necessary? Like, to land safely?"

"It's for the propwash," Thomas said helpfully. "Coming down or taking off, the lifters would blow air sideways. Dirt could go in folks' eyes. Those grilles lead into the storm drains."

"Also, when you get close to the ground, it's like you're resting on an air cushion," supplied Jericho. "It's called ground effect. Screws up control, unless you're ready for it. I've read about it. Choppers get it a lot." He pointed at the area beside the yellow rectangle. "Plus, that way people can be waiting right there, and kids don't get blown over. Clever."

"Huh." Bobbi nodded, looking thoughtful. "Learn something new every day." The grin she directed at Luke was infectious; Jericho knew that his pleased expression was echoing hers. "Flying cars are a really big deal for you, aren't they?"

"Well, they didn't used to be, but they friggin' well are now," Luke retorted. "Right, cuz?" Jericho wasn't overly surprised. Ever since Luke had gotten tall enough to see over a steering wheel, he'd been enthralled by the potential embodied in an engine and four wheels. Despite the fact that flying cars possessed neither engine nor wheels, it seemed he'd found a new interest.

Jericho was just as intrigued by the concept of a flying car, but he wasn't about to break the law to learn more about them. "They *are* pretty cool," he had to admit. "But it's just a thing. There's plenty of other stuff to look at here too, you know."

Luke shook his head, and Jericho felt his heart sink slightly. He knew that look all too well. Momentarily, he wondered if they'd let him post Luke's bail with his MagCard. Luke's next words confirmed his fears. "Nope. They ain't 'just a thing' no more. Not now I know they're actually friggin' *real*. I mean, I heard stories, but some things you jes' don't believe 'til you see 'em, y'know?"

Exasperated, Jericho shook his head. Luke could be remarkably single-minded when he wanted to be. "Still pretty sure you can't take one home with you. You heard the guy. They don't sell 'em for out of town use."

"He's right," Thomas supplied. "They really don't."

"Yeah, but—" Luke began, then broke off. "Oh, hey. It's the cops." His tone went immediately from earnest stubbornness to casual with a hint of caution. Even though Luke was (mostly) a law-abiding citizen these days, it was Jericho's experience that he never took attention from the police lightly.

18
Police Stop

Jericho and Bobbi turned toward the street, just as an odd-looking vehicle pulled over to the side of the road. It was utterly silent, which explained why they hadn't heard it. However, the lack of noise wasn't what drew his attention. The fact that it was hovering a foot above the road *was*.

The top half of it was a stock-standard police cruiser; four doors, paint job, bubble lights, the works. On the other hand, there were no wheels to hold it off the ground. He could see a flat plate under the closest corner, held in place by a framework of some sort, but what it did wasn't obvious. As the vehicle came to a halt, sturdy-looking struts folded down; the car lowered itself onto them. It hadn't been using any sort of gravity manipulation that he could feel, and there was no wind-rush from ground effect. Which left magnetic levitation, probably not unlike the train he'd ridden in from Savannah. They'd almost certainly covered these in the documentary as well, but he honestly couldn't remember it. *Hovering cop cars. Now I really have seen it all.*

The passenger-side door opened, and a police officer stepped out. He was fit and handsome, his uniform neat and tidy. Jericho didn't see a protective vest, but the cloth of the uniform did seem to be a little shinier and stiffer than it ought to be. The gun holstered at the cop's hip also appeared to be of a make that Jericho wasn't familiar with. Despite the fact that night was beginning to fall, the police officer wore what looked like high-tech sunglasses, about one widget short of being actual goggles.

The officer made a production of fitting his cap onto his head as he stepped forward, a hint of swagger in his step. From the corner of his eye, Jericho saw Luke's expression tighten up. Given his background, Luke's dislike of cops wasn't exactly unusual, but Jericho knew it was the self-important members of the profession who really drew his ire. Almost instinctively, he stepped forward a little, turning to the side so that he could keep an eye on Luke. This put him closer to the cop than Luke was, which would let him get in between if necessary. He hoped it wouldn't get that far.

"Good evening, folks," the cop said with a smile that looked friendly on the surface, but which Jericho would have bet didn't extend to his eyes. He took a few more steps forward, all but hooking his thumbs in his equipment belt. Jericho half-expected to hear harmonica music and see a tumbleweed roll past. "Welcome to Utopia City. I trust you had a good trip?" His words said one thing; his attitude, quite another. *This town ain't big enough for the two of us.*

Jericho couldn't decide whether this guy was just naturally an asshat or if he was just playing it up to get a reaction. Either way, Luke seemed happy to provide one. "With all due respect, what's it to y'all?" His tone was blunt, showing very little respect indeed. "We ain't done nothin' wrong."

At Luke's words, the cop smiled broadly, showing a set of teeth as neat and regimented as his uniform. Jericho waited for the other shoe to drop. It didn't take long. "No, Mr. Hansen, there's nothing amiss. This is merely a courtesy call to welcome you to our fair city. You have a good night now, sir. Ma'am." The words were delivered so smoothly that it took Jericho a couple of seconds to realize that the cop had addressed Luke by *name.*

Unfortunately, Luke was only marginally slower on the uptake. Even as the cop nodded toward Bobbi and began to turn back to his car, Jericho's cousin tried to move toward him. Not at all sure what Luke intended, but wanting to avert a legal catastrophe, Jericho blocked his way with his forearm. Luke allowed him to do this, but Jericho figured it was a near thing.

"Wait ... the *hell?*" Luke sounded like he was talking through clenched teeth. "How the *hell* did y'all know who I was?" The fact that he was still talking heartened Jericho. It was the only thing that did. Luke may have punched out a cop or two in his younger days, but that had been a different city with different rules on the street. Neither of them knew what the rules were, here and now.

"Why do you ask that, sir?" Jericho noted that as the cop turned back around, his attention was fixed entirely on Luke. *Probably watching him the whole time, and I didn't pick up on it.* The smartass know-it-all smile persisted. "Were you trying to keep it a secret?" The words were once again innocuous, but the attitude behind them grated at Jericho and it wasn't even *aimed* at him.

"What the frig's *that* supposed to mean?" *Oh, boy. Here we go.* Luke was usually even-tempered, but if anything got through his reserve, he got mad *fast.* While Jericho had never been on the receiving end of the full effect of Luke's temper—their spat on the train barely qualified—he'd seen the results from time to time. And now Luke was being deliberately provoked by an asshat cop, in such a way that the officer could claim full deniability.

"Do you think it should mean something, sir? Is there something I should know?" The officer's tone sounded friendly on the surface, but Bobbi glanced sharply at him. Jericho wasn't quite sure why she'd done it, but he was sure it had something to do with the cop's emotions.

He put his right hand on his cousin's left arm. "No, it's all fine, officer." Luke glanced at him, clearly ready to keep this going, but Jericho shook his head slightly. Lowering his voice, he hissed, "Luke, let it go. He's baiting you." Out of the corner of his eye, he saw Bobbi moving up on Luke's right side.

"If you say so, sir," the officer said. Once again, his voice was smooth, but this time Jericho thought he caught an undertone of satisfaction. "I suppose I'll ..." He paused as if searching for words, then smiled faintly and touched the side of his glasses in a way that didn't look accidental. "... see you around. Have a nice night, sir." *Is that a camera? Did he just take a photo of us?*

Luke opened his mouth to say something, but Jericho squeezed his arm in warning. "Leave it," he murmured, barely moving his lips. After a long moment, Luke shut his mouth again. The officer gave him another considering look, then got back into the car and closed the door. Unwilling to take a chance on Luke's self-control, Jericho stayed right by his side.

With barely a sound, the police vehicle lifted into the air and glided off down the street, the undercarriage folding back into place as it went. Jericho watched it go, while beside him Luke clenched his fists as if he wanted to run after it and beat the crap out of the officers within.

"Well, that wasn't creepy *at all,*" declared Bobbi firmly. She looked up at Luke. "You okay?"

"Pissed as hell," Luke replied bluntly. "That there asshole just walked up an' said he was watchin' me. Just outta the friggin' blue. What the livin' goddamn *hell?* Was that a black thing? I reckon it was a black thing." However, belying his tone, the scarred skin over his knuckles was fading to pink as his fists unclenched. Jericho began to breathe a little more easily. It looked as though Luke wasn't going to be celebrating his arrival in Utopia City by punching a cop. So far, anyway.

"He meant to put you on edge," Bobbi said thoughtfully. "The whole thing was deliberate. I got the impression that it's almost a routine with them." She put her head to one side and looked up at Luke again. "I'm guessing you've got a record."

Jericho stepped away from his cousin, giving him his space. *Yeah, you could say that.*

Luke grimaced, but her tone had been more speculative than accusatory. "Yeah," he admitted at last. "Minor shit. An' there's some stuff they couldn't make stick. Tried, though."

Jericho stayed silent. He was aware of most of Luke's record, at least from before he'd come out to his cousin with his powers. While he didn't approve of it all, he was pretty sure Luke had never hurt anyone who wasn't asking for it. *Stephen included.* And it wasn't as though selling weed was a capital crime.

"That'll be it, then." Bobbi nodded. "It wasn't about Jericho and me. It was about you, but it wasn't a, uh, black thing." She looked at Luke's cynical expression. "Well, think about it. It wasn't about the color of your skin, it's the fact that you've got a record. You're not in Georgia anymore."

"Nope, we're in Kansas." Luke's tone was definite. "Ever hear tell of 'Bleeding Kansas'? Even before th' Civil War started, back when this was still a territory, there was folks takin' up arms so's they wouldn't have to give up ownin' slaves. People *died* over it. Trust me when I say it c'n be a black thing here, too."

Bobbi nodded to acknowledge his point. "True. This is Kansas. But it's also Utopia City. I'm getting the distinct impression that inside city limits, it's a whole new ball game. That cop was way more interested in your criminal record than the color of your skin."

Her analysis sounded about right. Once again, Jericho decided that her powers were quite impressive. *She'd definitely make one hell of a therapist.*

"Jes' gonna say, that ain't much better." Luke looked at the both of them. "How'd he even know I *had* a record? We jes' *got* here." His expression was one that Jericho had seen before, a mixture of anger and bafflement. Fortunately, that combination was rare, because it generally preceded Luke punching something. Or someone.

Let's hope it doesn't come to that.

19
Checking In

"Wouldn't have mattered either way."

On hearing Thomas' voice, Jericho looked around. He didn't see him at first, but then he noticed a tree-lined walkway leading into the accommodation complex. The trees were thick enough that anyone entering would be hidden after just a few steps, and Thomas appeared to have taken advantage of that fact. He was just now moving back into view, looking as casual as ever. "They track MagCard use. The card connects back to a bank account that you own, so from there they can monitor all your MagCard use. Where you go, what you buy with it. The whole box of dice."

"They're tracking everyone's MagCards, all the time?" Bobbi's tone was less than thrilled. "That's a little frightening."

Jericho shook his head. The amount of effort involved with intercepting every visitor to the city would be untenable, even if the entire police force was dedicated toward just that. "No, I can't see it. I figure they just look at folks coming in from out of town. Anyone with a record gets tagged for a visit from the cops. Just to say hi, and let us know they're watching." *And maybe to push them a little, to see if they can provoke them into reacting. The way Luke nearly did.*

"Almost exactly that, yeah," Thomas agreed, snapping his fingers in apparent agreement. "But they check on residents, too. Anyone who looks like a potential problem gets the occasional visit. They call it 'pre-emptive policing'." There was a certain tone to his voice which indicated deep feelings on the subject. Jericho recalled that Thomas had absented himself quite handily when he saw the police car coming and wondered why the affable young man didn't want to be noticed by the police. *Then* he wondered why the officer hadn't realized Thomas was there; after all, he'd used his MagCard to help pay for the taxi ride as well. There was more to Thomas, he decided, than met the eye.

"Well, screw *them*," Luke said sharply, setting his jaw. "I'll just use cash everywhere. Let's see the assholes track *that*." If the police had intended to force his cousin to leave Utopia City, Jericho mused, they'd managed to achieve the exact opposite result.

"Might not be possible," Bobbi pointed out before Jericho could say the same thing. "Remember how the guy back at the terminal said basically everyone uses MagCards?"

Luke's expression turned abruptly sour. "Screw it. I'll work it out in the mornin'. Let's go git us a room." He started toward the accommodation complex.

"With you in a sec." Jericho turned to Thomas. "You'll be okay from here?" He wasn't quite sure what to make of the younger man anymore. The guy didn't seem to be an out-and-out criminal—Bobbi would've kicked him to the curb if that was the case—but neither did he come across as being totally on the straight and narrow. Over and above all that, there was something subtly different about him, and Jericho just couldn't put his finger on it.

"Sure." Thomas gave him a carefree grin. "Thanks for caring. And thanks for the meal." Lifting his hand for a moment, he brushed Jericho's cheek with his fingertips, so lightly that skin barely contacted skin. "See you around." Turning, he strode off down the sidewalk.

With a double blink of confusion, Jericho watched him go then turned to where Bobbi was waiting for him. Hoisting his overnight bag onto his shoulder, he went to join her. "Was that ... what I think it was?" he asked doubtfully. "Did he just hit on me?"

She chuckled indulgently. "Silly Jericho. Of *course* he did." As they started down the walkway, she looked up at him. "Doesn't that happen very often? Because I find that hard to believe. From a purely aesthetic point of view, I mean." The grin she gave him was filled with mischief.

"It might," he admitted. This wasn't something he talked about very often, because nobody really asked him, and it was kind of embarrassing. "I'm crap at telling if someone's interested in me. I had a bad experience a long time ago, and I can't help second-guessing myself. I mean, most of the time I'm good with people, just not with that. And any time I assume I know what's going on, I'm usually wrong."

"Huh, damn," Bobbi mused. "That's kinda sucky." She gave Jericho a smile. "Well, take it from me, he was definitely interested."

The walkway led through into a courtyard of sorts, with trees in planters to the left and right. Luke was waiting for them, backpack slung over his shoulder. "I didn't like the pretentious prick," he grumbled, clearly having overheard Bobbi's comment. "Who-all calls themselves 'Thomas', anyway? What's wrong with 'Tom'?" He gave Jericho a warning glance. "He's in the game, somehow. You see him again, don't trust him nohow."

"Is this because you don't want me rebounding on someone else before I give Stephen another chance, or something else?" Jericho asked bluntly. He'd found Thomas likable, if a little puzzling, and it was so emotionally *draining* to have his judgment called into doubt yet again. Besides, it wasn't as if he was actively interested in pursuing a new relationship; he'd only just met the guy, after all.

"Well, that too." Luke shook his head. "Let's drop it. I don't wanna fight over it." Turning, he led the way into the courtyard proper. It was wide and airy, and Bobbi's drag-bag jumped and clattered over the concrete pavers. The left side of the enclosure had an open door under a large LED sign that said 'RECEPTION'. The word 'VACANCY' was also displayed in a welcoming green; Luke headed in that direction.

On the point of following his cousin, Jericho began to wonder about the legalities of the cops' acquisition of MagCard information. Unable to figure it out for himself, he turned to Bobbi. "Wouldn't the cops getting that sort of information on us come under invasion of privacy? Against search and seizure laws or something?"

Bobbi shrugged. "Maybe. Or maybe the local by-laws allow it. This *is* a city with a high proportion of Enabled. I wouldn't put it past supervillains to come here and cause trouble just because they can. So, I'm guessing the local cops are extremely proactive as a result."

"Hmm." After a moment's thought, Jericho decided that if anyone could unpick the motives behind what had just happened, it would be someone who could read emotions like a book. "You're probably right. Good thing that none of us is a supervillain." He grinned and raised his voice slightly. "Hey, Luke. Still want a flying car, or would you prefer a cop car?"

"Depends on how far those assholes push me," Luke grumbled, and stomped ahead. Jericho shared a grin with Bobbi and followed on, glancing around with mild curiosity.

The perimeter of the courtyard was surrounded by a covered walkway lined with trellises, each entwined with finely dividing green vines bearing delicate indigo flowers. An open space in the middle held a dozen concrete picnic tables topped by broad umbrellas, apparently of a type that could be tilted to the side. It struck Jericho as a little strange that they were all tilted to the same angle, in the same direction. Which, as he realized a moment later, was due west. Toward where the sun had set, not so long ago.

"Jericho." Bobbi's voice held a tinge of mild exasperation. "What've you found to look at now?"

He looked around a little guiltily to where she stood in the reception doorway. "Nothing much," he admitted, gesturing at the angled sunshades. "Just that the umbrellas must be remote controlled or something. You see how they're all tilted the same way?"

"How you never came here as a tourist, I have no idea," she huffed. "Stop ogling the umbrellas and get in here. We've still got a room to book." He watched as she hauled her drag-bag over the step to get into the reception area.

With a chuckle, he followed her inside, to where Luke was already leaning up against the reception desk. Jericho wasn't too surprised to see a MagCard reader next to his cousin's elbow. In fact, it went a long way toward confirming what the food stall attendant and the cabbie had said about Utopia City. *Looks like everything* does *run on MagCard around here.*

The receptionist, a carefully presented lady whom Jericho gauged to be in her late forties, looked them over. Her nametag said her name was Helena. "And how many rooms will you be requiring?" she asked bluntly.

"Jes' the one, ma'am, if ya don't mind." Luke's tone was almost breezy. Jericho eyed him a little suspiciously, because the attitude shift was in direct contrast to the surliness he'd been showing just moments earlier. However, it didn't seem to be an act. Which was a little odd, given that in Jericho's experience, Luke was slow to anger but he was also slow to calm down again afterward. *Maybe he's on his best behavior for Bobbi. She did say that anger made her uncomfortable.* Whatever the reason, Jericho was grateful for it. A pissed-off Luke, best friend or no, was not the most pleasant of company.

Helena's reserve melted slightly at the combination of Luke's tone and his charming smile. "I meant *bedrooms,* young man," she said, not as severely as she might have. "Oaklands does not supply mere hotel rooms. We have short-stay apartments, with separate bedrooms. Now, will you still be requiring just the one?" One carefully manicured eyebrow lifted as she eyed the three of them together.

"Uh, no," Bobbi said hastily; Jericho carefully hid a grin. When she shot him a mild glare, he schooled his features into innocence. It didn't seem to fool her. "Three bedrooms, thanks."

"Y'know, if it's easier, we c'n take two bedrooms an' a sofa," Luke suggested. "I can bed down on a sofa easy. Or the floor, happen y'all got an air mattress." He seemed to be sincere, but Jericho wasn't sure if he was just offering out of a sense of personal obligation.

"We *do* have a two-bedroom accommodation with a fold-out sofa bed." Jericho heard the receptionist's tone loud and clear: *Though I have no idea why you'd choose that.* "I must advise you that the sofa bed is not as comfortable as the standard beds. It's very much for last-minute bookings."

Jericho looked at Luke and shook his head. "You don't need to do this," he said, making a bet with himself that his words wouldn't change Luke's mind. "We can get a three-bed place just as easily."

"Is the two beds an' a sofa cheaper than three beds?" Luke directed the question to Helena. "'Cause if it is, we'll take it." Mentally, Jericho paid out on the bet. *Called it.*

"It is, yes," the receptionist said. "A hundred per night instead of one-twenty." Jericho's eyes widened. ... *wait a second. How* much *was that again?*

"Wait." Bobbi held up her hand. "Okay, I don't get this at all. How the *heck* can you afford to run a place like this so cheaply? I mean, the prices for *everything* are way too cheap. Seventy bucks for the maglev ticket. Eleven bucks for a cab to get us here. One-twenty bucks a night for three people. Even *food's* cheap. How does that even *work?*" The tone of her voice said quite clearly that she wasn't going to let this go until she had answers.

She'd voiced almost exactly what he'd been thinking. "Yeah," he said slowly. "How *does* that work? Is there a hidden cost on our MagCards that nobody's told us about? A fine for leaving the city?" Neither of those options seemed overly likely. *What am I missing?*

"Or do we just hafta pay for walkin' down the street or somethin'?" asked Luke. "Or for breathin' the air?" That last one, Jericho had to admit, was somewhat imaginative but probably unenforceable.

Shaking her head, Helena smiled politely. "It's nothing like that. Our overheads are low, so we can afford to charge rock-bottom prices. Of course, we do charge a refundable deposit, and it *does* cost extra for sheets, pillows and towels, and to have the fridge stocked with alcohol. And to have food supplied." She handed Bobbi a laminated sheet. "It's all on here."

Bobbi examined the list; with an effort, Jericho stopped himself from peering over her shoulder. "One dollar per sheet," she read out loud. "Five dollars per pillow. Five dollars per towel. Alcohol supplied at cost plus five percent. Meals supplied with a five dollar surcharge." She looked up at the receptionist. "This still doesn't even *begin* to cover your overheads." With her free hand, she gestured at the courtyard. With full night beginning to come on, lights were now illuminating it brightly. "I mean, your electricity bill alone would blow through this in no time."

While Jericho didn't know what the power bill for a complex this size would come to, he was certain he didn't want to pay it. Just one apartment for a few nights wouldn't be a very large chunk of the total, but it would still add more to the cost than was already there.

"Ah." Helena's smile never dimmed. "I see your confusion. I'm sorry; I didn't mean to mislead. You see, when I said overheads in Utopia were low, I meant it. Electricity, for example, is free."

But that's impossible. "Wait, wait," protested Jericho. "Electricity has to come from *somewhere.* You can get it cheap, but you can't get it for *nothing.*" The idea just didn't make sense. Even if it was supplied by a solar farm or wind turbines — which, unless Force Majeure had a tornado in a cage somewhere, still wouldn't cut it for a city of that size — there was maintenance and so forth to be paid for.

"We do, sir," the receptionist said simply. "I moved to Utopia about eight years ago and I've been here ever since. Electricity's always been free, which makes everything that requires electricity to manufacture — or get — really inexpensive." Which meant, Jericho realized, that they could charge minimal prices and still make a profit. The only things that would cost a significant amount were those things that they had to source from outside. *Which I bet they're manufacturing more of all the time. It's what I'd do.*

With a wondering shake of his head, Jericho tried to imagine how Force Majeure had pulled it off. No wonder Utopia City had expanded so quickly, when they didn't have to worry about such a pervasive cost as electricity to hold them back. *I bet it was the Technologist. It sounds like something he'd do, just to prove to every other artificer that he's still the best around.* It made the flying cars look tame. Hell, it made the *maglev* look tame. Except that … *Wait a minute. Do they power the whole goddamn* maglev *system with their free electricity?* That epiphany, and the implications thereof, staggered him. *Jeez, how much power are they* generating? *And where's it* coming *from?*

"Hey. Cuz." The patiently amused tone of Luke's voice told Jericho that his cousin's normal good humor was fully back in place. "Getcher head outta the clouds. Gotta swipe for the room." As Jericho came back to earth, he saw Luke gesturing at the MagCard sensor panel. "We're still goin' thirds, right?"

"Yeah, of course." Reflexively, he pulled out his wallet and extracted the card. Swiping it across the sensor elicited a cheerful beep from the machine.

"Thank you." Helena gave him a beaming smile. "You're in one-two-oh-four. It's in Block One, just across the courtyard; go around the trellis to get to the passageway, then straight on through. The elevator's back under the building. Your apartment's on the second floor, northwest corner. Sheets, towels and pillows should be there by the time you get there. Feel free to ring me here at the desk to get meals delivered. Any questions?"

"Uh, yeah." Jericho was still a little dazed from the massive shift in his worldview of a few moments before, but something still seemed to be missing. "Room keys?"

"Already got 'em." Luke held up his MagCard. "These'll let us in, cuz. Keep up, will ya?"

"Ah, right." It made sense. After all, given the importance of the MagCard, it was definitely a good idea to keep it close by at all times. He hefted the overnight bag and headed out into the courtyard, with Luke and Bobbi right behind him. Halfway across, he stopped when movement caught his eye. Fascinated, he stared as the umbrellas began to return to their vertical positions, moving in eerie synchronization.

"What the hell?" Luke was also staring. "Y'all seein' that?"

"Yeah." It was just another weird thing in a day filled with high-tech strangeness. Relieved that Luke found it odd as well, he watched the umbrellas close themselves; the once-taut cloth drooping to hang in lazy folds. Just as he was about to walk away, the dull-black cloth itself caught his eye, something about how the unusual way light played across the repeating hexagonal pattern. He started toward the closest table, intent on examining it closer.

"Seriously. *Boys.*" Bobbi sounded exasperated. "What is it about automatically closing umbrellas that's got you so mesmerized? We got here in a *flying car.*" She stepped up alongside Luke and shook her head. "If you're going to stop and stare at *everything* new you see, we'll be here all night."

With a nod, Jericho turned away from the picnic table. "You've got a point. But if you saw something like this back home, you'd stop and look twice. I know I would."

"Well, true." With a roll of her eyes, Bobbi conceded the point. "Back home, something like that would be pretty amazing. But here? I've seen about a dozen cooler things since I got off the train. And that's not counting the train itself." She pointed at the now-motionless umbrellas. "That sort of thing doesn't even make the radar anymore."

"Jes' 'cause it ain't the coolest thing around don't mean it ain't cool." Luke snorted. "Bet you was the type ta tell the other kids there weren't no Santa Claus, too." Holding his backpack over his shoulder with one hand and the MagCard in the other, he moved past Jericho in the direction of the covered walkway. In another moment, he'd vanished from sight behind one of the trellises.

20
Home Comforts

After one last thoughtful glance at the umbrellas, Jericho looked around to discover that Bobbi had gone on to join Luke, though he could still hear her voice. "So what if I was? It's no favor to let them keep believing in a lie." He wasn't quite sure whether she was trying to convince Luke or herself.

Rounding the trellis, he found himself at the entrance to a well-lit corridor that ran under the building. He'd had a vague idea of cutting off the incipient argument, but it looked like he was too late for that; Luke had always had strong views on the subject. Resigning himself to the inevitable, he moved up to join the pair.

"Sometimes folks is better off believin' th' lie than knowin' th' truth." Standing in front of an elevator set into the side of the corridor, Luke swiped his card on the ever-present reader. The doors *dinged* musically as they opened. "If folks cain't work it out for themselves, might could be they wanna believe th' lie."

"But that's not *right*." Bobbi shook her head as she towed her drag-bag into the elevator. "People deserve to know the truth. Lying to them is just hurting them, in the long run. Jericho, *tell* him."

"Hey, don't pull me into this. I don't really care either way." Following Luke into the confined space, Jericho watched as his cousin pressed the button for the second floor. Apart from one odd button—bright green, with a white domino mask shape stamped into it—Jericho couldn't see a difference between this and any other elevator he'd been in, even down to the mirror on the back wall. He wasn't sure whether to feel relieved or disappointed.

Bobbi stared at him, her expression one of betrayal, as the elevator started upward. "But—" she began.

Shaking his head, Jericho raised his hand. "Let me stop you right there. I'm not a fan of keeping secrets that hurt people. But I've come to Utopia City because of a secret that I only share with a few people. So have you. You think we should be spreading those secrets around, too?" Half-turning toward the mirror on the back wall of the elevator, he deliberately distanced himself from the argument.

For a moment, Bobbi faltered before she rallied and tried again. "That's different. Secrets like that would hurt our families if they got out. I'm talking about secrets that *don't* hurt people when they get out."

"So, how's believin' in Santa hurt kids?" The tone of Luke's voice was derisive. "Lemme tell you a story. My li'l sis Serena was in th' first grade when Great-grandpappy Frank turned up his toes. First actual Christmas we ever had. Jericho's daddy got us all gifts, but fo' her he bought the reddest friggin' tricycle you ever did see, an' signed it from Santa." He grinned. "She rid that thing all day, every day. Went back ta school tellin' everyone what Santa got her."

"And wouldn't the other kids have made fun of her?" There was doubt in Bobbi's voice.

"They sho'nuff tried." The elevator stopped with a *ding* and the doors hummed open. "I was there. She stomped right up ta th' biggest one an' tole him that if *she* was Santa Claus an' he went around sayin' he didn't believe in her, she wouldn't bring him nothin' neither." Luke stepped out of the elevator; courteously, Jericho waited for

Bobbi to get out before him.

The argument, far from being brought to a halt, just kept on going. Jericho did his best to stay out of it by checking out the helpful signage which pointed them toward their apartment. It all seemed rather straightforward, although he did have to wonder why there was a strip of well-worn linoleum covering one-third the width of the oddly wide corridor.

He led them in the appropriate direction while they debated the matter back and forth. By the time they reached the appropriate corridor, Luke and Bobbi had reached the stage of 'what if' scenarios, positing more and more contrived scenarios to try to prove their points.

"Okay, I got one for you." Luke sounded pleased with himself. "Suppose you got hitched to an axe murderer—"

"Are we assuming I've got my powers or not?" Bobbi interrupted. "Because if I do, I'd know what he was the moment I met him." She tapped the side of her head.

"Lemme finish." Luke waited a moment, then kept going. "Yeah, you got your powers, but he doesn't wanna murder *you*. He likes you, you like him. He decides to drop th' whole axe murderer thing, you have kids with him, everythin's fine. Then, ten years later, after you got a good life, you find his diary or somethin' an' discover he useta chop folks into little bits an' pieces. Ya know that if ya turn him in, all th' good stuff goes away. Ya lose him, mebbe lose th' kids. But ya also know he's killed dozens o' people. What-all are ya gonna do?"

Jericho had other matters on his mind. They had passed the doorway for one-two-oh-two just a few moments ago and turned the corner. Directly ahead, the corridor ended in a window. Ahead and to the left was the door for 1203, while opposite it was the one they'd been assigned; that is, 1204. Where the door was standing wide open.

Before Bobbi could answer, Jericho held up his hand. "Whoa, guys, shut it for a second."

"What's up, cuz?" Luke's voice was curious, but he didn't try to move past Jericho. "Why'd you stop?"

"Someone's in our apartment." With barely a thought, Jericho dropped his overnight bag on the floor and curled his right hand to form a glue-tag. He didn't know exactly what was going on, but he didn't intend to be caught unawares. Cautiously, he edged forward, listening for untoward noises. The only thing he heard was an electronic humming, which didn't fill him with confidence. He trailed his left hand on the wall, trying to use his G-sense to detect any dense masses—such as guns—moving within the apartment. He was working on getting the sense to function as effectively as radar, but he had a ways to go on that. All he got was the sense of a single mass of mid-level density and uncertain size …

In the next moment, the hum became louder as a complex-looking boxy cart rolled out through the open door and turned toward them, trundling onto the strip of linoleum. Jericho held himself back from tossing the G-tag; while he'd seen Artificer-built killing machines on TV, this looked more like the maid's cart without the maid. On the front of the device was the Oaklands logo and the number sixteen. "What the hell?" he asked out loud.

"Greetings." The cart spoke with a synthesized feminine voice as it rolled to a stop a few yards away. Fortunately for Jericho's sense of the surreal, it sounded different to the one employed by UML for their announcements. **"I am Room Service one-six. May I help you?"** Behind it, the apartment door swung shut with an audible click.

"Wait." Luke found his voice first. "What was you doin' in our apartment?"

"Apologies. I am unable to formulate complex answers. Apartment one-two-zero-four has been supplied with towels, sheets and pillows. Beds have been made up. Does that answer your query?"

With a sigh, Jericho let the glue-tag dissolve into nothingness. "Yeah, it does. Is all the room service around here like you?" He wondered if it would even be able to answer the question. *What does it do if it gets a question it can't answer? Ring the front desk?*

"All room service in Oaklands Temporary Accommodation is carried out by units similar to myself," the cart answered. **"Does that answer your query?"**

Huh. It must get asked that a lot. "Yeah, you're fine," Jericho said, feeling a little embarrassed. "Carry on."

"Thank you. Have a pleasant evening." The cart started up again and rolled past them along the strip of linoleum, then came to a halt. **"Excuse me."** Looking back, Jericho saw that it had unfolded a mechanical arm from its side. When he'd dropped his overnight bag, it had fallen partly onto the linoleum; the cart was now lifting the bag by its straps. **"Does this luggage belong to you?"**

"Uh, yeah, sorry." Jericho hastened back to retrieve his bag. To his relief, the metal and plastic claw released the straps as soon as he took hold of them. "Thanks."

"You are welcome. Please take care of your luggage. Have a pleasant evening."

It rolled off again; as the humming sound faded into the distance, Bobbi looked at Luke and Jericho. "Well?" she asked. "Isn't someone going to say 'how damn cool was that'?"

Jericho shared a glance with Luke; with an effort, he kept a straight face. "Nah," he decided. "Seen one robot room-service cart, you seen them all. Luke?"

"What you said, cuz." For all the excitement he was showing, Luke could've been relaxing over a cup of coffee. "I mean, geez, we-all got us flyin' police robots. Why in hell do we need to git fussed over some room service cart?"

"Assholes." Bobbi tried to glare at them, but Jericho thought he saw a smile lurking on her lips. "You're forgetting one thing. I can read your goddamn emotions. You're not fooling me for one goddamn minute." Pausing at the door, she looked back. "And just so you know, I'd turn the asshole in anyway. My feelings don't matter; what *matters* is that he faces justice for what he's done." She swiped her card over the door reader, resulting in a soft beep and a click as the door unlocked. Pushing the door open, she entered the apartment.

Amused and exasperated in equal parts by the disagreement, Jericho turned to Luke. "Okay, *now* can you drop it? Seriously, I don't want to be listening to this shit all night."

"Sho'nuff, cuz." Luke's shrug was elaborately unconcerned. "So, what about that robot cart? How friggin' cool was *that?*"

Jericho grinned at the enthusiasm in his cousin's voice. "Oh, *hell* yes." He gave his cousin a warning look as he followed Bobbi into the apartment. "Just so long as you aren't fixing to try drag-racing it down the hallways."

The grin he got back from Luke didn't exactly fill him with confidence. "Hey. This is *me.*"

"I know," retorted Jericho, then he turned his attention to his surroundings. The apartment was … nice. Bland, with far less personality than the one Jericho shared with Stephen back in Savannah, but nice all the same. The main room, not exactly large, was dominated by a large-screen TV on one side and a picture window on the other. Below the window, which looked out on to the tree-lined street, there was a sofa with a neatly folded towel and set of sheets on it, as well as a pillow. Alongside the sofa was a small table with two chairs next to it.

Three doors on the far side of the room led to the bedrooms and bathroom as indicated by helpful symbols on the doors, while a dividing counter separated the kitchen nook from the rest of the room. It was equipped, as far as Jericho could see, with a counter-top stove, a microwave and a full-sized fridge. The only decoration in the living room was a large canvas print showing an aerial view of Utopia City by night, with the Spire front and center, illuminated by floodlights.

"Oh, thank God." Bobbi's voice was more of a groan. "I don't care that the maglev's clean and fast, I need a shower right now, so bad." She flicked a glance at Jericho and Luke. "I mean, if that's okay with you guys."

Gay or not, Jericho had learned respect for women at his father's knee. While he was already inclined to say yes, he sensed there was more to Bobbi's comment than met the eye. He was looking forward to a shower, and he suspected that Luke was as well, but there was the added factor of Bobbi being an empath. The constant proximity of hundreds of strangers during her train ride, and even the casual nearness of himself and Luke during the latter part of the trip, had to have left a lingering psychic impression on her. In her place, he suspected he'd be wanting to scrub his skin down to the bone.

"Go right ahead," he affirmed, with a glance at Luke. As he'd thought, his cousin was already nodding in assent. "Just don't use all the hot water, okay?"

She still had enough of her sense of humor left to grin at him. "I don't think that's possible. Free electricity, remember?" Pushing open the left-hand bedroom door, she disappeared inside with her drag-bag in tow. The door shut behind her and he thought he heard the complaining of bedsprings, as though someone had flopped full-length onto the mattress.

"Oh, yeah," he said out loud. "Good point." He dropped his overnight bag on the floor and headed for the TV. Taking up the remote, he retired to the sofa and flopped into it. "Luke, you wanna see what they got to drink in the fridge?" he asked as he levered at the heel of one sneaker with the toe of the other. Pressing the power button on the remote, he turned on the TV and brought up the channel menu. There were a *lot* of channels.

"An' what'd your *last* friggin' involuntary indentured servant die of?" asked Luke, already on his way into the kitchenette.

"Being a smartass," Jericho retorted. Even with the euphemism that Luke habitually employed, it was a measure of the friendship between them that they could make this joke, and they *never* used it around anyone they didn't trust. Especially in places where it could be taken the wrong way, which meant basically anywhere.

"Screw you too." Luke's answer was automatic. "Hey, ya know you c'n pick a channel an' stay on it. Nobody's gonna judge."

Jericho flicked past some more movie channels, paused at the mention of a couple of TV shows that he liked, then settled on a news channel out of Florida. "Just looking to see if anything happened to those two morons in Tallahassee." He was pretty sure they were both alive, though there was a very real chance they'd be charged with reckless endangerment. After all, those cops *had* been killed trying to save them from the Madness.

"Hope the cops throw the goddamn book at 'em," said Luke sourly. "There's a place an' a time for that sort of shit, an' that ain't it."

Jericho's second sneaker popped off at about the time the bathroom door closed behind Bobbi, and he took a moment to remove his socks as well. He turned the sound up as Luke got back to the sofa and handed him a bottle. It was chilled, with bubbles rising lazily inside, but the label was unfamiliar. *Utopia Gold*, he read. In smaller print, around the perimeter of the label it said *Brewed in Utopia City.*

"The hell?" he asked. "They brew beer here?" Utilizing a trick his Uncle Leroy had taught him once upon a time, he pushed his sleeve up and pressed the cap of the bottle hard against the underside of his forearm. Clenching his fist to flex the muscles in his forearm, he twisted the bottle and popped the cap off. After a cautious mouthful, he judged that it wasn't too bad, if a little fizzy. He took a longer drink then burped, the released gases burning sweetly in his sinuses.

"Looks like." Luke picked up the sheets, towel and pillow and dumped them on the table, then slumped down on the sofa, not even bothering to take his boots off. He held his bottle to his mouth and tilted it skyward; Jericho could see the air bubbles glugging up toward the bottom. When he took the bottle away and belched, it was a magnificent rolling eructation that should have rattled the window. Jericho felt like applauding.

The beer was very easy to get used to, but fortunately for his state of sobriety, Jericho couldn't be bothered getting up to fetch another. On finishing the bottle, he let out another burp and turned his attention back to the TV. It seemed the idiots had indeed fallen afoul of the law. They couldn't be named, or their faces even shown on TV, due to their being under eighteen, but he got the impression that the courts were going to come down heavily on them. *Well, good.*

When that story ran out, he turned the channel back to a more nationwide coverage. There was a spot on the Team Power press conference that Bobbi had mentioned, with Tess and Adam Power giving a no-holds-barred interview. The hostility from the reporters wasn't hard to spot; they were throwing question after question like sharks scenting blood.

Adam Power was ruggedly handsome, with blond hair. As befitted his age, he was going gray at the temples, giving him a distinguished appearance. At the moment, he was tight-lipped and strained, and answered relatively few questions. His wife Tesseract, a striking redhead, had always been cool under pressure. In this situation, she definitely needed it.

"How do you reconcile your daughter's accusations and continuing absence with your husband's claims of innocence?" demanded a solidly built woman as she thrust her microphone almost into Tess' face. Her accent—from Arkansas, if Jericho was any judge—was downright familiar. The hectoring tone he'd heard from dozens of 'concerned friends' since he'd come out, was (unfortunately) equally so.

From the look in her eye, the redhead wanted to punch her interrogator, but she restrained herself in an admirable fashion. "The physical evidence we had at the time was inconclusive," she shot back. "Adam says he was in his workshop at the time, and I believe him. It has to be a clone or an impostor."

That got the attention of several of the reporters. "Why not just call it an evil twin?" jibed the blocky woman. "That's just as likely, isn't it? Or mind control? We haven't had a real mind controller since Mindscrew. Do you think he's back?"

Tess Power shook her head fiercely. "It's not Adam's evil twin. Adam dealt with that bastard back in oh-four, while I tracked down the Clone Arranger and made him *eat* his duplicate-gun. As for Mindscrew, the FBI's had his remains in cold storage since 'ninety-seven. Forty-four caliber bullet to the back of the head." That was news to Jericho; it seemed that Team Power had access to better information than the average man on the street. "Anyway, he couldn't control minds. He just read them, then blackmailed people with the information he got."

"And where's your daughter now?" This was a smartly presented man with black hair that had been styled to within an inch of its existence. "Has your husband done away with her to save his own skin, or do you have her locked up in the basement? Are you helping conceal his crimes?"

It was perhaps fortunate that Adam Power didn't have an offensive Dynamic power rating; if he'd possessed destructive eyebeams of any kind, the man would've died then and there. "Listen, you," the hero snapped. "If you think for one *second* I touched Vanessa in *any* way, you—"

Tess put her hand on her husband's arm, and he shut up. "I believe that both my husband and my daughter are telling the truth," she stated, sounding far calmer than Jericho would've been in the same situation. "I don't know where Vanessa is right now, but she left of her own accord. She's very resourceful, and she can take care of herself, but I'm her mother and I *will* keep looking for her." Several of the reporters went to ask questions, but she talked straight over the top of them. "No matter what else happens, we're still Team Power. We got this. We *will* prove Adam's innocence, and we *will* get Vanessa back."

The camera cut back to the studio, where the immaculately presented news anchor was straightening the papers on her desk. "Well, there you have it," she declared brightly. "In other news, the New York based superhero team Manhattan Justice has announced—"

"Shower's free," announced Bobbi as she emerged from the bathroom. Jericho muted the TV and looked around. Now clad in brightly colored flannel pajamas, she was vigorously toweling her hair dry and looked somewhat more relaxed. "Whew, that's so much better," she said cheerfully. "Oh, and they've got a washer-dryer in there too. Which makes sense, seeing they had detergent on that list of stuff we could buy." She eyed the sofa dubiously. "Haven't you boys figured that thing out yet?"

"Later," Luke said lazily. Then his eyes opened as he came fully out of his half-doze. "Oh, hey, did ya say—"

Jericho knew what was coming and preempted his cousin. "Dibs on next shower!" He came to his feet in one smooth move, then took a single long step and grabbed up his overnight bag. Turning on his heel, he headed for the bathroom. Racing for the shower was a time-honored tradition from their younger days, but 'dibs' usually settled the matter.

"Not if I git there first, cuz." Luke quickly rolled off the sofa and landed on one knee, his hand already reaching out for his discarded backpack. Which changed things; this was now definitely a race. And while Luke was on one knee, Jericho was several feet farther away from the bathroom door. If Luke could get to his feet and beat Jericho there, the race would be over and done. Jericho watched his hand grasp the strap. "You snooze, you lose."

"My thoughts exactly." As he darted across the room, Jericho formed a glue-tag in his hand and loosed it at Luke's backpack, followed by two more. He was not a moment too soon, as Luke was already beginning to pull himself to his feet. With one hand on the table, Luke yanked upward on the backpack. The G-tags struck the pack and dissolved, imbuing it with an intense attraction toward the floor beneath it. Luke had put all his not inconsiderable mass behind the grab-and-heave; just as the pack began to leave the floor, it stuck and *stayed*, barely long enough to break Luke's momentum. The attraction granted by the hastily formed 'tags wasn't all that strong and the pack pulled free, but only after Luke had put too much force into pulling on it. He let out a startled yelp as he overbalanced forward, almost going ass over teakettle before he regained his balance.

With his mouth stretching into a grin that became a chuckle, Jericho dodged past Luke and got to the bathroom first. Grabbing the door frame, he hauled himself to a halt inside the room, just in time to hear Luke's outraged yell. "The *hell*, J? That's goddamn *cheating!*"

"So's ignoring dibs," Jericho retorted, laughing. He dropped his bag on the bathroom floor, then realized that the towel that the room service robot had left him was no doubt lying on his bed. Which meant it wasn't in the bathroom, where he needed it to be. The trouble was, if he left the bathroom to retrieve it, Luke was guaranteed to claim the bathroom in turn. If he glue-tagged the door shut, the 'tags wouldn't last long enough for him to get back. And while it was possible—kind of— to dry himself with glue-tags by making the water collect into a ball, it was also tedious as *hell*.

G-tags. Duh. His solution was staring him in the face. He leaned out the bathroom door and formed a push-tag in his hand. When it was strong enough, he tossed it at Luke's towel where it lay on the table.

Back in Savannah (and just now, with Luke's backpack), the 'tags had been hastily formed, leaving them barely strong enough to influence matters. But smaller items could be affected to the point that their entire mass was overcome by the faux gravitational forces involved, especially if he took his time powering the 'tags up. Case in point: Luke's towel. And while he couldn't steer things once he gave them direction—it wasn't quite telekinesis, after all—he could certainly *aim* them.

The G-tag hit the towel and imparted a temporary revision of local physics. Acting on this, the towel leaped off the table, moving on an upward angle toward where Jericho waited. Realizing too late what Jericho was up to, Luke made a hasty grab for the towel and missed it altogether. "Hey," he protested. "That's my friggin' *towel!*"

Jericho dismissed the 'tag when the towel was most of the way to him and heading for the ceiling; describing a perfect parabolic arc, it landed neatly in his hand. "Mine, now," he said cheerfully, slinging it over his shoulder. "Yours is in my room. Feel free to go grab it. Me, I'm gonna take a shower." Whistling off-key, he closed the bathroom door and locked it. He didn't necessarily think Luke was going to push his way in while Jericho was taking a shower—especially with Bobbi there—but there was no sense in taking chances.

21
Personal Issues

Wisps of steam curled around Jericho as he opened the bathroom door. He'd changed into the T-shirt and boxers that suited him as pajamas; after a good long shower and a proper wash of his hair, he felt beautiful again. Leaving his clothes in the laundry hamper, he brought his phone and wallet out into the living room with him.

"I got a riddle," Luke said at that moment. "What's the difference between a cape and a dynamic?"

Oh, shit. Answering, Jericho knew, was a bad idea. Luke's jokes usually reached a whole new level of horrific, all by themselves. "Don't—!" he called out warningly.

"Uh, I've got no idea," Bobbi replied. Jericho put his hand over his eyes, realizing she didn't have enough experience with his cousin to know better. "What is it?"

Luke's gleeful expression matched his tone. "A dynamic can wear a cape to go superheroing." Mercifully, he didn't carry on with the comparison.

"Oh, that was bad." Bobbi facepalmed as well. "And you should feel bad."

I could've told you that already. Jericho cleared his throat. "Shower's free," he announced, then winced internally. *Well, duh. Luke's right there.* Going to his bedroom door, he tossed his overnight bag inside and then headed for the sofa.

"Yeah, got that." Luke didn't look up from the TV, which seemed to be still showing the news, but with the sound turned down. Sitting with her legs tucked up under her, Bobbi was sharing the sofa with him; an open pizza box lay between them. "Ya lucky I didn't eat your share of th' pizza, asshole."

"Don't worry, I made him leave some for you." Bobbi unwound the towel from her hair, allowing it to fall down and frame her face, giving her a softer, more vulnerable air. She pushed aside a strand that had draped itself over her glasses, then looked up at Jericho. "Do you realize you spent longer in there than I did?" Her tone was more curious than accusatory, leaving him to believe that she hadn't spent much time around gay guys.

Jericho frowned. "I didn't spend *that* long … did I?" He looked over at the pizza box. Old knowledge from a long-ago summer job came back to him. *Family sized pizza, takes at least half an hour to bake and deliver … and it's not steaming anymore …* "Crap. I was in there for over an hour, wasn't I?"

The sour look on Luke's face was verification enough. "You sure as hell was, cuz. Don't look so goddamn surprised. That sort of thing's par for the friggin' course, for you." He rolled his eyes expressively in Bobbi's direction. "Why'd you think I tried ta git in first? Asshole always uses all th' hot water." He gave Jericho a mock glare. "An' I swear if you done that here, you're washin' your hair in th' sink from now on."

"Whatever," Jericho drawled, fully aware that Luke had plenty of experience to back up his complaint. "There's still plenty of hot water, so you can quit your bellyaching." Sketching an elaborate bow, he gestured in the general direction of the bathroom. "Now go get clean, you uncultured barbarian. And remember; the yellow stuff is called 'soap'. You're supposed to wash with it, not eat it."

Bobbi stifled an incipient giggle and held her towel out. "Uh, Luke, while you're up, could you do me a favor and hang my towel up for me, please?" She accompanied the request with a winning smile.

"Sure thing." Levering himself up off the sofa, Luke accepted the towel from Bobbi and headed for the bathroom, snagging his backpack on the way. His own towel—no doubt retrieved from Jericho's room—hung around his neck. "Outta the way. Time I showed y'all how it's possible ta have a shower in less'n three hours."

Jericho stepped aside as Luke went to barge past him. "Just because *you* don't know how to have a proper shower," he said with a grin. "I left my body wash and manicure set in there, just in case you want to try a civilized way to get clean."

Luke's answer was indistinct but contained elements of *bite me* and *cold day in hell* before the door banged shut. Jericho shrugged, unsurprised. "Shocker." He turned back toward the sofa where Bobbi sat. "What sort of pizza did we get?"

"Half and half meat-lovers and supreme," Bobbi said. This was kind of predictable; Luke had always had a serious hankering for meat-lovers pizza. Fortunately, it was a taste that they shared. Jericho had once made the obvious joke about 'loving meat' while they were sharing a pizza, causing Luke to shoot soda out of his nose. Still, it hadn't lessened his cousin's enjoyment of the delicacy. "Uh, do you have this hassle *every* time you two go for a shower?"

For a moment, Jericho didn't get her meaning, then the penny dropped. "Ah. No, Luke's got his place and I've got mine. But when we were kids and I was staying over at his place or he was staying at mine, it was always a race to see who got there first." Settling down on the sofa, he put his phone and wallet on the sofa arm and took up a slice of pizza. After the first bite, he came to the conclusion that he *had* to find the place that had made it. "Damn," he mumbled. "This is *good*." 'Good' wasn't really the word; his taste-buds lit up like fireflies on a summer evening as the sauces flooded his mouth.

Bobbi nodded at the pizza box. "Try one of the supreme slices. Even if I felt like finishing them, I don't think I could." She slumped a little farther down on the sofa with a sigh. "The news can be so damn depressing sometimes. Oh, yeah, did you hear? Another plane went down this afternoon, out of San Diego. They're looking for survivors now."

"Ah, *crap*," muttered Jericho. He finished the first slice of meat-lovers and decided to take Bobbi up on her offer of the supreme. "Did they say if it was human error or mechanical problems?" It was a tragedy; this sort of thing always was. But he *was* hungry, and that came first.

When Force Majeure commenced construction of the maglev across the United States, a very few far-sighted individuals had seen the writing on the wall and pulled their money out of domestic airline stocks. Unfortunately for the vast majority, the airline PR firms had done an exemplary job of keeping public faith going strong until it was far too late.

By the time the bubble burst, the public was fully aware that the maglev could transport people almost as quickly as a jet, in at least equal levels of comfort, and at far lower prices. Share prices dropped like rocks as most of the newly savvy investors tried to unload the unwanted stocks as fast as they could. Many people lost a lot of money as nearly all the larger airlines either cut out local operations or went bankrupt, sometimes almost overnight.

Some domestic airline companies were less affected than others, however. The maglev was good for passenger travel, but the few bulk transport cars in the system were used solely for Utopia City business. While ordinary trains could handle short-haul freight, if something needed to get across the country overnight, it usually had to go on a plane.

Of the airlines that kept flying in-country with passengers, there were two main types. The first was where their PR firms redesigned the 'flight experience' to attract the jaded traveler. They cited the boredom and the requirement to walk from one maglev car to the next, and offered an alternative. Every seat was now first-class, with legroom to match, while flight attendants—male and female both—were required to meet a much higher standard of physical attractiveness. They also had to cram themselves into skimpy outfits and wait upon the passengers' every need, to an almost embarrassing degree. For higher paying passengers there was 'super-first' class, for which (it was rumored) more intimate 'mile high' services were freely available from takeoff to landing.

The second type were the companies that couldn't upscale to the level of luxury needed to compete in the cut-throat new world of airline flight. They kept themselves flying on a shoestring budget, slashing costs when and where they could. Their fares were as cheap as they could afford to charge, but rumors abounded of shoddy maintenance and minimal training. Worse, bearing silent witness to these whispers, planes had begun to crash. Most were from the shoestring airlines but the super-first flights weren't coming out of it unscathed either, a clear indication that they also had problems behind the scenes.

Jericho considered them all idiots. It was clear to him that the day of the airliner was done, at least within the continental United States. Having traveled on the maglev, he couldn't consider going back to a lesser form of transport. In this, he was almost certainly in agreement with the vast majority of the American public. Despite its flaws, the maglev was clearly a superior form of mass transit to air travel.

"Too early to tell yet," Bobbi replied. "It was a super-first flight, so I'm guessing pilot error. Those planes are fairly well maintained, or at least that's what they say." She grimaced. "Why couldn't they just take the maglev?"

Jericho shrugged and took a bite out of the slice of supreme pizza; it was almost as good as the meat lovers. "Mffbe," he mumbled, then stopped talking until he could chew and swallow. "Uh, maybe they just wanted to get laid on the way to Chicago, or wherever they were headed." Which was, in his mind, a stupid excuse.

"Well, as insensitive as this is gonna sound, walking from New York to LA is still a lot better than dying in a fiery crash outside of San Diego." Bobbi nibbled at a piece of garlic bread. "I hear the FAA shut another airline down last week. How many does that make now?"

That newsflash only served to confirm Jericho's poor opinion on the matter. "I have no idea. But it's probably for their own good." He finished off the slice of pizza, then started on a third. "I mean, this is the reason Utopia City's got a no-fly zone around it, just in case some idiot flies a plane too close and it falls out of the sky."

"Or if someone decides that Utopia City's the reason their airlines are failing and attempts to crash a jet into the Spire like they tried with the Pentagon and the White House back in 'oh-two," Bobbi pointed out darkly. "I mean, sure, it didn't work then and it won't work now, but some people really are that moronic."

This was one of the few silver linings to come out of the 1990's. During that era, the terror villains had run roughshod over anyone who tried to curtail their activities, as shown by their repeated retaliation against any attempt by the government to rein them in. The death of Carnifex had marked the beginning of the end of this era, though said end had been long in coming and not without its tragedies. Along the way, precautions and safeguards had been developed via hard-earned lessons gleaned from the worst of the villain attacks. Ironically enough, these had served well to ward against more mundane attacks on the United States once the terror villains had been dealt with once and for all.

"Yeah, well, I bet the Technologist thought of that when he designed the place," Jericho said. "Doc Iridium isn't around anymore, but there's new villains popping up all the time. Force Majeure would've made sure that someone couldn't just drive a giant mech in and wreck the place. I mean, I know Raider's dead too, but someone like that." He looked at the canvas print on the wall, and shuddered, imagining the city on fire. Even knowing that the Minotaur and his ilk were all dead—some of them quite spectacularly so—the very idea of them being let loose on Utopia City was horrific.

"Yeah, true." Bobbi brushed the crumbs off her pajama top and dusted her hands clean, then picked up her phone from beside her. "Just going to make a call. Let my sister know I got in safely." She tapped in the code to wake it up, then dialed a number and held the phone to her ear.

There was a short pause, then her face lit up with a smile. "Hi, Mel. Yeah, funny thing, guess what, I'm in Utopia City." Wincing, she held the phone away from her ear. Jericho heard the *what?* from the other end of the sofa. "I know you were supposed to come with me, *but*—yeah, I know, I know, but your boss was being a dick and you might've lost your job ..." She paused to hold the phone away from her ear again. "But *look*, the press conference was *today*, and I know I should've called, but I was on the train before I really thought about it, and then I got caught up in the moment and bought a ticket straight through to Utopia City once the press conference was over."

Her sister must have managed to get a word in edgewise, because Bobbi went silent, except for a few interjections. "No, I'm *fine*. Yes, I *know* what my powers are like, they're *my powers*. I met a couple of guys on the train—*Mel!* It's not *like* that!" Her cheeks reddened. "*They're* not like that! They're total gentlemen. No, I said *gentlemen*, not sleazebags! Those words don't even *sound* the same! And if anyone can tell a sleaze, it's me, remember? We're sharing an apartment. You'd like them. If you can get here in the next few days, you can interrogate them yourself." She put her hand over the phone and glanced at Jericho. "You'll be gone in a couple of days, right?"

Despite himself, Jericho snorted with amusement. "Maybe."

She grinned at him and went back to the phone call. "Listen, we're in the Oaklands, one two zero four. Oh, hey, I might just have an inside line on joining Force Majeure ahead of time. One of the guys is setting it up for me. Isn't that fantastic? No, it's *not* a scam! You *know* I'd be able to tell that! Look, just get over here already because holy crap, you *have* to see what this place is like. It's *amazing*. I mean, remember that documentary we saw about flying cars that one—"

She broke off with a frown. "Hang on, I've got another call coming in. I'll call you back? Thanks, love you, mwah mwah." With one final kissy noise, she took the phone away from her ear and looked at the screen. Her smile dimmed a little and she muttered, "Oh, joy."

With a sigh, she tapped the phone and held it to her ear again. When she spoke, her voice was almost as animated as when she'd been talking to her sister, but her smile was strained. "Hi, Jack. It's so good to hear from you. How are you? No, of course I'm not angry with you. I never *was* angry with you." She paused. "Just hold on a second—no, hold on—no, *wait*, Jack. Just a *second*. Please." Covering the phone with her hand, Bobbi grimaced in apology to Jericho, then headed toward her bedroom. Once the door closed behind her, he turned the TV up a bit; the last thing he wanted was to listen in on any part of her phone call, even accidentally. An inane commercial for a furniture store began playing; he promptly ignored it, reaching across to tear off a piece of garlic bread.

The bathroom door opened and Luke emerged. Clad in a wife-beater and sweatpants, he looked a lot less stressed than when he went in. "Cuz," he grunted, wandering over to the sofa. "Bobbi gone ta bed?" He dropped onto the sofa and stole the last slice of supreme pizza, quite possibly more from habit than hunger; in Jericho's experience, Luke never turned down free food.

"On the phone," Jericho replied. "Boyfriend, I think. Way she was talking, anyway." He paused, then picked up his own phone from the sofa arm. "Shit, I never called Stephen back." He wondered how his boyfriend was taking the situation. The older man had always been a little highly strung, and to be cut off in the middle of an argument like that couldn't have helped his mental state. As Jericho went to hold down the power button to wake it up, Luke cleared his throat. Jericho looked at him quizzically for a moment, then the penny dropped as Stephen's betrayal caught up with him. Closing his eyes, he let his hand go slack around the phone as he slumped against the back of the sofa, wishing the world would go away.

He felt Luke put a hand on his shoulder. "Jes' now remembered the asshole's been cheatin' on ya, huh?" His cousin's tone wasn't vindictive or even triumphant, just … understanding.

With a sigh, Jericho dropped the phone in his lap and put his face in his hands. "Yeah." Just for a little while, he'd managed to block out the fact of Stephen's infidelity, but now the pain came back in full force. *What am I even gonna say to him? 'I know what you did'?* He ground the heels of his hands into his forehead, trying to get his mental processes up and running. "What the hell do I do, just call him or let him sweat? What does *anyone* do?"

Picking up the remote from where Jericho had left it, Luke aimed it at the TV. "Your call. Jes' don't make no promises you cain't keep, or *I'll* hafta kick your ass. Krav Maga or no Krav Maga." He hit the button to change the channel to the middle of an action movie. Someone was hanging upside down from a helicopter, firing a machine-gun at someone else. That didn't really help to narrow it down. Something must have occurred to him, because he muted the TV again and turned toward Jericho. "You wanna know what I figger you should do?"

Jericho gave Luke his full attention. His cousin may have grown up in the bad part of town, and he'd made one or two poor decisions in life, but Luke was still one of the most street-smart people Jericho knew. More to the point, Jericho trusted Luke to not deliberately steer him wrong. "Hit me."

"Don't call him yet." Luke gestured with the remote. "Wait'll you see what happens with th' interview tomorrow. Ya might bomb out, or they might offer you a full-time place right here in Utopia City. Work out what you wanna do as a superhero, *then* work out how Steve fits in with that. If he does. Doin' it th' other way 'round won't do you no favors nohow." He turned back to the TV and took it off mute. Dramatic music interspersed with explosions swelled through the room, leaving Jericho to his thoughts.

Luke's advice made a lot of sense. Jericho had no idea how to deal with the elephant in the room, but putting it off until he'd sorted out the other matters was in fact a way of handling it, at least temporarily. *It's all a matter of priorities.* Once he knew where he stood with Force Majeure, he could decide what to do about Stephen. Trying to deal with one while stressing over the other was a recipe for disaster.

With a feeling of accomplishment, Jericho settled back to watch the movie. He had no idea what was going on, but he guessed the good guy was the one rescuing the girl. *I wish real life was as easy to figure out.* After a tense stand-off, the bad guy was dealt with and the hero got to kiss the girl, who responded enthusiastically. Jericho didn't blame her; the guy had abs to *die* for.

"Hey, guys?" It was Bobbi who spoke, standing in the doorway to her bedroom.

"Just wanted you to know, that was my boyfriend on the phone. I told him where we're staying, so if he turns up in the next day or so, don't be too surprised." She bit her lip. "We didn't exactly part on good terms. He's had trouble understanding that it's my power that's been pushing us apart, and that I'm trying to fix things so we can get back together. But he's probably coming to see me anyway, so if he does show up, be nice, okay?"

Jericho shrugged. "Sure." He'd only known Bobbi for a few hours, but they had more in common than he would've expected from a stranger on the train, mainly to do with powers-linked relationship problems. Luke got along well with her too, which was a plus in Jericho's book. "We can definitely do that. Want us to make ourselves scarce when he shows, to give you two some privacy?"

From the relief on Bobbi's face, she'd been trying to figure out how to ask that herself. "That would be amazing of you, guys. Thanks. I appreciate it."

"So, what's he know about us?" Luke's question was pragmatic. "I'm guessin' you didn't tell him about Jericho bein' a Mask." The sly look he shot Jericho made it perfectly clear that he knew his cousin's views on the terminology and didn't give a good goddamn about them. Which, Jericho would be the first to admit, was his right and privilege. It was just also irritating as *crap*.

Bobbi shrugged. "I didn't really talk about you guys. Just that this is where he can find me, if he wants. I mean, I understand why he's upset, but I'm allowed to have feelings about this too." Despite her bold tone, she glanced at them, as if silently seeking permission to hold that opinion.

"Damn right," agreed Jericho. "It's not your fault if your powers are screwing with your head." It wasn't as though his powers had made his life any easier, even if they hadn't messed him around the way Bobbi's powers had with her. Without powers, he wouldn't have met Stephen, but then neither would he be facing his current drama.

When chatting with people on social media, it was easy to tell the power poseurs (or the newly Enabled) from the real deal. The fakers usually made extravagant claims about the latest cool thing they'd done with their supposed superhuman abilities, while the *actual* Enabled were usually a lot more low-key about it. Life with powers, as those in the know could tell anyone willing to listen, was never smooth.

Bobbi nodded. "Thanks again. You guys are the best. I'm going to brush my teeth and go to bed now. If you're going to keep watching TV, do me a favor and keep it down?" Her smile, though genuine, was tired.

"Well, I was about to catch some sleep myself," Jericho noted. He waved a hand at the TV. "This movie's about done. Just knock on my door when you're finished in the bathroom, okay?" He flicked push-tags at his sneakers where they lay on the floor. Like the towel, they were light enough that the permeating field was concentrated enough to overcome local gravity altogether. They leaped off the floor, and he caught them both on the rise. Turning, he saw both Luke and Bobbi looking oddly at him. "What?"

"That, cuz, is the single friggin' *laziest* thing I ever seen you do, an' that includes ridin' on the escalator," Luke declared. "You couldn't bend down an' pick 'em up like a normal person?" He was trying to maintain a tone of offended propriety, but Jericho was reasonably sure he could hear undertones of intense jealousy.

"I'm sorry, Jericho, but I have to side with Luke." The smile on Bobbi's face belied her words. "Surely you don't do that all the time when you're at home?" Amusement danced in her eyes.

Jericho tried to imagine Stephen's expression if he used his powers inside the apartment. "Yeah, nope. I don't. But I *do* have my tryout tomorrow, so I've gotta get in all the practice I can." He glanced across the room, trying to calculate angles. "Hey, you guys want to see lazy? Check this out." He dropped one shoe on the floor, then sent a 'tag across the room to nudge his bedroom door open. "Bobbi, you might want to step aside a bit. Just in case."

Eyes widening, Bobbi did as she was told. Then she looked between the doorway and Jericho, and backed up a little farther, pausing halfway inside the bathroom doorway. "Is this okay?" She had her hand on the door handle, ready to slam it shut at a moment's notice; Jericho approved of her caution.

"That'll do." He worked his fingers a little, then crafted a push-tag, his eyes flicking back and forth between the door and his shoe. While he had a certain innate understanding of the forces and vectors involved, he wasn't particularly skilled at this specific application of his powers. Taking a deep breath, he launched the G-tag at the shoe.

It hit the target cleanly and dissolved, imparting gravitational information to the footwear. The shoe leaped from the floor at the appropriate elevation for reaching his bedroom door, but he'd somehow managed to get the angle way off. Whipping past Luke's nose, it bounced off the wall, soared over the counter, ricocheted off the microwave, then came to rest with a dull thud somewhere within the kitchenette.

"Well, that was impressive, for an extremely narrow definition of the word." Bobbi's voice held amusement as she ventured from the bathroom door. "If, for instance, you had a grudge against your sneaker, that was very well done. Otherwise, not so much." With an airy finger-wave, she disappeared back into the bathroom.

"Great." Jericho's heart sank. Carrying the other sneaker, he headed into the kitchenette, to find his shoe protruding from the trash can. As he pulled it out, he glumly hoped that the interview would not be predicated on pulling off trick shots like that. "You okay there, Luke?"

"Just goddamn dandy." Rising from the sofa, Luke strolled almost nonchalantly over to the dividing counter, and leaned on it with his elbows. "Just between you an' me, you know what's gonna happen if you ever pull a stupid-ass stunt like that around me again?" His expression was as mild as his tone. It didn't fool Jericho in the slightest.

"I'm guessing something pretty drastic?" Almost instinctively, Jericho tried to hide the offending item of footwear behind his back. While he knew Luke wasn't about to do anything to hurt him, this didn't make him feel as complacent as it might have. Besides, he felt bad enough about the near miss as it was.

"Yeah, drastic. What I'm gonna do is take that goddamn shoe, an' shove it so far up your ass that you'll be able ta floss your goddamn teeth with the laces." Luke's delivery was quiet and measured, to the point that Jericho couldn't be totally certain he wasn't putting on an act. "Ya nearly took my head off with the goddamn thing."

Jericho couldn't work out whether Luke was genuinely angry or just horsing around. It *sounded* like a hundred fake threats his cousin had issued over the years, but this time had been a little closer than most. He thought he saw a twinkle in Luke's eye, so he took a chance. "Yeah, well, your head's a lot thicker than that shoe and you know it."

For a long moment, Luke held the forbidding expression, then it cracked as he let out a bark of laughter. "Friggin' asshole." Standing up straight, he reached across the counter and slugged Jericho on the shoulder. "Seriously, don't do that again. I thought the goddamn thing was gonna go right up my nose."

"Do my best." Frowning, Jericho brought the shoe around from behind his back and examined it. "Not sure if the G-tag hit it off-center or if the aerodynamics were out. Either way, I'm gonna leave off the trick shots 'til I know more about what I'm doing." Which wasn't a bad idea, he decided. "Though it would've been hella cool if I'd actually gotten it in my bedroom."

"Well, duh." Luke grinned at him. "This here's how normal folks do it." Before Jericho could react, Luke had snatched the shoe from him and hurled it in through the open bedroom door. "See? Worked first time. And I didn't have to guess." Turning back toward the sofa, he scratched his head. "Anyways, I gotta work out how this thing goes so's I can get me some sleep tonight." He gave Jericho a considering look. "You better fuck off ta bed too. Big day tomorrow an' all."

"Yup, just as soon as ..." Jericho paused as Bobbi emerged from the bathroom. "... that, I guess. Night, Bobbi."

"Night, guys." Giving them a nod and a smile, Bobbi headed for her bedroom.

As the door closed behind her, Jericho went to the bathroom and set about brushing his teeth. That done, he rinsed his face and wiped it dry with his towel. On exiting the bathroom, he saw Luke in the process of examining the sofa bed. "Need a hand?" he asked.

"Nah, I'll be fine. Night, cuz."

"Night." On entering his bedroom and closing the door, Jericho found his bed already made up, as the robo-maid had reported. More curiously, there was a TV-style remote on his nightstand. *Okay, that's weird.* Somehow, he didn't think the Oaklands would be so careless as to leave duplicate remotes in their apartments. Picking the device up, he looked it over. For all he knew, the bed might've had a vibrating function, or maybe projected holographic pornography into the air. This was Utopia City; he couldn't rule anything out.

To his minor disappointment, the buttons were the same as on a standard TV remote. When he pressed the power button, a whirring noise became audible. Turning, he watched as panels slid aside from a flat-screen the same size as the one in the living room. "Huh. That's pretty cool."

He hit the button again to close the panels, then put the remote down and climbed into bed. Lying back, he turned on his phone and took it out of airplane mode. Within a few seconds, it started pinging. When the alert tones ceased (taking longer than he'd hoped and less time than he'd feared) he checked his messages. There were seventeen missed calls and approximately four thousand text messages, all from Stephen, which served to wipe the smile off his face.

He didn't bother to listen to the phone messages; it was a good bet that he knew how they'd go anyway. The texts were variations on a theme, testing the waters with anger, guilt, whining and pleading. One by one, he deleted them, then sent back a single message.

'Not going to talk to you about this right now, Stephen. I'll call you after midday tomorrow.'

By that time, he hoped, he'd be done with the Force Majeure interview, and be able to worry about what to do regarding Stephen.

As an afterthought, he checked to make sure his phone had updated to local time, then set the alarm. Turning off the light, he closed his eyes.

22
Rooftop Encounter

Jericho opened his eyes and stared up at the darkened ceiling, a sense of inevitability nagging at him. While his Prodigy rating would let him get by with five hours of sleep on any given night, he could also sleep the night through if he chose. He had opted for the latter, leaving it to the phone alarm to wake him in time to make it to the interview. His Prodigy rating was also supposed to allow him to drop off to sleep in record time if he had to, but this wasn't happening. Forty minutes in, he was still stubbornly awake, and he was afraid he knew exactly what the matter was.

Five hours was his benchmark but he could get by on far less, especially under high-stress situations. He'd crash and sleep like the dead once the crisis was resolved but while it was ongoing, he was in no danger of oversleeping. If his Prodigy instincts demanded that he be awake to solve a problem, then he was awake.

The trouble was, the situation with Stephen was by definition high-stress, and his blithely worded text message didn't seem to be alleviating his inner turmoil. There was something going on that his back-brain figured he hadn't thought all the way through. Try as he might, he couldn't get a grip on it while lying in bed. No matter what he did, his brain just went in circles.

With a put-upon sigh, he pulled the sheet off himself and rolled over to put his feet on the floor. Moving slowly so as to minimize the creak of his bedsprings, he came to his feet and moved toward the door. *I can't handle this. I don't know what to do.* If he kept circling the drain like this, he might be awake for the interview in the morning, but he knew he would be in no way *competent* for it.

When he opened the bedroom door, he discovered to his surprise that the living-room TV was still on. Luke was lounging back on the sofa—which he still hadn't converted into a bed—watching it with the sound turned down to a murmur. He saw Luke's head turn, then the TV muted altogether.

"Thought you was goin' ta bed, cuz." Luke's voice was a soft rumble in the color-shot dimness.

"I thought so too," Jericho grumbled. "Can't sleep. Too much to think about." He indicated the sofa. "Thought you were going to fold that thing out."

Luke's shrug was visible even in the half-light. "Maybe later. Not tired yet. You *seen* th' movie channels in this place, cuz? There's stuff I ain't never even heard of before."

"I'll have a look after the interview tomorrow," Jericho decided. Padding into the kitchenette, he located the cupboard holding the few glasses, and filled one at the sink. The cool water was refreshingly welcome, but it didn't calm his disordered thoughts.

Leaving the glass on the side of the sink, he went back to his bedroom. Inside his overnight bag was a black nylon satchel, which he retrieved and unzipped. One item at a time, he donned the costume that lay within, starting with the cloth mask that that covered the top of his head and came down to his cheekbones; his hair was pulled through the hole at the back to make a ponytail. On went the dark jeans and long-sleeved shirt, and the black pullover on top of that. The knee-high soft leather boots were sized for women, but he needed the flexibility they afforded and they were very comfortable to wear. Next came the specially prepared jacket, then the utility belt. The gloves he pulled on were made of thin leather, more to protect his hands than to inflict any kind of extra damage with a punch. He focused on each item in turn as he put it on, mainly to make sure he didn't forget anything. As an afterthought, he slid his MagCard into an inside pocket of his jacket. *Don't want to lock myself out, after all.* The satchel, rolled up with its medium-length shoulder-strap wrapped around it, went into a long pouch at the back of his utility belt.

Part of what made his jacket special was a series of curved 3D-printed plastic plates sewn into the lining, placed so that they overlapped no matter how he moved. It wouldn't stop a bullet, but he'd already made sure it worked against a knife. The other part was the one good use that he'd found for spandex. He'd never wear it as a costume, but he had a double-thick layer of the elastic cloth stitched on to each side of his jacket. It was set up to stretch between his wrist and his hip on each side, with a tail of sorts hanging down farther. Each tail had a sturdy strap at the bottom end, which he hooked onto his belt for the time being to keep them out of the way.

When he checked the bedroom window, he found it wasn't designed to open any more than was necessary to admit night-time breezes, and it had a sturdy screen on the outside. *Front door it is, then.* He hadn't wanted to disturb Luke in case his cousin had gotten around to folding out the sofa bed and getting some sleep, but it seemed like he had no choice.

As he let himself out through his bedroom door, he saw that Luke was still watching TV. His cousin glanced around again, then did a double-take. "Jesus shit, cuz," he whispered. "You goin' out?"

Jericho nodded. "Guess so. I just need to get a breath of fresh air. I'll be back soon."

"That really a good idea?" asked Luke, concern obvious in his voice. "It's a whole new city out there. It ain't your turf. You don't know nothin' about it."

"If I get lost, I'll just turn on the locator for your phone," Jericho whispered with a grin. "I'll be ten minutes. Out and back. I just gotta clear my head."

Luke appeared to take this at face value. "Sho'nuff. You be sure an' take care now, cuz."

"Always do." Jericho shared a fist-bump with his cousin on the way past, then went to the front door and eased it open. Nobody was in the corridor; stepping through, he let the door shut silently then considered his next move. *I could've just gone out and gotten something to eat. Why did I costume up?*

But even as he asked the question, he knew the answer. The knowledge had been in the back of his mind all along. He needed to get out in the fresh air, on the rooftops, to truly be able to clear his head. Only then could he come to a final decision on what to do about Stephen. To get up that high, he needed to use his powers. And in order to use his powers without outing himself, the costume had been needed. It was good to know that his mind was still capable of working things through when he had no idea what to do next.

Moving with swift, sure strides, he made his way to the end of the corridor, where a closer examination revealed that the window was set on a vertical swivel system to allow it to open, though it was currently closed. *Well, well, well. Looks like Bobbi was right, and Oaklands really is set up for out-of-town Enabled to get in and out unnoticed. Let's see now …* Leaning close, he began to check out what exactly held the window shut. *If I wanted my guests to be able to come and go unseen, I'd leave a hidden escape hatch in plain sight.*

Moments later, his hunch proved correct. There was a MagCard reader discreetly concealed in a recess in the window-frame; swiping his card over it caused the window to swivel open like a revolving door. Even more interestingly, there was an equally discreetly placed ladder outside the window This was no doubt intended to perform double duty as a fire escape in a pinch; however, it also went *upward* toward the roof. Climbing out onto the ladder, he swiped the reader he found on the outside, causing the window to swivel closed behind him. After tucking the MagCard away again, he began to climb steadily. He was halfway up the ladder when he realized that the MagCard had worked even through his glove. Whatever biometrics it used, he decided, it didn't depend on anything so crude as a fingerprint scanner.

As he clambered up onto the roof, he saw a large glowing green and brown object hanging over the building. For a second he froze, wondering what the hell he'd just encountered. Then his forebrain caught up and informed him that the blocky object was just a holographic sign spelling out 'OAKLANDS' in twenty-foot-tall letters for all to see. Beneath the name of the establishment was the word 'VACANCY', in a smaller font.

Well, damn. That's what I call advertising. Allowing his heart rate to go back to something approaching normality, he looked around appreciatively. It was better up here, the cool breeze ruffling his ponytail and doing a lot to soothe his turbulent thoughts. The holographic sign threw out a muted glow, vaguely illuminating nearby buildings. Somewhere in the distance, a siren wailed briefly. He heard the thrumming as a flying cab went by, not so far away. Running lights blinked on and off, stitching its progress across the night sky. He followed it with his eyes until it went out of sight, then he tried to orient himself with regards to the city. Unfortunately, although he could see a lot of the skyline, he wasn't able to determine where the major landmarks were, such as the maglev terminal or even the Spire.

I must be too low down. Need to get higher. Looking around, he picked out the tall building he'd spotted from the street earlier—it looked like an apartment block—then started in that direction across the rooftop. As he came close to the edge of the roof, he noted that a couple of lower buildings stood between him and his destination. Pulling the spandex tails from his belt, he leaned down and wrapped the straps around his legs just above his knees, buckling them firmly into place. Then he backed up a ways and ran toward the roof edge. In the last few yards, he accelerated to a sprint, spread his arms to stretch the spandex taut, and leaped over the edge.

For a normal person, the spandex wouldn't have had all that much effect; the surface area thus gained was less than that of a commercial wingsuit. A normal person, however, wouldn't have first been able to reduce the effect of gravity on them—and everything they were wearing—to one-tenth normal. With his downward acceleration now a lazy three point two feet per second per second, the broad swathe of spandex worked just fine as a set of gliding wings.

His ears teased by the whisper of passing wind, he looked down at the buildings—apparently part of the larger Oaklands complex—sliding by underneath. Gliding like this was the closest he would ever come to real flight. He'd tried applying push-tags to himself for extra lift, but they didn't seem to be able to work on anything he'd altered the gravity on. No matter how hard he worked at it, he always had to come back down to earth in the end. Which, he supposed, worked well as a description of life in general.

The taller building before him was getting closer, and he was still moving with most of the speed gleaned from his headlong sprint. Eyes narrowed with concentration, he sent four glue-tags arrowing ahead, then prepared himself. Seconds before impact, he brought his arms up and his legs down, changing his angle of attack as he allowed gravity to have more of an effect on him. His forward momentum slowed, letting him hit the wall just right.

As opposed to the mishap with the shoe, he'd been dead on with the placements of the G-tags. They were right there to hand (and foot) when he impacted, securing him to the side of the edifice. It was built of neither concrete nor steel, as far as he could tell. The material was smooth and gently contoured, with the occasional window set into it. There were no visible joins, and his G-sense could pick out no structural beams within it. The outer surface was a light-gray material with a somehow-familiar hexagonal pattern layered on to it.

For just a moment, he wondered what it reminded him of. But now was neither the time nor the place for his innate curiosity to come out and play. The purpose of this rooftop-run was to clear his head and figure out what to do, not to investigate the local architecture. With that in mind, he started up the side of the building, creating and dismissing glue-tags with the ease of long practice. Gravity may have been the enemy of ninety-nine-point-nine percent of the human race; for him, it was a trusted ally.

It took him perhaps thirty seconds to ascend the seven stories to the top of the building. On the way up, he passed three balconies, each with a discreet set of mesh screens around it. *To keep out people with powers like mine, no doubt.* The third balcony held a couple, who were sitting and drinking what looked like wine while enjoying the city lights. They saw him and gave a friendly wave. Feeling that the night couldn't get much more surreal, he waved back. No words were exchanged; he kept climbing until he reached the top.

Instead of being flat as he'd expected, the roof continued upward in a step-pyramid configuration that had him puzzled, until he saw the hexagonal texture continuing onto the rooftop. The angle of the slope recalled the umbrellas in the Oaklands courtyard, and the pieces clicked into place. "Solar cells," he said out loud. "That's what they've gotta be." It kind of made sense. Even if Utopia City was able to produce electricity so easily that it could afford to give it out for free, why waste a potential energy source like the sun? Shaking his head at the amount of foresight that had gone into constructing the very buildings with solar collectors built into the walls and roof, he turned to look out over the city.

The breeze up here was rather brisk and had more of a snap to it. Even though he'd been climbing steadily, he was glad of his jacket. And now he could see across to where the Spire rose in the distance. Just as in the canvas print, it was illuminated from all sides, a visible message of hope shining across Utopia City. In a very real way, it *was* Utopia City.

The Spire itself bore no holograms; it needed none to show how impressive it was. However, they showed up here and there on the buildings surrounding it; some were static while others moved back and forth. He was too far away to see them clearly, but the overall effect gave Utopia City a fantasy air that he'd never seen anywhere else.

Seating himself on the roof-edge, he stared across the vast gulf between him and the culmination of his dreams. He'd started this journey armed with high hopes and idealism, seeking to bring a cherished dream to fruition. Even the initial break with Stephen was something that had an endpoint; three days, and he would be home once more.

But then came the revelation that his trust had *already* been betrayed, that any such triumphant return would reunite him with an unfaithful lover. Unable to go back and confront Stephen, both because he was already committed to moving forward and because he had no idea how to fix this (or even if it *was* fixable) he had continued on to Utopia City.

Now the looming specter of his return to Savannah (and Stephen) had him conflicted. On the one hand was his compassion and sense of fairness. All people were flawed; he knew this to be true, even of himself. *Especially* of himself. Guiltily, he thought back to his secretive fantasies about Relentless. That was never going to happen; he knew it for a fact. But if the celebrated hero ever *did* make a move on Jericho … *would I be strong enough to resist?* Even as a pure hypothetical, he had the uncomfortable feeling he knew what the answer would be. While this did not *excuse* Stephen his infidelities, it certainly went a long way toward helping Jericho to understand them.

On the other hand, there was the anger; an anger and a pain which cut bone-deep. *I gave him everything that was me, and he stabbed me in the back while smiling to my face.* Not even the knowledge of Stephen's beating at Luke's hands made him feel any better about that. After all, Stephen had chosen to do what he did, and he might choose to do it again.

Apart from all that … aside from the nagging feeling that *I know I never cheated on him, but under different circumstances it might've been me* and the certainty that *I can't trust him anymore* was yet another aspect which Jericho stubbornly refused to call the 'third hand'. Despite everything else, Jericho had an undeniable emotional attachment to the man. This was possibly what fueled much of the anger. Hate, after all, was often called the flip-side to love. But as much as he wanted to deny it, there it was; illogical, inconvenient, and impossible to crush.

He closed his eyes and took another long breath of the chill night air, letting it bottom out in his lungs. Slowly, he let it out again, feeling the knot of tension in his chest loosen slightly. By the time his lungs were empty once more, he thought he had a solution. It might not be the perfect solution to the situation. He wasn't even sure that such a thing even existed. It was, however, a solution he could implement, and maybe even make stick.

By the time I talk to him next, the interview will be done, and I'll know what's happening with Force Majeure. I'll give him the chance to come clean of his own accord. If he doesn't, then we're done. Finished. If he does, and he promises to make amends instead of offering excuses or denials … then I'll think about taking him back. Possibly.

Slowly, he nodded to himself. Hopefully, that would work. *Punching muggers,* he decided, *is a lot easier than this crap. I wonder if other heroes have these problems too.* He couldn't really imagine it. What were the odds of this specific set of circumstances cropping up at just the wrong time? Shaking his head, he stood up and dusted off the seat of his pants. *Guess it's time I went back and tried to get some sl—*

"Stop right there." The voice was feminine, firm, and accompanied by a double *click-clack* which sounded very much like a gun of some sort being readied. Overlaid on it was an oddly familiar thrumming noise. It was also coming from behind Jericho, which was a good trick, because there was nothing behind him to stand on but a lot of empty air. He froze, on the principle that people giving direct orders from impossible locations probably had a way to back up said orders.

"I've stopped," he said, somewhat redundantly. "Can I turn around?" Distantly, he was pleased to note that he'd remembered to use his 'G-Man voice', where he dropped his tone by about an octave and spoke with more emphasis than he did while in plain clothes. At his sides, he cupped his hands and generated a pair of glue-tags; while the unknown person was *talking* like a hero, it was always possible to get a false positive. Commencing a fight for his life while unarmed was a good way to die, very quickly.

However, it was also possible that this was merely a case of mistaken identity. Hero-meets-hero fights weren't *quite* as common as popular culture made them out to be, but they still happened from time to time. His G-tags were reasonably non-lethal as far as powers went, so even if he had to attack a hero with them, there would be no lasting harm. He really, *really* hoped that he wouldn't have to do that though, even in self-defense. No matter the outcome, bad feelings had a way of lingering. It had only happened to him once, and Pickup was *still* pissed at him.

"Go ahead," the woman said coolly. "No stupid moves. What are you doing up here?" She sounded bored and a little impatient, not the best combination of attitudes he would have picked for someone potentially pointing a weapon at him. The thrumming noise got a little louder, tickling at his memory. *That sounds almost like taxi lifters.* Something impinged on the edge of his G-sense; it was fairly dense, much larger than a person, and flying. It was also right where the voice had come from.

Slowly, he turned around. It was dark, but the glow of the city lights was adequate to illuminate what was before him. The vehicle hovering five or six yards away from the building was not in fact a taxi, though it *was* flying on ducted fans. It had one lifter at the front and two at the back, with a chopper-style saddle in between. While the handlebars were quite possibly just there for show, they indisputably turned it into something that would have taken Luke's general 'I want one' response and refined it into a burning passion; a flying motorcycle. Jericho didn't even ride that much, and *he* wanted one.

But what truly caught Jericho's attention wasn't the motorbike; it was the rider. The woman—her flight suit didn't quite have enough built-in technology to hide that particular fact—would've been instantly recognizable even if Jericho hadn't spent time looking up Force Majeure. Through sheer force of will, he managed to not let his jaw drop in amazement. "You're Transit!" he blurted.

"So noted," Transit replied, not sounding particularly impressed. The red and silver color scheme on her flying motorbike was repeated on her flight suit as well as her helmet. City lights were reflected in her full-face visor; he could see the shifting of the reflections as she tilted her head slightly. Paired gun muzzles, mounted just forward of the handlebars, were trained on Jericho. He noted absently that each time she moved her helmet, they twitched in response. "You still haven't answered my question."

"Uh, I'm a hero," Jericho explained hastily. "I'm called G-Man. I just came up here to … well, work my way through a personal problem. To find a solution." He let the G-tags dissolve into nothingness; while he was sure Transit wouldn't initiate lethal force at first contact, he didn't want her thinking he was about to attack.

To his relief, the gun-muzzles abruptly angled skyward with a *click-click-click* as something in the mechanism disengaged. "Well, that definitely sounds like 'brooding on a rooftop' to me," Transit replied, her voice becoming somewhat less hostile. "When villains have personal problems, they generally end up taking it out on their minions, not brooding. Did you get it figured out?" She did something with the controls and the sky-bike swiveled on its axis, skating sideways until it was mere feet from the roof-edge. The thrumming from the lifters was louder now, but he could still clearly hear her voice over it.

This close, Jericho could see the distorted reflection of his masked face in her helmet visor. "I think so." He glanced around. "Am I doing something wrong by being up here?" Normally, he knew that such a thing wouldn't be the case, but he'd already encountered more than one set of odd protocols in the rules that Utopia City worked by. It wouldn't be smart to assume that these were the only ones.

Transit replied with a snort that set his fears at ease. "Hardly. Night-time roof-running is practically a prerequisite for being part of the local Enabled scene. I just got a report that a guy in black was climbing this building, so I decided to swing by and check it out. Though I don't recognize your name or your logo. New in town?"

Holy shit, Transit is making conversation *with me!* With the strong feeling that she could read his thoughts off his face, he did his best to keep the fanboy-squee out of his voice. "Ah, yeah, actually. I got in today. I've applied to join, uh, your team. Force Majeure." *She* knows *what team she's on, you idiot!* "My interview's tomorrow morning."

"Hm." Her voice was non-committal. "Well, if you're going to go patrolling, we consider it a matter of courtesy to notify the police first, so this sort of misunderstanding doesn't happen." The reprimand was delivered so mildly that he barely registered it as such. "In any case, welcome to Utopia. See you at the interview. Don't be late."

Shit, if I don't come back with proof I met her, Luke's gonna call bullshit on this whole thing. "W-wait." Jericho forced the word out as he half-raised his hand to stop her.

The sky-bike, already turning away, stopped. She looked back at him. "What is it?" He was sure she was rolling her eyes. "Let me guess. An autograph?"

"Um, can I … can I just get a photo of you, on your bike? It's for my cousin Luke, not me." He knew he would *totally* keep a copy anyway. "He loves bikes and cars, and this would utterly blow his mind."

"Hmm." She paused, turning her helmet to look from side to side. "The lighting's terrible up here. You wouldn't get any details."

"Oh." His heart sank. "Sorry, I—"

"You're coming in for an interview tomorrow? I'll see what I can do then. No promises." With a sudden surge of noise, the lifters tilted forward and the flying motorcycle accelerated away into the night sky. For a moment, her darkened form occluded part of the Spire, and then all he could see was her running lights.

Seconds after that, the thrumming had died away into the distance, and Jericho was alone in the night once more.

23
Night Patrol

"Holy shit," he muttered. "Holy shit. That was Transit. I just got checked out by *Transit*." He heard the faintest hint of a high-pitched incredulous giggle in his own voice and tamped it down hard. The very last thing he wanted to do was hit that high note again tomorrow. Especially when he met Relentless. *I'm a superhero too*, he told himself firmly. *Just like them. I mean, not* exactly *like them, but* kind of *like them. They're what I want to be, someday.*

Taking a deep breath, which did very little to slow his still-racing heartbeat, he turned toward where the Oaklands' holo-sign glowed in the darkness and prepared to leap from the roof. Then he stopped and looked around. *I'm already out here*, he told himself. *I've got a couple of hours before I've got to be in bed, and I know damn well I'll be too keyed up to go to sleep right away if I head back now. Why not do some patrolling?* A grin spread across his face. *Transit as much as told me that I'm basically a member of the Utopia City Enabled scene now. May as well act the part.*

Recalling the Force Majeure hero's words, he reached into the pouch on his utility belt that held his prepaid phone. It woke up in a few seconds, and he retrieved the number for non-emergency police contact. Taking a deep breath, he pressed the call icon.

It only rang for a few seconds before someone picked up. "Utopia City Police Department," a bored feminine voice replied. "Sergeant Finlay speaking. How may I help you?"

"Uh, yeah, hi, this is G-Man. I'm an independent hero and I just wanted to let you know that I'll be patrolling in Utopia City tonight, in the Oaklands area." He had to fight to hold down the grin that threatened to spread across his face.

It may have been his imagination, but the voice seemed to become more alert. "Ah, okay. G-Man, is it? Can we have a basic description of your powerset and costume to pass on to our units?"

"Sure," he said. "I'm a prodigy/dynamic with gravity control; I get around by gliding. I'm wearing a black cloth mask over the top of my head, a black jacket with the letter 'G' on the back in white, black … well, basically, I'm wearing all black." He stopped short of telling her he was white. Back in Savannah, it would've been a notable detail. Here, he hoped that wasn't the case.

If it was, Sergeant Finlay didn't seem to think it worth commenting on. Faintly, he heard typing noises. "Okay, that's G-Man, DPR prodigy/dynamic, gravity powers, gliding, black costume with a jacket, white 'G' on the back. Patrolling in the Oaklands area. Thanks for the heads-up, buddy. I'll pass the word on. Take care, and good hunting."

"Uh, yeah, thanks," he said, then shut the call off. Again, the sensation of unreality washed over him. His interactions with the Savannah police department had been semi-cordial at best, with the notable exception of Detective Villanova. It had never occurred to him to call them up to tell him he was on patrol, and they'd never asked him to. *Different city, different rules.*

Turning, he moved to a different part of the roof, overlooking the street ten stories below. About a block to the west, the canal emerged from behind another tall building then meandered away into the distance. Squinting, he could see slender illuminated metal arches, their reflections glinting on the dark water, in between the rustic footbridges that spanned the canal. It was hard to make out more detail from this distance, but there seemed to be single-story restaurants and takeaway shops fronting the canal on both sides. In fact, the place where they'd gotten the pizza from was probably down there somewhere. He wasn't quite hungry again yet, but it wouldn't hurt to find out where the pizza place was, just in case they felt like dining out sometime before they left Utopia City. *That guy from the train station said something about living near the market. I wonder if that's what he was talking about?*

That thought in mind, he stepped up to the edge of the roof. As he leaned over to look straight down at the sidewalk, a wide grin spread across his face. For what he had planned, a clear drop was essential. There was nothing in his way; no awnings, no signs, not even a low-flying bird.

Adrenaline singing in his ears, he leaned forward. With his hyper-awareness of his own balance, he knew exactly where the point of no return was; in an instant, it came and went. Even then he could have pulled back but he chose not to, deliberately allowing it to happen. With the slightest push from his toes, he kicked off from the edge of the building and fell from the roof. Suppressing his slow-fall ability, he let himself plummet head-first toward the ground, feeling the wind-rush build up around his ears. For nearly two seconds he was at the mercy of gravity, just like every other person on the planet. Then he brought his personal gravity down to one-tenth normal and spread his arms wide.

As the wind filled the gliding wings and turned the death-dive into a swoop between the streetlights, he pressed his lips together to contain a yell of exhilaration. Until the momentum ran out, he could pretend he was flying. But even the sheer *rush* that filled his entire being from top to toe still paled before the feeling of amazement he had experienced just moments before, speaking to a core member of Force Majeure. And if things worked out, he wouldn't merely be speaking to them: he'd be working *with* them.

The cool night air buoyed him up, the slipstream making the tails of his mask flap gently as he glided down the street between the buildings. He watched as a police car slowly cruised along the street below. Directly ahead was a four-way intersection and then the canal, with the roadway leading in between two buildings. Like the boardwalk that Jericho could now see lined the canal's banks, the road ended abruptly at the bank of the canal, with only warning bollards to save an unwary driver from disaster. The road continued from the other side of the canal, but there was a good thirty-foot span of canal in between. Jericho was pretty sure that magnetic levitation wouldn't lift the car over the bollards. Neither would it work over water.

At least, he didn't *think* it would. The cops in the car seemed to believe otherwise, because the car slid silently through the intersection, heading directly for the bollards. Just as catastrophe seemed imminent, the bollards retracted into the road and he saw a rippling movement in the water ahead of the car. In a broad swathe leading from one bank to the other, the water heaved up and flowed to each side, revealing a metal grille just above the surface of the canal. The cop car never slowed or showed any sign that things were abnormal; keeping to the same steady pace, it cruised across the canal and onto the road on the other side. Behind it, the grille sank once more into the depths of the water as the bollards extended upwards again. Swirling currents arose, but these settled just as quickly. In seconds, he couldn't even tell that the bridge had been there.

Wow. Just wow. He wasn't sure what impressed him more; the retracting bollards, the submerging bridge, or the cool of the cops themselves to be completely certain that both things would work exactly when they needed it. *I know I'd be clenching up just a little.*

Descending slowly past the sixty-foot mark, he glided through the intersection. The canal lay ahead, lined on either side by restaurants and cafés. As he neared it, he took more notice of the slender metal arches spanning the canal. Occurring every thirty yards or so, they rose to about fifty feet above the water and seemed more decorative than anything else, with holographic murals of vines and flowers glowing in the night. While admittedly beautiful, he really couldn't see the point of them until he spotted what they were supporting. From the center-point of each arch, a single strut projected downward about three feet, where it attached onto a reflective cylindrical pipe about eight inches in diameter.

Even then he couldn't figure out what it was, until the resemblance to the maglev rail jogged his memory. Back in the station, they'd seen signs indicating the presence of a monorail. There was nothing else this could be. Banking gently to the left, he slid in parallel to the path of the rail, admiring the holographic decorations on the archways, each one different. The canal curved around to the right just up ahead, and he banked to follow that as well. Food smells drifted up to him from below, and he thought he heard soft music. There were no shouts or arguments; the occasional snatch of conversation went by, dozens of feet below.

A flash of movement in the corner of his eye caught his attention, so he turned his head briefly to glance behind him. There weren't many other things that would be moving at this height, the most likely among them being whatever it was that rode the rail he was gliding alongside. Sure enough, a monorail was just rounding the turn of the canal. Not unlike the maglev, there were three linked passenger cars, though they hung under the rail instead of riding on top. The method of locomotion was still the same; twinned brackets held curved metal pads that didn't quite touch the rail, propelling the train along with just a resonant hum to mark its passing. There was a gap between the pads to allow the support struts to pass between them. The monorail was much smaller than even a single maglev passenger car, each section consisting of a stubby cylinder about seven feet in diameter and twenty-five feet long, with half a dozen windows visible on the sides that he could see.

Jericho's top sustainable gliding speed was about twenty miles per hour, which was impressive considering the singular lack of aerodynamics inherent in the human body. His speed right then was a quite respectable fifteen miles per, but the monorail was going maybe twice that. Assured that it wasn't going to hit him, he turned his gaze ahead again. *There's probably a station up ahead somewh—* "Whoa!" The yell was dragged from his throat as the next support arch loomed large in his vision, the bright holographic colors coming straight for his face.

Pulling his arms back to his sides, he reversed the effect of his slow-fall as drastically as he could. Scientifically speaking, he didn't gain mass; instead, he vastly magnified gravity's hold on him. Three point two feet per second squared became *three hundred twenty* feet per second squared. He dropped, as the saying went, like a rock. Specifically, like a rock under the effect of ten times Earth's gravity. The increased downward movement let him miss the arch by mere feet, but it was a mixed blessing; now he was plummeting toward the canal, forty feet below.

Uninformed people would have decided that the danger wasn't so great; even at ten gravities, water was still water. Except that it wasn't. Under his current gravitational regime, he had less than half a second before he hit the water with an impact equivalent to falling four hundred feet onto concrete. Even if he survived the experience, he would then be unconscious, injured and at extreme risk of drowning.

Half a second, however, was far more time than he needed. As easily as he'd increased the effect of gravity on himself, he diminished it again just as fast. His effective weight went back to ten percent of normal, causing his death-dive to slow dramatically. Arms spread, he caught the air once more on the gliding surfaces, bringing himself back to almost level flight. As the monorail hummed by overhead, he banked toward the next support arch after the one he'd almost hit. Glue-tags shot out and he anchored himself to the leaning cylindrical pole without even thinking about it. The holographic vines continued to glow unabated even as they curled around and over his fingers, so he ignored them for the moment.

It was fortunate that he'd done this so often because the near miss had left him badly shaken, his heart hammering. He was good at what he did, but part of that was due to his knowledge of Savannah's rooftops and streets. Here he was the novice once more, at least as far as negotiating the terrain was concerned. And just as with Savannah, some of the terrain was dangerous, and it was up to him to keep his wits about him until he had it down pat. *Eyes front when you're flying between arches, dumbass!*

As he firmly berated himself, the adrenaline rush wore off and his heart rate slowed. Though he was unhurt, he made the choice to stay where he was for the moment. At three stories up, he was well below the monorail and yet still had a good view of both sides of the canal. Across the canal appeared to be a row of food vendors rather than actual eateries, while directly below him a small café had managed to squeeze itself in between a bakery and a fruit shop. Tables had been set up so that patrons could eat on the boardwalk. Fairy lights strung between the monorail poles glowed gently in counterpoint to the holograms, the lazy ripples on the dark water causing the reflections to twinkle.

Even at this late hour, there were more people out and about than he would've expected. Some strolled back and forth along the boardwalk, while others purchased food at the vendors. A few sat inside the café, while others ate at the tables overlooking the canal. *These guys must be coming off the late shift.*

From his vantage point, he could see a few people looking his way, their attention no doubt attracted by his involuntary yell. He essayed a tentative wave—*all good here, nothing to see*—and a couple of them waved back. After a few moments, they seemed to lose interest in him and went back to what they were doing.

And then he blinked, because someone strolling along the boardwalk had just caught his eye. He couldn't see the face, but something about the guy's stance and the way he walked looked familiar. *Is he the one from the station?* This wasn't a late shift worker, Jericho was certain. Nothing the guy said or did had given the impression of someone with a regular job. Instead of wearing the jacket from earlier, he had it folded over his arm. This seemed a little odd, given that it was now late in the evening and colder than it had been earlier.

What was his name, again? Todd? Tony? He couldn't remember off the top of his head, but it struck him as a mild coincidence that he'd encounter the guy again so quickly. Of course, the guy *had* said he lived in the area. His hair seemed to be just as attractively tousled as ever, which made Jericho suspect hairspray. *Nobody* looked that good all the time without help.

Releasing the glue-tags holding his hands and feet to the arch one at a time, Jericho moved around so he had a better view of the boardwalk. When he returned his attention to what was happening down below, he saw that the guy had stopped at the bakery and was loading a cloth bag with what looked like mini-pizzas. Jericho wondered if they were anywhere near as tasty as the full-sized ones he'd shared with the others earlier, and his mouth watered. The guy pulled out his wallet and produced his MagCard, which he swiped across the reader. After tucking card and wallet away, he took the bag of mini-pizzas and strolled off down the boardwalk with a jaunty step.

Once the guy was out of sight, Jericho turned his attention to the other people in the area. They seemed to be a mixed bunch as far as age, gender and ethnic appearance went. Clothes were neat and tidy, and while some were drinking what he suspected was alcohol, nobody seemed to be noticeably drunk.

The shops lining the boardwalk directly below him were all one-story constructions. Behind them, Jericho could see another street; this one was narrower than the one he'd glided down to get here, more like an alleyway. On the other side of the alleyway were taller buildings, in the two- and three-story range. Floodlights mounted on the corners of these buildings illuminated the building frontages clearly, probably to ensure that any security cameras had an unobstructed view of the roller-doors that he could see.

Jericho guessed that these were used by the boardwalk businesses for storage. Restaurants and food vendors would go through a lot of stock in a day, after all. Like the street outside Oaklands, the boardwalk and buildings were clean and clearly well-maintained.

Lifting his head, he looked around to re-establish his mental map of his immediate surroundings, then scanned the monorail support arches. He knew he could reach the next one along easily enough, even if he didn't have the opportunity for a run-up.

Scrambling up the arch for a little more height advantage, he gathered himself, then leaped and spread his arms. At the last minute, he chose to go diagonally across the canal instead of directly along it. This made the glide a little longer, but he was still pretty sure he could make it. Silently, he crossed the open canal, gradually losing altitude. When he reached the next arch, he'd dropped about ten feet, which he quickly remedied by scrambling up the angled metal pole until he was at a comfortable height above ground level. With his hands glued to the arch and his feet comfortably braced, he looked over the boardwalks again.

The short hop had renewed his confidence that he knew what he was doing. The leap, the glide, the landing; all had gone exactly to plan. He felt the knot of tension in his chest unraveling slightly. *Hey, I can do this.* Crossing the canal back and forth as he worked his way down it seemed to be the right way to go. Of course, he'd have to be careful to stay under the airspace owned by the monorail. He didn't know how often they came through and being hit by one would do him no favors at all.

That was when Jericho spotted the guy *again,* this time on his side of the canal. Moving with a very familiar jaunty step, this person definitely had the moves and mannerisms of the guy from the maglev terminal. *Tim? Goddamn it, what* was *his name?* He dismissed the question as not being important. What *was* important was that the guy had totally changed his appearance with a few alterations to his clothing. The tousled hair was now covered with a baseball cap, and he was once more wearing his jacket. And oddly enough, he was still carrying the cloth shopping bag, but it was now empty. *He wasn't out of sight for more than a few minutes. Did he stash the pizzas somewhere? Why? And why did he change his look?*

This was shaping up to be a mystery. He wondered if it had anything to do with why they'd been pinged in the train station for a free meal, or whether the guy had just chosen them at random. What *was* his deal, and why had he changed his look just to walk down the other side of the canal?

The most aggravating thing, Jericho decided, was that he'd probably never find out. It wasn't as if he could land in front of the guy and demand answers. That was the most direct way of blowing his secret identity to hell and gone that he could think of. And while it was *unusual* for someone to change up his look like that, it certainly wasn't illegal. *Hell, if I hadn't met him in the train station, I probably wouldn't even have noticed it was the same guy.*

Jericho frowned, wanting to let it go but at the same time unable to do so. *It's really none of my business.* Thomas had struck him as being nice enough (he mentally facepalmed as the guy's name finally popped up in his memory) even though he'd seemed unwilling to speak with the police. Which didn't surprise Jericho very much, as the police seemed to make it their business to know everyone *else's* business. The cheek-brush was something he hadn't forgotten, but it was a minor detail compared to everything else.

Then he recalled the single important fact that probably explained everything. *This is Utopia City. They do things differently here. What if he's a prodigy who's training himself to stay unseen in a crowd?* It made for a certain amount of sense. Being a prodigy as opposed to a dynamic or an artificer traded raw power and inventive genius for sheer bullshit resourcefulness, but that resourcefulness was useless if it wasn't utilized and trained. Thomas had certainly been personable enough to talk to, but that was probably just *one* of the things he was good at.

As Jericho turned over the possibility in his mind, he watched Thomas approach one of the decorative footbridges that allowed easy passage over the canal. There was a gap between the shops at that point, probably to allow pedestrian traffic through to the street beyond. Coming across the bridge was a guy in his late teens, maybe a few inches shorter than Thomas, with a positively lanky frame and hair so blond it was basically white.

As they passed one another, the pair slowed a little; they didn't look directly at each other, but he could've sworn their lips moved, as though they'd exchanged a few words. Jericho's lip-reading skills were rusty, and he could barely see their faces from where he was, so he couldn't make out what was being said. However, it was all clear now; those two knew each other, and this was almost certainly Prodigy training. Which meant it was none of his business. Satisfied, Jericho nodded and began to turn away—just as two men lunged out of the pedestrian alleyway and smashed the lanky kid to the ground.

24
Learning Experience

Jericho stared as one of the men knelt on the kid's back and wrenched his arm up between his shoulder-blades. *Wait, what the hell?* Nobody else seemed to take this amiss … well, given there weren't all that many people nearby, he was unsurprised that barely anyone had noticed, apart from Thomas.

"Hey!" Thomas objected. "Leave him alone!" He tried to pull the first attacker off the lanky kid, only to be grabbed by the other one. A small dark object was shoved into Thomas' ribs and Jericho heard a distinctive crackling sound. Thomas convulsed and fell to the ground; the man stepped back and held the device at the ready.

Before he really knew what he was doing, Jericho had launched himself from the pole toward the fight. Arrowing down toward them, he watched as the first man jabbed the blond-haired kid with another such device, his knee still jammed into the kid's back. *Probably a stun-gun,* Jericho surmised. They were harder than firearms to deal with in some ways, and easier in others.

In the time it took to think about it, he'd covered thirty of the forty-five feet to the site of the attack, G-tags already forming in his hands. Just as one of the men looked up and spotted him, he brought his hands forward and sent the 'tags flickering through the air.

The guy who was kneeling on the blond kid's back had short-cut sandy hair. His buddy was balding with black hair and a ratty vanDyke beard. Both were wearing dark jackets over jeans. The push-tag was the first one on target; it hit Sandy Hair, imparting a sideways shove. "Hey!" the guy yelled, just as the glue-tag hit him on the shoulder. If he'd been standing up, the push-tag wouldn't have done more than make him stumble slightly, but his current position wasn't very stable. He lurched sideways, falling off the lanky kid. In the process, his shoulder impacted the boardwalk and *stuck* there. Once again, the attractive force was relatively weak, but in the absence of leverage it would serve to hold him on the ground for a precious few seconds.

"What the—" Baldy McBeardface looked around to see Jericho swooping down toward him and reached into his open jacket; Jericho figured he wasn't going for a hip flask. Without giving the guy the chance to pull the gun that he presumed was there, Jericho loosed two more G-tags.

Once again, he used a glue-tag and a push-tag in rapid succession, but this time they went in the opposite order. Striking the jacket, the glue-tag dissipated into the cloth, with the effect that everything touching it was bonded to it and each other. Thus, anything in a shoulder holster would *stay* there until the effect wore off. A split-second later, the push-tag arrived, with the effect that the guy lost his balance and stumbled. Then Jericho reached hand to hand range, and things happened very quickly thereafter.

Even as he did his best to yank his right hand from inside his jacket, the bearded man brought the stun-gun around in an attempt to tag Jericho when he got close enough. Under normal circumstances, Jericho would've had to either trust to the plastic plates to protect him or stop short to avoid the impact. He chose to do neither, pulling off a move that only someone with total control over their effective weight even had the option to try. Taking hold of McBeardface's left wrist with his right hand and the man's collar with his left, he guided himself *over* the device and brought his legs around in a move any circus acrobat would be proud to own. As intended, he swung all the way around the guy, wrapping him up with his own arm. His G-sense pinged, confirming that there was indeed a dense metallic mass within the man's jacket. Bringing his weight up to normal, he let his feet drop to the ground and prepared to send the bald perp on a short flight of his own.

He didn't have the benefit of glue-tags on the ground to aid in leverage, but they weren't essential for what he wanted to do next. The moment he had solid footing, he pushed his own weight up to one and a half times normal and reduced Baldy's to one-tenth. Setting his stance properly, he pressed against the guy's back with his shoulders, and *heaved.* The resultant yell sounded quite startled, which didn't surprise Jericho in the slightest. Being thrown around like a rag doll was never a pleasant experience.

As he brought McBeardface up and over, he turned with his leverage points so his opponent was going to land face-up. Bracing himself, he heaved outward and around, then let go. Still weighing one-tenth of his normal total, Baldy was flung toward the canal like a particularly ungainly Frisbee. As the guy crossed the edge of the boardwalk, Jericho removed the gravity alteration. Baldy yelled again as his ballistic arc angled abruptly downward and he fell seven feet into cold water.

"Mother*fucker!*"

Jericho turned toward Sandy Hair just as the man wrenched his shoulder free of the glue-tag holding him down. The guy began to get up, but Jericho got there first. A single light touch made the guy three times as heavy as he was used to being, and he collapsed face-first onto the boardwalk. Jericho rarely used that many Gs on a standing target except in a fight against multiple opponents, but it worked well on someone who was already on the ground.

"What the holy living hell do you think you're doing?" blurted the sandy-haired perp as Jericho removed the stun-gun from his grasp. Suppressing the impulse to use it on its owner, Jericho tossed it to one side and wrenched the guy's wrists up behind his back. "You're in so much trouble right now, you've got no idea, you son of a bitch!"

"What I'm *doing* is performing a citizen's arrest," panted Jericho as he dug a zip-tie out of the pouch on his utility belt. "The charge is assault and battery, committed on these guys right here. Soon as I call the cops—"

"We *are* the cops, you moron!" snapped Sandy Hair. "We're undercover!"

Jericho paused. He'd heard any number of excuses as to why he shouldn't secure someone for the cops before but strangely enough, the perpetrators claiming to be police officers themselves wasn't one he'd run into before now. *Well, there's always a first time.*

"You'll excuse me if I don't just take your word for it," he said as he expertly threaded the zip-tie around into itself. Wrenching the guy's wrists a little higher, he settled the looped tie around them and pulled it tight. "Got anything resembling proof?"

"Yeah." The word came out as a painful grunt. "Call the fuckin' precinct. Give 'em my badge number and ask for my name. It's Chuck Gleeson." He rattled off a series of digits.

"Hold that thought." Keeping a careful eye on the other man, currently splashing in the canal, Jericho took his phone out and hit redial on the last number.

"Utopia City Police Department." This time, it was a man. "Sergeant Donovan speaking. How may I help you?"

"Yeah, this is G-Man. I called earlier and told you guys I'd be patrolling near the Oaklands. I'm at the Market right now; there's a couple of guys here wearing civives and carrying stun-guns, who attacked someone out of the blue. I was doing a citizen's arrest, but they said they're undercover cops. One of them's given me what he says is his badge number." He carefully repeated the series of digits.

"... yeah, that'll be Gleeson. Detective Charles Gleeson. He's working in that area, along with his partner Detective Forrester. He's got kinda red hair; Forrester's bald with a beard." There was amusement in the operator's voice. "You can let them go. They're ours."

Jericho winced and got up from Gleeson's back. "No problems. Thanks for your help." Ending the call, he put his phone away then reached back to the pouch next to the one with the zip-ties. From there, he retrieved a seat-belt cutter, which also worked well to cut the plastic restraints without having a potentially dangerous exposed blade. It was the work of a moment to slice the tie free, while he let the man's weight go back down to normal. While this held a slight element of risk, he considered himself safe if the guy tried to physically attack him. "So, why *were* you attacking that kid, anyway?"

A splashing sound drew his attention and he saw the guy who had to be Forrester climbing out of the canal, dripping wet and with a nasty look in his eye. "That's none of your business, asshole," the second plainclothes detective said. "You've interfered with us in our lawful operations. You're under arrest, and so are those two." His glare cut past Jericho. "Well, don't just *stand* there. Stop them!"

Reminded of Thomas' presence, Jericho flicked his eyes sideways to where the kid had been lying. Thomas was helping him up; the kid was wobbly but moving on his own. Raising his head briefly, Jericho caught the younger man's eye for a fraction of a second. In that instant, he could've thrown G-tags and glued their feet to the ground ... but he didn't. Thomas' eyes widened slightly; with the kid in tow, he stepped into the alleyway and disappeared.

"I thought you said it was none of my business." Jericho was fully aware that he was channeling Luke's smartass nature, but the bald detective was seriously rubbing him the wrong way. "Come on, make up your mind. What's so special about him, anyway?"

"He's wanted as a person of interest, you idiot," Gleeson retorted as he got up onto one knee, then reached not for the stun-gun lying nearby, but his ankle; a moment later, Jericho was looking down the barrel of a snub-nosed revolver. "It took us *hours* to get into position to grab that little shit, and then you had to foul it all up. Which means *you're* under arrest for obstruction."

"*Seriously?*" Jericho was pretty sure there wasn't much benefit in arguing with them, but it wasn't like he had many other choices that didn't involve beating them up again, which wouldn't help matters beyond his immediate satisfaction. "You jumped him out of nowhere, and you're in plain clothes. For all I knew, it was a straight-up mugging, or worse."

He knew *now* that it wasn't, but he was still trying to figure out why he'd let the pair get away. It had been a reflexive move, almost instinctive. Maybe it was because he liked Thomas as a person, or perhaps because he just didn't like the way the officers had jumped them with no warning. It might even have been all those factors combined. Whatever the reason, done was done.

"If we'd verbally challenged, the little shit would've made a bolt for it," the sopping-wet Forrester snapped. "Him and his friends are slippery like that. We're law enforcement, and you obstructed us in the execution of our duties. That's an indictable offense."

First off, no it isn't. Not when I didn't know you were cops. But Jericho decided not to quibble the finer points of the law at that moment. Both cops were on their feet now, Gleeson pointing his pistol directly at Jericho. Neither one had moved within arm's reach, which only proved they were able to learn. Forrester didn't have a weapon to hand, but Gleeson was perfectly capable of shooting Jericho if he tried to either attack or flee. While it was technically possible to glue-tag the revolver before Gleeson got a shot off, going up against someone of unknown skill when he really didn't have to would be the height of idiocy. Likewise, he could G-shake both cops into puking helplessness, but that wouldn't stop Gleeson from firing at least once. The shot might miss … or it might hit anyone behind Jericho. In any case, he held on to the faint hope that this could be sorted out with diplomacy.

"When you first hit the guy, I was across the other side of the canal," Jericho said carefully. "It's not as if you're in uniform. Call the precinct yourself if you don't believe I'm a hero. You just heard me confirm that I checked in with them earlier." He tried to remember the name of the sergeant he'd spoken to, but her name eluded him.

"Bullshit," snapped Forrester, but Jericho thought he detected a quick glance between the two of them. "I don't believe that for a hot second. You just helped a potential criminal escape. That's not what a hero does."

Jericho looked at Gleeson, who appeared to be the brains of the operation. "If you don't want to call the precinct, you can ask Force Majeure directly. For God's sake, I came here to interview for a place with them! In fact, I was talking to Transit about five minutes ago, just up that way." He pointed back toward where he thought the building was. "Seriously, just *ask* them. The name's G-Man. I talked to her. She was riding a flying motorbike."

This time, the glance that the two detectives shared was more pronounced. "Check it out, Forrester," Gleeson ordered.

"I can't," Forrester objected. "He threw me in the water, remember? My phone's screwed. You make the call." As he spoke, he reached into his jacket, where the glue-tag had already dissipated. The pistol he produced was only a small-caliber automatic, but this didn't make the situation any more tenable. "I got him covered."

"So long as *someone* makes the goddamn call already." Jericho was starting to get a little sick of being held at gunpoint, but if it got this sorted out, he was willing to stand it. If they kept this up much longer, though, he was seriously considering taking matters into his own hands.

"Yeah, yeah, don't get your tights in a twist." Gleeson replaced his pistol in its ankle holster, then pulled out his phone. Activating the phone only took a few seconds, then he tapped a number in. Seconds later, he got an answer.

"Hi, yeah, this is Gleeson. We got this guy calling himself G-Man, who just blew a bust wide open and chucked Forrester in the canal. He's claiming he talked to Transit about interviewing for a spot with Force Majeure tomorrow. You got anything on him?" There was a pause. "Yeah, G-Man. Black costume. Just flew in out of nowhere."

While he waited, Jericho replayed the conversation in his head. Hopefully they wouldn't try to arrest him now, but if they were still intent on it after the phone call, his only hope would be to talk to someone in authority and convince them it was just an unfortunate misunderstanding.

"What?" Gleeson's voice took on a note of unhappy surprise. "Can you check again? Okay … yeah, understood. Thanks." He shut the call down then glanced at Jericho. His expression was more than a little worried as he put his phone back in his pocket.

It was apparent that Gleeson was on the back foot. Jericho tamped down an upswell of hope as the police detective cleared his throat nervously. "Uh, G-Man, it looks like it was just a misunderstanding after all. Your story checks out. You're, uh, you're free to go."

Both Jericho and Forrester stared at Gleeson, then the penny dropped; for Forrester, at least. Jericho was still confused as the bald cop let the automatic droop until it was pointed at the boardwalk between them. Forrester moved a few steps away from Jericho, until he was beside Gleeson. "They backed him up?" he asked out of the corner of his mouth, in the worst prison-yard whisper Jericho had ever heard.

"Every word." Although he glanced at Jericho, Gleeson didn't bother lowering his voice. "Interview's tomorrow morning, and Transit logged the encounter with the duty officer." His entire attitude and stance had changed, making him look as though he'd wilted in the sun.

"So that's it?" Jericho looked at the two men dubiously. "We're done here?" The about-turn had him puzzled and suspicious. Surely it couldn't be this easy.

"Yeah, we're done." Gleeson nodded jerkily to underline his words. "What you did, intervening like that, it was an honest mistake, like you said. So, we're good if you are. And, uh, sorry about pointing guns at you like that. No hard feelings, yeah?"

Jericho stared at the man. *What the hell just happened?* This was literally what he'd been saying earlier, and still they'd drawn down on him. Looking from Gleeson to Forrester and back again, he shook his head. "Next time, if the guy in the costume cuts you free and backs off, get a clue as to which side of the law they're on."

It was time, he decided, to make a dramatic exit. There was a monorail support arch about forty feet to the left and another one fifty to the right, but he wanted to be more definitive than that, so he picked an arch pole on the other side of the canal. Vaulting onto the footbridge rail, he ran lightly up it until he reached the highest point, then launched himself into the air. The moment his feet left the wooden rail, he reduced his effective weight as far as it would go and spread his arms to let the elastic cloth catch the air.

As he glided across the water away from the cops, he heard Gleeson let out a long sigh. "Well, *that* was a fuckin' close one. Were you *trying* to get us fired?" Forrester's reply was inaudible, but Jericho didn't much care anymore. His heart was still hammering from the stress of the situation. Less from the fight than from the subsequent confrontation, if he was honest with himself. He knew his capabilities in hand to hand combat, but this was a whole different battlefield. If this had happened anywhere else, and it had come down to a legal stand-off between him and two undercover cops who were technically in the right, he'd probably would've lost out big-time.

The archway pole he'd aimed at loomed ahead of him, and he reflexively threw out a couple of glue-tags. Once he came into contact, he wasted no time in climbing higher up the pole to get a more elevated kickoff point. At forty-five feet off the water, he was basically level with the maglev rail, and the pole was beginning to angle inward. In addition, he noticed that people were starting to look up and point again. He didn't know how many had seen the confrontation with the undercover cops, but it probably wasn't the best idea to make even more of a spectacle of himself on the night before his big interview.

Poising himself, he leaped over open air once again, heading away from the canal. The sloped roofs of the shops passed beneath him, then the narrow street. When he came to the first storehouse, he was still higher up than the roof of the building, so he spiraled down for a landing. Ten feet up, he deliberately stalled out, spilling the air from his gliding wings, then dropped easily to the rooftop.

There wasn't much light here, but the rooftop had the same sort of hexagonal pattern that he'd seen elsewhere, along with a waist-high safety rail. Utopia City, it seemed, was particularly dedicated toward solar energy collection. Still, he wasn't there for that.

"That was too goddamn close," he told himself severely, pacing along the edge of the rooftop, inside the rail. "What the crap were those asshats even thinking, roughing up those guys like that? I couldn't have known." Taking a deep breath to try to settle his racing nerves, he went through the action again in his head. Unless there'd been some signal or warning that he hadn't seen or heard, they really hadn't identified themselves as police officers until he'd taken them down. And right up to the point that Gleeson had made his phone call, they'd been all set to have him arrested and charged for obstruction. At worst, if Gleeson had been more trigger-happy, he might even have been shot. Then, between one minute and the next, they'd inexplicably chosen to take him at his word.

No, he realized as he turned and paced the other way. *They only got interested in my credentials as a hero once I name-checked Transit and said I was interviewing with Force Majeure. That's when they started to change their tune.*

He stopped and leaned on the rail, looking out over the narrow alleyway. It was silent and deserted, quite at odds with what he'd just gone through one block over at street level. Despite his agitation, one corner of his mouth quirked up in a half-grin; if that wasn't a metaphor for the life of a superhero, he didn't know what was.

But getting back to more serious matters: what *was* it about Force Majeure that could make even the cops decide not to arrest him? He hitched his butt up onto the rail, then swung his legs over so he was sitting with his feet against a post and knees out over the drop. Slowly, he began to put the pieces together.

It was a fact of life that things were done differently here in Utopia City. The free electricity, the better wages (and side benefits), the amazing technology; that was all in the 'plus' column. In the 'minus' column was the fact that the cops tracked the MagCards of people they considered undesirable and made subtle attempts to provoke them into reacting in an illegal fashion. And apparently … this. Undercover cops smashing a teenage boy into the sidewalk because he was (or they thought he was) a person of interest. This wasn't exactly unknown even in Savannah, but he'd had higher hopes for Utopia City. Though there was the fact that Thomas had stepped into hiding when they'd been talking to that last cop. *I never asked them why that blond kid was a person of interest.*

And now it seemed that the UCPD quite blatantly bent over backward for Force Majeure members, even going so far as to defer to people who were merely trying out for the team. This was almost certainly because nobody wanted to upset the superheroes who had built the city. Was that good or bad? He frowned, trying to pin it down as being in one column or the other. On the one hand, it meant he still had a chance to make it into the team. On the other …

"Why did you do it?" The voice came from directly behind him.

25
Survival Mode

Jericho spun around, stifling a yelp of surprise. He recognized the voice almost at once, but it was still something of a shock to see Thomas standing in the middle of the rooftop. His sudden movement overbalanced him backward off the rail; instead of using his powers to recover, he turned it into a twisting flip that left him on his feet on the roof, facing Thomas.

"Geez!" he exclaimed. "Don't *do* that! What the *hell?*"

At first, Thomas didn't answer. The light up here wasn't the best, but Jericho got the impression that the younger man was regarding him with a steady intensity. Thomas' whole attitude was a lot more defensive than on the other two occasions when Jericho had seen him; here, he seemed ready to fight or run at a moment's notice. Slowly, he folded his arms. "You're a hero." His voice was flat. "Even when you knew they were cops, you didn't stop us from getting away. Why?"

Oh, god, don't talk to me in that tone of voice. Jericho felt a distinct flutter in his chest as all his buttons got hit at once. *Tall, well-built and standoffish.* Clenching his fists inside his gloves to remind himself to keep things on a professional level, he took a deep breath. "They didn't strike me as being exactly on the level," he said, telling most of the truth. "Good cops don't taser the living crap out of someone without at least giving them a chance to surrender."

Thomas' lips tightened. "Depends on your definition of 'good'. They tell you why they're after us?"

"Something about the other guy being a person of interest. I didn't stop to ask any more details." Jericho paused, frowning. "How'd you know I was up here, anyway?"

That won him a snort from Thomas. "Credit me with *some* intelligence. You're a prodigy. I could see it in how you fight. Prodigies gotta brood." He spread his hands, indicating the rooftop. "And here we are."

Coming on the heels of the fact that he'd been snuck up on *twice* in one night, the implication that he was so predictable jarred Jericho to his heels. "Crap, I gotta up my game."

Thomas shook his head briefly. "Wasn't all that easy; plus, I cheated. I've got a Prodigy rating, too. Anyway, I just wanted to say thanks. And to tell you if you're gonna keep pulling that sort of crap, keep your head down. Force Majeure will land on you like an orbital strike if they find out. They aren't real keen on new heroes who show up in town and start shaking things up. Especially ones who interfere with undercover police operations." His message clearly delivered, he turned and headed for the far side of the building, his sneakers somehow making no sound on the rooftop.

Huh, I was right. He really is a prodigy. "Wait." Before he realized it, Jericho had taken a step forward. "What's going on? What did they want you guys for, anyway? Why—" He paused, rethinking what he was going to say. "Why were they so rough on you?" Asking Thomas why he was so eager to avoid the notice of the police would do his secret identity no favors at all.

Thomas stopped and turned. Slowly, he made his way back to where Jericho was standing. He had a calculating expression on his face. "I'll tell you that if you tell me how you got them to let you go like they did."

"I …" Jericho paused for a moment, then decided it was going to come out anyway, one way or the other. "… as it happens, I'm interviewing to join Force Majeure in the morning. Apparently, that gives me protected status."

"Ah." It might have been his imagination, but it seemed that Thomas eased back half a step. "Maybe I made a mistake then. My bad."

"No!" Jericho flinched at the sound of his own voice. "No, it's not like that," he insisted more quietly.

Thomas' gaze was a challenge in and of itself. "So, what *is* it like? Force Majeure is Force Majeure."

Jericho ran several answers through his head, but none of them sounded good. "Uh … can you tell me what you've got against Force Majeure? What've they done to *you?*"

Slowly, Thomas folded his arms again. This wasn't a great sign, but he was still standing there, so Jericho waited.

Eventually, Thomas sighed. "You already know I'm a prodigy," he said. "What I'm about to tell you isn't exactly a secret, but I'd really rather you kept it to yourself. All right?" His gaze on Jericho's was firm and forthright. Oddly enough, it reminded Jericho of Bobbi for a moment.

"Absolutely," Jericho said. "You don't know me, so I can't back this up, but I don't break promises."

Thomas' hard expression wavered for a moment. "I've heard that before," he murmured. "But I believe you. I don't know why, but I do." He took a deep breath and unfolded his arms. "The first thing you've got to understand is that if you're an Enabled in Utopia, you toe the line as far as Force Majeure is concerned, even if you're not a member. Independent heroes follow their lead, the cops follow their lead, *everyone* follows their lead. 'Law and order' isn't just a phrase, here. If you're not doing things their way, you're invited to leave, then you're told to leave, then you're *made* to leave. And that's if you're a *hero*. With me so far?"

"Yeah," Jericho said slowly. He was doing his best to concentrate on Thomas' words, but the flutter in his chest was back in full force. *Damn it, why couldn't you have been a girl, or short and weedy?* With an effort, he focused on the issue at hand. "So, where do you come into it?"

Thomas chuckled humorlessly. "We're the closest thing you'll find to supervillains in Utopia right now. It's not by choice. There's more than me and Ray. That's not his real name, just so you know. Right now, there's six of us, all Enabled, and we all came to Utopia looking for … well, to be honest, I don't know *what* we were looking for, not anymore. Everyone else lost one or both parents to supervillain attacks." He frowned. "Which feels like it *should* be significant, but I don't know how."

"Everyone else?" asked Jericho. He tilted his head. "What about you?"

Thomas looked away, patently uncomfortable with the question. "I was attacked by an Enabled, and it didn't end well."

"Jeez," muttered Jericho, without really knowing why. "I'm sorry. I really am." Up until now, Thomas had presented a façade of careless confidence; this was the first crack Jericho had seen in it. He wanted to ask more questions, but he didn't want to push too far or too fast.

Impulsively, he took a step forward, but Thomas backed away. It took Jericho no time at all to realize that the younger man was on the cusp of bolting. Seeking to look less threatening, he moved back and lowered himself to the railing. "Sorry. I'll just sit here, okay?"

Thomas nodded jerkily. "Okay, that's fine." He seemed to be breathing quickly, almost hyperventilating. "Just … keep your distance, all right?"

"Whatever you want." Showing off just a little, Jericho shifted his weight slightly until his balance was just right, then lifted his legs and assumed a cross-legged posture on the rail. Resting his hands palm-up on his thighs, he looked up at Thomas. "So, do you want to tell me why you and your friends are on the outs with Force Majeure if you came here looking to be heroes? Because I can't see anyone with half a brain coming here to be a *villain*."

The little bit of theater seemed to disarm Thomas' paranoia, or at least distract it for a while. "No, that's true. I never chose to be a villain. When I got here, I tried to join Force Majeure. We all did. But there's something about them …" He shook his head. "During the interview … there was a vibe. I can't describe it. We all just changed our minds. Opted out. Walked away to be independent heroes in Utopia. But we weren't that good at it, and because we weren't even paying lip-service to Force Majeure, the cops didn't cut us any slack when we screwed up. So now our Enabled identities are on the wrong side of the law, which technically makes us villains." He snorted self-deprecatingly. "I never even got around to picking out a name or a real costume."

Jericho tilted his head. "Surely you can just leave? Be Enabled somewhere else?" There had to be more to this than what Thomas was saying.

"No." Thomas grimaced. "We *could* have, back before the cops dropped the hammer on us, but after that it was too late. We're all minors, or close enough to it. We all came here, hoping that our powers could give us a fresh start in life, because our families just weren't there for us anymore. None of us has a credit rating. No paper trail, no way to get a job and earn money. We're runaways, so any bank accounts we had are well in the red by now. We can't just give ourselves up to the cops and hope for fair treatment, because the *best* case would involve being sent back to what we had before, and I'm never going back to that." He took a deep breath. "The trouble is, everything in Utopia's done by MagCard. Money as a physical thing barely exists here. Even if we had any cash, you can't use it to buy a ticket on the maglev. They only take MagCards, and *those* need a bank account with money in it."

"What, really?" That didn't sound right. "I'm pretty sure that it's illegal not to accept cash money as payment of debt, or something like that." He recalled reading something about 'all debts, public and private'.

Thomas shook his head. "I wish that was the case, but no. Cash money's legal tender, but there's no Federal law that says anyone's got to accept it. Utopia passed legislation a few years ago that gives all commercial shopkeepers access to MagCard readers. In *theory*, they could accept money, but in practice nobody wants to hold cash on their premises."

"Okay, sure. But the maglev's not the only way in or out of the city," Jericho pointed out. "I-seventy goes past just to the south of the city. I saw it on the way in. How did you get *into* the city in the first place, if it's so hard to get out?"

"I rode the bus in from Omaha," Thomas explained. "The plan was to get a MagCard as soon as I got on to the team. With the membership backing me up, I would've been able to open another bank account, one that—" He broke off. "Anyway, it didn't work out. Some of the others came in on the bus like me while it was still stopping here, or hitched in. A couple had MagCards, but after they were branded as villains, they couldn't use them. By the time we realized we were trapped, it was too late."

Jericho shook his head. "There's got to be a way to get out of town without using a MagCard. You make it sound like someone set things up so there'd be no way out, and I absolutely refuse to believe that."

Tilting his head and looking up at the night sky, Thomas chewed on his lip for a moment. "I don't think this is deliberate. It's more of a collection of unrelated situations with an unintended consequence. Greyhound was the last interstate bus line that had a depot here, but that closed down four months ago because the maglev's faster and cheaper. They were the last legal way to get out of town using cash money. There's a fleet of electric shuttle buses that do morning and afternoon runs to local towns, but they only take MagCard as well."

"Can't you just walk out along the interstate, or one of the other roads, and hitch a ride on the way?" While Jericho had never done the hitchhiking thing himself, it wasn't a difficult solution to arrive at.

Thomas shook his head. "All the roads out of town have surveillance on them. The local laws allow for anyone hitchhiking or even just walking alongside the road to be intercepted by the cops and given the third degree. And that's if you're an adult; if you're a minor, they've got the power to straight-up detain you for your own protection until they can hand you over to whoever *they* recognize as your legal guardian. Force Majeure *will* check the MagCard accounts of the ones that have them, which will bust any Enabled identities wide open. They're really intense about bringing down anyone who's been tagged as a villain in their area of operation. I heard of this one dynamic who could do super-speed, called Lightfoot. He tried hacking into the city's systems, using his speed to overwhelm the firewalls. Didn't help. They pinged him and he made a run for it. Got all the way to Eskridge, a hundred miles out, but they were waiting for him when he got there."

"How about tourists?" asked Jericho. "If you flag down someone leaving town, the cops wouldn't care about you, would they?" He hadn't seen any ordinary cars driving around, but he hadn't been in the city for very long. There had to be *some* places where tourists went.

"Ordinary cars don't get to drive into Utopia proper, or didn't you know that?" Thomas must have seen something in Jericho's expression. "Huh, you really didn't know that. Wheels aren't allowed on our roads, especially since they're literally made from solar panels and all." His voice held a curious mixture of pride and bitterness. "No, cars on the interstate can pull in at Southside Parking and fuel up with biofuels that Utopia produces, but their roads don't connect to our roads. People *in* Utopia can own cars, but they're the same as the cop cars, only slower, so they can't drive on regular roads. As for hitching a ride straight out of town, the Southsiders have got that all sewn up."

Jericho was startled by the solar panel revelation but before he could comment, he was distracted by the reference Thomas threw in at the end. "Southsiders? Are they the people who work at Southside Parking?"

"Well, yes and no," Thomas said. "They're the closest thing Utopia's got to an actual criminal underworld. See, Southside Parking is a big multilevel structure that caters for anyone off the interstate who wants to spend more time than the few minutes it takes to gas up. People can go right through to the South Side Mall and get a meal, do some shopping, whatever. The Southsiders are infiltrated through the business and into the mall. They've got connections, and they're the only ones who really handle cash in Utopia. Anything illegal that comes into the city, it comes in through them. That's where anything being smuggled into or out of the city gets handed over, in the parking structure. And when they leave is when anyone sneaking out of Utopia goes with them."

It sounded a little too pat to Jericho. "That sounds like something the cops would love to bust in a heartbeat, to be honest."

Thomas nodded. "Yeah, they do their best. But any time official suspicion starts to fall on one of the actual Southsiders, he gets swapped out for someone who's not in on it, while the guys in charge never show their faces. If the cops try to slide someone into the organization, the mole just ends up doing dead-end work until he gets reorganized out of the sensitive area again." He spread his hands expressively. "It's a sweet setup, but while they do offer passage out of town on the interstate, you've got to pay up front. If they get even the slightest suspicion someone might be a ringer, the whole deal drops through. You never see your cash again. It's a whole lot easier to stay in town and look for another way out."

Jericho held up a finger, suspicion flooding through his mind. "Wait a minute. I saw you using a MagCard to buy stuff earlier. You've clearly still got an active account that the cops don't know about, so it can't be all that difficult for *you* to get out of town."

"Yeah. I was, I do, and it's not." Thomas' frank statement took Jericho aback. He'd expected defensiveness or backtracking, not a flat-out admission. Further confusing him, the younger man smirked slightly. "That wasn't my original account. There's a little trick I can pull, but I can't do it too much or too often. I think people are starting to suspect, which would explain why the cops are on our asses so hard."

"Well, if it's not all that hard for you to buy a ticket out of town, why don't you just get one and go?" asked Jericho. "I mean, it's obvious you don't like it here."

Thomas gave him a hard glare. Paradoxically, this sent a flush of warmth clear through Jericho's heart. "If you're anything like me, you already know the answer to that. I'm not about to leave the others in the lurch." The younger man shook his head, regret clear on his features. "I just didn't know they'd made Ray as one of the Survivors, or I would've told him to keep his head down."

"Survivors?" Jericho wished he could hug Thomas for his reply but he didn't want to scare him off, so instead he put his hand on the rail and shifted his posture so he was sitting sideways with his legs folded beside him. "What's that?"

Thomas tapped himself on the chest. "Us. We all survived what happened to us. Like I said, we're the closest thing you'll find to supervillains here right now, and that's only because we're Enabled and we kinda break the law. Anyone who tries to go full-bore villain here gets hammered down *hard*, but we do our best to stay under the radar. All we really do is steal food and other necessities of life. Nobody gets hurt. Except when the cops spot one of us." His face closed up. "I should've been more careful."

"Well, that sucks." It was unpleasant to find out that even Utopia City had a dark underside. "Are you going to be all right? That one asshat stun-gunned you pretty good there."

Thomas' hand went to his ribs. "I'll be fine. I'm tougher than I look." Which, if he was a prodigy like he said, was quite possibly nothing less than the truth. The cautious look he gave Jericho only underlined the veracity of what he'd been saying. "So that's me. What are you gonna do about it?" The tension evident in his voice was echoed in his posture. By all appearances, he was preparing to bolt if he had to.

On the one hand was the fact that Thomas and the rest of the Survivors were breaking the law every time they stole something. They were at odds with Force Majeure, in Utopia City, the very team he'd come to join and still held in high regard. If he turned the Survivors in, not only would he get a pat on the back from local law enforcement, but there was also a good chance they'd be reunited with whatever family they had, which would get them out of Utopia City. And it might even give his chances of joining Force Majeure a significant boost. If he looked at it purely from a selfish standpoint, it was the right thing to do. It was certainly the *legal* thing to do.

On the other hand, he did feel a certain amount of attraction toward Thomas, and sympathy toward him and his friends regarding the rough hand they'd been dealt. That wasn't nearly enough to tip the balance, but the issue of morality *was*. Growing up in Savannah, Jericho had always been aware that legal did not necessarily equal moral. Discrimination against minorities, against homosexuals, against women, had long been legal. It had even been thought of as moral for the longest time. But it wasn't legal anymore and, in all truth, it had never *been* moral. What was happening to the Survivors now was basically the same thing, under a different guise.

If he turned Thomas and his friends in, subsequent events would be out of his control. He'd have no way of guaranteeing their well-being once they were in the system. Worse, if he did it right now, he'd be betraying the trust, however tenuous, that Thomas had vested in him by telling him what was going on. That, above all else, decided him.

"Well, I'd *like* to try and help you if I can," he said frankly, deriving a certain amount of amusement from Thomas' start of surprise. "But I don't ... whoa, *wait* a second." For the second time that day, he felt an almost physical burst of light in his head as the pieces of a puzzle slotted together. "Maybe I *can* help. Or at least, I know someone who can." It was all so clear now. Luke had almost certainly come to Utopia City to contact the Southsiders. With that as a starting point, the elements of his plan fell into place like dominoes.

"You know someone?" Thomas didn't sound overly thrilled by the idea. "Can you narrow it down a little?"

"Not right this second. Operational security." Jericho's mind was working overtime. *How the hell do I get Luke back in contact with Thomas without outing myself in the process?* "I'll figure something out. Right now, how about I give you my number so we can work out details later?" He dropped his feet to the rooftop and sat up straight. Flipping open the appropriate pouch on his belt, he pulled out his phone.

"Shit, no." Thomas shook his head. "Text messages are routinely monitored in Utopia, and I'm almost certain voice calls are too. If we're going to do this, we need to use codewords that still sound normal, and we just plain don't make voice calls. Voiceprints are a thing, after all. I usually keep my phone turned off until I want to check my texts, just in case they're trying to track it."

"Sonovabitch," Jericho muttered, shaking his head. "The way you're talking, Utopia City is about one step away from being a full-on police state. Why doesn't Force Majeure do something about that?"

"You've got the wrong end of the stick there," Thomas said, his voice tired. "Officially, Force Majeure has no hand in city politics. *Un*officially, if they want a local ordinance passed, it gets rubber-stamped before the ink's had time to dry. They've even got some say about what goes into state law. Everyone knows it; nobody talks about it. All these laws? Their idea."

"But ... that ... I don't understand." Jericho shook his head, trying to make sense out of Thomas' words. With this latest revelation, he was beginning to second-guess his decision to apply for membership. "They're *superheroes*."

"Yes. They are." Thomas gave him a sympathetic look. "But their job is to protect the public, not to coddle them, and you have to admit Utopia constitutes an almost irresistible target for hostile Enabled, as well as anyone else who has a bone to pick with Force Majeure. Enabled can be kids as well as adults, and Force Majeure is totally aware of the danger posed by teenagers with all the power but none of the judgement, especially in a target-rich environment like Utopia. To counter this, back when they were first starting up, they had a whole slew of local laws passed, all deliberately aimed at making it as hard as possible for anyone to get close enough to do serious damage without showing up on the radar *somewhere*. This included reducing the chance of hit-and-run attacks by making sure that sneaking in or out of town, or slipping through the cracks once they were here, became a whole lot harder. So basically, while we got caught up in it, it wasn't directed specifically at us. It just turned out that way."

Jericho's incipient outrage slowly ebbed away as he took in the younger man's words. "God damn," he muttered. "I'm not sure which to be more concerned about. The fact that the end result is screwing you guys over so hard, or that I can actually understand the reasoning behind it all." He shook his head. Well, at least it explained why Utopia City cops were such hardasses. They were *literally* guarding against hostile incursions, every hour of every day. Bobbi's speculation back at the Oaklands had hit the nail right on the head. "Maybe I could put in a good word for you guys when I go to my interview with Force Majeure tomorrow?"

"Shit, no, don't do that." Thomas put both his hands up defensively. "We've gotten by so far by staying under their radar. If they decide we got to you, you lose your spot *and* they come after us in force. There wouldn't be a corner dark enough for us to hide in."

"You don't know they'd do that." Jericho's elevated view of Force Majeure was taking a beating, but he had to believe that America's premier Enabled team would give the Survivors a fair hearing. "They're *heroes*. That's not what they do."

"No." Thomas shook his head. "They're *people*. People with powers, but still people. They've been running the show here for fourteen years. Sure, they're superheroes. But there's no way in hell they'd allow kids like us to challenge their authority or make them look ineffectual and weak. It's not the way they do business. This is their hometown, and they aren't about to step back for *anyone*." He threw up his hands. "I mean, it's not like they're gonna do anything illegal. They don't have to. The laws are all on their side. They *wrote* them that way. And if you think someone like Relentless is gonna give someone like me a break when he's got no reason to, then you don't know the guy very well."

"Crap." It was an admission of defeat, rather than a denial of Thomas' words. "Okay, I won't say a word. We'll do it your way."

"And you've got to be careful." Stepping forward, Thomas took Jericho's hand in his own. His grasp was warm, even through the leather of Jericho's glove. "If you get caught helping us, you'll be in serious trouble. At the very least, you'll lose any chance of ever getting into Force Majeure. Maybe go to jail. I can't allow you to risk yourself or your future like that."

Slowly, Jericho stood up. He was very aware of the nearness of the younger man, and the intensity with which Thomas was regarding him. Distantly, he realized that his heart rate had picked up again. As a prodigy, he had a certain innate ability to power through the effects of such things as fatigue and poison much more quickly than normal humans could manage. It seemed that his own hormones fell outside that category. But no matter what his body thought of the matter, this was not the right time or place for him to start awkwardly flirting. *Down, boy.*

He cleared his throat, trying to keep his voice steady. "I'll write your number down rather than store it in my contacts list, and I'll be careful about what I say when I do contact you." *Low-tech for the win.* He was quite pleased with the idea, and with the fact that he carried a notebook and pen in his utility belt for just such an occasion.

The glance Thomas shot Jericho, and the momentary grin that tugged at the corner of his mouth, suggested that the act wasn't totally convincing. Taking pity on

Jericho's sensibilities—or perhaps simply deciding he needed the use of both hands for the moment—Thomas let go Jericho's hand and retrieved his own phone out of his pocket. "Okay, what's your number? And more importantly, what's your plan?"

"Well, the plan's relatively simple." Jericho kept his eyes on Thomas' face to remind himself to stay on track. *One thing at a time.* "My friend's going to be meeting with the Southsiders tomorrow to arrange some business of his own. I'm pretty sure he'll be willing to help arrange passage out of town for all of you. Once we both go back home, I'll dip into my savings for however much cash they want and then my friend returns to Utopia City with it. He pays half up front, waits with the Southsiders until you're all safely away, then he pays them the other half. One week, tops. Figure you can hold out that long?"

Thomas blinked. "You'd *do* that? Just to help us get out of town?" His expression was an agonized mix of hope and incredulity, teetering toward the former. If Jericho had thought his expression was intense before, by now it was downright laser-focused. He searched every visible inch of Jericho's features with his eyes, clearly seeking any sign of deception or misplaced humor.

"Well, yeah," Jericho began. He didn't get any further, because Thomas impulsively grabbed him by the front of his jacket and kissed him, hard. Surprise exploded in Jericho's mind, driving all other thoughts away. His eyes widened, but not as much as Thomas' did.

The kiss ended far sooner than Jericho would've liked, but he wasn't arguing with the fact of being kissed in the first place. Trying to collect his whirling thoughts, he swayed in place as Thomas stepped back, staring at him. *Oh, come on,* he thought fuzzily. *It wasn't* that *bad a kiss, was—*

"Jericho?" blurted Thomas. "What the *hell?*"

26
Changing Plans

Jericho stared back at Thomas. "Wait, *what* now? How did you—" Far too late, he realized he should've played dumb, and abruptly shut his mouth. The cat was out of the bag by now, but at least he could avoid spilling any more of the beans. A random part of his mind asked, *wait, he remembered me? Wow. I did not expect that.*

"That's not important right now," Thomas said firmly, not helping Jericho's state of mind. "How come you're *here*? Have you been stalking me? Are you *following* me?" His stern gaze sent shivers down Jericho's spine.

"No!" protested Jericho. "You came with us in the cab, remember? You told us about the Market. I decided to check it out, and that's what I was doing when those asshats attacked you and Ray." He chose not to mention the fact that he'd been watching Thomas stroll up and down the Market before that point. That part did sound a little stalkerish, even inside his own head. "I couldn't let that shit fly, so I stepped in."

"You certainly managed *that*," agreed Thomas with a grin, before his expression turned thoughtful. "I guess I did tell you about it, yeah. And I'm glad of it. Ray would probably be on the way to jail if you hadn't stepped in. Or I would've had to beat them up, which would've opened a whole other can of worms."

"Well, I'm pleased I could help." Jericho knew it sounded lame, but he couldn't think of a less awkward way to say it. "I, uh—"

He stopped himself before the words *I'd like to see you again maybe, once things settle down* came out. This would sound too much like *I did you a favor, would you like to go out with me?* and would probably be the exact *wrong* thing to say right now.

"You, uh …?" prompted Thomas, hitching one eyebrow up slightly. Jericho got the distinct impression that the young man knew exactly what he was thinking. What he had no way of knowing was Thomas' *opinion* of this line of inquiry. Which inspired another question. How Thomas would respond to this one, he had no idea.

"Um, I was wondering, now that we're kind of sharing information … *how* did you know it's me?" Jericho gestured at his mask. "I know you said it isn't important but it kind of *is*. I'd like to know how I screwed up. If you can figure it out, so can other people." Especially given that he'd spent less than half an hour in Thomas' company, all told. The kiss had definitely changed matters up, though.

Thomas sighed. "I guess you've earned this one. Don't tell anyone, and I do mean *anyone*, but I'm not just a prodigy. I've also got a Dynamic rating that lets me read and replicate the biosignature of anyone I come into physical contact with." He eyed Jericho carefully. "There's exactly five other people who know I can do this. Don't spread it around, please?"

This was news to Jericho, but not in a huge way. In fact, it made Thomas just a little more relatable, as a fellow prodigy/dynamic. Considering this, he smiled wryly. "Sure. You keep my secrets, I keep yours. Isn't that the way it works?" He blinked as something occurred to him. "Wait. When you kissed me, was that so you could get my biosignature data or because you wanted to kiss me?"

Thomas smirked in return. "Yes."

"Oh, ha ha." Jericho gave him a dirty look, but felt his smile widening anyway.

He'd walked into that one, and Thomas had delivered. The younger man was turning out to almost be as much of a smartass as Luke, which Jericho kind of liked. Of course, the stolen kiss was something he needed to think about. But before he could get into that, another question occurred to him. "Um, don't you need someone's MagCard to use their bio data with?"

"Ah." Thomas held up a finger. "As it happens, no. You see, the MagCard doesn't store data. Only *you* can access your account, but you can use any MagCard to do it with. The 'Card's just the interface."

Jericho's eyebrows shot up at his news. "Wait, *what* again now? You can hit anyone's account, once you've got their biometric data? And they'll never know?"

"Well, yeah, they'll know, especially if I'm using their account at one end of town and they're using it at the other end. The system flags little anomalies like that and brings them to the users' attention. Also, it lets the authorities know. It's how I pull that little trick I told you about, and why they're starting to come down on us. If word gets out that MagCards can be hacked—which they can't, not really—confidence in the system will take a big hit. So far, they've kept it under wraps, and I've done my best to keep it discreet, but if I splurged on something like a ticket out of town, I'd blow my cover big time. Plus, I'd have to really be on my toes to get away with it at all."

"Shit." Jericho shook his head. "Like the saying goes, it's a great trick but you can only do it once." He took a deep breath. "And of course, once you're away from Utopia City, you can't really do it at all."

"That's right. Of course, once I'm away from this shithole, I can start earning money the proper way. All honest and above board." There was a wistful tone in his voice that Jericho didn't think was faked. "Every time I do it, I feel like I'm digging a hole just a little deeper."

"Well, I'm here to help you out of that hole," Jericho declared, trying to inject surety into his tone. He had no guarantee that what he was saying was what would happen, but he was damn sure going to try.

"Thanks. I really appreciate it." Thomas' expression transformed into a smile. "Actually, are you busy right now?"

Jericho blinked and looked around. Nothing seemed to be demanding his attention right at that moment. "I … well, I *was* going to patrol a bit longer before I went back to the Oaklands, but I'm open to suggestions." He wasn't quite sure how the conversation had gotten to this juncture, and he certainly didn't know where it was going. Far from making him uneasy, the sensation that flooded through his mind and set his blood fizzing was excitement. *This* was the mysterious (dare he say it— *romantic*) side of being a superhero that he'd daydreamed about in Savannah but had never experienced. Until now, anyway.

Thomas grabbed him by the hand and pulled him toward the far edge of the roof. "Let's grab a cab, and I'll show you the South Side Mall. Trust me when I say you've never seen a mall like it."

"Wait, grab a *cab*? Go to a *mall*?" Jericho looked down at himself. "I'm in costume, here."

"So, change," Thomas said pragmatically. "I already know what you look like. Or go as you are. Cabbies don't care, so long as the MagCard's good."

Jericho was intrigued by Thomas' enthusiastic description of the South Side Mall. He'd been to a few and was reasonably sure that he knew how they worked. One might be a little larger than another, but a mall was a mall. He was also sure that walking through one in costume might draw a little too much attention, even at this time of … "Wait. It's fairly late. Won't it be closed?"

"Pfft." Thomas rolled his eyes expressively. "The South Side never closes. Some of the shops do, but most of them go all night, because Utopia never sleeps." He tugged on Jericho's hand again. "Come *on*."

His enthusiasm was infectious. Jericho was strongly reminded of Serena, who'd dragged both Luke and himself to mall openings and movie showings, persuading them with sheer sisterly persistence and strategic use of puppy-dog eyes. Luke had gone along with her reluctantly, occasionally grumbling but letting her have her way. For his part, Jericho had enjoyed the outings considerably more, much to Luke's disgust.

Reaching behind himself, he opened the long pouch at the back of his utility belt and extracted the satchel before removing the utility belt itself. The coiled-up belt went into the satchel before he turned his attention to the jacket. Taking care to unbuckle the straps from around his legs—he'd forgotten to do that once, which had made the whole operation awkward as hell—he unzipped the garment and let it slide off his shoulders. Then he paused and shrugged it back on for a moment.

"What's the matter?" asked Thomas. "Is something wrong?"

Jericho gave him a rueful smile. "Just realized I might want this." Reaching into the inside pocket of his jacket, he extracted his MagCard and slipped it into his pants pocket.

"That's definitely true," the younger man agreed, sounding amused. As he watched Jericho take the jacket off for a second time, a spark of mischief danced in his eyes and he pretended to wolf-whistle.

Ducking his head to hide the warmth in his cheeks, Jericho folded the jacket and stashed it in the bag. *If Luke saw me blushing like this, he'd be laughing himself sick.* After the jacket, he put the gloves in the satchel, followed by the mask as the final item. With each removal, he felt a little less like G-Man and a little more like Jericho Hansen, though the difference was hard to quantify. As Jericho, he supposed, he was more relaxed and laid-back, less worried about how he was presenting to the public and whether his mask was on straight. Jericho was definitely more likely to go checking out a mall in the middle of the night than G-Man. Turning to Thomas, he gave the younger man a firm nod. "Let's go."

It was only about twenty feet to the pavement. Jericho slowed his fall and landed lightly, as was his usual practice. Thomas jumped down without needing assistance, absorbing the impact by flexing his knees and ankles. Jericho wasn't perturbed; prodigies tended to be good at calculating falls like that. Either they could handle it, or they didn't try it.

He couldn't help wondering what it would be like running the rooftops of Savannah with Thomas at his side. It wouldn't be beyond the bounds of custom for G-Man to acquire a sidekick (or even partner) with whom to fight crime. And Thomas definitely wanted to get out of Utopia City.

Two obstacles immediately came to mind; Stephen, and Force Majeure. Taken in reverse order, Force Majeure was a problem best dealt with by walking away from it. *He* wanted to join, but Thomas didn't. If he simply failed to show up to the interview, then he'd be free to go back to Savannah and resume his heroic career there, with Thomas at his side.

Of course, Stephen would raise a huge stink. He'd accuse Jericho of all the things he himself had done and reiterate his claim (with some justification) that Jericho had only gone to Utopia City to meet good-looking Enabled. Which wasn't true, but if it was what had happened, Jericho would never be able to prove his intentions otherwise. He and Stephen would be through, but the process of separation would be neither short nor sweet.

As they strolled from one pool of light to another, Jericho glanced at Thomas, wondering if it was fair on the younger man to drop him into that sort of hot mess. Then, as Thomas looked back at him, he realized something important. At no point in making any of these plans had he consulted Thomas on what *he* wanted.

"What?" Apparently embarrassed at the scrutiny, the younger man ducked his face away. "Do I have something on my nose?"

"No." Jericho hesitated, then took the plunge. "Listen … uh … when this is over, and you're out of Utopia City, if I'm not in Force Majeure … I was wondering if …" He trailed off. "Never mind. I'm just being stupid."

The look of enlightenment on Thomas' face was almost comical. He stopped and turned toward Jericho. Reaching up, he cupped Jericho's cheek with his hand; the warmth of his fingers on Jericho's skin was almost intoxicating. "No, you're not," he said softly. "If you were going to ask if I wanted to come back to Georgia with you, I think that's really sweet."

Jericho felt his heart lurch. "But you're saying no." *Because my life is shit like that.*

"I'm not saying no." Thomas slid his fingers into Jericho's hair, a profoundly intimate gesture. "But I'm not saying yes, either. I'm saying wait and see. Let's not make plans past tomorrow until we see what tomorrow brings, okay? You came here to join Force Majeure, so you owe it to yourself to give that your best try. If you don't make it, then we can see about making plans. If you do, then I can travel to wherever you get posted. It's no big deal. Either way, we got this. Okay?"

That wasn't a yes, but it was a hell of a lot better than a no. "Okay." Jericho nodded tentatively. "I'm good with that." To be honest, he would've been good with any plan Thomas put forth.

"Good," Thomas said briskly. His fingertips trailed down Jericho's jawline, then he smiled in a way that coiled warmth in Jericho's chest. "Let's go get that cab."

27
South Side

The first air-cab stand they found was empty, but when Jericho pressed the button, an operator answered immediately. He gave the relevant information and was told that it would be a minute and a half before the air taxi arrived. This, he presumed, meant that it probably had to be called in from another area. In any case, Jericho found no great hardship in waiting, especially in Thomas' company.

"So, you haven't been to the South Side Mall yet?" Thomas seemed to be gleefully holding on to a secret of some sort.

"You know I haven't." Jericho shook his head in mild exasperation. "What's it like?"

"Oh, you'll see."

It was a quiet night, but Jericho still didn't hear the cab coming until it was decelerating to land. With a whoosh of air and a thrum of lifters, it settled down over the landing grille. They climbed on board and strapped themselves into the back seat; there was a space between them, so Jericho put his costume satchel there.

"Evening, folks." The cab driver, a woman, sounded chirpy enough. **"You're heading for the South Side Mall?"**

"Apparently so," Jericho confirmed. He tugged his MagCard from his pocket. "I got this one, okay?" With his new awareness of how Thomas was paying for things, he had no problem with covering the entire fare. A swipe across the reader paid the amount on the screen, and they were airborne a moment later. With a smooth banking turn, the cab headed in what Jericho supposed was a southerly direction.

It was quite restful in the taxi as they wove their way between the buildings, the noise of the lifters barely audible. The Spire was intermittently visible out the right-hand rear window, but while it was the most striking thing in the Utopia City landscape, it was far from the only beautiful thing. Quite apart from the glittering lights outlining the buildings, what really underlined the futuristic appeal of Utopia City were the holograms that hovered over and between them. He'd seen them before, from a distance, but they were quite another thing up close. Advertising, illustrations and sculptures of pure light abounded. A hundred-foot long dragon, red and gold in color, looked up from where it was wrapped around a structure that could have been lifted straight out of a Tolkien novel and opened its jaws wide to roar soundlessly at them. It was utterly magical in a way he hadn't seen in a long time.

"Like it?" murmured Thomas. "I love being up here at night."

"Me too," Jericho said promptly. "I've seen a bit already, but this is absolutely gorgeous."

Jericho had his hand on top of the costume satchel, the strap wrapped around his wrist. In the next moment, he felt Thomas' hand resting on his, the fingers curling over to grasp his palm lightly. He didn't move, save to shift his hand slightly for easier access. With all the turmoil that was his life right then, he was content to sit there and enjoy the human contact. From the way Thomas' hand settled into his, it was a mutual decision.

"We're nearly there, fellows." The cabbie's voice sounded over the speaker all too soon. **"Where do you want to be dropped off? Mezzanine or footpath level?"**

Thomas didn't hesitate. "Mezzanine level, please."

"Mezzanine level, no problem." The cab adjusted its heading slightly as it came around a building, and Jericho saw their destination for the first time. With blue-green holographic lettering rippling over the frontage to form and reform the words **SOUTH SIDE MALL**, it was astonishingly tall with a gracefully rounded exterior. About ninety percent of the way up, half the area of the building became an expansive rooftop park. The rest of the building continued upward, tapering to a gracefully curved summit. Beyond the mall was the parking structure Thomas had mentioned, which was an impressive building in and of itself. The raised highway of the interstate could be seen in the background, cutting between the buildings of Utopia City on its east-west track. Jericho was at the wrong angle to see the offramp that led to the parking structure but as the vehicles raced along, he did spot a weird glinting of light just above the freeway, where no such reflection should be visible.

"What's that?" he asked before he realized the cabbie probably had no idea what he was referring to. "The flash of light off the interstate, I mean."

"Oh, the whole time the interstate's inside city limits, and particularly inside the Greenway, it's covered over."

"Greenway?" asked Jericho. At times, it felt as though his brain was filling up with all the details that made Utopia City unique. "What's that?"

"Big-ass park. It goes all the way around the city. You would've crossed it on the way in."

That rang a bell; while the maglev had still been two or three minutes out from the station, it had passed over an expanse of parkland. The greenery had blurred past in just a few seconds, too fast to see anything of note. He'd been impressed at the time, though since then his threshold for 'impressive' had been raised somewhat.

"Okay, I remember something about it," he said. "It goes all the way around the city?"

"That's right. The freeway goes under it, then comes up to give them access to Southside Parking. But the whole time it's inside Utopia there's a transparent cover over it that stops the exhaust fumes from spreading into the city and cuts down on traffic noise. They've got pollution precipitators in there to filter out the particulates, so they don't build up. We have to let them drive through, but we don't have to breathe the crap they leave behind."

"What about the parking garage itself?" asked Jericho. "Driving around in one of those places, the air's half goddamn fumes."

"No, they don't park their own cars or trucks or whatever. It's one of those big automated gigs. Drive onto a platform and park your car, and it gets stored like a book on a shelf. Then you just go through to the mall and have a meal, check into a short-stay, watch a movie or do some shopping. It's all right there." As the driver explained, the cab swooped in toward the park. Jericho picked out the air-cab stand on the edge of the flat area, just a few seconds before the cab decelerated and came in for a smooth landing. **"Here you go, fellows. Have a nice evening, and enjoy South Side."**

"Oh, we certainly will." Thomas popped his door open and climbed out. Jericho was just a few seconds behind him, holding on to the strap of his satchel as he closed the door behind him. The taxi took off in a rush of displaced air and a thrumming of lifters.

Jericho paused and looked around. "How many floors has this thing got, anyway?" he asked. "I mean, it's not all shopping, is it?" A low rail curved around the perimeter of the park, then gave way to the roofed-over area from which the rest of the building kept on going upward. There didn't seem to be any actual doors preventing entry; it was well-lit in there and he could see people moving around. Faint music came to his ears.

The park itself was composed of brightly colored rubberized concrete paths winding between discreetly placed garden beds, with well-manicured grass in between. Real grass, too. In Jericho's opinion, no matter how realistic they tried to make the artificial stuff look, it always came out just a little bit wrong. Here and there were placed concrete picnic tables, with the same sort of automated umbrellas he'd seen in the courtyard of the Oaklands; all furled away, of course.

"Whole thing's twenty-four stories," Thomas informed him as they began to stroll toward the main part of the building. "This is level eighteen. Everything below us is shopping, movies, and short-stay apartments; everything above us is privately owned."

Jericho shook his head in amazement. "Twenty-four stories? This is the eighteenth floor? I could've sworn it was five times that. How high up *are* we?"

Thomas waggled his hand from side to side. "Nine hundred feet, plus or minus. The ceilings are high, here. You'll see." He smirked, as if at a private joke.

"I guess I will." Jericho looked around. Distant sounds of splashing indicated that the swimmers were having fun in the pool. The playgrounds were sitting idle, probably because the kids who'd normally be using them were in bed. All in all, if it weren't for the absurdly tall hologram-clad buildings in the near distance or the six floors still looming over them, he could've mistaken this for any small-town park in America.

As they walked under the roof overhang, Jericho felt the same subtle popping sensation that he'd experienced walking out of the maglev station. He ignored it, gazing around to see what new wonders he would face. After all, a rooftop park probably wasn't the reason Thomas was looking so pleased with himself.

Within was well lit, as he'd already noticed. Several restaurants lined the interior space, which had remarkably few pillars standing in to support the rest of the building above them. Each restaurant had a holographic sign out front and tables and chairs placed in the public area, which was broad enough that it didn't feel cluttered. The other two things to look at were a fountain which sprayed bursts of water on what had to be carefully calculated arcs to miss the ceiling above ... and, a little way beyond the fountain, an open shaft going down into the floor, maybe thirty feet across.

Jericho's attention skidded off the fountain and fixed on the downward shaft. The closer he got, the farther down into the building he could see. About twenty feet below the level he was standing on was a holographic number '17' in glowing green, about ten feet high and slowly revolving in midair. Behind it, the shaft opened into another level, and he thought he saw the bottom edges of shopfronts set back maybe twenty feet from the edge of the shaft.

He'd seen light-wells before, but this one was a doozy, especially since it lacked both an overhead skylight and anything resembling a safety rail. In fact, the only visible safety feature was a low curb around it, more a gentle upward slope than any real attempt to stop people from getting too close. As Jericho watched, a guy got up from his table and strolled over to the shaft ... then stepped straight off the edge.

He spotted the discreet sign at about the same time as his G-sense kicked in. Gravity, his power told him in no uncertain terms, was going absolutely *nuts* in that hole. Not only was it *not* behaving itself, but the *type* of misbehavior was in constant flux. Seeking sanity out of the madness, he focused on the sign. It was a series of diagrams, essentially explaining that the direction of travel depended on which way the arms were held. Raise one or both arms, and he would go up. Lower them, and he would go down. Aim them in any given direction, and he would move in that direction. For those with bulky objects to carry, one arm would do. *Sounds simple enough.* It was, after all, a more effective version of what Jericho himself had been doing since he'd gotten his powers.

Beside the sign was a simple metal podium with a handprint embossed on top, and the words 'YOU ARE HERE' engraved below the handprint. He paused to glance at that, but Thomas tugged at his arm. "Come *on,*" the younger man urged. "Haven't you ever wanted to go flying?"

Well, of *course* he had. Keeping a careful grip on the satchel strap—the absolute last thing he wanted to do was accidentally drop it and have some curious person open it to find out who the owner was—he moved up to the edge of the vertical drop and leaned out to look down.

As far as he could tell, the cylindrical shaft went all the way to ground level. The distance from the floor of one level to the ceiling of the next was about thirty feet, as near as he could estimate. As Thomas had pointed out, the floor-to-ceiling space for each story was only about five feet less. He wasn't sure why they needed such high ceilings or so much space in between, but there was probably a good reason for it *somewhere.* Utopia City was like that.

This close to the edge, he could see that the number '17' was repeated on the near side of the shaft. Off-set by ninety degrees and about fifty feet farther down, the number '16' showed up on either side of the shaft, this time in blue. *Odd floors in green, even in blue. Got it.*

The size of the numbers, and the thickness of the floors, were about the least impressive thing he was seeing right now. The *most* impressive thing was the sheer number of people darting every which way through empty air, seemingly at random, like fish inside an insanely expensive aquarium. He could only imagine that it became *more* crowded during daylight hours but even as it was, he had no idea how people were not colliding with one another.

This close, he could feel the G-field affecting his body. His powers could 'see' about the first fifteen feet or so and determine which way the artificial gravity would allow him to go. The problem was, as far as he could tell, if he stepped over the edge, he'd be buoyed up like a ball on a waterspout.

"Come *on,* scaredy-cat!" Beside him, Thomas let himself fall forward into the shaft, arms pointed downward. Jericho watched as the artificial gravity reshaped itself around the younger man, adjusting itself second by second so that he could travel in that direction. In another instant, Thomas was beyond the reach of Jericho's G-sense.

Oh, well, he thought. *If he can do it …* Holding the satchel to his chest just in case, he stepped over the edge and fell feet-first. According to the sign, if he kept his free hand down, he would travel downward, so he did; the gravitational field almost miraculously adjusting to let this happen (at a maximum rate of fifty feet per second, his power helpfully informed him). Experimentally, he raised his arm so his free hand was above his waist, and he felt his downward travel slow. Raising the arm to shoulder height brought him to a stop.

All around him, he could feel the local gravity twisting into a pretzel as it boosted some people upward, allowed others to 'fall' downward or moved yet others around the outside perimeter of the cylindrical shaft; all according to which way they were holding their hand relative to their body. *We're being scanned, all of us,* he realized. *Somewhere in this building, a computer is modeling every single person here in real time, deciding which way to move us, and ensuring nobody collides with anyone else.* That level of processing power was a sobering thought.

Reaching out with his G-sense, he took hold of the local gravitational field. It felt … soft. Pliable, even. People were darting past him, both up and down, so he didn't mess with it, but he was pretty sure he could make the field do what *he* wanted it to, rather than the controlling computer. A slow smile spread across his face. *I'm gonna have to come back to this place.*

"Isn't this the best thing ever?" asked Thomas, coming up from below and drifting to a stop beside him. "I've always wanted to fly like Challenger or Lady Quantum. The building spits you out if you play around in here *too* long, but it's a lot of fun until then."

"It's definitely worth it," Jericho agreed. "Thanks for inviting me."

"You're welcome." Thomas grinned and tapped him on the shoulder. "Tag; you're it." As Jericho turned in surprise, he raised his arms and 'flew' upward.

"Hey!" protested Jericho, but Thomas was already far out of reach. "So, it's like that, is it?" Jericho felt an irrepressible grin spreading across his face. "You're on." Throwing his free arm out with his fingers pointed Superman-style, he gave chase.

The younger man had obviously been doing this for some time, as his finesse with the moves soon showed. Jericho's experience with gliding stood him in good stead, but he was unused to the freedom inherent in not having to worry about stall speeds. The result was that while his caution made him technically a better flyer than Thomas, he was still outclassed by the flamboyance that his new friend brought to the ad-hoc aerial playground.

All that aside, he fell in love with the whole sensation of powered flight within the first thirty seconds. Being able to climb, dive and turn with impunity was what he'd dreamed of since first getting his powers. While he knew he'd probably never get the ability to fly under his own steam, this was a very acceptable second best. As he pursued Thomas, and was chased in turn, he found himself laughing from sheer exuberance. Of all the things he'd thought he would be doing when he came to Utopia City, this was not one of them.

Eventually, Thomas veered off from their game, and angled over to land on what turned out to be floor twelve. Following him, Jericho landed easily on his feet. "That was *amazing*," he gasped, almost out of breath from laughing.

"I know, right?" Thomas was red in the face, quite possibly due to his own laughter at Jericho's initial midair clumsiness. He fanned himself theatrically with his hand. "I'm glad you like it. It's one of my favorite places in Utopia."

"I can see why. That was the most fun I've had in … well, ever." As Jericho caught his breath, he took the time to look around and for the first time noticed something else that would normally have had his jaw falling open with astonishment.

There were people walking on the *ceiling*.

Upside-down shoppers, nearly fifteen feet over his head, were strolling in and out of the corridors that led off the open area, pushing levitating shopping carts as if what they were doing was perfectly normal. He would've taken it for the effect of a spectacularly impressive mirror image, except that what the people were doing at his level *didn't match* what he was seeing overhead.

There were only three explanations for this: one, it was some kind of holographic art. Two, he was seeing things. Three … he consulted his G-sense. Immediately, he got a result. From about twelve feet up, the local gravity field was reversed, so that people beyond that boundary considered 'down' to be 'up', and vice versa. Basically, it seemed to be a vastly more powerful version of what his push-tags did. His eyes weren't playing tricks; there really *were* people walking on the ceiling.

"That …" he said faintly to Thomas. "… ceiling thing. Is it all over the mall?"

"The shopping levels, yes." Thomas grinned. "Pretty cool, hey?"

"Yeah. Cool." Jericho shook his head. The ceiling heights made a lot more sense now. With people walking both on the floor and the ceiling, possibly carrying unwieldy purchases, having a lot of excess headroom could be useful for avoiding accidents.

As for the corridors themselves, they were built on a hexagonal cross-section with holographic signage floating halfway between the floor and what his brain insisted on calling the 'other' floor; some upright, some upside down. He watched as one shopper approached a doorway angled downward into the corridor wall. The doors slid open, but as the woman stepped over the threshold, her entire body swung forward to an angle that looked entirely unbalanced to Jericho's eye. Then she walked downward into the shop, still tilted forward at that absurd angle.

"Gravity adjustment?" asked Jericho.

Thomas nodded, having followed his line of sight. "Gravity adjustment." He indicated the angled shopfronts. "Twice as many shops, twice as many people shopping at once. Whatever floor you're walking on is normal to you. After a while, I think people just stop noticing."

Jericho blinked and shook his head again. It was all too reminiscent of an Escher painting, or perhaps that David Bowie movie with the crazy puppets. He watched, bemused, as a man with a briefcase stepped off the ceiling into the drop-shaft and was immediately reoriented into a feet-down posture before rising out of sight. He still didn't really know what the rules for moving within the gravity-controlled shaft were, but he was happy so long as the monitoring computer did.

"This city," he said. "Wow." He gestured at the corridors then at the drop-shaft. "That's just weird, but *this* is way too much fun. I think I'm addicted."

"Me too." Thomas sighed. "It's one of the few things I'm going to really miss when I leave."

The comment, offhand though it was, reminded Jericho of the serious discussion earlier, and of his own responsibilities. "Yeah," he agreed. "And I'd really love to spend more time with you right now. Explore the place and check out your favorite shops."

Thomas nodded soberly. "I sense a 'but' coming up." His hand found Jericho's and squeezed it.

An unhappy smile crossed Jericho's face. "I'd be happy to stay out all night with you. But … I really should be getting back to the Oaklands and getting some sleep. If I'm not up bright and early for the interview in the morning, Luke'll be fixing to barge into my room, drag me out of bed and toss me in the shower on full Arctic."

"Oh, God. I'd pay money to see that." Thomas let out an unseemly snort of amusement. "But you're right. I could chat all night too, but I really should be heading back to the others. They're likely to get into all sorts of trouble if I'm not there to keep an eye on them. Besides, I want to make sure Ray made it back okay." He patted his hip pocket. "I turned on my phone when we got the cab. Someone would've texted if he *didn't* make it, but I just want to be sure anyway."

"I hear that." Jericho nodded toward the drop-shaft. "Shall we go up and get a cab?"

Thomas' smile held a tinge of sadness. "Yeah, let's do that."

Clasped hands raised together as in victory, they stepped off the edge. Gravity bore them upward, side by side.

Around them, unheeding, the business of the South Side Mall went on.

28
Post Mortem

Jericho and Thomas climbed out of the cab, then moved away from the stand as the flying car took off again. It wasn't the same taxi stand they'd left from, but Thomas had assured Jericho that he wouldn't have far to walk. The street was deserted, save for hover-cars 'parked' here and there at the curb, powered down and resting on their landing struts.

"I guess this is good night, then," Jericho said awkwardly. "I had a really good time. Thank you for showing me the Mall." He had a hard time correlating the technological masterpiece that he'd just seen with the fact that the Southsiders did business literally next door (as opposed to lurking in an abandoned warehouse somewhere) but he supposed that criminals could handle high-tech just as well. Besides, he didn't want to think about that right now.

"Me too." Thomas seemed reluctant to let his hand go. "I'm glad you were there to rescue Ray. And the rest of it. Thanks for, well, everything."

"Well, I haven't *done* the rest of it yet." Jericho reluctantly patted the satchel. "Gimme a second to costume up, and I'll get your number, okay?" He inclined his head toward a nearby alleyway; it was better to get out of sight than risk being caught on a street camera.

"Okay." Thomas flushed a little as he let Jericho's hand go, fingers trailing against one another. They entered the alley, and Jericho unzipped the satchel.

The mask went on first, then the jacket. His heroic identity in place, Jericho took a little more time getting his gloves and utility belt on right. Then he opened the pouch that held his notepad and pen and took them out.

"Are you sure Luke will be up for this?" Thomas still seemed uncertain about this.

"Sure as I can be." Jericho essayed a grin. "I'll just have a talk with him before I go to the interview. If I know him, I'll only need to drop a few hints about how this'll piss off the local cops." He flipped back the cover of the notepad and clicked the pen. "Ready."

Slowly, Thomas read his number off his phone, and Jericho copied it down. In return, Jericho recited his own number from memory, giving Thomas time to tap it in.

"He's pretty damn big, as I recall." Thomas gave Jericho a grin. "If anyone could get the Southsiders to pay attention, he could."

"Luke is good at that," agreed Jericho as he tucked the pen and pad away. "Well, I'll see you tomorrow night, and let you know how it went." Going by reflex, he held out his hand to shake. He was unprepared for Thomas to pull him close again.

"I had a *really* good time tonight," whispered the younger man, and planted a firm kiss on his lips.

"Uh, I did too," stammered Jericho, feeling his cheeks heating up all over again. He watched a sly grin dance on Thomas' lips, and wondered if the guy was deliberately trying to fluster him. If he was, it was working. "I'll, uh, I'll see you later."

"See you then," said Thomas, taking a few steps back. "Say hi to your cousin for me."

"I will." Taking a deep breath, Jericho reduced his personal weight to its minimum, and jumped upward, reaching for the edge of the roof overhang above them. Grasping it, he swung up and landed on his feet. When he looked down again, Thomas waved once, then turned and headed out of the alley. Jericho watched him as long as he could, then looked around to center himself.

A lot had happened in the last hour or so, and he needed time to think it all through. But he could do that once he got back to the Oaklands. It only took a few seconds to secure his wing-tails, then he took a run-up and leaped lightly into the air, aiming for the next building. Not even bothering to glide across the gap, he covered the thirty feet and touched down on the next rooftop with ample room to spare. This was the sort of roof-running he'd practiced when he first made up his mind that he was going to be a superhero, and he could almost do it in his sleep.

Running, leaping, landing, he crossed two more rooftops in the same manner. Deciding that he'd earned a little goofiness, he pulled a somersault on the way across to the third one, taking care to keep his arms in close to his sides so he wouldn't accidentally catch the air and stall out in mid-leap. He would've repeated the stunt at the next jump, but there was a wider road coming up and he didn't want to screw up in view of the public.

Buildings two and three times as tall as the warehouses dominated the skyline across the road, with the ten-story apartment building visible behind the nearest ones. *And the Oaklands is just past that*. Along with most of the high-rise architecture in Utopia City, each building (along with its attendant holographic signage) looked like the architect had been aiming to make the cover of *Science Fiction Weekly*, or some similar publication. He honestly wouldn't have been surprised if most of them had succeeded.

Accelerating to a sprint, he kicked off and arrowed into the air, angling slightly upward. His much reduced effective weight let him go farther before he would need to deploy the gliding surfaces and thus introduce extra drag. This street was seventy feet wide if it was an inch, and he made it about thirty before he began to angle downward. Unlike when he'd jumped off the apartment building earlier, his momentum consisted solely of what he'd supplied himself, and there was only about twenty-five feet between himself and the smooth surface of the street below.

Spreading his arms, he caught the breeze and farther flattened out the already-shallow parabola he was describing through the night air. Below him, moving as silently as he himself was, civilian maglev cars cruised along the street on their own business. None of them seemed to react as he glided overhead, which proved that the citizens of Utopia City either didn't look up, or they were far more used to seeing Enabled out and about than he was.

Seconds later, he arrived at his target building. His glue-tags performing their duty efficiently, he ascended the sheer wall with little in the way of effort. By the time he reached the roof, sixty feet up, he was barely breathing hard. All the same, he stopped to admire the view and review his churning thoughts.

When I set out to go patrol the Market, did I expect to see Thomas? It was a valid question. After all, Thomas *had* said he lived near there. *Did I go there to see him?*

No, he decided. He'd even forgotten the guy's *name* momentarily, which would've been embarrassing at the best of times, even if he wasn't a mental-based prodigy like some he'd heard of. Transit's words had inspired him to go patrolling, but he'd been more interested in discovering the city than meeting anyone in particular.

Of course, seeing Thomas had led to Jericho beating up on two undercover cops—he was still internally cringing over *that* little exercise in crossed wires—and then finding out about the Survivors. And offering to help them escape the city.

Which had led to the kiss from Thomas, and then the side trip to the South Side Mall. And the second kiss.

Any one of these incidents, twelve hours previously, he would've dismissed as highly unlikely. Looking at the entire chain of events, his credulity would've been strained to the breaking point and beyond. But they *had* happened, and he wouldn't take any of it back, except maybe when he'd tossed Forrester in the canal.

A grin creased one corner of his mouth. *Nah, he was being an asshat. He deserved it.*

But even taking that into account, there was still the issue with the Survivors, and what he'd pledged to do about it. On the one hand, they were breaking the law; on the other, they weren't being given the option *not* to. So, while his plan to sneak them out of town was almost certainly illegal in and of itself (he wasn't sure about the specific details) he considered it the lesser of two evils.

There was definitely a chance this would get back to Force Majeure and screw with his chances of joining. On the other hand, the only commitment he'd made in that regard was to attend the interview. He *wanted* to join, but he'd already said he'd help the Survivors out. If events ended up with him being kicked to the curb over something like this, it would be a sign that he wasn't a good fit for them. Which would hurt a lot; he wasn't denying that. But just like he would never act against the best interests of Force Majeure once (if) they let him join, he couldn't turn his back on the Survivors now. And whether he got into Force Majeure or not, there was still the other thing to think about. Specifically, the Thomas-shaped elephant in the room.

He kissed me, twice. And I liked it, a lot. The trouble was, he wasn't done with Stephen quite yet (even though he definitely wanted to be) and so following up on anything like that was right off the table. No matter *how* much he wanted to go back for thirds. *If I did that, Stephen could definitely say I was cheating on him.* He knew how his boyfriend thought. The slightest impropriety on his own part, in Stephen's mind anyway, retroactively excuse every single time he'd stepped out on Jericho. *I refuse to give him that satisfaction.*

Steering clear of any chance for Thomas to get that close again would be a little unpleasant, but his own personal honor demanded it. Of course, once he'd spoken to Stephen, he'd know where he stood. Taking a deep breath, he mentally dusted his hands off. *Okay, that shit's dealt with. So long as I don't run into any other crises between here and my bed, I should be able to enjoy a few hours of sleep.*

Moving around the rooftop until he had a view of the sign over the Oaklands complex, he let his back-brain handle the calculations. It was about fifty yards away, half-obscured by the ten-story apartment block, but the other rooftop was twenty feet lower; the glide was definitely doable. A police hex thrummed overhead as he took his run-up and leaped out into empty air. Fortunately, it seemed that the Utopia City PD had gotten the message about him, as the blocky drone didn't react to his apparent suicide attempt.

This late at night, the air was still and cool for the most part, making it steady and reliable to glide in. He arrived on the roof of the Oaklands less than ten seconds later, his soft-soled boots barely making a sound as he touched down. With a feeling of almost coming home, he glanced around to make sure nobody was watching. The rooftop was broad and clear, making it easy to check, especially with the overhead glow from the holographic sign. There were only a few shadows around, and they weren't all that deep.

Reaching behind himself, he opened the long pouch at the back of his utility belt and extracted the rolled-up satchel once more. In a somewhat more leisurely fashion than he'd done with Thomas, he stored the belt and jacket in the satchel, then took his gloves off and stowed them in afterward. His phone, he figured, could stay in his belt pouch until he got inside. A tap of his finger reassured him that his MagCard was still in his pants pocket.

"Whew," he muttered as he glanced around one more time. An irrepressible grin flitted across his face as he reviewed the night's events. Thomas was definitely someone he wanted to get to know better, once he'd dealt with the Stephen problem. But that was something he was going to have to sleep on. And of course, there was the interview tomorrow. *Time for bed.*

Moving to the edge of the roof, he leaned over to look for the top of the access ladder. As he did so, he heard the unmistakable sound of a police siren. It was in the distance but getting closer. It sent a thrill through him, and just for a moment he was tempted to go see if he could locate the unit and offer assistance. Regretfully, he decided that his ignorance of the city's geography and the fact that he was going to need *some* sleep before the interview meant that he'd have to give this one a miss.

Locating the ladder, he climbed down to the appropriate floor, cheating a little with the satchel's weight so it wouldn't dangle too awkwardly and pull him off balance. There was a necessary pause while he pulled out the MagCard and swiped the exterior reader; the window swiveled around and allowed him entry. Stepping through, he swiped it closed once more. Only then did he remove his mask and stash it in the satchel. Challenger Act or no Challenger Act, illegal surveillance cameras were still within the realms of possibility, even in Utopia City.

His apartment door was only a few yards down the corridor. As he came up to it, a musty odor reached his nostrils. *Oh, great. Did I step in something?* If he had, it wouldn't be the first time. *I'll put my boots in the bathroom and clean them in the morning.* But even as he formed the thought, he frowned. *That almost smells like—*

Reflexively, he swiped to unlock the apartment door. As it opened, a wave of the same smell hit him, and he recognized it for what it was.

29
Worst Case

Blood.

It is a smell that strikes to the very core of the human subconscious. Even people who have never experienced it before, and don't know what it is, feel a sense of unease when they first scent its distinctive metallic tang.

Jericho already knew it well, and terror surged into his throat like a living thing. The last time he'd felt fear on this scale was the night he'd been thrown from a building in downtown Savannah and gained his powers, but on that occasion he'd only had himself to worry about. Now, with the cloying odor of fresh carnage in his nostrils, he knew beyond all doubt that something terrible had happened within the apartment.

"*Luke!*" he screamed, eyes widening in a desperate attempt to discern more detail from the pattern of light and shadow that came in through the window. The satchel's strap slipped from nerveless fingers and thudded to the floor as he lurched sideways, scrabbling frantically for the light switch he knew had to be there. "Luke! Bobbi! *LUUUUKE!*"

The lights flickered, as if reluctant to reveal the full horror of the scene to him. By the time they came on, Jericho was already moving forward, staring glassy eyed from one spot to another in search of what he already knew he didn't want to see. His pulse thundered in his ears, and red tinged the edge of his vision. A tightness in his chest made it hard to breathe.

Some part of his mind registered that Luke's sofa-bed had still not been unfolded, but the cushions were lying in rags. The sheets were shredded and torn on the floor, and liberally stained with crimson. Feeling as though his feet were mired in concrete, he stumbled onward. "Luke!" he sobbed, trying to draw air into his lungs. Tears of anguish rose in his eyes, putting a haze over the room. "Bobbi!"

Swiping the back of his hand over his eyes, he scrubbed the tears away and cleared his vision. A cry of animal pain burst from him as he finally saw Luke, sprawled on the floor outside Bobbi's bedroom door. The worst of his fears had been realized; his vision narrowed until all he could see was his cousin. In another instant, barely aware that he'd moved, he was kneeling next to Luke. The spreading pool of blood began to soak into the knees of his pants, but his entire attention was focused on his cousin's face. One eye was obscured by a mass of gore, but the other was open. For a single heart-stopping moment, Luke met Jericho's agonized gaze.

"Luke," Jericho croaked, taking his cousin's large hands in his own. The cooling blood was sticky against his hands, and he saw that Luke was still clutching splintered lengths of wood. "Luke, I'm here." But with that movement, Luke's head lolled to one side, his single visible eye now staring sightlessly at the far wall. The brief flash of hope drained away, leaving a dreadful certainty in its place.

"No ..." keened Jericho. "No. No. No. Not you, Luke. Not *you.*" Leaning forward, he cupped Luke's head in his hands, lifting it up again, searching vainly for any signs of life. Looking down at Luke's body, he tasted bile in his throat as he saw the many stab wounds and slashes that had been inflicted on his cousin. Luke was soaked from head to toe in his own blood; his previously off-white wife-beater was stained dark red with it. A coil of blue intestine protruded obscenely through one of the larger wounds. When Jericho tried for a pulse—knowing he would never find one but hoping against hope anyway—he discovered that Luke's throat was one huge gash from side to side. There was no heartbeat, no breath, no hope of a miraculous last-minute rescue. The agony of wrenching loss behind his breastbone doubled him over, until his forehead pressed against Luke's. *"No ..."* It was a primal plea.

Bobbi. Driving back the shrieking voices of horror in his head, he forced himself to stumble to his feet. Despite everything he might hope to the contrary, Luke was dead; Bobbi may yet be alive. Leaving Luke's side was the hardest thing he'd ever done, but a hero's duty was to the living. Dimly, he was aware that his most extreme emotional responses were being blunted, probably by the same Prodigy abilities that let him push through physical trauma. The pain was worse than anything he'd experienced in his life to this point, but he found himself able to remain somewhat functional instead of curling into a ball of pain and loss and howling his agony to an uncaring universe.

This awareness didn't make it any easier to stumble into Bobbi's room, but he managed it somehow. "Bobbi?" he called, the sound barely making it past the painful lump in his throat. When he put one hand on the sagging door, it fell off its one remaining hinge onto the floor behind him; such was the intensity of his focus, he barely noticed the muted *boom*. "Bobbi?" he rasped again.

There was no body on the bed or the floor; all he initially saw were her glasses, bent and crushed into the carpet. *Did she get away somehow?* For one cruel moment, hope assailed him until he kicked something and saw it was the door to the closet, ripped clean off its hinges. Grimacing as tears ran freely down his cheeks again, he took one more reluctant dragging step toward the closet and saw her.

She hadn't been able to arm herself, and his heart lurched to see the desperate fight she'd put up anyway. The tattered and gore-soaked sleeves of her pajama top revealed that she'd taken defensive wounds, and he thought he saw a darkening under her fingernails in the dim light. Through the overwhelming waves of grief and uncomprehending disbelief that assailed him, a tiny spark of satisfaction glowed sharp; even facing certain death, Bobbi had marked her killer, had snatched his DNA.

Her face had borne the brunt of the attack. A wave of nausea passed through him as he saw that the attacker had sliced her eyes and slashed her across the mouth until her lips were no longer recognizable. It was no consolation at all that her suffering had been ended with a single efficient stab up under the breastbone.

Ignoring his own tears, he knelt before the closet and reached inside. With trembling fingers, he tried for a pulse, but it was no more present than it had been in Luke. Whoever had invaded the apartment during Jericho's sojourn away had achieved their goal, though Jericho's grief-numbed mind could make neither head nor tail of *why*. Why these two? Why this apartment? Why this night? It wasn't, couldn't be, a simple robbery gone wrong. Whoever had come in here had done so with the specific aim of killing everyone in the apartment. Most criminals, in Jericho's experience, shied away from murder. This was more like the act of a terror villain, or one of the Madness, than a startled burglar.

And then, as anger began to take over and clear his mind, Jericho realized one more thing. While Bobbi's skin was cooling, it was still warm to the touch. This meant that whoever was responsible had left the apartment mere minutes before Jericho arrived. *I can still catch them!*

The paralysis of the pain he felt was replaced by crimson rage and a razor-sharp need to hunt down whoever had done this and make them *pay*. Staggering to his feet, he lunged out of the bedroom. He wanted desperately to stay with his cousin, but nothing would bring Luke or Bobbi back to life, while catching their killer would let him do *something*. As he vaulted the length of the room, he fancied he heard what he would forever after consider to be Luke's last words: *Go git th' sumbitch, cuz.*

Oh, I intend to. The way Jericho's emotions were roiling right then, the asshat would be lucky to live long enough to stand trial. He didn't have an exact plan for what he intended to do to the guy when he caught him, but it was going to be extremely violent and probably fatal. He flicked a push-tag at the MagCard where it lay on the floor, then reached down for the strap of the costume satchel as the card smacked into his palm.

The front door to the apartment burst open with shocking abruptness, almost in his face. Uniformed cops filled the doorway. Beyond them, more crowded in the corridor. He could see guns in hands, already beginning to angle toward him. Adrenaline surged, slowing the world to a crawl. He left the bag where it lay and straightened up fast, a G-tag forming in his hand. Shouts rang in his ears.

"Down on the floor!"

"Don't move!"

"Hands in the air!"

Thoughts seemed to ooze through his head with the slowness of molasses.

These guys are never going to listen to reason.

I'm going to have to go through them or past them.

There's too many to get past.

Through them it is.

Wait, what the hell is—

One officer squeezed the trigger on something shaped like a pistol, but made of plastic and lacking a muzzle aperture. It gave an electronic chirp; the acrid scent of ozone abruptly overrode the cloying effluvium in his nostrils. Whatever this was, he didn't like it. He tried to throw himself aside, but it was too late.

tac-tac-tac-tac

White fire lanced through his nervous system, turning his world into a tracery of agony. The first jolt seized up every muscle. The second dropped him to his knees. The third left him twitching face-down on the carpet.

His last coherent thought was: *but I'm one of the good guys—*

tac-tac-tac-tac

- End of Part Two -

PART THREE

MURDER, MOST FOUL

And the hunt begins.
- Sgt Diane Finlay, UCPD (DL)

God *damn* it, Independence.
- Relentless

Problems solved; solutions expedited …
- inscription on a business card

30
Presumption of Innocence

When Jericho's mind started functioning again, he found himself face-down on the carpet. A cuff had been tightened around his left wrist, and his right arm was being pulled up and back, no doubt to complete the act of restraining him. "No!" he shouted, twisting and bucking to try to free himself.

"Whoa, crap!" Clearly caught off guard, the police officer who'd been kneeling beside him went sprawling. "He's active, he's active!"

Fully aware that he wasn't masked, and that he was probably pushing the envelope on being outed with his faster-than-normal recovery from the electric shock, Jericho nevertheless knew he had to get the upper hand. He didn't know how long he'd been down, but it couldn't have been long. *If I can get out of this right now, I might have half a chance at catching up with the killer.*

Rolling away from the cop onto his back, he came to his feet fast; the way he'd been trained in his Krav Maga lessons. Still, the cuff dangling from his left wrist reminded him that he was far from out of the woods. He could certainly fight his way out, but this would assuredly destroy his secret identity in the process. If he could just talk to them and make them *listen,* he'd be home free.

The officer who'd tasered him before—it had to be some kind of taser, even without the trademark wires—looked taken aback at what was going on but began to swing the weapon back toward him anyway. Another one started pulling an identical weapon out of its holster. Events were rapidly spinning out of control. There was no way this was going to end well. He doubted they were of a mind to pay attention to anything he said. Nevertheless, he had to try.

"I'm not—" Jericho reached the first cop and stepped past the taser, inside the officer's reach. Taking control of the taser, he removed it from the cop's grasp. As a continuation of the same move, he grasped the officer's collar and turned with him. A vague idea that electricity could go straight through one person into another made him push the cop toward the second officer. "—the bad guy here!"

tac-tac-tac-tac

The police officer he'd shoved convulsed and went down, which meant that the uniforms weren't particularly insulated against electricity. Just for an instant, Jericho considered firing back; after all, it wasn't as though he could really hurt anyone by doing so. But attacking cops who were specifically doing their jobs went against the grain, even if it was *him* they were trying to arrest. He'd screwed up enough with the undercover cops at the Market; this time around, he wouldn't even have the excuse of a misunderstood situation to fall back on.

"Hold *everything!*" he yelled, tossing the liberated taser on the floor in front of him and raising his hands in surrender. "I didn't *do* this! I just got home! I was on patrol—"

Too late, he bit the words off, a sinking feeling manifesting behind his breastbone. *Patrol.* That was a word used by law enforcement, by the military ... and by superheroes. *All this, and I managed to out myself anyway. I am such a goddamn moron.*

The room went still, then someone pushed past the police officer who'd tried to taser him. Jericho tensed, but the man simply held up a wallet with a badge attached.

Heavy-set and grizzled, he wore plain clothes and had a certain air of competence about him. "Detective Sergeant Stirling. Did you just say 'patrol'?"

Jericho stared at the badge. It seemed to be genuine, as far as he could tell in this situation. Surrounding an image of the Spire with the sunrise behind it were the words UTOPIA CITY DETECTIVE SERGEANT and a serial number.

The detective sergeant tried again. "Is this a Challenger Act situation?"

Crap. Definitely outed myself. The sinking feeling intensified. The thought of denying it crossed his mind very briefly, then he reminded himself that everyone in the room had heard it and they almost certainly had recorders running, if not actual bodycams. Slowly, he nodded. "Yeah." A memory stirred in the back of his mind. "I'm gonna need a Designated Liaison." To his relief, the officer who'd been tasered groaned and sat up, shaking his head groggily.

"Shit," muttered Stirling. Turning his head, he looked toward the bedroom door. "Hey, guys—"

The moment Stirling's attention left him, Jericho made a move for the door. *The killer's got to be close by, and if I can get past these idiots—*

"Whoa, hold up there, champ." The detective sergeant interposed himself in front of the doorway, showing more situational awareness and faster reflexes than Jericho had anticipated. As he was too solidly built for Jericho to easily slip past, this brought the incipient escape attempt to an immediate halt. "At least 'til you get a chance to talk to that DL you just requested."

"Get out of the way!" shouted Jericho. "We can deal with the Designated Liaison later! The guy who did this is out there! He can't have gotten far!"

Stirling shook his head. "No can do. Until we get this cleared up, you're a suspect. We can't let you go anywhere." His voice was firm and fatherly, but it was the last thing Jericho needed to hear right now.

"But he's getting *away!* You *know* he is!" Jericho fought down the desperate impulse to disable the guy anyway and make a break for it. The trouble was, they were at least listening to him now; decking one of them would make all that effort null and void. If he was going to chase down Luke's killer, he knew he'd find it much easier without the police chasing *him* down.

The detective sergeant let out a short aggravated huff of breath, then raised his voice. "Someone find me a Designated Liaison, right *now.*" His eyes never shifting from Jericho, he reached up and clicked a button on a rectangular object clipped to his lapel, then pressed a finger to the low-profile earpiece he was wearing. "Stirling to Hotel X-Ray Three-Four-One Actual. Report status of drone, over."

A crisp voice emanated from the tiny speaker on Stirling's shoulder. *"Hotel X-Ray Three-Four-One is orbiting Oaklands complex, as per orders, detective sergeant. UV, IR and low-light scanning. No unknowns spotted on street or nearby rooftops, over."*

"What the hell does that even *mean?*" demanded Jericho. "What's Hotel X-Ray ... oh." It wasn't until he said the words out loud that the meaning became clear. "You've got a *hex* up there?" He hadn't even considered that they might use them for more than enforcing air-traffic rules.

"We do. And there's more." Detective Sergeant Stirling raised his finger to cut off further protests, then pressed the earpiece again. "Stirling to Three-Four-One. You were recording from the moment the drone showed up, right? Over."

"That's an affirmative, sergeant. We have all the imagery, over."

"Good." Stirling showed his teeth in what might have been a smile. "Run the infrared back as far as it goes. If our perp walked out, he would've left an IR trail. Find me that trail, over." Turning to Jericho, he shrugged. "It won't be a strong one but if he left on foot, it'll give us a line on which way he went, rough shoe size, stride length, the whole nine yards."

His throat tight with several conflicting emotions, Jericho nodded. *He* wanted to be the one to catch the killer, not the cops! In his current state of mind, it was a toss-up whether the guy would survive to stand trial, and right now Jericho was perfectly okay with that. *Luke was kin. You mess with my kin, you mess with me.* It had always been that way.

The radio speaker crackled. *"Roger, rolling back IR recordings. And … we have a hit. Footprints, leading out to the curb. Looks like the guy was favoring his left leg, over."*

"Which way do they go from there?" pressed Stirling. "Across the street? Left? Right?"

"They don't. They stop at the edge of the street, like he got in a car, over."

"Excellent. Three-Four-One, have someone follow that up for me. Stirling, out." The detective sergeant released the earpiece and dusted his hands off, looking satisfied. Almost as an afterthought, he turned the lapel speaker off.

Jericho stared at Stirling, wondering why he seemed so pleased. "Got in a car? He just walked out … and got in a *car?*" He couldn't believe it. Visions of chasing down the perpetrator were fading as he took in the new information. "Do you have street-cams covering the area? Can you find out where it went? Who owns it?" It seemed improbable that a city so technologically advanced *wouldn't* have camera systems in use on its streets.

Stirling put his hand up, bringing Jericho's questions to a halt. "There isn't any public surveillance directly outside this complex for several reasons, but they couldn't have gotten off this section of street without being imaged from at least three directions. Plus, cars pull power from the municipal energy net via inductance from the street, so they can be tracked to a certain extent. We can get back results from both of those in just a few minutes, once we put in the request, which I just did. And the farther the perp goes in the car, the higher the statistical chance that one camera or another will get a good look at his face. We're likely to get the 'who' and the 'where' at the same time."

"So, you know the killer just walked out and how to catch him." Jericho spread his hands. "I'm right here, so I'm not the killer. Can I go already?" He gestured with his left arm meaningfully, making the cuff hanging from his wrist swing back and forth.

"We know *someone* walked out," Stirling corrected him. "It may have been the perp, but it could just as easily have been some guy visiting his girlfriend." Jericho opened his mouth to protest, but Stirling talked over him. "Personally, I believe you. But regulations are regulations; cutting corners will drop *both* of us into a whole world of trouble. Talking about that …" He looked around. "Where the *hell* is that DL? Don't we have one on site?"

From the way people were looking around and shrugging—even the cop Jericho had used as a human shield, who was otherwise giving Jericho a dirty look—it quickly became clear that there were no Designated Liaisons in the vicinity.

"Because of *course* not," sighed the detective sergeant. "Okay, everyone but the paramedics back in the corridor. This whole apartment's a crime scene until proven otherwise. CSI's on hold 'til this is cleared up." He rubbed his forehead with finger and thumb for just a moment, then pressed the earpiece. "Control, this is Detective Sergeant Stirling, attending ten-forty at Oaklands. We have need of a Designated Liaison. I say again, this is a Delta Lima situation, over." Despite the aggravated expression on his face, his voice remained calm and professional.

Jericho of course did not hear the reply, but the sergeant nodded as if by habit. "Copy incoming DL, fifteen mike. Will wait out." Releasing the earpiece, he turned to two guys who were peering in the door, wearing paper booties and protective coveralls. As a mildly interesting detail, each of them sported a slimline backpack with a hard-shell cover. "Sorry guys, you know the drill. This shouldn't take long." Then he looked back toward the bedroom door. Toward Luke. "How's it going over there?"

Jericho's attention was drawn that way despite not wanting to see Luke in that condition, and for the first time he noticed the two paramedics with his cousin. They were also wearing hard-shell backpacks, appropriately marked out with red crosses. The one on the right was holding an oxygen mask over Luke's face, with a tube leading back into the pack. Spidery arms extending from the other paramedic's pack were doing *something* to Luke, but Jericho couldn't see what.

Before he could begin to raise his hopes again, the paramedic on the left shook his head. "Vic's deceased, I'm afraid. Unresponsive to resuscitation, catastrophic organ failure due to multiple penetrating trauma, blood pressure is basically zero, and core temp is dropping." At some unseen command, the arms began to retract into the backpack. His colleague released the oxygen mask and it automatically reeled back into his pack via the hose. "Same deal with the female vic in the bedroom. I'm calling it. We're going to need a second Rover."

I didn't even see them go in the bedroom. Events were moving too fast for Jericho now. At that point, he was past caring who or what a 'Rover' was.

"Son of a *bitch*," muttered Stirling, shaking his head. "Okay, once the DL gets here, it shouldn't be too hard for you to prove that you aren't the perp, and then we can wait for the street boys to bring him in so you can ask him why."

"Yeah," muttered Jericho. Not twenty-four hours earlier, Luke had caustically pointed out that Jericho had never even solved a murder. Now, he was setting out to solve the motive behind *Luke's* murder, and he was barely able to string two thoughts together. Luke would've appreciated the irony; Jericho had a harder time doing it.

And of course, Bobbi was dead as well. He felt bad for not having thought of her earlier. While he'd liked her and considered her a nice person, his connection with her was nothing like it had been with Luke. But he wasn't about to forget her altogether. *I swear to the both of you, no matter how long it takes, I* will *make sure this asshat goes down for what he's done.*

When he took a deep breath to center himself, the rank odor of blood filled his nostrils. He'd thought that his exposure to the smell had deadened his senses to it, but he was badly wrong. Worse, the harder he tried to force control over himself, the more a massive tide of grief and anger threatened to sweep him under and the more his heartbeat thundered in his ears. "I gotta get out of here," he mumbled, covering his nose and mouth with one hand.

He made it three hasty steps into the corridor before his legs gave out. Falling to his hands and knees, he threw up everything in his stomach.

31
Clearing the Air

Jericho had no idea how long he spent hunched over in misery, his stomach muscles still cramping and heaving even though there was nothing but bile to bring up. Slowly, he brought them under control; that, at least, he could still do. "Oh, god," he groaned softly.

"How you feeling, champ? You all done?" Stirling patted him on the back, then offered him a plastic canteen and a handful of alcohol wipes. "Here, clean yourself up and get the taste out of your mouth."

Squatting back on his heels, Jericho first wiped his mouth clean then took a hefty swig of water from the canteen. Swirling it around in his mouth, he looked for someplace to spit.

Divining his need, Stirling indicated the noisome mess on the floor before him. "Go ahead. It's not like you're gonna make it any worse."

It took two more rinses before Jericho was no longer tasting his own stomach acids. Then he took another mouthful and deliberately blew it out through his nose, flushing the water through his sinuses to get rid of the residue there. It stung like all *crap*, but that was at least something he could handle as a prodigy. There were a few spots on his arms and hands, which yielded easily to the alcohol wipes. However, this still left the problem of the mess of vomit in the hallway. He was keenly aware that all the cops in the vicinity had withdrawn to a discreet distance.

Detective Sergeant Stirling, who'd winced at Jericho's rough and ready approach to clearing out his sinuses, raised his eyebrows. "Better now?" At Jericho's nod, he gestured toward the wall of the corridor. "You're gonna want to step back a bit." Looking down the corridor, he made a beckoning gesture and raised his voice. "Okay, sixteen! Cleanup time!"

Jericho looked around to see one of the automated room-service carts approaching. As far as he could tell, it was the same one that had welcomed them to the Oaklands. He backed away from the mess on the floor, watching incuriously as spinning brushes unfolded from the front of the cart.

"Spillage detected. Cleaning in operation. Please stand clear." The cart moved up to the mess, brushes deftly directing all the stray splatters into the center of its path. It kept rolling forward steadily, and he heard a gurgling noise from beneath. Where it went, it left a clean path behind.

Back and forth the cart tracked, doing a far more thorough job than Jericho would have under the circumstances. By the time it was finished, the floor was pristine; a couple of jets of air freshener had even disposed of the last of the smell. **"Spillage removed. New spillage detected within apartment one-two-zero-four. Permission requested to enter apartment one-two-zero-four and clean spillage."**

"Ah, no. Permission not given." Stirling watched the cart carefully, as if he were worried that it would charge past him and start mopping up evidence anyway. "You can go now. We'll call for a cleanup when we need one."

"Permission to clean spillage not given. Room Service one-six requested to leave vicinity. Is that your requirement?"

"Yes," the detective sergeant replied firmly. "That is my requirement."

"Thank you. Have a pleasant morning." The cart rolled onto the strip of linoleum and trundled away down the corridor from whence it had come.

Jericho watched it go. "Handy," he observed, unable to muster more interest than that.

"Yeah, they are. A bit eager to please, but you learn to deal with that. That's the Oaklands all over," Stirling pointed at a discreetly placed air vent. "Air intake for climate control. They've got molecular filters inside, with real-time analysis going on twenty-four-seven. If certain molecules get past a given concentration, a call gets automatically placed. For puke, one of their cleaning carts shows up. For blood, we show up. But you don't care about that right now, do you?"

"Not particularly," Jericho conceded. He realized he could've made a break for it any time the cart was working, but what was the point? The cops were tracking the murderer down without requiring assistance from him. It helped to know that the guy would soon be behind bars (if they even *used* cells with bars in this goddamn city) but his mind kept circling the drain with a single heartbreaking mantra: *Luke's dead. Luke's dead. Luke's dead.* He had no idea how Olivia was going to take the news, or Uncle Leroy and Aunt Ellie, or Serena. Hell, he still didn't know how *he* was going to cope. It was too much, too *big* to handle all at once.

Slumping back against the wall, he let himself slide down until he was sitting on the floor, his elbows resting on his knees. Bowing his head forward, he covered it with his arms, the handcuff on his left wrist pressing cool against the skin beside his ear. He had no idea what he was going to do now. What he was *supposed* to do. It was his fault Luke had come to Utopia City. His fault Luke was dead. *If I'd just let myself be happy in Savannah, Luke would still be alive.* Could he even *do* this anymore? Did he deserve to be in Force Majeure? Eyes open or closed, it didn't matter; all he could see was Luke's face in that instant after he realized his cousin was dead.

A fumbling at his wrist distracted him and he looked up to see Stirling unlocking the cuff. "Can't have you walking off with this, champ," the detective sergeant pointed out. A click, and the heavy metal came free. He moved away then, but didn't go too far.

Jericho was acutely aware that the guy was keeping a close eye on him, even as he stood chatting with the CSI crew. Nobody tried to talk to Jericho, which he counted as a blessing. *If I'd come straight back here after meeting Transit,* he raged at himself. *I would've been here when the murderer showed up. Things would've gone a whole lot differently.* Round and round his mind went, driving his thoughts in ever-tighter spirals. *Why did it even happen? Was this guy after Luke, or Bobbi ... or me? Or was it a case of mistaken identity?* He simply could not comprehend the level of savagery in the attack being directed against a total stranger.

A thought struck him, and he raised his head. "Detective Sergeant." His voice was scratchy; in anticipation of what was to come, his throat already felt raw. Tears were threatening to fall. Many, many tears. But he couldn't let it happen; not yet.

Stirling turned toward him; compassion written across his features. "Yeah, what's the problem?"

Jericho nodded at the door to the apartment. "You didn't kick it in. How did you get it open?" He asked the question, not *despite* the fact that Luke lay dead in the apartment beyond, but *because* of it. If Luke's killer was to be brought to justice — whatever form *that* took — then he needed to understand more pieces of the puzzle. How the police had gotten the door open possibly had a bearing on how the killer had let himself in.

Stirling tapped a flat pouch on his belt. "Police override card. We all carry 'em. Biometrically coded like the MagCards, so only authorized police officers can use 'em. Why do you … ah." He looked over at the door, then at Jericho. "You're wondering if whoever did this used a card like that." He rubbed his neatly trimmed gray-shot beard reflectively. "Well, it's *possible*. But using a cop override card automatically sends a complete report of what door was overridden and who was holding it at the time, back to the UCPD headquarters. We've got people whose job is to find reports like that and link them to ongoing cases. Nothing like that's popped up for us. However that door got opened, it wasn't with a legal override."

"How about an *illegal* override?" persisted Jericho. "Your tech's amazing, but what one person can program, another person can hack. What if someone made an override card that acted like the ones you use, except it didn't report to anyone?" The idea was scary. In fact, it was terrifying. A cold-blooded murderer loose in Utopia City, able to walk through any electronic security? Nobody would be safe.

Stirling raised his shaggy eyebrows. "Son, I'm gonna give you the benefit of the doubt, and assume you're not thinkin' straight. The guy who designed the overrides is the same one who designed the MagCards." He paused expectantly.

Jericho stared back at him until the penny dropped. "Oh. The Technologist." It was obvious when he thought about it. Equally obvious was the fact that he *hadn't* been thinking about it, until right now.

"You got it." Stirling nodded. "A lot of artificers build stuff that us normals scratch our heads over. The Technologist builds stuff that other artificers go nuts trying to duplicate. He gave us the MagCard and the override about thirteen years ago, and if they were in *any* way hackable or able to be duplicated, we woulda heard about it by now. Unless *nobody* used the hacked version, ever, there'd be quirks and glitches in the system that we could backtrack. And can you imagine someone building something like that and *never* using it?"

"Damn it, no. I can't." Jericho shook his head. "Okay, it wasn't an override card, and nobody busted the door in. Which means it was opened from the inside. Pretty sure none of us knew anyone in Utopia City. Which means they either let the killer in, begging the question of *why*, or there's an Enabled in town who can bypass locked doors without leaving a mark on them. And you'd know more about that side of things than I would."

"That was something I was going to ask you later but sure, this works." Stirling was holding an electronic pad, made small by his beefy hand. His fingers tapped nimbly over its screen, then he looked over it at Jericho. "I can check on the Enabled thing but for now, you're certain neither of your friends knew anyone in Utopia? Or had someone meeting them, or joining them?"

Jericho blinked. The question had cleared his mind, leaving potential answers he didn't like. "I …" Luke *had* to have been here to meet with the Southsiders. There weren't many other reasons for his presence in the city. But how did he even admit that he knew of his cousin's criminal leanings? And why would *they* have even come to the Oaklands to kill him? "… I have no idea."

"Damn." Stirling folded the pad over like a wallet and slid it into a pouch on his belt. "Still, it's something we can look at. Anything else?"

"Yeah, actually." Jericho looked up at the burly detective sergeant. "Where exactly is my Designated Liaison?"

"That would be me." The voice, coming from farther down the hallway, sounded vaguely familiar. Jericho looked around to see a Hispanic woman in her early to mid-thirties approaching them, flanked by a pair of Enabled. She wore a police uniform with sergeant's insignia and a severe expression. Flicking a glance at Stirling, she indicated Jericho with a tilt of her head as he climbed to his feet. "Finlay. You called for a Designated Liaison. This the guy?"

The Enabled to Finlay's right was one Jericho had never seen before. The man was of moderate height and more than average bulk, though a certain amount of that was probably due to the heavy bulletproof vest he was wearing, along with what looked like tactical SWAT gear. The only thing that really clued Jericho in that he was wearing a costume rather than a uniform was the large white 'C' with the number '2' inside it, printed on the front of his vest. His helmet faceplate was tinted to hide his features, which was another indicator.

On Finlay's left, however, was someone with whom he was definitely familiar. Independence wore a form-fitting costume in muted reds and blues with SWAT-style goggles to conceal her identity; he'd already known that bit. Likewise, her waist-length platinum-blonde hair was pulled back and secured by a tie at the base of her neck. This close, however, he could tell her outfit was definitely bulkier than spandex, with strategic padding that shouted 'body armor' to him, as well as black straps crossing over her chest. These probably supported the harness that held her sword—he could see the hilt protruding from behind her left shoulder—and her assault rifle, the stock of which was visible over her right shoulder. A belt, also black, held pouches of varying size and shape, including some that almost certainly held spare magazines for the assault rifle.

An unexpected reminder of her humanity and fallibility came in the form of a low-profile brace on her left knee, not unlike the one Nighthawk had been wearing on the train. From the irritated look on her face, she would much rather have been resting up with an icepack than attending this kind of do-nothing duty. He empathized, while hoping that she wouldn't hold it against him.

"This is the guy," Stirling confirmed. "Need us to pull back out of the corridor?"

Finlay shook her head. "Nah, we're good." Jericho frowned, wondering where he'd met her before, especially since her name also sounded familiar. The woman's expression sharpened. "Hey, feller, you okay with me as your DL? Because I can just go if you're not. No skin off mine."

"Well, I just want to get this over with so we can get on with catching the *actual* goddamn bad guy," Jericho said candidly. "And to be honest, I'm just trying to figure out where I know your voice from."

"Huh. That *is* funny." She tilted her head. "I could swear I've heard your voice somewhere too. But that doesn't matter right now." Her gaze shifted to Stirling and her frown deepened. "Seriously? You attended a serious assault call without a DL on hand?"

"Hey, you guys don't grow on trees," Stirling said defensively. "Anyway, there was no word of an Enabled being involved."

"Any call to the Oaklands means there's a good chance of an out-of-town Enabled being involved *somehow*," she pointed out with an air of strained patience. Turning back to Jericho, she let out a sigh. "Sorry about the mix-up." Reaching into her pocket, she pulled out a folding wallet. When she flipped it open, Jericho saw a card embossed with the Great Seal of the United States, the image surrounded by the title DESIGNATED LIAISON. It included the woman's picture, and informed Jericho that her name was Diane Finlay. Again, the name rang a bell but before he could follow up on it, she was talking again, in a tone of voice that suggested she was giving a memorized speech. "I'm a Designated Liaison to the UCPD, authorized for this position by the US government, the state government of Kansas and the Mayor's office of Utopia City. My function is to evaluate the potential involvement of Enabled identities in crimes, without revealing those identities to the public at large. I am legally bound to maintain absolute confidentiality about any information I learn in the execution of my duties. If I were to betray this trust, I would suffer substantial legal penalties under the Challenger Act, including but not limited to incarceration in Federal prison." She dropped the robotic act and kept talking as she put the wallet away. "Basically, my job is to find out who you are when you're in costume and ascertain where you were when this crime was being committed. Once I'm satisfied you weren't involved with this, I tell the guys and they drop you as a suspect so they can move on with the case."

Jericho nodded. "Yeah, I've already been told about that bit. Just not how it worked."

From her expression, this wasn't the first time Finlay had explained this aspect as well. "That card I just showed you gives me the equivalent of a Top-Secret clearance. Trust me when I say that people will believe me when I say you're in the clear. But hey, if you want to get arrested and processed and go through the whole nine yards, it's your choice. Nobody's forcing you to do this."

Jericho glanced at Stirling, as the closest thing he had seen to a friendly face so far. The detective sergeant gave him an encouraging nod. "She's on the level, champ. This is the way we handle this sort of shit."

For what Jericho suspected would not be the last time, he wished Luke and Bobbi were still alive to advise him. *Or just plain still alive.* Despite the bone-deep pang it caused him, he put the thought aside for the moment. He had to see this through, and breaking down in front of all these cops would do nobody any good at all.

"Yeah." It was more a sigh than a word. "Let's do this thing."

"Good." All business once more, Finlay indicated the dead-end section of corridor that ended at the window. "That opens up?"

Jericho nodded. "Yeah. There's a reader."

"Good. Independence, could you please secure the perimeter?"

Jericho stepped aside as Independence moved up to him. Despite the situation, he felt a tinge of awe at being in the presence of such a famous Enabled. Coming in just behind Castellan and just ahead of Tesseract Power, she was one of *the* prodigies everyone wanted to emulate. Her eyes raked down his body in a single scathing assessment and dismissed him in that same moment—*not worth my time*—before she passed him by. This neither surprised nor dismayed him; he had years to go before he could even hope to be as good as she was. So smoothly that he hadn't even seen her palm the card, she tapped the reader and the window swiveled open for her. Stepping out onto the ladder, she tapped the outside reader and the window closed once more.

Finlay turned her attention to Jericho and lowered her voice. "Your costume's on site?"

It wasn't like he could exactly deny it. "Yeah, it's in a zipper bag just inside the door. Black nylon."

She nodded. "Got it." Raising her hand, she gestured at the waiting CSI guys. "There's a black nylon bag with a shoulder-strap just inside the front door. I need it now."

The closest CSI guy glanced at Stirling, who gestured impatiently. "You heard the lady. Get it."

Jericho watched as the guy fetched the satchel and brought it over to Finlay. She took it, then turned to the second Enabled. "Okay, bubble us. Usual parameters." Before he had a chance to wonder what that meant, a silver-gray field descended around the pair of them.

Reaching out, Jericho pressed on the curved surface; it gave, but only a little. "Okay," he said dubiously. "Um ... I have to ask. Is it actually a good idea to put you into a force field bubble with a murder suspect?"

She gave him a tolerant chuckle. "Yes, it actually is. This bubble's permeable to me but not to you. I can walk out any time. Even if you attacked with overwhelming force and killed me before I had a chance to escape, Second Chance could wind back events in the bubble to before I got hurt, then freeze everything and pull me out. And *then* Independence would kick your ass into next week. But that's not going to happen, is it?"

Which explained why the guy was called 'Second Chance'. "Well, no. I don't have any plans to hurt you," admitted Jericho immediately. "What are the 'usual parameters'?"

She tilted her head to acknowledge the question. "Nobody can hear either of us. I'm the only one they can see, and only in silhouette. Which means they can't overhear us and they can't lip-read through the bubble, but they *can* keep track of my well-being."

Jericho knew he had no way of verifying her words, but it seemed Designated Liaisons came with some pretty harsh penalties for playing fast and loose with information. On balance, he decided, she was probably telling the truth. "Okay. So where do we go from here?"

Her voice was crisp. "Step one. Anything else in the apartment that might out you?"

Jericho had to take a moment to think about this. "Just my phone. Call logs and stuff."

"Got it." Finlay nodded firmly. "You have it on you right now?"

The phone usually resided in a pouch on his utility belt, which was in the satchel she was holding. He pointed. "In there."

"Good. Step two. You need to tell me the sequence of events before you came on the scene, and anything you can tell me about your superhero identity." Finlay looked at him expectantly.

"Okay." Jericho did his best to get his chaotic thoughts into order. It felt beyond bizarre to be telling a near-total stranger his deepest secret, so he held off on that until he had no choice. "I was patrolling over at the Market. Well, to be honest, I kind of interceded with a couple of undercover cops for getting rough with a kid. Tossed one of them in the canal. Then I—"

"Wait." The woman held up one hand. "G-Man? You're *G-Man?*" The smile that spread across her face was as unexpected as it was welcome. "Hah. This is gonna be a slam-dunk."

Jericho's brain skidded to a halt. "Wait, how did you know my name? I hadn't even got that far yet." Paranoia added itself to the swirl of thoughts in his head.

She snorted with laughter, then shook her head. "We spoke on the phone. I was on switch room duty until they called me in on this. I *knew* your voice was familiar. You called and said you were going to be patrolling. Remember what I said just before we hung up?"

Finlay. Holy crap. Now it was evident where he'd heard her voice. It was an effort to push back past all the events of the night to the phone conversation on top of the apartment building. He frowned, concentrating. "Wait ... you said ... good hunting?"

A satisfied smile crossed her face. "Exactly. When I heard about you dumping Forrester in the canal, I laughed my ass off. So, we just need one more thing."

"What's that?" he asked.

"Power demonstration." She turned her hands palm-up. "Just something small, to make sure that the G-Man I spoke to then is the G-Man I'm talking to now."

"Right." He took a deep breath, then reduced his own effective weight to its minimum. Jumping lightly into the air, he tucked his knees into his chest and drifted through a slow-motion backflip before landing lightly on his feet once more. "Good enough?"

"Definitely good enough. The 'G' stands for 'gravity', I take it?"

She was clearly guessing; it was equally obvious that she'd never heard of him before. He successfully quashed the twinge of disappointment at his lack of fame. Right then, it wasn't important. "That's right. I can make myself or other things fall slower or faster."

She nodded. "Okay, that checks out." Her expression was focused as she pulled out what he took to be a standard smartphone, right up until he saw the holographic interface dancing above the 'screen'. "We're already cutting the timing fine with your stunt at the Market, but if we can nail you down as being someplace else when the crime was under way, you're home and dry. Now, where did you go from the Market?"

He didn't want to talk about Thomas; fortunately, the conversation he'd had with the young prodigy wasn't part of this situation. "Went across the street and sat on top of a warehouse for a bit while I thought about exactly how I'd screwed up." He paused, thinking about how to word the next bit. "Then I changed out of my costume and took an air-cab to the South Side Mall, to see what it was really about."

"Air-cab," murmured Finlay, flicking holo-icons on the phone. "All right then … yes, found you. Air-cab to South Side. And then, twenty minutes later, you take one back to near the same location. No record of using your 'Card to purchase anything at the Mall itself. What were you doing in that time?"

"Playing in the gravity shaft," Jericho said with a blush, recalling the thoughts he'd had about Thomas at the time. "I can only glide on my own, but I'd give anything to be able to fly."

With a tolerant smile, Finlay shook her head and rolled her eyes. "Most of us can't even glide. So, the air-cab let you out a few blocks away from the Oaklands, just about the time the filters picked up the smell of fresh blood in your apartment and we got the alert. What did you do then?"

"I went back, rooftop-running." He snapped his fingers. "A hex went overhead just as I started my glide back to the Oaklands, if that helps."

"It does. Even when hexes are running patrol patterns, they're recording everything they see." She manipulated the interface for a few moments, then nodded. "Got it."

Leaning forward, he stared at the unfolding image. He'd seen the holographic screen on the kiosk in the maglev station but on something the size of a phone, it was even more impressive. It showed the top of the building he'd climbed onto after gliding across the street. A tiny person, arms outstretched, leaped outward and began to glide out of frame. Finlay did something to pause the action, then expanded the image until only the gliding figure was in the field of view. It was very clearly him, the wing-surfaces outstretched and the white 'G' showing up vividly against the black of his jacket. This was the first time he'd seen a picture of himself gliding from that angle; or from any angle, really.

"This is you?" she asked, as if there were many others in the city for whom gliding was a natural act. "And what's that cloth under your arms? Is that what you use to glide with?"

He was impressed; most people took a little longer to come to that conclusion. "That's me and yeah, the extra surface area and the slower falling rate is what lets me pull that off." He didn't bother going into how much trial and error had gone into making the gliding surfaces *work*.

"So, if I opened this bag, I'd find elements of the costume you're wearing in this image?" she pressed.

"Yeah." Now Jericho knew what she was pushing toward. "My jacket, mask, gloves and utility belt."

"Noted." Tucking the satchel under her arm, she undid the zipper and reached inside. The first thing she pulled out was the sleeve of the jacket, which she kept on tugging at until half the garment was out of the bag. "Emblem checks out," she murmured, half to herself. "Gliding surfaces, too." She turned toward him as she squeezed part of the jacket between thumb and forefinger. "What's this stuff I can feel inside it?"

"Plastic plates to stop knives," he said, suddenly shy about the fact that he was showing off makeshift body armor to someone who probably made a practice of wearing the real thing.

"I see." Her voice was devoid of judgement, for which he was grateful. Stuffing the jacket back into the satchel, she zipped it up and handed it back to him. Turning her attention back to her phone, she began to page through settings on the holographic file. "Okay, given these timestamps, you were all the way over at South Side when it was going down. You're cleared." She put away her phone and offered her hand. "Sorry for your loss."

"Thanks." He shook it with a grimace at the reminder. "What happens now?"

Raising her other hand, she snapped the fingers twice. The bubble faded away, leaving Second Chance and the others watching them expectantly. "He's in the clear," she stated firmly. "Carry on." Her expression was sympathetic as she put a hand on Jericho's shoulder. "I know it all sucks right now, but Utopia's got the best CSI department on the *planet*. They'll catch the bastard who did this and bring him down."

"Thanks," he said again, knowing how inadequate it was. In about one minute, she'd sliced through what would've been an insuperable obstacle of red tape anywhere else. For her, it was all in a night's work.

"You're welcome," she said lightly. "And when they find out who he is, I hope you get to hunt him down and kick his ass." As she turned away, he heard the window behind him open and close again. A moment later, Independence brushed past him once more.

He watched as Finlay, flanked by the two heroes, headed off down the corridor. Then he turned to Stirling. "Okay," he said. "What do I do now?"

"Nothing," the detective sergeant said bluntly. "Sorry, champ, but all we can do now is stay out of the way while the experts do their job." A moment later, he blinked as something seemed to occur to him. "Well, unless you happen to know a superhero with, uh, special senses or something?" He paused, eyeing Jericho significantly.

A moment later, Jericho got the hint. *He's asking me if my Enabled identity can do anything to help.* "No, I don't know anyone like that," he admitted. He could read a basic crime scene reasonably well, but only up to the level of a talented amateur. Next to trained experts equipped with Utopia City's level of technology, he'd be so far behind the curve it wouldn't even be funny. Besides, as much as he wanted to help, he wasn't sure how long he could maintain his current act. Sooner or later, things were going to break free and he was going to crash, hard. Once that happened, he'd be worse than useless.

"Copy that," Stirling replied. "We've contacted the Oaklands management, and they've offered you use of another apartment on this floor, free of charge. Number one-two-one-two. You okay with that, or would you rather come back to the precinct and spend the night there?"

No matter what happened, he was going to have a bad night of it. He knew that for a fact. And while he knew the police would be sympathetic, he really wanted to be alone for this. "I'll stay in the Oaklands, thanks."

"Whatever suits you." Stirling handed him something. "You're gonna need this." It was his MagCard. He didn't even remember dropping it.

"Thanks, I … what the *hell?*" His upcoming ordeal temporarily forgotten, he stared at the pair of mechanical apparitions which had just rounded the corner and were proceeding along the corridor toward himself and Stirling. About four feet high and seven feet long, each of them moved with a mincing gait on four efficient-looking legs, emitting only the faintest of humming noises. While the legs were black and metallic, each curved upper body had a white carapace with a red cross displayed prominently in the middle. They moved with a subtly inhuman grace.

"Those are Rovers," Stirling explained quietly. "The medics use them all the time. Semi-autonomous gurneys. Gyro-stabilized and able to cover just about any terrain you can find. They can both monitor the patient and administer treatment on the move. It's a licensed variation of an experimental military robot that they've been working on out East for a few years." Hometown pride was evident in his voice as he added, "But our version's smarter and faster and a lot more versatile."

Jericho shook his head, which was starting to develop an ache between the eyebrows. He watched as each Rover, placing its round-ball 'feet' with the precision of a dancer, entered the apartment, and a lump arose in his throat. He knew what they were there for, and he didn't want to think about it.

Stirling, watching him keenly, slapped him on the shoulder. "Listen, you're d— uh, you look like shit. Go get your head down. We'll talk in the morning."

"Right." Jericho let out his breath in a sigh. He could already feel the stinging behind his eyelids which told him tears were not all that far away. This time, he wouldn't be able to hold them back. "Which way's the apartment I'm staying in?"

"I have no goddamn idea," Stirling admitted. He held up a hand and gestured to one of the other officers. "Clancy, walk this guy up around the corner, will you? There's a room service cart that can take him the rest of the way. Apartment one-two-one-two."

"Sure thing, detective sergeant." The officer called Clancy nodded to Jericho. "Come on, sir."

"Thanks," said Jericho. He moved past Stirling, then stopped and turned. "And thanks for …" Words failed him. "… everything."

Stirling nodded; his expression sympathetic. "You go get some sleep. I'll see you in the morning."

Oh, crap. Jericho suddenly recalled that in the morning, he was due to go and attend his interview with Force Majeure. He had no idea how he was going to manage that, or *if* he was going to be able to manage it.

I'm a prodigy. We do the impossible on a regular basis. If he could just convince himself he was capable of it, he could do it. *Besides, Luke would want me to follow through. He didn't make me get on the maglev just so I could wimp out now.*

He followed Clancy down the corridor and around the corner, clutching his MagCard and costume satchel like talismans. His feet wanted to stumble, both from fatigue and reaction to what had happened, but he didn't let them. Sure enough, one of the room service carts had parked itself on the linoleum strip. The numbers one and three were painted on the front of the cart.

"Room service one-three," Clancy said out loud. Jericho couldn't have spoken, even if he wanted to. The painful lump in his throat was back. Tears welled in his eyes and he blinked them away.

"Greetings. I am Room Service one-three. May I help you?" The voice held the same synthesized feminine tone as the other room service robot had.

"Yes. This man needs to go to apartment one-two-one-two." Clancy spoke in a matter-of-fact tone.

"You wish to be guided to apartment one-two-one-two. Is that your requirement?"

"Yes." As Clancy spoke, more tears were flooding Jericho's vision to the point that he was having trouble even reading room numbers now.

"Understood. Apartment one-two-one-two is in this direction. Please follow me." The cart didn't bother turning around; it merely motored off along the strip of linoleum as if 'front' and 'back' were interchangeable concepts for it. At Clancy's encouraging nod, Jericho followed along, concentrating on putting one foot before the other.

The little room service cart rolled down one corridor after another, weaving its way through the building without pause. Eventually, it slowed to a halt. The mechanical arm unstowed itself from the side of the cart and pointed toward a particular door. **"That is apartment one-two-one-two. Do you require further assistance?"**

Jericho didn't answer; he couldn't. Moving past the cart, he swiped the MagCard blindly across the reader and lurched in through the door as it swung open. The immediate impression he got of the apartment was that it was smaller than the one he'd been in before, with a different canvas print on the wall. But he wasn't worried about that. Dropping the satchel and MagCard on the floor, he began pulling his clothes off as he headed for the bathroom.

"Your clothing has suffered contamination from potentially infectious biological material. Would you like me to clean it for you?"

"Whatever," he choked out. Right then, he was at the end of his rope.

The bathroom door opened before him, and he more or less fell into the shower cubicle. An unaimed shove at the shower control lever brought the water pouring down on top of him, just hot enough to be painful. Uncaring, he slumped to the floor of the cubicle, knees drawn up to his chest. As the shower pounded on his head and back, his own floodgates opened. The stark, sterile white tiles echoed back his racking sobs as he gave way at last to the bone-deep grief that had been tearing at him ever since he realized that his best friend, his closest friend, was dead.

"Luuuuuke!" he howled in anguish, hot tears running down his face and mingling with the water from the shower. *"LUUUUUUUUKE!"*

No answer came. Alone in a city of over a million people, he screamed his pain and loss until his voice cracked and his throat ached.

Utterly bereft, Jericho Hansen grieved.

32
Coming to Grips

Jericho stood atop the Spire, impossibly high in the sky. The Oaklands was far below him. He was master of all he surveyed. Utopia City spread out before him in all its glory. He could reach out, look into any of the homes, ensure that everyone was safe. He was a hero. It was what he did. He kept everyone safe.

"Cuz!" It was Luke's voice, coming from the Oaklands. "Cuz! Help!"

That was odd. Luke had never needed help before, for as long as Jericho had known him. He looked, focusing his vision, and saw that Luke was under attack by a shadowy form. The man held a knife of living flame that darted and slashed at Luke even as his cousin shielded Bobbi from the attacker. Already, blood flowed from Luke's wounds. There was so much blood.

"I'm coming, Luke! I'm coming!" Jericho leaped from his elevated perch, spread his arms, and prepared to plummet to the rescue. But something was wrong with his powers. He couldn't speed himself up. Luke came no closer. Jericho found himself forced to land on the side of the Spire. He spread his arms again, leaped off, and dived to the rescue.

"Help!" called Bobbi. "Save us! I'm not a superhero yet, so you have to save us!" The shadow man darted past Luke and slashed at her, and Jericho screamed as he saw blood flowing from her gouged-out eyes.

The air was like tar. He strained to reach them faster, but even putting his arms to his sides only increased his speed by a tiny amount. "Luke, I'm coming! Hold on!" he called out desperately, as if saying so made it more likely to happen.

And then he was standing in the same room, watching helplessly as Luke took the knife-blow to the throat. Blood sprayed out, coating the room, coating Jericho, coating everything and everyone except the shadowy man. The man whose face Jericho couldn't see. The man who laughed as Luke fell to the floor so slowly, blood still spraying from his throat like a fire hose.

"I'll kill you!" screamed Jericho, leaping toward the man with his fist drawn back to punch. But no matter how he flailed and swung and kicked, the man ducked and dodged every blow. And every time he dodged, he slashed at Bobbi. More slashes hit her, cutting up her face.

"You're supposed to save us," she said calmly through her ruined mouth, even as the killer plunged the grotesquely long knife into her heart. "You weren't supposed to run off and leave us alone." She fell backward into the closet that had always been behind her, and Jericho leaped at the killer once more with a bellow of rage. The man dissipated like a shadow made of spider-webs, leaving behind just an echo of mocking laughter.

"It's your fault!" shouted the bearded police detective from the Market, waving a pistol in his face. "You're no hero!"

All the shoppers from the Market turned and sang in chorus, "You're no hero! You're no hero!" Even the cop he'd thrown into the canal, floating face-down and drowning, blew bubbles in time with the words.

"I am a hero!" shouted Jericho desperately. "I save people!"

"Didn't save your buddy, champ." Detective Sergeant Stirling entered the room riding a Rover like a horse, chasing a room service cart that was mopping up all the evidence. "You got here too late and got arrested for the murder." He clamped thick, shiny handcuffs on Jericho's wrists, then galloped off in pursuit of the room service cart as it took the corner on two wheels.

"Cuz." It was Luke's voice. Jericho dropped to his knees beside Luke. He tried to pick his cousin up, but the pieces of wood Luke was holding were too big and got in the way.

"Luke," sobbed Jericho. "Don't die. Stay with me. Don't go away." He got his arms around his cousin and started to drag him. He was in Utopia City, and they had the best hospitals anywhere. He could save Luke's life if he could only get him to a hospital.

"They don't know how to save him." It was Sergeant Finlay, trapped in a silver-gray bubble like a snow globe ornament. *"I'm a Designated Liaison and I'm the only one who knows how."*

"Then tell me!" begged Jericho. *"Tell me how to save him!"*

"That's easy," she said. *"All you have to do is—"*

Independence drew her sword and popped the bubble. It vanished, leaving nothing behind.

"Tell me!" pleaded Jericho of the veteran superhero. *"Tell me what I have to do!"*

She looked him in the eye and shook her head then turned and hobbled off, an arrow sticking out of her knee.

"Cuz." It was Luke's voice again. He grasped Jericho's hand. *"Cuz. Why'd ya do it?"*

"Why did I do what?" asked Jericho. He looked down as Luke's last breath rattled in his throat, meeting his cousin's one good eye, and discovered that his hand was wrapped around the hilt of the knife that was sunk deep into Luke's chest.

"No!" he shouted, opening his eyes and sitting bolt upright on what turned out to be a sofa. A blanket slid off his chest into his lap. Silence greeted his outburst, and darkness filled the apartment.

Slowly, he forced his breathing to ease off, as he could feel the light-headedness of hyperventilation coming on. His heart hammered in his chest, and he was drenched with sweat. There was a dull ache in his forehead that he recognized as a sign of dehydration, aided and abetted by a monumental case of dry mouth.

"Son of a *bitch*," he mumbled. He could only remember snatches of the nightmare even now, but it took a lot to raise his heart rate this much. Every time he closed his eyes, he saw Luke's face with his single staring eye and for the life of him, he could not figure out if it was a real memory or a remnant of the dream.

Whichever one it was, it brought home the brutal truth to him. Luke was dead. Nothing was ever going to change that. Luke had accompanied Jericho to Utopia City, and now he was dead. While his death could not be totally laid at Jericho's feet—nobody had ever been able to tell Luke what to do, or what not to do—Jericho felt responsible enough that it made him sick to his stomach. *If I hadn't come to Utopia City, if we hadn't come here, he'd still be alive. How the hell am I supposed to live with that?*

He put his feet on the floor, more of the blanket sliding off and making him aware that he wasn't wearing anything under it. *Who put this over me?* In the state he'd been in, he could see himself making it to the sofa, but there was no way he would've had the presence of mind to find the blanket and cover himself with it. If he'd been that together, he would've woken up on the bed.

Stumbling to his feet, he wrapped the blanket around himself. The last thing he wanted to do was find out that a cop had been assigned to watch over him by giving them a full-frontal flash. There was just enough illumination coming in through the window to let him find his way to the kitchen nook, alongside the closed bedroom door. His questing hand found what his eyes had missed, brushing across a light switch. A sharp click sounded, and light flooded through the small apartment. The glare-blindness only lasted for a moment before his eyes adjusted.

As in the previous apartment, there were glasses in the cupboard under the counter. Awkwardly holding the blanket around himself, he took one out and filled it at the sink. The first glass took care of the dryness in his mouth, and the next three took the edge off the dehydration headache. The fourth was half-empty when he tipped it out and placed the glass in the sink. Leaning back against the counter, he looked around at the apartment, taking stock of his surroundings for the first time.

As he'd seen when he came in, the living room was smaller than the one in the other apartment. Instead of the Spire at night, the canvas print portrayed a wider view of Utopia City at either sunrise or sunset; he was insufficiently familiar with the city to determine which. Aside from the sofa (which wasn't a fold-out model) there was the kitchen nook, the bedroom (which he had yet to see inside) and the bathroom (with which he was altogether too familiar). A flat-screen TV of identical make to the one in the last apartment took up a good chunk of the wall opposite the sofa. This, then, was his living situation until something better could be arranged.

He opened the bedroom door to find it unoccupied. There was one queen-sized bed, made up neatly, with his costume satchel sitting beside a small pile of folded clothing, on the end of the bed. At the foot of the bed rested his boots. He ignored the phone, the MagCard and the TV remote on the bedside table in favor of more important matters. On closer examination, the clothing on the bed was either what he'd been wearing before, or a set of unreasonably precise duplicates. Presuming it was his original clothing, at some point it had been laundered and dried, and he *knew* he hadn't done that. Likewise, his boots had been meticulously cleaned and polished.

Holding the blanket around him, he stuck the pile of clothing together with a couple of glue-tags so he could pick it all up in one piece. Then he headed for the bathroom. As he'd guessed, there was a clean, dry towel hanging on the rail, where he almost certainly *hadn't* left it. Dropping his clothes onto the lid of the washer-dryer, he tossed the blanket out into the living room and stepped into the shower. He retained enough fragments of the nightmare that he had no intention of going back to sleep, but at least he could shower away the outward evidence.

As the hot water cascaded down his body, he mused over the fact that his clothing had been laundered and his boots cleaned. Then there was the fact that the towel had been hung up (or washed and *then* hung up) and the blanket spread over him as he slept. Either someone (probably a cop, given that the Oaklands didn't seem to have any human cleaning staff) had tended to his needs … or the room service robot had done it all, without him telling it to.

By the time he got out of the shower, he was leaning toward the latter theory, but he wasn't quite sure how he felt about it. On the one hand, he'd undoubtedly needed the assistance. On the other … asking permission would've been nice. *Unless saying 'whatever' gave it enough wiggle room to do all this? I think I'm gonna need to be careful what I say around them.*

After drying himself off, he got dressed, trying to ignore his reflection in the mirror. The few glances that he did catch proved that he looked more haggard than he had in years. But with all that, putting his clothing on was a transformative act. Naked, even with a blanket for cover, he'd felt vulnerable and exposed.

Clothed and ready for action, he headed back to the bedroom. A check of the satchel confirmed that the contents were all present and correct. Taking the MagCard, he tucked it into his pocket. The phone he kept in his hand as he walked out into the living room.

The TV had a remote sitting next to it; Jericho took this and settled back on the sofa, then dragged a cushion on to his lap and wrapped his arms around it. With that little bit of extra comfort dealt with, he began looking for an early morning news channel. With luck, the cops would've caught the asshat, and he'd be able to ask some questions and get closure for himself and Luke's family. With better luck, they'd have leads that he could follow and catch the guy first. Not that he had much in the way of hope for that scenario.

Of news channels there were many, but most of those were broadcasts from other cities or even other states. He cycled between the two local channels, *UC/24* and the unimaginatively named *Utopia News*, and found … nothing. No breathless reporting from the scene with red and blue lights flashing in the background, no armchair detective work into the identity or motives of the killer. On the one hand, he was pleased that there would be no microphones thrust into his face while a reporter yammered questions about how he felt regarding the death of his best friend. On the other … he scrubbed his hands over his face, trying to put words to his emotions. It just didn't feel *right* that Luke and Bobbi's passing had garnered such little attention. Not that he wanted a media circus, but there had to be a compromise between 'no attention' and '*all* the attention'.

He flicked back and forth between the two channels a few times, then found a menu button. Scrolling through the list of channels, he paused as he reached one simply called *Police Alerts.* When he pressed the Enter button, he found an interactive list of peoples' names. The one at the top showed an update time of only a couple of hours.

Jack Portman, he read. There was a face-on image of a guy with brutal good looks, and a few seconds of looped footage exhibiting a clarity and sharpness of detail surpassing every security camera he'd ever seen before. In the footage, the same man as in the picture hobbled into frame with his hands jammed into his pockets. When his face came into view, he seemed to notice the camera for the first time, and brought his right hand out of his pocket, far too late to conceal the vivid scratches down one side of his face where Bobbi had gotten him with her fingernails. A splash of crusted brown showed up dramatically on his knuckles as he rubbed at his forehead, the move clearly an excuse for concealing his identity. Then he limped jerkily onward, definitely favoring his left leg. With a sense of shock, Jericho recognized the background as the courtyard of the Oaklands. *Okay, that settles it. This is the guy. I bet I know exactly how he got that limp. And he didn't get it out and about, kicking ass and taking names.*

He studied the man's features intently, then scrolled down to find what the cops were saying about him. Wanted for questioning about a double homicide. Do not approach. Inform police or Force Majeure if seen. Last seen at … Jericho didn't know the location, but there was a low-detail map that showed it to be on the southern side of the city.

There were only a few ways to interpret that. This 'Jack Portman' guy had left the Oaklands just before Jericho had gotten back. On the security footage, he'd shown signs of having been in a fight, including fingernail gouges on his face and blood on his knuckles. The cops evidently hadn't caught up with him yet, but it looked like they'd tracked the car to some place near where the Southsiders held sway. But what was the connection? Was Portman a hitman? Someone who resented Luke's presence in the city? The timing didn't make sense. They'd barely been in the city six hours, and Luke hadn't even had the chance to get out and annoy anyone. And what sort of assassin went in after two people with a knife? Admittedly, he'd *won,* but a stupid winning move was still a stupid move. It left far too much leeway for the other target to call for help, to *run* for help, to join in the fight … anything, really. The fact that it *hadn't* happened didn't mean it *couldn't* happen. Any hired killer worth his salt would know this.

He grimaced, recognizing that he was avoiding thinking of one other possibility. *Is this Portman guy Enabled?* While this would go a long way toward clarifying how he'd succeeded in killing them both, it didn't help with the *why* at all. In fact, unless the criminal activities Luke had been involved in were a magnitude or two more profitable than Jericho was aware of, there was no way paying for an Enabled hitman would be worth the price.

Or did one of Adam Power's enemies somehow find out what Bobbi was planning to do, and take steps?

Which brought the questions around full circle. Who was Jack Portman? Was he Enabled, or a normal who just got lucky? What was Luke to him? Or Bobbi? Why did they let him in, or *did* they let him in?

And, most importantly: *Where can I find that sonovabitch?*

33
The Ugly Truth

He was still sitting on the sofa, the cushion on his lap and the few seconds of footage rolling over and over on the TV in front of him, when there came a knock on the door. With a blink and a start, he looked around. He'd been brooding, out of costume, in the living room of the apartment. This indicated just how screwed-up the situation was, and how desperately he needed to resolve what had happened. Which hadn't happened, of course. He was lacking in both information and the opportunity to get more.

The knock came again, and he tossed the cushion to one side and jumped to his feet. Just for a moment, he imagined it was the killer and he clenched his fists. He'd smear the guy into the ground and break every bone in his body if it was. "Who is it?"

"Stirling," called a familiar voice. "Can I come in?"

"Just a second." Forming a glue-tag in his hand, he approached the door. There was a sturdy-looking security chain on the frame, and he slid it into place. He hadn't noticed if there'd been one in 1204, but he was willing to assume it was there. Which made it even harder to puzzle out. If someone unknown to both Bobbi and Luke had knocked on the door, why hadn't they taken this most basic of precautions?

Keeping the hand with the 'tag out of sight, he opened the door. Stirling stood outside the apartment; as far as Jericho could tell, there was nobody with him. The door hit the limit of travel of the chain, so Jericho closed it slightly and took the chain off again. Without dissolving the 'tag, he opened the door.

"Getting a bit paranoid there, champ?" Stirling strode into the apartment as if he didn't have a care in the world.

Jericho closed the door, and finally allowed himself to relax far enough to dismiss the glue-tag. "I've been worrying at the problem for hours and I can't see how or why this even happened. For all I know, the guy was after *me*, not Luke or Bobbi. But I've never seen him before in my life. And how did he get inside? Was he Enabled? Have we got another Darksider on the loose?"

Stirling shuddered. "Don't even joke about that shit."

Most of the terror villains of the nineties had been dynamics, with a few artificers. Mutilator, Guillotine and the Darksider had been the only potential prodigies among them, each with a very impressive kill count to their name. The difference was that Mutilator had Devastator for backup, while Guillotine would've needed either an Artificer-created weapon or a Dynamic ability to produce the molecule-fine cuts that had removed heads and arms with such ease (not to mention the billowing clouds of fog that made it so much harder to target her in combat). The Darksider, with neither resource to fall back on, had been terrifying enough in his own right. No lock could hold him out, no amount of security could prevent his entry. And once he made it inside … he'd secured the exits so nobody could get *out*, then gone hunting. There had rarely been survivors.

"We know who, we know how, and we know why." Stirling put the discarded cushion back into place and settled onto the sofa, then looked at the TV. "Ah. You got the 'who' as well. Good."

"Yeah, but I don't know who this guy *is*," Jericho pointed out, trying not to take his frustration out on Stirling. "What's his game? Why Luke?"

"Before we get into that, how are *you* feeling?" asked Stirling bluntly. "Because you still look like ten miles of bad road. You're gonna need to sleep *sometime*, you know."

"Tried it." Jericho shook his head. "It's worse than staying awake. I can handle it, though. Done it before."

"Hmm." Stirling looked unconvinced, but he moved on all the same. "Okay, there's some stuff I'm gonna be filling you in on, but you need to be discreet about it and you definitely don't tell anyone where you got it from." He glanced around the room almost theatrically. "Normally I wouldn't even be doing this, but you look like a stand-up guy to me and … well, special circumstances and all that shit." Which was a roundabout way of saying he knew Jericho was a superhero, even if neither one of them was going to admit it.

Jericho nodded. "Understood. Anything you can tell me, I'll totally appreciate." *Holy crap, Stirling's actually going to Gordon me on this one?* He hadn't *expected* anything like this to happen, but he was definitely going to take it.

"Oh, this is nothing special," Stirling said. He was lying through his teeth, and they both knew it. "I'm just carrying out a welfare check on a private citizen. Aren't I?" He stared long and hard at Jericho to make his point, then took a deep breath. Despite his outward bravado, he still apparently had to brace himself to break the rules even this little bit. "So."

"So," echoed Jericho, encouragingly.

"So, a guy called Jack Portman came in on the maglev from Indianapolis last night." Stirling's casual tone was almost convincing.

With that simple statement, much fell into place. "Bobbi," Jericho said, enlightenment almost blinding him. "He's Bobbi's boyfriend. She *said* he might be coming in. I didn't make the connection 'til just now." Jack was a pretty common name, after all.

Stirling nodded, more firmly in the groove now. "We had information that they were a couple, but it's always good to get corroboration. When he got into town, he took an air taxi to the south side of town and dropped out of sight for a few hours. After that, we've got him taking another cab to the Oaklands, where he walked into reception and asked which room Ms. Reynolds was in. Then he took the elevator up, went to the apartment, and knocked on the door. When they let him in, he attacked them."

"But why?" asked Jericho. "I get it that there was tension between him and Bobbi, but I still don't see the motive."

"Two things," Stirling said. "I presume your cousin was going to be sleeping on the foldout sofa bed?"

Jericho nodded. "Yeah, he was. Why?"

Stirling didn't answer the question directly. "Second thing. Portman was on meth when he came into the apartment. The lab reported traces of it in the blood samples we took off … uh, in the blood samples they found in the apartment."

The evasion didn't escape Jericho's notice, but he chose not to comment. "Meth? Oh, crap." As G-Man, he'd had to subdue a meth-head once. The guy just wouldn't go down. He'd also been attacking a lamppost that had apparently said unkind things about his mother.

"Filthy stuff." Stirling grimaced. "The working theory is that he showed up and they let him in. He saw the sofa, didn't know it was a bed, and maybe jumped to the conclusion that Ms. Reynolds was sleeping with your cousin. If he was high, it wouldn't have been a big jump."

"Crap. Luke was probably still watching TV when he got there." It was another piece to the puzzle. Unfortunately, it fit all too well. "When she was on the phone with this Jack guy, she said she was sharing with two guys. So, you're right. He comes in, the sofa's not a bed, and Luke's right there."

Meth didn't, as far as Jericho knew, make the user super-strong or impervious to pain. But it could easily cause users to react in a delusional fashion, and it did go a long way toward making them very difficult to put down. If they were armed, things got bloody, very fast. Luke had clearly gotten a hit or two in—the limp proved that—but the guy had just kept attacking. And he'd had a knife, which would've made it much harder for Luke to defend himself. Bobbi's power would've been worse than useless in this situation; from what she'd told Jericho, the rage radiating off her boyfriend would've almost paralyzed her.

Recalling the footage, he glanced at the TV, then his eyes narrowed. "He was on meth, all right," he said. "Look, right there. He's tweaking." He gestured at the screen, focusing on the way Portman's hand jittered back and forth in the fakest-looking attempt at rubbing his forehead he'd ever seen. The jerky way Portman hobbled offscreen also took on a whole new meaning. Compulsive, twitchy movements were a hallmark of the drug and its aftermath.

"Wondered if you'd catch that." Stirling showed his teeth briefly before the expression dropped away again. "We haven't caught up with the asshole yet. Him and the guy who was driving abandoned the car in a parking garage where all the security cameras had been mysteriously vandalized." As if his meaning wasn't already clear, he rolled his eyes as he said the word 'mysteriously'. "He's gone back down the rabbit hole for the time being. But we've shut down every avenue out of the city we can. We know he didn't take the maglev, and he can't use his MagCard now without raising a flag."

Jericho recalled Thomas' impromptu lesson on how MagCards operated. "And he can't steal someone else's identity to go on the maglev, because MagCards don't work that way."

Stirling gave him a measured nod. "Correct, though most people don't know that. We don't advertise it, because it's *amazing* how many people try that trick and wonder why they get caught anyway. But it looks like he's wise to it, 'cause it hasn't happened yet. The only other real way out of the city's the interstate, but we've shut down the off-ramp for the time being so he can't just hitch a ride."

"That's gonna piss off the Southsiders." Jericho grimaced internally when Stirling gave him a sharp glance. *Probably wondering where I heard about them.* The comment had just slipped out, but he couldn't exactly take it back. Besides, considering that the maglev didn't allow passengers to carry illegal drugs, the Southsiders had probably been the ones to supply Portman with the meth in the first place. He could muster very little in the way of sympathy for them.

"If you're referring to the employees of South Side Parking, they'll be adequately reimbursed by the city for the loss of business." From his tone of voice, Stirling knew Jericho didn't mean the business.

"Yeah, that too," agreed Jericho, deadpan.

Stirling snorted with amusement, then heaved himself to his feet. "Well, that's all I had to say. It's time I was going. We'll be in touch about releasing the body, probably sometime this afternoon. His parents have been contacted, and his father said he'd come in to help identify the body."

They need two people for that, Jericho realized. *Uncle Leroy's gonna need me there as well.* He didn't *want* to do it, but this was a situation where there was no comfortable way out. Luke had backed him up all his life; this was the absolute least he could do in return. "I understand," he said awkwardly. "I'll be there too."

Stirling offered his hand to shake. "Good talk. And, uh …" He glanced sideways at the TV. "… if you happen to be out and about, and you run across this joker, call me before you do anything rash, huh?" The unspoken message was clear: *At least give us a chance to arrest the guy before you do something drastic to him.* He pulled a card out of his pocket and offered it to Jericho.

Jericho took it, then shook his hand firmly. "I have no idea what you're talking about. I'm just a private citizen." Sensing that Stirling wanted a little more, he added, "But on the off-chance I do happen to find him, I'll definitely try not to do anything that you wouldn't do." *No promises.*

"Good." Stirling looked as though he might have been repenting of his decision to share so much information with Jericho, then he shrugged ever so slightly. "You didn't hear any of this from me, okay?"

Stirling had offered Jericho his trust in this matter; given Jericho's views on loyalty, there was only one answer he could give. Meeting Stirling's eyes, he spread his hands in a parody of innocence. "Hear what?"

Some of the tension went out of the detective sergeant's shoulders. "No idea what you're talking about, champ." He headed for the door, then stopped. "Oh, yeah. Nearly forgot. Once they've cleared your stuff and your cousin's personal effects, you'll be able to pick them up from the precinct house."

"Yeah, that'd be good." The last thing he wanted was for Luke's possessions to languish in police storage a moment longer than necessary.

Stirling nodded. "I'll let the guys know." He tapped his lower lip with his finger. "I don't know exactly when your uncle will be getting in, so I'd really try to get some sleep if I was you." A little humor crept into his tone. "Because seriously, you do look like shit."

"Yeah." Jericho was fully aware of that, but he wasn't exactly looking forward to trying to sleep again. It would happen eventually. He didn't have to like it.

"Good." Apparently taking his agreement for acceptance, Stirling opened the door and stepped through. "See you around. Take care of yourself."

As the door closed behind the detective sergeant, Jericho slowly sat down on the sofa, barely aware that he was doing so. Stirling's visit had turned his entire view of the situation upside down. The nebulous castle of speculation he'd constructed regarding a criminal conspiracy employing Enabled assassins against either Luke or Bobbi had collapsed and evaporated like the morning dew. *Luke wasn't being targeted. I wasn't even being targeted. There was no grand plan. It was all about one stupid goddamn meth-head asshole with a knife, and Luke was just in the wrong place at the wrong time.* He had trouble believing that such a horrific event could come to pass from such a mundane confluence of events, but there it was. The facts were in, and he had to accept them.

There just remained two burning questions.

Where is Jack Portman, and how soon can I get my hands on him?

<h1 style="text-align:center">34
From the Shadows</h1>

Now that Jericho knew what had *really* happened, he found that his thoughts had ceased to churn in ever-decreasing circles. Confusion no longer clamored in his head and tangled up his wits. He took up the remote and turned off the TV. There was no need to keep it on any longer; by now, Portman's features were indelibly burned into his memory. They would stay that way until he got his hands on the man, one way or the other.

A glance out the window reminded him that it was still dark. By the clock, it was just after six in the morning, so he still had an hour or more before sunrise, and three hours before the interview.

He paused. *Can I still do the interview? Should I still do it? Is attending a job interview really the best way to show respect for Luke and Bobbi, for their memory?*

Again, he reminded himself that Luke had put significant effort into making sure he got to Utopia City in the first place. *He'd be seriously disappointed in me if I backed out now.* There was just a tiny niggle at the back of his mind; his thoughts were steadier than they had been before Stirling's visit, but he still wasn't entirely certain he was up to going through with the whole affair. *What would be worse; if I went to the interview and bombed out, or just didn't go?*

That, at least, was something he could work out. He still had no way of knowing where Jack Portman was (unless he counted the extremely vague descriptor 'with the Southsiders') but that could be shelved until he had more information. Right now, he needed to nail down what he was going to do about the interview.

As he unzipped the satchel and started donning his costume, he realized that he didn't know how to get out of this area of the Oaklands quickly. In fact, given his state of mind when he'd gotten to the apartment in the first place, he wasn't even certain *where* he was in the Oaklands. It was, he decided, something he would figure out as he went.

Tapping his face with his gloved fingers, he made sure he wasn't about to head out without his mask on. Normally, this wouldn't be an issue but in his current state of distraction, anything could happen. Then, just to be sure, he did a quick visual and tactile check to verify he was fully costumed up with the satchel in its rear pouch. Once again, he tucked his MagCard into an inside pocket then zipped his jacket up. On the point of opening the door, he paused. If he didn't turn his head, he could still see Luke sitting on the sofa in his mind's eye, just outside the limit of his peripheral vision.

"See you later," he murmured under his breath and opened the door.

You be sure an' take care now, cuz. The voice was in his head, not in his ears. Tears sprang to his eyes and he had to force himself not to turn around. Not because of what he might see, but because of what he wouldn't.

"Always do," he whispered as the door closed behind him.

Outside the apartment, he leaned against the wall and took several deep breaths. *I'm good*, he told himself. *I'm a hero. I'm strong. I'm capable. I'm not going to fall apart again.*

Once he'd talked himself into believing that, he straightened up and looked around. Corridors led to the left and right, but just a few yards down the hallway, he saw a you-are-here sign. A few seconds of study allowed him to work out where he was in relation to the rest of the Oaklands, and where to find the nearest window exit.

The longer he hung about inside the building, the more likely someone was liable to poke their head out of their apartment and wonder why he was prowling around in costume. Thus, as soon as he worked out where he was going, he didn't waste any time. Down the corridor to the left and around the corner he went, his long strides covering the distance quickly. There was a window ahead of him just where the diagram said it would be, and he hurried toward it. Taking his MagCard out, he tapped the reader as he'd seen Independence do. It worked just as well as swiping the card across the reader, and he tucked the knowledge away as the window swiveled open. *Learn something new every day.*

Climbing out onto the discreetly placed ladder, he tapped the outside reader to close the window, then put the card away, zipped up his jacket again and started climbing. As he crested the edge of the roof, he saw the by-now familiar rooftop with its holographic sign hanging overhead. Nothing seemed to have changed, except perhaps for the faintest glow in the sky to the east. He amended that thought as he clambered onto the roof proper; nothing had changed except him.

It was amazing how thoroughly perceptions could shift in the span of a night. Before, he'd surveyed the futuristic buildings with their holographic decorations and the moving lights in the sky with an almost childlike sense of wonder, but now he saw Utopia City as a darker and more savage place. Somewhere within this high-tech wonderland lurked an amoral killer, a malevolent serpent defiling what Jericho had come to see as a post-scarcity garden of Eden.

Breathing the night air in deeply, he tried to flush the loss and pain out of his heart through sheer force of will. It diminished slightly as he allowed himself to drink in the fact of *being*; of merely existing without thought or motivation. Spreading his arms, he turned slowly in a complete circle in an attempt to recapture his earlier mood. It eluded him, mocking his idealism with the harsh realities of the world.

The breeze had sharpened from the last time he was up here, and the air traffic had diminished. He watched what he thought was a hex thrumming across the sky, a circle of blinking lights made elliptical by perspective. Running lights still flitted here and there, though he wasn't entirely certain if they all belonged to air-cabs. He turned his head and stared up at the apartment building that towered over the Oaklands. *Maybe I'll be able to get my head in the game again if I go back up there.* It had worked before, so it should work again.

He eyed the edge of the rooftop between himself and the apartment building, then prepared for his run-up. Taking a deep breath, he started forward, pushing for the speed that would glide him across the gap. But just as he hit his stride, a chilling thought destroyed his focus.

The last time I did this, Luke died.

He stumbled to a halt, just a few yards from the edge. Looking up at the apartment building, he shook his head. *There's no reason to think that way*, he told himself. *That murdering sonovabitch was always going to come to Utopia City.* Slowly, he retraced his steps.

Once he got back to the starting point, he flung himself forward once more. His feet pounded against the rooftop, driving him toward his goal. He needed to get up to the top of that apartment building. That was where he'd be able to clear his head. There was *no correlation* between him going out as a superhero and something terrible happening to a loved one.

He barely made it halfway along the rooftop before the chaotic swirl of his thoughts brought him to a stumbling halt. Leaning over, he rested his hands on his knees while he dragged air into his lungs as if he were exhausted, though this was nowhere near the case. Inside, a bone-deep fear began to well up as he realized just how off-balance he was. *I can't even get this right. What am even I doing here?*

"You okay there?"

The voice came out of nowhere, startling him badly. He snapped upright and spun around, searching for whoever had spoken. It had sounded like a young woman, one who was close by. But he was alone on the rooftop, or at least he'd thought he was. "Who's there?" he snapped, forming a G-tag in each hand.

"Sorry." What he'd taken to be a discoloration on the waist-high parapet and a patch of haze in the sky beyond took a step toward him; a human form fading into existence. Slim hands emerged from long sleeves and a hood was lifted out of the way, allowing a woman's face to emerge from the dimness. More precisely, her face was visible from the cheekbones down, while her eyes were still shrouded by the hood. "Didn't mean to bother you, but I was wondering if you were okay."

Temporarily shocked out of his funk by the adrenaline singing in his veins, Jericho stared as she walked closer, her feet making absolutely no sound on the rooftop. The light from the sign moved oddly across her costume, to the point that he could almost swear he was able to see through her. "Where did you come from? I *looked* there!" After Luke, Transit and Thomas, and now this woman, he was starting to detect a pattern. He'd gotten complacent in Savannah with no other prodigies to match his wits against. *I really do need to up my game.*

"Don't beat yourself up," she said, as if reading his thoughts. "Not being seen is kind of my thing. The name's Smokeshadow." She held out her hand; reflexively, he dissolved the G-tag in his right hand and shook it.

"G-Man," he replied. "So, invisibility? You're a dynamic?" He nodded toward her costume. Even so close, he had trouble focusing on its details. "Or are you wearing Artificer gear?"

She tilted her head in acknowledgement of his insight. "Not quite invisibility. I don't have a Dynamic rating. I'm mainly prodigy, with a low-end Artificer rating. My outfit's made from a programmable hyperweave. Variable refractive index with adaptive camouflage. It makes me hard to spot, and skill takes care of the rest." As he watched, the costume altered color and form to become a comfortable-looking hoodie and a pair of jeans. The translucent effect faded, giving it the appearance of ordinary clothing. "But you're not up here to talk shop. You're hurting really badly right now, and you want to go somewhere to either vent or brood, or both." The tone of her voice, her stance, what he could see of her expression; all radiated understanding of his plight.

Slowly, Jericho let the other G-tag dissolve. Folding his arms, he turned away and moved toward the roof's edge. Smokeshadow's feet still made no sound against the rooftop, but she was close enough that his G-sense just barely registered her presence behind him. She didn't speak, which gave him time to gather his thoughts.

"I came to Utopia City to try out for Force Majeure," he said roughly, fixing his gaze on a distant building and addressing his words to it rather than the woman behind him. Normally he wouldn't have been spilling his guts like this, but she was very easy to talk to. "My cousin and I met a lady on the train, and we were sharing an apartment. I went out on patrol." His fists clenched inside the gloves. "When I got back, they'd been murdered."

"Jeez." There was a catch in her voice, then her hand rested on his shoulder and squeezed supportively. "I'm so sorry. I can't imagine."

Between her touch and her words, he felt a little of the tension leaving his body.

He was obscurely grateful that she wasn't saying anything stupid like *you must feel so terrible* or *it'll be all right*. Of *course* he felt goddamn terrible and no, it would never be all right. She hadn't tried to hug him either, which was another point in her favor. While he wasn't averse to physical contact under the right conditions, a hug from a stranger under these circumstances would feel incredibly awkward.

Lifting his anguished face toward the night sky, he drew deep lungfuls of the chilly air. "The cops know who did it. They've made sure he's not getting out of the city. I'd be going after him myself right now, but I'm new in town. This isn't my city." That was true in more ways than one. He didn't know the layout, he didn't know the customs, and the people didn't know him. At least the citizens of Savannah knew *of* G-Man, even if they ignored him most of the time.

"And you got that other thing you said," she pointed out. The hand on his shoulder was a physical reminder of her presence, comforting without being intrusive. "Trying out for Force Majeure? That's pretty damn important. I'd be conflicted too."

"Yeah." He dropped his head. "Luke—my cousin—made sure I'd get here in time to try out. The last thing I want to do is disappoint him. But if I attend the interview in this state, there's every chance I'll screw it up anyway. I have no idea what to do." *Which is why I'm up here,* he didn't have to say.

"You and him were pretty close, huh?" Somehow, she hit just the right note so that it didn't feel like she was being patronizing.

"Brothers couldn't be closer." It was nothing less than the truth. He could barely remember a time when Luke *hadn't* been a part of his life. "He was set on me coming here and doing this. But I don't know if I can face up to it right now."

"So, call 'em and ask to reschedule," she said bluntly. Her voice was brisk now, no-nonsense. It was a total contrast from the solicitous tone she'd been using up until now. "And if they won't, then go anyway."

"But I'm a mess—" He wasn't sure why he was protesting. This was exactly what he needed to hear.

"And if you *can't* reschedule and you *don't* go, then you're one hundred percent guaranteed to lose your slot." Her grip on his shoulder tightened and she pulled him around to face her. "But if you *do* go and you *do* make it, then you're in. Not everything's a sure winner. Sometimes you've got to just roll the dice and hope you don't come up snake eyes."

He blinked. The logic was simple and inescapable. It was what his mind had been fighting back against; somewhere deep inside, he'd been trying to hold out for a guaranteed success. She was right, of course. There were very few sure things in life.

"Goddamn it," he muttered. "You're right." It was a wrench to let go of the notion that he could somehow wrangle a miracle out of the situation, but he managed it. *I'm just gonna have to do it the hard way.*

"Mm-hmm. And you do realize that if you do make it on to the team, you've got a lot more chance of being in on the bust when they do catch up with the guy who did this, right?" Her tone was matter-of-fact. "So straighten up, get your head together, and come out swinging. Nobody's gonna hand you this win. You've gotta grab it with both hands and make the best of it."

"Yes, *ma'am*," he replied, only half-jokingly. He marveled that he was capable of even making a joke at a time like this, no matter how feeble. "Thanks, I … that helps a lot."

She gave him a half-smile. "You're welcome. It's not like I told you anything you couldn't figure out for yourself. What time's the interview?"

"Nine," he said. "But I want to get there early, just to be sure." The air-cab had been very prompt the previous evening, but he didn't want to automatically assume this would always be the case. And it would be the height (or the depth) of irony to decide to attend, then be late anyway.

"Good thinking." She dropped her hand from his shoulder. "Dunno if you're up for getting some sleep, but you're not in the best of shape right now. So I'd try if I were you. Even an hour would do you good."

He rolled his head on his neck, recalling the nightmare he'd woken up from. "I … really don't know how well that's going to work. Right now, sleep and me aren't on the best of terms."

She didn't argue the point. "Caffeinate yourself, then. Have a hot shower, or a cold one. Close your eyes for twenty minutes. You're a prodigy; you *know* there's a dozen ways to recharge your batteries."

"Yeah." Jericho nodded. "Yeah, you're right." This was a first in his experience. He'd never before managed to get past the need to brood without actually brooding. "Sometime, when I'm in a better headspace, you're going to have to tell me how you pulled that off."

"Sometime, when you're in a better headspace, I will," she agreed. "For now, you need to go deal with you."

"I'm going, I'm going." He headed toward the edge of the roof. As he got there and prepared to climb down onto the waiting ladder, he turned back toward Smokeshadow. "Quick question. What are you doing here anyway?"

"Here in Utopia City, or up here on this roof?" she asked, a grin quirking the corner of her mouth.

Jericho had originally meant to query her presence on the roof, but her question had opened a wider field of interest. "Uh, both, I guess. If you're okay with telling me."

She nodded. "Well, I'm on the roof to see what can be seen." She held up a hand as Jericho went to speak. "Not finished. We're both prodigies. You go to a rooftop and brood; I find a good vantage point and watch. The street, cars going by, people, the sky, the city. I like to get in a few hours of watching in the morning to freshen me up for the day." She gestured to the east. "And in an hour or so, I'll be watching the sunrise. I understand it's pretty good."

"Whoa, wait!" He held up his hands to stop her as the possibilities burst upon him. "How long … were you … did you see …" If she'd seen Portman go in and come out again, she might be able to afford him some insights that the police didn't have access to.

"Sorry." She shook her head, a regretful tone in her voice. "I've only been up here since about four. Everything's been quiet, so I'm guessing the action was long done by then."

"Oh, okay." He tried not to feel let down. It wasn't her fault, after all. "And in the city? Are you here to join Force Majeure too?"

"Pfft, hardly." She gestured, as if to wave his suggestion away. "I'm a tourist. I'm literally here to sightsee." The pause was just long enough for the pun to register with Jericho. "So to speak. Though …" She drew the word out thoughtfully.

"Though, what?" he asked.

"Though, did you want to see something interesting before you try to get your head down?" Her expression was lively, inviting him to reply in the affirmative.

He hesitated, but knew he had to answer at some point. "Yes?" he ventured, not at all sure if he had the willpower right then to say no.

"Cool." She grinned conspiratorially and gestured to him. "Come over here, and check this out. Try to stay as quiet as possible."

He went over to her and stood, looking from the rooftop down onto the street. "What am I looking for, exactly?" he murmured from the corner of his mouth. From her attitude, it seemed she was going to show him some kind of wildlife. Maybe a bird nesting in one of the trees?

"You'll see," she breathed, and dug in her pocket for a notepad. One page, ripped out, became a paper airplane after a minute or so of careful folding. Then she pointed at a manhole situated under a streetlight. "See anything weird about that?"

He peered in that direction. "It's a manhole. Or rather, a manhole cover." Looking more closely, he added, "It's got a kind of spiral pattern on it." Apart from that, it seemed perfectly normal.

"Good eye. Now, check this out." She grinned and threw the paper plane. Not at the manhole, but out toward the street. It got about a third of the way before a contrary wind gust put it into a dive. Rather anticlimactically, it crashed into the sidewalk about a yard from the curb. She sagged. "Crap. And I was going to do the big dramatic reveal, too."

"What did you want to do with it?" asked Jericho practically.

"Get it onto the street." She dug out her notepad again. "Gimme a minute here. The next one should fly better."

"Don't bother." He formed a push-tag in his hand and flicked it toward the paper airplane lying forlornly on the concrete below. The target was small but unmoving; his aim was good. The 'tag hit the plane and flicked it sideways four yards, right into the middle of the road. Jericho dismissed the effect before it could go any farther, then glanced at Smokeshadow. "Now what?"

She looked from his hand to the plane, then she nodded. "That works too. Now, we wait." Grinning in anticipation, she leaned both hands on the parapet of the roof, and fixed her attention on the street below.

"For what?" He couldn't see anything happening. Even if a maglev car came along, it wouldn't so much as touch the paper airplane.

"Shh. Just wait. And watch."

He stilled his impatience. This was far too elaborate to be the setup for a simple practical joke. With the occasional glance to ensure that the roof behind them was clear, he settled down to observe the scrap of folded paper in the middle of the road.

Time ticked by. One moment stretched into the next. He'd done this before, staking out an area for criminal activity, but before now, it had always been his choice when to start and when to finish. And normally, he had something more interesting to look at than a paper airplane. He began to wonder what Smokeshadow would do if the wind blew it off down the street.

Then he heard … something, he wasn't sure what. Beside him, Smokeshadow murmured "Here it comes." He followed her eyes and saw that the manhole cover was opening. Not lifting, as he would've expected, but *opening*, the spiral pieces sliding apart like a camera iris. It was a strange and compelling sight to see on a deserted street at oh-dark-thirty in the morning.

When he saw what came *out* of the manhole, his sense of the weird ratcheted up a dozen notches. Covered in a glossy black carapace, it was about six feet long and thoroughly articulated. His first thought was *mechanical lobster*, but it had too many legs and no pincers. Apart from that, it was about the right shape. As if a mechanical horror climbing out of the sewers in the early hours of the morning could have a *right* shape.

He opened his mouth to ask a question, but her hand on his wrist quieted him. Together, they watched as it scuttled over to the paper airplane. He didn't see exactly what happened next, but when the thing turned away, the plane was gone. A rounded brush polished the spot on the roadway where it had rested, then the thing scuttled back toward the manhole. Seconds after the cover irised shut once more, a car rounded the corner, gliding smoothly over the now-empty street.

Jericho looked at Smokeshadow, his eyebrows raising under his mask. "Well, crap. What was that?"

She shrugged. "Street cleaner, I guess. I'm thinking things like that handle routine maintenance and cleaning, as well as trash collection. All without letting the regular public see them." She chuckled. "Explains why there's no litter or graffiti, doesn't it?"

"It does." He shook his head. "I'm beginning to think there's a lot more going on behind the scenes in this city than I'll ever know about."

She snorted with laughter. "You're only just getting that now?" Shaking her head, she made a shooing motion with both hands. "Go sort yourself out, already."

"Okay, and thanks." He went back to the ladder and started down it. He appreciated Smokeshadow's attempts to distract him from his problems, but he still didn't know how well his efforts to get ready for the interview were going to go.

In the end, however, he didn't just owe it to himself to try. He owed it to Luke and Bobbi as well.

35
Making the Calls

Jericho finished off the bowl of cereal and rinsed it in the sink. *Captain Utopia's Breakfast Crunch* wasn't too bad, though it was a brand he'd never seen before. Befitting the name, the front of the box portrayed a ridiculously square-jawed Enabled wearing both spandex *and* a cape, swooping through a stylized version of Utopia City. Entirely unsurprisingly, the box also advertised something called *Captain Utopia's Cartoon Hour*, which was probably just as hokey as the image suggested. Imagining Luke's sarcastic comments on the matter—which, to be fair, would've been entirely justified—brought a pained smile to his face.

Which brought him to the next matter at hand. On returning to the apartment, he'd showered, which had helped to clear his head a little. The subsequent bowl of cereal had put much-needed food in his stomach, but now he faced a nearly impossible decision. There were two calls he had to make and while he knew which one he *should* be doing first, he just couldn't face up to it right now. With a grimace, he bit the bullet and selected the number that would merely dictate his career for the foreseeable future.

The phone rang exactly once before it was picked up. "Relentless' office; Samantha Colburn speaking. Please state your name and business." Ms. Colburn, presumably the same person who'd sent him the email confirming his interview, sounded like the very epitome of an executive assistant; specifically, someone who it was exceedingly unwise to mess with. Relentless and his colleagues in Force Majeure might have the final say as to who joined the team, but that required Jericho to get in to see them in the first place.

"Hello, uh, this is G-Man," he said hesitantly. "I'm just calling … I just had …" He stopped, realizing that to tell her about Luke's death would give her significant clues to his identity. While being a superhero's executive assistant *might* garner her appropriate clearance, he couldn't be certain. "I, uh, I was just wondering if it was possible to reschedule."

"G-Man." Ms. Colburn's voice was sharp with disapproval. "You're due to be interviewed at …" There was the most minuscule of pauses. "… nine o'clock this morning."

He could already hear the 'no' in her tone, but he forged ahead anyway. "Yes. I've had a … family issue since arriving in Utopia City, and I don't know if I can …" *if I can deal with this crap on top of everything else right now.*

Ms. Colburn's reply was firm, professional, and utterly unhelpful. "I have every sympathy for your situation, G-Man, but Force Majeure is a very busy organization. Their time is booked for these interviews for months in advance, just as yours was. Two hours before your appointment is hardly an appropriate point to petition for a change in schedule."

"But … but I …" The sheer injustice of it all overwhelmed him. He wanted to scream at her down the phone, but he recalled just in time that she wasn't aware of the situation with him and Luke. For all she knew, he was bailing because of the split between him and Stephen. It was even partly his fault for using such mealy mouthed wording. But he couldn't be certain if she was cleared to know his secret identity, or if she'd even change her stance once she knew about Luke. *Is there such a thing as a Designated Liaison for executive assistants?*

"Whatever your problems are, G-Man, I am restricted to following procedure." Ms. Colburn's voice seemed a little less chilly than before, but she wasn't giving an inch. "Rescheduling is no simple matter. Many others have calls on Relentless' time. To displace someone else from their interview merely because you want to reschedule would be the height of unfairness to them. Now, do you still wish to cancel your interview and reapply, or are you going to be attending?"

No matter his own feelings on the matter, it was time to follow through on Smokeshadow's advice. "I'll be there," he said. *I don't know how well I'm gonna do, but I'll damn well give it everything I've got.*

"Commendable," she replied. He was reasonably certain she wasn't being facetious. "I wish you all good fortune with it. Now, was there anything else?"

"No, ma'am," he replied. Unlike with Smokeshadow, he wasn't joking even a little bit with the honorific. "Thank you for your time."

The phone went dead in his ear before he was quite finished saying the word 'time', but that didn't matter a great deal. Even if he rang her back, he doubted he could convince her to change her mind. Unfortunately, he was now out of excuses to delay making the other phone call. Given the opportunity, he'd have put it off indefinitely, but that way promised disaster. The trouble was, if Uncle Leroy's reaction was anywhere near what Jericho thought it might be, trying to head him off was just as likely to be problematic. Leroy was the type of man who never let other people dictate his choices without a fight. And while the Savannah cops knew when to look the other way, his personal brand of retribution would never fly in Utopia City.

Leaning with his back to the kitchenette counter, Jericho located the name he needed in his Contacts list. On the verge of pressing the call icon, he paused, trying to figure how to word things so Leroy didn't just go at the problem in his customary bull-headed fashion.

Well, don't jes' sit there, cuz. Shit or git off th' pot.

His finger still hovering over the phone, Jericho deliberately didn't look over his shoulder at the sofa. He *knew* Luke wasn't sitting there, but he could quite clearly hear the kind of earthy advice his cousin had given him many times before. Figment of his imagination or no, Luke was right. He was just stalling. Taking a deep breath, he touched the icon.

This time, the phone rang twice before it was answered. "Hey," Leroy's voice answered, sounding about as grim as Jericho had ever heard him. "Jericho boy, you heard yet? About Luke?"

Jericho's heart tore in half right down the middle. *Aunt Ellie. Olivia. Serena. Luke meant the world to them.* "Yeah, I … I'm here in Utopia City too." Leroy tried to ask a question, but Jericho talked over the top of him, not wanting to break down in the middle of what he had to say. "I'm the one who found him."

"Jesus motherfucking Christ." Leroy's voice was raw with pain. "How'd it happen? Who murdered my boy? The cops there ain't tellin' me shit." A moment later, Jericho's words must have registered on him, because he asked, "An' what are *you* doin' there?" In the background of the call, Jericho caught a fragment of an automated announcement, referencing Chattanooga. *That sounds like he's just passing through Atlanta, on the way to Chattanooga. He'll be here in two hours.*

Hunching over the phone, Jericho squeezed his eyes shut. "I'm really sorry. I came here looking for work. Luke and me were sharing a place with someone we met on the train. I went out for some air. While I was away, her boyfriend showed up, doped to the gills on meth. When they let him in, he went crazy with a knife. Luke tried to stop him, but the guy killed them both." *If I'd been there, I could've stopped him and saved them.* The guilt from that, he knew, was going to stay with him for the rest of his life.

"Fuuuuck." As Jericho had suspected would happen, Leroy didn't query Luke's presence in Utopia City. "Who did it? The cops catch the motherfucker, at least?" Shock was giving way to anger. Leroy had always espoused the 'get even, not mad' point of view, except he also got mad. He also seemed to have skipped straight past the 'denial' stage of grief, probably because life had shit on him so often that he didn't question it when bad things happened.

Jericho wanted to tell Leroy what Stirling had passed on to him, but that information was almost certainly confidential; if it got out, the burly detective sergeant could get into a lot of trouble. "The cops know who he is, but they haven't caught up with him yet. I'm pretty sure the Southsiders are hiding him." This wasn't betraying Stirling's confidence, because he'd already figured that out of his own accord.

Tellingly, Leroy didn't need to ask who the Southsiders were. "Those motherfucking cocksucking backstabbing assholes!" he exploded. He paused as what Jericho had said sank in. "Now, you're sure he was her boyfriend and not someone sent to put Luke outta the way?"

From the sounds of it, the chances of Leroy doing any further 'business' with the Southsiders had just taken a dive into the negative numbers. This was probably a good idea from the point of view of both Utopia City and Savannah. Jericho decided to sink the final nail into the coffin. "I'm certain of it. The cops got a solid ID from security footage. But it looks a lot like the Southsiders sold him the meth he was strung out on when he did it."

"That's fucking *it.*" Leroy was snorting like a bull, which was what he usually did just before he punched something. Or someone. It was never hard to tell where Luke had inherited his temper from. "I need a name. When I get there, I'm gonna find this cocksucker and put him in the ground myself, along with any other sumbitch gets in my way."

"Bad idea, Uncle Leroy." Jericho liked his uncle and aunt a lot. He'd been aware for some time that his uncle's side of the family occasionally performed illegal activities, though he'd never seen any kind of proof until now. So long as he didn't encounter them breaking the law while he was out and about as G-Man, he'd chosen to leave that source of potential awkwardness well alone. The very last thing he wanted was his uncle fixing to apply Savannah-style vengeance to Utopia City's criminal element. Besides, he wasn't quite sure where Leroy would find live 'gators in the middle of Kansas. Hogs, yes; 'gators, no. "The cops here know their shit. They're really on top of their game."

"They haven't caught the motherfucker that murdered my boy," Leroy shot back. "They can't be *that* goddamn good at it."

"They've got him trapped in the city," Jericho argued. "It's only a matter of time. And you think Aunt Ellie really wants to see you getting arrested again? Trust me, they'll know who you are and they'll figure out what you're up to if you try to go out and about. Put one foot out of line and they'll be all over you like a cheap suit. You won't be able to take a shit without a cop handing you the toilet paper." He recalled the way the cop had confronted Luke. For someone as far up the underworld food chain as he suspected Leroy was, they wouldn't send just one car.

"Sum*bitch.*" It didn't quite sound like defeat, but Jericho suspected it meant agreement to not go charging around Utopia City like a wounded bull. The heavy sigh confirmed it. "Anyway, how are you handling things, boy? The cops didn't try to pin it on you, did they?"

"Briefly, but I proved it couldn't have been me. Still, everything could be a lot better," Jericho admitted. *Luke and Bobbi could still be alive, for one thing.* "I'll be coming back to Savannah with you and Luke for the funeral." The words *of course* went unspoken. He didn't want to leave Utopia City with Portman still on the loose, but kin *always* came first and he'd been closer to Luke than most.

Leroy hadn't totally given up yet. "That druggie cocksucker still needs to pay, along with the assholes that sold him the fuckin' ice. I'm just saying."

Jericho didn't approve of this for the simple reason that murder, even of a well-deserving sonofabitch, was still murder. He may have had inclinations of his own toward that end, but he knew that if Portman gave himself up peacefully, he'd hand the guy over to the cops alive.

On the other hand, if Portman put up a fight … Jericho honestly didn't know which way that would go. There were many things that could go wrong in a fight. If someone was actively using lethal force, especially when under the influence of a drug like crystal meth, there was no sense in taking chances.

Deep down, he knew quite well he was preemptively justifying the possibility of having to kill the man who'd murdered Luke and Bobbi. Right then, he just didn't *care.*

"Well, I just want to see him face justice." *Whatever form it takes.* "I'll see you when you get here."

"Yeah." Leroy was still brimming with anger; it came out in the tension of his voice. "You take care now, boy. Don't you go chasin' after that murderin' sumbitch all by your lonesome."

"You know me, Uncle Leroy. I'm not stupid. This is a job for cops and superheroes." All of which was true, and none of which precluded him from taking a hand.

"Uh huh." The tone of Leroy's voice showed his opinion of doing things legally, but he didn't say anything directly, for which Jericho was grateful. If his uncle didn't say it, he didn't have to take notice. "See you soon, boy."

"See you soon." Jericho shut down the call, then began to pace up and down the tiny living room. Far from calming him down, the call to Uncle Leroy had ramped up the anger he'd already been feeling, and now it roiled in his guts.

Abruptly, the small apartment felt claustrophobic around him. "Screw this," he said out loud. "If I stay here, I'm gonna go nuts. I'm going in now." Galvanized into action by the sound of his own voice, he shoved his phone into his pocket and scooped up the costume satchel by its strap. Pausing only to double-check that his MagCard was in his pocket, he headed for the door. Behind him, on the sofa, a memory of Luke waved goodbye. *Kick ass, cuz.*

He didn't look back. *I intend to.*

36
Sharing a Cab

As the elevator started downward, Jericho began to wonder where he was going to complete the change into his G-Man identity. Once he was in public, it was going to be almost impossible to find a secure location to revert to his heroic identity. *Oh, for crap's sake. I'm such a dumbass.* The last thing he wanted to do was go back to the apartment.

As he glanced around, his eye fell on the domino-mask button he'd spotted the night before. *Wait a minute.* Its significance dawned on him, and he pressed it. As he'd suspected, the elevator pulled to a halt, while subtle lighting came up around the mirror. At the same time, a tiny LED readout appeared next to the button.

2:00

1:59

1:58

Timer. Huh. Still, more convenient than a phone booth. Not that he'd ever tried to change in a phone booth. He wondered if anyone had ever attempted that outside the comic books. A ridiculous mental image went through his mind of Pickup's vehicle idling at the curb while the man himself struggled and cursed in the confined space of a phone booth, trying to change into the jumpsuit he wore for his superhero work. It was worth a brief chuckle, but the experience still wasn't something he wanted to test out.

Unzipping the satchel, he went through the same ritual as before; jacket, utility belt, gloves, mask. His phone went into a pouch on the utility belt and the MagCard into an inside pocket of his jacket. Rolling up the satchel, he reached behind him to open the long pouch that went right across the back of his utility belt. Once the satchel was safely stored away, he secured the wing-tails to his legs.

The timer still had a good thirty seconds to go by the time he'd finished costuming up, so he hit the button again, zeroing out the counter. Using the lights around the mirror, he double-checked every detail of his costume as the elevator moved the rest of the way down to the first floor. This was, he had to admit, quite handy.

When the doors opened, he stepped out and headed down the passage that let out into the courtyard. The sun had been up for maybe half an hour, so it wasn't shining down between the buildings yet, but it was definitely bright out. He noted with interest that the umbrellas were all open again and had aligned themselves toward the east. But he had more important things to worry about than automated umbrellas. Specifically, he wasn't the only one in the courtyard. As a point of fact, he could see about two dozen people, three in costume like himself. Those three were heading into the reception office, while most of the others were going out toward the street. It struck him that this was only the second time he'd encountered more than one other Enabled at a time, and the first instance had been on the maglev. *How the hell did I only run into one of these guys last night?*

Following the others into the reception office, he found a younger woman behind the desk this time, wearing a nametag that read 'STACEY'. Stacey was in her twenties, and just as immaculately dressed as her counterpart from the night before.

Of the three Enabled, one was a teenage girl in a black domino mask, barely tall enough to come up to his shoulder. She had short blonde hair, and a sleeveless top and tights in the same shade as her mask, as well as a backpack. There was a teenage boy wearing an elaborate helmet, a circuit-board patterned costume and a metallic backpack; and a tall, well-built guy in wave-patterned blue and green spandex. He wasn't sure about the girl, but circuitry-boy was almost certainly an artificer and spandex-guy was probably a dynamic.

Although all three of the Enabled newcomers were apparently bombarding Stacey with questions simultaneously, she didn't look overly fazed by the rush. In her place, he would've punched someone by now. It seemed the Oaklands knew what they were doing when they hired people. Then again, he supposed that he shouldn't be surprised; people who moved to Utopia City seemed to have a very can-do (not to mention, laid-back) attitude.

"Lady and gentlemen, your attention please!" called out Stacey, clapping her hands once. Miraculously, the group quieted. "Thank you. Now, is anyone seeking to book into Oaklands, or book out?"

That got a non-response, though the probable artificer looked around to see if anyone was raising a hand. Nobody was.

"Oh, good," Stacey said, with a brilliant smile. "That makes this easier. I'm going to assume that you're all looking for the best way to get to a specific location. The Spire, perhaps?"

Along with the other three, Jericho put his hand up. A girl in a hoodie, who must have wandered in behind him, raised her hand as well. There was a good chance that at least one of the Enabled was also trying out for Force Majeure membership. He experienced a surge of doubt as he looked around at the other contenders. *What have I got that these people don't?* Two of the three even had proper costumes, though Jericho only awarded half marks for the one in spandex.

Firmly, he tamped his qualms down again. *Luke and Bobbi had faith in me. I haven't got time to piss and moan about how the odds are stacked against me.* Setting his jaw, he focused on the receptionist again.

"I'll keep this brief," she said brightly. "There are three ways to get anywhere in Utopia. A taxi would be most expensive, but you'll get there in five to ten minutes, and you can split the cost. The monorail will take ten to fifteen minutes, and it's only a few dollars. The bus costs less than a dollar, but it could take twenty minutes to half an hour, depending on which line you take."

Jericho frowned. *That can't be right.* The memory from last night prodded at him, of looking over his shoulder as the monorail came up behind him. He'd been traveling at fifteen miles an hour, and the monorail had been doing twice that at best. He didn't know the exact distance to the Spire, but the cab ride the previous evening had covered a little over thirteen miles, and the Spire was farther away than the maglev station.

"I'm sorry, sir?" asked Stacey. "What was that?"

Belatedly, Jericho realized he'd inadvertently spoken out loud. *Well, let's sort this out, one way or the other.* "I saw the monorail last night," he said, not bothering to explain what he'd been doing when he saw it. "It wouldn't have been traveling faster than thirty miles an hour. I could be wrong," —he knew damn well he wasn't— "but I'm pretty sure that wouldn't get us to the Spire in less than half an hour."

"That's very true, sir," Stacey agreed. "But the monorail has two services. One travels at a relatively slow speed for sightseeing purposes. The other moves a lot faster, to get passengers to their destination quickly and efficiently. Most weekend and night-time runs are tourists, so they'd pick a sightseeing route. That's what you would've seen."

Belatedly, Jericho recalled that the monorail had been cruising down the middle of the canal when he saw it. The boardwalks on either side had been very pretty, and it was likely there were equally scenic places elsewhere in the city. "Right. How close is the nearest monorail station?"

"One block north of here, sir," she replied crisply. "On the corner of Oppenheimer Street and deLesseps Avenue."

"Thanks." Jericho nodded to her. In any other city, he would've tipped her for the assistance, but that apparently wasn't an option here. He had what he needed; turning, he left the reception office, then headed out along the path to the street.

The monorail sounded vaguely interesting, but right now he just wanted to get to the Spire as fast as possible. According to Stacey, the bus would take even longer to get there, so there really was only one option left. He'd have to hail a cab.

However, there was the matter of everyone *else* also wanting a cab. By the time he got out onto the sidewalk, there were about twenty people waiting at the cab-call post. All of these were dressed in suits or more casual clothing, nothing that would be mistaken for a costume. As he watched, a taxi came in for the same type of go-to-hell landing that he'd seen yesterday outside the maglev station. Half a dozen people moved forward and climbed in; within thirty seconds, the cab was airborne again. As soon as it was clear, another cab descended at the same speed, from the same angle. That indicated either a very impressive level of piloting skill, or a high-end auto-landing system.

Shading his eyes, he looked up and saw three or four more cabs orbiting the landing point. Nobody appeared to be jockeying for position; in fact, they seemed to be moving in eerie unison. *Yeah, thought so. They're letting the autopilots do the heavy lifting.* Utopians seemed to be very pragmatic, in that regard. As the cabbie had noted on the ride in, the locals knew the rules, and nobody cowboyed it up; it just looked like they were.

Someone jostled his elbow and he looked down to see the costumed teenage girl. What caught his attention was an extremely realistic tattoo on her upper arm, about the size of his hand; it consisted of shiny black scales that he could've sworn were real. Until they moved, and he realized that they *were* real. Or rather, the patch moved and the scales stayed where they were, fading back to normal skin once the patch had moved on. *Okay, that's not something I've seen before.* As he watched, the patch of shiny black scales moved down her arm and transformed her hand into a wickedly taloned appendage. While the texture of the scales was more like 'gator hide than snakeskin (he was familiar with both), the claws looked exceptionally sharp.

"Watch it with that," he said. He normally wouldn't have spoken so curtly, but it would only take one wrong move for her to slice his leg open.

"Ah, shit, sorry, man." Glancing at her hand, she flexed it and the scaled effect moved back up her arm, leaving pink skin and closely bitten nails behind. He watched as the texture disappeared from her shoulder under her top, causing an odd traveling wave of motion beneath the cloth. "Don't mean to go all slasher on you."

"I'd prefer you didn't either." Belatedly recalling his manners, Jericho offered his hand. "G-Man."

She shook it, revealing that whatever the scales did when they were present, they didn't make her any stronger when they went elsewhere. "Black Dragon. You're headin' for the Spire too, huh?"

Jericho inclined his head toward the other Enabled. "Looks like we all are." The current taxi left in a gust of wind, and he moved forward alongside the Enabled girl as another landed in its place. There weren't many people left; he figured they'd catch the next cab, or the one after.

"Oh, yeah, point." She wrinkled her nose. "So, what's *your* power?"

This was a question he usually faced from normal people, not Enabled; mainly because there was only one other Enabled in Savannah, and Pickup knew his powers quite well. He wasn't feeling very chatty right then, so he went with, "Gravity control."

She looked impressed. "No shit? That mean you can fly and stuff? I can fly if I push myself hard enough, but it rips the shit out of my clothes, and sometimes I lose the backpack so I'm better off not flying right now."

Jericho was pretty sure she'd said all that in one breath. "Flight, no. Other effects, yes." He wondered what she meant by flight ripping her clothes. If she grew wings from her back that were anything like those claws, or if her arms transformed *into* wings, he could definitely see how it would have that effect. But he didn't know enough about her powers to judge, one way or the other.

"Oh well, all G." Her tone was placid. He glanced at her sharply, wondering what she meant by that. *Was that a joke on my Enabled codename, or was she abbreviating 'all good'? I need a teenage whisperer. I wonder if there's an app for that.*

They were at the air-cab stand now, the painted rectangle still fluorescing red. With a rush of wind and a thrum of lifters, the latest cab landed precisely on the rectangle. He was the first to step forward and open the door; it hinged upward, allowing him to climb in. This time, he took a seat at the back while Black Dragon sat in one of the side-on seats. "We're headed for the Spire," he said out loud. "And the Challenger Act applies."

"Gotcha, buddy," the cabbie replied. **"Anyone back there not know how to pay for the fare or do your seatbelts up?"** As he spoke, the words CHALLENGER ACT RECORDING OVERRIDE displayed themselves in prominent red letters across the top of the screen.

Taking the MagCard from the inside pocket of his jacket, Jericho swiped the reader on his seat before fastening the five-point restraints. It seemed his fellow passengers were equally conversant with the mechanics of travelling in an air taxi; the guy with the elaborate helmet had taken off his metallic backpack before sitting down. Within moments, everyone was strapped in.

When the cab took off from the stand, he was able to see an immediate difference from the flight of the previous evening. The sun was rising rather than setting, so the city had a brighter and more optimistic look about it. He could see more of the buildings, most of which would have overshadowed any of the skyscrapers in Savannah. But even these were all dwarfed by the singular structure that they were bound for. Even after they got up to cruising altitude and turned in that direction, the still-distant Spire dominated the skyline on the small corner-screens.

But he had other matters to occupy his attention. As unexpected as it had been to run into the three Enabled at the reception office, he was now sharing a *taxi* with them. That was definitely something he had never done before. Not that socializing with his fellow Enabled was right at the top of his to-do list right now; he was more focused on the upcoming interview.

"So, introductions," said the guy in the blue and green spandex; because of *course* he wanted to be sociable. Jericho thought he was moderately handsome, but the guy was trying way too hard to look and sound more impressive than he really was. "I'm Wavefront. I create and control water. What about you guys?"

The kid in the circuit-board costume looked up from fiddling with his helmet, which he was currently holding on his lap. In its place, he was wearing a low-profile set of goggles. He looked about seventeen and had messy brown hair. "I got the idea for this from a movie, but I can't call myself Cybug because copyright laws suck. So, you can call me Cyberswarm." He put the helmet back on, and hundreds of tiny skittering metallic creatures began flooding out of the backpack. Each one was silver in color and had a tiny round body with multiple legs, along with a single glowing red eyespot on the front. They climbed all over Cyberswarm in just a few seconds, then interlocked with each other to form something that looked like scale armor. It looked impressive, but Jericho wondered just how durable it really was.

"Holy shit," said Black Dragon. "That's cool as fuck. Can they do anything else?"

Cyberswarm shrugged. "I can make blunt weapons, but edges are still a bit difficult. I can climb walls if I take it slowly, and I can tie down muggers if they're not too strong. Still working on all the applications, to be honest." He gave no visible signal, but the 'bugs' suddenly unlocked from each other and retreated into the backpack again. Despite his current level of distraction, Jericho had to admit that they were creepy as hell.

"Well, I'm Black Dragon," the girl said cheerfully. She held up her hand and concentrated; a second later, the black scales appeared on her hand and spread down her arm. The razor talons were just as impressive the second time around. "If I really, *really* work at it, I can turn into a dragon."

"Can you breathe fire?" It was the fifth person in the cab, a drab young woman in a baggy hoodie and faded jeans. Somehow, she'd managed to get on board and pay for her share of the cab without Jericho really registering her presence. Up until this point she'd been slouching in the corner seat, effectively fading into the background. He vaguely recollected her being in the admissions office, but beyond that he had nothing. Then she gave him a slight smile and he realized that the hood hung down just far enough to make it hard to see her eyes. "Hey, G-Man. How you doing?"

Recognition burst on him all at once. "Smokeshadow?"

Wavefront looked at him, then at the woman in the hoodie. "You know each other?" He addressed himself to Smokeshadow. "How did you *do* that? Can you turn invisible?"

Smokeshadow shook her head and pushed back the hood of her jacket, which was the sort of dull gray color that came about from too many washes. As she did so, it became clear that she was wearing a domino mask under it.

Now that she had his attention, Jericho recalled that when she'd gotten into the cab, her shoulders had been hunched forward and her head down. Her blank expression and body language had marked her as someone who was just too boring to want to talk to. At the time, it had seemed perfectly natural not to pay her any notice; in hindsight, it was hard to believe how thoroughly she'd hoodwinked all of them.

As she sat up, animation came back into her face and her body seemed to fill out as she lifted her shoulders and pushed them back a little. It was amazing how much difference a few minor changes in her posture made. "Nope," she said in a matter-of-fact tone. "I'm just really, *really* good at not being there, even when I am. Hiding, sneaking, being invisible in a crowd. It's my specialty."

"Prodigy," concluded Cyberswarm, earning Jericho's approval. "Nice. On the downside, anyone who really wants to see you will still see you."

"Mental prodigy with a little bit of artificer, but broadly speaking, that's true." agreed Smokeshadow. She slumped her shoulders again and tucked her mousy brown hair back into her hood, which seemed to inch forward to put her eyes in shadow. Her face went slack and her voice became a toneless mumble. "Of course, I can also talk so blandly and boringly that people just stop listening ..." Her head turned until she was looking out the window, making Jericho feel as though he didn't need to be paying attention to her anymore. Even though he'd specifically been watching to see how she did it, he found it hard to focus on her.

"That's ... kinda scary," Black Dragon admitted. "I know you're there, but my brain keeps trying to ignore you. How the fuck are you doing that, and how come your clothes can shift around if you're a cowl and not a cape?"

"Body language and smart cloth," Smokeshadow explained, turning back to them and becoming interesting again. "Or if you want to be more technical, programmable hyperweave. All those little tricks that public speakers and celebrities use to be noticed in a crowd? That works both ways. It all comes naturally to me; plus, I've worked at it." As she straightened up once more, the hood retracted to show that the mask was an extension of her collar. The jacket took on a much sharper cut, changing color to a gorgeous sky-blue. At the same time, she ran her hands through her hair, took a deep breath and leaned forward. Her face went from forgettable to vivacious in a transformation so smooth it looked natural even when it had to be calculated. Although he wasn't attracted to her in the slightest, she was suddenly *the* most intriguing person in the cab. Her attention focused on Black Dragon. "But enough about me. *Can* you breathe fire?"

"Pfft, nah," the teenager replied, waving her now-normal hand. "That would be awesome as hell, though." She looked at Smokeshadow's jacket with clear envy in her eyes. "And holy shitballs, so would a costume made outta that smart cloth stuff."

Wavefront cleared his throat, sounding offended. "Black Dragon, you shouldn't be swearing. It looks bad to the public—"

"—and you can fuck off until I give a shit," she interrupted him. "You're not my dad, you're not my big brother, you're not my probation officer, and you're sure as shit not the boss of me."

Under any other circumstances, Jericho would've said something, but today wasn't the day. Fortunately, Smokeshadow chose to intervene before things escalated. "Hey, Wavefront, weren't you in Tallahassee yesterday, going up against the Madness? I'm pretty sure I heard your name on the news."

"I wish," grumbled Wavefront. "I got there too late to do anything. And it was a *perfect* setup for my powers, too." He shook his head, a sour expression on his face. "They had a *fountain*. Do you know what I could've done with a fountain?"

"Well, at least Relentless and Independence stopped the Madness before anyone else got killed," Cyberswarm said helpfully.

"There's that, yeah." Wavefront sounded as though he wasn't overly worried about the casualties. "I just wish I'd had the chance to show them what I could do."

Jericho wasn't sure if Wavefront had any idea exactly how insensitive his words had just sounded; nobody else seemed to want to comment on them. Before the resulting silence could stretch out for too long, Black Dragon piped up with a question. "Hey, anyone know what the piggies were doin' at the Oaklands last night? Woke up an' looked out the window, an' there was a couple of cop cars on the street outside. An' I thought there mighta been something big flying around outside."

Talking of insensitive ... Jericho clenched his teeth so hard they hurt and folded his arms. Fortunately, the only one who seemed to pick up on this gesture was Smokeshadow. She gave him a sympathetic look before speaking up. "Someone got attacked and killed in one of the rooms, I think. The police are still looking for the perpetrator."

"Damn, that's some kinda ballsy," observed Black Dragon. "Goin' after someone inside an Oaklands apartment? You'd never know if it's gonna be an Enabled on the other side of the door."

Jericho turned his head to look out the window. *She didn't mean it* that *way … she didn't* mean *it that way … she* didn't *mean it that way …*

"Not *everyone* in the Oaklands is Enabled," Cyberswarm objected. "Most people staying there are probably normal."

"Yeah, but a one in ten chance of gettin' your ass handed to you by some guy who can put his fist through a brick wall? That's just fuckin' *askin'* for trouble." Black Dragon gave Cyberswarm a challenging look. "It's a stupid idea, is what I'm sayin'."

"Yes, but most of the time you'd get away with it," Cyberswarm argued earnestly. "And that's what people would see. Not that they'd get caught."

Jericho could feel the last vestiges of his self-control starting to slip away. He gritted his teeth, not wanting to yell at them for something they didn't even know about.

"So, did anyone go out patrolling last night?" It was Smokeshadow again. "Not saying I did, and not saying I didn't, but the sunrise was nice from the roof this morning."

As a diversion, it was patently transparent to Jericho, but it seemed to work. Wavefront, at least, took it at face value. "I'm more of a daytime hero," the spandex-clad man said. "Besides, I'm stuck with walking, unless I want to totally soak everything around me."

"Spent most of the night working on my bugs," Cyberswarm said. Taking off his helmet again, he popped open a panel and examined the intricate circuitry within. Holding a tiny tool like a pencil, he prodded something. Jericho thought he saw the spark of a tiny welding arc. A wisp of acrid smoke drifted across his nostrils.

Black Dragon shrugged. "Got in way late and I didn't want to get lost." She eyed Smokeshadow's costume. "What else can your hyperweave shit do, anyway?"

"Not much more than ordinary cloth, really," Smokeshadow admitted. "It can't protect me from bullets or turn me truly invisible, but it can change color and cut to provide active camouflage or give me whatever clothing style I want." She looked toward Black Dragon. "If you tear it, it'll slowly mend itself, but too much damage will destroy the smart aspect. And I'm the only one who can repair it." As she spoke, the jacket reverted to the gray washed-out hoodie from before.

Black Dragon wrinkled her nose, apparently deciding that programmable hyperweave was less useful than she'd thought it was. Or perhaps her attention span really was that short. "So how tall *is* the Spire, anyway?" she asked. "And are people allowed to climb it?"

"Nearly eight thousand feet, I believe," stated Wavefront authoritatively. "Driver?"

"Seven thousand nine hundred eighty feet from top to bottom," the cabbie stated through the intercom. **"Tallest man-made structure in the world. Hell, it's taller than some *mountains*. If you were standing on top and fell off, you'd reach terminal velocity before you hit the ground. Not that you'd ever be standing on top. Nobody's allowed up there."**

"What if someone climbed it anyway?" persisted Black Dragon.

"It's been tried. They were caught before they got off the main slope."

"Okay, what if someone hired a cab to fly real close and they jumped out—"

"Cabs don't fly that close to it. Nobody does. There's a flight exclusion zone all the way around the Spire, so people don't do that exact thing." Despite the cab driver's lack of inflection, Jericho could've sworn he heard a disgusted undertone.

"And secondly, cab doors are locked while in flight so nobody can just step outside."

"Oh." Black Dragon slumped back into her seat, her expression clearly saying *you people are no fun.*

Privately, Jericho disagreed. There was a time and a place for crazy antics. On top of an eight-thousand-foot building was not it. Utopia City was evidently set up to run like a finely tuned machine, which meant that any kind of Wild West attitude was strictly proscribed. This wasn't to say the way the undercover cops had mistreated the blond kid last night was *excusable,* just that he had a better idea of their motivations now. To those officers, Enabled kids presumably stealing stuff and coloring outside the lines were like grit in the machinery, making them look bad and distracting them from going after *genuine* threats. Of course, the fact that there was a murderer currently at large in Utopia City didn't make the uniformed police look very effective, either. *The sooner I help them nail Portman's ass to the wall, the better for everyone.*

He watched as the Spire came closer and closer, then something the driver had said occurred to him. "If there's a no-fly zone around the Spire, how close can we get before you have to land?" It would be the creamy icing on his shit cake if he had to walk a mile just to get into the building.

"Minimum one thousand feet from the base of the structure," the cabbie replied. **"It's all good. There's a row of air taxi stands on the outer edge of Challenger Plaza. I've already got one on hold, so I can drop you off there. ETA ninety seconds."**

Which merely served to confirm yet another one of Jericho's suspicions. What had seemed like fortuitously good flying was simply the result of careful forethought and good management. It was looking more and more like the takeoffs, landings and holding patterns were all accomplished by dedicated computer systems rather than fallible human pilots. He shuddered at the idea of attempting to accomplish all this without the aid of computers. It just wouldn't happen. *There'd be bits of air taxi raining down all over Utopia City.*

And then the G-forces were building again, which meant they were coming in for a landing. He could've adjusted his effective weight so as not to feel the deceleration but chose not to. While the system *might* be adaptable enough to handle changing weights within the car during the delicate operation of landing, he didn't want to bet his life on it. So, he sat it out and let the extra half-gee press down on him, just the same as everyone else.

The deceleration let off for a moment, dropping all the way to half a gee—the cabbie must have pulled up the nose to bleed off the forward speed—and he caught the familiar flash of a maglev rail out the window as they passed over the top of it. *That must be the east-west line.* A few seconds later, the extra weight cut in again as the thrumming of the lifters ramped up for a moment. With a by-now familiar four-way *clunk,* the cab came to rest on the ground. Feeling like a veteran at this, Jericho was on his feet and reaching for the door handle while the others were still fumbling for the release catches on their restraints.

Popping the door open, he climbed out and looked around.

37
Sense of Wonder

There was a world of difference between flying toward something as massive as the Spire and looking up at it from ground level. More than perspective could account for, the contrast was deeply conceptual. In the air, Jericho could accept that the Spire was 'just' a building. He could see the base from above, just as he could see the top from below. It gave him a sense of proportion that he could grasp, the same as he felt while gliding past tall buildings.

Standing where he was at the edge of the expanse of multi-colored paving stones, looking past the statue of Challenger to the awe-inspiring grand sweep of the Spire, he found himself simply incapable of grasping the immensity of the building all at once. While aware of the proportions, his mind could not handle them at that moment. Upward, ever upward it reached, the distant tip rendered unreal by the fact that clouds were parting to drift around it.

"Hey, is that statue *floating?*" Black Dragon's voice jarred him out of his reverie as she started forward at a trot. He followed along, mainly out of an awareness that the cab had already lifted off again and he didn't want to be in the way of any arriving newcomers.

But as he got closer to the imposing likeness of the world's first superhero, carved to twice life-size by someone with a great deal of talent, he realized that she was right. The statue, shaped as though the force-field-clad hero were just coming in for a landing, was slowly oscillating back and forth on its base—or rather, *above* its base. There was a clear foot of separation between the statue and the circular marble plinth above which it hovered. Below the brass plaque that bore Challenger's name, words had been carved into the marble itself:

HE PAVED THE WAY FOR THE REST OF US.

This close, he understood perfectly what was going on. "It's a gravity effect," he said, pointing at the focal points of what his G-sense could pick up. "There's field generators there, there and there. They keep it stable and in the air." He was pretty sure the oscillation was deliberate, but he couldn't be certain. Neither did he care all that much, right then.

"Niiice," she said with satisfaction. "Here they are, able to turn gravity into their bitch, an' they've used it to keep a chunk of carved rock in the air. Great *going,* guys." Her talent for hiding sarcasm until the last moment came as no great surprise.

Jericho frowned, forcing down his irritation at the suggestion that any use of anti-gravity technology might be seen as trivial. "They also use it to keep the maglev stable, if you didn't know." He gestured at the base of the Spire, well over two hundred yards distant, and at the other Enabled, who were still crossing the expanse of Challenger Plaza. People wearing civilian clothes were also getting out of taxis and heading for the Spire. "I'm thinking we need to go in before the lines get too long." Just from the shades of skin color and idiosyncrasies of clothing around him, he could see that ethnic and cultural diversity was alive and well in Utopia City, even within the subset of the population who worked in the Spire. *Good to see.*

"Lot of people comin' in," Black Dragon commented as they started toward their destination. "They all got powers, you think?"

The plaza, far from being a simple flat paved area, had a fountain in the middle as well as picnic tables with more of those self-adjusting umbrellas. He had no eyes for the fountain or even the sunshades, though; they were positively *ordinary* compared to the building he was walking toward.

"I doubt it," he decided. "Remember, a lot of administration goes on in the Spire too. Running a city this size would take a lot of people." He tried to estimate the internal volume of the immense structure before them, but his brain flaked out and delivered 'hell if I know' as its best result. The irony was, at this distance he literally couldn't take in the whole thing at once. The closer he got, the more it resembled a gigantic sloping technological hillside, leading to a steeply ascending mountain.

"No shit, Sherlock." Her reply sounded like more sarcasm to him. He wondered if she used it as a defensive mechanism, or if it just came naturally. Or if there was a difference, with her. Or if he even cared.

"So, about your power." Apart from the swearing and sarcasm, she hadn't been offensive to him, so he phrased the observation in a noncommittal fashion.

"What about it?" she responded warily.

He paused while he thought about his next words. "Why are those scales traveling over your body like that? Are you just playing around, or is there something else going on?"

She made a rude noise with her lips and he thought that was going to be it, until she shook her head. "My power sucks big hairy donkey balls. I can't turn it all the way off, and I have to concentrate super hard to turn it all the way on. When I'm not paying attention, it just moves around. If I'm really scared, or really pissed, or really *anything,* I go all the way dragon without meaning to. But usually, I can only do head and arms and stuff. Dragon-me kicks ass but getting myself all the way there is nearly fuckin' impossible unless shit's going down in a major way."

"So, do you get any larger?" asked Jericho, deciding not to call her on the swearing. He'd seen how well that had worked for Wavefront, and he didn't need *another* source of aggravation in his life right now. "Because I can see you going through costumes on a daily basis if that happened."

"Not any bigger, no," she said dismissively. "But I'm a lot tougher an' stronger. Knives don't hurt me, though bullets sting like fuck. Ripped the shit out've a cop car once."

There was a story there, if Jericho was any judge, but she didn't seem to want to expand on it. "And because you can't turn your emotions all the way *off,* you can't turn your powers off either," he guessed. "That's gotta suck for your secret identity."

She rolled her eyes behind her domino mask. "Fuckin' *tell* me about it. I useta love going to the beach. Not any fuckin' more. Now it's *why are you wearing your sweater, it's hot out* an' stuff." She pitched her voice to a screeching falsetto for the parental (he guessed) impression.

"I can see how that could be a problem." While her problems weren't on the same scale as his, he could definitely sympathize. Although she *did* have a serious potty mouth for someone who looked about fourteen.

"Well, duh." She gave him a steady look. "So how about you? How do your powers suck?"

He shrugged. "I already told you. I can't make myself fly, no matter what I do."

"You said something about that, yeah." She gave him an appraising look, her head tilted to the side. At that moment, the patch of scales roved up from the neck of her top and passed over her face, momentarily giving her golden cat-slitted pupils under scaled eye-ridges, and the beginning of a snout. "Can't fly at all, huh?"

"Well, I can *glide*," he said, holding out his arm to show the elastic cloth. "It's almost as good. Or at least, that's what I tell myself."

"Eh," she said doubtfully, waggling a hand back and forth. "Gliding's cool and all, but it doesn't pull the chicks, get what I mean?" Elbowing him in the ribs, she gave him what was probably supposed to be a leer.

He cleared his throat firmly. The swearing was one thing, but that was going over the line. "Okay, first? I don't go out as a superhero to 'pull the chicks'." *Or the guys. But you don't need to know that bit.* "Second? You're far too young to be even *talking* about that sort of thing."

"Hey, I'm eighteen!" she protested. "I'm plenty old enough!"

Jericho may have been the merest novice when it came to figuring out if someone was interested in him but he had long experience with seeing through people in other ways, mainly thanks to his long association with Luke. "Pull the other one," he said dryly, repeating one of his father's favorite sayings. "It whistles Dixie in three-part harmony."

Which only served to prove that while she was adept at handing out sarcasm, she was as bad as him at understanding it. "What?" she asked.

"I'm calling bullshit on you being eighteen. You're sixteen at *best*," he clarified. "And even then, I'd want to see some sort of photo ID. There's no way in hell you're eighteen."

"Bite me, asshole," she responded. "You're not a cop. And there's no age limit on joining Force Majeure. I checked."

"I never said there was," he said, but she loftily ignored him, triggering irritation on his part. "Whatever," he snapped and lengthened his stride, outpacing her. He didn't *need* this shit, on top of everything else. If she wanted to be a bratty teenager, she could go and be one somewhere else.

Over the course of their conversation, they had drawn close enough to the Spire to determine where under the rim of the broad curved frontage the actual entrance was. As it happened, it was at the closest point to the statue of Challenger, consisting of a wide expanse of tinted glass, punctuated at intervals with sliding glass doors. Probably acting on some impulse about not wanting to be beaten, Black Dragon trotted past him without a single sideways glance and entered the closest set of doors. He followed her inside.

Within was a lobby of considerable proportions, hosting no fewer than six reception desks. These were flanked by security scan-locks that might have been lifted directly from the maglev station, although the sliding doors were brushed metal rather than glass. The far wall was thirty feet high, with a huge Mercator projection of the world set into it. Bronze represented land while black shiny metal showed up as water, and etched lines pointed out time zones. Across the map, tiny lights were inset where he knew capital cities were located; even before he looked, he knew there would be one for Utopia City as well. This also drew his attention to the silvery spiderweb of lines spreading out from that light, covering the entire United States, with a spur line running up along the Canadian west coast to link to Alaska's meager network. *Wow, I had no idea the maglev went that far.*

At the bottom of each time-zone column was a sweep-hand clock showing what Jericho assumed was the current time in that zone. One additional clock, rimmed in gold, showed that the local time was three minutes past eight. As a final touch, hidden floodlights in the ceiling cast a glow that seemed to mimic daylight across the map.

People were lined up at five of the six desks, swiping their MagCards on readers as they reached the front of the line. Each one stepped into the scan-lock as it opened. He couldn't see what was going on inside, of course, but he presumed the steady inflow meant nobody was being stupid enough to bring contraband *into* the Spire, at least not this morning. Stopping for a moment, he looked around, trying to get a feel for what was going on. There was no impatience, no frustrated glances at watches. People were stepping forward in an orderly fashion, forming into queues without requiring any kind of guidance. It seemed the lines were moving through quickly enough that there was no backlog, at least for the moment. He tried to estimate how many people were coming through and got lost at 'thousands'.

The sixth desk had a prominent sign over it reading 'VISITORS', so he figured that was for him. Black Dragon was on her way over there, while the other three Enabled were already clustered in front of it. People stepped out of his way to let him through the queues as he moved in that direction; he got there just in time for the raised voices. Or rather, voice.

"What do you *mean*, I can't go in and show 'em how awesome I am?" demanded Black Dragon. "I'm kick-ass. Force Majeure would be *lucky* to have me on the team."

"Yes, miss, I understand," the receptionist said patiently. "But there's a procedure for this. If you want to join, you send in an application. We review the applications and send out return emails in due course. We can't just accept—"

"I put in my application a *month* ago," interrupted Wavefront. He was still trying to sound impressive, but his annoyance gave him an unfortunately petulant air. "Why is it taking so long?"

"Because mine took five weeks to come back," Jericho said, then turned to the receptionist. "Speaking of which, I've got an appointment for the name of G-Man. Nine o'clock this morning."

She seized upon the opening with barely concealed relief. "Just let me check," she murmured. Lacquered fingernails rattled on her keyboard briefly, then she looked up again. "I have you down for the nine o'clock, though it seems that you're almost an hour ahead of schedule, sir. Would you like to visit our gift shop or our café?" Something on her screen caught her eye, and she blinked. "Or … would you like to take a tour while you're waiting?"

It shouldn't have surprised him that they had both a gift shop *and* a café, but it did. Jericho had just started to turn around and look for these facilities when the last part of her statement caught up with him. "Tour?"

"You're *shitting* me." Black Dragon stared at Jericho. "They're actually letting you *in*? For a *tour*?"

"G-Man has an appointment," the receptionist said. "He's been accepted for an interview. Would you like me to put in an interview application for you?"

Black Dragon's reply was immediate. "Would that get me a tour?"

This was a different side of the girl. At the possibility of a tour of the Spire, she'd gone almost fangirlish, her tone and expression showing eagerness for once. The contrast with the don't-give-a-damn teenager he'd had words with outside couldn't have been more glaring.

"Not ordinarily …" The receptionist typed something, then looked over the result. She glanced up at Jericho. "… but he's got the option of bringing along a plus one, if he so wishes."

If Jericho thought the change in Black Dragon had been dramatic when she found out about the tours, he quickly learned that he'd seen nothing yet. Her puppy-dog eyes might have been more effective if she'd ever practiced them. As it was, she reminded him of a pit bull he'd once seen attired in a pink tutu and fake eyelashes.

He deliberately ignored her and turned to Smokeshadow. "You want to come up?"

She paused, long enough to make Black Dragon start bouncing on her toes in anguish. "Tempting," she mused with a smile quirking the corner of her mouth, "but I think I'll pass this once."

"Please!" Black Dragon burst out. "I won't say a word! I'll be extra good! You'll never know I was there!" She clenched her hands together so tightly, the skin over her knuckles turned white.

"I don't believe that for a second," Jericho said flatly. Normally he would've been a lot more tolerant of her behavior, but since the phone call with Uncle Leroy his temper had been on a slow boil, mainly because anger was easier to deal with than grief. He was just self-aware enough to understand that he was at least partially projecting his irritation onto Black Dragon, which had the potential of causing him to treat her unfairly.

On the other hand, she *was* an exceedingly annoying self-absorbed teenager. Nobody would blame him if he said no.

"Please!" insisted Black Dragon, her tone desperate. "I'll do better! Gimme a chance! You'll see!"

Jericho pursed his lips, ready to turn her down on general principle. *I just don't need this.* But then Smokeshadow caught his gaze. Behind the domino mask, her eyes briefly flicked sideways toward Black Dragon, while the mask itself flexed as though she were raising one eyebrow slightly. It wasn't a demand or a plea; as best he could tell, it was just a suggestion. Something along the lines of: *Hey, why not? You never know.*

He hadn't known Smokeshadow long, but she'd already impressed him with her perspicacity and insight. If she considered it to be a good idea to bring Black Dragon on the tour with him, then he figured it wouldn't be too much of a hardship to go along with that. Still, it didn't mean he had to be *nice* about it.

"Dragon," he said bluntly. "You want to come on the tour?"

She blinked. "Hell *yes*, I do."

"Then you can come. But there's conditions. Break those conditions and you're off the tour. Got it?"

"Fuckin' A!" She fist-pumped the air hard, her hand momentarily becoming a draconic claw once more. "What do I gotta do?"

"First, you're going to offer at least basic respect to me and whoever's running the tour," Jericho stated flatly. "You listen to what we say, and you do it. No half-assed BS."

Part of him expected her to balk at that, but instead she came to a parody of attention and threw something that was probably an acceptable military salute *somewhere*. "Sir, yes, sir!" she proclaimed, then spoiled the effect by rolling her eyes.

"Good," he said. "Second condition, no F-bombs. Otherwise, keep your language as clean as you can. Three strikes, you're out. Got it?"

"Wait, what the f—" She trailed off as he raised a finger. "Right, got it. No swearing." She paused, tilting her head. "So, is that three strikes and *then* I'm out, or out on the third strike?" The hopeful tone of her voice left him in no doubt as to which she would prefer.

"Third strike." Jericho mentally shook his head. *Should've realized she'd go for that loophole.* "You've got two chances. Strike three, you're out. Understood?"

She nodded. "Got it. Two chances, three strikes." Clasping her hands in front of her, she gave him the most innocent look he'd seen on her yet. He didn't trust it for an instant. "Like I said, I'll be good."

Wavefront shook his head. "Sucker," he said with a smirk. "You've got to know she's playing you like a fiddle."

"Hey!" protested Black Dragon. "Keep your, uh, stupid nose outta my business, okay? He said I could come. Right, G-Man?"

"Back off," Jericho said without heat. He'd made his decision and he was sticking to it.

Wavefront stared at him, then rolled his eyes. "Yeah, well, whatever," he muttered. "I'm not the one who just let a teenager pull the wool over my eyes."

The guy just didn't know when to quit. Jericho felt his fists clench at his sides but forced himself to relax. *He's not worth it.* "See you after the tour." With the specific inference that Wavefront wasn't going on the tour.

"Woo hoo, *fuck* yes!" Black Dragon punched the air. "Let's *kick* this puppy!"

Jericho opened his mouth, then closed it at Wavefront's smirk. *I'm not gonna give him the satisfaction.*

"Before you get too excited," the receptionist said, "I have to issue your visitor passes." Pulling open a drawer, she removed two plastic rectangles on lanyards, each one four inches by six inches, and about a quarter-inch thick. Embedded in the plastic was a holographic image of the Spire, with the word 'VISITOR' written across it in black, bordered with bright yellow. "G-Man, this one's yours." Putting the first one on the counter, she beckoned Jericho closer. "Hold one hand flat on the pass while you swipe your MagCard on the reader."

"One second," he said. Unzipping his jacket a little way, he retrieved the MagCard from its inside pocket, then did as he was told. When he tapped it with the card, the reader beeped agreeably.

"Good," she said with satisfaction. "You're now in the system. Put that on, and don't take it off while you're on the tour. If you take it off, or if you leave the area you're supposed to be touring, it will set off an alarm and you *will* be apprehended. If you're lucky, you will then be ejected from the building. If you're not lucky, criminal charges will be preferred against you. Do you understand this warning?"

"Yes, I do." Matching her serious tone with one of his own, he put his MagCard away and zipped up his jacket before slipping the lanyard over his neck. The oversized visitor pass made it feel like he was wearing half a sandwich board.

"Excellent," she said. "And finally, I'm going to need you to hand over your phone and any other electronic devices you have on you. These will be returned to you when you leave the building." She gave Jericho a quick, tight smile. "Security. You understand."

That aspect hadn't occurred to Jericho before this point. In his opinion, it verged on paranoia, but it was their building and their rules. "You got it." Opening the pouch where he kept his phone, he held in the button to shut it all the way down then handed it over.

She peeled a Post-it note off a pad, attached it to the phone, and wrote 'G-MAN' on it in marker pen before putting the phone in a drawer behind her. "Okay, that's you done. Black Dragon, was it?"

Jericho stepped back to allow the teenager access to the counter, while the receptionist repeated the instructions. Black Dragon carefully followed them. As unconcerned with societal norms as the girl usually was, Jericho wasn't surprised at her focus here; she clearly didn't want to screw up her one chance to tour the Spire. If he was being honest with himself, he couldn't imagine that anyone would. Except Smokeshadow, apparently; but the enigmatic Enabled was clearly someone who marched to the beat of a different drummer.

The receptionist finished her litany then looked directly at Black Dragon. "Do you understand this warning?" She was definitely conscientious at her job. Although the teenager had been right there to hear what had been said to Jericho, the woman had repeated it verbatim for her sake.

"Yeah, got it. No taking the thing off, no sneaking away, here's my phone." Having said that all in one breath, Black Dragon slapped her phone on the counter. Then she pulled the lanyard over her head, letting the pass slap her in the stomach. "Come on, let's *do* this thing already!"

"Certainly." The receptionist repeated the labeling process, though Jericho suspected she only wrote 'BD' on this one, then hit a key on her computer. The metal doors of the scan-lock slid open. "Go on through."

Black Dragon darted into the scan-lock, with Jericho following more sedately. The doors closed behind them, and lights came up to bathe them in a gentle glow. Not entirely to his surprise, the doors at the far end stayed closed for the moment.

"Hey, what's the dealio?" The teenage girl was standing about three inches away from the far doors, nose a hair's breadth from the dividing line, almost vibrating with impatience. "Why don't they let us through already?"

Jericho tried not to regret bringing her along on the tour. Folding his arms, he leaned casually against the wall to convey a relaxed pose. "Maybe because this isn't the maglev. This is the *Spire*. They're not just looking for guns, drugs or explosives. This thing's going to be scanning us down to the microscopic level."

Black Dragon gave him an incredulous stare. "What do they think we are? Morons?"

He shrugged. "They'd be the morons if they didn't check every person, every time. It just takes one." He raised a finger. "And by the way, when you swore before? That was strike one. I'd have said something then, but I didn't want to give Wavefront any more ammunition."

Incredulity gave way to indignation. "*What?* No way! That just slipped out. And anyway, we hadn't started the tour yet. That doesn't count."

Jericho wasn't in the mood to take any shit; not from her, not from anyone. "You swore after you agreed to the terms. We can make it strike one or strike two. Your choice." The only way to deal with her, he'd learned, was to leave her absolutely no leeway.

Just for a moment, he thought she was going to tell him to go to hell, but then her face creased up as the realization of her situation bit deep. "Fine, strike one," she muttered. "Not fair." As if on cue, the doors at the far end of the scan-lock slid apart.

"Woo!" Her bad mood evaporating on the instant, Black Dragon charged forward out of the scan-lock, only to skid to a halt almost immediately. "Whoa!"

Jericho couldn't see what she'd reacted to, so he straightened up and stepped away from the wall. When he exited the scan-lock, it was into a room surrounded on four sides by frosted glass. Black Dragon was face to reflective faceplate with none other than Transit. "Be careful there, miss," the flight-suit clad woman said firmly. "Hello, G-Man. I see you're on time."

38
Within the Spire

It hadn't been twelve hours since Jericho had last seen Transit, but he felt as though he'd lived a lifetime in the interim. In the normal course of events, the fact that she remembered his name would've been a cause for internal fanboy squeeing, but right now he cared far less than he should have. "Well, you did say not to be late."

He hadn't thought his change in attitude was that blatant, but from the way Transit tilted her head slightly—a mannerism evidently developed to replace facial cues when using an opaque visor—she'd almost certainly picked up on it. Black Dragon was less subtle about her response: "Okay, that's just cold."

He slowly turned his head toward her, making a production of it. She hastily subsided.

"Hello, Transit," he said, returning his attention to the Force Majeure hero. "It's good to see you again." He inclined his head toward the teen. "This is Black Dragon. She showed up, looking to try out."

"I see." Transit nodded to acknowledge his words. "So, Black Dragon, have you put in an application yet?"

"Not yet," mumbled Black Dragon, dropping her eyes to the floor. "I will, though."

"It's a good idea." Transit's voice never lost its tone of measured calm. "As much as I admire your eagerness, we simply can't take the risk of accepting just any walk-up off the street. Potential recruits must be vetted before we ever send the email. And of course, there's always a backlog of worthwhile applications."

"You had me checked out." Jericho wasn't totally surprised, though he was impressed that he hadn't spotted any part of the investigation into him.

"Certainly." Transit turned her head toward him. Her tone held warmth, which may have meant she was smiling. Or not, of course. "Joining Force Majeure is a serious business. It's not for just anyone. We don't want to bring someone in only to find out that they lied about their powers, or their basic principles are utterly incompatible with ours. Or worse, they were joining under false pretenses to spy on us or commit sabotage from within. A rogue operative with full Force Majeure clearances could do untold damage before they were stopped."

Jericho shook his head. "I don't even want to think about that. Have there ever been saboteurs?" He'd already been inclined to accept the stringent security precautions, but this put the icing on the cake.

"Or spies? What do you do with spies, anyway?" asked Black Dragon. "String 'em up by the nuts 'til they say who sent them? Dangle 'em off the top of the Spire?"

Jericho frowned. "That's a bit bloodthirsty. Besides, torture's illegal." Personally, he blamed the violence on TV and in video games for the younger generation's attitudes.

"Well, we don't do *that*, no, but we do question them rather thoroughly before we hand them over to the Feds," Transit allowed. "Now, saboteurs are another problem altogether. If someone wants to steal our secrets, we're essentially unharmed in a physical sense, if not corporate. But doing damage to the maglev network or to the Spire itself could kill any number of people, so we nip that in the bud *hard*. To this end, we have explicit permission from the government to defend our properties and our persons with immediate lethal force, even if it's only attempted sabotage."

"Uh huh." Jericho recalled the incidents where people had attacked the maglev line. Force Majeure had not been gentle with their response, either time. "So has anyone tried to do that sort of thing from the *inside* yet?" While he suspected such an action would be harder to pull off, it also had the potential to wreak far greater havoc.

"Nobody's come close to succeeding," Transit said, with a hint of satisfaction in her voice. "We've had several runners-up over the years, though. We usually let them get to the final interview before we spring the trap on them. The footage of their faces when they realize just how screwed they are is always amusing. However." She clapped her hands lightly together.

"However?" asked Jericho, as she seemed to be waiting expectantly.

"However, you've signed up to take a tour, and I'm your designated tour guide." She looked from Jericho to Black Dragon. "Let's get this show on the road, shall we?"

There were two other exits from the room. One was a set of double doors to the left, and the other an obvious elevator recessed into the wall opposite the scan-lock. Transit turned toward the elevator and waved her hand over a blank metal panel. In response, the door slid aside. Jericho hadn't seen her use a MagCard but that meant nothing when there was an artificer involved.

Inside, there was another blank panel where there should have been buttons or a floor counter, or both. That didn't seem to faze Transit, who gestured toward the panel, not even bothering to make physical contact with it. As the doors closed, Jericho wondered how much of this was for actual security and how much was to impress visitors with Force Majeure's technological capability. He suspected the answer was 'yes'.

When the elevator started moving, it nearly took his breath away. The last time he'd felt this level of smooth but tremendously powerful acceleration was on the maglev. Also as with the maglev, he could tell they were using gravity generators to counteract the effects of acceleration and deceleration. He felt it all, of course, through his G-sense if not his inner ear. In just one second, the elevator car moved thirty feet vertically then stopped on a dime, leaving him with the feeling that he wanted to get off the world until it stopped spinning around him.

"Are you all right, G-Man?" asked Transit as they stepped from the elevator.

He wasn't sure what sign he'd given of his inner discomfort, but he shrugged. "I'll be fine. That was … fast."

Her tone was amused. "We don't believe in wasting time here in Force Majeure. None of our elevators have music piped in, because you're never in there long enough to need it." Stepping forth, she turned left out of the doors.

Following along as he shook off the final effects of the elevator ride, Jericho found himself in a ten-foot-wide corridor, lined with doors and the occasional window. Black Dragon joined him a moment later and glanced around. "Looks a bit like a hospital, doesn't it?" she murmured, indicating the broad lit-up colored stripes on the floor and softly glowing light panels in the ceiling. The fact that the doors had MagCard readers next to them barely spoiled the illusion.

"Only a bit." He pointed at the floor. "Those aren't painted on." Which was true; the stripes were *moving*, rearranging their relative positions from second to second. How it was done, he wasn't sure, but the floor certainly wasn't made of hospital-standard vinyl floor tiles.

Then he noticed something else. Specifically, that up ahead, the corridor looked like it curved subtly around to the left. Glancing over his shoulder, he saw that the corridor extended back behind them with the same curve, this time to the right. "Does this go all the way around?" he asked, raising his voice to address Transit.

"Good eye," Transit confirmed. "We're currently in a circular corridor, or what we call a circuit."

"Wait," said Black Dragon, turning her head from left to right. "This is a *circle?* How *big* is it?"

"If you follow the center-line of the corridor, exactly four thousand feet," Transit said. "I occasionally use one like it as a running track." She pointed at the nearest door. "If there's any sort of emergency and we get separated, press your visitor pass to any reader and follow the flashing blue line. It'll lead you to where you need to be. But as we're *not* under emergency conditions right now, you can follow me instead."

She set off, power-walking down the corridor as if she had a long way to go and a short time to get there. Jericho lengthened his stride to keep up, while Black Dragon trotted along behind. "What're all these doors about?" asked the teenager. "What's this level do?"

"Research and development, mainly. Research and Development Sierra-Five is just up to the left. We can look through the observation window." Transit led the way forward, until they passed a door marked 'R&D S-5' and came to a large picture window. Subtle distortions in the light coming through told Jericho the 'glass' was probably some kind of complex polycarbonate. The window-frame, as far as he could tell, was equally reinforced.

Within was a combination laboratory and engineering space. Workstations with what looked like holographic displays were interspersed with benches containing lathes, drill presses and other mechanical devices he suspected Luke would've been far more at home with than he was. The window darkened momentarily as a welding arc sparked up at the far end of the room. After it cleared, he spotted bits and pieces of technology that he had no way to identify on some of the workbenches.

Black Dragon pressed her nose up to the window, so that her breath fogged the surface. "Holy fuck, it's a mad science laboratory."

Jericho cleared his throat and raised two fingers. *Strike two.*

The look on Black Dragon's face as she turned around would've made Jericho burst out laughing if he'd been in the mood for laughter. He could tell her natural instinct was to cuss out anyone who told her what to do, but in this case her innate caution would've been screaming at her *don't do that!* Or at least, that was the impression he got from her facial contortions. Finally, she muttered, "Sorry."

"That's all right. Just don't do it again." Transit's tone was mildly amused. "But you were close. They're designing technology that *almost* works."

Jericho turned his head to look at her. "How's that again?"

"It's simple," Transit said as she started walking again. Black Dragon lingered a moment, but once they were a few yards away, Jericho heard the teenager's visitor pass let out a warning buzz. Startled, she hurried to catch up with them. Transit went on as if oblivious to the interruption. "We have three artificers on the main team, but—"

"But—" Jericho began, then shut up as Transit looked his way. "Sorry, never mind."

"What?" she asked. "If you have a question, feel free to ask."

He frowned, trying to make sense of her words. "I thought you and the Technologist were the two artificers. Who's the third?"

"Silent Knight, of course." Her tone said *duh.* "But his power is based around improving and maintaining his own armor."

"Wait, wait," Black Dragon interrupted. "About Silent Knight. Is that whole silent thing an act, or can't he talk at all? Is it a birth thing, or was it an accident?" Her eyes gleamed with prurient interest. "Is he horribly scarred under all that?"

All of which, Jericho understood, was fodder for endless debate on the internet message boards. But this was definitely not the right time or place. "Dragon—"

"Silent Knight's armor supplies more than mere physical protection," Transit stated firmly, cutting Jericho off. "It's a completely self-contained life-support system. He says that if he built in external communication apparatus, it would compromise the integrity of the armor."

"Does that mean he's built himself *into* his armor?" persisted Black Dragon, her expression twisting into horrified delight. "Ew!"

"No." Transit's tone was final. "That's a ridiculous concept. There are far too many things that could go wrong. His life support is simply … comprehensive. Total isolation from all external factors. He once suggested integrating a similar system into the core systems of the Spire, but that would've meant removing all communication with the outside world, so the move was voted down."

Jericho nodded in agreement. "I can see how that could be a problem."

"No kidding." Transit huffed a sigh inside her helmet. "*As* I was saying, the Technologist and I each have a more comprehensive field of capability than Silent Knight, which means we're *the* go-to people for technology in the team. Now, we could spend all our time in the workshop coming up with new designs, but then we'd be doing nothing else all day. Instead, we employ people to come up with designs that *almost* function. Ideas that are both valid and worth developing, but which need better than modern technology to translate into working models. Once they've pushed it as far as they can, we review their work to that point and decide which ones to carry on with. It saves us a huge amount of drudge engineering."

Which was not only ingenious, but also reminded Jericho of something. "You called that lab back there R&D lab five," he said. "Does that mean there's four other labs?"

Her laughter sounded odd inside her helmet. "There's *nine* other labs. Five more in the Spire, and four out at UCIAT; or as we call it, 'you-see-it'."

"You see it?" Jericho repeated the last three words, not sure what she was talking about.

"Utopia City Institute for Advanced Technology," she explained. "Did you not know about this?"

Jericho paused for a moment to think before he spoke again. Hearing the acronym pronounced was far different from seeing it on paper. "I've *heard* about it. I just didn't make the connection." He vaguely recalled looking it up when he was scouting colleges out of high school. It turned out the scholastic requirement was too high and the waiting list far too long for him to even consider applying. "So, they actually do R&D for you?"

"They get extra course credit if they design something that we end up using. Quite a lot of it has military applications." Transit's voice picked up a tinge of pride. "Aside from our superhero activities, Force Majeure's been in the business of supplying specialty equipment to the military for nearly a decade. Our market share's steadily growing all the time. For about the last eighteen months, the only military contracts we haven't owned wholesale are things we don't want to do or aren't equipped to supply. But we also do individual items." She hooked her thumb over her shoulder. "Relentless' mace came out of a lab like that one. I studied Lady Quantum's powers and figured out how to make the gravity motor work to a point, and the Technologist improved on my design."

Gravity, of course, was a subject near and dear to Jericho's heart. "Gravity motor? You can make things *fly*?" He'd been aware of the gravity stabilization on the maglev—he couldn't *help* but be aware of it—and he'd seen the floating statue out on the plaza, but the flight aspect was one he hadn't considered. Especially since his own powers didn't include flight. But of course, once he thought about it, there weren't many *other* ways that the mace could be made to fly without adding rockets or something similar to it.

"Oh, easily," Transit said, then paused. "Well, not *easily* easily. Gravity generators which don't result in free flight are relatively simple to make. It's a little harder, though entirely possible, to make gravity motors that *can* fly on their own, but they run the risk of becoming unstable."

That word sounded ominous to Jericho. "Unstable how?"

Transit's voice was serious. "The chance of them spontaneously developing a self-propagating gravity well is non-negligible. The Technologist has to add his own touches to negate that possibility, which means that any such design can't be mass-produced."

While Jericho mulled this over (and tried to think of a way to say 'self-propagating gravity well' that didn't sound like 'runaway black hole') Black Dragon stuck her oar in. "But if *you* build something on your own, it can be mass produced, yeah? Like this non-flying gravity generator thing?"

Transit nodded. "The Technologist and I have to design and build the machinery to do the production, which itself can't be mass-produced. However, it can then mass-produce *my* technology, without any further input from us."

"Wasn't the maglev something you collaborated on?" asked Jericho. He couldn't imagine Transit having the time to personally build every single maglev car.

"The proof of concept version was, yes," Transit admitted. "But we refined the design so it only needed gravity generators for stabilization and counteracting inertia. That allows them to be mass-produced and maintained without our input, freeing us up for other work."

"Oh." Jericho felt obscurely let down. He'd been personally convinced that the maglev was the most advanced technology in the world, and meanwhile it was only the *second* most advanced technology, behind Relentless' mace. And of course, Force Majeure had a huge advantage on virtually every other team with an artificer on it, because the Technologist's assistance meant mass production was possible. Very few, if any, artificers could match that. He'd heard somewhere that Adam Power was capable of it, but the man had his own problems at the moment.

"So, who designed the Spire?" asked Black Dragon. "You or el Techmeister?"

Transit turned to face Black Dragon directly as they came to a corridor leading off to the right. Also ten feet wide, it had no curves and seemed to go a very long way into the depths of the building. "Do not *ever* call him that in his hearing," she said, an instant before Jericho could say something similar. "Seriously, do *not*."

"Okay, fine," grumped the teenager, quite possibly having caught the look on Jericho's face. "I won't."

Jericho considered calling a third strike anyway but chose to let it slide; she hadn't sworn, after all.

"Good." Transit led the way down the new corridor, with Jericho and Black Dragon following. She waved her hand to encompass the building around them. "Just so you know, every level of the Spire is divided into four quadrants by radial corridors like this one. Circuits go all the way around, radials go into the center, and there's a maximum of three circuits to a level."

She turned to Black Dragon. "Now, to answer your question, we collaborated with a third party on the design. In fact, the entire city was designed with their input." As Black Dragon opened her mouth again, Transit raised a finger. "No, I'm not going to tell you who. They prefer anonymity, for obvious reasons."

Within the infrastructure of Utopia City, much less the Spire itself, Jericho figured there had to be secrets that any antagonist of Force Majeure would give an arm and a leg to possess. Capturing a team member to interrogate would be painfully difficult. Getting hold of the mystery third party, with no clue as to their identity, would be virtually impossible.

"Well, I know it's a guy, anyway," Black Dragon said blithely. She blinked as both Transit and Jericho turned to look at her. "What?"

"Why does it have to be a guy?" Jericho had no idea why Black Dragon would even make a statement like that. "Why can't a woman have designed it?" He gestured at the building around them. By any metric he could imagine, it was a marvel of engineering.

"Because it looks like a dick, that's why," retorted the girl. "Phallic, that's the word. Every phallic building ever, a guy designed it." She held one hand down near her waist and the other up level with her shoulders, like a fisherman boasting about his catch, only vertically. "It's like they're saying to the world, 'I got one *this—*'"

"Stop. Talking." Jericho didn't shout, but it was a near thing. He felt his teeth gritting together. Once again, he began to regret allowing her on the tour. He couldn't even imagine the mindset that would jump straight to phallic imagery as a go-to for explaining architecture.

"Sure, but you know I'm right." She gave him a smug look, then turned to Transit. Jericho was suddenly appreciative of the fact the Force Majeure hero was wearing a full-face helmet. He wasn't sure he could've met her eyes about then. "I'm right, aren't I?"

"I can neither confirm nor deny." The amusement had returned to Transit's voice. "Though I'm sure the designer would be *fascinated* to hear your theories as to why the building is shaped like it is."

"Yeah, well, I bet I'm right." Black Dragon stuck her chin out. "Why'd you guys build it so tall, anyway? Half a mile woulda got the point across just as good."

"Several reasons." Transit was back to being a tour guide. "First, it's an advertisement." Black Dragon opened her mouth with a look of glee, but Transit raised a hand quellingly. "Not *that* kind of advertisement, and if you ever want to get onto the team, I would strongly suggest you leave that sort of joke at the door." She waited until the teenager subsided, then went on. "Force Majeure is a strong, diverse team with a powerful core leadership. We can do things no other team can. Building the Spire only half a mile high would've invited other artificers to try to beat it. A mile and a half, on the other hand, puts the bar so far out of reach that the smart ones give up and compete for second place. We are paramount, and this proves it." The pride was apparent in her voice.

Jericho nodded. "Understood. But why did you stop where you did? Seven thousand nine hundred eighty feet? Was there some sort of architectural reason you couldn't cover that last twenty feet?"

Somewhat to his surprise, Transit chuckled. "I was waiting for one of you to ask that question. I'll give you one back. How high above sea level do you think the base of the Spire is?"

While Jericho didn't know that offhand, her wording gave him a clue. "No idea, but the number ends in twenty." He was absolutely certain of it.

"*Now* you're thinking." She sounded approving. "Precisely one thousand twenty feet."

It was the last piece of the puzzle. Had Jericho been thinking more clearly, he felt he would've figured it out earlier. "Plus seven nine eighty makes nine thousand feet." It was beyond his comprehension. Not only had Force Majeure pulled off this incredible feat of engineering in only a couple of years, but they'd even built in a math riddle for shits and giggles. There was architecture and then there was *architecture*. This was definitely the latter. *Sonovabitch. Nine thousand feet.*

Black Dragon, predictably, couldn't let matters rest there. "Okay, so it's the tallest building in the world. Good going. You know it's also a f—a really huge target. What's to stop some ass, uh, clown from hijacking an air taxi, loading it with explosives, and flying it into the side? It probably won't knock it over, but there'll sure as hell be a hole in the side afterward. Or a plane. I bet if you flew a plane or even a f—a, uh, cruise missile into the side of this thing, it might do some damage. And there's a lot of people out there who don't like Force Majeure. Just saying."

It was kind of impressive. The girl apparently used F-bombs as punctuation, but with that third strike hanging over her head, she was doing her best to catch them before they came all the way out. *I gotta admit, she's making the effort.*

"This is true." Transit led them to an elevator, then paused. "I *was* going to take you down to show you the power core, but I think I'll take you on a detour first." She turned her helmet to face each of them in turn. "You will keep your hands to yourselves. Touch anything at all, and you will be summarily expelled from the Spire. Any membership options will be *finished*. Are we understood?" The tone of her voice was uncompromising.

"Definitely." Jericho shoved his hands into his jacket pockets to show his good intentions.

They both looked at Black Dragon, who didn't seem to have any pockets to put her hands in. Finally, she folded her arms tightly across her chest. "This good enough?"

Transit nodded. "That should do." The elevator opened at her gesture, and she led them inside. Again, she merely waved at the wall where a button panel might've been, and the doors closed. *Oh, wait a minute. She's a mechanokinetic. Of* course *she doesn't need to hit any buttons.* Not a moment too soon. Jericho braced himself. They rocketed upward with an acceleration only he could feel.

"So, what's up here, anyway?" asked Black Dragon. "Or aren't we allowed to know that?"

"Part of the Spire's defensive systems," Transit said. "Note that I will not be answering questions about how it works, or even how to get clearance to access it. For today, you're with me. And while what we do up here is an open secret in Utopia, we usually don't spread it around."

Halfway through her speech, the elevator began to decelerate just as abruptly. As with the maglev, it wasn't something he thought he'd ever get used to, but he could endure it. The sheer convenience was undeniable, considering they'd just ascended half a mile in about twenty seconds. The doors opened, and she stepped out into a corridor that looked identical to the one they'd just come from. Jericho figured there was probably some way to tell which floor he was on, but it wasn't immediately obvious.

"So, what happens to the air in the elevator shafts?" he asked to distract himself from the lingering discomfort. "Is it pumped out of the way?"

"We keep them at near-vacuum, with vents to the outside on the longer shafts," Transit replied at once. "It serves to expedite high-speed movement from one floor to another, and also ensures that any hypothetical intruders can't use the elevator shafts to get around." She pointed at a discreetly placed air vent on the wall. "Also, all air conduits are a maximum of six inches square and are regularly patrolled by lethally armed semi-autonomous drones of my own design."

Which removed *that* aspect as a potential entry route. The amount of forethought that had gone into the design of the Spire had officially gone far past 'comprehensive' and was bordering on 'insane'. "*Has* anyone ever made it inside?" he asked. "Apart from the ones trying to join so they could sabotage or spy on you, I mean?"

"Well, we *do* have secure holding facilities," Transit said. "Anyone who tries to go anywhere in the building without specific permission is likely to end up there." Jericho noted that she'd neglected to answer the actual question. For a moment, he wondered if the lack of an answer was a subtle hint, then decided that no, it wasn't subtle at all.

"Or in pieces, right?" Black Dragon smirked. "Any assclown who tries to break in here deserves whatever they get."

"I couldn't have put it better myself." Transit strode along the corridor without looking back at them. "And that brings us to the second reason we built the Spire the way we did. It's here to serve as our base, our citadel and our bastion. If we're ever attacked by an enemy we can't immediately beat—and only an idiot assumes they won't be—this is where we fall back to, a place where nobody can simply burst in and attack when our guard is down." She paused at a door. "One more time: touch *nothing*."

Jericho nodded, his hands firmly in his jacket pockets. Black Dragon grasped her opposite elbows. Transit nodded, and the door beside her slid open.

They entered a large room dominated by half a dozen holographic consoles. Unlike the kiosk in the maglev station, these were flat and round, and extended their imagery from waist level up to head height. Technicians with intent expressions and headsets that could almost have doubled as helmets studied the holograms. From time to time, someone reached into the depths of an image with a gloved hand and did something that Jericho couldn't make out. An undercurrent of murmured conversation was all that kept the silence from being oppressive.

Five of the consoles were just big enough to reach across, while the sixth looked more like a display than a workstation. Fully fifteen feet across, it held a stunning holographic view of Utopia City. A narrow green band, just inside the periphery of the map, caught his eye. Only two or three inches wide, it went all the way around the city. *Is that what the cabbie called the Greenway?*

By comparison, the Spire (proudly situated in the middle) was only eight or nine inches tall. As Jericho watched, clouds drifted across the map. It took him a moment to realize that some of them were well below the tip of the Spire. He could see now that the streets were laid out in the same way as the corridors in the building he was standing in, with concentric circles crossed by radial lines spreading out from the center.

"Okay, so it's pretty as, uh, anything," Black Dragon said eventually. "But what's it *do*?"

Transit cleared her throat. "Johnson."

One of the technicians straightened up and looked her way. "Ma'am?"

"What's the weather like over Memorial Park?"

He didn't even have to look at the displays. "Clear with some high-altitude clouds, ma'am."

"Give them a light rain shower for fifteen minutes," she said as casually as if she were ordering coffee. "G-Man, Black Dragon, this way."

"Light rain shower, Memorial Park, fifteen minutes, yes ma'am." The technician turned to the nearest console. Jericho kept one eye on the man as Transit led the two of them toward the large display. He seemed to be fiddling with controls around the edge, as well as reaching into the middle of the hologram, but Jericho had no context that let him figure out what the guy was *doing*.

Transit pointed into the large holographic map. Obediently, a red flashing arrow sprang to life above a small green patch on the map which was overlaid by a yellow-orange cross. It took Jericho a moment to realize that the cross was an integral part of the landscaping. "That's Memorial Park. Everyone should visit at least once. It's got walled pathways engraved with the names of every person who died when the bomb went off." She didn't have to explain which bomb. "Except for one, of course."

"Doc Iridium," Jericho guessed.

"Correct." Transit primly clasped her hands behind her back. "His name doesn't belong there."

Silently, Jericho agreed. *Let the sonovabitch rot in obscurity.* As he watched, the view enlarged, pushing first the green band and then the Spire itself to the very edge of the map and beyond. The reduction in scale revealed more of the rich and varied detail available with this unique method of representing the city. The canal he'd seen the previous night, or perhaps another one, meandered around the western perimeter of the park, widening at one point to form a pond in which a tiny island had been placed. Small footbridges, like the ones at the Market, linked the island to both banks of the canal, giving access to the western entry to the park.

There were three other entrance points to the park, but they lacked the canal and the pond. From each one (including the one from the west) broad pathways led inward and upward. While the rest of Utopia City seemed quite flat, Memorial Park was built up to form a gentle hill, with just enough rises and hollows to make it look natural. Secondary pathways spider-webbed between the four main ones, with shade trees and bright dots that he presumed to be garden beds here and there.

The four primary paths converged on the summit of the hill (such as it was), but were covered by a continuous canopy of shade trees for nearly all of the climb, their orange-red foliage providing a striking contrast against the green of the grass (and incidentally, forming the cross which he'd registered earlier). At this scale he was unable to get a look at the memorial walls he supposed would be under the tree cover, though he was definitely able to admire the exquisite landscaping that had gone into making the park a thing of beauty. Because the park was oddly shaped, the path leading down toward the western edge was longer than the other three, and the tree-cover persisted almost to the very edge. He walked around the holo-table and saw the reason for this; when viewed from the western side, the trees lining the four pathways formed a Christian-style cross. *Well, it is a memorial.*

"What's the scale on this?" he asked, interested despite himself. "I mean, how big's the park?"

"Two hundred acres," Transit said at once. "It's about half a mile by three-quarters."

Jericho knew he shouldn't be surprised, but he was anyway. *That's bigger than Forsyth Park, back home.* From what he'd seen of the city map before it zoomed in on Memorial Park, it was just one of many greenspaces in the city, including the rooftop parks such as the South Side Mall sported. Though he hadn't seen anything as impressive as the Greenway. *When they planned this place, they didn't mess around.*

And then he saw the clouds gathering above the park, thickening as he watched. "Oh, no way," breathed Black Dragon from the other side of the table. "You have *got* to be f—funning with me."

"Oh, yes way." Jericho had always wanted to say this. "They literally *can* make it rain." The dirty look she gave him would've made him smile, if he'd been up to smiling right then.

He watched as the first wispy streamers of rain began to descend from the clouds. Keeping his hands in his pockets, he leaned down to study the display. Tiny vehicles crawled along the streets nearby, while motes that may have been aircars drifted across the sky, their paths already curving to avoid the incipient shower. There was no doubt in his mind that this was a real-time representation of what was going on out in the city.

"Do you have cameras or something out there, watching everything?" asked Black Dragon. "I mean, if we zoomed in close enough, could we see people walking down the road?"

Transit shook her head. "No. Every building's got a regularly updated computer map, and most vehicles can be location tracked in one way or another." She indicated the rain shower. "That, and places like the park, are the only things that need to be directly observed and modeled by the system."

"Huh." Jericho did his best to take in every element of what he could see. The amount of detail was staggering. He couldn't even begin to address the absolute technological capability that this represented.

"Time to move along," Transit said briskly after far too short a time. "Let's go."

Reluctantly, Jericho straightened up and turned away from the display map. Black Dragon followed, though she looked back at the large hologram table more than once. Silently, they left the room, leaving the technicians to their esoteric tasks.

"Well, holy, uh, feces," Black Dragon said flatly once they were in the corridor again. "That was frickin' *amazing*." She paused. "Though it still doesn't explain how you're gonna stop some ass, uh, clown from flying an air-car packed with C-4 into the side of the Spire. I mean, yeah, you can make it rain, but windshield wipers are a thing, right?"

"They are," Transit agreed. "But rain's not the only thing we can generate. Transonic gale force winds, targeted lightning strikes and pinpoint tornado cells are also extremely viable options." She pointed upward. "A full thousand feet of the Spire is packed with the technology that makes all this possible. And that's not the *only* defensive measure we can bring to bear."

Black Dragon's jaw dropped open in what appeared to be honest astonishment. It was impressive that Transit had managed to render the teenager speechless, though Jericho wasn't surprised. Using the weather as a weapon was a novel concept for him, too, but he had a concern of his own. "Are you sure you should be telling us all this? I mean, we're not even *members* yet. And even if I get in, I doubt I'd get clearance for stuff like this."

They stopped at the elevator and the doors opened for Transit. "You've seen less than you think you have," she said. "What floor are we on? How do you access the elevator to get here? How do you get in that door? What defenses are in the corridor itself? And how do you make the weather controls do what you want them to?"

As they stepped inside, Jericho considered her words. It was true that he knew exactly how far upward they'd traveled, but that didn't translate to giving him the floor number. And of course, given the care taken to maintain security elsewhere in the Spire, he would've flat-out laughed in the face of any attempt to convince him that this area was any less safe. On the other hand, if he passed off the information he already knew to a hypothetical third party, it could supply targeting data for a potential surprise attack. Which he never intended to do, or even let anyone know he *could* do.

Better for all, he concluded, if he simply did his best to forget about it. Besides, he had other issues to concern him.

"Okay, so that's all G." Black Dragon seemed to have gotten over her stunned silence. "But what about something bigger? What if someone chucks an ocean liner at you, or sends a dozen tac nukes at once? All you gotta do is miss one, and your whole day's ruined."

"Nobody can pick up an ocean liner and throw it," Transit pointed out. "They're just too fragile. But even if someone could, the answer would still be the same. You saw the Greenway on the map, right?" She turned her head, looking at them each in turn, then sighed. "You could hardly miss it. It's half a mile wide and goes right around the city."

"Saw it, yeah," Black Dragon answered. "What's so special about it?"

Transit sent the elevator plummeting toward the base of the Spire again. Jericho gritted his teeth and endured the cognitive dissonance between what his powers were telling him and what his inner ear reported. "It's special because it's half a mile wide and it straddles the fifteen-mile circuit. If Utopia ever comes under serious attack, a force field will snap into place, covering the city all the way out to the Greenway. It's rated to take a one-megaton airstrike."

As the elevator came to a halt (about fifty feet underground, if his power was reporting accurately), Jericho took a deep breath and powered through the disorientation. "I'm guessing you haven't tested it against a one-megaton warhead in real life." It didn't even occur to him to dispute her assertion of the force field's strength, much less its actual existence. Every time he thought he'd hit his limit of wonder for the day, Transit pulled another technological rabbit from the hat. *Weaponized weather. A force field thirty miles across, rated to take a nuclear blast. No wonder these guys are top of the heap.*

Transit's voice was amused. "No, but we're very good at running tests with scaled-down models. That rating is conservative, by the way. Anything that can break the force field would also destroy everything from Omaha to Wichita."

"Talking about being in Kansas and destroying stuff, what about tornadoes?" It appeared that Black Dragon just wouldn't let things go. "Or earthquakes. You get those here too, don't you?"

Stepping from the elevator, Transit nodded. "Our range for disrupting extreme weather events is much greater than for creating them. Since we constructed the Spire, no tornado has gotten within a hundred miles of the city. In real terms, that's a quarter of the state. As for earthquakes … well, you've heard of Seismic."

This wasn't a question. While not in the same league as the Minotaur or Doc Iridium, Seismic had become infamous in his own right for his 'earthquake machines', which he'd used to hold entire *cities* to ransom. His practice was to target two different cities at once, then allow them to hold a bidding war for the amount they were willing—and able—to pay. The loser would be devastated by Seismic's machine; if the winner failed to pay the promised amount, they would also fall.

"Well, yeah," Black Dragon said, then her eyes lit up. "Did he attack you guys? Did you kill him?"

Transit shook her head. "He dropped out of sight before Force Majeure had the chance to deal with him, but we did manage to acquire one of his decommissioned devices. The Technologist repurposed it and built it into the foundations of the Spire. As a result, the land beneath Utopia is the most tectonically stable in the world. This locality could be hit with a magnitude ten quake, and we wouldn't feel a thing."

"So why doesn't he build more of them?" asked Jericho pragmatically. "There's plenty of places around the world that suffer from earthquakes."

"He can, and he has." Transit turned to look at him. "We don't advertise it, because Seismic's name is not a good thing to have attached to something like that, and they're not as powerful as the one under the Spire. Also, a sufficiently capable artificer might be able to retro-engineer one of them and start triggering earthquakes again, so we've had to install safeguards. However, we do have units installed in most of the world's problem spots by now. When was the last time you heard of a major quake on the west coast, or in Japan?" Leading the way through a doorway, she pointed at an observation window ahead. "And here's our final destination. You don't get to go inside, for reasons that will become obvious."

"What's in there?" asked Black Dragon. She moved ahead of the other two. "Whoa, holy crap. I dunno what that is, but I *want* one." Light splashed across her face as she spoke.

Jericho moved up alongside her and looked through the observation window. This one was angled down over a larger room, giving them a clear view of the whole space. The room beyond was hexagonal in shape, with conduits going in and out of the walls. Control panels lined the perimeter of the room, some with holographic readouts and some with normal-looking buttons and dials. It was hard to make out many details, because the glass (most likely polycarbonate again) was strongly tinted.

However, all that was secondary to what was in the middle of the room. A pit twenty feet across and three feet deep, also hexagonal, was situated below an armature reaching down out of the ceiling. Cradled between a trio of metal brackets at the end of the armature, about ten feet above the pit, was a sphere made of midnight-black material, about two feet across. Jericho wasn't entirely sure that the sphere was touching the brackets. Metal and ceramic beam guides, three feet long, extended inward from the corners of the pit. Actinic streamers of violet energy crackled between them and the sphere, so bright that Jericho had to shade his eyes despite the protective tinting on the window. Black Dragon didn't seem to care. When he glanced her way, her eyes had become dragonish again, and were staying that way. *Showoff.*

When he turned his eyes to the sphere itself, he couldn't see its surface, just its existence. No matter how hard he tried to focus on it, it could've been a hole a thousand miles deep, as opposed to something that was *right there.*

"Whoa ..." he breathed. "What *is* that?" For the second time on the tour, he'd encountered something that pushed past the emotional numbness he was feeling. The hairs on his arms were trying to stand up in sympathy with the spectacular lightshow within the room.

"It's the power core," Transit said simply. "The Technologist calls it negative-point energy, but he always makes those stupid air-quotes when he says it, so I'm not sure if it's just a nonsense phrase he made up or if it really describes what's happening in that room. It's not my field of expertise. All I know is that it's what powers the Spire and Utopia, along with everything else."

Tornado in a cage, hah. Jericho stared through the thick window at the power core and wondered exactly how much energy the sphere was generating. Though that then begged the question of where the power was coming *from.* However it worked, it was so far out of his comprehension that he may as well have been an ant crawling across the page of a physics textbook. "The maglev system too?"

"Like I said, it powers *everything,*" Transit confirmed. "He installed it shortly after the first couple of floors of the Spire were completed. It took the mother of all jolts to jump-start, but ever since then it's been giving us all the power we need. And it's not running at anywhere near full capacity yet."

"Perpetual motion," Black Dragon said, her voice flat. "He invented perpetual motion, didn't he?"

Transit gave the slightest of shrugs. "He says it'll be good for at least ten thousand years, so maybe?" She paused for a moment, then chuckled lightly. "The amusing part is that there's a power drain somewhere in the system. It's delivering about half a percent low, and he doesn't know why."

Jericho could read between the lines easily enough. Transit was a capable artificer in her own right, but she was continually overshadowed by the Technologist when it came to building devices that made physics go and cry in the corner. It was only human to take amusement from the evidence that the man didn't know everything, after all.

"So why doesn't he just shut it down, fix the problem and start it up again?" asked Black Dragon pragmatically.

"Because he can't work out where he went wrong." Transit said. "And he's not going to shut it down until he does. The alternative is to rebuild the system from scratch. Which would take at least a week. And while we've got backup power, there's nothing in our inventory that would power the Spire for a full week, much less everything else. Not to mention, we'd be horrifically vulnerable during that time. And *then* we'd have acquire a single-use power source capable of jump-starting it all over again. It was hard enough the *first* time." She didn't sound as though she relished the idea.

"When you put it that way, half a percent sounds like something I could live with," Jericho decided.

"Exactly." Transit looked at Jericho, then at Black Dragon. "So, you've seen the technical side of things. There's a lot more to the Spire than that, of course. Anything else you'd like to know about?"

"You guys all live up in the Spire, right?" Black Dragon's comment wasn't really a question. "Can we go see Relentless' place?"

Jericho shook his head, and saw that Transit was doing the same thing. "You can't be serious," he said, part of him wanting the same thing and the rest of him wondering when he'd made the transition into being an adult. "There's no way we'd ever be allowed up there."

"Correct, G-Man," Transit said firmly. "Force Majeure quarters are only accessible by personal invitation. As the only Force Majeure member on the spot, I don't feel like cleaning up my mess to show guests around. Did you want to see anything *else*?"

"Well, okay. What's the health plan like here?" asked Jericho, not quite on a whim. Career-ending injuries were a perennial bugbear for dynamics, though less so for prodigies (who would usually do the equivalent of walking it off) and artificers (who had effectively re-pioneered the field of prosthetics). "You guys got a sickbay or something?" He doubted that a place the size of the Spire would send its unwell or injured employees out to fend for themselves in the public health system.

"You might say that." Transit sounded more than a little amused. "Come on." She led the way back to the elevator. Black Dragon hung back as long as she could, though she came trotting along when the pass let out its warning buzz.

They traveled upward about thirty feet, letting out onto yet another corridor while they were still some twenty feet underground by Jericho's calculations. Another trek through the broad, hospital-like hallways took place, until they reached a door marked MEDICAL-1. Transit knocked and opened the door without pausing, to reveal ...

"Okay, I was wrong," Black Dragon said. "What I said was a mad science lab before? That wasn't it. *This* is it."

Jericho sighed. "You can't just go calling everything a mad scientist's laboratory." Besides, it was more of a hospital than a laboratory. The sterile *everything* was already something he'd come to expect from the Spire, though the surgery tables were new. There was really nothing else he could call them, equipped as they were by a proliferation of waldos coming down from above, and the oxygen masks hanging up out of the way. He could even see notches where IV trees could snap into place. The one major difference from the R&D lab was the way the waldos came equipped with surgical implements. From the looks of it, they were equipped to perform everything from the removal of a hangnail to open-heart surgery.

"Can I help you?" He looked around at the voice, as a woman appeared through a door on the other side of the room. "Oh, hello, Transit. Who are these people?"

The woman was clad in a full-body coverall, strongly reminiscent of what the techs up in the weather room had been wearing. Her hair was concealed under a hood that seemed to be part of the coverall. With only her uncovered face to go by, she appeared to be in her late thirties, with fair skin. A nametag on her chest read 'CHANDLER HoS'.

"Hi, Merry," Transit said. "This is Black Dragon and G-Man. I'm just giving them a tour before G-Man goes in for his interview. Guys, this is Doctor Meredith Chandler, our head of surgery. If you come seriously unstuck out in the field, Merry here is the one who'll be in charge of putting the pieces back together."

Doctor Chandler rolled her faded blue eyes. "It's always a team effort and you know it."

Jericho bobbed his head respectfully. "It's a pleasure meeting you, ma'am."

"Yeah," Black Dragon said. "Likewise." She waved at the surgery tables. "You ever get anything really nasty come through here? I mean, blood everywhere, stuff like that?"

"It's not unheard of," the doctor replied primly. "But I take pride in doing my work properly. Nobody dies on my watch if I can help it."

A sharp pang shot through Jericho as a thought seared across his mind. *If Force Majeure had managed to get Luke and Bobbi here when I found them, she might've been able to save them.* The medical equipment certainly seemed advanced enough. In his dream, he'd assumed that Utopia City hospitals were the best in the world. If they had anything like this, he'd been entirely warranted in thinking so. *If only.* Surreptitiously, he leaned against the nearest table, trying to conceal his grimace.

"Are you all right, young man?" Doctor Chandler eyed him perceptively. Apparently, he'd been less subtle than he thought.

"I'll be fine." Clearing his throat, he stood up straight and did his best to compose himself. It wouldn't help anything if he broke down in front of Transit.

The Force Majeure hero turned her reflective faceplate toward him. She didn't speak for a moment, and he wondered what she saw when she looked at him. "Maybe we'd better be moving along from here. I'll see you around, Merry."

Doctor Chandler didn't shift her gaze from Jericho, even as she answered Transit. "Definitely." Her eyes flicked to Black Dragon, then back to Jericho. "If you do get onto the team, G-Man, feel free to come down and say hello. We don't just treat physical injuries here."

As opposed to when Transit looked at him, Jericho wondered how *much* Doctor Chandler had seen. He nodded politely. "I, uh, thanks. I might take you up on that." Along with Transit and Black Dragon, he headed for the exit; though in his case, it felt like a full-scale retreat.

"Was there anything else you wanted to see?" asked Transit as the door closed behind them. "We've still got about twenty minutes."

"I'm hungry," Black Dragon said immediately. "Got anything to eat around here?" Jericho wanted to snap at her, but he restrained himself with difficulty. What had happened wasn't *her* fault.

Transit shrugged. "Sure, I can take you to a commissary." She turned her head toward Jericho. "If you're okay with that?"

While food was the last thing on his mind right then, Jericho wasn't going to take it out on the teenager. He took a deep breath and tried to clear his head. "I don't mind."

"Hell, *yes!*" Black Dragon said immediately, then froze and looked at Jericho with a stricken expression.

As swearwords went, 'hell' wasn't too bad, and she'd definitely been working at curbing her speech so he decided to cut her a break. "That one's fine," he assured her. "Just don't overdo it, okay?"

"Sweet!" she exulted and turned back to Transit. "I don't give a crap what they got to eat there, just so I can say I ate in the Spire's eatery." She slapped her pocket. "Wish I had my phone so I could get selfies."

"There are many reasons we don't allow non-issued phones within the Spire." Transit's voice was bland. "Taking selfies in the commissary is not in the top ten." She led the way down the corridor.

"So why don't you allow outside phones in the building?" asked Black Dragon, trotting alongside Jericho. "Is it so nobody can bring in a virus from the outside and infect the computer systems?"

"While the possibility of that exists, it's not very high," Transit observed. "Our systems are extremely robust. They have to be; there are people trying to hack the maglev/MagCard system more or less constantly."

Not only was this a good way to get his mind off Medical-1, it was also something Jericho hadn't given much thought to before that point. Now that the idea had been raised, he found it worrisome, not least because he'd spent several hours the previous day entrusting his life to the maglev. "Has anyone ever succeeded?"

Transit chuckled as she waved her hand to open the elevator door. "To the level of gaining access to any kind of control or sensitive information? No. To the level that they raised red flags and drew our attention? Yes. Very briefly." She didn't elaborate on what had happened next. He suspected that it hadn't turned out well for the hackers.

"Good." He wasn't very surprised by the definitive reply. Before he could say any more, the elevator had moved upward half a dozen floors and the doors were opening again. *One of these days I'll get used to that. Just not today.* "I guess you've had fourteen years to work on your computer security."

"Physical *and* digital, yes," Transit confirmed with quiet self-satisfaction. "But to answer Black Dragon's earlier question, the main reason we don't allow phones in the building isn't about viruses. It's to do with information gathering. They don't have to be programmed to deliver malware, just to record everything they come into contact with. Any recordings that leave the Spire are analyzed and redacted as necessary so that if they fall into the wrong hands, nobody can get anything out of them. It's only common sense to assume that the instant anything hits the cloud, it's in the wrong hands, so we make sure that only *our* recordings leave the building."

She led them along a curving corridor, then turned toward a set of sliding doors marked 'COMMISSARY #3'. The doors opened as they approached, and Jericho found himself looking at a large room at least half-full of people. It was a semi-standard mess-hall layout, with hexagonal tables spread out across the room. People were seated at the tables, laughing and chatting and generally socializing. Rolling between the tables were things that looked remarkably like the room-service carts back at the Oaklands.

The décor also came as a surprise. Murals covered all four walls ... *not* murals, he realized a moment later. Each of the walls was a giant holographic display screen, the gradually shifting landscapes showing just enough three-dimensionality to make them look unnervingly real. The tables were made of metal and plastic, but the chairs looked much more comfortable than the standard industrial model of cafeteria seating. In the center of each table was a napkin dispenser.

"Where do you get your food?" asked Black Dragon, pointing at the far wall of the room. "There's no serving counter." She was right, Jericho realized a second later. There was only the ever-shifting holo-mural. As he watched, one of the service carts deposited a steaming plate on a nearby table then removed a bowl and a cup. It stored the items within its boxy body, then rolled off again. A moment later, it disappeared into the back wall, no doubt via an aperture concealed by the holographic display.

"We sit down and order," Transit said. "Or rather, you order. I ate before I came down, in our private commissary." By way of explanation, she waved at her visor. "I don't open this in public."

"Well, that sucks." Black Dragon pointed at a vacant table. "Let's sit there." Marching over to the table, she pulled out a chair and sat down. Immediately, a hologram sprang to life in front of her, in the form of text hanging in the air with informative images rotating alongside. "Whoa, what the crap?"

Jericho pulled out a chair for Transit. It took her a moment to realize what he was doing, then she seated herself with a pleased murmur. Momentarily distracted from the hologram, Black Dragon watched the byplay with a look of puzzled fascination, as if observing the rites of a lost tribe of jungle savages.

When Jericho took his own chair, he found a hologram triggering in front of him as well. "Huh. Menu." Reaching out, he tapped the section that said 'Sides', and a whole new page opened in front of him. With that cue, Black Dragon started playing with hers. She quickly learned that she could swipe it from side to side in order to get from one page to the next.

Transit already had a menu in front of her, but her dismissive wave made it go away. "Any questions so far?" she asked.

"Yeah, can I really get chicken drumsticks in ranch sauce?" asked Black Dragon. "Because if I can, that would be awesome."

"Yes, you can," sighed Transit. "Did you have any *important* questions?"

"How many people work in the Spire?" asked Jericho, thinking back to the incoming crowd he'd seen earlier. "And how do they all get to work on time?" Even one hiccup in the system would throw everything into chaos.

"Between fifteen and twenty thousand, depending on the day of the week and the time of day," Transit replied. "Shifts are staggered so that everyone doesn't have to arrive or leave at once. Some people have private apartments in the building that they stay in over the week and only go home on weekends."

Black Dragon's jaw fell. "Fifteen to twenty *thousand?*" she repeated, her face blank with astonishment. "What the crap do they all *do?*"

"Municipal administration," Transit answered, then began ticking off points on her fingers. "Police force. Emergency services. Public transport. Civic works. Infrastructure." Having run out of fingers, she waved her hand at the walls of the commissary and by extension at the city around them. "You didn't think this place works so smoothly by *accident*, did you?"

Black Dragon's attention was already back on her menu. She tapped several options, which rewarded her with musical notes apparently generated by the table. When she tapped the 'ORDER' button, the menu was replaced by the UML symbol. "I gotta swipe to get my meal?" she asked.

"Swipe with your visitor pass," Transit advised her. "That way it's billed to us rather than to you."

"Oh. Right." Black Dragon did as she was told, and the hologram blinked out of existence. Glowing green numbers, starting at '1:43', faded into view and then commenced to count downward.

Jericho dismissed his menu and looked across the table at Transit. "I was under the impression it would make the place run less smoothly, not more. That's the way things normally go, right? Bureaucracies typically expand out of control until half of what they're doing is political infighting rather than making things work." At least, that was how his father had explained it once.

"Usually, yes," agreed Transit. "But we studied the problem when we first came up with the idea of building Utopia as an integrated entity. We have safeguards in place. Productivity across the board is monitored as a matter of course. If anything seems to slow down or come to a halt, we have people whose job is to find the logjam and unjam it. And of course, they have access to our computer systems to keep track of which people are on point but are being held back, which ones are being pointlessly obstructionist, and which ones are trying to enrich themselves by manipulating the system. The first type get promoted, the second get demoted to the level of their observed competence, and the third get shown the door. It seems to work."

"Huh." That was a more detailed answer than he'd been expecting. It also showed up a whole new level of competence on the part of Force Majeure and Utopia City. "So how does this work with outside corporations opening offices in the city?" he asked. "Do they get to do business their way, or do they have to fall into line?"

Transit snorted. "What do you think? Utopia's been *the* fastest-growing concern in the continental US for the last fourteen years. Outside interests have been falling over themselves to get a foothold here for the last ten, which means it's a seller's market. If they want to do business here, they meet our standards or they go elsewhere. Usually, they meet our standards."

A service cart trundled up to the table. When the panel in its side opened, delicious-smelling steam billowed out. **"Order for Black Dragon,"** announced the cart in a bland masculine voice. **"Chicken drumsticks in ranch sauce. Vanilla shake."** From the aperture, a mechanical arm extended with the plate of drumsticks on the end. It placed the plate on the table, then returned and emerged with a tall glass, complete with a waxed-paper straw. **"Please enjoy your meal."** The mechanical arm retracted, the panel closed, and the cart trundled off.

Jericho watched it go, noting that it had 'SC3-02' painted on the sides and back. *Spire Commissary three, robot two?* "Those robots really get around."

"They do," agreed Transit. "It's one of my better designs. We license them out for handling menial jobs that don't require much in the way of human judgment. This frees people up for more fulfilling work."

"God *damn*, these are good," Black Dragon said indistinctly, taking another bite out of her chicken drumstick. Jericho noted that her lips had taken on a scaly appearance, and her teeth were rather sharper than before. She took a drink from her shake, a look of bliss crossing her face. A bright purple tongue flickered out to wipe up a dribble of ranch sauce from her chin. "Can I come here to live?"

"First you have to apply to join, then you have to be accepted, and then you have to be assigned to Utopia," Transit said. Jericho thought he heard humor in her tone. "But certainly, do all that and it's a possibility."

Black Dragon's reply was muffled by chicken drumstick, and Jericho gave Transit a measured nod. "I think you've got a convert. I mean, if she wasn't already set on joining."

"I suppose so." Transit's voice had that amused tone again. "Aren't you going to be ordering?"

Jericho shook his head. "I can't even *think* of eating right now." Just sitting and looking around at everyone else talking, laughing, enjoying themselves, he felt a sudden stab of anger toward all of them. It wasn't their fault; they'd done nothing wrong. But they were alive and well, and Luke and Bobbi ... weren't.

"Nervous?" Now she was sympathetic. "That's natural. Just remember, every auxiliary member of Force Majeure had to go through the same interview process. And the others must think you've got *something* to bring to the table, or you wouldn't be here."

Pissed, yes. Nervous, no. But he suspected that saying as much to one of the people who would later be interviewing him would only lead to more questions. Ones he wasn't prepared to answer. Even if he did bare his soul on this, he suspected that Black Dragon simply wouldn't understand what he was feeling. He envied her ability to live in the moment and not worry about the consequences of her actions. After an uncomfortable pause, he nodded. "I guess."

Transit leaned back in her chair. "All right, then. Tell me, what made you decide to apply to join Force Majeure?"

Jericho watched the slowly scrolling landscape on the wall across from him as he considered his reply. "I want to be a hero," he said eventually. "I mean, a *professional* hero. I'm pretty good at it, and I want to do it full-time. At the same time, ever since I got powers, I guess I've wanted to be a part of something bigger. Force Majeure is as big as it gets." That was true enough, even if he had to fake the emotion behind it.

"We definitely are," Transit agreed. "So, is there anything more, or is that it? 'For the greater good' and all that?" There was definitely a mocking tone to her voice, and Jericho wondered how much of his pretense she was seeing through.

"There's more," he admitted in an attempt to deflect her attention, ducking his head slightly. "I mean, I'm not in it for the glory, but I want to be *recognized*, you know? As a gay superhero who works alone, it's like my Dynamic ability's invisibility instead of gravity control. Once I'm with you guys, they can't ignore me anymore. Does that make me a bad person?" He'd only ever said this to one person before, and that person was now dead. *Luke, I am so goddamn sorry.*

Transit snorted, clearly unaware of his emotional turmoil. "It makes you human, is what it makes you. But it's nearly time for your interview. Which means I need to get Black Dragon back to the lobby." She turned her head to face the girl, who had just finished off the last of the drumsticks. "Time to go." Standing up from the table, she pushed her chair back and turned toward the door.

"Can we go back to the power core?" asked Black Dragon as she got up from the table. Jericho was already standing. "I could watch *that* crap all day. It's better than one of those lightning balls."

"I know what you mean, but that's not going to happen." Transit's tone was brisk and professional. "Once you're back in the lobby, you'll need to arrange for an application, and we'll email you our answer in due course."

"Yeah, yeah, I know." Black Dragon sighed and tossed the bone into the bowl. "Lucky asshole." Reaching out, she slugged Jericho in the arm.

Deciding to let her have that one, Jericho spread his hands. "The application form was online." Unspoken were the words: *if you'd ever bothered to look.*

The teenager's only reply was to give him the finger on the way out of the commissary. Jericho glanced at Transit, shrugged and followed.

When the elevator arrived, Transit held Black Dragon back with one arm. "This one's yours, G-Man," she said. "You go up to your interview. I'll be escorting Black Dragon back to the lobby and ensuring that she fills out the application form correctly."

Stepping into the elevator, Jericho turned to face her, unsure as to what was going on. "But … won't you be interviewing me, too?"

She chuckled. "What do you think I've been doing for the last forty-five minutes?" Reaching into the elevator, she gave him a firm slap on the shoulder then stepped back. "Follow the blue line when you get there. And remember: don't say anything to the Technologist about the missing half percent." There was a smirk in her words.

Before he could respond, the elevator doors had shut, and he was hurtling up into the Spire once more.

39
Interviewing; Superhero Style

The elevator stopped short of the half-mile mark this time, but only by about fifty yards. Jericho stepped out into the corridor, looking for the correct line to follow. It made itself immediately apparent, drawing his eye with sequential pulses of bright blue light, streaming down the corridor to the left. Taking a deep breath, he followed the flashing line around the … circuit, that was what Transit had called it.

Normally, he knew, he'd be terrified. The very thought of facing up to an interview with the heroes whom he idolized above all else should've had butterflies the size of B-52 bombers breeding in his stomach in plague proportions. But instead he only felt a deep burning anger, aided and abetted by the fatigue now scratching at the back of his eyeballs.

The blue line led up to a closed door, which of course slid open as he approached it. Taking a deep breath, he stepped into the doorway itself. Within was a large room. Peripherally, he registered a wrestling mat off to one side, but most of his attention was nailed down by the sight of Force Majeure. Sitting. Waiting. Looking directly at him. His nerves chose this moment to rebel against his resolve and he froze, staring into the room.

"Well, come in," ordered a feminine voice impatiently. "We haven't got all day." Jericho blinked, and the blur of indecision resolved into seven people. Six of these were seated on the other side of a horseshoe-shaped desk, while the seventh sat back against the wall behind the others with her hands folded in her lap.

He recognized the one who'd spoken; he'd met her not so long ago, after all. *That's Independence.* Jericho could see the hilt of her claymore beside her, the sword apparently removed for comfort and propped up against the desk. For some strange reason, that settled him slightly. It was such a *human* thing to do. The grip of the sword was wrapped around with alternating red and white stripes, while the pommel was dark blue with a single white star. Her assault rifle was nowhere to be seen; he surmised it was down behind the desk.

Stepping into the room, he moved forward until he stood in the center of the arc of the desk. Behind him, a faint *whoosh* signaled that the door had closed behind him, trapping him in the room with—well, with his heroes. The people he wanted most in the world to emulate. His nerves rose up, constricting his throat, while he fought to relax it again. The last thing he wanted to do was sound like an idiot in front of these people.

It didn't help that he had no idea who the seventh person in the room was. The only one in the room not in costume, she wore instead a well-cut pantsuit and looked to be in her fifties. She returned his gaze appraisingly but did not offer to speak.

"Uh, hello," he said, addressing the room at large. His voice sounded horribly artificial to his ears, but there was nothing for it but to push on anyway. Shortly after getting the confirmation email, he'd tried to compose a speech that he could use when he finally got to this point. After a dozen attempts, he'd given it up as a bad job. Now he wondered if he shouldn't have kept trying. "This is a huge honor, I, uh—"

"We know," Independence interrupted him. "So, Transit's already made her assessment of you. If we don't have to wait for her, let's get this thing started. Relentless?"

The Olympian presence seated at the midpoint of the horseshoe desk shifted slightly. Even sitting, Relentless was *huge*. The armor probably made him look larger than he really was, but there was only so much bulk it could add. Each of his forearms, resting on the desk, looked larger than one of Jericho's thighs. At his elbow, placed there like an exclamation point, was his mace. Which, Jericho now knew, had a gravity motor in the head. This didn't make it any less awe-inspiring. Quite the opposite, in fact.

"G-Man." Relentless' voice rumbled, deeper than thunder. In one large gauntleted hand, he held a piece of paper, which he glanced at before folding it and placing it on the desk in front of him. "First question: are you the only one using this name? Is there another G-Man out there that we're going to have to consider?"

"Uh, no, not as far as I know." Of all the questions Jericho had been expecting, this wasn't one of them. "I couldn't find anyone online with this name, which is why I settled on it."

"Understood." Relentless barely paused. "In your opinion, are there any circumstances under which betraying a trust is acceptable?"

What—? But before he could begin to parse that question, a deeper impulse took over and he found himself speaking, his voice firm and harsh. "No. Trust is sacred. Inviolable. I will *die* before I willingly betray someone else's trust in me." The words spoken, he looked to the heroes around the table.

"Hm." He couldn't interpret Relentless' wordless comment, or the man's expression under that helmet. "Are you affiliated with any other Enabled?"

"Uh, no." Jericho did his best not to sound confused by the rapid shifts in topic. The veteran hero's gaze on him seemed neither interested nor dismissive. Merely analytical, as if he were already dissecting Jericho's motives and inner workings. This did absolutely nothing to alleviate Jericho's incipient crush on the man. "I've never been part of a team."

"Hrmm," mused Relentless. Jericho could almost swear he felt the vibration through his feet. "Do you associate with any other heroes on a regular basis?"

Jericho had no idea where the leader of Force Majeure was going with this. "Not really. The only other Enabled in Savannah is Pickup, and we don't … associate." The truth was, Pickup hated his guts. He could think of no polite way to put the point across, so he left it at that.

Now Relentless' helmet tilted to the side slightly. "Pickup? What's his powerset?"

Still mystified, Jericho shrugged. "Artificer, I guess. His pickup truck turns into a twenty-foot-tall robot, with him as the pilot."

In the quiet of the room, he heard a quickly stifled snort of laughter from someone else at the desk, but he couldn't tell who'd made it. Relentless either didn't hear it or ignored it altogether. His gaze was still fixed on Jericho. "And can this robot do anything other than turn back into a pickup truck? Does it possess any unusual … travel modes?"

What was Relentless fishing for? Jericho knew very little that was important about the truck. The leader of Force Majeure probably wasn't interested in the rifle rack or the truck-nuts that Pickup's ride sported. "No, just legs or wheels, I guess. It, uh, it gets nineteen miles to the gallon?" It was something he'd once read in an article about his fellow Enabled.

The explosive snort of laughter came again. Once more, Relentless pretended it had never happened, but Jericho thought he saw Lady Quantum cover her mouth with her hand. "Next question. Name as many terror villains as you can. Twenty seconds. Go."

Jericho's mind went blank. He *knew* this. All the names were common knowledge. Why was it so hard to settle on one? "Uh, Minotaur," he forced out. That was a name *everyone* knew. Another one popped into his head, then another. "Carnifex. False Flag. Seismic. Mindscrew. Guillotine."

"Stop." Independence leaned forward slightly. "What was that last one? Before Guillotine?"

Jericho grimaced. He knew exactly what she was talking about. "Mindscrew. It's what they called him."

She rolled her eyes. "For Christ's sake, his name was Mind-Fucker. Just say it. It's a *name*. It won't kill you."

It wasn't in Jericho's nature to make snap judgments about women, especially when it came to negative impressions. He was overwhelmingly inclined to give people the benefit of the doubt. But in this specific instance, he was quickly coming to the conclusion that either Independence disliked him personally, or she was a raging bitch in general. Perhaps it was both; he couldn't be sure.

His options were limited. Either he did as she said, or he made a stand. And right now, with the way things were going, he was less and less enamored with the idea of compromising his morals and beliefs to become a part of this group. He met her gaze squarely. "The *news* called him Mindscrew." He switched his attention back to Relentless. "Also, Singularity. Charnel. Mutilator and Devastator. Kraken. Doc Iridium." It pained him that he'd forgotten even *that* name in his panic. "Darksider. Raider." His mind went blank again. "Does Cherenkov count?"

Relentless shook his head, apparently amused by the byplay between Jericho and Independence. "No, he does not."

Which was only fair. While Cherenkov *had* killed hundreds, it wasn't deliberate. Neither was he American. The second Enabled to emerge, Cherenkov had gotten his powers as a result of the Chernobyl disaster. Glowing an eerie blue with the radiation for which he was named, he'd been unable to approach people without killing them. No longer fully human, or even altogether sane, he'd roamed the area around the ghost city for the next seven or eight years. Attempts by the military to detain or destroy him had gone … poorly. Long-range photography had shown that his powers were literally flaying the skin and flesh from his bones, bit by bit, so it was no surprise that he eventually ceased to show up on satellite surveillance of the area. It was a sobering lesson that not all powers were beneficial to everyone around them.

"Wasn't there a rumor going around that he figured out how to get control over his powers and came to America, boss-man?" asked Lady Quantum. "I mean, the dates match. He stopped showing up there in 'ninety-three and Devastator joined up with Mutilator in 'ninety-four." From the tone of her voice, she didn't take very much in life seriously.

Raven-haired, with looks that had often been described as 'stunning', she was the only one at the table who wore both spandex and a cape. Over and above these sartorial transgressions, the front of her costume sported a circular hole exposing a little of what promised to be an impressive cleavage. While the boob window was an unfortunate fad occasionally taken up by those who also favored the use of spandex, all too few were able to pull it off effectively.

Jericho was about to reluctantly dismiss her costume choice as irredeemably tacky until he realized that in this specific instance, the window was surrounded by a depiction of elliptical electron orbits from a classic (though incorrect) model of the atom. With the window representing the nucleus, it made up her Enabled logo: an atom caught in the act of splitting. Grudgingly, he admitted it was a clever design.

Truth be told, even Jericho (not usually an expert on the female form) was aware that she filled out her costume in all the right places. While the rest of it didn't quite emulate the American flag in any overt detail (Jericho recalled there were laws against that) it certainly incorporated stars as well as stripes; all in red, white and blue. A pair of blue wrist-bracers decorated with white stars set off the skintight spandex.

All in all, it looked patriotic as hell, though any red-blooded (read: straight) male would be hard-pressed to remember specific details of the costume after spending any time at all with her. As he recalled, she was able to fly and generate a protective force field (as well as devastate enemies with powerful energy blasts), so the normally idiotic costume choices wouldn't detract from her safety in this case.

As for her question, he'd read something like that on a not-quite conspiracy-theory website, but just as he was starting to nod in agreement, he caught the wink she sent him, followed by a sly glance at the Technologist. A moment later, he grasped the notion that she was baiting the artificer for her own amusement.

"With an entirely different appearance and power signature." The Technologist's tone was acid. "I assure you, I've investigated the matter closely, and the dates are the only correlation to be found. Coincidences happen." Turning to Jericho, he spoke as if the side-commentary had never occurred. "Well, it appears you know your history … mostly." He wore an outsize pair of goggles with retro-tech flip-out lenses, though when it came to the most well-known artificer in the world, Jericho would've bet against them being an affectation. The rest of his ensemble consisted of a light metal exoskeleton over a white costume that strongly resembled lab-wear. In reference to the fact that this was indeed a superhero team, the coat aspect had become a cape. "Let's see if you know your science. Explain to me in your own words the Proximity Principle."

"Proximity Principle." Repeating the words didn't make the phrase any more familiar. *Are they deliberately setting me up to fail?* It was certainly beginning to feel that way. He gave the artificer a defiant glare. "I have no idea what that is." *Like you didn't know this already.*

"What?" The word was almost a hiss. "Are you jesting with me, boy?" The Technologist looked around almost theatrically at the rest of Force Majeure. "What are they *teaching* people about powers these days?"

"I'm *sorry*." Jericho barely restrained himself from rolling his eyes sarcastically. "They don't teach Enabled electives where I'm from."

"From what I hear, they barely teach the theory of evolution," the white-clad artificer retorted. Jericho didn't argue; the man wasn't far wrong. "Very well, then. We shall back up a little. What do you know of how Enabled attain their powers?"

Jericho paused. The only power origin he had any familiarity with was his own, and a baseline of one wasn't very helpful. Well, of course there was Bobbi's, but he had virtually no information on that one, except that she'd been cheated on and broken up with the guy in question. "Shit happens, and you get powers." It wasn't quite a question.

"God save us all from backwoods rednecks." The Technologist let out a long sigh. "Allow me to elucidate for you, boy. Theoretically, there exists a subatomic particle which has been given the working title 'Enabler boson', an imprecise term at best. CERN has yet to isolate one, though they have some promising leads. I will not go into its specific properties right now …"

Just for a moment, Jericho thought he saw the other members of Force Majeure relax slightly. Independence may even have mouthed the words *thank fuck.*

"… but suffice to say that it only interacts with the nervous system of a sapient being, when that being is under considerable stress. That interaction, so the theory goes, links the being to another state of reality which is possessed of an overabundance of energy. Being the fragile vessels that we are, we're limited in the amount of this energy that we can channel, and of course the expression of said energy is curtailed and shaped so that we don't simply explode on first contact." He paused, eyeing Jericho severely. "Am I boring you yet, boy?"

This was the first Jericho had ever heard of such things. However, the Technologist didn't seem to be bullshitting him, so he gave a civil reply. "No. So … if these Enabler bosons interact with us when we're under stress, we get powers. But we can't just mainline it. It's gotta be limited so we can handle it. Yeah?" He reflected for a moment that Cherenkov had been a perfect example of a power not being limited *enough.*

The Technologist pursed his lips. "Close enough for a first try. Several books have been written on the many and varied factors which shape the expression of the power, but we won't go into that now. However, the conditions which define the *powerset* usually follow certain patterns. Dynamic powers tend to manifest if the person is in imminent physical peril. Prodigies are brought about by severe emotional stress; especially grief, fear and anger. Artificers, on the other hand, are the result of a need for action or a change in circumstance that is urgent but non-immediate. Are you following me so far?"

Despite his irritation with Independence, Jericho was fascinated by what the Technologist had to say. For all the older man's acerbic nature, he was clearly well-informed on the subject matter. He nodded. "Yes, sir."

The Technologist smiled thinly. "Good. Now we come to the Proximity Principle. This is an observed phenomenon that sometimes overrides what I just mentioned about which powerset fits which stimulus. If someone is placed in a high-stress situation in which they encounter an Enabler boson, *but there is another Enabled in close proximity*, then a very significant chance exists that the powers of the new Enabled will be patterned off those of the original. This is especially likely if the stimulus resembles what the original went through, but that need not be the case." He paused, eyeing Jericho like a particularly severe schoolmaster. "There is more to it than that, of course. Would you care to hazard a guess as to what the second part of the Proximity Principle involves?"

This was far outside Jericho's understanding. He looked from one face to another, seeking inspiration. The lady at the back of the room was still watching him closely, as if dissecting his every move. When he looked at her questioningly, she shook her head a mere fraction of an inch. *I'm not here. You're on your own.*

A moment later, his attention was drawn by the muted tapping of hard fingers on a keyboard. He looked around to see Silent Knight steadily typing. Jericho was impressed at the flexibility that the artificer had built into his armor, though he wasn't sure what it was made of. The outer carapace, patterned after medieval plate mail, was a deep, glossy black, though the baldric looked as though it had been added after the fact. Made of black enamel-painted metal, the flexible belt ran diagonally up across Silent Knight's chest and helped affix a metal guard in place over his right shoulder.

Interrupting Jericho's inspection, the ebony-armored hero took the low screen before him and turned it first to face the Technologist and then Jericho. On it, in letters large enough for him to read from where he was, Silent Knight had typed,

WE'RE SUPPOSED TO BE THE ONES ASKING HIM QUESTIONS ABOUT HIS POWERS. TALKING ABOUT THAT, WHAT DO YOU BRING TO THE TEAM? GRAVITY IS A VERY BROAD TERM.

It looked like they were back to picking at him. He'd about had enough of this. "My Prodigy rating has let me pick up Graduate level in Krav Maga, and my Dynamic rating lets me control how heavy or light my opponent is. *That's* what I bring to the team."

"Hrmm." Relentless stirred, then came to his feet. "Let's see how you do with a physical challenge. Do you believe you can subdue me with your powers?"

Well, I sure as shit couldn't do it without *my powers.* Jericho stared up at the leader of Force Majeure as the meaning of Relentless' words became clear. "Wait, you actually *want* me to—"

Moving away from the desk, Relentless strode toward the wrestling mat. "Yes." His reply was uncompromisingly blunt. "If you can't use your powers to subdue an ally before they do something stupid, then you might freeze at the wrong time, and we don't need someone like that on the team. Remove your visitor pass, then come here and use your powers to subdue and restrain me."

Jericho heard the words 'restrain me' and his mind went places it really shouldn't have gone, right then. He wrestled it back on track. "I, uh, you're really strong, but your armor's heavy. I don't want to overestimate what you can take and hurt you by accident."

"Listen." Relentless scowled, sending a tremor down Jericho's spine. The big man's anger was even more intimidating in real life than on TV. But the tremor was about more than just fear. Right then, he was more attracted to the leader of Force Majeure than ever before. "If I can survive the Blood Rose, I can take anything you can hand out. *Come. Here.*" He pointed at the mat before him.

Pure reflex took over and Jericho slipped the pass off over his head. Putting it on the end of the desk, he crossed the floor to the mat. *He survived the Blood Rose?* His internal monologue gibbered to itself and ran in circles. *He fought the Minotaur and lived?* This was something he *hadn't* known about. It elevated Relentless to a whole new level again. There were always rumors about Blood Rose survivors, of course, but—

"Ready? Go."

He pulled his head back into the game just as Relentless reached for him. The metal-clad gauntlet looked big enough to wrap around his head and pop it like a grape. While he didn't *think* Relentless would do that, it wouldn't look good to get tapped out within seconds of the test starting.

This was *not* something Jericho had envisaged doing when he got the email. The last thing he wanted to do was fight Relentless. But the veteran hero had given him his orders, and he really did want to punch someone right now.

Ducking under the grab, he dived and rolled past Relentless' tree-trunk legs, slapping one of them on the way past. Two gravities tended to be enough to put someone on the ground (especially if he caught them off balance) but this was *Relentless,* so he pushed it up to three instead. Rolling to his feet, he backed up to make sure Relentless didn't fall on him. The guy had to weigh three hundred pounds *without* his armor; being crushed by half a ton of superhero would be painful if not fatal. Face to face, Jericho could attest that even without the camera angle to add height, Relentless was nearly seven feet tall in his armor and about four feet wide in the shoulders. That last bit was perhaps an exaggeration, but not by a lot. Relentless didn't just *loom,* he *towered.*

Footfall by deliberate footfall, Relentless turned to face him. "I'm not down yet," the big man grunted, then advanced on him. Every step crashed against the floor, even through the thick matting.

There was every chance that Relentless was waiting for him to try the duck-and-roll maneuver again, so Jericho went upward instead. Reducing his own weight to a fraction of its normal value, he leaped lightly over Relentless' grasping hands, pulling a twisting somersault as he did so. Relentless began to turn again, but even his monstrously inhuman strength was slowed by the extra weight he was fighting against. Jericho got another hit in, pushing Relentless' effective weight up to seven times normal. *Come on. Fall down. Any day now.*

This time, he had managed to catch Relentless with one foot off the floor, and the iconic hero was caught off-guard by the increase in weight; he went down on one knee, using both hands to catch himself from falling the rest of the way. But then, incredibly, he straightened up and looked Jericho right in the eye. Jericho could see the strain he was under from the shuddering in every movement. Inch by inexorable inch, Relentless began to stand up. *Sonovabitch. Whoever gave him the name Relentless wasn't joking.*

"No," muttered Jericho. "No." He *didn't* want to pile on the last three gees—falling at that level of acceleration would injure *anyone*—but there was something else he could do. Clenching his teeth, he grabbed the local gravity field and *shook.*

Only Jericho and Relentless were within the area of effect; the room was wide enough to manage that. Jericho himself was immune to the power, but Relentless was not. Still, Relentless' resilience was astounding. The big man didn't fall flat on his face or puke up his lunch, as Luke had done once upon a time. But he did subside to the mat once more, bracing himself with his arms. His head hung down as he panted harshly. "Congratulations," he rasped. "Consider me subdued."

Immediately, Jericho dropped the gravity enhancement. He couldn't do much about the nausea that came about from the G-shake, but that would pass. Still, as Relentless began to climb to his feet, it seemed he was throwing it off more quickly than most. Jericho wondered if that was a case of pure brute stubbornness, or if Relentless had a Prodigy rating to go with his more apparent Dynamic rating. "Sorry about the G-shake," he said awkwardly. "I didn't want to use that, but you weren't going down."

That earned him a glare. "You should've used that *first,* then tagged me while I was disoriented," Relentless rumbled. "As it was, I could've hit you several times while you were dancing around, but I wanted to see how you planned to put me down. Do better next time."

Jericho winced internally. *Oh, for crap's sake. Can I do* anything *right?* "Sorry, yes. I will." He paused. "Uh, next time?"

"Me." It was Independence; as Relentless stepped off the mat, she stepped on. "You're fighting me. No powers." She prowled closer to him, all lithe movement and deadly promise. Her knee had clearly recovered in full, because there was no sign of the brace from the night before. "No tricks, no gimmicks, no weapons. Just guts and skill."

A whimper tried to climb out of his throat, but he suppressed it ruthlessly. "I can't beat you," he said flatly. If facing Relentless had been a uniquely terrifying experience, this ramped it up to eleven. *Fighting Independence without using my powers? Craaaaaap.* "It's just not going to happen." There was no shame in admitting defeat before the fight if it was a foregone conclusion.

"Well, of *course* not," she snapped. "That's not the point of this exercise. The point is to see what you're capable of, and what you need instruction in. Too many

Enabled try to coast by on their powers. Yes, I'm going to beat the snot out of you. It's up to you to defend yourself and try to get at least one hit in on me. You're a prodigy; you'll live."

Which was cold comfort. He knew all too well that he was going to be in a world of hurt in just a moment, but not once did he even consider using his powers to cheat. Force Majeure was giving him this chance to prove himself, and he was going to do it on his own merits or not at all.

"This is the problem with small-town heroes," Independence observed with a curl of the lip as she watched him get set up. Unlike Relentless, she didn't immediately jump to the attack, but that meant absolutely nothing. "You get comfortable in your own little niche, and you start thinking you're something. Because you've had no serious opposition. Then you decide you're good enough to join a team like this one, and that's when you run into a cold hard dose of reality. Are you ready?"

Her words stung, but he had to admit she had a point. Specifically, the way that more than one person had snuck up on him since he'd arrived in Utopia City. "Ready," he responded.

Barely had the second syllable left his mouth before she came in with a hard and fast attack. Shocked by her speed, he barely parried it, then slipped aside from another strike, and totally missed the leg-sweep that put him on the mat. He rolled frantically to get out of the way, then tried to extend the move to regain his footing. Reducing his personal gravity would've let him get there faster, but Independence had specified no powers, so he didn't.

Neither did he get all the way to his feet, because she was right there again, targeting his face with a lightning-fast palm strike. He defended, and almost got a grip that would've led to an arm-bar, but he had to abandon it to avoid letting a knee hammer into his ribs. This time, he went down willingly and was able to use the momentum to roll all the way to his feet … just before she kicked him squarely in the chest and sent him sprawling on to his back. The plastic plates sewn into his jacket spread the impact, but not by *that* much. She didn't give him the chance to recover; by the time his vision cleared, she had one knee on his chest and another on his left arm. Her left hand was holding down his right—*son of a* bitch, *she's strong!*—and her right was poised to drive into his face.

"One," she noted. "Up. Again." With her trademark litheness, she came upright and stepped back away, giving him room to stand. "Body armor? I felt something when I hit you."

"Yeah," he grunted as he got up gingerly. His chest hurt, as did a few other places, but he didn't think she'd cracked any ribs. He shaped up again, watching her eyes. When she came in again, he tried to slip past her attack to get a hit in of his own, and almost succeeded. Or, to put it another way, he failed. That earned him an elbow in the ribs, which the plates absorbed nicely for once. This was followed up by a palm-strike to the jaw, which rang his head like a bell. Instinctively, he covered up, trying to block and evade her attacks while his head cleared.

She didn't give him that luxury. Just as his reeling thoughts crystallized again, he realized too late that he'd held the same stance for an instant too long. His left arm was taken in an iron grip, and the room whirled in a tight circle. Despite the thickness of the mat, the impact drove the breath from him. His wrist ended up in a highly uncomfortable position behind his shoulder-blades, and there was a weight on his back that he guessed was her knee.

"Two," she said. "Okay, we're done here." The weight vanished, and his arm was released. "Up."

This time, he was a little slower to get to his feet, but he managed. The grogginess was draining away as he stood up—*Prodigy rating for the win*—though the aches and pains would linger for a little while yet. "We're done?" he asked, hoping he'd heard right and that she wasn't going to keep whaling on him for shits and giggles. He also hoped that Silent Knight wouldn't take this as *his* cue to start beating on Jericho. There was a limit to what he'd be able to do against the armored Enabled without using his powers.

"We're *done*." Independence was already seated in her place at the desk. "No time to laze around. More questions to ask."

Oh, good. Though to be honest, the incisive questions were just as draining as the fighting had been. Which, he supposed, was the point of this, despite the way Independence's tone raised his hackles. Squaring his shoulders, he did his best to stride confidently back to the center of the horseshoe. On the way, he took up the visitor pass and slipped the lanyard back over his head.

Lady Quantum raised her hand. "Ooh, me next." She leaned toward Jericho slightly, her eyes bright with curiosity. "So, G … G-dude? G-guy? Mr. G? What makes you want to be a hero? What do you personally expect to get out of it? Fame? Fortune? Romance? The letter H?"

He hadn't expected this whimsical line of questioning, but he chose to play it straight. Tests within tests were a thing, after all. "Uh … because, um, I want to be a hero because it's the right thing to do." He paused, trying to work out what she wanted to hear, then decided to go for broke. "I, uh, I come from the South. I see discrimination and people being crapped on by authority for no other reason than skin color or religion or politics. Some of my own kin have had that happen to them. I want to show that people can be better, that it's not so hard to do the right thing." He gestured in an effort to get his point across. "Helping people makes things better. Hurting people makes things worse."

"So why did you attack the police officers at the Market last night?" asked Independence. The question caught him off guard again. While he'd been halfway expecting to be spoken to about it, they hadn't raised it when he walked in. It was beginning to look as though she specifically didn't like him. Or maybe she was just irritated about being called in to do guard duty for the Designated Liaison, even if she *didn't* know it was him behind the mask.

Tamping down his growing anger, he made a conscious choice to follow his father's adage of 'when in doubt, be honest'. "I didn't know what was going on," he admitted. "They weren't in uniform. I saw them knock a teenage kid down and use a stun-gun on him. There was another guy that they stun-gunned as well, just for trying to help him. I didn't know if it was a mugging, an abduction or something else, so I stepped in."

"In the process, you threw one of them into the canal, shorting out his stun-gun and destroying his phone," observed Independence. "That's nearly a thousand dollars' worth of damage, and potential exposure to a drowning hazard, over a *misunderstanding*." She leaned forward, eyes intent behind her goggles. "The punk they were trying to apprehend goes by the street name Razor-Edge. He's a dynamic who controls the shape and size of his own bones. This lets him grow bone from his hands and arms and potentially other parts of his body, to use as weapons or armor. Stun-guns are about the only non-lethal option the police have for taking him down. Now, thanks to *you*, he knows we're onto him, so he'll be keeping his head down. Which means we're going to have to find some other way to get a line on the gang he runs with."

"I didn't *know* that," said Jericho, clenching his teeth to avoid saying more. *Ray,* he thought. *Razor-Edge. Okay, so Thomas was telling the truth. Just not all of it.* There was absolutely nothing he could do about Razor-Edge being on the loose, at least as far as they knew. (If they *had* known about his subsequent meeting with Thomas, he was certain they'd be hammering him on *that* subject). But when it came down to it, he'd taken on the responsibility of getting Thomas and the Survivors out of Utopia City, which included Ray. "Has he actually hurt anyone?" he asked, unable to avoid asking the question. As he understood things, the Survivors didn't attack people; they just committed minor larceny as a survival tactic. If this basic claim was false, it would be a deal-breaker, at least as far as Ray was concerned.

"Not as yet," admitted Independence. "But it's only a matter of time. He's caused quite a bit of property damage with his powers."

In other words, 'no'. Jericho decided that his original stance had been vindicated. Of course, there was still his own property damage to deal with. "Do you want me to pay the UCPD back for the gear? Because I can—"

"No." It was Relentless. "Force Majeure has a fund for that. Rule number one: never accept liability before talking to a lawyer." He settled back into watchful silence, a gesture from one gauntlet-clad hand indicating that the interview should continue.

"And anyone stupid enough to try suing a member of Force Majeure deserves what he gets." Tourbillon, clad in a hooded robe of charcoal gray, was Force Majeure's teleport specialist. Jericho couldn't get enough cues from the enigmatic Enabled to determine whether he was looking at a guy or a girl. Even the voice was androgynous, though there was a noticeable French-Canadian accent. "G-Man, you are gay, yes?"

"Well, yes." Yet another question coming in from left field, while Jericho was distracted with the mention of the Survivors. "I don't exactly make a secret of it."

"No, you don't." Tourbillon pushed back the hood and met Jericho's eyes. Even that didn't help, as the top half of his (or her) face was covered by a mask not unlike Jericho's, while the bottom half could've belonged to a strong-jawed woman or a delicate-featured man. A silvery circlet holding a black gem in the middle of Tourbillon's forehead completed the ensemble. "But the question is this: are you expecting this fact to get you onto the team to satisfy some kind of affirmative action policy?"

"What the hell?" To say Jericho was offended by the insinuation was an understatement. He'd *never* attempted to use his sexual orientation to gain an advantage in that way, and he never would. (The fact that Savannah offered very few opportunities for such an abuse of his minority status was beyond the point). "Not just no, but *hell* no! I'm here to join on my own merits!"

Tourbillon nodded. "Certainly. But if you get on to the team, is it your intention to politicize your status? Raise awareness for gay rights, using your position on the team for publicity?"

"Maybe you weren't listening," Jericho snapped. "I just *said* I wouldn't be bringing my orientation into this." With an effort, he maintained control over his temper.

"Why not?" Independence took over the line of questioning. More aggressively than Tourbillon had, she leaned over the table, eyes locked with his. "Are you ashamed of being gay?"

Jericho stared disbelievingly until he finally found his voice. He couldn't *believe* how insensitive she was being. Even discounting the rumors that she was a lesbian; the fact that she had the nerve to ask a question like that, even in a private setting, just floored him. "No … that's not it at …" All the anger and pain and frustration that had beset him ever since returning to find Luke and Bobbi dead rose up and overwhelmed him. "You know what? Screw you! Screw you and your whole goddamn team! I did *not* come here for this sort of passive-aggressive *bullshit!* You don't want me on your team? Well, *good!* I wouldn't join now if you goddamn *begged* me! I'm *out!*"

Turning on his heel, he stomped toward the door. As it slid open before him, some part of his mind told him that he was letting his emotions control him, but the larger part said *so goddamn what?* All they'd done was badger him and push his buttons until he pushed back. *Well, screw them.* He didn't *need* to be a part of Force Majeure to find Portman.

And if anyone thought otherwise, they were in for one *hell* of a surprise.

40
Passing the Torch

Jericho was still fuming as he exited the elevator into the frosted-glass visitor enclosure. He'd left the blue line behind when he got into the elevator two floors up, but now he knew where he was. The scan-lock opened as he approached, which once again proved that whoever was tracking his progress knew exactly where he was within the Spire. He stepped inside and headed on through, barely needing to pause before the outer doors opened as well.

His temper, already beginning to cool, gave way to self-recrimination. *What the hell did I just do that for?* In one fell swoop, he'd comprehensively sunk any hope of joining Force Majeure, once and for all. Worse, he'd cussed out Independence and the rest of the team before storming out. He was just grateful that the door out of the interview room had opened for him. Had it remained shut, he would've looked like even more of an idiot than he'd already proven himself to be.

He was self-aware enough to be thankful that the bustle of the lobby had died off somewhat. The fewer the witnesses to his ignominious retreat, the better. Turning toward the Visitor desk, he pulled the pass off over his head and handed it back to the receptionist. No sense in not being polite, after all. It wasn't her fault he'd just lost all control over his emotions in front of the people he'd wanted to impress more than basically anyone in the world. "Thank you, sir," she said with a smile. "Here's your phone."

"Thanks," he muttered, accepting the device. A large envelope came with it, which he hadn't expected. He held it up questioningly. "Uh, what's this?" For all he knew, it was a restraining order blocking him from ever approaching the Spire again.

"Transit left it for you," the receptionist said patiently. "Apparently it was a request?"

His eyes widened. In all truth, he'd utterly forgotten the conversation from last night. Far too much had gone on since then. "Oh. Oh! Thank you."

She smiled widely. "You're welcome, sir."

Moving away from the desk, he opened the envelope—the flap hadn't been sealed—to reveal a glossy eight-by-ten of Transit, perched sideways on the seat of her sky-bike, airborne with the Spire in the background, one hand raised in a wave. Scrawled across it in neon red marker was the dedication: TO LUKE. BEST REGARDS, TRANSIT.

Oh, God. It's perfect. Luke would've loved it. He felt tears starting in his eyes at the thought that his best friend would never get to meet Transit or even see the picture. It would, if he had anything to do with matters, be going into the coffin.

Tucking the envelope under his arm, he turned his attention to his phone and the fact that it still had the Post-It note affixed to its face. The note peeled off easily enough and he slid the phone into a pouch on his belt then took hold of the envelope again. He crumpled the note up in his other hand as he walked farther away from the desk, then looked for the nearest trash can.

"There's one just over there." Smokeshadow appeared at his elbow as if by magic. She glanced at his face and her expression turned serious. "Oh, boy. That bad?"

"The only way it could be worse is if I was literally under arrest." He formed a push-tag with the scrap of paper in the center. When he made the throwing motion, it whipped across the intervening space and impacted the can with a high-pitched *ting*. "I basically told them to go screw themselves. So, yeah. Even if I applied again, I'm pretty sure they wouldn't even consider me. Or if I got in, I'd get posted someplace like northern Alaska. Or Death Valley." He looked around in search of a less gloomy topic. "Where'd everyone else go?"

She gave a one-shouldered shrug. "Wavefront went home to wait for his email, I guess. Black Dragon came out, handed her application to the receptionist, and left as well. She was cursing up a storm when she went out the door. They let Cyberswarm through right after that. Me, I browsed the gift shop, then had a coffee and a muffin at the café. They make pretty good muffins, but the coffee's not great. What'cha doing now?"

Jericho hadn't thought this far ahead, but it wasn't hard to work out the next move. "My uncle will be hitting town sometime soon. He'll be expecting me to be at the Oaklands so we can go and officially identify the body. After that ..."

"After that, you've got a funeral to go to," she said perceptively. They headed out of the lobby, through the sliding doors into the morning sunlight. Challenger Plaza stretched out before them. Here and there, pigeons fluttered and pecked at the paving stones. Water droplets from the fountain sparkled in the sun. The rush had died off out here as well, but there were people occupying some of the picnic tables. Over the tables, the auto-adjusting umbrellas were performing their duties flawlessly: just one more tiny detail of life in Utopia City. "Will you be coming back here, afterward?"

He paused, thinking about how to phrase his answer. "Yeah," he said eventually. "I think so. Not to stay. Just to get business done."

"You're going after the murderer." It wasn't much of a guess. A five year old child could've come to that conclusion.

"Well, yeah." That *was* part of his reason for coming back, of course. The other part was the plight of the Survivors. His initial plan to help them was no longer viable—not that he felt comfortable working with the Southsiders after everything that had happened anyway—which meant he was under pressure to come up with an alternative idea. That part, he was still working on.

"You do know the cops and Force Majeure are likely to be hunting this joker down, right?" She reconsidered her words. "Well, the cops, anyway. Force Majeure probably won't consider it worth their time."

"That's the real problem." Jericho clenched his free hand inside its glove. "The cops aren't exactly going to be tearing the city apart, and they'll have to reopen access to the freeway at some point. If he's smart enough to keep his head down, sooner or later he'll be able to just slip out of the city. The only superhero in town who's got a personal motive to keep looking for him is me."

She winced. "Wish I could say you were wrong. If you ever need any help with that, let me know, okay?" She produced a business card from somewhere and passed it over. With her hands back in her hoodie pockets, she strolled alongside him. She seemed content just to be out in the open air, tilting her head to let the sunlight slide across her face.

"I'll do that." He tucked the envelope under his arm again, then took his phone back out and hit the power button to start it up. While he was waiting for the sequence to complete itself, he looked the card over.

Smokeshadow, he read. ***Enabled extraordinaire. Problems solved; solutions expedited; cards sharked; red tape sidestepped. Very affordable rates.***

"Different," he observed as he tucked the card into his pocket. "I can't help but notice that these services you're offering have the potential to be extremely dodgy, legally speaking."

"Meh, I'm more of a morality over legality type of girl," she retorted dismissively. "If a law hurts people, then the people who drafted it clearly had their heads up their asses and it's up to clear-thinking people to redress the balance."

On the one hand, that kind of statement went directly against everything Jericho stood for as a superhero. On the other, it resonated precisely with how he felt about what was happening with the Survivors. Of course, this then opened up queries about Smokeshadow herself.

"If you don't mind me asking … are you a hero or a villain?" He could've kicked himself for his automatic presumption, earlier, that the former was the case. Just because someone was friendly and approachable didn't mean their motives were pure. Every scam artist ever was proof of that concept.

"Yes." She smirked at him.

It took a few seconds for the realization to dawn on him that she'd given her answer in full. "What?"

"Short answer: yes. Long answer: both at the same time." Her tone challenged him to make something of it.

He frowned. "That … doesn't make any sense." How could she break the law and uphold it, all at the same time?

"Depends on context." She shrugged. "All the laws in the world are useless when there's people who are willing to twist the intent to get what they want out of them, and they've got the money to pay lawyers to support that interpretation. Court cases take months or years, long enough for someone with a medical condition to die because they can't afford the treatment they need. Let's just say, matters got expedited in a not entirely legal manner. I had to leave town afterward, but it was worth it in the end."

"Ah." This raised a new concern. "So, when you said you were just here as a tourist, were you being serious or …" He turned and walked backward for a few steps, shading his eyes with the envelope to look up at the Spire, trying not to wince as he recalled his dramatic exit from the interview in vivid detail. But once he got past that, the mere knowledge that he'd been up into the highest occupied reaches of the astounding edifice still amazed him just as much as the revelation of what the technology within was capable of doing. From this perspective, it looked slender and fragile, but he knew just how much of an illusion that was. More concerning to him right now were the multifarious security measures designed to keep intruders out. *If Smokeshadow tried to sneak in there, I'd hate to think what would happen to her.*

"Oh, shit, you thought I was casing the *Spire?*" Her delighted laughter rang across the plaza, setting some of the pigeons to flight. "Oh, hell nope. I deal in audacity, not idiocy. No, this is me being a bona-fide tourist."

"Oh, good." Sincere relief washed over him as he turned to move forwards once more. "So; you're a tourist, Black Dragon was a walk-up and Wavefront was jumping the gun. Any idea what Cyberswarm's story was?"

"He had the ten o'clock appointment." Her voice was amused. "Showed up early just to make sure he didn't forget to be there on time. I gathered he's got a habit of that."

"Hah. Nice." He guessed Transit was giving Cyberswarm the tour. *How much of his tech did she allow him to take in?* Considering how stringent the Spire's security protocols were, he was pretty sure the answer was somewhere around 'zero'. "So, did you ever consider joining?" Force Majeure, he meant.

"Pfft, nope." For emphasis, she shook her head. "I make my own rules. Always have, always will."

"I can respect that." Jericho was more of a by-the-book person, but he also believed that each person had to make their own way in life. "So, uh, why did you wait to walk out with me?"

She shrugged. "Well, I like you. You're a nice guy, and you're not about to make moves on me. Plus, you're interesting enough for me to want to stick around."

"But … what makes you think I'm interesting?" he asked. "About the only thing that people find interesting about me is the fact that I'm Enabled, but you're Enabled as well, so that shouldn't matter."

They were nearing the statue of Challenger now, and she veered off to inspect it. "You don't have to be Enabled to be interesting," she said over her shoulder. "But it helps. What makes you interesting is your issues. You've got a few, but not so many that you're liable to do something stupid. Now, Black Dragon, there's a girl with a few too many issues. Just saying."

The truth of that statement was self-evident. He joined her at the marble plinth. "How can you tell someone's got issues? I thought your thing was body language, not mind reading." Looking up at the statue slowly oscillating back and forth in mid-air, he felt a renewed sense of awe at the tradition that Force Majeure was carrying on.

"Tells." Her tone was casual. "Everyone's got them. I just take more notice than most people." *Because she's a prodigy, duh.* Not twenty-four hours previously, Jericho had carefully explained to Luke how prodigies were able to consistently surpass the peak of human ability in any given endeavor. Admittedly, prodigies usually leaned toward physical capabilities than mental, but evil super-geniuses were no less a thing than their two-fisted adversaries. (The geniuses tended more toward monologuing than brooding, but that was only a matter of detail).

"I see," he said dryly. "Remind me never to play poker against you." *Cards sharked*, he recalled.

"Funny thing," she said cheerfully. "That's exactly how I expedited matters. And it's also why I had to get out of town in a hurry." She grinned disarmingly. "Some people have *no* sense of humor."

"I'm sure." His tone was dryer than he'd thought he could manage, but simply walking and talking with her had taken away a lot of the tension left over from the debacle that the interview had devolved into. Still, he had to get away and meet Thomas before Uncle Leroy got into town, so they could work out how to get the Survivors out of Utopia City.

Before he could work out an excuse, his phone rang. He pulled it from its pouch and checked out the screen. It was Uncle Leroy's number. Swiping to accept the call, he held the phone to his ear. "Oh, hey. How far out are you?" He began working the numbers in his head. If Leroy was still half an hour away, he could go and see the Survivors and still get back in time …

Leroy's voice cut through his musings like a hot knife through soft butter. "I'm in town now. I just got off the train. Whereabouts are you? I kind've expected you to meet me at the station, boy."

"Oh. Oh, shit." Jericho took the phone away from his ear and looked at the time, only now realizing just how badly he'd miscalculated matters. When he'd thought Leroy was passing through Atlanta on the way to Chattanooga, the maglev had been coming into Chattanooga itself. So instead of having half an hour up his sleeve, he had no time at all. Leroy was here *now*.

"Yeah, *oh shit* is right, boy. So, you gonna come get me or am I gonna have to figure out this place all on my lonesome?" Right now, Leroy sounded more irritated than pissed, but he was getting there.

"Uh … just hang tight," Jericho temporized. "I'm near a cab stand. I'll come get you. Ten minutes, tops."

"See you then." Leroy ended the call, leaving Jericho staring at the phone. He'd counted on having *some* time to work out how to help the Survivors, but that time was now gone. There was no way he could get a cab to that area of town, locate Thomas and his friends, thrash out a new plan *and* pick up Leroy in time.

"You've got the look of a man with more problems than he can handle," observed Smokeshadow with a knowing grin. "Anything I can help you with?"

Jericho hesitated. With Smokeshadow's assistance, he could sort everything out *and* pick up Leroy with the older man being none the wiser. The big question was, of course, did he trust her? *Could* he trust her? If he told her what was going on, she would inevitably gain access to his secret identity.

Should I just bite the bullet and tell her? She's enough of a smartass and a boundary-pusher that she'll probably go along with it for shits and giggles.

He shook his head, not in negation but to settle his thoughts. Events were moving too fast for him. He had to make a leap of faith. "I've got a question for you and I need an honest answer."

"I'm listening." Her tone was non-judgmental, her posture open. He found himself *wanting* to tell her all. It came as a mild shock to realize that his trust in her was stronger than it probably should've been. It was probably her body language at work, he knew, but it just *felt* right to confide in her. His earlier worries about scam artists returned. There was no doubt at all in his mind that she could be a superlative member of the fraternity, should she so choose.

He just had to hope that she wasn't scamming *him*.

Unfortunately, it wasn't like he had many other options right now.

He took a deep breath and made the leap of faith. "Okay, suppose there was a bunch of teenage kids in Utopia City who were basically stealing to live, and they just wanted to get out of the city. Would you be more inclined to turn them in to the cops or help them get out of town?" He held his breath, waiting for her answer.

She didn't hesitate for a moment. "Help them get out of town, duh. Sounds like a lot more fun than turning them in." While this fit with what he'd seen of her to this point, it was still a huge relief to hear her say it. But she wasn't finished. "What are these kids to you, anyway?"

"I know one of them, kind of," he admitted. Even as he said it, he was aware he was fudging matters more than a little. But there was something about that personable young man. Whatever it was, it was more than his artless good looks, the fact he was also a prodigy, or even the stolen kisses. Something deeper than all that.

He met Smokeshadow's gaze and knew from the quirk of her smile that she was picking up at least some of what he was thinking from his expression. "Kind of, huh?"

"Yeah, kind of," he said awkwardly, firmly repressing the impulse to look away from her knowing gaze. "I've got to go pick up my uncle, but … hold on one second." He put his phone away and pulled out his notepad and pen. Flipping to the page where he'd written Thomas' number, he copied it to another page and scribbled his own email address on it as well. Tearing out the second page, he handed it to her. "The cops here monitor text messages. Cellphone calls are probably checked as well. His name's Thomas. Get in touch, meet up and let him know that I sent you. Can you do that?"

"Bears, woods," she retorted, looking over the page. "That's the easy bit. Though you do realize you're taking a chance with your secret identity here, right? With information like this, I could do *anything*." She gazed at him guilelessly, though he thought he spotted a twinkle in her eye.

"I'm trusting you not to," he said firmly. "I don't believe you're that sort of person."

"Pft," she muttered, rolling her eyes. "Save me from heroes who put their faith in the morally ambiguous because their hearts are pure and their cause is just. You're no fun. What do I do after that, and what's the email address for?"

"For you to send some stuff to me," he said. He spent the next thirty seconds explaining in detail exactly what he did need, according to the plan that was now unfolding in his head. It wasn't going to be easy and it definitely wasn't going to be cheap, but it was preferable to the Survivors being imprisoned for crimes they'd had no choice but to commit.

"Got it," she said once he finished. "Shouldn't be too hard. When do you think you'll be getting back?"

He shrugged elaborately. It seemed so much easier to do that with the metaphorical weight off his shoulders. "Three, maybe four days, I guess?" He'd never been involved in the planning of a wake and a funeral before, much less the other preparations he had to make. "I really, really appreciate this."

"*Look to my coming on the first light of the fifth day; at dawn, look to the east.*" Smokeshadow smirked as she quoted the line from the movie, then she slapped him on the shoulder. "Go deal with your family business. I'll handle this end."

"Thanks." Turning, he headed for the air taxi stand. It was time for him to go and fulfill his *other* obligations.

Fortunately, changing in the cab on the way over was going to be the least of his problems.

41
Best Laid Plans

Smokeshadow

Tapping her finger against her chin, Chelsea watched as G-Man climbed into the nearest cab. A moment later, it spun up its lifters and vaulted skyward in a blast of air-wash. Banking hard, it turned toward the east and accelerated in the direction of the maglev terminal.

Poor guy, she mused. He was so very *earnest* about being a superhero, even when life seemed determined to shit all over him. As a fellow shit-magnet, she had to admire his dedication to the cause. To deal with *her* problems, she'd had to abandon all pretense at being a 'good' person and settle for just being 'all right', to quote a TV show she'd seen once upon a time. She could never go home again, but at least her sister would be getting the treatment those assholes had been withholding from her.

Moving out of state had removed the threat of arrest; she'd made sure not to pull anything that had a potential Federal indictment attached to it. But this had in no way solved all her issues. When she called herself a shit-magnet, she was speaking no less than the truth. No matter where she went, no matter what she did, she invariably encountered screwed-up situations which required her inimitable capabilities to unscrew.

Why this was, she had yet to figure out. Either she was really good at predicting where trouble would be ahead of time, or trouble was basically everywhere and she was better at spotting it than the average idiot. On balance, she tended to prefer the second explanation, because the first one made her look like a glory hound.

This didn't mean she'd been lying to G-Man about being a tourist. She *was* one, in a manner of speaking. She tended to go places and see the sights, because she did like to visit new locations and meet new people. This served to keep her occupied between bouts of 'what the hell is it *this* time?'.

Sight-seeing (for her, at least) was a somewhat different occupation from before she'd gotten her powers. As a prodigy, she needed to settle down with a good vantage point and watch her surroundings. Almost immediately, she would be able to pick out significant patterns of movement and behavior; keeping it up for several hours would imprint that area on her awareness. During this time, if there was anything odd or unusual to be seen, she'd usually spot it and get an idea of what was going on. For instance, as she'd shown Jericho, the mystery of why there was no litter or graffiti to be seen anywhere had been neatly solved. She wasn't quite sure *what* she'd do with her knowledge of the street-cleaning bugs, but there it was.

Utopia City, in her estimation, was remarkably devoid of screwed-up situations. In fact, she'd been in the city for just over twenty-four hours before she had her fateful encounter with G-Man on the rooftop. He'd exhibited all the signs of someone with a serious problem, though when she found out what it was, she'd been hard put to figure out how to fix it. Bringing dead family members back to life didn't fall under her purview, after all. If it had, she would've been charging much higher rates.

Still, he was a nice guy. She liked nice guys; they gave her hope for the future of the human race. So, she gave him some basic advice for free, boiling down to 'don't let the bastards wear you down'. But even after she sent him on his way, every instinct she had was telling her that there was more to the situation. She knew he was going to the Spire though, so she'd decided to tag along on the principle that whatever the *other* problem was, it would come out sooner or later.

And so, it had. Which left her where she was now, with the collective fate of a bunch of Enabled teenagers resting in her (if she said so herself) capable hands. She spread out the piece of paper G-Man had given her and examined it. A phone number with the name 'Thomas' scribbled next to it, and an email address for a 'j_hansen_90'. When she factored in the half-assed plan he'd come up with on the fly, it definitely fit the pattern of the screwed-up situations she regularly found herself embroiled in. Mentally, she cracked her knuckles. *This* was more like it.

Taking out her phone, she tapped in the number. The floating statue of Challenger was only a few yards away; moving in that direction, she held up her phone as though she were taking pictures and made a complete circuit of the monument. In doing so, she got a complete three-sixty degree visual of her surroundings, including everyone nearby. As far as she could tell, nobody in her line of sight was close enough to listen in on a casual phone conversation. Neither did anyone's body language indicate they were anyone paying her more than the usual amount of attention. Reaching up under her collar, she ran her fingers over the small device she found there.

While her outer costume, the part made of programmable hyperweave, could 'grow' pockets wherever she wanted them, they were only as permanent as the current shape of the garment. The workaround, though not obvious, had been simple. Underneath the hyperweave, she wore a form-fitting one-piece, complete with pockets that didn't disappear when she forgot why she needed them.

Clipped to the collar of the one-piece, concealed beneath the hyperweave, was a subsonic voice-scrambler. Pressing the button on the side, she turned it on. Her voice wouldn't sound any different to the untrained human ear, but computers would go nuts trying to analyze the signal. As a bonus, the subsonic carrier wave also set up sympathetic vibrations in the lenses of any nearby cameras aimed at her, making it exceptionally difficult to capture a clear image of her face.

As a last line of defense, she went into 'ignore-me' mode. Unlike many Dynamic manipulation powers, this worked perfectly well over a video link, mainly because it didn't require special conditions to make it work. Purely digital surveillance was a semi-hard counter for her skillset, but it suffered from the drawback that humans had to review the imagery. So long as she wasn't doing anything blatantly illegal on the footage, it was possible to be overlooked. Hunching over her phone, she hit the call button and held the phone to her ear.

Normally, she would've started with a text message, but it would be easy for a bunch of skittish teenagers to misinterpret her intentions and cut off all contact before she had a chance to gain their trust. So, a voice call it was.

The phone rang once, twice, three times. She took the time to consider what sort of tone she wanted to set for the call. Jericho was clearly interested in Thomas and she doubted he'd pursue someone who wasn't reciprocating in some way, so she was dealing with a guy who probably wasn't heterosexually oriented. *Leave off the seductress.* These were teenagers she'd be dealing with, almost certainly runaways; otherwise, they would've called their parents or other guardians for assistance. *Nix the authority figure.* Thomas knew G-Man by his costumed identity and trusted him, so that might be a way to gain his confidence.

"Hello?" The voice was that of a young adult, probably eighteen or nineteen. Male, wary, on edge. "Who's this? How did you get this number?"

"Hello; am I speaking with the T-man?" She kept her voice calm and professional, but not so robotic that he'd think he was speaking with a cop. "I was given this number by a man in black, first initial G. He's got family issues, but he's asked me to pass on a message."

There was silence on the line. It persisted long enough that she began to wonder if the call had dropped out. "Tell me something that only he would know," the young man said.

She paused for thought. "He had his tryout this morning, and he bombed. Right now, he's headed for the maglev station to meet with someone. The message I was told to pass on is that the old plan is out but there's a new plan in place. We need to meet in person so I can brief you on the new plan."

"Why can't we go with the old plan?" the young man asked, almost accusingly.

"Things have changed." She projected surety and honesty into her speech, as much as she could without visual cues. "If everything was okay, I wouldn't even be contacting you."

Again, there was hesitation on the line. "Are you the friend he told me about?"

This time, she let the snort go through loud and clear. "I sincerely doubt it. The last time he spoke to you, I hadn't even met him. No, I suspect this friend of his is the subject of the family issues. Now, are you okay with meeting, or not? If you want to blow me off, that's your right and privilege. But if you do that, I have no other way to contact you."

"I … I'd rather not meet, not without getting word from him." She had to hand it to the kid. He knew how to be persistent.

As it happened, so did she. Injecting every ounce of firmness and patience she could into her voice, she spoke again. "You won't get it. He asked me to pass on this message because he won't be in contact for a few days. Now, like I said, there *is* a plan. But for it to go forward, we have to meet face to face. It's your choice. It's not like I can exactly force you, but unless you can meet me halfway on this, I won't be able to help you." Then she waited. If she pushed any harder, her instincts said, she would drive him away. *Time to let him decide for himself.*

He hesitated for the longest moment. "Okay, I'll meet you." Even now, she could tell that he was teetering on the verge of ending the call. "Come alone. I'll know if you don't."

"Whatever you want," she assured him. "When and where?" This was going to be the tricky bit, she knew. Neither one of them could count on their communications being secure. He knew Utopia City better than she did; that was a sucker's bet. It was up to him to arrange a meet where the authorities wouldn't also be waiting when they showed up.

"Thirty minutes," he said. She approved; that would give her the time to get there (wherever 'there' was) while also making it hard for the forces of law and order to muster an appropriate response. "As for where … you know where he's staying?"

"I do." It would be hard for her not to; she'd met him on the roof. "I'm staying there myself."

"Good. Go in and speak to the receptionist. Leave a message there for me, by name. Let me know what you're wearing and go to the Market. You know where that is?"

She rolled her eyes at his unintentional parody of a dirty phone call. *Oh, yeah. He's definitely gay.* "I know of it. Haven't been there yet." *Where is he going with this?*

"Okay, go there, wander around a bit, and wait for me to contact you. That sound okay?"

"Sure, we could do that." But even as she said it, several problems with the scenario occurred to her, starting with drone surveillance and ending with impostors pretending to be her. "Or … I'll give the *receptionist* a neutral location and wait for you there."

"Oh. Yeah. Right." He paused, the tone of his voice indicating that he'd just seen at least some of the flaws that she'd previously spotted. "We could do that too, I guess."

"See you when I see you," she said lightly, and ended the call. Nudging her phone at the seam which pretended to be a pocket in the 'jeans' she was wearing caused a slit to open in the hyperweave, and she slid the phone into the actual pocket within. Her MagCard was in the same pocket; taking it out, she headed for the cab stand.

On the flight over to the Oaklands, the cab driver didn't speak much. That suited her, because she needed to make contingency plans. What to do if Thomas didn't show. What to do if he showed and was hostile. If the police showed up instead. If the police showed up while Thomas was there … there were many ways this could go.

Most of her plans boiled down to combinations of 'run away', 'load on the charm' and 'hide in plain sight', but that was the nature of being a prodigy with an emphasis on mental capabilities rather than physical. She was fully aware that her powerset did not make her into an action hero, but she was confident in its ability to get her out of most predicaments with her skin intact. Now, if only she could work devise a way to avoid getting *into* said predicaments in the first place …

When the air taxi landed outside the Oaklands, she was once more an anonymous young woman in a hoodie. Heading in through to the courtyard, she approached the desk. "Excuse me, Stacey?"

It was always a good move to take note of the names of counter staff, after all.

"Oh, hello," Stacey greeted her politely. "Can I help you?"

"Yes. Yes, you can." Chelsea shifted her aspect toward 'I am the most important person you're going to meet today'. Immediately, she saw the young woman straighten her back slightly, her eyes becoming alert. Even more important than making sure that people correctly delivered the messages you left with them was the trick of getting them to remember to pass on the message in the first place. "Could I ask you for a favor, please?"

"Oh, of course," gushed Stacey. With an internal wince, Chelsea dialed back the intensity of her body language. Some people were more impressionable than others.

Leaning in, she lowered her voice, hopefully to the point that any sound pickups would fail to register her words. "I'm waiting for a friend of mine. His name is Thomas." She paused to make sure Stacey had taken that in. "If he comes in and asks, could you please tell him I'm waiting on the roof?"

Stacey nodded earnestly, though the light of something akin to hero-worship still shone in her eyes. "I will absolutely do that for you," she promised.

"Thank you." Even though it was technically unnecessary, she gave Stacey a beaming smile guaranteed to give her the warm fuzzies for at least the next ten minutes. Just because her skills were all about manipulating people didn't mean she had to be a bitch about it.

Once Chelsea got up to the roof, she pulled out her phone and fiddled with it for a moment. Setting the stage was important; if she was going to convince Thomas to let her assist with the well-being of his friends, she had to gain his trust from the get-go. And while her skills and abilities were impressive by any normal metric, at the end of the day she was still a prodigy, not a dynamic. She was still dependent on physics and human neuro-anatomy, not on powers beyond the ken of mortal man.

Which meant making use of psychology, a field in which her Prodigy rating had long since granted her a serious grounding, ignoring the minor fact that she lacked formal training qualifications (at least, any that would be recognized by an institute of higher learning). Humming a light tune, she finished her preparations and set about waiting. And watching; always watching.

Fifteen minutes later by her phone readout, the stairwell door opened and a tall young man in a baseball cap and sunglasses, wearing a jacket and jeans, stepped cautiously onto the roof. Behind him came someone in black-and-gold power-armor that was configured to a feminine form, complete with a gold-tinted faceplate. Rollerblades built into her boots made her tall and slender despite the inevitable bulking effect of the armor. Which left Chelsea wondering how Thomas had smuggled his friend in past the security cameras in the courtyard.

She hadn't doubted for a moment that Thomas' Enabled friends were the real deal and not a bunch of pretenders, but it was good to get corroboration.

Her phone was already set up, and she pressed the 'play' icon. The young man (she figured it was Thomas, but she didn't have any proof yet) turned and frankly stared. This wasn't surprising, as she'd arranged for her hyperweave to take the form of a classic spy-movie trench-coat and fedora. Standing where she couldn't be seen from the street, she folded her arms and tilted her head so the sun's shadow fell across her face, a trick she was a past master at pulling off. Right on cue, her phone cut in with the number one tune on her playlist.

As the music hit its first strong bars, the guy lowered his sunglasses slightly, allowing her to see his dramatically raised eyebrows under the brim of the baseball cap. "Are you shitting me right now?" he asked in tones of patent disbelief.

"What?" The armored girl rolled a yard forward, to stand beside the guy. "What's that tune all about?"

Chelsea stared at her incredulously. "Seriously, you don't know the *Mission: Impossible* theme? What rock have you been hiding under?" Her thumb hit the icon to turn off the music. At a subtle command (transmitted more via body language than anything else), the hyperweave reformed into her more usual hoodie-and-mask.

The guy sighed. "It's a long story. Call me Thomas. This is Blades. And you are …?"

It was in anticipation of precisely this question that she'd stored a card in a temporary pocket in the sleeve of her costume. As a prodigy, she was well-versed in basic and advanced legerdemain; a flick of the wrist produced it as if from thin air, and she handed it over to him. He accepted it gingerly, as if it might explode. Which, considering what dynamics and artificers were capable of, was not an entirely unwarranted concern.

"Smokeshadow," he said, reading the card, then glanced up at her. "Problems solved?"

"And solutions expedited," she added. "Also, cards sharked, but I'm reasonably sure that won't help with anything right now."

"Well, cards *are* an integral part of our problem, but not that type, no," he agreed. "So, G-Man's asked for your help?"

"He has." She generated a warm smile, calculated to engender trust and fellow feeling. "And I've agreed to help him out, because screw bureaucracy. Which means I need to get together with you and your friends, sooner rather than later." It only took a moment or so to go over the salient points of the plan G-Man had come up with, which had the overwhelming merit of being relatively simple in execution. Easy it wasn't, given that it required two separate and distinct areas of collaboration in two different cities, but she lived by the principle of 'good: fast; cheap: pick two' and it had never let her down yet. *You can never have everything you want.*

Once she finished, Thomas and Blades looked at each other, then back at her. "Well, crap," said Blades. "Think you can pull it off?"

"I'm not the one you've got to ask that question of," Chelsea pointed out. "But unless we get our end done, it's dead in the water."

Blades huffed irritably. "Okay, *fine*. Think *he* can pull it off?"

Raised her hand in a 'stop' motion, Chelsea shook her head. "You're asking the wrong question. Is he going to try his damnedest to get it done? Hell, yes. Is it guaranteed to work, no matter what happens? Of course not. But do I think there's a good chance of success?" She tapped her chin with her finger. "I can't judge that one. All I know for a fact is that if you kill the plan now, it's dead."

"She's right," Thomas intervened. "I trust G-Man not to pull shit that might hurt us. But it's not just up to him or me, *or* you." As he spoke to Blades, his tone was firm. "Everyone else gets a say, too. The Survivors as a whole deserve the option to make this choice."

"And not to put too fine a point on it, but he's working on a limited timetable." Chelsea didn't know how much Thomas had told Blades, but it was worth repeating. "On top of prepping for this plan, he's got a funeral to go to. After *that*, he's got issues back home to deal with. So, let's not screw around the nice superhero who's sticking his neck out to save you guys from being pummeled into the ground by Force Majeure, hmm?"

"Wait, *what* again now?" Blades stared at Thomas. "You didn't say G-Man was a *hero*. Me and Ray thought he was some newcomer villain butting in to mess with the cops."

Thomas sighed. "You never asked. If you'd asked, I'd have told you." He pointed at Chelsea. "You can tell *she's* not exactly the heroic type, right?"

"Hey!" Chelsea mock-protested with a smirk. "I'll have you know I resemble that remark."

She couldn't see Blades' expression, but the pun got a face-palm from Thomas. The armored girl shook her head. "Seriously? She's gotta be a villain, after a joke like that."

"Morally ambiguous," Chelsea corrected her. "Get it right." She gestured at the two Enabled before her. "Listen; if you didn't have to steal to eat, if you had the chance to earn money normally, would you still steal?"

"Of course not!" Thomas' voice was sharp. Blades' headshake came only half a second later.

"Exactly." Chelsea tapped herself on the chest. "I don't steal for the sake of theft or profit. If I take things away from people, it's because in my opinion they've forfeited their right to own them. You guys are a sight more heroic than me. Now, I'm looking to give you guys the chance to get back to *being* heroic. So's G-Man. How about we go put this to the rest of them?"

This level of persuasion was a lot easier to pull off than when she'd been talking to Thomas over the phone. Posture, expression and tone all combined with the fact that Blades was already half-convinced in the matter.

"Yeah," said the armored girl in tones of enlightenment. "That's a great idea." She looked from Thomas to Chelsea. "We gonna go together, or …?"

"How about you go on ahead?" Thomas suggested. "That way, you can let the guys know we're coming."

"Sure, I can do that." Again, Blades looked between the two. "You can kick her ass if she pulls anything, right?"

Chelsea wrinkled her nose. "I don't do the ass-kicking. If and when I find it necessary, I get someone like you two to do it for me."

"Right. See you two back at base. Don't be too long." Blades threw what might have been a salute toward Thomas and headed back toward the roof entrance. When she tugged on the door, it refused to open. "Crap. Forgot about that."

"Here." Thomas pulled something from his pocket and tossed it to her. "Gimmick loaned it to me."

"Oh, cool. That'll work." Blades applied the device to the door, and it came open almost immediately. "Thanks." She tossed the thing back and stepped through the doorway.

"What *is* that?" Chelsea leaned closer to look at the object. Small enough to fit in her palm, it had the unfinished look of a typical Artificer prototype, with bolt-ends and random extrusions protruding in different directions. "Did she just pick the lock on a safety door with it?"

"Well, it's a Gimmick universal lockpick, so yeah." Thomas tossed it in the air and caught it. "She makes useful stuff like that." He grinned at her surprised expression. "I know, I know, the name's kind of a cliché. Don't look at me; I didn't choose it."

Raising her eyebrows, she gave him a dry look. "It's still a pretty generic name for an artificer."

"And 'the Technologist' isn't?" Thomas shook his head slightly. "Let's face it; there are only so many unique and interesting names available before we start repeating ourselves. And that way leads down the Nighthawk path."

She shook her head quizzically. "The Nighthawk path? I'm not familiar with that one."

He snorted. "I'm not surprised. It's a pretty obscure case. Five or six years ago, a Prodigy hero in Detroit using the name Nighthawk joined Force Majeure, and of course got mentioned in the news. About one month later, a comic book company which had a character not dissimilar in looks, and who was also named Nighthawk, sued her for copyright infringement. Force Majeure's lawyers did their research, and discovered that two other heroes and five villains in different parts of the country were also using the name, three with hyphens and two using it as two separate words. A couple of them had been going for quite some time without anyone noticing. Prodigies flying under the radar, so to speak."

"Holy shit." She put her hand over her mouth to muffle the giggle. "That's amazing. What happened?"

"About what you'd expect." Thomas made a movement with his head that suggested he'd just rolled his eyes behind his sunglasses. "The company dropped the case, on the proviso that the various Nighthawks made sure not to emulate the comic character in costume or catchphrases. Mainly because they had no desire to piss off a bunch of villains who didn't care much about the legalities of the situation. And of course, going after the heroes without doing anything about the villains would've sent entirely the wrong message."

"And let's not forget the bit about Force Majeure's lawyers," Chelsea noted. "Pretty sure they were the eight-hundred-pound gorilla in this situation."

"That might've had *something* to do with it, yes." He looked around and nodded. "Okay, we've given her enough lead time. Let's go."

Heading over to the door, he pulled the device from his pocket again and applied it to the gap in the door about where the lock-tongue would engage. Chelsea watched in bemusement as he pressed an apparently random lever; there was a click from the door, and he pulled it open. "Handy," she mused. "Does she do commissions?"

"You'll have to speak to her about that yourself." Stepping in through the door,

Thomas led the way down the stairs to the top floor of the Oaklands. She followed, wondering how much the artificer would charge for such a device. She herself was skilled in picking all sorts of locks, of course, but some took a lot more time than others.

They took the elevator the rest of the way to the first floor and strolled out through the courtyard in the manner of two people who were coincidentally going in the same direction. Again, Chelsea was led to wonder how Blades had gotten out through there without showing her armor off to the courtyard cameras; she couldn't imagine that the Survivors had lasted so long without internalizing the habits of basic caution. And while the teenage artificer could no doubt have removed the armor, transporting it then became a problem of trying not to look conspicuous while hauling around sixty pounds or more of metal.

Once they got out on the street, Blades was nowhere to be seen, though Chelsea had no way to determine how fast the girl could move on those (almost certainly motorized) rollerblades. There were a few pedestrians here and there, none of whom were exhibiting the sort of reaction to be expected after a passing encounter with an Enabled. Granted, this was Utopia City, but given the respect shown to those with powers here, the people should've reacted *somehow*. And yet, they hadn't.

She restrained herself from asking the obvious question. Leaving people wondering exactly what had just happened was *her* thing, and she was determined to unravel the mystery by herself. With that in mind, she kept her own counsel, and watched the street and sky as they walked.

By the time they reached the turn in the road that preceded the Market, they'd passed forty-three pedestrians and two people on bicycles. Nobody in sight looked in the least bit like someone trying to conceal a suit of armor. However, there was activity going on in the sky overhead which raised dark suspicions about something else altogether. She would have mentioned it, but she didn't know how good his self-control was, so she kept her mouth shut for the moment.

They went down the dead-end road that fronted onto the canal, barricaded from the water by a row of bollards. Turning to the left once they reached the water, they walked along the boardwalk alongside the canal. Brightly colored fish flickered and darted in the gently rolling depths beside them. Overhead, a monorail whisked silently past on the gleaming rail suspended over the canal by slender archways, curving away from them to follow the canal between the busy shops of the Market.

Continuing southward rather than turn west again, they crossed the road for a second time and went down a side street. The first buildings they encountered were two-story storehouses, almost certainly intended to service the shops of the Market.

By now, her suspicions had crystallized into a certainty. Picking her moment, she grabbed Thomas by the arm and spun him into a recessed doorway, flattening herself against the door beside him. "We're being watched," she said. "Followed, even. There's been at least one hex in line of sight forty seconds out of every minute since we left the Oaklands."

"That's not totally unusual, is it?" But he was already scanning the sky overhead.

"You tell me," she replied with a certain amount of snark. "I *do* know there's not enough hexes in Utopia City to surveil every square foot of the city at all hours, no matter how much the cops might wish otherwise. To have consistent hex oversight after your friend showed off her armor on a rooftop, and to not lose sight of us for more than five seconds at a time afterward, goes far beyond 'coincidence' and straight through into 'enemy action'." She rapped her knuckles on the door they were pressed up against, then handed him the universal lockpick she'd lifted from his pocket while he'd been distracted with looking up at the sky. "We've got about ten seconds before the closest one reacquires us. Think fast."

He stared from the lockpick to her and back again, then her words got through to him. "Right," he said, turning and hastily putting the little gadget to use. She counted seconds in her head; the door clicked just as she reached 'six'. He pushed it open and they tumbled through into the darkened building. The door slammed shut behind them.

"Think they saw us?" whispered Thomas, crouching in the gloom and removing his sunglasses.

She stood up, brushing herself off, and pulled her phone out. Activating its flashlight mode, she waved it around to get an idea of the room they were in. "They either did or they didn't," she said in a normal tone. "Either way, the operator's going to realize he's lost us any moment now. We're out of sight right now, so we need to get outside the search perimeter. Which means we need to find a different exit and keep moving, before he calls in reinforcements."

Thomas nodded. "You've done this before," he observed. He added his phone light to the effort to illuminate the area. Long rows of shelves stretched away to the left and right, though the lights didn't do nearly enough to eliminate the pervasive darkness.

"Once or twice." Chelsea looked around to see if there were any flashing red lights in evidence. "The alarm on that door must be silent." There was an aisle between two shelves, directly ahead. She started down it, flanked on both sides by identical crates, their ranks leading off into the darkness ahead.

Thomas hurried to catch up. "The lockpick wouldn't have set it off. Gimmick knows her stuff."

"Hmm." She didn't argue the point. Artificers pulled impossible tricks like that, all the time. "Good."

They hustled through the dimness, their phone lights creating a double circle of illumination around them. Despite her personal certainty that they were alone in the building, she kept a lookout all around; it only took being mistaken once to come unstuck.

Still, a feeling began to creep over her that they'd made a totally different mistake. Thomas voiced it first. "Uh … do you know where the way out *is?*"

"I guess I was hoping for a fire evacuation sign," she admitted. This was a bad thing. They were out of sight right now, but if the forces of law and order decided to surround the building they'd last been seen next to and search it comprehensively, evading capture would become very tricky indeed.

That was when she heard the faint sound and caught sight of movement out of the corner of her eye. Something big was bearing down on them from behind, fast. *I thought there was nobody else in here, dammit!*

"Look out!" she shouted, squeezing herself into the gap between two of the crates. The bulky machine that whispered past a second later would've flattened her if she'd stayed where she was. Cautiously, once she was sure it wouldn't come back, she peered out. The machine wasn't there. Neither was Thomas.

Shit, shit, shit. "Thomas!" she shouted. There were no blood splatters or any other evidence that the young man had been injured; he was just … *gone.*

"Here!" she heard, up the row and around the corner. "Come on! Hurry up!"

Not sure what was going on, swearing under her breath at the fright he'd given her, Chelsea ran after the sound of his voice. The light of her phone bobbed and weaved and threw crazy shadows everywhere, but she had the basic surefootedness afforded to all prodigies. Grabbing the frame that supported the shelving, she swung herself around the corner and ran on. "Where?" she yelled, between gasps for breath. Being a prodigy also gave her a certain minimum level of fitness, but a marathon runner she wasn't.

"Here!" he shouted again, and she saw him waving his own light. It was considerably higher off the ground than she'd expected; in its glow, she saw, he was sitting on the back of the thing that had nearly run them down.

It was an automated forklift, she realized, riding on large, soft wheels. The movement of those wheels over the concrete floor was the only thing that had warned her in time. At that moment, it was moving to align its tines with a crate on one of the higher shelves.

"What the hell are you doing?" she called as she slowed to a jog. "Get down from there!"

He flashed her a manic grin. "No, I've got a better idea! You get up here!"

"What? Are you nuts?"

"Possibly!" His grin never went away as he lay flat on top of the thing and extended his arm downward.

He's a lunatic. I'm sticking my neck out for a bonafide … wait. Prodigy. He's allowed to be insane if he can actually pull it off.

Running up at her best pace, she jumped into the air with her free hand outstretched. For the first time since she got her powers, she wished her Prodigy rating had been inclined more toward the physical than the mental. Missing his hand altogether, her fingers scrabbled uselessly on obdurate metal. She felt herself slipping back, just as the creaking noise from the front of the forklift indicated that the machine had acquired its load and was now about to reverse.

A powerful grip slapped around her wrist and she was hauled upward. Thomas was a husky young man, but she was still impressed by the level of strength he was exhibiting; one-handed, lacking any kind of serious leverage, he was still dead-lifting her entire body weight. *His Prodigy rating must be higher than I thought. Or maybe helping me up fits into his sweet spot.*

In another moment, she was safely (for a given definition of 'safe') on top of the unmanned vehicle as it began to roll backward. "Okay," she panted, trying to catch her breath. "What's this in aid of? Going for a joyride is not going to get us out of here."

"On the contrary, it's going to do exactly that." He wasn't even out of breath, the smartass show-off. His grin twinkled at her, daring her to challenge his assertion.

She drew an aggravated breath. For a physical prodigy, he certainly knew how to push her buttons. "Okay, one: how's it going to do that? And two: how do *you* know it's going to do that?"

"To answer your second question, I've been in these places before." He pointed forward at the crate that was now supported on the tines of the forklift. "And to answer your first question, where do you think it's going with that? These things don't just move crates around the warehouse for the fun of it."

"Oh. Right." It only took her a second to figure out his meaning. "It's fetching it for transport?"

"Got it in one." He made a show of leaning back nonchalantly. "It's gonna take us straight to the loading dock. Soon as we get there, we jump off and make our daring escape."

"Okay, I get that bit." Moving cautiously, Chelsea readjusted her position until she was sitting upright on the rolling forklift. "But if you've been in these warehouses before, why didn't you warn me about the damn forklifts *before* one of them nearly ran us down?"

"Partly because I forgot in all the excitement," he confessed. "And partly because from the way you were looking around, I thought you knew about them already." He gave her a sheepish shrug. "I'm sorry. It won't happen again."

She tried to give him a hard glare, but her heart wasn't in it. "It better not."

"I'll do my best," he promised, then glanced over his shoulder. "Starting right now. You might want to brace yourself. These things have been known to turn pretty fast."

She followed his advice before turning to look for herself, so when the forklift abruptly slowed and turned to exit through a large roller-door, she wasn't caught off-balance. Unfortunately, any hope that they would simply be able to jump off and start running withered and died when she took in the fact that the loading dock itself was enclosed, with another roller-door guarding it from the outside.

Their unusual transport came to a halt and began to lower its cargo to the concrete paving of the loading dock. "Now!" said Thomas, but Chelsea was already on her way down to the floor. She landed easily, flexing her knees to absorb the impact, then went straight over to the wall of the enclosure to get as far away from the forklift as she could. Thomas joined her a few seconds later; they watched as the monstrous machine turned nimbly on the spot and went back into the warehouse, its soft rubber tires whispering on the smooth concrete. The roller-door began to rumble back down into place, but she ignored it. They needed to get *out*, not back in.

"Okay, there's got to be an easy way out of here," she said, holding up her phone and feeling quite pleased with the fact that she hadn't dropped it the whole time. The light showed the outer roller-door, firmly shut … and another door beside it, of a shape and size suited to people rather than forklifts or trucks. "And there it is."

Fully aware of the passage of time—for all she knew, the cops could be moving to surround the warehouse right now—she headed for the smaller door.

"Wait!" called Thomas. "If you open it, you'll set off the intruder alarm!"

Oh, yeah. This normally hadn't been an issue for her, because in the general run of things she could rely on being gone before the forces of law and order showed up to make problems. She'd already known she would have to be more circumspect in Utopia City. This merely served to highlight that problem. "Can you disable it?"

"I've never actually tried to use the lockpick from inside a building, to disable an alarm that's in here with me." He looked at her expression. "What? It's not like that's a common situation. Usually it's more like 'disable the alarm to get inside'. Gimmick showed me how to do it from the outside, but never told me if it would even work from the inside."

"Okay then, what's the plan?" She hated to ask the question. Usually, *she* was the one with the plan. But Thomas was the expert in this situation, so she was willing to go along with whatever he had in mind. Unless it was ludicrously suicidal, of course. She hated ludicrously suicidal plans, from personal experience.

"We wait, just a minute or so." He moved closer to the outer roller-door. "Come on, but stay out of the way of the door itself."

She did what he said. "You think the truck coming to pick up the crate is going to be here that quickly?"

"Sure I do. This is an automated system. The forklift wouldn't have put the crate out there unless the truck was on its way." He pressed up against the wall alongside the roller-door. "Which gives us a way out."

"Personal experience again?" She followed suit.

He nodded. "Personal experience again."

She was opening her mouth to ask another question when the roller door started rumbling upward. Daylight intruded, the ambient light within the loading bay becoming brighter by the instant. Directly outside was the rear end of a truck, virtually identical to dozens he'd already seen on the road. Backing directly toward the open roller-door.

By this time, the fact that it didn't have wheels was only a minor detail. Moving as silently as the police cars had, it glided over the smooth concrete toward the opening. She saw the opportunity and acted on it, darting toward the open roller door before the truck reached it. If the software driving the truck was as uncaring as the forklift's, she figured, she could be out and away before anyone was the wiser.

"No—!" shouted Thomas, but it was too late. As she stepped out through the roller-door opening, she felt the subtle *pop* of the delicate force field they used in the maglev terminal. This time, alarms *did* go off; lights flashed and sirens blared, and the roller-door began to close, thundering downward at about five times normal speed.

Thomas came rolling out, almost at her feet, half a second before the door crashed into place. She helped him up. "Run?"

"Run," he agreed. They sprinted away from the warehouse; or rather, Chelsea ran as fast as she could, and Thomas kept pace with her. She wanted to head back to the Market where she could lose any pursuers in the crowd, but Thomas led the way farther south, deeper into the maze of warehouses.

They ran past one row, then another, then he abruptly dodged down a side-alley between buildings and they flattened themselves to the wall as a hex thrummed past overhead. "They're gonna saturate the area," she warned him. "Then they'll probably check the programming of the doors to see if they've been hacked. That's what that thing does, isn't it?"

"That's what I'm guessing. But we aren't going to need it anymore." He reached out to the door beside him and rapped sharply in the tune of 'shave-and-a-haircut'. Before she could do more than wonder what his game was, the door clicked. He pushed it open and went in, with her following close on his heels.

As he pushed the door shut behind them, she turned to him. "You *knew* I didn't know about that alarm system. Why didn't you stop me?"

"I tried," he protested. "But if they can't have motion sensors, which the forklifts would set off, they have to have *some* way of detecting when people get in or out. The only way to get through the forcefield safely is to go in or out after it's been breached by something that's supposed to be there." He sighed. "And once again, I really didn't think you'd just run out there."

"And I'm not used to working with people who know more about a particular situation than I do ..." She trailed off with an awkward shrug, fully aware that she'd screwed up. "Sorry. I should've followed your lead." Frowning, she looked back at the door they'd come in by, then re-ran the last minute or so of action through her head. "Wait. *How* did you get that door to open for you just now?" Turning her phone light, she shone it on the back of the door, illuminating a weird-looking device built around the lock. "Okay, what's *that?*"

"That's the mechanism that recognizes the rhythm and opens the door." The voice came from back in the darkness. "Don't touch." As Chelsea turned in surprise, a teenage girl came stomping out of the shadows, hefting what looked like the sort of gun used in laser sports. She wore overalls and a visor that concealed the top half of her face, though it didn't hide the fact that she had Asian ancestry. "This her?" The last words were directed toward Thomas as the plastic gun rose to cover Chelsea. Any inclination to dismiss the 'weapon' as an innocuous prop was dispelled by the ominous red glow from the end of the barrel.

"Put the Zarkinator down, Gimmick," Thomas said soothingly. "She's a friend. She's here to help G-Man get us out of Utopia."

"For reals?" Lowering the weapon, the artificer (if that wasn't at least part of the girl's powerset, Chelsea was prepared to do the can-can in a clown costume in Times Square) took a few steps closer to her. "If you can pull that off, that'll be goddamn amazing."

"Well," Chelsea said with a shrug, "I've got the easy part. G-Man's going to be doing the heavy lifting. Gimmick, huh? Your little lockpick-thing is pretty effective." She held out her hand. "Smokeshadow. Pleased to meet you."

"Yeah, I know." Gimmick pushed her visor back to show her face and shook hands. "Blades told us." An electronic ping distracted her, and she slung the 'Zarkinator' over her shoulder then took something that looked like a repurposed calculator out of a pouch on her hip. "Holy shit, the hexes are going batshit around a storehouse just a couple of blocks away. What the hell happened out there?"

Thomas cleared his throat awkwardly. "Miscalculations were made. Nobody was hurt, and we got out of it in one piece." Theatrically, he dusted his hands off. "Well, let's go introduce you to the others. And see what we've got that'll pass for a photo booth."

"Holy shit, are you getting us *fake IDs?*" asked Gimmick delightedly. "Shit, yeah!" She paused. "Wait, who are you and G-Man going through? Because the Southsiders'll gouge us for an arm and a leg before—"

Thomas shook his head. "Not the Southsiders. In fact, they're currently losing a lot of business because their access to the interstate throughpass has been shut down due to that murder last night. No, this is someone else."

"Good." Gimmick didn't sound as though she liked the Southsiders at all. "I hope they choke. Come on through and meet the guys."

Chelsea followed her along a row of shelving, this time keeping a much more wary eye around for roving forklifts. The light level improved as they went along, until they turned the corner and entered an open area with floor-lamps and folding tables and chairs, arranged in an imitation of rooms in a house. Low partitions divided the 'lounge' area from the 'kitchen', while a row of sleeping bags lay off to the side on inflatable mattresses. She counted five people in the area; two doing the cooking, three watching TV. One of the people watching TV, a girl with short blonde hair tied back in a ponytail, was sitting in an electric wheelchair. The other four were boys, two alike enough to be twins.

"Home sweet home," Gimmick said cheerfully, then raised her voice. "Hey, guys! We got company!"

"Oh, hey," the girl in the wheelchair said as she somehow made it turn on the spot without touching the joystick. "You made it. I was beginning to wonder when you'd get here."

Chelsea blinked. "Wait … *Blades?*" She suddenly began to understand how the girl had gotten in and out of the Oaklands without attracting notice. If she recalled correctly, she'd spotted the wheelchair at least once and dismissed it from consideration. *Assumptions. They'll bite you in the butt.*

"That's me." The girl gestured at her legs. "This isn't an act, you understand. I'm pretty sure it's why I can do what I do. But enough about me." She gestured to the others. "Meet Sidestep, Razor-Edge, Photonic Avenger, and Sidestep."

"Yo." The tall white-blond teenager at the camp stove waved a hand. "Call me Ray."

"That's *the* Photonic Avenger," grumbled the red-haired boy who'd been watching TV. "You always get it wrong."

"Sure thing, PA," retorted the blonde girl with a smartass grin. "Whatever you say."

"You also said 'Sidestep' twice," Chelsea said carefully. It felt like a joke was being played on her, somehow. The number of names had matched the number of people … but there were only six sleeping-bags, not seven.

"Yup." One of the twin boys had been on the sofa watching TV, while the other assisted Ray with the cooking. They spoke in eerie unison, which she'd seen twins do before. Then the one on the sofa popped out of existence, which she *hadn't* seen twins do before. The other one grinned at her. "That's me. It's always me."

Her vision briefly seemed to double as he stepped *out* of himself in an eye-watering manner, then there were two of them again. The new duplicate headed over to a folding table in the 'dining' area and took an apple from a bowl of fruit. At the same time, the other one came toward her. He held out his hand to her; between one instant and the next, he was holding the apple. "Want one? They're pretty good."

She blinked, noting that the one next to the table, who was grinning at her, was now empty-handed. "That's a neat trick," she managed, and accepted it from him. It looked and felt like an apple, and even smelled like one. She took a cautious bite and confirmed that it also tasted like one.

"Thanks!" he said. "It's great to meet you. Are you really getting us out of here? Can we go to New York? I've always wanted to see New York. Is there really —"

"Okay, guys, enough." Thomas laughed. "Let her get a word in edgewise. Everyone, this is Smokeshadow."

At Chelsea's signal, the hyperweave pulled back from her face, and she gave them a finger-wave. "Hi. I'm here to help you get the hell out of Utopia City."

42
Leroy in Utopia

Utopia City Maglev Station
Monday, October 7, 2013
10:37 AM Central Daylight Time

Walking out of the maglev station, Leroy Hansen did his best to ignore the faint popping sensation of whatever it was he'd just stepped through. His head was already on a swivel as he took in his surroundings. This was the city that had taken his son's life, after all. He didn't intend to let down his guard for a single goddamn minute until he was on the way home with three things. One: Luke. Two: his brother's son, safe and sound. Three: the head of Jack Portman. He was willing to stretch the third one into the figurative sense, at least a little. But not too far. Portman had messed with his kin, so he was going *down*.

He looked around, shading his eyes against the late-morning sunlight. The most normal aspect of the situation was the fact that there were people moving all around him. He was used to crowds and because of this, he checked to make sure his jacket was securely zipped up, with his wallet in an inside pocket. Locations like this were prime hunting grounds for pickpockets, though nobody had even made an attempt yet. This might have been because they could see he wouldn't be an easy mark, or something else; he couldn't tell.

A few yards away, there was a row of parking meters. Some of these were occupied by the weirdest-looking cabs he'd ever seen. At least, he assumed they were cabs, given that they were shaped roughly like cars and were painted bright yellow — holy *crap!*

His internal monologue came to a screeching halt as one of the 'cabs' leaped skyward with a thrumming sound and a rush of wind. For something that was nowhere near as loud as a chopper or even a car revving its engine, its vertical acceleration was downright astounding. He was just getting over the surprise when another one descended into a vacant spot. The same bone-deep noise accompanied this one, making him wonder exactly how those things got around.

The side door of the latest arrival hinged upward as it opened, and Jericho stepped out. Leroy could tell the exact moment the boy spotted him, as a certain tension went out of his shoulders and his face took on an expression of relief. Leroy had been there a time or two himself, when shit was piling ever higher and someone who was better equipped to handle matters showed up to take over. *Thank God*, that expression said. *Now I can step back and let someone else deal with this.*

More cabs arrived and left as Leroy moved forward to greet his nephew, but he wasn't watching them anymore. His earlier irritation was gone, and he was now more concerned over Jericho's well-being than his tardiness; the boy's eyes were red-rimmed and there were lines on his face that hadn't been there before. Leroy had never seen him looking so beaten-down, and that was a fact. But he was alive and healthy, which was the crucial detail right then. Utopia City had done its worst, but it wasn't getting Beau's boy as well. Not if Leroy had anything to say about it.

"Jericho," he said roughly, opening his arms to embrace his nephew. Hugging wasn't a big thing for him, but the boy looked more than a little shell-shocked and Leroy figured he needed this. Hell, they *both* needed this.

He was big and hefty enough—it had been a long time since he'd worked as a longshoreman, but the years of heavy manual labor had left their mark—to weather the impact as Jericho came in to hug him. The boy's wiry arms wrapped around him tight enough to make his ribs creak, and he returned the gesture with his left arm. He used more care in putting his right arm around his nephew, because he didn't want the clasp-knife up his sleeve to come loose.

His time doing the hardest, dirtiest work on the docks—quite often the only employment he'd been able to keep, in the face of his grandfather's unreasonable wrath at his marriage to Ellie—had led to him forming connections with the local underworld. These had expanded in subsequent years, though they'd never quite proven lucrative enough to allow his family to subsist on the profits alone. Beau had helped them out where he could, but it was only since his brother inherited the family business that Leroy had been able to rely on a steady income from year to year.

Still, his less-than-legal activities had kept the family afloat during the lean times. They'd also led him over the years to this point, the irony of which did not escape him. A long-standing habit from the early days on the docks ensured that he never went unarmed when he felt threatened. And right now, in a city he did not know, one which had claimed the life of his only son, he felt very threatened indeed.

"Uncle Leroy," mumbled Jericho into his shoulder. "I'm sorry. I shouldn't have gone out." From the catch in his voice, Leroy got the notion he was holding back tears. For all that the boy was his nephew, Leroy had harbored a sneaking suspicion for years that he might be a bit of a sissy. Finding out that Jericho batted for the other team hadn't done anything to dispel the idea, but he did his best to not think any less of his brother's boy for all of that. Family was still family, after all, and Beau had stood by him when it counted.

But sissy or not, he surely couldn't blame his nephew for breaking down over Luke's loss. He'd already shed tears of his own, and he'd be dropping more before this was over.

"You couldn't have known," Leroy assured him. There were questions he wanted to ask about *why* Jericho had gone out for a walk in the middle of the night, in a city which had proven itself to be so fundamentally dangerous, but those could wait. "Like as not, if you'd been there, the sumbitch woulda killed you too." Leroy knew how well Luke could handle himself in a tussle; if his son couldn't take the guy, then his nephew *definitely* wouldn't have stood a chance.

For a moment, it felt like the boy was going to argue, then his shoulders slumped as he sighed. "Yeah." He let go of Leroy and looked his uncle in the eye. "What do we do now?"

"Now we go talk to the cops." This was a sentence Leroy didn't often employ. "Get Luke's stuff back, arrange for 'em to release his body to us, then figure out how to get it back to Savannah." He wasn't even sure if ordinary trains ran through Utopia City, but he'd work *something* out. "The problem is, I dunno where the precinct house is, or the morgue, or how to get to either one."

Jericho's expression firmed up. "I know how to do that bit, anyway." He nodded toward the row of 'parking meters', where those *goddamn flying cars* were still landing and taking off like it was a perfectly natural thing to do. "Let's take a cab. Pretty sure the driver will know where the precinct house is."

"A cab." Leroy looked again at, if he were to believe the evidence of his eyes, the flying taxicabs that seemed to be a fact of life in Utopia City. "How do those things stay up, anyway? Jets?"

Jericho's reply was remarkably concise for the subject at hand. "Ducted fans running on high-density batteries."

Leroy's eyebrows climbed toward his thinning hairline. Every word in that explanation was understandable to him but as a whole, it painted a picture that he had trouble fitting into his worldview. "Ducted fans. Batteries."

His nephew's shrug was the epitome of *don't shoot the messenger*. "Well, that's what I got told."

Sumbitch. This goddamn city. Leroy wanted to protest that this sort of thing was flat-out impossible, but it was hard to do when he was looking right at them. Finally, he huffed and said, "Okay. You say so, boy."

Improbable flying cars or no, Jericho was acting like he knew what to do in this situation, so Leroy let him take the lead. For the first time since he'd arrived, he took a good hard look at his nephew. The boy was carrying a black zipper bag and an eight-by-ten manila envelope, neither of which he'd explained, and Leroy wasn't going to ask about. His all-black clothing was also new; a long-sleeved pullover, jeans and soft leather zip-up boots. Leroy knew he hadn't seen Jericho in a little while, but the hipster look was different. Or maybe it was emo or goth; Leroy neither knew nor cared. *Not important. He's alive. That's what matters.*

The *other* thing that mattered was getting his hands around the throat of the sumbitch who'd killed his son, but that was going to have to wait.

43
Reclamation and Identification

Plate glass doors, thick and heavy, hissed open in front of Jericho and Leroy as they entered the precinct house. Contrary to Jericho's expectations, it wasn't in the Spire. If his guess was right, the overall administration went on in the central building while the day-to-day running happened closer to the street. Not that the precinct house was small or out-of-the-way; it took up nearly half a city block and went up for several stories, while the local morgue took up most of what was left. Flagpoles overhung the pavement, proudly flying the national and state flags, while a row of air-cab stands at the end of the block serviced both buildings.

Within, the precinct house was high-ceilinged and airy, with plenty of what looked like brushed aluminum and plate glass. Jericho was disinclined to trust appearances; if the same technology had gone into this building as had been used to construct the rest of Utopia City, then its construction would never have involved anything as frangible as mere aluminum or glass.

With this in mind, he further assumed that the wood paneling on the front desk was just that; paneling. On top of the desk, he was unsurprised to note, was a MagCard reader. What the desk lacked was any kind of barrier, bullet-proof glass or otherwise, between them and the sergeant behind it. Jericho's G-sense prodded him as they neared the desk, indicating a much denser core to the counter. He suspected a mechanism to generate a force field but there was no real way to tell, apart from by actually trying to go over the desk. Which, for several reasons, he was reluctant to do.

"Can I help you?" asked the sergeant. Her nametag read RICHARDSON. In her late forties or early fifties, she had once-vibrant red hair now showing silver highlights, though from the set of her shoulders, she still kept in shape. Jericho wouldn't have been surprised to find out that she still went out on the beat occasionally. He was reminded of Stirling; she exuded the same air of competence.

"Yeah," grunted Jericho's uncle. "Leroy Hansen, with an 'e'. I called ahead from the air-cab."

Sergeant Richardson tapped on something out of Jericho's sight, then raised her head. "Leroy and Jericho Hansen. Reclaiming personal effects, correct?"

"That's us," Jericho offered. "Black backpack and gray overnight bag."

"All right, I've got you here." She indicated the MagCard reader. "Swipe your cards, then I can let you through."

Leroy looked at the reader, then at Jericho, as if to ask, *is she serious?* Jericho reminded himself that Leroy was extremely new in town. His uncle had yet to experience the sheer *ubiquity* of MagCard use around Utopia City. Taking his own card out, Jericho tapped the reader and it beeped agreeably.

With a shake of his head, Leroy tapped his card on the reader as well. It beeped a second time, and Richardson nodded. "IDs check out," she said. "Put these on and come on through." She slid two plastic visitor passes on lanyards over the desk. They weren't as chunky as the ones from the Spire, but Jericho was still pretty sure they were laced through with electronics. He didn't see what she did next, being occupied with sliding the lanyard over his head, but a door set into the wall beside the desk clicked audibly.

Leroy led the way. Jericho followed on, wondering if there was going to be a problem with the clasp-knife up Leroy's sleeve. He'd spotted it early on; Leroy's tentative hug hadn't been enough to conceal the metal object in his sleeve from Jericho's G-sense. It didn't feel dense enough to be an iron bar, but it was just about right to be a large folding knife. Which, as it happened, he'd already known that Leroy carried from time to time.

No alarms blared. Leroy was not stopped. A uniformed officer—young, Hispanic, male, clean-cut—showed them to a back room, where Luke's backpack and Jericho's overnight bag sat on a table. Leroy went straight to the backpack and started going through the contents. More sedately, Jericho checked out the overnight bag. It contained nothing of any real intrinsic value, but his body wash and shampoo had been of a similar brand to Bobbi's and he had no desire to inflict even the tiniest indignity on her family at a time like this.

"Everything there?" The officer's tone made it clear that he considered it a redundant question.

Jericho nodded, somewhat impressed. "Yeah. I even got the right shampoo and deodorant back. How did your guys manage that? Has Bobbi's family already come through?"

"No, sir." The officer shook his head. "From what I hear, they just fingerprinted everything in the bathroom and matched the prints to the deceased." He tilted his head, indicating ... something, Jericho wasn't quite sure what.

"Huh." It was definitely a solution, Jericho had to admit; just not one he would've thought of. None of the toiletries had even a residue of fingerprint powder on them, which he just decided to put down to Artificer bullshit technology. Of course, it would've been nice if they'd repacked his bag as neatly as he'd left it. As it was, he was going to have to carry the satchel over his shoulder until he had a chance to repack the thing. For now, he unzipped the side pocket and put the envelope with the photo inside.

Leroy looked up from Luke's backpack, the grim set of his mouth at odds with the tears standing in his eyes. "I hear that right? You got my nephew's fingerprints without his permission? Y'all need to delete that shit, right now. That there's unlawful search an' seizure."

"Sir, the prints were evidence gained at a crime scene," the police officer said patiently. "They were used strictly to determine which property was his and which wasn't."

"Let it go," Jericho advised his uncle. "Prints like that go into the FBI database, and they don't ever delete them." It was something he'd learned from one of his infrequent conversations with the hopeful Detective Raul Villanova. In any case, he strongly suspected that entry into Force Majeure would involve collection of significantly more biometric data than simple fingerprints, so the point was probably moot.

"Hm." Leroy gave him a stern glance. "You gotta learn to protect your rights better, boy. Never know when someone's gonna sneak up behind you and f—uh, mess you up, 'cause you didn't keep an eye on things."

Jericho eyed his uncle, reasonably sure he knew what Leroy had been about to say and why he'd changed his wording. Despite the surroundings and the solemn purpose for which they'd come here, he had to quell a twitch of his lips at the dark humor of the situation. Leroy was given to crude jokes at the best of times, but he was censoring himself because he didn't want to offend Jericho. The irony was that Jericho wouldn't have been offended. Still, he appreciated the effort.

Leroy slung the backpack carefully on one shoulder. "Come on," he said to

Jericho. "We still gotta get to the morgue, which means walkin' three sides of a square for no good reason." He gave the officer a dirty look, as if the layout of the two buildings was a plot by the police just to aggravate him personally.

"You *could* go that way, sir, but there's also a through connection," the officer said politely. He gestured down the corridor. "Follow me. They've already been notified you're on the way."

"Won't we need to sign in there?" asked Jericho.

"No, sir." The officer led the way along the hallway, to a large set of double doors marked 'CITY MORGUE. AUTHORIZED PERSONNEL ONLY'. "We already transmitted your credentials across. Someone will meet you." Turning to Leroy and Jericho, he held out his hand. "Passes, please. You won't need to come back through."

Leroy took the lanyard from around his neck and handed it over to the officer. Jericho did the same. The officer swiped his MagCard across the reader; the doors beeped in response, then slid apart. Side by side, Leroy and Jericho stepped through.

The room they entered didn't look like any morgue Jericho had ever seen on TV. Of course, he'd never seen one in real life before, either. Detective Villanova's recently revealed interest in getting to know him notwithstanding, his relationship with the Savannah PD was not at the level that he'd ever been invited to the morgue to view a body. Even so, he strongly suspected that Utopia City's version was far and away more advanced than anywhere else in the United States. Or the world, for that matter. The closest comparison he could come to was Medical-1, in the Spire; only in this case, there were no IV trees or oxygen masks on standby, and the equipment looked more suited for taking bodies apart than putting them back together.

A nearby door slid open with a sibilant hiss, and a young woman stepped through. As high-tech as the surroundings were, she fitted right in. Her scrubs resembled the work gear worn by the weather control techs and the Spire head of surgery, and she wore safety glasses that seemed to flicker with internal lights. Jericho suspected a heads-up display. "Hi, sorry to keep you waiting. I'm Eliza Thompson. First, let me say how sorry I am for your loss. Mr. Leroy Hansen, was it?"

"That's me," Leroy replied. Anyone else observing him would've taken him to be comfortable with the situation, but they'd have been wrong. Jericho, with the advantage of years of association with his uncle, could see that the man didn't want to be there; not the morgue, not the building, not even the city. The reasons were not hard to understand. Most important was Luke's death, but Leroy would always be uncomfortable in any city not his own. Neither would he be in any way at ease with the conspicuous display of what Jericho presumed to be Artificer technology around them. It wasn't a reaction that Jericho shared, but he could understand it after a fashion. "Luke's my boy."

"Yes, I understand. Let me just fetch him, so that you and your ... nephew? ... can identify him." At Jericho's nod, she smiled briefly and turned her attention to the holographic tablet she was carrying. Her fingers tapped the surface, seeming to pull up menus that stood away from the screen, allowing her to flick one and then another with gloved fingertips.

About twenty seconds later, a nearby door slid aside to admit an unsettlingly familiar form. Consisting of a curved white carapace above—featuring a large red cross right on top—with black mechanical legs below, it was an automated stretcher like the ones he'd seen during the horrific events of the previous night. Rovers, he seemed to recall Stirling calling them. For all he knew, the thing that approached them was one of the two he'd observed entering the apartment on their grisly task. It was certainly identical in every way, moving with the same elegant, almost mincing gait he'd seen them using before.

"What in goddamn hell *is* that thing?" muttered Leroy as the Rover stopped before them. The gleaming white surface reflected distorted versions of their faces back at them.

Jericho didn't answer; he was too busy staring at the far wall, bracing himself for what they were going to see next.

"Medical transport robot," Ms. Thompson said off-handedly, as if it was perfectly normal for a machine the size of a big dog or a small horse to just walk up to them. Which, to her, it probably was. "They're very useful. Are you ready to view the body now?"

"No," gritted Leroy. "But I won't never be. Hit me."

She let out what sounded like a sympathetic sigh. "Yes, sir." When she tapped something on her tablet, one end of the carapace split open and slid away.

Leroy's face crumpled with grief as he looked down at Luke, unshed tears shining in his eyes. "Yeah." His voice was thick with emotion. "That's my boy. That's my son." He turned his head away.

The medical tech nodded. "Thank you, sir," she said, her finger ticking the box hovering over her holo-tablet. She turned toward Jericho. "Do you concur with the identification?"

Jericho grimaced. He didn't want to look at Luke's face and suffer yet another reminder of his cousin's death. But this was what he'd come here for. Reluctantly, he turned his gaze downward for the first time since the carapace had opened up. Instead of resting on a metal tray, his cousin was cradled by a molded-plastic support that held him rock-solid. They'd done a good job tending to the body; it almost looked as though Luke were asleep, lying there with his features at peace and his eyelids closed. The only jarring notes were the cold that radiated from within the enclosing carapace and the wisps of vapor drifting toward the floor. The wounds inflicted on him by his killer were still visible, but not as horrifically apparent. Still, he was never going to wake up. Never again would he open his eyes and utter one of his smartass comments. It was more painful, not less, to see him like this.

Shifting the satchel to his right shoulder, Jericho grasped the edge of the Rover with his left, curling his fingers underneath so tightly that the blunt metal edge of the chassis pressed painfully into his palm. Faint vibrations came to him through his fingertips. It was something to focus on as he nodded jerkily then looked away. "Yes. That's Luke." A tear rolled down his cheek, and he let go to brush it away. "Is that it? Can we go now?"

Ms. Thompson ticked a second box. "I'll just need you both to swipe your MagCards to sign off on the identification." She held out the tablet, a red rectangle blinking above the screen of the device.

Jericho swapped the overnight bag to his left hand, then fumbled his card from his pocket and swiped it through the rectangle; half of the holographic icon turned green. When Leroy followed Jericho's lead, the other half did the same and the tablet beeped softly.

"Thank you, gentlemen." The woman swiped her fingers through a few more icons, then looked up at them. "You raised a query about transporting the body when you came in. The Utopia City medical examiner's office can arrange transport back to your home town—Savannah, wasn't it?—on the maglev. Unless you've got another preferred means of transport?"

"Savannah, yeah." Leroy's tone was even more gruff than normal. "Rode on the maglev coming in. Cain't see folks being too pleased with us carryin' a coffin on board on the way back. Just saying." He inclined his head at the patiently waiting Rover. "Doubt they'd be much happier with one of them things."

"Oh, no," she said at once. "You wouldn't be required to carry the coffin on a regular car. UML has special cargo cars that we make use of in this sort of situation." She poised her hand over the tablet. "All we need is your preferred departure time, and you can ride back with it."

"How much is it gonna cost to ride back on a special maglev car?" asked Leroy suspiciously.

"Free of charge, sir," the medical tech assured him. "The UCPD has already notified us that they'll be footing the bill. This happened in their city on their watch, after all. They say it's the least they can do for you."

Leroy took a deep breath and leaned forward, a strong hint of his habitual aggression coming out in his manner. "No, the *least* they can goddamn well do is catch the sumbitch who murdered my boy. *That's* the least they can do for me, right now." Anger vibrated in his voice.

Ms. Thompson seemed utterly unfazed by his harsh words. "I'm sure the UCPD is doing its best, Mr. Hansen, but it's a large city for him to hide in. However, they *will* catch him, and they *will* bring him to justice."

Letting out his breath, Leroy rocked back on his heels and seemed to deflate a little. "Fine. You say they're payin' for the transport home?"

"Of course, sir."

"Right, then." Leroy looked over at Jericho, then back at the medical tech. "How about two this afternoon?"

She tilted her head slightly. "We can make it earlier if you want, sir."

"Nah." Leroy shook his head definitively, the firmness back in his tone. "Got business here in town. Two'll do."

"Certainly, sir." The medical tech made some notations on her holo-tablet. "Take the two PM maglev to Savannah. Once the train leaves the station, go to the back of the last car and tap the door button with your MagCard. That will give you access to the cargo car. It'll convey you directly through to Savannah."

"What happens when we get off at Savannah?" asked Leroy.

"There's a secondary station for cargo," she informed him. "The car will stop there for fifteen minutes, and the coffin will be offloaded onto the platform. You'll have to arrange your own transportation from there." Her attitude said, *Once it's off the maglev, it's out of our hair.*

"Hm," grunted Leroy. "That's fair." He nodded to Ms. Thompson. "Thanks, I guess."

"You're welcome, sir. I hope your business goes well." She did something with the tablet and the Rover's carapace slid closed once more. It left the room by the same way that it had entered. Ms. Thompson gestured to the far end of the room. "Out this way, gentlemen."

Leroy and Jericho followed her along a corridor, from which they exited into the foyer of the morgue building. To Jericho's unspoken relief, they didn't encounter any police officers for Leroy to vent his anger at. Just before they reached the exit (plate glass like in the precinct house, but tinted instead of clear) the doors opened to admit three people.

"It should never have happened," sniffled the youngest of the group, a woman a few years older than Jericho. Blonde and delicately built, she probably would've been pretty if her eyes hadn't been swollen and her nose reddened from crying, but Jericho was no kind of judge of that sort of thing. He turned his head away, uncomfortable with the feeling that he was intruding on her grief.

Jericho had almost caught up to where Leroy was waiting at the sliding doors, when he heard the name, slotting into one of those odd pauses in the background noise that happen occasionally. The desk clerk had just said, "Reynolds?"

He knew that name. It had been Bobbi's surname. The chances of someone with the same name as Bobbi, coming in at this time, clearly distraught, and *not* having some connection with her? It was possible, he guessed, but highly unlikely.

"Give me a second," he said to Leroy, and headed back toward the trio. On the way, he tried to recall what Bobbi had said about her sister. They were close, she'd said. He seemed to recall that the sister had been unable to accompany her because of work issues, or something. Jericho guessed that faced with a family bereavement, her sister's boss had caved.

What did Bobbi say her name was, again? He couldn't remember. It might've started with 'M', but that was it. He came up behind the group and cleared his throat. "Uh, excuse me?"

The crying blonde turned, as did an older woman to whom she bore a marked resemblance. The third member of the group, an older man with broad shoulders, was speaking to the desk clerk with his back to them. Jericho could hear the rumble of his voice, but not the sense of his words.

"I'm sorry, can I help you?" The younger woman was wary, but polite anyway. This close, he thought he could see Bobbi's features in hers, but that could still be wishful thinking.

"Uh, I'm Jericho Hansen," he said awkwardly, and put down his overnight bag to free up his right hand. "You're Bobbi's sister?"

She stared, eyes widening. "Hansen ... were you *there*? You can't have been there. They said he killed everyone."

"I'd gone for a walk." He hated the lie, but it was the best one he could manage. "Luke was my cousin. He, uh ... he did his best to protect her. I'm sorry I couldn't have been there, too. I'm sorry we couldn't have done more."

"I was allowed to see a portion of the police report." It was the older woman. "Your cousin confronted an armed man to try to save someone he barely knew." She put her hand on Jericho's shoulder. "He was a very brave young man. You must be proud."

Embarrassed, Jericho ducked his head. "He's always been my hero." Which was true, though he'd never quite seen it like that before. "I just wanted to offer my condolences, and say I'm sorry."

"Thank you." The younger woman offered a watery smile. "It means a lot." Her face twisted once more in grief. "But it never should've happened. It wasn't *possible*."

Silently, Jericho agreed. It *shouldn't* have been possible, if Bobbi's power had been able to read emotions through a door (which he was entirely unsure about). Unless, of course, Portman been in a drug-induced calm before she opened the door, and then gone into a rage thereafter. After the fact, conjecture was all Jericho had. Bobbi's sister had known about her powers, but he suspected her parents didn't, and the last thing he wanted to do was spring that information on them unexpectedly. Still, there was nothing more he could do about it. He offered mother and daughter a nod of farewell, then turned away to rejoin Leroy. The plate glass doors slid open before them, and they stepped outside.

"What was that about?" asked Leroy as they started back along the pavement. Ahead of them, air-cabs dropped in toward the landing zone and took off from it in a steady aerial ballet that was a beauty to watch.

"The lady who was staying with us, her name was Bobbi Reynolds," Jericho replied absently. "That was her family." Seeing her sister's face had almost been like seeing her again, and it was messing with his head. She'd been determined to push past the problems that her power threw in front of her and do some real good in the world. He felt mildly ashamed that his greatest goal boiled down to not much more than 'become a professional superhero'.

How can I finish what she started? No matter how he worried at the question, he couldn't see a way to pull it off. It didn't matter that *he* believed her about Adam Power's integrity; her word on the matter would be nothing but hearsay if he repeated it because he had no way of proving how good (or ethical) she'd been with her abilities.

I'm just gonna have to be the best damn hero I can be, and keep my eye out for anything else that can help him. And in the meantime …

Up until now, with everything else that was going on, he'd been willing to let the police handle the manhunt for Jack Portman. But for all their vaunted technology, the murderer was still in the wind. Bobbi's sister had been absolutely correct; this should never have happened. Not only that, but Portman should have long since been captured.

Kin had to stand by kin. With Leroy, he would accompany Luke's body back to Savannah for the funeral. But after that, after he'd returned to Utopia City and concluded his business with the Survivors, he *would* get back in touch with Stirling and do his best to help the cops out any way he could.

<h1 style="text-align:center">44</h1>

Test of Wills

Leroy didn't speak again until they neared the cab stand. From the look on his face, his thoughts were just as dark as Jericho's, if not more so. Jericho hoped he wasn't fixing to bring in his in-laws to settle the matter, Savannah style. Even aside from the authorities taking a dim view of this, it would likely devolve into a hot mess, putting innocents in danger. The last thing he wanted was to have to choose sides against his own blood.

"Is that everything you brought?" Leroy asked abruptly, indicating Jericho's overnight bag and the costume satchel.

"Yeah," Jericho said. "I was never gonna be staying long." *Three days*, he'd promised Stephen in the letter before all this happened. It had taken less than *one* day to turn his world entirely upside-down. "I'm currently in a short-stay apartment, but I don't need to go back for anything."

"Good." Leroy clasped Jericho's shoulder, then nodded toward the air taxi stand. "Go to the train station. Get a ticket for Savannah. I'll be along at two, with Luke."

"What? No!" Jericho's suspicions, already alerted by Leroy's vague allusion to 'business' in Utopia City, flared to life. "What are you gonna be doing?" He figured he already knew, but he needed Leroy to say it.

Leroy shook his head. "Ain't nothin' you need to be worryin' about. I'm just gonna be a little while, okay? No big deal."

"You're going to look for *him*, aren't you?" That was the obvious conclusion. For a newcomer to the city, especially one who didn't know the local rules of engagement, it was a bad idea. He couldn't work out a way to dissuade his uncle, so he took the next best option. "I'm coming with you."

"Like absolute *fuck* you are!" Leroy seemed on the verge of an explosion. "You're takin' your shit and gettin' the hell out of this shitty goddamn town before it kills you too!"

It didn't matter that Jericho was Enabled, or that G-Man was an established hero; he absolutely *hated* going against the will of anyone he held in deep regard. It had been hard enough arguing with Stephen over the phone outside the maglev station; here and now, it was even more difficult to make a stand and defy his uncle on this. But that didn't mean he wouldn't. "No. I can't let you do this alone." He took a deep breath to bolster his nerve. "Someone needs to watch your back."

"And what are you gonna do if shit goes down?" demanded Leroy. "We both know you can't fight your way out of a wet paper bag. Luke's always hadda bail your ass out of trouble, ever since grade school. It's too goddamn dangerous and you know it!"

Jericho felt tears rising to his eyes, but whether they were from grief for Luke or frustration at his uncle's obduracy, he couldn't tell. "Luke was my kin too!" he yelled. "He died because I wasn't there to help him! I've gotta do this!" He considered revealing that he was indeed able to take care of himself but decided not to. Doing that would open him up to far too many problematic questions.

"I am *not* goin' back to Beau an' Dahlia an' tellin' 'em I let their boy get killed too!" bellowed Leroy. He grabbed Jericho by the upper arms and shook him hard. "Don't you get it, boy? It's *too goddamn fucking dangerous!*"

"Which is why I can't let you go alone!" retorted Jericho. He dropped the overnight bag, then brought his arms up and over, breaking Leroy's grip; a use of his skills he hoped Leroy would overlook in the heat of the moment. "*I'm* not going back to Aunt Ellie and telling her you *and* Luke got killed 'cause I wasn't there to help!"

They paused then, both breathing heavily with the emotion of the moment. Jericho glared at Leroy, who glowered right back. Passers-by avoided them carefully, then hurried onward.

"Listen, boy," Leroy said. In contrast to the shouting of a moment before, his voice was low and dangerous. "If I hafta drag you back to your goddamn apartment by your goddamn ear and tie you up for your own goddamn safety, then so help me God, I will do just that. Do *not* goddamn push me on this."

Jericho stared defiantly at him. "The guy who killed Luke came through a goddamn locked door to do it. Do you honestly think I'd let you leave me tied up while you go out looking for him?"

It was a low blow. Jericho *knew* it was a low blow. But if that was what it would take to win this argument, that was what he was going to have to do. The knowledge didn't prevent him from feeling sucky about kneecapping his uncle.

He could tell the moment of Leroy's surrender by the way the older man clenched his eyes shut in a slow grimace. "Jesus *shit*," Leroy grated. "You're not gonna let this go, are you?"

"You're goddamn right I'm not," Jericho agreed. "I don't know this city much better than you do, but I do know a little bit of it. I also know more about how it operates than you do." And there was no *way* he was going to let his uncle go off and take on the Southsiders and Jack Portman without some sort of backup.

Leroy gave him a side-eye glance. "I think I might surprise you there, boy," he muttered. "But if you're gonna be comin' along, come on." He indicated the cab stand, with three of the eight landing spots currently occupied. "Those the only way to get to the southern side of the city?"

"Fastest way, yeah. Only way, no," Jericho answered. "There's buses and the monorail as well. But this is probably the best way to get to a certain spot in a hurry." Bending down, he retrieved the overnight bag; the satchel still hung on his shoulder.

"Yeah, I saw the sign for the monorail in the train station," Leroy said absently. "Okay, cabs are probably the best for—"

He was interrupted by the sound of a police siren, very loud and very close. It was the standard 'pay attention now' BWARP the cops did when they were right behind the car they were interested in. Startled, Jericho turned to see a cop car gliding up level with them. There were no empty parking spots at the curb, so it came to a halt and (he guessed) lowered its struts to park where it was. Both doors opened; two officers got out.

Given that the street had three lanes of traffic going each way and the cop car was now blocking one of those lanes, Jericho would've expected a certain amount of traffic congestion around the obstruction. But, as if by magic, the vehicles in the lane behind the police vehicle began to merge toward the outside lanes … and those in the outside lanes slowed and separated to let them do it. Jericho couldn't tell if this was civic awareness or something else at work, but he didn't have time to observe the situation and figure it out for himself, because the cops were already approaching. Beside him, he sensed that Leroy was ready to unleash his frustrations on the officers of the law. Barely moving his lips, he murmured, "Stay cool. They like to push buttons."

"Good morning, gentlemen," the first officer greeted them, a faint smile on his lips that Jericho guessed did not extend to his eyes. As with the first cop he'd met outside the Oaklands with Luke and Bobbi, both officers wore heavily modified sunglasses. The cop on the left was the one who had spoken; he was tall and wiry, while his partner was shorter and more heavily built. Both were immaculately turned-out, and this time Jericho could identify the wireless tasers they carried, opposite what looked like actual firearms. "Do you know why we stopped you?"

Leroy eyed them sourly. "Why don't you tell us?" His tone wasn't quite non-confrontational, but it was a lot less curt than it could've been.

"We stopped you," the shorter cop said, "because we had reports of two men having a physical altercation, shouting about people being killed, on the footpath outside the morgue *and* right around the corner from the precinct house. You can see why we felt some concern. Wouldn't you feel the same way, Mr. Hansen?"

Jericho saw Leroy twitch at the blatant name-drop, and he suspected his uncle was likely to bite just as quickly as Luke had. But before Leroy could answer and get himself in trouble, Jericho spoke up. "Of course I would. But as you can see, the altercation is over. We've reached an agreement, and we're not about to resume."

Both cops turned to look at him, taking the pressure off Leroy. "My partner was speaking to your uncle, not you." It was the taller cop who spoke.

"My bad," Jericho said smoothly. Leroy shot him a sharp glance, which he ignored. "It was an honest mistake. My name's Hansen too, and I thought you were talking to me." He waited until the cop opened his mouth again, then kept talking. "I didn't think you'd even be interested in him. He only got into town an hour ago. I'm the one who found the body last night, after all." He felt his throat constrict at the thought but forced himself not to show any outward signs of his ongoing grief. He was *not* about to let these asshats hassle his uncle just for setting foot in their pristine city.

"Body?" With that one word, he had their attention. "What body?" It was the taller one who'd spoken.

"My son." Leroy stepped back into the conversation then, having regained his metaphorical balance. "He was murdered last night. I came here to identify his body. Either of you ever had to do that? Go someplace you wouldn't normally set foot in for a million bucks, just so's you could verify that yeah, your only son was dead? Your firstborn child?" His voice was rough but steady and while his fists were clenched at his sides, he wasn't standing like he intended to throw a punch. Jericho figured he was digging his nails into his palms to keep himself focused.

"No, sir. I have not." The shorter one took over the conversation. "What are your intentions now you've done that?" His tone, while not in the least bit conciliatory, lacked the implicit challenge that it had held earlier. It seemed he recognized when he was on the back foot, so he wasn't pushing nearly as hard. This didn't mean he wasn't pushing *at all*, though.

"Dunno." Leroy made his tone speculative. "I've come all this way. May as well take in the sights. Might could even do some business, now I'm here."

"What sort of business would that be, sir?" The taller cop leaned in slightly. Nothing that could be taken as aggression, but definitely an encroachment on Leroy's personal space. A subtle provocation to put him on the defensive, or to spark some kind of offensive action that they could capitalize on.

Fortunately, Leroy was too savvy to fall for it. "Mine." There was no way he could see the cop's eyes, any more than Jericho could. But he locked gazes with the cop anyway. The phrase *wanna make something of it?* was quite apparent from his manner, though he didn't say it out loud.

"You aren't intending to do something stupid like try to track down the man who murdered your son, are you?" asked the shorter cop. "That might not be a good idea, especially if you impeded an ongoing investigation."

"Yeah," said the taller cop. "Because if you did that, we might just have to take you into protective custody. For your own good, you understand."

Leroy's eyes narrowed. "You wanna try that again, son?" Implicit in the tone was the understanding that Leroy had tangled with the forces of law and order more than once before and had usually come out on top. "Last I heard, false arrest was still a crime."

"Nobody needs to get arrested today," the shorter cop said in what wasn't quite a reversal of their position. "What my partner's saying is, this guy's already committed two murders so he's clearly a dangerous man. The last thing we want is more dead people because someone decided to go looking for him without backup."

"Yeah," the taller cop said. "It's tough enough doing our jobs without having to worry about untrained idiots from out of town trying to do them for us."

Jericho took this as evidence of two things. First, the taller cop was proving Thomas right (yet again) by indicating to Leroy that he wasn't welcome in town, by attitude if not with words. Second, both cops were being fed information in real time, either via earpiece or through heads-up displays in their glasses. Neither he nor his uncle had mentioned Bobbi, after all.

"Well, if y'all had done your *goddamn jobs* by now instead of harassin' innocent visitors to your goddamn city, I'd be already on th' way home," Leroy retorted. "You're so quick ta come down on folks like us, where in hell were you when my son an' his friend was gittin' their throats cut in their own goddamn apartment?" His hackles were well and truly up by now, so much so that his normally careful diction was beginning to slip.

Oh, for crying out loud. I'm trying to calm things down, *not heat them up again.* Jericho moved his overnight bag to his left hand and put his right on Leroy's upper arm. "Whoa, okay, let's dial this down a notch," he said hastily, speaking both to his uncle and the cops. "Let's not take this places it doesn't need to go."

"That's not such a bad idea," said the shorter cop. He turned toward his partner and flicked his head in a gesture which, if Jericho was reading the body language right, indicated a chewing-out in the near future. "Let's all step back and take a breath."

"Let's do that." Jericho focused on that officer. "Look, is it okay if we just go? It's been a trying day for the both of us, and we've still got to get back home."

"Go ahead," the shorter cop said.

"Thanks." Jericho nudged his uncle toward the air taxi stand. Leroy didn't budge. Jericho shoved a little harder. This time Leroy allowed himself to be moved, taking a reluctant step backward. Manufacturing a smile for the benefit of the cops, Jericho injected a friendly tone into his voice. "See you 'round."

"Count on it," said the taller cop just as they turned away, but just quietly enough that they could pretend not to have heard it. Leroy stiffened, but kept moving under the impetus of Jericho's hand.

After a few paces, Leroy muttered, "Assholes," under his breath.

"Well, yeah," agreed Jericho. "I did warn you. But giving them a reason to arrest you isn't exactly gonna help anyone."

"Mmm," grunted Leroy, then turned to face him. "Anyway, what the hell was that 'my bad' crap about?"

Jericho glanced back at the cops. They were getting into their car again, too far away to overhear the conversation. "Psychology," he clarified. "If they'd said sorry and backed off, you would've felt friendlier toward them, right? You wouldn't have gone as hard at them as you did?"

"Well, yeah, but cops never say sorry," Leroy said with a frown. "It just don't happen."

"Not the point. When *I* said it, they went on the back foot for a bit. Nobody wants to argue with someone who's agreeing with them." Jericho shrugged. It was perfectly clear to *him*.

He was just glad the shorter cop had been on the same wavelength about de-escalating matters. On the other hand, Leroy was neither under arrest nor talking about leaving him behind anymore, so that was a plus.

Leroy stared at him. Jericho wasn't quite sure what he saw before he finally gave a grudging nod. "Okay, fine. Let's take that damn cab."

They walked in silence for a moment or two, then Jericho turned to his uncle just before they reached the nearest cab. "You okay?"

"I'll be fine." Which by implication meant he wasn't, but Jericho had few options to deal with that right then. Leroy gestured impatiently. "Well, go on. Git in the damn cab. We got places ta go."

Jericho reached out and opened the cab door. All he could really do was wait until Leroy either calmed down enough to talk about it or decided to drop the matter altogether. Knowing his uncle, the latter was more likely to happen ... eventually.

He climbed into the cab, with Leroy following. They dropped their bags into the cargo net in the middle then settled down in their respective seats before Leroy spoke again. "Like to see how long those two sons of bitches'd last in Savannah with that kind of attitude."

Such an incidence would probably be entertaining to watch; for a specific definition of 'entertaining'. Jericho didn't want to dwell on it, given that he'd probably end up having to rescue the cops from the results of their own arrogance. A change of subject was in order. "Probably not long. So where *are* we going?"

"Still figurin' that out." Leroy turned to face the partition separating them from the cab driver. "Actually, screw it. Driver, how much is it to the South Side Mall?" He pulled his MagCard out. "I'm payin', boy. No arguments."

"But—" Too late, Jericho reached for his own card.

"I *said*, I'm payin'. You're comin' along with me on this, you're doin' it by my rules. Got it?"

"Got it." Leroy was set on his course, and Jericho didn't want to reopen the debate about him coming along, so he didn't argue.

The driver spoke up then, quoting a price only a little higher than Jericho had paid on the previous night. They'd be traveling a little farther, which explained the larger fare. With their five-point restraints secured and the fare paid, the cab took off and headed in what Jericho judged to be a southerly direction. Leaning back in his seat, he tried unsuccessfully to relax.

"Now, these folks we're goin' ta see are serious about their business." Leroy's words were innocuous, but the tone said something else altogether. "Everything you hear stays with us. Got it?"

"Got it," Jericho said again.

It went against the grain to meekly agree to meet with underworld figures—not counting his uncle—without making any plans to take them down. However, there were bigger things at stake here. Locating Jack Portman and bringing him to justice was paramount. After the run-in with the police, he was finding it harder and harder to justify stepping back to let them deal with the matter. Luke's restless memory demanded no less of him. The Southsiders were criminals, but if they could steer him to Portman, they would keep. For the time being, anyway.

45
One Small Step

It was Jericho's second time visiting the South Side Mall, but there was no sense of familiarity as the cab thrummed over the city. The buildings passing by didn't look the same as he'd seen the night before, probably due to the lack of holographic scenery. They didn't seem to run those during the day, almost certainly because direct sunlight was too bright for them to show up properly.

Leroy wasn't in the mood for talking, which suited Jericho, as he wanted to do some thinking. Matters weren't quite serious enough to require brooding time, but they might get that way soon. Whenever he turned around (or so it seemed), Utopia City threw him a new curve ball. On this specific instance, it was the recurrence of the subtle harassment that the other cop had tried on Luke. The shorter cop had toned things right down once he understood the reason Leroy was in town, but his partner had wanted to keep pushing. Jericho couldn't help but wonder how things might have turned out if Leroy had been facing the cops alone.

There were ways for cops to say things that, while not technically a violation of someone's rights, might easily spark a reaction in the unwary. If the reaction could be construed as threatening violence against a police officer, arrests would then take place. This was nothing new; certain members of the law-enforcement profession had been using variations on the same ploy to 'keep them uppity blacks in their place' for well over a century. And not just in the South, though it was more endemic there than elsewhere. Similar tactics were employed on the homeless just about everywhere, to 'encourage' them to move along. Utopia City, Jericho was learning, was not quite as perfect as the name suggested. While the harassment wasn't solely (or even mostly) targeted at ethnic minorities or the impoverished, it was still unjust and unfair to anyone with a prior criminal record coming into the city and looking to be taken on their own merits.

The trouble was, *here* such action was supported by local legislation, as far as he could tell. From what Thomas had told him during their rooftop conversation, all this folded back into the need for Utopia City law enforcement to keep track of *anyone* who might be coming into the city with an ulterior motive in mind. The fact that people with criminal records were undoubtedly being targeted even if they had no intention of committing crimes in the city was problematic, and he had no idea how to fix it.

He chased the idea around inside his own head for about half a minute, looking for something to work with, then realized the answer was (metaphorically) staring him in the face. Stirling had already Gordoned him with non-public information about Portman. If Jericho could make use of that data to bring the murderer to justice, Stirling would owe him one. The canny detective sergeant struck him as having a finger on the pulse of the city; if anyone knew whether the attitude of the police was a specific policy or just an accidental byproduct of the legislation, he would.

"We're nearly there, guys." The cabbie's voice cut in on his musings. **"Where do you want to be dropped off? Mezzanine or footpath level?"**

Instead of answering the question immediately, Leroy turned his head and looked out the rear window of the cab; an instinctive move, checking for a tail. In most places, that would've been an adequate precaution. Utopia City wasn't most places. Instead of looking back, Jericho checked upward as well as to the left and right, making good use of the improved field of view offered by the cab's windows. A few seconds later, his suspicions were confirmed as he spotted a familiar object coasting along on a parallel trajectory.

"What's that over there?" he asked, feigning both ignorance and innocence. "Are we going to hit it?"

Leroy looked where he was pointing, and his eyebrows rose. He opened his mouth to say something, but Jericho discreetly nudged his foot to keep him quiet.

"That's a hex, buddy. A semi-autonomous police drone. Don't worry. They've got to follow flight lanes just like the rest of us. Even if it wanders out of its lane, these cabs come with some pretty sophisticated collision-avoidance software."

"So, what do these hexes do?" Leroy managed to keep most of the suspicion out of his voice, but Jericho was pretty sure he'd picked up on the implications. "Surveillance and shit like that?"

"Well, mainly traffic control but the cops sometimes use them for surveillance, yeah. You're lucky that you're even getting this good a look at one. Most times I see 'em, they're goin' someplace *fast*. The operator for this one must be off getting coffee or something."

Jericho watched as Leroy took another look at the UFO-like object. "Right," his uncle muttered. "Gotcha."

It wasn't hard to follow Leroy's train of thought, given that Jericho had already arrived at the same conclusion. The police were aware of Leroy's presence in the city and the hex was traveling in the same direction at the same speed; ergo, they were under surveillance. Under virtually any other circumstance, he would've welcomed the chance to bust the Southsiders in the act of making a criminal deal, but again he ran headlong into the inescapable fact that he wanted something much more important. As much as it rankled him, at that moment he had a vested interest in making sure the meeting with the Southsiders went off without a hitch.

So, of course, did Leroy. "Driver? Drop us at the mezzanine level."

"Mezzanine level, you got it." The cab slowed as the South Side Mall loomed in the middle distance. The building looked both familiar and strange to his eyes; its overall shape and the layout of the park were the same, but the sign was fixed and unmoving rather than sliding over the frontage with rippling letters.

"Holy shit," muttered Leroy. "That's one big sumbitch of a mall."

"I know, right?" Jericho looked past the mall to the interstate, where cars flashed past in both directions under the transparent cover. Hopefully, the UCPD's shutdown of through-traffic access to the Southside offramp was holding. *Not getting out that way, Portman.*

The cab's approach and landing were identical to that of the previous night; this merely served to heighten his sense of cognitive dissonance. They climbed out of the cab and moved away, hunching their shoulders in unison against the windblast as it took off once more. Leroy looked around at the park, shading his eyes against the overhead sun. As he turned in a circle, he tilted his hand up discreetly to get a look at what Jericho presumed was either the same hex or another one the cops had brought in.

Leroy then pretended to yawn and covered his mouth with the hand that had been shading his eyes. Using the other, he gestured toward the entrance to the undercover area. "Okay, now we gotta get down to ground level. Footpath exit E-five is where they told me to go."

"Know how to find it?" Jericho hadn't considered the idea that the hexes might be able to focus their cameras closely enough to allow for lip-reading of surveillance subjects. Leroy had either thought of it ahead of time or was just that paranoid.

"Nope, but I'm guessin' between us we can figure it out."

It was odd to retrace the same pathways he'd strolled along with Thomas on the previous night. Once again, some things were different, but the underlying structure of the surrounding area was the same. Children climbed and swung on the playgrounds, high-pitched shrieks and shouts of enjoyment drifting across the immaculately groomed lawns. Solar umbrellas were spread wide over the picnic tables, at which couples and groups were sitting. The splashing and squealing from the Olympic-sized pool was even more pronounced than it had been before. Insects buzzed here and there in the garden beds alongside the path.

Leroy pulled out his phone as they headed for the entrance to the mall proper. Jericho nodded at it. "Remember what I said about those?"

"Go teach your mamaw to suck eggs, boy." Leroy snorted and tapped in a number, then held the phone to his ear. "Yeah, it's me. I'm at the mall. Need a meet-up. Place we agreed on. Two of us. Jeans, jacket and white shirt for me. The guy with me is wearin' all black. We're carryin' luggage. Five minutes. Got it? Good."

As Leroy put the phone away, Jericho looked up into the sky, shading his eyes as Leroy had done before him. After a few moments, he spotted what might've been the same hex again, loitering unobtrusively some distance away. The irony was that Utopia City locals probably didn't even register the presence of the drones anymore, whereas he and Leroy were being forced to actively query their motives. *It sucks, being on this side of the fence. Being a superhero is a lot more fun.*

"Okay, we need to go in there," he said, gesturing toward the overhang. "From there, I'm pretty sure I know how to get directions."

Leroy gave him a suspicious look. "You been here before?"

"Last night." Jericho left it at that. He didn't know how Leroy would react to being told about his growing attraction to Thomas, so the easiest course of action was to not mention the other Enabled at all.

"Right." Leroy brought his hand up to his face, ostensibly to scratch his nose. "They got stairs down?"

"Better than that." Despite everything that had happened, Jericho couldn't hold back his smirk. Leroy gave him a suspicious look but couldn't press him on it for obvious reasons. "You'll see."

When they reached the overhang, Jericho felt the gentle *pop* as the force field gave way before him. Beside him, Leroy hunched his shoulders a little and glanced around with a frown on his face but kept going. "This goddamn city," he muttered.

Jericho personally thought the Artificer technology was kind of cool. His uncle clearly thought otherwise but he didn't want to start an argument, so he kept his mouth closed while he looked around. The fountain was still just barely missing the ceiling with its seemingly random sprays of water, and the restaurants were doing more business than ever. He noted that the drop-shaft had a steady flow of people stepping into it or emerging from it, but that wasn't what he was after. There'd been a sign on how to handle flight within the drop-shaft, he recalled, and beside it … "There," he said with some satisfaction.

Stepping up to the metal podium with the 'YOU ARE HERE' engraving, Jericho placed his free hand flat on the handprint embossed on top. Immediately, a three-dimensional model of the South Side Mall sprang into being in front of him. It was fully four feet across and eighteen inches high from the first floor to the mezzanine level, which was all it seemed to portray.

The rest is private property. Not on the map. Right.

Most importantly, the holomap made it possible to examine the mall's internal structure. As a helpful aid, green and blue layers seemed to denote the top and bottom layer of each shopping level. Red, yellow and orange sections were also visible within the image. A flashing red dot was visible in the appropriate area of the mezzanine level, near a tiny representation of the fountain. It was even possible to see the narrow cylinder, less than an inch wide, that represented the drop-shaft drilling through the hologram from ground level up to where they stood. He noted what looked like other drop-shafts in the building, but they only went two or three floors at a time.

The embossed handprint had a little give to it, so he pushed it in. When he felt a faint click, he let go; the holographic image persisted. Red digits appeared in the air above the podium, counting down from sixty. He tried to reach into the image but as his fingertips came into contact with it, he felt it pressing on his skin. Pushing harder, he watched it slide away from him.

"Okay, that's new," he murmured. It seemed the 3D map was composed of 'hard light'; from what he'd seen before, this was probably a shaped force field overlaid by an interactive hologram. *No interface gloves needed. Nice.* When he pulled his hand away, the hologram eased back into place. Dropping his overnight bag on the floor, he hitched the satchel up on his shoulder. Then he took 'hold' of the representation of the South Side Mall, feeling the integral force field press back at the skin of his hands, and turned it bodily in mid-air until he was facing the northern side of the structure.

"Where are we going to again?" he asked Leroy.

Leroy reached up again to rub his nose. "Footpath exit E-five," he said, his lips barely moving.

"Right." On a hunch, Jericho let go of the image with one hand, then flicked away the mezzanine level with a dismissive gesture. That floor slid off the image and vanished. *Okay, that works.*

He worked his way down through the South Side Mall, examining each level in turn and touching minuscule shops at random. With each touch, a two-dimensional image emerged of the shop itself. While doing this, he was careful to keep an eye on the timer over the podium. With ten seconds to go, he reached across and pressed the handprint to reset it, then continued his virtual exploration of the mall.

Some sections were in red; when prodded, they popped up a notice stating, 'Non Public Area'. He discarded those as well as the orange and yellow sections, which turned out to be the short-stay apartments and cinema complex that Thomas had mentioned the previous night.

When he'd worked his way down to ground level, he tapped a selection of the shops and then the exits themselves, taking care not to stop when he found the egress marked Footpath E-5. If the police were monitoring his use of the holomap—and he had no reason to assume they weren't—he'd just laid a trail of two dozen false leads, any of which could be the meet-up point. *Hopefully, they don't have enough assets to cover them all at once.*

Having done all he could, he stepped back from the much-reduced holographic map. It popped out of existence as he picked up his overnight bag. "Time?" he asked Leroy.

"Mebbe two and a half minutes," his uncle replied.

That's gonna have to be close enough. "Okay, let's go." He started toward the drop-shaft.

"Wait, we're goin' down *there*?" Leroy caught up to him, his expression dubious in the extreme. "What if somethin' goes wrong? It's a long way down." He looked around. "Mebbe we should see if they got a real elevator around here someplace, or even stairs."

"We're nine hundred feet up," Jericho reminded him. "If all they got is stairs, we'd never make it to the meeting point in time." When he walked over to the edge of the open shaft, the G-field enveloped his body while he was still a couple of yards away from the edge. It wasn't doing anything specific with him, and he knew people without his powers wouldn't even notice its presence, but it was there. Glancing around, he made sure Leroy was still at his side. "Remember to keep your arms at your sides," he said, and stepped off the edge.

As he dropped down into the shaft, he found himself being nudged sideways until he was occupying the airspace closer to the center of the cylindrical void. The previous night, he'd been too overwhelmed by everything else—including, if he was being honest with himself, Thomas' presence—to take much notice of how the computer system handled traffic in the drop-shaft. But with his situational awareness on high alert, he could see people being moved to the left or right around the perimeter of the cylindrical space, while those toward the center (like him) traveled vertically.

The new understanding didn't prevent him from noticing something else, which was a very distinct potential problem. Specifically, Leroy wasn't with him. Looking up as he passed the eighth floor, he didn't see his uncle anywhere nearby. *Oh, crap. What's happened?*

Bringing his free hand up to chest level, he found himself moving to the very center of the drop-shaft as he came to a halt. People to his left dropped past him, while those on his right floated upward. Nobody paid the slightest bit of attention to him as he looked around for Leroy. The older man was nowhere to be seen.

With an aggravated sigh, he raised his hand and started moving upward, scrutinizing the downward flow of people in search of his uncle. However, it wasn't until he reached the top that he located Leroy, still standing on the edge.

"Come *on*," urged Jericho, fully aware of the irony inherent within the situation. Here he was, a superhero, in the position of encouraging his uncle to attend a meeting with members of a criminal organization. *Can my life get any more surreal?* With a gesture, he indicated where he wanted to go; obediently, the G-field directed him over to where Leroy stood and placed him on solid ground beside his uncle. "It's perfectly safe, and we're running out of time."

If they missed the meeting with the Southsiders, they'd lose their best chance of laying their hands on Portman before the cops did. And while the UCPD had (for the most part) impressed him with their technical capability, he had yet to see if they were as good at catching any given criminal as they were at the rest of their police procedure.

Leroy grimaced. "Don't look safe. Sure as hell don't feel safe." He waved his hand over the yawning gulf before them. "What's keepin' everyone up?"

"Directed gravity fields," Jericho answered before his brain caught up with his mouth.

"And how the hell do you know *that*?" Leroy eyed him suspiciously, as if under the impression that Jericho might be spinning a line of bullshit.

Jericho shrugged. "I've done research on the subject." Which, for a broad interpretation of the term 'research', was true. "It's what they use to stabilize the maglev, and make sure you don't feel the acceleration."

"I *wondered* about that," Leroy conceded. "You're certain-sure it's safe?" He didn't look convinced, not yet.

"Absolutely." The combined engineering skills of Transit and the Technologist were the closest thing Jericho had to a rock-solid guarantee for that. If the worst came to the worst, he could use his powers to save them both, even though he couldn't exactly tell Leroy that.

"Now I know why them sumbitches said ta land on th' mezzanine level," grumbled Leroy. "Assholes wanted ta rattle me afore the meeting."

"Probably." As far as Jericho was concerned, it was almost a certainty. Power games were just as prevalent among the criminal fraternity as anywhere else, if not more so. "You gonna let them win?"

Leroy's back straightened and his head snapped up. Injured pride echoed in his voice. "Screw that. How do I get down, again?"

"Close your eyes, arms by your sides, step off the edge." Jericho figured his uncle was much less likely to flail around and screw up his descent if he couldn't see what was going on around him, especially the shoppers walking upside down on the ceilings. "I'll tell you when to open them."

Leroy nodded stiffly. "Screw this for a motherfucking joke," he muttered under his breath. Then he took a deep breath and did as Jericho had told him; closing his eyes, he clenched his fists by his sides and took one pace forward. Jericho mimicked the action, though he kept his eyes open.

This time, with both of them in the G-field, it was easier to see how they were guided toward the middle of the drop-shaft. Side by side, they descended smoothly to ground level. All told, even with the deceleration at the end of the drop, it took a shade under twenty seconds. In the event, Leroy didn't need Jericho to tell him when the trip was over; when his heels contacted the ground, his eyes popped open and he let out his breath in one long gust. Jericho hadn't even been aware he was holding it.

They were standing in a circular plaza, lined with shop fronts. It was not unlike the open space around the drop-shaft at each level, except that there was no hole leading farther downward. Furthermore, the corridors that led off in all different directions had a normal shape, not hexagonal, and the black reflective ceiling was only fifteen feet up instead of twenty-five. Neither was anybody walking on it. *Must be because this is the ground level.* There were still holographic signs outside the shops, though.

The floor was composed of a glossy vinyl-like material (though Jericho would've given long odds that it something much more sophisticated) which exhibited seemingly random colored lines against a white background, not unlike what he'd seen in the Spire. Directly beneath their feet was the edge of a thirty-foot-wide circle, delineated by a foot-thick blue line, which followed the perimeter of the drop-shaft overhead. The G-field extended outside the line by a yard or so.

"Well, that was easier'n I thought," Leroy decided, though he glanced upward warily as he spoke, and took a definitive step away from the blue circle.

"So, when we leave, you want to go get a cab the same way?" Jericho couldn't resist the dig.

Leroy gave him a dirty look. "Hell with that. If they've got taxi stands at ground level, I'm takin' one of them."

"Fair enough." Jericho looked around at the corridors leading off the circle. The map he'd studied had shown them dividing and rejoining on every level, but they only let out into the open on the first and second floors. 'Footpath' was the ground level, while 'Public Transport' was the second floor; the impression Jericho got was that the monorail and bus services both had pickup points there. These only served 'N', 'E' and 'W' exits, of course; 'S' exit led through to the Southside Parking complex.

Jericho pointed at the corridor leading to the eastern series of exits. As built up as it was, the South Side Mall still had a sizable footprint. He saw another 'YOU ARE HERE' podium, but he didn't bother stopping to recheck his calculations. If his estimate was anywhere near correct, they had very little time to reach the rendezvous point.

Even without the hexagonal cross-section corridors, the first floor held a great many shops. Normally, he would've slowed down to browse, but under the current circumstances he had neither the time nor the inclination. With Leroy keeping an eye on the time while Jericho made sure they were going in the right direction, they hustled along the main thoroughfare in the direction of exit E-5.

The east entrance consisted of an atrium of sorts, about a hundred feet across, lined with shops and with a curved outer glass wall. Five sets of automatic doors were set into this wall, each with a number above it, from 1 to 5. Jericho and Leroy glanced at each other, then hustled toward the far-right door.

"How long we got?" asked Jericho as they neared it.

"Thirty seconds ago." Leroy didn't look happy.

Jericho could understand his uncle's disquiet; if Leroy hadn't balked at the drop-shaft, they probably would've been there on time. But, as the popular saying went, shit happened. He couldn't blame his uncle for reacting badly to an unexpected situation that played into one of the most basic fears of mankind.

The doors slid open and they walked through, unexpectedly encountering another near-insubstantial force field that popped as they breached it. It was a measure of Leroy's urgency that he made no comment about this. They moved on, heading out under a large overhang onto a broad stretch of sidewalk with an air-cab stand, beside which a pick-up lane had been set up for private cars. Nobody was standing there with a sign saying '*Hansen*' or even '*This way to the criminal conference*'. While Jericho would've expected the former rather than the latter, the lack of either one didn't overly surprise him. There were cars waiting at the curb, but nobody was pointing at them or even staring in their direction.

The buildup of tension in his body, preparing him for a potentially dangerous encounter, began to bleed off. Crushing disappointment replaced it; he'd been banking on this meeting giving him a lead on Portman, and now they had nothing. "Goddamn it," he muttered. Beside him, he heard Leroy say something quite a bit stronger.

"Hansen?" The voice came from behind them. Deep and masculine, it was pitched quietly, so as not to be heard more than a few yards away. "Don't turn around."

Jericho repressed his natural impulse to do just that, as Leroy answered, "Yeah, that's us."

"Who's this one?" Despite not looking, Jericho knew he was the one the voice was referring to. "He wasn't in the original agreement."

"My nephew." Leroy's voice was flat and uncompromising. "He's solid. If I can hear it, he can hear it."

Once again, Jericho repressed an impulse born of surprise; this time, he managed not to turn and stare at his uncle. He'd never thought Leroy had that much regard for him.

A moment later, he realized what was really going on. Saying anything that indicated a lack of trust in him may have sparked a negative reaction with the Southsiders. Leroy was determined not to let *anything* stand between him and Jack Portman, so he was playing it this way.

Which also, Jericho realized a second later, put the kibosh on any intention he might have had of using information from this meeting against the Southsiders later on. Once given, his word was absolute. It didn't matter that Leroy had given his word for him; if he didn't speak out against it, he was tacitly agreeing to keep whatever was said to himself.

Goddamn it. He'd had an idea of coming back later after dealing with Portman, and helping clean up the Southsiders. Now, whatever he learned here would be useless to him. He'd be starting with a totally blank slate.

"Fine." The person behind them gave him a nudge in the small of the back. Leroy had been treated in the same manner, from the way he also took a step forward. "The car at the curb. Get in. Do anything stupid and shit *will* go down."

Leroy grunted in what might have been agreement as he led the way to the hovering vehicle that had just pulled to a halt. It was painted a nondescript brown color. Jericho followed, wondering if any other superheroes ever got into situations like this.

The car windows seemed to be tinted or polarized in some way; even under the shade of the overhang, it was hard to see inside. Leroy opened the back door of the car and got in. Jericho climbed in afterward and settled his bags on his lap. The car moved off.

46
An Unintended Consequence

There were two people in the front of the car, but that was all Jericho could tell. Anything more was hidden by a barrier between the front and back seats, tinted so strongly he could only make out silhouettes. A black padded cloth bag, maybe six inches wide by a foot long, was hanging on a hock attached to the barrier.

By the time Jericho had his seatbelt fastened, the car was already moving in traffic. There was no engine noise; in fact, there was no vibration whatsoever. The smoothness of the ride was comparative to the maglev itself. Somewhat to his relief, the belts were of the standard over-the-shoulder type, which (he hoped) meant the vehicle wasn't also configured to fly. Not that he had any problems with flying, such as in air-cabs. The problems would emerge if they went airborne in an illegally modified vehicle. He suspected that being caught doing so would result in a somewhat more stringent penalty than merely voiding the vehicle's insurance policy.

"Phones, any other electronics." The voice, flat and metallic, came through a speaker. Jericho recognized the tell-tale distortion of a voice modulator. While the words were intelligible, there was no way to identify the person on the other end, or even tell if they were a man or a woman. **"Put 'em in the bag in front of you."**

Thankful that he'd taken the time to remove the phone from his utility belt while changing in the air-cab on the way to meet Leroy, Jericho took it from his pocket and slid it into the bag. As he did so, he noted that the receptacle had a silvery liner. *A Faraday cage, or something like it?* Leroy's phone went in as well, then they both sat back again. "Done," Leroy reported. "What now?"

There was a pause. **"No signals. You're clean. All right, Hansen. What did you want to talk about?"**

Jericho remained silent; this was not the time to pull the same stunt as he had with the cops. His uncle was running this show.

"Well, I *was* gonna talk to y'all about openin' some kinda trade agreement between us, but somethin' more important has come up." Despite being unable to properly see the people he was talking to, Leroy's voice was as firm as any CEO addressing a potential business partner. "We git this outta the way an' we can talk turkey. But not 'til then."

"The people I work for wouldn't be averse to cutting a deal with Savannah," allowed the voice from the front, after another brief pause. **"But what's the more important situation?"**

"Jack Portman," Leroy's voice was hard. "Last night, he killed my son. Word is, he's hangin' with your crew. Hand him over an' we can deal. I'll even do y'all a discount."

This time, the pause was much longer. Jericho got the impression that it was due less to hesitation than to a silent conversation with a third party.

"We're aware of Portman." The lack of inflection in the voice made it hard for Jericho to determine whether the person speaking was regretful or uncaring. **"He's got a prior arrangement with us. He's paid us quite a bit of money to keep him safe until we can ship him out on the interstate. Once he leaves the city, he's all yours.**

But while he's inside Utopia, he's under our protection. You understand how it goes."

"*Screw* any deal he's made with y'all," Leroy snarled, his fists clenching. "That sumbitch killed my close an' dear kin. I'll meet an' beat whatever he paid y'all, an' I'll look him in the eye while he dies screamin'.'"

"I'm sorry, but that's not going to happen." Once again, the synthesized voice made it hard to tell whether the regret was sincere. Jericho suspected it wasn't. **"When we make a deal, that deal is set in stone. It's the way the Southsiders work. How would you like it if you made a deal with us that someone else came along and undercut, just because they had more money?"**

Leroy showed his teeth. "If Portman wants to bitch about it, jes' point him my way. I'll listen to whatever he's gotta say, right after I've carved his guts out an' tied a goddamn bow-knot around his neck with 'em."

"Once again, apologies." It may have been Jericho's imagination, but the voice sounded more abrupt. **"I've already said we don't do business that way. Now, did you still want to discuss a potential trade arrangement?"**

"Screw you an' your 'potential trade arrangement'," Leroy snapped. "If we can't do a deal about Portman, then we're done here." Reaching into the bag, he retrieved the two phones. "Stop the goddamn car."

"If you say so." The car slowed and pulled over to the curb. **"If you change your mind, you've got our contact information."**

"You can shove your contact information up your ass," Leroy growled as Jericho climbed out of the car, lugging both bags with him. Once they were on the sidewalk, he slammed the door so hard Jericho feared for the window glass. But it held, and the car pulled away from the sidewalk and vanished off down the road.

"Well, crap." Jericho couldn't exactly blame Leroy for blowing the negotiation. There hadn't really been anything to negotiate. What they'd wanted, the Southsiders had been unwilling to give them at any price. He found that he could admire the Southsiders for sticking to their principles while at the same time being utterly pissed that they had those principles in the first place. If they were honest about not breaking their deals when offered a greater amount of money (and he could think of no reason for them to lie) then they would've no doubt been a lucrative trading partner for the Savannah underworld.

It was just that right then, those principles were all that was standing between Jericho and Leroy ... and Jack Portman.

"Sorry about that." Leroy seemed to be calming down. "Self-righteous little asswipes. No respect for a man's own kin. You'd think something like that'd be a deal-breaker. Here." He offered Jericho his phone back.

"Thanks. It's probably never happened to them, personally." Jericho accepted it and tucked it into his pocket. He was trying to be reasonable about the whole thing, as difficult as this might be. "I read somewhere that principles are easiest to stick to when they're not challenged."

"If somethin's easy to stick to, it ain't a principle, it's an opinion." Leroy fiddled with his phone. "Lemme git my phone turned back on an' see if I cain't find us one of them taxicab landing zones. Don't feel like walkin' all th' way back to th' maglev station."

"Yeah, no, that might be a bit of a ..." Jericho trailed off as a hex whipped overhead, moving in the same general direction as the car had gone. "... uh, that might be the least of our problems. I'm thinking we're gonna have company in a minute."

"Company?" Leroy looked up from the phone too late to spot the hex, but then his gaze fixed on something past Jericho's shoulder. "Crap damn it."

Jericho turned. Just as he'd expected, not one but two cop cars were gliding down the road toward them. "Wow, they got on our trail pretty damn fast." He suppressed the instinct to run; he'd done nothing wrong, and he was a superhero, goddamn it!

"They probably got access to security footage back in the Mall, an' as soon as we left they woulda been pingin' my phone, if they're as good as you say they are," Leroy decided. "I mean, I had it turned off, but that don't mean nothin', these days. Especially in this goddamn city." He watched the cars as they got closer. "You got anythin' illegal on ya? 'Cause we're about ta be stopped an' searched. How ta be an asshole cop, one-oh-one."

"Well, no." The only thing Jericho wanted to keep out of the public eye was his costume, but he had an idea about that. "You?" He couldn't believe he was actually asking his uncle that. It was the closest he'd ever come to acknowledging that Leroy wasn't an upright and honest citizen ... well, if he ignored the entire episode where they'd just made contact with a criminal organization, of course.

Leroy raised his eyebrows as if he couldn't believe it either. "Nope. But I'm gonna miss my knife. They're gonna confiscate it for sure." He grimaced. "I liked that knife."

"Maybe not." Jericho assumed the cops knew about the knife already; they'd just chosen not to do anything about it. Taking it away from Leroy just before he left the city sounded like the sort of screw-you an asshat cop would pull if they couldn't pin anything more damaging on him.

He paused to re-examine that last thought. Before he came to Utopia City, he never would've thought of the police in those terms. Even back in Savannah, the worst attitude he'd seen them exhibit was indifference, not outright hostility. It seemed his trip to Utopia City was involving a lot of firsts.

"Whaddaya mean?" Leroy turned to look at him.

Instead of answering him, Jericho stepped around so that Leroy was between him and the oncoming cop cars. "Give it here." He dropped his overnight bag on the ground and held out his hand.

For a moment, Leroy looked like he was going to argue, then he visibly changed his mind. Shaking the heavy folding knife from his sleeve, he handed it over. It wasn't hard to understand why he was reluctant to give it up; the knife was a beautiful piece of craftsmanship, featuring a six-inch blade (no doubt razor-sharp, knowing Leroy) with a Bowie-style clip point.

Jericho unzipped his costume satchel a little way, then slid the knife inside and closed it again. Leaving the overnight bag on the ground at his feet, he pulled the strap all the way over his head and tucked the satchel itself under his arm. He didn't care if the cops searched the overnight bag; they'd no doubt been through it with a fine-tooth comb in the station. The satchel was the one thing he wanted to maintain control over.

"You know they'll search that too," Leroy warned him out of the corner of his mouth as the two cop cars pulled up. There was only one parking space free nearby, so one stopped on the road while the other came to a halt directly next to the space and moved *sideways* into it before folding down its struts. Hovering cars apparently had their advantages.

However, Jericho wasn't thinking about that. His attention was on the four officers who were climbing out of the two cars. "We'll see," he said quietly.

While the officers didn't approach them quite as aggressively as the one cop had done with Luke, or even the two had done earlier with him and Leroy, there was a certain purposefulness in their advance. Two moved toward Jericho, and two toward Leroy. In each case, one took the lead while the second moved up in a flanking position, hand near his holstered taser but not yet touching it.

"Good morning, gentlemen," announced the lead officer approaching Leroy. "I am hereby informing you that you have been observed meeting with individuals suspected of criminal activity within Utopia City. As such, we have reasonable grounds to perform a stop-and-frisk. If we find any suspicious items on you, we may find it necessary to confiscate those items and take you into custody for questioning. Do you understand?"

"I understand but I don't give y'all permission to search us." Leroy's tone was uncompromising. "Neither does my nephew."

"That's all right, Mr. Hansen. That's you, isn't it? Leroy Hansen?" The cop never lost his friendly tone. "I could quote the appropriate statutes, but rest assured that at this point due to the aforementioned reasonable grounds, we do not require your permission. Of course, if you choose to be non-cooperative, we can take you back to the station and conduct this search under much less congenial conditions. It's your choice."

Leroy's jaw muscles hardened. "Sure, go ahead. But it's jes' me you're after. We all know that. You goddamn well leave the boy outta this."

It was a weak ploy; Jericho knew it. So, apparently, did the officer. "It doesn't work that way, Mr. Hansen, and you know it. Your nephew was there as well." He reached Leroy and steered him away from Jericho, leaving the other two free to move in.

"Okay, son," said the first one. "First off, I'm going to need your name, for the record." He gestured toward his sunglasses. "Just say it out loud."

Jericho frowned. "Don't think I'm being uncooperative," he said, "but how is it that you know Uncle Leroy's name but not mine? Did you single him out or something?"

"Your uncle's name is in our records as a person of interest," the officer said. "Yours is not. Name, please."

"Jericho Hansen." He looked at the two officers. "Was that it?"

"Not hardly." The lead officer looked down at his costume satchel. "What was it your uncle palmed to you when you saw us coming, Jericho?"

The police force was an organization that Jericho had a lot of admiration and respect for. Certainly, there were corrupt and abusive cops, but they were in the minority. As a taxi-driver acquaintance of Luke's liked to say, there were assholes in every uniform. He had no reason to believe that these officers were on the take or intended to plant evidence to incriminate him in something, so he was inclined to cooperate with them.

However, there was still Leroy's knife to worry about. According to his uncle, the officers would confiscate it under whatever pretext they could. From what he'd seen of how Utopia City officers treated people with criminal records, it seemed like something they'd do. No matter that the knife had been used in no illicit activity whatsoever during Leroy's time in Utopia City, the chances were strong that it would be seized on the grounds of suspicion. And given that both he and Leroy were leaving the city that afternoon, his uncle's chances of reclaiming the confiscated property would be minimal.

"I don't believe that's any of your business," he said evenly. He didn't want to lie to a cop, so he'd told the absolute truth; he didn't believe that it *was* their business.

"Wrong answer, son." The cop stepped forward, reaching for the costume satchel. "Hand it over. I need to search that to make sure it doesn't contain contraband."

Jericho shook his head. "Incorrect. You can search me. You can search my overnight bag. But you don't get to search this one." He held it a little closer to his chest, feeling the extra weight of the knife inside.

"Son, do you know the penalty in this city for obstructing a police officer in the execution of his duty?" The cop made an impatient motion. "It isn't pretty. Go on, hand it over."

Clearing his throat, Jericho lowered his voice. "Before you get yourself in trouble, I'd advise you to contact Diane Finlay. Sergeant Diane Finlay. Ask her if it's a wise idea to search a black nylon bag belonging to Jericho Hansen." He paused, eyeing both the cops facing him. In all honesty, he had no idea if this would work or if the Challenger Act even worked the way he hoped.

The two cops looked at each other, then at Jericho. "How ... do you know Sergeant Finlay?" asked the lead officer.

"We met briefly last night, in the execution of *her* duties." Which was absolutely true, while at the same time being vague enough that anyone not in the know would remain ignorant of the actual state of affairs. Or so Jericho hoped.

He couldn't see their eyes, but their very manner indicated that Sergeant Finlay was more than just a random name to them. "Isn't she ...?" began the backup cop.

"Yeah." The lead cop made a *go-on* gesture. "Make the call."

"Right." His partner took a step back and pressed his finger to his ear. Jericho assumed he was wearing the same sort of earpiece Detective Sergeant Stirling had made use of, the previous night. As he began mumbling to himself, Jericho looked over to check on Leroy. At that moment, one of the officers had his uncle in the search position and was in the process of professionally frisking him while the other stood back and watched.

"Listen, son." It was the officer who'd first approached him. "You've got nothing on your record worth talking about. Not even a speeding ticket. It's clear that you keep your nose clean. Why are you hanging around with the old man over there? You've got to know he's trouble. He's got a rap sheet a mile long."

First off, screw you. Jericho swallowed that response and looked the cop directly in his reflective shades. Raising his voice just far enough for Leroy to hear, he said, "He's kin. Where I come from, we don't walk away from kin." *Try and turn me against my own goddamn uncle, will you?*

"Yes, but—" The cop broke off as his partner gestured to him. Jericho watched as they went into a huddle, talking in lowered voices. It went back and forth a few times, then the lead cop came toward him. The guy's attitude had altered in a way that was indefinable and yet somehow familiar. Then it hit him; at the Market, Detective Gleeson had reacted in the same way after the phone call. After he'd found out that Force Majeure had an interest in Jericho as a hero.

"So, what'd she say?" Jericho asked, keeping his voice neutral. "Bad idea?"

"Yes, sir," said the cop. "Bad idea." He turned toward the other two and raised his voice. "Okay, pull it up. We're done here."

"What?" It was the lead cop of the other pair. "But we haven't—"

"We were acting on incomplete information," the officer insisted, making a cut-off gesture with his hand. "Delta Lima." He turned back to Jericho. "Sorry to have bothered you, sir. Have a nice day."

From 'son' to 'sir', huh? Yeah, sounds like she laid it out for him. "You too, I guess." Jericho kept his voice neutral.

The phonetic code for 'designated liaison' had gotten the attention of the other two cops. They stepped away from Leroy, even leaving Luke's backpack unopened beside him. "You sure about that?" asked the guy who'd been searching Leroy.

"Absolutely." The cop who'd made the call got back into his car. "This is a wash. Call it in. No result."

Leroy stood there while the other three got into their respective cars as well. He waited until they'd headed off down the road and disappeared around the corner before he turned to Jericho. "Okay, what the hell?"

Jericho pulled the satchel strap over his head so he could get to the zipper. Opening the satchel a few inches, he tilted it so the folding knife slid out through the gap into his hand. He passed it over to his uncle, then zipped up the satchel again. "I convinced them it wasn't worth their time to search me."

"No." Leroy shook his head as he stared at the knife, then slid it up his sleeve again. "That shit ain't how it works. There ain't no goddamn way on God's green Earth you jes' talked two cops into not searchin' you. An' what's Delta Lima mean, anyways?"

"It's clearly a police code of some sort," Jericho hedged. He didn't want to lie to his uncle, but if Leroy kept pressing, something was going to give. "You've got your knife. It's all good, right?"

"No, it goddamn well ain't all good." Leroy fixed his attention on the satchel. "It's somethin' to do with that thing." He held out his hand and snapped his fingers twice. "Give."

"Uh, no." Jericho tightened his arms around it. "This is private." He didn't want to fight his uncle on this, but it didn't look like Leroy was going to let matters go.

"Private don't mean shit when you've pulled off somethin' I ain't never seen before. I'm your uncle, boy. Now give." Reaching out with one hairy paw, Leroy took hold of the satchel.

Even then, Jericho could have broken his uncle's grip (or, with the application of a little more force, the older man's arm). But he was between a rock and a hard place. His carefully fostered illusion of being a wimp would be utterly shattered if he fought back and prevailed against his larger and vastly more experienced uncle. That he could kick Leroy's ass, he had no doubt. He was really that good. But in winning the battle, he would lose the war. His uncle would have very strong grounds for suspecting his true nature after that, just as he would once he saw the costume. The only real difference would be whether or not the older man got hurt in the process.

All of that passed through his mind in an instant. "Fine," he sighed, and let go of the satchel. "Don't say I didn't warn you."

"Warn me about what, boy?" Leroy took hold of the zipper and pulled it open. The first thing he encountered was the sleeve of the jacket, which he pulled out. The shoulder of the garment followed, then part of the back. When Leroy saw the insignia on the jacket, he stopped. He stared at it, then at Jericho. "What the living hell are ya doin' carryin' *this* thing around with ya?"

Jericho knew quite well that his secret identity was now irretrievably compromised. There were very few examples in popular culture of events ending well after a superhero's alter ego was uncovered by any kind of criminal. He could think of some unpleasant incidents involving real-world heroes as well. In the comics, this sort of situation was usually resolved by either a fortuitous case of kiss-related amnesia or a totally unconnected accidental death. He was pretty sure his kisses didn't inflict memory loss (and Leroy would probably deck him if he tried) and there was no way he was going to hurt his uncle over this.

So, keeping one eye on Leroy's reaction and the other to watch for oncoming pedestrians, he offered a half-shrug. "I'll give you one guess."

Leroy stuffed the jacket back into the satchel, then rummaged around and pulled out Jericho's mask. "How long have you been …?"

"Going around as G-Man?" Jericho took the mask and satchel away from him, shoved the mask back where it belonged, and zipped the whole thing up again. "Well, it's not like I took over from anyone. It's been me, from day one." He raised one eyebrow appraisingly at Leroy. "What're you gonna do, now you know it's me?"

Leroy seemed to be in a state of shock, his eyes flicking from the satchel to Jericho and back again. "Sum*bitch*, boy! You got the slightest idea how shit-scared my guys are of you? They spend half the time watchin' the rooftops when they should be watchin' the road."

Jericho blinked. This had not been what he expected to hear. "What?" He paused, trying to process that. "Isn't Pickup …?"

"Screw Pickup." Leroy made a rude noise. "We can hear that shit-heap of his comin' a block away. Especially with them wide-mouth exhaust pipes he installed last month. Looks good for the news but gives us plenty of time to scatter. Meanwhile, *you* …" He prodded Jericho in the chest with a hard forefinger. "… *you* don't make no noise comin', an' the first anyone knows of you is when you're glidin' overhead. It makes you look creepy as *hell*. That purse snatcher you chased down an' beat up last month? Asshole never stopped talkin' about you the whole time he was in police lockup."

Slowly, Jericho face-palmed. "He snatched an old lady's bag, and broke her wrist when she fought back. So, I had to explain why he shouldn't do that."

He'd been fairly pissed about the whole situation, which had led to him going a little further than he normally would've. It turned out that dangling someone upside down off a rooftop by one ankle was easy with the right Dynamic ability, and it left quite an impression. By the time he'd turned the purse snatcher over to the authorities, the guy had been twitchingly eager to confess every crime he'd committed, just so long as the cops put him in a nice safe cell away from Jericho.

"Don't matter. By the time he got moved on, everyone had heard an earful and *nobody* wanted to mess with you." Leroy shook his head, then another revelation crossed his face. "Sum*bitch*. You come here to join Force Majeure, didn't you?"

"That was the general idea, yeah." Jericho's head was still spinning from what Leroy had told him. *I was actually making a difference?* "They wouldn't let me postpone the interview, so I went in. I'd just finished when you called."

"So, how'd it go?" Leroy tilted his head. "I figure you aced it. You always was the smart one."

Jericho grimaced as he slung his overnight bag over his shoulder and the satchel over the other. "Not so great. They pushed my buttons pretty hard, and after what happened to Luke, I didn't feel like taking any shit. I tolerated it so far, then I snapped back and kind of cussed them out a bit before storming out." Even now, he wanted to cringe every time he recalled what he'd yelled at them.

"Holy shit." Leroy's eyes opened wide. "You cussed out *Force Majeure?* Shit, now I definitely wanna hear details."

As they headed off down the street in search of an air taxi stand, Jericho considered his next words. There were some details he was never going to tell his uncle, but he needed to say *something* after that bombshell. And if he was being honest with himself, he wanted to tell at least some of it.

"Well, you know how I don't use the 'b' word about women?"

Leroy nodded "Uh huh."

"Let's just say if I was ever gonna start, Independence would get first dibs."

"Huh?" Leroy looked confused for a moment, then his brow cleared. "Oh. *Oh*."

Jericho set his jaw. "Yeah. '*Oh*'."

As he walked on, his thoughts were stormy.

It won't be today, and it won't be tomorrow. But I will be back, and I will find you, and I will get to you, even if I have to go through the Southsiders to do it.

Force Majeure or no goddamn Force Majeure.

- End of Part Three -

PART FOUR

JUSTICE FOR THE FALLEN

Don't go messin' with the quiet ones. They'll surprise ya.
- Leroy Hansen

Invisibility isn't a power. It's an art form.
- Smokeshadow

He's just one man!
- minion facing G-Man

… what just happened?
- Jericho Hansen

47
To Remember the Departed

Jericho sat across the aisle from Leroy, on the lower deck of the maglev. They were heading east, toward Savannah. As the train cleared the last of the tall buildings, Leroy heaved himself to his feet and picked up Luke's backpack from the seat beside him. Jericho got up as well and fetched his overnight bag down from the storage bin.

After locating a restroom in the maglev terminal, he'd taken the time to change into ordinary civilian clothing—blue jeans and sneakers, nondescript T-shirt and jacket—and repack both his costume satchel and overnight bag properly. The former had gone into the latter, which increased his load but reduced his anxiety level now that he only had one bag to manage.

With Leroy leading and Jericho following, they went back along the train, through the doors to the next maglev car. This proved to be another passenger car, so they kept going all the way to the rear of the car. This time, the doors refused to open when Leroy pressed the button.

"Nothing back there, buddy," said a guy sitting in the last row. "I thought I heard something connecting to the train so I checked, but the doors don't open."

"You say so," Leroy said, and tapped the button with his MagCard. The doors hissed aside, and he stepped through. Jericho followed along, hearing the man's startled exclamation cut off by the closing of the doors.

"That was kind of mean," Jericho noted as they traversed the short passage between cars. The next set of doors opened before them and they stepped through into a quiet, echoing space. Initially, it was pitch black, but lights started coming up along the length of the car. Whatever else the cargo car had, Jericho realized, there was a distinct lack of windows.

Fully the length of a standard passenger car, there were shelves stretching from one end of the car to the other, and from the floor almost all the way to the ceiling. These started at the left-hand side of the car and extended halfway across, leaving the right-hand half clear. They contained box after anonymous box, all clamped down hard. The right-hand side of the car featured a triple-width door. A few seats, of the same approximate quality as the ones in the car they'd just left, were lined up at the far end of the side door with their backs to the wall. Next to them was some sort of terminal.

"Was it?" asked Leroy absently, already scanning the shelves. Most of them were over his head, so he stepped back to the right-side wall and craned his neck to look. Then he gave Jericho an annoyed glance. "You're good at climbing, right? You gotta be, seein' as how you spend all your time on rooftops as G-Man, scarin' the crap outta my guys. Get on up there and see if you can find Luke's coffin."

"Okay, yeah, I can get up there." Jericho headed over to the seats and dropped his overnight bag on one. "But one: I'm not your trained monkey. And two: wouldn't it be easier if we used this terminal to locate it first?"

Leroy glared at him and the terminal both, but he stopped trying to look at what was on the upper shelves. "Fine. Do it your way."

"Thought you'd never ask." Jericho examined the terminal. There was no keyboard and the screen was dark, but a MagCard reader was set into the top right-hand corner. He pulled out his card and tapped the reader. The terminal lit up, and text scrolled up the screen.

WELCOME [JERICHO HANSEN].
YOUR CARGO IS IN [BAY 5 SHELF 6/3].
AUTO-UNLOAD OF CARGO HAS BEEN [AUTHORIZED].
WHEN TRAIN REACHES [SAVANNAH, GA] CARGO WILL UNLOAD.
ETA [SAVANNAH, GA] IS 2 HOURS 24 MINUTES.
IS THIS SATISFACTORY? [Y] [N]

He read through the text twice, then tapped the [Y] with his finger. The terminal beeped to acknowledge this, then the text scrolled up and off the screen. The words 'THANK YOU' faded into view for about ten seconds, then the screen shut itself down again.

"Well?" asked Leroy impatiently. "Did you find it?"

Jericho ignored him for a moment as he turned and scanned the shelving. A moment later, he saw what he was looking for; the notations 'B1', 'B2', 'B3' and so forth along the sections of shelving. "Yeah," he said as he paced along to what had to be Bay 5. Peering through the stacks, he could see that it wasn't just one set of shelves; there were items stored *behind* other items.

On a hunch, he went to the end of the shelves and checked for more notations. Not at all to his surprise, he found 'S1', 'S2' and 'S3', going from right to left. The shelving sections went up to six levels, the cargo on the top ones only a few feet away from the travelling gantry that hung from the roof.

"Okay, then ..." He went back along the shelving bays until he reached the fifth one. "Six up, three across." In other words, right at the back. Reducing his weight to its minimum, he crouched slightly and jumped fifteen feet straight up, then caught the edge of the top shelf and swung himself up onto stable footing. Staying in a crouch, because the roof wasn't all that far over his head, he looked back to where he thought his quarry should be. Right enough, there was indeed a crate there, easily big enough to contain a coffin. Like everything else on the shelves, it was securely clamped down, so it wasn't going anywhere until they got to Savannah. Climbing over the top of the shelves, he laid his hand on the crate.

Hey, Luke.

At the back of his mind, he imagined Luke's response. *Hey, cuz. See ya 'round.*

See you 'round.

With a lump swelling in his throat, he moved back to the edge of the shelves, then let himself drop to the floor. His power took over and he drifted downward, landing with all the impact of jumping off a stepstool. "Found him," he announced, then noticed the way Leroy was staring at him. "What?"

"That was the most bullshit thing I ever seen." Leroy shook his head. "No *wonder* you been scarin' the beejeebers outta the guys."

Witty banter with his uncle was about the last thing Jericho wanted right then, but he could not let that stand. "Oh, come *on*." He rolled his eyes. "You just went to

Utopia City. You rode in *flying cars*. In the South Side Mall, you landed safely after falling nine hundred feet with your eyes closed. And you call *my* power bullshit?"

"Yeah, but Utopia City's *supposed* to be like that," Leroy argued. "*You're* s'posed to be … *you*. Not jumpin' three times your height straight up. Not puttin' on a black costume and makin' my guys piss their goddamn pants."

Jericho let his knees sag, dropping him into one of the seats. He looked up at his uncle. "So, you weren't pulling my leg? I really scare your guys? Nobody ever said that before. Even Luke thought I was a joke as a superhero."

"Luke?" Leroy shook his head. "No, that ain't right. Luke was even more scared of you than any of the other guys. Especially when you beat the crap out of him, that one time." He paused, staring at Jericho accusingly. "I know you needed to maintain your secret identity an' all, but did you hafta do that to your own cousin?"

"I did what again now?" Uncomprehending, Jericho stared at Leroy. "I never laid a finger on him. Like, ever." He tried to figure out the sense behind what Leroy was saying and failed. "It's not like he thought I was someone else. I told him about my powers long before I ever went out as G-Man."

"You goddamn what?" Leroy looked more confused than ever. "Shit, he's been spreading stories about how scary you are for more'n a *year*, now. That's why I was so surprised it was you. To hear him talk you up, G-Man was some grim avenger of the night that they didn't wanna cross if they liked havin' their kneecaps in one piece. An' it was *definitely* a bad idea to try shootin' at you. Him bein' my boy, they listened." Tilting his head, he eyed Jericho carefully. "You're sayin' you never tuned him up?"

"Not even once," Jericho assured him. "In fact, he thought I was still a wimp 'til I told him how I knew Krav Maga on the train coming in."

Leroy shook his head, then chuckled wryly as he dropped into the seat beside Jericho's. The joke didn't seem *that* funny, but it managed to raise a brief smile on Jericho's face. *All this time, I've been keeping away from Leroy's area of operations so I wouldn't have to mess with his guys too much. Meanwhile, Luke's been putting the fear of God into them, so if they did see me, they'd run instead of fighting.* He would never have considered asking his cousin to do something like that on purpose, but it seemed so very … *Luke.*

"No," he said, shaking his head slowly. "That was all Luke building me up. Behind my back, I might add. Though I can just see him sitting in on that sort of thing and listening to the guys repeat the stories, then embellishing them for shits and giggles."

"He totally woulda done that," agreed Leroy. "Seriously, the amount of shit he put the guys through on your account, if he was here right now, I'd kick his ass."

Jericho snorted. "No, you wouldn't. I'm a superhero. I'd have to stop you." He paused, tilting his head thoughtfully. "To be honest, I'd probably get popcorn instead and award points for style."

"Hah!" Turning in his seat, Leroy slapped Jericho on the shoulder. "I still have trouble believin' it was you all this time. Didn't even fuckin' *suspect*."

"What, really?" Jericho looked askance at his uncle. "Even though I was dating the same guy who did the online writeup on G-Man?"

Leroy looked blank. "Who did what again now?"

Well, that answered *that* question. "Never mind." He shook his head and moved on to the topic he'd known he would have to deal with at some point. "So, now you know I'm G-Man, what happens now?"

It took a few seconds for Leroy to get his point. "What, you think I'm gonna try blackmailin' you or some such? *Hell*, no. Like you said to that cop back on the street, we're kin. Kin don't pull that shit on each other. Anyway, Luke'd haunt me forever if I even thought about it."

"Granted." Jericho raised his eyebrows. "But there's still a lot of options between 'do nothing' and 'threaten to out me'. Just knowing this is gonna affect the way you do things. I'd feel a lot better knowing where you're going to be on that scale."

Leroy shrugged. "Who says we gotta change things up? I mean, if you'd been hittin' my guys every night, it might be different. But if we keep right on th' way we been doin', the guys stay properly worried about superheroes, you do your thing, we do ours, no harm, no foul."

This seemed very weird to Jericho. Heroes and criminals usually didn't sit down and have polite discussions about areas of demarcation … did they? "I guess, sure. Just so you know though, if your guys start going into hard drugs or hurting people, I'm gonna have to take notice."

"Yeah, no. Hard drugs are a good way to get noticed by the big syndicates. I like bein' my own man, an' not goin' swimmin' with concrete shoes." Leroy leaned back in his seat. "So, you'll be stickin' around Savannah, then?"

"Well, I'm pretty sure I just shit all over my chances of joining Force Majeure, so I guess I will be, yeah." Jericho paused, remembering the Survivors. "But I'm gonna need to go back to Utopia City after the funeral anyway, just for a bit. There's some folks there that need help." He explained the situation with Thomas and the others, trying not to go into too much detail, especially about Thomas.

"An' from the fact you're tellin' me about this, you need me to help you git 'em outta there." It wasn't a question.

It was time to bite the bullet. "Yeah. I was originally gonna give money to Luke to pay their way out with the Southsiders as a part the deal you guys were making with them, but …" He didn't have to finish.

Leroy grimaced. "Yeah. That. Plus, right now, I wouldn't piss on them Southsider sumbitches if they was on fire. So, you got a plan B?"

"I do." Jericho took a deep breath and outlined the plan he'd come up with. He didn't *like* breaking the law, but there was such a thing as the lesser of two evils. His feelings for Thomas *probably* didn't factor into the decisions he'd made but even if they did, he wasn't about to step back now. *I'm in this for the long haul. So long as Leroy can come through with his side of things, of course.* "So, can you help?"

Leroy snorted. "'Course I can help. You're my goddamn nephew. 'Sides, if you can forget you're a superhero long enough to sort out this shit-show, so can I."

"Thanks. I'll owe you one for this. They all will."

"An' of course, if that sumbitch Portman's still out an' about when you git back, you c'd mebbe track him down an' pass on my regards." Leroy cracked his knuckles.

"That's the general plan, yes." Jericho raised his eyebrows. "I'm honestly surprised you're leaving me to it. I've never known you to let something like this go before."

"I ain't lettin' it go." Leroy looked at Jericho's skeptical expression and his face hardened. "I *ain't*. But like you said, I cain't do nothin' in a town where th' cops are breathin' down my goddamn neck all the goddamn time. So I figure either you'll git him, the locals'll finally pull their fingers out and git him themselves, or you'll spook him enough that he skedaddles outta town. They won't be able ta keep th' offramp access shut down forever."

The latter option didn't seem likely to Jericho. "The cops might be pushy as crap, but surely they'll have laid hands on him by then."

Leroy shrugged. "Well, I'm gonna be puttin' feelers out anyways. He gits outta town, I'll find him. He goes ta prison, I'm gonna find out everythin' I can about who he's in with, an' how ta git a message in to 'em. Then all I gotta do is pay for a carton or two of cigarettes—"

"Stop right there," Jericho interrupted. "You might be my uncle and all, but I'm not at all comfortable with listening to you planning to commit a crime."

"Mm." Leroy rubbed his chin, a calculating look coming into his eyes. "Talkin' about crimes bein' committed, don't s'pose I could git you to pay some of the other guys a visit sometime, right when they're sortin' out their product …?"

Jericho cleared his throat meaningfully and gave his uncle a hard look. "Really?" As tempting as it might've been to get an inside line as to when and where things like that would be happening, he was fully aware of the slippery slope that kind of bargain represented. "I'm not here to clear out your rivals and make life easier for you."

His uncle didn't even bother looking embarrassed. "Hey, it was just an idea. Ya know it'd make you look good for the cops an' the papers."

"Until someone dug deeper and noticed that some people were being smashed while others were barely being touched. Then they'd start asking why. Once that happens, my credibility takes a nosedive, especially among the type of people who are just looking for an excuse to make my career crash and burn." Jericho shook his head. "I decided a while ago; if I'm gonna do this, I'm gonna do it right. If I catch them at it, I'll hit them. If I catch your guys committing a crime out and about, I'll hit *them*. All square across the board."

"Can't fault you on that one." Leroy hesitated. "So why ain't you been hittin' my boys more often, anyways? Ain't like you don't know what part of town we operate out of."

"Same thing, other way around." Jericho took a deep breath and let it out. "I didn't want to risk running into you personally."

Leroy's forehead wrinkled. "You thought I might recognize you? Figure out who you were?" He snorted. "Not a chance. Until I saw that there costume, I didn't have the first goddamn suspicion."

Jericho wasn't so sure. "Face to face, it might've gone a bit differently." Leroy had known him for nearly twenty years; no matter how carefully he used his 'G-Man voice' to disguise his speech, there was always the chance his uncle would recognize him behind the mask. "Plus, I didn't want to have to hurt you *or* turn you over to the cops, and I couldn't bank on being able to 'accidentally' let you escape if there were witnesses when we ran into each other." He shrugged. "So … I made sure to concentrate my movements a little farther away from where you do business than I might otherwise have done so."

Leroy raised his shaggy eyebrows. "You must think you're pretty damn good if you reckon you c'n whup *my* ass, boy."

Jericho sighed. "I'm a *prodigy*. Plus, I'm pretty sure I mentioned Krav Maga. So yeah, I can whup your ass. It's just that I don't want to have to."

"Ah. Right." Leroy blinked, and Jericho watched his expression change. It was not unlike what had happened with Luke back on the train, under much the same circumstances. "Got it. You ain't jes' pretendin'."

"No, I'm not just pretending. I'm a for-real superhero." It was odd how both Luke and Leroy had needed this to be made clear more than once. On the upside, it meant his secret identity was as secure as it would get, if the people who knew him best *still* had trouble believing it.

"Right. So. Two goddamn years. Right under my nose." Leroy shook his head wonderingly, then something clicked in his expression. "So *that's* how you knew about the gravity stuff in that motherfucking death-drop. Research, my ass."

Jericho smirked, choosing to ignore the snide comment. "That, and I met Transit and the Technologist in the Spire today. They've got elevators there that clock about ninety miles per hour, going straight up. If they're the ones who designed that drop-shaft, and I can't see anyone else doing it, then it'll work come hell, high water or meteor strike."

That got Leroy's attention. "The Spire? You actually got to go inside? What's it like?"

"In a word?" Jericho tilted his head, wondering how much he could get away with telling his uncle. Then he decided to play it safe. "Classified."

Leroy gave him a dirty look. "Smartass."

"You can always go back and sign up for a tour." Jericho shrugged. "They might even let you in."

"Yeah, *that's* gonna happen." Leroy leaned back in his seat. "So, talk to me. Tell me about the trip, an' what you did that you *can* talk about. Tell me about what Luke did, an' that woman who was with you ...?"

"Bobbi," Jericho supplied.

"Yeah, her." Leroy gestured expansively. "How'd ya meet? What was she like? How'd Luke get along with her?"

In those last words, Jericho heard an echo of the loss and pain that he'd felt ever since he walked into the apartment. Leroy wasn't just looking for a story of the trip. He wanted to know of his son's last hours. Everything Luke had said and done; all the details Jericho could recall.

It was the very least he could do for his uncle. "Okay, so picture this. Here I am before this trip even started, standing outside the maglev station in Savannah, arguing with Stephen over the phone. And there's Luke, sneaking up behind me ..."

48
Where the Heart Is

Savannah, Georgia
Monday, October 7, 2013
5:31 PM Eastern Daylight Time

"**Your attention, please. This car has now arrived at the Savannah auxiliary station. Your cargo will be automatically unloaded. Please vacate the car for your own safety. Do not forget your luggage. Utopia Maglev Lines takes no responsibility for luggage left on the train. We hope you have enjoyed your trip. Your attention, please. This car has now arrived …**"

Jericho roused himself and stood up, taking up his overnight bag and slinging it over his shoulder. Flashing lights had activated up and down the interior of the bulk cargo car, bright red rather than the yellow lights that would've been used in the passenger cars. Beside him, Leroy snapped to wakefulness with a snort.

"We there already?" he asked. "That was quicker'n I thought it was gonna be."

"That's because you slept half the way," Jericho said, giving him a hand to get up. "Now we gotta get off so it can unload our cargo." Stepping around the terminal, he eyed the flashing MagCard reader on the door. With a sigh, he pulled out his wallet. Sometimes, security was a *pain.*

"Really?" asked Leroy. "We gotta swipe ta get off?" Leaning down, he picked up Luke's backpack from where he'd left it on an empty seat.

"No." Jericho extracted his MagCard and tapped the reader. The doors unlocked and slid apart with barely a hiss of rubber on steel. "We've got to swipe to open this up so we can claim our cargo. Us getting off is just a bonus. If I'm right …" He stepped out onto the enclosed loading dock and pointed at a matching reader on the outside of the car. "See? If we'd been waiting here for the train, we'd still have had to swipe to open it. I'm guessing this is to make it harder for people to hide in the cargo car and then let themselves out the main doors with whatever stuff they've managed to steal."

"Sumbitch." Leroy shook his head. "Whoever worked out this security setup's got a mind twistier than a pretzel in a tornado."

"*I* figured it out," Jericho reminded him.

Leroy gave him the side-eye. "Fine. A *weightless* pretzel in a tornado."

"Ha ha. Asshat." Jericho was about to make another comment when he heard the whirring and clunking from within the cargo car. "Oh, hey. It's unloading."

From the outside, the cargo car looked almost identical to a passenger car; Jericho surmised that this was yet another security feature. However, the 'windows' were little more than mirrored glass. This meant that Leroy and Jericho couldn't see what was happening without stepping in front of the open doors; a potentially hazardous act. Patience, Jericho decided, was a virtue.

The mechanical noises increased in volume, then an apparatus resembling a forklift suspended from the overhead gantry emerged from the doorway. On it was the crate that Jericho had located. The tines set the crate down and slid from underneath it, then the entire apparatus retracted into the doorway. As soon as it did so, the doors slid shut and clicked into place.

"Please stand away from the edge of the platform," the synthesized voice announced. **"The cargo car is secured for travel. This train will leave in twelve minutes and thirty-two seconds."**

"Why wait around for twelve minutes?" asked Leroy. "Why not go now?"

This was something Jericho thought he could answer. "The maglev system's timed like a goddamn Swiss watch. One lone car on the track, out of sequence, would screw everything up. So when the next train leaves in twelve minutes and so many seconds, this thing's gonna be attached to the back end, like it was with the train from Utopia City." He had to admire the system. They had their shit *nailed*.

"Oh." Leroy eyed Jericho as if wondering how he knew that, then shook his head and dropped the subject. "So where are we, anyways?"

"This is probably part of the Savannah maglev complex." Jericho peered out through the open loading bay doorway into the yard beyond. He could see a high fence with a gate in it, and what looked like a small parking lot, but those weren't the details that clued him in. "North side of it, at a guess."

Leroy eyed him askance. "Lemme guess. Your powers act like a compass."

Just this once, Jericho couldn't resist a little dig. "Yeah, as it happens. If I focus hard enough, I can feel the earth's rotation. That way, I always know which way east and west are." He waited to see if Leroy twigged. There was a compass stored in one of the pouches of his utility belt, but that wasn't how he'd known.

"What, really? That crap must be so goddamn hardy." His uncle didn't sound like he was being sarcastic. *Holy shit. Hook, line and sinker.*

Jericho snorted, and gestured toward the yard visible through the opening. "No, not really. The shadows are falling from left to right. Sun's going down, so we're facing north."

"What the goddamn ...?" Leroy looked out through the doorway in his turn. "Sum*bitch!* You really had me goin' there." Shaking his head, he pulled out his phone and made a call. "Hey ... it's me. I'm back in Savannah, but I'm not at the main station. Don't rightly know ... listen, I'm telling you. You know the maglev? Good. Go cruise around the north side of the fence. Look for a gate. Yeah, a *gate*. Bring your truck. We brought Luke back. Me and Jericho, that's who. Yeah, he was there too. Look, don't ask damn-fool stupid questions. Just bring the goddamn truck."

Leroy killed the phone call and shoved his phone back in his pocket. "Daryl's on his way. Go see if you can get that gate opened for him when he shows."

"Sure thing." Jericho lightened his overnight bag and tossed it off the loading dock. He didn't bother doing the same for himself as he jumped down; that sort of drop he could handle in his sleep. He caught the bag as it drifted down into his arms, ignoring Leroy's derisive snort. On a hunch, he got his MagCard out as he headed up the slope of the loading dock toward the gate.

When he got outside with his bag over his shoulder, he headed over to the gate and found the reader almost immediately. *Called it.* Dropping his bag at his feet, he settled down to wait.

Daryl was Leroy's brother-in-law and (Jericho suspected) a part of Leroy's underworld operations. A big man, ten years younger and about fifty pounds heavier than Leroy himself, he and Jericho were vaguely acquainted. They shared no direct blood, but Jericho considered him and the rest of Aunt Ellie's family to be kin just the same. Truth be told, his aunt would've pitched a hissy fit with a tail on it if anyone from her side of the family had thought of snubbing him. His close friendship with Luke had gone a long way to help matters as well.

He knew Daryl well enough to recognize his pickup truck, so when he saw it rolling slowly up to the gate about fifteen minutes later (the cargo car had taken itself off a few minutes before), he tapped the reader with his card. The gate rumbled aside, and Daryl drove in with a nod to him. Jericho was ready to give him directions, but Daryl was clearly on the ball. Performing a passable three-point turn, the big man reversed the truck down into the loading dock. Jericho stayed by the gate as it rumbled shut again; his assistance wouldn't be needed to get the crate into the back of the truck, he had his overnight bag with him, and he was pretty sure only he or Leroy could open the gate to get out.

It didn't take long for the two men to get the crate containing the coffin in the back and secured with a strap across the top. On the way out, Daryl pulled the truck up alongside Jericho, and Leroy opened the door. There wasn't enough room in the front for two big men, his overnight bag and him as well, so he tossed the bag in the back and climbed into the front. Leroy, he noted, still held Luke's backpack on his lap. The truck rolled forward to the reader and he leaned out the window and tapped it with the card. This opened the gate, and they headed out onto the street.

"Your place, Jericho?" asked Daryl.

"I guess," he said without thinking, then pulled himself up. "Wait, no. My folks' place. Mama's gonna want to make sure I'm okay." That wasn't the only reason, but it would do for now. He didn't have anything in his overnight bag good enough to wear to a funeral, but he'd deal with that later. Right now, he didn't want to confront Stephen. Not with everything else that was going on.

"Sure thing." Daryl changed gears, and the truck rumbled off down the street.

"How's the arrangements going?" asked Leroy. Jericho kept quiet, knowing damn sure the question hadn't been directed at him.

"Ellie's handlin' it all," the big guy reported. "From what I hear, we're fixin' ta have th' wake tomorrow night, dunno where, an' th' service at First African Baptist on Thursday."

"Family?" asked Leroy next, in that sometimes-annoying shorthand that close relatives acquired.

"You an' Jericho jes' got in. Li'l Serena's takin' th' maglev down from New York tonight. Ellie's told Beau an' Dahlia, an' they-all's reachin' out to everyone else."

Jericho tuned the conversation out after that. He was holding up reasonably well, all things considering, but after Leroy had dozed off on the train, he'd had a lot of time to think. To indulge in recriminations. Smokeshadow's words had stuck with him, but a tiny insistent part of his mind kept telling him that he was still responsible for the death of Luke and Bobbi. Never mind that Luke was normally capable of taking care of himself; Jericho was the superhero in the family. He should never have left them alone in a strange city. Their deaths were a tragedy, one he could have prevented. *Should* have prevented.

On top of that, if he didn't have enough on his mind, there was the looming confrontation with Stephen. Only the day before, he'd fervently assured his boyfriend that he'd be back in just a few days, and all would be normal again. He'd even been looking forward to it; not the recriminations, but the eventual return to their previous closeness. Stephen would've held it over his head for a few days or weeks; that was a given. In the end, he liked to think, all would have been forgiven and forgotten.

However, in light of Luke's revelation, his entire relationship with Stephen had become irretrievably tainted. What should've been a return to a sanctuary promising comfort and support was instead horribly awkward and promising to get worse. It didn't help that along with the knowledge of Stephen's infidelity came an unpleasant awareness of how manipulative his boyfriend had been all this time. Which was why he wanted nothing to do with Stephen right at that moment, not even to make him face up to his transgressions. It was all too much effort, and he was so very *tired*.

When the truck pulled up outside his parents' house, he turned to Leroy. "I'm gonna want to talk to you about that other thing later, too. How long is it gonna take, once we've got what we need?" He was careful to couch his comment in general terms, not because he thought Daryl would be shocked by the idea of criminal activity, but because the big guy just didn't need to know.

"Couple-three days," Leroy said consideringly. "Thursday, mebbe Friday. They need to be able to pass a basic background check, yeah?"

Jericho nodded. "At least that, yes." Once he got to Utopia City, shoddy preparation was the *last* thing he wanted to have to contend with.

"Yup. Git me th' stuff an' I'll see how we do."

Jericho opened the door and extricated himself from the vehicle, then retrieved his overnight bag from the flatbed. Giving Leroy and Daryl a wave goodbye, he opened the front gate and trudged up the front path of the house he'd grown up in. It was large, inviting, prosperous; everything about it spelling out 'success'. This was not a word Jericho would have used about himself, right then.

There was a saying that went 'you can never go home again'. Jericho was beginning to see the truth in that as he neared the front door of the house. He'd moved out of home a month after he debuted as G-Man; a little over six months later, Stephen had contacted him for the photo shoot. Jericho being as skittish as he was, it had taken them a few weeks to officially start dating, and they'd been together a year before he finally accepted Stephen's invitation to move in together. In all that time, nothing had caused such a major shift in his perspective as the last twenty-four hours of his life. He didn't feel like himself anymore, and he wasn't at all sure where he belonged in his old life, if he belonged anywhere at all.

Climbing the steps onto the broad front veranda, he took a deep breath to gather his nerve. Reaching out, he pressed the doorbell. Solemn tones resounded within the house, vaguely audible through the imposing door. Re-settling the overnight bag on his shoulder, he waited.

Heavy footsteps sounded, then the door opened. His father stood there in shirtsleeves and slippers; as tall as Leroy, he wasn't quite as wide in the shoulders, while being slightly heavier in the gut. Such was the effect of living an easier life than his brother. His black hair was thinning and going gray at the sides.

"Who is it, Beau?" his mother called out, from farther back in the house.

"Jericho." It was both a greeting and a way to inform Jericho's mother. "Jericho's home." Much like Leroy, Beau Hansen wasn't a hugger, but he stepped forward and held his arms out anyway. "Welcome home, son."

Jericho needed this. He hadn't realized until this moment how *much* he needed it. "It's good to *be* home." Dropping his bag to the veranda decking, he let himself be enveloped in his father's strong arms. The tears started in his eyes once more as he returned the embrace, then was hugged in turn by his mother.

"Can you stay for dinner?" she asked as she reluctantly let the hug go. "We can always set another place." Her gaze was sharp with concern as she looked him over. Dahlia Hansen may have been a hard-nosed New Yorker born and bred, but she was a mother through and through.

"Yeah, about that," he said, trying to surreptitiously wipe away the tears spilling from the corners of his eyes. On the one hand, he didn't want to impose on them, but on the other … there was no way in *hell* he'd be able to face Stephen right then. "Can I … stay here? Maybe a few nights?"

"Of *course*, honey." His mother's features, as lean and finely boned as his own, creased with worry. "Stay as long as you like. Have you got troubles … where you're living?"

As he'd told Luke on the maglev, his parents knew about his orientation, though (as far as he knew) they were unaware of his precise living arrangements. There were several reasons for this. All his life, his mother had been deeply scathing of any relationship where one member was more than five years older than the other. His father, more entrenched in the conservative attitudes of the South, was grudgingly accepting of his son's lifestyle, but still got twitchy when he heard about men living with men. And then, of course, there was Stephen and his attitude to mixed-race relationships; this didn't apply to Beau and Dahlia, but it *did* apply to Leroy and Ellie, of whom there were pictures up around the house. All of which added up to a potentially explosive outcome, assiduously avoided by the simple expedient of never mentioning Stephen to his parents.

"In a way," he hedged. "Is my old bedroom free?" He didn't hold out much hope; it *had* been a little over two years. If they'd repurposed it, he figured that in a pinch he could bunk down in any one of the several spare rooms.

"Of *course*," she said again, and led the way into the house. Taking up his overnight bag, he followed her. As they went up the stairs, he was still not entirely sure what he would find. Everything from his adolescent years would've been packed away, no doubt. It would be just as familiar-strange as the rest of the house; looking the same, but not quite as he recalled.

She opened the door and gestured him in. He took two steps over the threshold then stopped dead, blinking. Those two steps had been like walking through a time warp into the past. The feeling was so strong that he had to glance back over his shoulder to make sure his mother was still there. She made an encouraging *go-on* gesture. "We kept it just the way you had it."

This was not an exaggeration. Letting the bag drop to the rug with a muted *thud*, he looked around, trying not to stare too obviously. The drama and swimming trophies sat in pride of place on his dresser, reminders of a more innocent time in his life. His posters still hung on the wall; these were mostly of boy bands, though there was one of Adam Power and an early one of Relentless that featured the hero's kinetic sledgehammer instead of the more recent gravity mace. The room was essentially unchanged from when he'd last slept there, even down to the coverlet on the bed.

"Is it alright?" his mother asked anxiously.

The tears finally broke free, spilling down over his cheeks as he turned and went back to her. He hugged her again, enjoying the closeness and the warmth of the embrace. "It's *perfect*," he said, trying not to choke on the lump rising in his throat.

The pain of losing Luke was almost bearable when taken on its own, but if he'd had to deal with too many other problems, he wasn't sure he how he would cope. This one simple gesture ensured he didn't have to worry about where he was going to be staying until the funeral arrangements were complete. Other issues, such as internet access, he'd worry about in the morning. The only thing he wasn't sure about was whether or not he'd be confronting Stephen before he went back to Utopia City. That was definitely something he wanted to leave on the back burner for as long as humanly possible.

Either way, it was now up to Smokeshadow to keep the Survivors out of trouble until he got back.

49
Of Mice and Men

Earlier, in Utopia City
Smokeshadow

Carefully, Chelsea lined up her phone at Gimmick. With a solemn look on her face, the teenage artificer stood before the white sheet they were using as a photography screen. The phone clicked, and the image stored itself away.

"Okay, that's that," Chelsea announced. She imported the photo into the dossier she'd assembled of the Survivors, and prepared it for emailing to G-Man.

Over the past hour, she'd gotten to know Thomas' five friends. Thomas himself intrigued her, because once the younger prodigy got home again (or as close to home as a warehouse could be) he'd let go some of his hyper-caution and begun to show more of a domestic side than she would have expected from him. After greeting them all, he'd made sure that Ray was recovering well from an attack they'd suffered the previous night at the Market, then he'd taken over the cooking.

Thomas and Ray had been saved, according to Sidestep's enthusiastic description, when G-Man swooped dramatically out of nowhere and threw half a dozen undercover cops in the canal. She'd noted both Thomas and Ray expressing reservations at this telling, but listened politely to the story until Sidestep ran out of superlatives to describe the black-clad Enabled. Once the younger boy became distracted by the TV again, she'd checked privately with the other two and gotten the real story.

While they were figuring out what to use as a photography screen and what information to put in for each of them, she'd taken the opportunity to chat casually with each of the Survivors, getting as much information from their body language as from what they said. It had been a rewarding experience, making her all the more determined to get these kids out of Utopia City to a place where they could be themselves without getting into trouble.

Blades was an artificer, of course. She'd gotten her powers when (or shortly after) a villain drove the equivalent of a main battle tank over her family car … with her family still inside. Her parents had been killed, and her legs crushed beyond any hope of recovery. While she had relatives who were willing to take her in, they had control of the medical insurance money, and weren't willing to spring for the full price of a PowerTech Industries mobility frame; settling instead for a third-party knockoff at a fraction of the cost. And, it turned out, a fraction of the utility, given that it lacked the high-end neural-induction circuitry that made the PowerTech product so versatile. When she complained, they bought her a regular electric wheelchair to shut her up.

Undeterred, she made use of her brand-new Enabled abilities to develop her own version of neural induction and build it into the frame. Then she'd gone one step further (so to speak) and reconfigured both wheelchair and frame so that they could connect together, allowing her to control the former using the latter's synthetic proprioception rather than relying on clumsy manual controls. From there (according to her), it hadn't been hard to engineer the hybrid so that it could reshape itself from chair into a set of power armor and back again. She'd been careful to keep the chair aspect looking like the standard commercial model it had once been, the exterior camouflage panels giving it a worn and battered appearance. When clad in her armor, she was able to rollerblade literally anywhere her heart desired, including up walls and across ceilings. She confessed with a hint of amusement that, while the frame gave her the full range of mobility if she needed to use it, she rather enjoyed the comfort of the wheelchair.

Chelsea had already met the other artificer in the group; Gimmick. Part of the girl's specialty was building small but versatile items, such as the universal lockpick and the gun she called the Zarkinator. "Because of the way it sounds when I fire it," was her explanation for the name. She hadn't hit a limit yet on what she could build, just that it had to be small and easily portable.

The other part of her specialty was her ability to understand technology on an almost supernatural level. This allowed her to look at any machine and analyze its primary function at a glance, and to disable, repair or subvert it for her own use with almost frightening ease. Thus explaining the mechanism on the door lock, and why they weren't worried about the forklifts in the warehouse running them down by accident. Her talents even extended to Artificer creations, though (according to her) the Technologist's inventions were pure hell to work with.

Sidestep was a sweet kid. His powerset was purely Dynamic in nature, letting him duplicate himself and teleport things from one version of himself to the other. When split like that, he was in control of both bodies at once; neither one was the 'main' body. At any time, he could dismiss either body and recreate it from the other one. When he duplicated himself, anything basic he was wearing or carrying (such as clothing) also got duplicated, but vanished when that version of him did. He was effusively friendly, leading her to wonder when he'd last had an actual mother figure to relate to.

On the other hand, the Photonic Avenger (usually referred to as 'PA', much to his disgruntlement) had powers that were much more aggressive. Red-haired and more reserved than Sidestep, he was also a couple of years older. He could levitate slowly from one place to another, and release blasts from his hands that ranged from blinding light all the way through the damaging energy spectrum to a full-on EMP. To conceal his identity, he had a motorcycle helmet which he'd painted in bright primary colors, with a tinted visor.

Of all the Survivors, Ray (it wasn't his real name, though he preferred it to 'Razor-Edge') seemed positively embarrassed by his power, to the point that he didn't enjoy using it. The bony plates he extruded from his body could wrap around him as armor or angle outward to act as weapons. Either way, they ruined his clothing with the hooks and slashing edges that were an integral part of their formation. When he was armored up, he was much stronger and more durable, though he didn't consider the cost to be worth it. He'd privately confessed to Chelsea that he'd deliberately chosen not to armor up while the undercover cops were manhandling him, mainly because he didn't want to hurt them.

She believed him, too. That was the odd part of it. The original offer to help out the Survivors had been made on a whim, mainly because she liked G-Man and he honestly needed the assistance. More to the point, this definitely fitted in with her prior experience of being a trouble magnet. But what she hadn't expected was the way she was able to relate to them. Not to put too fine a point on it, they were nice kids who'd had an absolutely shit turn of luck through no fault of their own.

It reminded her of herself and Marni in a way, though it had been her sister who'd suffered all the bad luck. Marni's problem had involved a particularly nasty form of lymphoma and a medical insurance company that decided to change its guidelines to exclude pre-existing conditions just in time to avoid honoring her policy. A lawsuit (that their parents couldn't afford) may have changed matters, but Marni would've been dead by the time it was settled. Chelsea hadn't been Enabled when that mess started, but she'd ended up as one by the time it was over. The insurance company now accepted pre-existing conditions and Marni was getting affordable treatment. On the downside, Chelsea was wanted for gambling fraud in the state of Ohio. She couldn't go home anymore, so she went everywhere else. Such as Utopia City.

"Okay," she announced. "I've got your pictures, your names and the personal details for your IDs here. Is there anything else anyone wants? Because I'm about to email all this away. Once it's done, it's done. I doubt very much that G-Man will be able to handle a do-over."

"Uh, one problem," Gimmick said. "Back when we moved into this place, I connected one of my gadgets up to the internal rebar structure in this place and used that as a basis to turn the walls into a Faraday cage. Phone signals aren't gonna get through."

"Ah." Chelsea frowned. "Wouldn't that basically make this into a black hole, electronically speaking? And how do the forklifts get their orders, if signals don't get through? I can see that going very wrong, very fast."

The artificer waved her hand dismissively. "Electronic invisibility, for the first problem. I tuned the Faraday cage so any signal that hits one side of the cage skates all the way around and then re-transmits. For the other thing, I've already got scanners on the roof to keep an eye on any hexes in the vicinity. There's a cable that runs down the wall and under the door, then connects to a re-transmitter unit on the wall inside. All I really had to do was reconfigure them to pick up the signals that communicate with the forklifts as well. But it doesn't work with phones. Totally wrong frequencies. You're gonna have to go outside and see if you can get a signal."

"What about the hexes?" Thomas came over, wiping his hands on a towel. "They were getting pretty thick in the air for a while there. She's not going to want to step out right in front of one."

"Oh, good point." Gimmick retrieved the scanner display device from her belt. "Nope, looks like they've given up. There's one still orbiting that storehouse, but there's nothing else moving in the air nearby. So long as we keep at least one building between us and the active one, we should be good."

"Police chatter?" asked Chelsea. She'd made good use of police band scanners in previous escapades, and she would've been astonished if Gimmick didn't have something similar in her repertoire.

"Already covered." Gimmick tapped the display unit. "This puppy even analyzes their speech to see if they're talking about us, and if they're excited or bored. Currently, there's nobody talking about us, and the few that are nearby are bored to crap."

"All right then." Chelsea pointed in the general direction of the door that she knew about. "If I stick to the outer wall, I'm not gonna run into any forklifts, right?" Nearly being run down by one had left her distinctly wary around them.

"Nope." Gimmick smirked. "They know not to come out this way. But if it'll make you feel better, I'll come with." Taking up her visor, she fitted it over her eyes.

Chelsea nodded. "Thanks. I appreciate it. Besides, I want to make sure I can get out and back in."

"Gotcha covered." Reaching into a pouch on her belt, Gimmick produced a small electronic item. "Earbud radio. It's linked to the re-transmitter." She handed it over to

Chelsea. "I can make a dozen a day. When you're done with it, drop it on the ground and step on it. It'll just be random junk then."

"Huh, cool." Chelsea fitted it into her ear. Almost immediately, she could hear the static produced by the earbuds that the others were wearing. "Thank you." She was able to build something of the sort herself, but they rarely lasted more than a day, and the range was less than half a mile. Nobody had ever intercepted the signal though, so there was that.

"Can I come too?" asked Sidestep. "I never get to go out."

Thomas gave him a dry look. "You came out with me last night to the Market."

"Yeah, but the Market doesn't count. You made me stand out of sight while you passed me food to send back here." Sidestep jutted his chin out stubbornly. "I wanna go outside too!"

"Me, too." PA got up from where he'd been watching TV. "I'm bored."

"Fine." From Thomas' tone, he just wanted to end the argument before it began. "Just mask up. We don't want some random passer-by seeing your faces."

"Do *you* ever mask up?" asked Chelsea. "Because I haven't seen it yet."

Thomas shrugged and pulled a red cloth mask out of his pocket. "I've got one, but I'm kind of the public face of the Survivors, so wearing it would defeat the purpose most of the time."

"Ah, good point." She looked around and saw that PA was wearing his helmet and Sidestep had acquired a pair of goggles. At her silent bidding, part of her hood flowed over her face to form a domino mask. "Okay then, let's go."

She headed along the wall toward the door, with the other three following. "Once I send this, your entire job will be to stay in here and keep your heads down 'til G-Man gets back with the finished products." She paused, looking at Gimmick. "How are you off for food reserves?" There had been a beer cooler beside the camp stove, but she had no idea how well-stocked it was.

"Figure we could hold out for a few days," the artificer said. "If we had to, I mean." Stepping past Chelsea, she knocked firmly on the inside of the door, the same shave-and-a-haircut that Thomas had used to get in. Obediently, the door lock clicked open. Gimmick pulled on the handle and it opened.

Eyes on her phone, Chelsea stepped out into the alleyway. As she cleared the building, she saw the no-signal icon pop out of existence, to be replaced by several bars. "All *right*," she said, and hit the icon to send the email. It would take a few seconds, she knew; six photos and a chunk of text made for a serious block of data.

Ping ping. And of course, any incoming alerts would light up her phone as well. Though the alert tone wasn't one she recognized, off the top of her head …

"Oh, shit," whispered PA, from beside her.

"Crap, crap, crap." That was Gimmick, on the other side. Chelsea felt a hand on her shoulder. "We gotta get back inside, *now*."

"What? Why? The email hasn't …" She looked around. At the end of the alley was a hex, but this one was sitting on the street corner. Something made her turn her head, and at the other end of the same alley was another hex, doing the same thing. As she watched, it spun up its ducted fan and lifted off the ground, struts folding into place underneath it.

"Too late. They never went away." If disgusted admiration was a thing, Gimmick's voice was a perfect example of it. "They landed and went to low-power mode, then waited for us to show ourselves."

"Tell the others," PA said quietly. "Tell them we're blown. We're blown *so* wide open."

"I'm telling them, I'm telling them." Sidestep sounded shaky. His hand crept into Chelsea's, and she squeezed it. "What are we gonna do?"

"Okay, they can't grab us, right? They can only harass us?" She hated not having all the answers at her fingertips.

"Yeah, but they can follow us 'til the cops catch up." Gimmick's tone held dire certainty. "Blades can probably outrun them, Sidestep has half a chance of out-dodging them, and you and Thomas could probably pull some Prodigy bullshit to get away. But me and PA and Ray don't have those options. We'll have to fight our way out, and that's gonna get real loud, real fast."

"No blowing stuff up," Chelsea said firmly. "We need to keep this quiet."

"We might not get that choice."

She turned at PA's voice, to find that the young dynamic was pointing at the hex at his end of the alley, which was now cruising down the alleyway toward them. Despite herself, she was impressed. With no more than two feet of clearance on either side of it, the drone was holding rock-steady within the miniature windstorm that it was generating.

In the next second, she realized its intent. "It's gonna dust us!" she shouted. "PA, drop it!"

'Dusting' was a term she'd picked up from a novel once, where a helicopter hovering in ground effect caused so much dust and wind to kick up that the people under it were unable to fight back effectively. The hexes were nowhere near as large as a full-sized chopper, but the narrow confines of the alley would magnify the effect dramatically. If it could force them back inside, that would allow the police to bottle them up until appropriate reinforcements (specifically, Force Majeure) could be brought in.

PA didn't need telling twice. He held out his hands toward the oncoming drone and did … nothing, as far as she could see. But the hex lurched to one side, hit the alley wall, then fell to the ground with a tremendous crash.

"What the hell was that?" Thomas came out through the door, his cloth mask tied around his face. When he saw the downed hex, he turned to PA, his eyes narrowing. "Did you …?"

"I told him to." Chelsea pointed at the far end of the alley, where the other hex was approaching. "Can you get that one, too?"

"Watch me." PA reached out toward that one as well, just as a small turret emerged from the under-surface. In the next second, he convulsed and fell to the ground. Chelsea's nose wrinkled from the smell of ozone.

"You mechanical asshole!" Gimmick dropped the scan display into its belt pouch and unslung the Zarkinator. Bringing it to her shoulder in one smooth move, she fired. The ominous red glow emanating from the end of the barrel erupted in a beam that lanced out toward the hex, accompanied by an onomatopoeic *BZARK*.

Chelsea hadn't been sure what to expect, but she wasn't disappointed. Even as the hex tried to dodge, Gimmick's shot punched clean through it and out the other side. Trailing smoke, the drone lurched away, rebounding off the alley walls, its ducted fan making a discordant clattering sound.

Blades, fully clad in her armor, came out through the door next, with Ray right behind her. "What the hell … oh, shit."

"Oh, shit is right." Thomas took a deep breath. "Blades, go find out what's out there. Ray, armor up. We need you hard to hurt."

"Roger that," replied Blades crisply. With a screech of wheels on concrete, the armored girl accelerated off down the alleyway, leaving lines of light where her wheels had touched. When she reached the fallen hex, she went briefly up onto the wall, her wheels acting as though the vertical surface were flat ground.

Thomas turned toward the tall white-blond kid. "Ray?"

"Not in this alley." Ray pointed at the confining walls. "If I even bumped into one of you, I'd do serious damage."

"Does anyone need anything?" asked Sidestep. "I'm still inside."

"Grab our inch bags," Thomas advised him. Crouching down, he helped the groaning PA to his feet. "That's the important stuff."

"Inch bags?" asked Chelsea, moving to give him a hand.

"It's short for I'm Never Coming Home," explained Thomas as he got his shoulder under PA's. She did the same on the other side, and he nodded his thanks for her assistance.

The redhead's helmet had saved him from a nasty knock when he went down, but his knees were still wobbly. "Tased me," he slurred. "Jus' before it shot me, I tasted ultraviolet."

"Heads up, people. By the numbers," Thomas declared. With Chelsea helping him support PA, he followed the way Blades had gone. Ray darted ahead and jumped up onto the downed drone, then down the other side. As he moved ahead to check out the mouth of the alley, she saw bony growths shredding his clothes from the inside.

"Here," said Sidestep, handing Thomas a backpack. As soon as he was relieved of his burden, another one appeared in his hands and he offered it to Chelsea. "It's PA's."

"Oh." She accepted it with her free hand. It was heavier than she'd expected, but she had no problem slinging it over her shoulder.

"Thanks." Sidestep gave her a wide smile, then moved back to where Gimmick was bringing up the rear with the Zarkinator at the ready.

By the time they got to the mouth of the alley, Chelsea was carrying a second pack and so was Thomas; apparently, they belonged to Ray and Blades, respectively. But the extra burdens weren't the biggest problem. This came in the form of two more hexes, sweeping down the street toward them; another one, just visible over the rooftops, was thankfully moving *away* from them at speed.

"They're painting us!" warned PA. He brought up his hand and pointed at the hex to the left. "I've got this one!"

"Out of the way!" Gimmick pushed through the crush and tried to get her weapon lined up on the right-hand one.

Instinctively, Chelsea pulled Sidestep out of the way. "Is that really the best—"

BZARK.

Again, the almost-solid beam erupted from the barrel of the weapon. It may have been the result of better aim or just better luck, but the outcome was somewhat more dramatic than before. Instead of smoking dismally and meandering off to crash in an undisclosed location, the drone exploded. Fiery debris flew in all directions as it crashed to the street and rolled over and over. One piece hurtled in their direction, until a large arm clad in solid bone came up to take the impact. It shattered against the obdurate surface. Chelsea ducked as shrapnel struck the building they were standing next to.

"Everyone okay?" asked Ray. His voice was deeper and louder, but that wasn't the only change in him. He was now covered from head to toe in wickedly barbed bony plates. The remains of his clothing hung in rags from the edges of his armor. There was a scorch-mark on his right forearm, but Chelsea had other things to worry about. The hex PA had taken on was nowhere to be seen.

"What the hell was that?" she yelled at Gimmick. "Didn't I tell you not to blow stuff up? I'm pretty sure I told you not to blow stuff up!"

"It's not my fault!" the artificer retorted. "They were gonna tase us! It was that or wake up in a cell!"

"Shut up and run!" yelled Thomas. "And no more shooting!"

Running seemed like a good idea, so Chelsea followed his lead. Or rather, she ran as fast as she could, and he kept pace with her. In her expert opinion, people who used their Prodigy ratings to show off like that just plain sucked.

The air rasped in her lungs, but she pushed herself onward. While her powerset's sweet spot centered around manipulating and deceiving others, she couldn't figure out how to use that aspect of it to stay out of the hands of the law at this point in time, so she had to fall back on the old favorite of 'run away'. Running away was *always* a solid plan B.

They pelted down the street and turned a corner; when (not if) more hexes were due to arrive in the vicinity, it would be a good idea to not be in their line of sight. However, this plan did not account for a hex coming in the other direction.

It swooped down toward them. Gimmick raised the Zarkinator. Once more, with a loud *BZARK*, the ominous red glow emanating from the end of the barrel erupted in a beam that sliced toward the oncoming drone. However, just before the attack would have made contact, the hex's centrally placed ducted fan cut out for no apparent reason. The massive police drone began to fall out of the sky, its inadvertent course change causing it to avoid Gimmick's shot altogether. The real problem with this was that its projected impact point was far too close to Chelsea, who was a couple of yards away from the rest of the Survivors.

"Hey!" Gimmick pointed accusingly at PA. "No EMP'ing my targets!"

He didn't get the chance to answer before the hex hit the street about four yards away from Chelsea. Fortunately, it didn't explode. It *did,* however, break up on impact. She shrieked and ducked, covering her head with her arms as fragments flew in all directions.

"Watch out!" A moment later, she was shoved to the side as the youngest member of the group cannoned into her. While he didn't move her very far, she was out of the way when the largest piece of the hex tumbled past. He was directly in its path; she heard the sickening crunch of bones breaking as it mowed him down without pausing.

"Sidestep!" she cried out. *Is he—*

"I'm fine!" the thirteen-year-old assured her from the other side of the group, giving her a thumb's up. As she watched, he split into two again, his aspects moving to get as far apart as possible. Only one of him was now wearing his pack. She didn't need to look in order to know that the version of him that had been hit by the piece of crashed hex had already vanished.

The momentary danger over, everyone glared at the Photonic Avenger. "What?" he asked, spreading his hands in a show of fake innocence. "That wasn't me. It probably ran out of power."

"Bullshit!" Thomas glared at PA. "Next time, blind its sensors. The last thing we need is bits of machinery falling from above." Turning, he looked toward Chelsea. "But there'll be reinforcements incoming soon. We need to get out of sight, and fast. Any suggestions? And where the hell is Blades?" He pressed his finger to his ear. "Blades, report location."

Chelsea's radio earpiece crackled suddenly. "Incoming!" It was definitely Blades' voice. Panting hard like she was running a marathon, she nevertheless sounded like she was having the time of her life. "Comin' in hot, three bogeys!"

As Chelsea's mind began to catch up with what she'd just heard, Blades rocketed out of the side street in front of them, the rollerblades built into the boots of her fully invested power armor leaving glowing lines on the roadway behind her. Right behind her, about ten feet off the ground, came three more hexes, just as the girl had reported.

PA and Gimmick both reacted at the same time, but the boy was a shade faster on the draw. He extended his hands and the front hex suddenly lost power, just as the other one had. As it slowed and dipped, the second hex swerved to miss it, right into Gimmick's sights.

BZARK.

Once again, there was no messing around with clattering ducted fans and smoke trailing off into the distance; Gimmick's aim was getting better, detonating the hex in a ball of flame. Undeterred, the third hex blew straight through the explosion, zeroing in on Blades.

The armored girl went across the T-intersection without slowing down; for a brief heart-stopping moment, it looked as though she was going to crash headlong into the building in front of her. But then she pulled an insane S-turn maneuver that somehow had her weaving *up* the wall, still trailing the lines of light. Kicking off, she executed a flawless backward somersault that landed her on top of the last hex, just as it applied upward power in an attempt to climb and avoid the building. With the extra weight on board, it dipped rather than rising. Somehow using that for extra momentum, Blades bailed out just before impact. She hit the wall sideways, skating away *along* it as if it were flat ground, then swerved down to ground level. With no chance of stopping, the hex smashed in through the wall; a moment later, there was the dull thump of a muffled explosion from somewhere inside.

As if she did this sort of thing every day (and for all Chelsea knew, she did) she came in for a flashy sideways skid that brought her to a halt about a yard from the rest of the group. "Clear that way," she reported, pointing down the street she'd just come from. "Not sure for how long, though."

"Right." Thomas scowled at Gimmick and PA. "Now, if you've got that out of your systems, maybe we can get back to escaping. We're out of options, here. I don't even want to know how many thousands or millions of dollars' worth of police property we just destroyed. That's gonna put us very solidly on their radar. They're not going to stop coming after us now. It's only a matter of time before Force Majeure gets called in to deal with us. We need to find a hole they won't think to look into and pull it in on top of us."

Now that the action was over, Chelsea was already planning for exfiltration. Almost immediately, she spotted what she was looking for; a manhole cover with a spiral pattern built into it. "This way," she said, heading for it.

"Okay, I trust you, but why this way?" asked Thomas as he caught up with her.

She pointed at the manhole. "Pretty sure that leads to the maintenance tunnels. Gimmick, think you can get that open? Or do you need your little lockpick?"

The Asian girl looked it over, and snorted. "In my sleep. It's barely even Artificer tech." She slung the Zarkinator over her shoulder and pulled a complicated-looking tool off her belt. When she pressed a button, LEDs rippled up and down the length of it. "Behold; my master key and my traveling toolbox, all in one convenient package." Crouching beside the manhole, she reached out to the center of the circular plate with her tool. Even before it came into contact, the cover started to open outward, its spiral leaves sliding into slots around the rim.

Thomas nodded. "Okay, yeah. I'm impressed."

Oddly enough, Gimmick pulled back and grabbed for the Zarkinator. "Wasn't me! Something's coming out!"

Before she managed to get the weapon off her shoulder, one of the six-foot (and far more than six-footed) cleaning bug-things emerged from the open manhole. This close, Chelsea could see that it had *amazing* articulation, allowing it to flow upward over the edge like water.

With a grunt, Gimmick landed on her butt and almost fell over backward, staring up at the giant mechanical lobster-spider hybrid. It waved a couple of sensor antennae at her, then scuttled past her and down the street toward the intermittently burning rubble that had once been a group of hexes.

"What the hell was that?" Thomas stepped forward and helped Gimmick to her feet.

"Street cleaner," Chelsea said in unison with Gimmick. They looked at each other, then nodded firmly. Great minds thought alike, after all.

For a frozen moment, everyone waited for more bugs to come up, then Ray pointed. "Uh, guys? It's closing!" And so it was; the metal leaves were emerging from the rim of the manhole once more, sliding in together to make a coherent whole.

"Screw that," Gimmick muttered. "Give *me* a fright, will you?" Getting up onto her knees, she adjusted the multitool and tapped the center of the manhole cover with it. Without any fuss, the cover opened once more.

Chelsea nodded. "Nicely done. Now get down there." With some relief, she handed PA his INCH bag. It had been dragging her arm out of its socket the whole time. "And I think this is yours." Letting the other pack slide off her shoulder, she handed it to Blades.

Thomas turned to look at her. "What about you?"

"I'll be fine," she assured him. "Get to the Oaklands. I'm in room—"

"Don't tell us," he interrupted. "Take Sidestep with you."

She glanced at Sidestep, who nodded enthusiastically. "That works," she said. "Now *get down there.*"

Blades put on her pack and went down first, followed by Sidestep's other version. PA, looking much recovered from before, shrugged on his pack and climbed down as well.

"Uh, I'm sure I'm being stupid or something," ventured Ray, still wearing his bone encrustations. He gestured at the open manhole. "But are we gonna be running into more of those spider-things? I don't like spiders at the best of times."

She grinned. "You saw the way it ignored Gimmick. Right now, they're dealing with that mess you guys made. Anything else?"

"Yeah. Clothes." Ray gestured at himself. The bone armor afforded him modesty for the time being, but Chelsea could easily see him becoming considerably more R-rated once he put it away again. "How am I gonna get around?"

"Gotcha covered," Sidestep announced. "Got everyone's INCH bags." He pointed at the second backpack Thomas was holding. "Yours is right there."

"Oh, good." Ray started down the ladder.

Thomas frowned. "So, what else do you think might use those tunnels?"

"Cops incoming," warned Gimmick, looking at the readout on her handheld display. "We got less than a minute."

"No idea," Chelsea admitted. "The cleaners, maybe traveling electronic shops to keep stuff working? Probably some kind of roving guard to make sure people don't sneak down here and mess with the cleaners or whatever. So tell PA to EMP anything that comes at you."

"Got it." Thomas didn't sound thrilled, which Chelsea approved of. She wanted the Survivors on their toes. "See you at the Oaklands, I guess. We better get moving; whoever's driving those drones is gonna think of the tunnels sooner rather than later."

She totally agreed. "Better move fast, then. You'll be able to keep track of direction underground?"

Thomas nodded. "PA can see magnetic fields. It's a handy trick he has."

"I'll bet." She looked around as sirens echoed off nearby buildings. "Now get your ass down there before someone sees you."

Thomas scrambled down the ladder, followed by Gimmick. As the manhole cover irised shut, Chelsea took her phone from her pocket. On the fly, she reconfigured her clothing as a floral dress, with an extension to the top of her head that became a wide-brimmed hat.

"What do we do?" asked Sidestep nervously from beside her. "Why aren't we running? They'll catch us."

Chelsea smiled reassuringly; this was a game she knew how to play. "They'd catch us whether we ran or not," she said, and passed him her phone. "The trick is to not make them chase us. Lose the goggles and follow my lead." Out of the corner of her eye, she saw the eyewear flicker out of existence. "Alright, now crouch down and pretend to be taking pictures of the manhole like it's the most interesting thing you've seen all day."

"Okay," he said doubtfully, but did as he was told.

The first police car came around the corner then, siren still blaring. She waved her arm, beckoning them over. While the lights didn't cut out, the siren did. The car slid up to them silently. "Excuse me, ma'am!" called an authoritative masculine voice. "I'm going to need to ask what you and the boy are doing here."

Making sure the sun dropped a shadow across her face, she turned toward the car. Her entire demeanor radiated 'total innocence' and 'utterly forgettable' as she moved forward to block Sidestep from the view of the cop car's side-mounted camera. "Oh, hi, officer! We're from out of town, so we decided to take a walk, but then there were people in costumes running around and stuff started exploding, so we hid, then something weird came out of that manhole and we thought that was so cool, so I wanted to take pictures and—"

"Okay, okay," the cop interrupted. She was mildly impressed. He'd endured more of her way-too-enthusiastic monologue than most people would have. "People in costumes? Did you see which way they went?"

"They ran that way," she said, pointing down the road Blades had said was clear. "But listen, I wanted to tell you—"

"Stay here," he said hastily. "Someone will be here to interview you soon." The car tilted forward slightly, then shot off down the road. She noticed they didn't turn the siren on again.

"Okay, that worked." Sidestep sounded like he couldn't quite believe it. "What do we do now?"

"Now, we walk away," she replied. "Briskly, but without quite looking like we're running away."

"I can do that," he said, and they started off down the street together. She checked the sky for hexes—none were immediately in evidence—then altered her clothing again, this time to blouse and slacks, and adjusted her gait to give herself an extra thirty years of age. The hyperweave couldn't mimic hair exactly, but she made it form a close-fitting cap that resembled graying hair in a conservative cut, at least from a distance.

Then she looked down at Sidestep. "Is there any way you can change your clothing to look different?" At the moment, he was wearing a T-shirt and jeans. The shirt, she figured, could be turned inside-out, but that was just a stopgap. She'd done her best to make sure the cops got no pictures of his face, but if they'd captured any imagery of his clothing, they could zero in on him before she could get him back to the Oaklands.

"Sure," he said at once. "Give me a second."

She waited, not sure what he was about to do. Ten seconds passed, then twenty. Suddenly, his T-shirt flickered, going from light green and short-sleeved to red with long sleeves. This was something she could do in a moment with her hyperweave, but it was impressive to see someone else pull off the same trick, especially so quickly.

"Let me guess," she said. "You had a spare shirt in your INCH bag?"

"Uh huh," he said. "Thomas made sure we all had changes of clothing."

"So what is it with Thomas, anyway?" she asked. "I'm guessing he's a prodigy, but there's more to it than that. Something deeper."

Sidestep shrugged. "I dunno about that. I just know he's really cool. He knows everything about being Enabled, and he knows first aid and cooking and how to put together a good costume, and he's been teaching us how to fight and stuff. We woulda been caught a long time ago if it wasn't for him." His hand crept into hers; she squeezed it reassuringly.

Which certainly confirmed Thomas' status as a prodigy but didn't answer her question. There was something about the young man that piqued her curiosity. While she had nothing against secrets in general, she objected to not being in on them.

A cop car came around the corner ahead of them. Sidestep tensed, his grip growing tight on hers. She gave the police officers a sedate wave—*we're unimportant, nothing to see here*—and watched as it cruised on past.

The sound of sirens faded behind them as they walked. She made sure to turn a few corners so that when (not if) the cops in the first car discovered they'd been steered wrongly, it would take them longer to cover all the possible ways she and Sidestep could've gone. It didn't take long before they came out from between two shops into the Market area proper. Enough people were walking back and forth here that a woman and a teenage boy were entirely unremarkable.

She made sure to keep an eye on the sky as they headed back toward the Oaklands. The occasional hex showed up, but they were all moving fast, heading across the sky in the direction of the debacle outside the warehouse. To her expert eye, nothing swerved in their direction or even slowed to look at them.

"So how are they doing?" she asked in a low tone as they neared the entrance to the Oaklands courtyard.

"Getting pretty close," he said. "PA's had to EMP two of those bug-things, but Gimmick wiped their memories so's they don't recall sensing anything strange after they wake up. She says they're real stupid, anyway."

"Good." As she led the way into the courtyard, she adjusted her clothing to become a brightly patterned T-shirt and stylish jeans. Considering her options, she went into the reception office. "Hi, Stacey," she said cheerfully, using the same body language as before.

"Oh, hello again." Stacey beamed to see her. "That's a nice outfit. How can I help you?"

"Thanks. Just so you know, I've invited a few friends up to my apartment, if that's okay?"

"Oh, sure." Stacey nodded earnestly. "Just so long as you don't have any loud parties or stuff like that, mmkay?"

Chelsea chuckled. "Oh, you'll hardly know we were there." Giving Stacey one of her feel-good smiles, she left the office and gathered in Sidestep by eye. Together, they crossed the courtyard and took the elevator up to her floor.

It was odd to know that their every step (more or less) was being relayed to the Survivors by Sidestep's other aspect. Fortunately, it was well within her capabilities to ignore that knowledge and act normally until they got to her door. Swiping the reader, she led the way inside, then let the door swing shut. "How long?" she asked. While she was tempted to plop down on the sofa and let the tensions of the day drain out of her, she knew all too well that it wasn't over yet.

Sidestep tilted his head slightly. "Thomas says five minutes. It'd be less, but Ray still needs to change."

She bit her lip. It would be heartbreaking for things to go catastrophically wrong, this late in the game. They didn't even need someone to screw up; an eagle-eyed police officer at the wrong place or time could make all the difference. This was why she preferred to work alone. Any problems were hers and hers alone to deal with.

Time ticked by. She restrained the impulse to pace back and forth, or to ask Sidestep for an update on the situation. If something went wrong, he'd tell her. If nothing was amiss, she'd just be needlessly bugging him.

Something else occurred to her. Blades, at least, would need to come in through the courtyard. The artificer had come in before with Thomas; that was easy enough. But while having the other three come through as well probably wouldn't raise any immediate red flags with the staff at the Oaklands, it would definitely jump out at any pattern-matching software the police put it through.

Thomas would be more careful than that ... wouldn't he?

There was a knock on the door.

She glanced at Sidestep. He headed over and yanked the door open. His other self was standing there, with Thomas beside him. Behind them both was Blades in her chair, with her INCH bag on her lap. Gimmick and Ray, both in ordinary clothing, filled out the group.

"Excuse me, ma'am," Thomas said politely. "I'm looking for an international woman of mystery?"

Chelsea rolled her eyes, a flood of relief washing through her. "Oh, get in here, you clown."

50
This, Too, Shall Pass

Hansen Family Home
Savannah, Georgia
Tuesday, October 8, 2013
5:45 PM, Eastern Daylight Time

Jericho held still while his mother ran a concerned eye over him. "Are you sure you're up to this, honey?" A slender, fine-boned woman, Dahlia Hansen was still good-looking at forty-five. Jericho had gotten his build, most of his features and his hair color from her. His height and jawline had come from his father, who was as heavy-set as Leroy, if not as broad across the shoulders.

"I'm sure, Mama." He didn't mean to be so curt, but he'd had enough of the thousand subtle hints that he should be locking himself in his bedroom and suffering in silence, rather than coming out in public to hurt himself all over again. Everyone knew how close he and Luke had been, but secluding himself out of sight and mind was not the way to fix the ever-present ache in his chest. That could only be done by going back to Utopia City and getting his hands on Jack Portman. "I need to go. Show myself. I heard there's folks that think I was killed too. This is the best way to put that sort of thing to rest."

"All right." Again, he heard the doubtful tone. "Just remember, you can leave at any time if you think it's getting too much for you." Manufacturing a smile, she laid a gentle hand on his shoulder. "Nobody will think the less of you for it."

Except that everyone is already judging me in some way. "I have to go. Show my face. Be there for him, like he'd be there for me." It was the simple truth. No matter what else they thought of him—sissy, wimp, whiny kid, whatever—if he did not show up to his kinsman's wake and pay his respects, they would all think the less of him afterward. *He* would think the less of himself afterward. They'd smile to his face and make excuses about the ordeal he'd gone through, but word would get around that Jericho Hansen had folded when it came to the crunch. *They'd say I couldn't even man up and go to the wake. And they'd be right.*

He adjusted his tie, making sure that his collar sat correctly around it. While he would not be alone in sporting such neckwear—his father would be wearing one, along with several other attendees—he would be in the minority. That didn't bother him; he'd been in a minority for a good portion of his life. He wasn't wearing it for them, and he wasn't wearing it for himself. Luke deserved all the respect Jericho could show him, and taking pride in his appearance for the wake was a good start toward showing that respect.

There was a knock on his door, but it opened before he could make any sort of reply. His father leaned in, already speaking. "Hey, boy, have you seen—ah, there you are, honeybunch. Been looking high and low for you." His eyes went to Jericho. "Ready to go, son?"

A smile creased Beauregard Hansen's face as he looked at his wife and son, but Jericho could still see the pain in his eyes. It was the same pain he saw when he looked in the mirror.

"Yeah, Pa. I'm ready." Jericho stepped aside to allow his mother to precede him, then pulled his hair back and slipped a neat black tie over it. On the way out of the room, he took up the large envelope and the USB drive that lay on the dresser. The latter he slipped into his pocket, while he kept the former in hand. It had taken him all of five minutes that morning to download the email Smokeshadow had sent him and load the files onto the drive; an empty one he'd found in his father's desk drawer. Then he went further afield and did some research into the movements of Enabled in surrounding cities; one in particular. What he found saddened him but didn't surprise him, not after what Luke had told him.

He took one last look around the room before he closed the door behind him. In the year and a half he'd been living away from home, they'd kept it exactly the same, leaving everything precisely where it was. The suit he was wearing had been hanging in his closet, likewise untouched. It wasn't the best he owned, but his best was at Stephen's apartment, and he didn't feel up to that specific confrontation quite yet.

As if in response to his thought, his phone began to buzz. He took it from his pocket and checked it. Stephen again. He didn't know who'd told his boyfriend he was back in town, but he had declined a dozen calls and chosen not to read three times that many text messages since getting off the train.

In point of fact, not dealing with Stephen was becoming more stressful than dealing with his parents. They were aware he was gay, but not that he'd been living with someone, much less an older man. Whichever reason they'd had for not pressing for any details, he was grateful.

Yet again, he swiped left to decline the call, and put the phone back in his pocket. He didn't know what he was going to do about Stephen, or even what he was going to say. *I know you cheated on me. You cheated on me; we're through. Stop calling me; you're no longer my boyfriend.* It was all true, but none of it felt *right*.

"Who was that calling, boy?" Walking ahead, Beau Hansen directed the question back over his shoulder.

"Nobody important." Jericho couldn't figure out how to answer the question in such a way that would satisfy his parents without opening a whole new can of worms. All other things aside, neither one of them was likely to react well on hearing that their son had been cheated on by his boyfriend. For no other reason than to avert the inevitable shitstorm, he felt justified in not telling them anything at all.

"Suit yourself." Beau led the way out to the car and opened the passenger side front door for Dahlia. Jericho opened the rear door and got in, then fastened his seat belt. Truth be told, he wasn't looking forward to attending the wake, but he knew he damn well had to. He *needed* to. Grieving for Luke wasn't a once-and-done proposition; he would be missing his cousin for the rest of his life. He'd heard the pain of such a loss faded over time, but he had yet to see the truth in that.

Few words passed between them for the first few minutes. Jericho leaned back and looked out the window, trying to relax in peace and quiet. Once they got there, he knew he'd have precious little time to keep himself centered.

In the driver's seat, Beau cleared his throat in his inimitable 'I have something to say' manner. "Son, I have to ask. Why in blue blazes did you even go to that goddamn city—"

"Language, dear," interrupted Jericho's mother.

"Sorry, hon." Beau tried again. "Son, why did you go along to Utopia City, and why did you take Luke with you?"

Jericho took a deep breath. He didn't want to lie to his folks, but while he'd tried to inform them in the past that he had powers (failing mainly due to nerves), now was definitely not the time to heap that information on top of everything else that was happening. The fact that he didn't want to talk about it at *all* didn't help.

"I told you before, I wanted a change of scenery," he said. "There's jobs going there all the time." He carefully did not disclaim responsibility for dragging Luke to Utopia City; he *was* basically the reason Luke had gone, even if his cousin had had his own reasons at the time.

"Hm." Despite Jericho's desire for Beauregard to let the matter rest, his father only paused for a few moments before speaking up again. "If you wanted a better job, you could've come to me. The head of our social media news division has been looking for an intern. I can move some people around—"

"And I'd be the guy who got his place 'cause his daddy owns the company." Jericho shook his head, not caring that his father couldn't see him. "I'm not about to push someone else aside who's more qualified, just because I'm related to you. I don't want to be known as the boss's son. I want to make my own way." *And how's that working out for me right now?* Biting his lip, he stared out the car window. Feeling stifled, he buzzed the window down.

"He has a point." His mother's voice was gentle but firm. "It's always a risk to break away and go where you think you'll do better, but sometimes the risk is worth the reward." It wasn't as though his father could argue; after moving from New York, his mother had used her own money to establish a now-thriving law firm in Atlanta. "Which reminds me, honey. I do have some entry-level positions opening up if you wanted—"

Jericho sighed. "Thanks, but no thanks, Mama." Far from neglecting him, his parents seemed intent on inflicting on him a surfeit of support, most of which involved keeping him safe, right where they could see him. The trouble was, it wasn't the kind of support that he needed right then. "I appreciate it, but—"

"I understand." His mother turned in her seat to smile back at him. "The offer's open if you ever change your mind."

"Let the boy be, Dahlia," Beau stated from the driver's seat. "He needs room to make his own decisions." He seemed sublimely unaware that he'd been just as ready to chart out Jericho's life for him, only a few moments before.

Diplomatically, Jericho chose not to point this out. He leaned back in his seat and looked out the window again as his parents chatted in low tones about inconsequential matters. In an effort to distract himself from where he was going, he found himself comparing Savannah to Utopia City.

Until he'd been shown the alternative, he hadn't known there could *be* an alternative. Just as he was picturing how Savannah would go with having solar-panel paved streets and cars with magnetic levitation, a truck passed them with gray-black exhaust belching from its smokestack. Even though only a little got to him, he coughed as the harsh fumes stung his throat. *If I'm like this after one day there, what would it be like for someone who decides to visit friends after living there for years? They'd think they're back in the nineteen twenties or something.*

It was a sobering thought, and probably another reason that people who lived in Utopia City preferred to stay there. Just taking the maglev there was the best possible advertisement the city could have.

The car left the main road and cruised down quiet tree-lined streets to a house with which Jericho was already very familiar. It wasn't the house Uncle Leroy and Aunt Ellie had moved into when they first returned to Savannah; *that* one had been partially subsidized by Jericho's parents. This one, a sight larger, had been purchased when Jericho was fourteen. Though the bank loan they'd taken out to buy it was still being paid off, the house itself was theirs. Leroy had adamantly refused to allow his brother to help pay for the house, though he'd grudgingly allowed Beau and Dahlia to stand as guarantors for the loan.

Black streamers had been fastened all the way along the front fence, with sprays of flowers at each post providing a sharp contrast. The simple front gate had been transformed into an archway, with more streamers and flowers. Jericho wasn't familiar with this aspect of funeral preparation, but he suspected that some florist somewhere had been cleaned out of a certain type of bloom.

Cars were parked up and down the street, and Jericho wondered exactly how far they'd be walking to get back to the wake. His mother murmured something that he didn't catch, but it must have been something along those lines, because his father shook his head. "I called ahead," he said confidently. "Leroy said we could park in the driveway."

Suiting action to word, Beau turned the wheel and eased the car into the driveway that led up alongside the house, behind the 4×4 that already stood there. Once his father had pulled to a halt and turned off the engine, Jericho got out and opened his mother's door for her. With murmured thanks, she emerged from the vehicle as gracefully as a movie star climbing out of a limousine.

"Dahlia, Beau, Jericho. So good y'all could come." The voice belonged to Aunt Ellie, Luke's mother. A handsome middle-aged African American woman, she was dressed all in black with a tiny matching veil over her eyes. She hugged Dahlia, then embraced Jericho in his turn. Just for a moment, the achingly familiar scents of powder and perfume transported him back to younger and happier days, being greeted at the door with a hug from Aunt Ellie before going to play with Luke. The association was so strong that he choked up all over again.

"Is it true?" she whispered; her voice ragged with unshed tears. "Did he really throw hisself in the way of the knife to save you?"

Barely able to speak, he shook his head. "No," he managed. "I'd gone out for a walk. It was Bobbi. He tried to save Bobbi."

Slowly, she released him then took him by the shoulders and looked him in the eye. "Who-all's this Bobbi, anyways?" she asked, eyes narrowing slightly. "Leroy mentioned her name, but I couldn't get no kind of a straight answer out of him about her."

Jericho shook his head again. "A lady we met on the train. She was going to Utopia City too, so we went thirds in temporary accommodation to save money. That's all." With the back of his hand, he scrubbed at the tears standing in his eyes. "Listen, can I just go inside for a bit?"

"You go right on ahead." Ellie was all concern now. "If you need to lie down a spell, feel free to use the master bedroom."

Jericho didn't think he'd quite need that, but he thanked her anyway. As he headed past his aunt toward the house, he saw several of his younger cousins talking among themselves. Like him, the teenagers were all gussied up for the wake; boys and girls both. Unlike him, he was willing to bet it was parental decree and not personal choice that had led to their careful grooming. While he knew and got along with all of them fairly well, he didn't feel overly sociable at the moment, so he gave them a nod and murmur of greeting as he went on into the house.

Ellie had always been house-proud, but the level of cleanliness that greeted him as he stepped over the threshold went all the way to the next level and beyond. The floor had been swept and mopped, the walls scrubbed and the silverware on display polished to a fine gleam. The curtains looked as though they'd been laundered and possibly ironed as well. But that wasn't what gave him pause.

What hit him right between the eyes was that virtually every flat surface in the living room held a picture of Luke with a black ribbon folded over one corner: a grinning gap-toothed Luke at age ten, proudly astride his brand-new bicycle; Luke at age twelve with his arm around a seven year old Jericho; Luke at thirteen, hamming it up behind the wheel of Leroy's truck; a sixteen year old Luke leaning on the door of his own car; Luke graduating from high school at seventeen; the selfie he'd taken with Luke at his own graduation, five years later; Luke's wedding photos with Olivia …

Jericho stumbled away, fighting against the treacherous tears. Everywhere he looked was another memory, striking to his heart. He'd been there for every photo, either in it or pulling faces to try to make Luke laugh. Luke had been his confidant, his stalwart defender, his cousin and best friend. It was too much. *I was wrong. I'm not ready for this.*

Entering the dining room, he saw that the table was cluttered in a way entirely foreign to Ellie's normal neatness, though apropos to the current situation. As a centerpiece was a photo of Luke, taken not so long ago outside the garage where he worked. This picture, blown up to letter size, was housed in a gleaming gold-plated frame, against which the black ribbon stood out starkly. Jericho's heart seized up all over again at the look of carefree happiness on his cousin's face as he clowned around with his workmates.

Around the picture were tributes to Luke from his friends and relatives. A small teddy-bear, one he thought he recognized as coming from Serena's extensive collection, lay next to a blank car key attached to a magnificent Ford Mustang keyring, probably from Leroy. Cards littered the table here and there, reminding him of the envelope he was still holding in his hand. With a spasmodic motion, he put it on the table, tucking it under the teddy-bear.

When Leroy spoke from behind him, he jumped. "What's that, boy?"

Jericho shook his head as he turned to face his uncle. "I … it's something … when I went out, I met … I asked for it. Before everything happened." He felt wretched, just trying to explain the sequence of events.

"Lemme see." Taking up the envelope, Leroy opened the flap and slid the photo out. As he took in the picture, his eyes widened. Slowly, he whistled. "*Dang*, boy. You jes' *full* of surprises. She sign that herself?"

"Yeah, she was nice. Pretty sure she signed it." Jericho shrugged. "She left it at the desk for me. I just thought … well, I knew Luke would've liked it. I got it for him, so it's his. It should go with him."

"Damn straight he woulda liked it. It woulda been framed and gone up on the goddamn wall, is what he woulda done with it." Leroy looked the photo over again and shook his head slowly. "Want I should leave it in the envelope, or out?"

"Leave it in," Jericho said hastily. "Too many questions, otherwise. I don't want to show it off; I just want Luke to have it."

Leroy sighed, quite clearly torn between the desire to display the photo of Transit, and his understanding of Jericho's need for privacy. "Yeah, you're right," he said eventually. "Pity, though. There's men in this town would give their back teeth to get their hands on that sweet piece." Reluctantly, he slid the photo back into the envelope and put it back where it had been.

"Are you talking about her or the bike?" Jericho was pretty sure he knew what Leroy's answer would be, but he asked the question anyway.

"Pretty much whatever you think, boy." Leroy eyed him keenly. "You look like shit. You git any sleep last night?"

"Some." Jericho half-shrugged. He knew the twenty minutes of sleep he'd managed wasn't enough, not by a long shot. But it was all his churning brain had allowed him, once he was alone.

It was the downside of being a prodigy. His sense of duty toward Luke was pushing him toward resolving what had happened to his cousin, and not letting him rest until he did something about it. While his powerset allowed him to function without the missed sleep, it was in no way pleasant. The fact that he considered the need to attend Luke's funeral to be more important in the short term cut no ice with his subconscious. In the end, he'd costumed up and gone out and about, patrolling the neighborhood just to do *something*. It hadn't really helped, though he'd gotten in some quality brooding time on a convenient rooftop.

Back home after spending a couple of hours scouting the local area (and finding nothing worth taking out his inner turmoil on) he'd spent the rest of the night sitting up and reading from the selection of books he'd kept in his room. This had served to pass the time, though he couldn't help but wonder how he'd ever considered those books his favorites. The plots were shallow, the protagonists vapid and naïve, and of course he already knew how they ended.

But there was no way he could explain any of this to Leroy. For one thing, it would take too long and someone might overhear the wrong thing at the wrong moment; for another, he wasn't at all sure Leroy would understand the inner conflict of being a prodigy. Of always feeling as though there was a certain level of competence he was expected to meet, that he was forever failing to achieve.

Leroy eyed him keenly. "Seems to me—" But whatever observation he was about to make went by the wayside as Olivia entered the room, with Serena close behind her.

"*There* you are." Dressed all in black, with a veil that did nothing to hide her resolute expression, Olivia marched up to Jericho. Serena, a year younger but just as determined, matched her pace. "There's folks out there sayin' stuff that just cain't be right. I want to know the truth."

"Absolutely," agreed Serena. Reaching out, she tapped Jericho in the middle of the chest with a single knuckle, her signal for as long as he'd known her to show how serious she was. "I *know* you, Jericho Hansen. Give it to us straight."

Faced with the girl he'd considered his sister in all but name for most of his life, and the one who'd begun to aspire to that status since her marriage to Luke, Jericho had no way out. He looked to Leroy, who grimaced.

"Listen, girls, mebbe this ain't th' right time—" his uncle demurred.

"If it's not the right time, Daddy, when's it ever going to be?" demanded Serena. "When stuff like this happens, it's always *oh, it's too soon to do anything about it* and then *it's too late to worry your pretty little head about it.* We want to know, *now*. Before it starts spreading too far."

Jericho took a deep breath. Serena had always been his best gal pal. They'd watched chick-flicks together, traded observations on boys (once he came out), and generally been there for one another in the ways that Luke was unequipped to handle. If anyone deserved the truth, whatever she wanted to know about; she did. And Olivia was Luke's widow; he wasn't going to lie to her about anything substantial. "What do you want to know?"

Olivia set her jaw in a way that made it look as though she were bracing herself for an unpleasant revelation. "They's sayin' Luke was shacked up in a motel room with a strange woman. That her husband came in and found 'em together, so he killed 'em."

What the—how in God's name did that *crock of shit get out there?* Unfortunately, Jericho felt he knew the answer. The group of cousins he'd seen talking together must have overheard some of what he said to his aunt, then filled in the gaps for maximum shock value. There was no meanness to it—at least, he *hoped* it was down to sensationalism and not meanness—but he had to lock this shit down *fast*.

"He wasn't cheating on you," he said bluntly. "Luke and I were saving money by sharing an apartment with a lady we met on the train; two bedrooms and a fold-out sofa. Luke had the sofa. I went out for some air. The lady's name was Bobbi. Her asshat boyfriend showed up, high on meth. He had a knife. Anything else you want to know?"

They both blinked at him, and he realized with a start that he'd been using his 'G-Man voice', the one he habitually utilized to make him sound more impressive when in costume. Thinking back, he tried to recall if he'd ever had a TV interview that had made it all the way to the nightly news. Of course, he had no way of knowing if the girls even watched the news with any sort of regularity. Or if they'd noticed the change in his voice at all.

"Right, wow. Okay." Serena tilted her head, as if looking at Jericho in a new light. "Yeah, I'm satisfied. Livy, you good?"

"Uh huh." Abruptly, Olivia hugged him. "Thanks. For giving me the truth."

"You deserved to know." He returned the hug. Warm tears soaked through his suit coat from where her face rested against his shoulder. This wasn't something he could blame her for; his own tears were threatening to fall again, soon. "I'm sorry I couldn't have been there."

"You need to cut that shit out right now, boy." Leroy's large hand closed over Jericho's bicep. "'Scuse me, ladies. Need to go talk some sense into this dumbass bonehead."

Jericho let Olivia go and allowed Leroy to haul him away down the corridor, toward where Jericho knew Leroy had his office. The girls watched him go, concern etched on their features.

"Now you listen to me, boy." As they reached the office door, Leroy raised his voice; Jericho figured this was to ensure Serena and Olivia had no doubt he was being thoroughly read the riot act. "Some meth-head psycho comes at you with a knife, he don't care if there's two or three or *ten* of ya ..." Opening the door, Leroy dragged Jericho inside, then shut the door behind them. Letting the rant trail off, he released Jericho's arm and heaved a sigh, looking as though he'd just aged twenty years. "Think they bought it?"

"Guess so." Jericho shrugged. "Serena'll probably be snarky at you for yelling at me, but she'll get over it. Why did you need me in here ... ah." Remembering, he dived into his pocket and retrieved the USB drive.

"Thank Christ. For a second there, I thought you'd forgotten all about it." Leroy took the drive and went around behind his desk. From what Jericho could tell, his uncle's office was less richly appointed than his father's study, but only by a matter of degree. There was a computer, a printer and a bar fridge. Which, as far as Jericho could tell, covered the essentials.

Dropping into the chair with a sound of air escaping from upholstery, Leroy hit the button to boot up his computer. Jericho hooked a chair over with his foot and sat down as well. It was nice to be in a quiet place again; one where he didn't have to think about what was going on in the outside world.

The computer didn't take long to get up and running, and Leroy inserted the drive. He pulled the files off it, then looked queryingly at Jericho. "What did you want done with the thumb drive?"

"Wipe it for me, please." If he put it back where he'd found it, with no signs of the files that had been on it, nobody would be the wiser.

"Easy peasy." Leroy clicked the mouse. "Huh. Dunno who it was that sent you these files, but they know their shit. Got pictures, details, the whole nine. This is gonna be a fuckin' cakewalk."

"Good to hear." A moment later, the printer on the end of the desk started whirring as a sheet of paper extended out of the slot. Just touching the edges, Jericho took it up, only to find that it was stiffer and glossier than he'd been expecting. The pictures of the Survivors, taken against a white background, looked remarkably sharp and detailed. He'd seen genuine ID photos that looked less professional. All Leroy was going to have to do was cut them out. And in fact, there was a professional-looking paper guillotine on the shelf behind him. "Nice paper."

"Photo quality." Leroy's tone was off-handed. "Comes in right handy, on occasion."

"I bet." Jericho dropped the sheet onto the desk and stood up, choosing not to speculate as to why his uncle just happened to have high-quality photographic paper on hand to load into his printer at short notice. "Did you need me for anything else?"

"Nope. I got this handled." Leroy pulled the drive from its slot and handed it back to Jericho. "All yours, boy."

"Thanks." Jericho slid it into his pocket and made a mental note to replace it in his father's desk drawer. "I appreciate this."

"No problems." Leroy looked up at Jericho, his expression speculative. "Jes' make sure you don't go usin' that there tone o' voice where any of my guys can hear it. Some o' them mighta run into G-Man once or twice, an' I can guarantee you they will *not* have forgotten the experience."

So, of course *Leroy* had picked up on his slip. "Yeah. Won't happen again." Jericho opened the office door and stepped out into the corridor. Drawing a deep breath, he started toward the front of the house, steeling himself against the impending emotional pit-traps he knew were awaiting him.

At the last minute, in a ploy to put off the inevitable for a little longer, he detoured to the bathroom and splashed water on his face. Leaning on the basin, he stared at himself in the mirror. *Stop being such a chickenshit*, he told his reflection, echoing Luke's voice in his head. Shit had happened. There had been consequences. As much as he might want to turn back time, he couldn't. He didn't want to be here, but he couldn't *not* be here. He owed it to Ellie, he owed it to Leroy; but most of all, he owed it to Luke.

Feeling a little more on top of his problems, he ventured out. More people were arriving now, and food was being ferried through the house into the backyard. He followed along, to find that a long table had been set up under a pavilion for the food, with a couple of barbecues beyond. The latter had already been fired up, and aromatic smoke was wafting through the evening air. Folding chairs and tables were arranged around the back yard under the darkening sky, so that people could sit and eat at their leisure.

But the black streamers were omnipresent here as well, and pictures of Luke had been affixed to the upright pavilion poles. Every time he looked at them, he was reminded once more of the many good times he'd had with his cousin. These memories led inexorably to what had happened next and he had to turn away, sick at heart.

Soft music began playing over portable speakers. It matched the mood of the gathering; somber, though leavened with a tinge of lightness. Everyone knew Luke was gone, but at the same time as they were mourning his loss, they were also celebrating his life. Intellectually, Jericho knew that; in time, he knew he'd probably come to accept it. But right then, he was too close to matters to be able to look away from the darkness and be comforted by the light. *If I'd just been there, Luke would be alive now.*

From a distance, he watched as Olivia moved through the gathering. She seemed to be effortlessly in control, but under her veil he could see the tightness around her eyes that bespoke a deeper hurt than even Jericho held in his heart. Around her clustered family and friends, offering comfort and assistance; none of which would do her a damn bit of good right now, but which she'd need in time.

Feeling like the ghost at the banquet—and wasn't *that* an appropriate metaphor—Jericho lingered at the edges of the throng. The few people who approached him only seemed to want to talk about Luke's supposed infidelities; he was polite to them, but he squashed those rumors hard.

The food smelled good; folks had brought over all the staple delicacies, and eventually his rumbling stomach pushed him to have some. There were several jugs of iced tea, so he picked one at random and poured half a glass full. Drinking it, he detected a bite which suggested someone had added a custom kick, possibly tequila. He was more a beer man, but anything that put more distance between him and the rest of the world seemed a good idea, so he refilled the glass and loaded a paper plate with devilled eggs, chicken casserole and a large dollop of goulash.

Sitting and eating was a mundane enough occupation that he managed to stave off the darkness threatening to permeate his every thought. He also didn't mind the spiked iced tea; his Prodigy rating gave him a good head for alcohol, but with a little effort he was still able to get a pleasant buzz on. Sitting, eating, drinking, looking around at his assembled family and friends, he was almost starting to feel at ease when Daryl approached him.

"Hey, Jericho," he said diffidently. "Don't wanna bother ya, but do you know some fat little git with a faggy little red beard? 'Cause there's someone like that at the front gate lookin' for you."

Oh, for crying out loud. There wasn't anyone else it could be. Just for a moment, he considered disclaiming all knowledge of Stephen, knowing full well that the guys on the gate would probably rough him up a mite before tossing him out on his ear. But he didn't want to find out how far Stephen would push things; he, of all people, knew how persistent the older man could be. If the cops got called on the gathering, for instance, it probably wouldn't go anywhere but it would certainly disrupt the proceedings.

Jericho sighed and stood up. "I'll go see what he wants." His gaze met Daryl's. "Just by the way, seriously? 'Faggy'? You do know I'm gay, right?"

From the look on Daryl's face, he'd known but had not yet made the mental connection between that and what he'd said. "Oh. Shit. Sorry."

"Don't be sorry. Be better." Jericho patted Daryl on the shoulder and moved past him, leaving the food and drink on the table. With the advent of Stephen at the wake, his appetite had vanished anyway. If it was there when he got back, it would be there. If not, it didn't matter.

He'd spent the longest time going over this confrontation in his head, figuring out how and where he'd approach Stephen on the topic. It had to be handled with the utmost of delicacy, he knew, or Stephen would fly right off the handle. The last thing he'd expected was for Stephen to bring the confrontation to him. *But if it's gonna be, it's gotta be now.*

Rather than draw attention by going through the house, Jericho went down along the side fence. As he emerged into the front yard, he heard Stephen's voice;

normally high-pitched and querulous when he was agitated, it seemed as though his boyfriend was going for a record.

"I know he's in there! If you don't let me in to see him, I'll be calling the police! Do you really want that?"

As Jericho got closer to the gate, he recognized Leroy standing there. The big man's entire posture shouted that he desperately wanted to punch someone. "One more time," Leroy was in the process of saying, clearly working to keep his temper. "This here's a private party. Who is an' isn't here ain't none of your beeswax. Now *fuck off*, before I really get mad."

"But I—" As Jericho got closer, Stephen leaned around Leroy's bulk and spotted him. Immediately, his tone changed, becoming more imperious. "Jericho! Tell this Neanderthal to let me in! I have to speak with you!"

Leroy turned to look incredulously at Jericho. "You *know* this little shit?"

Jericho sighed. "Yeah, I know him. Uncle Leroy, this is Stephen LaMonde, Stephen, meet Leroy Hansen. Leroy, I'll deal with this." Moving up to the gate, he opened it and stepped through.

"That's your *uncle?*" When not dealing with prospective subjects for **Gay!Power**, Stephen's social skills were sometimes rather hit and miss. "But he's—"

Jericho cut in before Stephen said something that *would* get him punched. "He's Luke's daddy. Now, come on. You didn't come here to talk about him." Taking hold of Stephen's elbow, he steered his boyfriend (or ex-boyfriend, once it became official) away from the gate. Lowering his voice in the hopes that those behind him would not overhear his words, he hissed, "What are you *doing* here? This is a private function, and I know for a *fact* you weren't invited."

Far from being offended by the question, Stephen puffed his chest out proudly. This made him look faintly ridiculous, but Jericho wasn't paying attention to that. "I've got contacts everywhere," he boasted. "I knew you'd come back for the funeral, and I knew there'd be a wake first, so I asked around. And here I am." He turned his attention to Jericho and his expression hardened, as much as it was able to. "What *I* want to know is, why didn't you invite me? Aren't I good enough to be here with you? Are you here with someone else?" His eyes opened wide, almost theatrically so. "I was right, wasn't I? You met someone there! Did you bring him back with you? How did you sneak him back into town? I was waiting outside the maglev station for *hours* yesterday!"

Prior to his experiences in Utopia City, Jericho would've been on the defensive at this point. He could never argue with Stephen without feeling as though he were somehow in the wrong, even when he wasn't. But the sheer amount of projection involved with Stephen's wild accusation made him grit his teeth. *He did it, now he's saying I'm doing it? Where the hell does he get off with that?*

"Okay, first, that's just a little bit stalkerish, isn't it?" Jericho could tell that Stephen had been expecting him to back down and apologize for basically everything; instead, his harsh tone rocked the older man back on his heels just a little. Not giving Stephen a chance to muster a response, he kept talking. "Second, Leroy and I came back with Luke's coffin, and we got off on the cargo platform. Yeah, the maglev's got a cargo platform. Nobody else came back with us. And third, I did not goddamn well hook up with anyone while I was there!" He'd done his best to keep his voice down but from Stephen's expression of shock, he may as well have screamed the last few words at the top of his lungs.

"But ... *why*, then?" pleaded Stephen. "Why haven't you been answering your phone? I've called you, I've texted you, I've put messages on all your social media. Why are you shutting me out? Why are you cutting me off like this?"

Jericho shook his head slowly. He hadn't even considered looking at social media since he'd gotten back. Now, knowing what would be waiting for him, the thought made him cringe. "Because I can't deal with it, right now. I can't deal with …" *The fact that you cheated on me.* "… us." It was the last hurdle he had to cross, and he just couldn't make himself go there. On the one hand, he *knew* Stephen had been unfaithful, but on the other, he'd had eighteen months of happiness with the man. Undoubtedly some of that happiness had been counterfeit, while Stephen screwed around behind his back, but still …

"Well, when *will* you be able to deal with it?" demanded Stephen. "After the wake? After the funeral? You can't put us on hold forever, you know. Whatever's bothering you, we can deal with it. Together." His expression softened and he held his hand out. "Come home. After this is over, come home."

Jericho grimaced. It was almost tempting, but his resolve was rock-solid. His Prodigy rating wouldn't let it be any other way. "After the funeral, I'm going back to Utopia City." He hesitated, not wanting to say *to hunt down the bastard who killed Luke* out loud.

Before he could think of something to say in its place, Stephen took advantage of the opening. "No! You can't! I won't let you!"

"You won't *let* me?" Jericho stared at the older man. He had no idea how Stephen intended to prevent him from going. The idea of physical force was laughable, and his inconstant lover had long since squandered any claim to the moral high ground.

Stephen jutted out his chin. "If you go back, we're *through!* I'll know you don't love me anymore!" Folding his arms, he took on an expression of triumph.

Despite his own resolve, despite knowing how this had to go, Jericho felt a lurch in his stomach as Stephen threw the words at him. This, then, was the nuclear option. In all their arguments, even in that last phone call before he got on the maglev, Stephen had never gone quite so far as to threaten to break up with him. Never in his wildest imaginings had he thought the other man might go there. Still, this was his best chance to do what needed to be done.

"No." He shook his head, fully aware that Stephen's words had only been a bluff. What he said next … wasn't. "We're already through. We were through the day you stepped out on me. I just didn't know it at the time."

It wasn't the first time he'd said those words; he'd rehearsed them over and over in private, trying to find a way to say them that felt *right*. But speaking them out loud to Stephen's face and *meaning* them was a whole new ball game. The knowledge of this sent a chill over his skin, as though he'd just plunged into a pool of icy water. Adrenaline surged through his system and his heart rate increased. *What's going to happen now? How's he going to take me knowing about it?*

Stephen took no more than a moment to react. Staring at Jericho as if he'd gone insane, he shook his head. "What are you talking about? I've *never* done that."

He was better at lying than Jericho had ever given him credit for. If it was anyone else who'd spilled the beans about Stephen's infidelity, doubts would have overtaken Jericho at the sheer sincerity inherent in the denial. But it had been Luke and, as he'd assured his cousin himself, no matter what other bullshit the man had ever pulled, Jericho trusted him implicitly to not lie about the important stuff. *And Luke knew how important Stephen was to me.*

"Really." By now, Jericho was treading ground he'd never thought he would have to cover. His brain felt divorced from the rest of his body, as if he were operating his mouth via remote control. "Three days, Stephen. You took *three days* for each trip out and back. On the bus, I can maybe see it. But on the maglev? Eight hours to cross the *country*. What were you doing the rest of the time? Cruising gay bars? Spending all day in bed with them? Nude photo sessions?"

He'd just been shooting in the dark, but he caught the fractional shift of Stephen's eyes. "My God, you *were* taking nude photos of them, weren't you? What the *hell*, Stephen?"

That minor point of contention between them had been long since resolved, or so Jericho had thought. He recalled Stephen's efforts to try to get him to pose for photos like that; efforts he'd turned down. Stephen had accepted his decision (albeit with bad grace), and he'd thought the matter closed. Apparently, such had not been the case.

His problem wasn't with people, Enabled or otherwise, choosing to have such photos taken. What people did with their bodies was their business. It was with Stephen, choosing to take risqué pictures of other men without so much as giving Jericho the heads-up that he was doing it. *Why* Stephen had done it that way was abundantly clear; he was cheating on Jericho at the same time. But even if he hadn't been, it would've still amounted to a huge betrayal of trust. Now, it was just the icing on the infidelity cake. *When your house is on fire, you don't worry about the firemen trampling your prize flowerbed.*

Stephen was definitely rattled now, from the way his eyes flicked from side to side more noticeably. He was still in control of his wits, though. "I have *no* idea what you're talking about." Leaning forward, he sniffed at Jericho's breath. "I *thought* so. You've been drinking. Come on; you don't know what you're talking about. Let's go home. You'll feel better in the morning." Reaching out, he took Jericho by the arm, gently trying to guide him away from the house.

"You have to be kidding." Jericho pulled free of Stephen's grasp. "One drink is not gonna cut it." He shook his head. "You're not getting it. I *know* you've been stepping out on me. Luke caught you at it, or don't you remember the time he near on put you in the hospital?"

That got a reaction. Just for a moment, Stephen's concerned act slipped, and Jericho saw the residual anger and fear. Then the older man's expression closed up again, and he blinked at Jericho. "I'm sorry? *Luke* said he put me in the hospital? I'm sure I would've remembered *that*."

Jericho leaned in, invading Stephen's personal space in a way that he hoped was intimidating. "Cut the shit. I said 'near on'. Luke told me where he was and what he was doing when he caught you fooling around on me. He *also* said he had his guys beat the crap out of the other guy. Fly Boy. Remember him?" It was what he'd been checking up on, earlier in the day.

Stephen stepped back. "I remember the name," he huffed, transitioning to 'affronted'. "I wrote up an article on him the day before I was attacked. By people who were *not* Luke."

"Funny thing." Normally, Jericho would've been smiling as he closed in for the kill. Right now, he didn't feel like it. "I checked up on that. Fly Boy was off the streets for a good month following that night. Only started showing up again about a week ago. Almost as if he'd had the shit kicked out of him, and he took a while to recover. That's a pretty strong coincidence, don't you think?" He pointed back into the houseyard. "I figure I could ask around and find four or five people who could give me all the details of what happened that night. But I won't. Because you're just the sort of vindictive asshat that would have them arrested and prosecuted, even though they never laid a hand on you. Or I could go to Augusta and ask Fly Boy myself. But I don't have to. I believe what Luke said, implicitly. And I've just realized one other thing."

Stephen's lips were pressed together so tightly that they were showing white. "What's that?" His voice was barely audible.

"You're not my Vicki Vale. You never were." Jericho shook his head slowly. "I can't believe it took me more than a year to work it out. You've been Trevoring me, the whole time. Luke could see it, but—"

He caught a flicker of motion in the dim light; Stephen's open hand, moving in a swinging motion, aiming for his face. In that moment, he could've evaded the blow or caught it, but he couldn't bring himself to accept the concept that his boyfriend might go so far as to strike him. *Not Stephen. He's bluffing. No matter what else he's done, he'd never—*

The *crack* of palm meeting flesh was loud in the still night air. Jericho felt the sting of the impact, but like everything else, it was remote. Something he was experiencing from a distance. His brain reeled; not from the force of the blow, but from the *fact* of it.

"Wha … *what?*" he asked incredulously. "You *hit* me! I don't believe—"

Stephen tried to slap him again, but Jericho had had enough of that shit. He intercepted the blow before it got close and took control of Stephen's arm. With sharp, practiced motions, he turned his now-very-ex boyfriend and applied a compliance hold. If he used a little more force than precisely necessary, that was neither here nor there.

Domestic violence wasn't a crime he'd had to deal with much in his time as a superhero on the mean streets of Savannah, mainly because it was rarely perpetrated in public. He'd long since disapproved of the act as a matter of principle; after what had happened to Bobbi, 'disapproval' was far too mild a word.

Never in a million years, though, would he have imagined Stephen to be capable of such a thing. The clarity of hindsight reminded him that the writing had been on the wall all the time. *If he'll cheat on you, he'll hit you.* It was accepted wisdom; somehow, up until that point, he hadn't realized that it applied to him as well. He wondered how many other people without his resources had learned that unhappy lesson the hard way. Far too many, he suspected.

Compliance holds, by their very nature, were painful when struggled against. Stephen struggled against it. "Ow!" he complained, "You're hurting me!"

Right then, Jericho couldn't have cared less. A deep, dark part of him wanted to pop Stephen's shoulder clean out of the socket and make it so he never used that arm again. He restrained that urge; there were some lines that should never be crossed.

Dark figures loomed on either side of Jericho. "We saw this little shit hit you," rumbled Daryl, to his right. "Why don't ya go back inside? We c'n take it from here." Inherent in his tone was a promise of dark bayou water and hungry 'gators.

"No, thanks." Jericho felt a slight easing of tension. His kin had been watching out for him, even when he hadn't known they were. "I've got this. He's gonna be leaving now." He glanced to the left, into Leroy's face. His uncle was glaring at Stephen in a way which boded ill for his ex-boyfriend in the very near future. "This is over and done. We're finished. Got it?" Though he was speaking to Stephen, he pitched his voice to include the pair flanking him. No matter what Stephen had done, the last thing Jericho wanted was for him to end up with broken kneecaps out in the bayou somewhere.

Sullenly, Stephen said nothing. Jericho increased the tension on his trapped joints just a fraction. "I said, *got it?*"

"Ah! Yes, I've got it." Stephen's voice was more high-pitched than before, and he was standing on tiptoe. "We're finished, yes."

"Good. I'll be over to get my stuff later. It'd better be all there." Jericho released Stephen and gave him a shove; the shorter man stumbled a few steps forward. "Go home. Don't come back here. Don't try to call me again."

Stephen moved a few more yards away, then turned. To his shock, Jericho saw tears streaking the older man's face. "I know what happened! They got to you, didn't they? F—Utopia City got to you! They turned you against me!"

Jericho was pretty sure he knew what Stephen had been about to say. *Force Majeure turned you against me.* But to say *that* would be to out Jericho in public, and that particular act had serious legal penalties attached.

The adrenaline was wearing off now, and Jericho felt his hands trembling slightly. He had to work to ensure that his voice wasn't shaking as well. "Don't be a goddamn idiot. What happened is you cheated on me and got caught."

Daryl took two steps forward, menacingly. "Go on, just fuck off."

"I'll find the truth!" The defiant cry would've been more impressive if Stephen hadn't been retreating down the sidewalk at the time, rubbing his shoulder. "I'll show everyone what they're really like!"

Yeah, good luck with that. Jericho didn't bother watching him out of sight. He turned to Leroy. "Sorry about that."

"Ah, weren't nothin'." Leroy shook his head. "Cain't believe you went ahead an' let that little shitheel hit you."

"I didn't really think he was going to go through with it. Still can't believe it even now, to be honest." Jericho rubbed his cheek. "Everything else I expected. The lies and denials, sure. Hitting me, no. You think you know someone, but ..." His voice trailed off. There really wasn't anything else to say. He started back toward the gate, Leroy alongside him.

"Yeah." Leroy's voice was quiet. "Kinda know what you mean." His glance at Jericho was filled with wry humor.

"So ... what? You an' him? You was a thing?" It was Daryl, on his other side.

Jericho angled his eyes sideways toward his kinsman. "Yeah ...?" he ventured. Daryl *seemed* to be okay, but the 'faggy' comment was still fresh in Jericho's memory.

The big man shook his head wonderingly. "Jes' gonna say. You coulda done a *lot* better'n him."

Tension gusted out of Jericho in a shaky laugh. "Yeah, I'm starting to think that way myself."

Leroy clapped him on the shoulder. "You'll be fine, boy."

Jericho wasn't so sure, but he was willing to take it one step at a time.

Side by side, they walked back to the wake.

51
Holding Back the Tide

Hansen Family Home
Savannah, Georgia
Wednesday, October 9, 2013
8:35 AM, Eastern Daylight Time

"Honey, are you all right?"

Jericho stifled a yawn and tried not to blink in response to his mother's question. He'd refrained from looking too closely at his face in the mirror when he got up, but he was pretty sure that whatever Leroy had seen back in Utopia City was twice as apparent now. To borrow his uncle's extremely blunt phrasing, he looked like shit.

He refrained from rubbing his eyes, despite the persistent feeling that there was sand trapped behind his eyelids, mainly because he knew damn well it would do no good. This wasn't the longest he'd been awake without proper sleep, but it was certainly getting there. Just like the previous night, he'd spent twenty minutes in restless sleep and the rest of the time tossing and turning in a fruitless quest for peaceful slumber. This time, however, he hadn't gone out and about, not wanting to inflict his current mood on any hapless muggers he might encounter. He'd thought the confrontation with Stephen would have settled part of his mental turmoil, but his luck just didn't run that way. What he *needed* was to get back to Utopia City and hunt down Jack Portman once and for all—presuming the UCPD didn't already have the man in custody by the time he got back, of course—to get closure for Luke.

However, there was still the funeral to attend on Thursday, so once they'd gotten home from the wake, he'd gone straight to bed. This was partly a futile attempt to get some sleep—*any* sleep—and partly to avoid immediate parental interrogation regarding the incident with Stephen. They didn't know his ex-boyfriend directly, and they hadn't seen what had happened, but the way that they were now looking at him oddly over the breakfast table meant that *some* rumors must've gotten back to them.

He had no idea how everything was going to turn out; it would, of course, invariably get worse before it got better. That was how life worked. If he had his druthers, he'd have preferred to shut out the world until the fallout ceased to be a problem, but he knew his parents wanted the best for him and he felt bad about keeping anything from them.

"I'm fine, Mama." He tried to sound convincing, but it was a weak attempt even to his own ears. He had trouble with any kind of lie at the best of times; this wasn't the best of times.

Politely ignoring the feeble untruth, his mother tried again. "Is there anything you want to talk to us about? Anything at all? You know we're here for you."

"Let the boy be, Dahlia," his father said gruffly. "He's young. Whatever it is, he'll get over it." He poured sorghum molasses over his pancakes. "If he wants to talk about it, he will."

"You spoke to Leroy before we left last night," she said, switching her attention to her husband. "What did *he* say about what happened?"

"Nothing," grumbled Beau. "Nothing at all. He said it was Jericho's business, and that it was over and finished." He eyed Jericho, as if considering overturning his own stricture against pushing for more information. "What I don't know is what sort of business you'd have with Leroy that you can't tell me about, son." His gaze narrowed; apparently connecting a series of dots within his own mind, he took on a troubled expression of his own. "Do you owe people money? Is that what you were talking to him about?"

It was a polite fiction within the family that Leroy had never been engaged in any sort of criminal endeavors, either before *or* after Beau reached out to him. It wasn't that Beau and Dahlia denied such a thing had happened; they simply never acknowledged the concept. As far as Jericho could tell, this was so they could continue to associate with him while ignoring any rumors of such activity as the scurrilous fabrications that they surely must be. Beau, after all, had been forcibly cut off from his brother for ten years; since that time, he'd never let anything get in the way of maintaining their family ties. Kinfolk, as he'd impressed on Jericho from a young age, was kinfolk. It was simple as that.

All that aside, it was acceptable to admit that Leroy might possibly know how to contact people on the shadier side of the law. This did not specifically suggest that Leroy himself was in any way connected to criminal activity. He simply knew how to deal with such matters before they became an issue.

Still, Jericho knew his father wasn't an idiot. Beau wouldn't need to make many connections before a picture emerged; the trouble was, lacking any significant clues to the puzzle, the conclusions he reached were likely to end up being both misleading and problematic. The time Jericho had spent with Leroy in his office, and the confrontation with Stephen (for which Leroy had also been present), would likely have both reached his parents' ears and been conflated into one event. This could easily lead to complications, despite the fact that they were totally unrelated, save that they both involved him returning to Utopia City.

The worst part was explaining that the two incidents *were* unconnected would inevitably lead to requests for him to clarify the situation. Which he was wholly unwilling to do, for reasons he considered to be entirely compelling. The idea of explaining about Stephen and his infidelities was only outstripped in unpalatability by the concept of filling them in on the tangled web of events that had led him to approaching Leroy to get fake IDs made up for the Survivors. Inevitably, he would have to admit that he'd been going out as a superhero for the last couple of years. Not only did he have *no* idea how they'd react to such a revelation, but this was a discussion that he really, really didn't need right now. At least until he'd dealt with the current mess, once and for all.

They wanted answers. His unwillingness to lie to them threatened to become a problem. The scratchiness in his eyes wasn't helping in the slightest; neither was the feeling that he was made of brittle glass, liable to shatter into a thousand fragments if he moved too quickly. He took a deep breath in through his nostrils, seeking some sort of inspiration.

Jes' tell 'em somethin', cuz. Don't hafta be all the truth, jes' enough that they're satisfied.

He froze for a second. For some reason, he'd thought the interjections from his memories of Luke would go away once he left Utopia City. Not for a moment did he consider the idea that Luke's ghost had taken up residence in his head, offering gems of wisdom when needed. On the contrary, all of this was stuff he'd heard his cousin say at one point or another; right then, he was desperate enough to take advice from a memory. Especially since Luke had been on to something. Of course, this meant that he was going to have to open up a little.

"It was my boyfriend," he said reluctantly. Saying it even now brought back hurtful memories of the ugly emotions that had twisted Stephen's face and voice; the words his ex-boyfriend had thrown at him in a blatant attempt to cause pain. Scarcely less unpleasant was his memory of the shocked realization that Stephen intended to go through with the slap, just before it physically landed. It wasn't the pain of impact; that barely registered. What had wounded him far more deeply was the emotional shock, the betrayal of trust. *I still can't believe he actually hit me.*

Even in his less-than-optimum mental state, he registered his parents' reaction to the simple statement. His father leaned back slightly as if attempting to escape the reality of what Jericho had said, while his mother leaned forward, eyes bright. Gathering all the available information. Building a case. Absently, he wondered if all lawyers acted like that with their families.

"Well, *this* is the first I've heard of a boyfriend," she said with an encouraging smile. "What's he like? Why haven't you brought him around to meet us?"

"I can't." It was the simple truth, on every level. "Last night was when I broke up with him. I was asking Uncle Leroy for advice, earlier." This was where he knew he'd be treading fairly heavily on the line between truth and falsehood. While he *had* asked Leroy for help and advice earlier, that particular 'earlier' had been in Utopia City, and it hadn't been about Stephen. "I didn't want to worry you with my problems." And *that* was the absolute truth, even if he wasn't being totally honest with his implied meaning.

"Ah. Right." Beau seemed to be unsure of what to say to that. "Did he advise you to break up with … with your boyfriend?"

Jericho didn't even try to unpack all the emotions loaded into that statement. There seemed to be a little bit of relief and a little bit of guilt in there, but he wasn't sure which one inspired the other, or if they were a mutually supporting loop. At least he seemed willing to accept Jericho's story at face value. Or perhaps he was just unprepared to ask for any kind of supporting details.

Not so his mother. "*Why* did you break up with him? And why didn't you come to me about this? Or Ellie? We'd know more about dealing with men; it's not as if we haven't been married to them for years." She gave Beau a gently exasperated look, infused with love. Jericho was pretty sure she'd noticed the 'with your boyfriend' hesitation as well.

"We had … differences," Jericho said. The differences had been plain to see, he figured. Stephen believed he could cheat on Jericho, and Jericho disagreed. He tried not to grimace as the pain caused by that betrayal dug into his heart once more. "Uncle Leroy gave me some straightforward advice. When my boyfriend showed up at the wake, we discussed the problems with our relationship, and now we're not a couple anymore." Which was leaving out almost all the details but was still effectively the truth, however stretched out of shape it may have been.

"Oh, *honey*." His mother got up and rounded the table then gave him a hug, smelling gently of soap and powder. "I'm so sorry to hear that. If you're ever having problems like that again, come and *talk* to me. We can probably work something out, so you don't have to be so drastic as to break up with whoever it is."

He awkwardly hugged her back. "Thanks, Mama. I'll remember that."

"Make sure you do." Planting a kiss on his cheek, she ruffled his hair fondly then went back to her chair. "And if you ever decide you want to talk about the *rest* of it, I'm right here."

"Uh, yeah." Jericho concluded that trying to hide an omission from her was futile. "I'll do that."

"Thank you, honey." She gave her husband a sideways glance. "We'll both be here for you. Isn't that right, darling?"

Even Jericho could pick out the subtly warning note in that question. There was only one right answer that his father could give. The other answer undoubtedly involved an extended stay in the doghouse.

"Of course, honeybunch." Beau Hansen may have been a little uncomfortable with Jericho's preferences, but he wasn't *stupid*. And of course, he'd been married to Dahlia for more than twenty years, so he would've had no excuse for not knowing the signs. Clearing his throat, he turned to Jericho. "Son, you know I haven't always been on board with ... well, the way you are." Beside him, Dahlia coughed meaningfully. He took a deep breath. "You being gay, I mean. But I do know what it's like to go through a breakup, so if you ever want to talk about that ... you know, man to man ... well, I'm here too."

The intense warmth that suffused Jericho's chest almost overshadowed the guilt he felt for misleading his parents about what had happened. He'd known his parents loved him and cared about him, but this was going to the next level, especially for his father. And just to make the emotional mix even more complicated, relief colored everything else. He wasn't exactly *thrilled* with Stephen's actions, but being able to even hint at a bad breakup had been sufficient to focus the discussion away from more sensitive matters.

"Thanks, Pa," he managed. "I appreciate it." He took up another forkful of his omelet, but even the savory taste of what was normally his favorite breakfast food seemed dead in his mouth. Still, he swallowed the mouthful then pushed back his chair. "I'm not hungry anymore. I think I'll go up to my room."

"All right, honey." With troubled eyes, his mother watched him get up from the table. "We'll put some by for later, when you're feeling better." Inherent in her tone was an absolute refusal to countenance the idea that he might not feel better later.

"Okay. Thanks." He pushed his chair back in and left the room, pretending not to hear the low-voiced discussion that sprang up behind him once he was out the door.

That had been close; very close, indeed. Between his distaste for subterfuge and his parents' need to know what had happened, he'd come closer than he liked to spilling the beans about everything. His mother had clearly spotted the way he was eliding over some details but thankfully she'd chosen not to push too hard. Leaving any kind of real loose end to his story would've been as good as inviting her to pull that thread and unravel the whole narrative. And while he wanted them to know the full truth about him and his powers eventually, there was a time and a place for that sort of thing. *Not here, and not now.* He wasn't sure about much else, but he was certain about that.

Climbing the stairs to the second floor, he went along the corridor to his room; pushed open the door and entered. Once again, it was like stepping into the past. The illusion wasn't as perfect as it had been on his first night, imperfections revealed by the light of day. The poster of Relentless was a case in point; Jericho could now see a little fading around the feet where the sunlight angled in and caught it, first thing in the morning. But it was close enough to raise memories of days gone by, both good and bad.

Closing the door behind him, he sat down on the bed with his elbows on his knees and his face in his hands. *This isn't going to work much longer.* He'd initially gone to his parents for refuge because he couldn't bear to face Stephen. That bridge was now well and truly burned; not that he'd ever intended to cross it again. He didn't really have anyone else in town that he could call a close enough friend to be able to crash on their sofa for a few nights.

Uncle Leroy and Aunt Ellie would take me in if I asked.

While that was true, it was no solution to his problem. If he was having difficulty sleeping here, in the room he'd slept in for nearly all his life, he didn't want to know how many reminders of Luke he'd encounter if he went over to Leroy's house again. His self-imposed duty tugged at him—it *called* to him. The urge to return to Utopia City was stronger than ever. But he couldn't go; not until he'd attended Luke's funeral, and collected the fake IDs from Leroy. He had duties there, too, and he couldn't leave until he had fulfilled both. In the meantime, sleep refused to come to him and even food was losing its taste. As a prodigy, he knew that was the least of his problems; he could skip a few meals without any significant downside. A few bites here and there would suffice to sustain him in the short term.

But if he didn't get back on track *soon*, he wasn't sure how long he could hold out. *A couple of days. That's all. I can handle a couple of days.* If he tried to push it much past that, he suspected he'd wake up from a sound sleep to find himself on the maglev back to Utopia City. Possibly even in costume. Being a prodigy was cool and all, but sometimes the push to act accordingly with his focus was a real *pain*.

Which then raised the question of what he was going to do to pass the time until the funeral was done, and he had the fake IDs firmly in hand. If he was going to *make* this work, he couldn't just sit here in his room for the next day and a half. That would be a sure and certain way for him to go steadily insane. Sleep was almost impossible to get a handle on, and he'd utterly failed to lose himself in books.

There's just one thing I can do, right now.

Standing up from the bed, he went to the closet and retrieved his overnight bag. It was mostly empty; the clothing and toiletries that had been in it were residing in their appointed places in his dresser or the bathroom cabinet. He'd handled the unpacking himself, to avoid the potential of his mother finding and opening the costume satchel. This was what he now took from the overnight bag and unzipped.

The black jeans and long-sleeved shirt didn't shout 'superhero', so he put them on. Leaving the rest of the costume in the satchel, he donned a pair of worn sneakers and shrugged on a light tan jacket that he'd found in the closet. A dark green Sand Gnats baseball cap, along with a pair of scratched sunglasses, completed his ensemble. He wasn't sure what he looked like but it certainly wasn't G-Man, scourge of the Savannah underworld.

Zipping up the satchel again, he slung it over his shoulder then took his phone and wallet from the dresser and slipped them into his pants pockets. When he left his room and headed downstairs, he found his parents just finishing up breakfast. Either they'd heard him coming or their discussion about him was over, because when he entered the dining room all was quiet.

His mother looked up and smiled. "Feeling better, honey?"

"A little," he said. "I was thinking I might go out to the mall. Walk around for a while. Maybe catch a movie."

He hated lying to his parents like that, but he figured they'd be a lot more accepting of his need to go out if they thought he was doing normal things like shopping or catching a movie. Not putting on a costume and running across the rooftops or gliding over the city. The trouble was, there was no good way to explain to them that he had to do this just to settle himself down long enough to get some worthwhile sleep.

Beau looked up from his paper and nodded. "That might be a good idea, son. Did you want me to give you a lift on the way into the office?"

"Thanks, but I think I'll just take a cab." The satchel felt horribly conspicuous on his shoulder; he had a nervous impulse to hitch it up a little but refrained. "I'll see you both tonight, I guess."

"See you later, son. Have a good day." Beau went back to reading the paper.

"Take care, and have fun," his mother added.

He almost smiled at that. "I'll try."

52
Drama in the Park

While Jericho's eyes still felt as though they'd been packed with sand overnight, the view from the top of the southern steeple of the Cathedral of St. John the Baptist was spectacular. The breeze was refreshing, and he ignored what he considered to be offended looks from the local pigeons, having usurped their eyrie. His civilian clothes were stashed in the satchel on a rooftop several blocks away, from where he could retrieve them on his return trip. He didn't often come out in the daytime (his costume and modus operandi being tailored for night work) but this was something he needed to do. While this wasn't getting him back to Utopia City, it seemed to scratch the itch a little.

Kicking off gently from the spire, he spread his arms. The gliding surfaces of his costume stretched and caught the air beneath them, translating his falling motion into a long leisurely swoop. Few people looked up and pointed, which wasn't totally surprising; two hundred feet of altitude made him relatively hard to spot. The tails of his mask flapped in the breeze as he worked at finding his optimum gliding angle. If he'd wanted to give people heart attacks, he would've done a death-defying dive as he had in Utopia City, but for the moment he was going for distance. Savannah didn't have a surfeit of buildings over ten stories, and even fewer over fifteen. It was warmer during the daytime, so the air wasn't as heavy. He could feel updrafts coming off the blacktop here and there, giving him a minor boost in lift.

Seven blocks from the cathedral, he'd dropped maybe a hundred feet. He'd been originally aiming for Chatham Apartments, but he just didn't think he was going to make it. Banking a hard right over Calhoun Square, he spilled air and lost another twenty feet in altitude before gliding in for a landing on the taller of the Wesley Monumental steeples. Affixing himself to it with glue-tags, he ascended the spire with quick, sure movements. His muscles wanted to complain from the sudden exertion, but he told them to shut up and do their job. Once he reached the top, he launched himself off again, aiming once more for the huge apartment block. It was well within his range now; as one of the tallest buildings in the city, it would give him serious gliding distance. A much taller nearby radio tower promised even more range, but he didn't want to damage any of the equipment attached to it.

That was when he saw, alongside Forsyth Park, the pickup rumbling down the road. Or rather, Pickup. The garish paint job was easily distinguishable, even from a hundred and fifty feet up, through gaps in the trees. And while the Confederate flag was by no means an unusual decoration on vehicles south of the Mason-Dixon line (and sometimes north of it) he hadn't seen many other vehicles of that size and make in the city with one plastered clear across the hood.

Still, it might be a false positive. Pickup had his fanbase, just as Jericho hoped to have someday. This may well be some good ol' boy who'd taken a standard truck and slapped on the same paint job in imitation of his hero. And besides, all he was doing was driving down the street.

He held on to that hope right up until the oversized pickup truck slowed to a halt and rearranged its chassis into a twenty-foot-tall robot that stomped across the road—holding out one oversized hand in a 'stop' gesture to the oncoming traffic—and into the park itself. Almost immediately, the robot vanished between the trees.

Jericho maintained his forward motion for a few seconds, trying to decide what to do. Technically, Pickup was a hero. He certainly enjoyed more popular support in Savannah than Jericho did as G-Man. But Jericho couldn't see why he'd suddenly taken the notion to head on into the park, and that was worrisome. While they both upheld the law as best they could, they had very different styles in doing so.

Sighing with aggravation at his own indecision, he banked to the right. *One overflight, just to see what he's up to,* he promised himself. *If it's nothing, I'll just keep right on going.* He wasn't sure what he was going to do if there was actually something going on. *I'll just have to play it by ear.* Criminals he could deal with, but since his last clash with Pickup, he'd resolved to handle his next interaction with the man in a less confrontational manner. Humiliating a fellow hero just felt so *wrong.*

Gliding over the park, he peered down through the foliage. For a long moment, he thought he'd lost Pickup, then he spotted the garish paintjob ahead of him and to the right. *He's heading for the fountain. Why is he heading for the fountain?* Carefully, he angled over to follow the robot's line of travel.

And then all became clear. Clustered around one side of the fountain was a bunch of youths in garish clothing. All of them, as far as Jericho could see, were black. For a moment, he thought they were vandalizing the water feature but then he saw that some had phones in their hands and others were performing a series of stunts on skateboards. At least, until Pickup stomped into their midst. They scattered to make way for the twenty-foot-tall robot, save for the one kid intent on doing a perfect grind along the rim of the fountain, inside the ornamental wrought-iron fence. Leaning over the fence, Pickup grabbed the boy with one large metallic hand and tossed him thirty feet into a garden bed. Then he picked up the kid's skateboard from where it had fallen into the garden surrounding the fountain. Plywood crumpled as the robotic hand easily crushed it to splinters. One wheel came off and bounced a few times before rolling away.

The boy's yell was still sounding in Jericho's ears as he swooped overhead, then spilled air from his gliding wings to come in for a landing on the fence itself. Balancing easily, he called out, "Hey! Leave them alone! They weren't hurting anyone!"

The hulking mechanical head turned toward him. Jericho knew the robot's pilot, probably seated somewhere inside the torso, was studying him. He'd never met the man face to face, but they were in no way friends.

"Fuck off, G-Man. Ain't no nevermind of yours." The speaker that passed for the robot's voice-box was scratchy and distorted the pilot's speech, but Jericho picked up a distinctly annoyed tone.

"I'm making it my business, Pickup. Why are you harassing them? They're not causing a problem. It's a public park."

"They was trespassin' inside the fence, an' causin' a public nuisance!" boomed the speaker. **"That right there's against the law."**

Internally, Jericho sighed. *Same old, same old.* He doubted very much, given Pickup's prior behavior, that the man would've come down this hard on a bunch of white kids doing the same thing.

"They were shooting a video, am I right, guys?" He turned to the nearest of the black youths, who nodded. It wasn't the first time he'd seen this sort of thing, and he'd even stopped to watch from time to time. Some of these guys—and girls; he didn't want to be sexist—had seriously sick moves going on. "Hey, buddy. You okay?"

"'m fine," grunted the kid who'd been tossed into the shrubbery, pulling himself to his feet. He looked intact, though scratched and probably bruised. "What the motherfuck—my fuckin' *board!* What'd you do to my board, you cocksucker?" He started forward, only to be held back by two of his friends. Which was probably a good thing; Pickup wasn't known for going easy on anyone he could claim was a credible threat.

"You was trespassin' with it. I confiscated an' destroyed it." Pickup let the fragmentary remains of the skateboard clatter to the pavers. **"Suck it up. Next time, don't go trespassin'."**

Jericho could see what he was referring to—the fence was there for a reason, after all—but destroying the board had been nothing but a dick act. "Destruction of property's also illegal," he snapped. Holding out his hand, he snapped his fingers twice. "You owe him for his board. Pay up."

Pickup took a step closer. For all that Jericho was balancing easily on the fence, the robot still loomed over him. At this distance, Jericho could clearly hear the rumble of the turbocharged diesel engine that powered the Artificer creation. Gray smoke billowed out of the chromed exhaust pipes protruding up behind the robot's shoulders. **"I ain't payin'** *shit.* **He was usin' it to commit a crime."**

Jericho raised his voice, trying and failing to tamp down his growing anger. "I don't give a shit! Even the cops need a court order to destroy stuff! You broke his board; you goddamn owe him for a new one! Now you're gonna hand over money for his board, or I'll—"

"You'll do what?" Pickup's voice was full of derision. **"Attack me?"** The twenty-foot-tall robot raised its hands in a parody of surrender. **"I'm the hero, here. You can't make me do fucking** *shit.***"**

Jericho clenched his teeth with irritation and frustration. The last time he'd clashed with Pickup, the man had tried to use his robot to swat Jericho out of the way. He'd paid for his arrogance; where Jericho would've had reservations about inflicting his full power on Relentless, he'd suffered no such problem with making the robot feel all ten of those Gs. It seemed that having to rebuild his entire ride from scratch had been a learning experience for Pickup.

"You're just harassing them because they're black," he shot back, unable to think of anything wittier to say. There it was, out in the open.

Pickup shook his head. **"You sayin' I'm racially profilin' 'em? That's slander. Go ahead and prove it."**

Oh, he's definitely learned from his experience, goddamn it. Jericho kept his voice steady, despite the growing urge to vault up onto the robot and bring it crashing to the ground. Dumb opponents were a lot easier to fight. "Fine. Why don't you quit swinging your dick around and go fix that piece of shit you're riding around in?"

For the first time, he heard uncertainty in Pickup's voice. **"It don't need fixin'."**

Jericho generated a push-tag, then held it up between finger and thumb so that the sunlight refracted through it. "If it's not out of my sight in thirty seconds, that's gonna change."

"G-Man!" he heard from behind him. Turning his head, he saw a police officer approaching the confrontation. Behind him, between the trees, he saw a parked police cruiser. The officer pointed at the fence Jericho was standing on. "I'm going to have to ask you to get down off that fence."

"Sure thing." Letting the 'tag dissipate, Jericho jumped down lightly, then pointed at Pickup. "You need to—"

The cop raised his hand in the classic 'stop' motion. "No, *you* need to stop giving me orders. Pickup, what's going on here?"

"Those little shits were skateboardin' all over the fountain an' causin' a public ruckus," the artificer claimed, sounding smugly self-satisfied. **"I was just bustin' their chops for it when G-Man interfered."**

"He broke that guy's board and—" Jericho began hotly.

"G-Man, I'm talking to Pickup. You can wait your turn." The cop's voice was firm, brooking no disagreement.

Gritting his teeth, Jericho nodded sharply. He'd learned long ago; arguing with the police was a losing proposition. Folding his arms, he settled down to wait.

"Did you destroy that skateboard?" At least the officer was following up on the question.

"Sure did. The little shit was breakin' the law with it." Pickup's voice was proud, even boastful.

"An' then he chunked me right over there in the bushes!" shouted the kid who'd lost his board. "Ask him about that!"

The officer sighed and pushed his cap to the back of his head. "Pickup, what the hell have we told you about manhandling suspects?"

"He was trespassing." The giant robot shrugged. **"You want a crime, G-Man there threatened to bust up my ride."**

"Is that true?" The officer looked over at Jericho.

There was a trap in his words. Jericho wasn't about to lie, but neither was he obliged to fall tamely in line. "These guys were shooting a video, not bothering anyone. Pickup came in all heavy-handed, chucked that kid in the bushes, crushed the kid's skateboard for no good reason, then refused to pay for it. Hell *yes*, I told him if he didn't haul ass I'd wreck his shit."

The cop sighed again, and pinched the bridge of his nose in the classic *I'm not paid enough for this* move. "Okay … everyone here's banned from Forsyth Park for twenty-four hours. All of you. That's an official police directive." He pointed at Pickup. "Don't go pickin' at those kids unless they're committing an indictable felony, you hear me? And no more tossing them around like rag dolls." His attention turned to Jericho. "As for you, threatening to destroy Pickup's vehicle is just antagonizing the situation. Don't do it."

"What about that guy's skateboard?" pressed Jericho. "Pickup still needs to pay for it."

The cop shook his head. "Y'all can sort that out between yourselves. I can tell you now, the DA's office is not going to support a lawsuit against a superhero over a *skateboard*." He gestured toward the road. "All y'all, clear on out of this park. Now."

Pickup turned, then swung his arm so that he pointed at each of the youths in turn. **"If I hear of you little shits causing trouble again, I *will* be back."** Before either Jericho or the cop could say anything, he changed down into the truck again and drove off across the park, swerving between the trees. Jericho wondered if anyone would even chip him for the wheel-tracks he was leaving in the carefully tended grass. The cop didn't seem to be about to.

Shaking his head, he gathered the youths in by eye and led the way out of the park. He noted that, for all the 'official police directive' verbiage, the officer had not yet even pulled out his notebook. Of course, the cop's body-cam would've recorded the whole affair, unless that too had been turned off.

"So, everyone's okay?" he asked, paying particular attention to the kid who'd been hurled into the garden bed. "What about you? He threw you pretty hard, there."

"Nah, I'll be fine." The kid was brushing himself off, though there were rips and stains in his clothing that Jericho figured were going to need professional attention. At least none of the stains looked like blood. "He fucked up my board pretty good, though." Mournfully, he looked at the one wheel he'd been able to salvage. Around him, his friends muttered unkind things about Pickup; most of which Jericho privately agreed with.

"Yeah, sorry about that. He's an asshat." Jericho shook his head. "Though I am a bit curious. How come y'all's not in school? It's not even midday yet."

"School's out," said the kid whose board had been wrecked. "Busted water main. Not busted as bad as my board, though."

"Ah, gotcha." Jericho recalled seeing something about that on the news. "You guys were doing pretty good there 'til Pickup showed."

One of the older boys in the group, a lanky guy of about sixteen or so, stepped up in front of Jericho. "Yo, G. Why din't'cha throw down with the sumbitch? You coulda owned his tinfoil ass easy."

"Three reasons." Jericho held up his index finger. "One, he's technically a hero, and if I started something with him, the papers would grab it and make up all sorts of shit." Bobbi's explanation of mainstream media politics had been an education in more ways than one. Up went his middle finger, alongside the first one. "Two, you guys were right there. If he started flailing around, someone might've gotten hurt." He raised his ring finger to complete the set. "And three ... you never know where the cops are, like we just saw. If that one had seen me start shit, it would've made my position as a superhero a lot dicier." If he got branded as a villain, he knew, the Challenger Act would no longer protect him against being unmasked.

"That tin-plated douchebag needs a good kick in the ass," groused the owner of the broken board. "How the hell am I gonna afford another one, if the cops won't even make him pay for the old one?"

Knowing a decent board cost at least a hundred, Jericho reached into his utility belt and took a couple of twenties off the roll he kept there. His stash hadn't been worth much in Utopia City, but out in what his brain insisted on calling the 'real world', people still accepted cash money. "Screw Pickup and the truck he rolled in on. Here's forty toward a new one."

"Shee-it, G! You da *man!*" The lanky kid high-fived his buddy with the busted board, who was looking at the money like he couldn't believe it. "You our hero, G. You *the* hero."

"Thanks. You guys try and stay out of trouble, all right?"

He shook hands with a few of the guys and endured shoulder-slaps and back-pats from the rest before he left them to it.

The tension in his chest felt as though it had eased slightly. He still needed to get back to Utopia City as soon as he could manage it, but it seemed that the urgency was mitigated by going out and helping people. Or at least, attempting to do so. At best, the standoff against Pickup had been inconclusive; more realistically, he'd failed to do more than give the kids a token level of support. Still, their effusive thanks lingered in his memory and helped offset the sour taste in his mouth.

How can I hope to make a lasting difference if the cops won't even back me up?

53
Gone, But Not Forgotten

First African Baptist Church
Savannah, Georgia
Thursday, October 10, 2013
3:35 PM, Eastern Daylight Time

"But that was the kinda boy my Luke was. He didn't have no meanness in him nohow, and he always tried to help folk out." As Jericho watched from the front row, Leroy took a deep breath and gripped the podium with both hands. Around him, the congregation murmured variations on 'Amen' and 'Rest his soul'. He thought for a moment Leroy was going to go on, but then his uncle looked directly at him. "There's one more story about him that needs to be told. But it ain't my place to tell it. My nephew Jericho was there when it happened, so he can tell it to y'all now." Leroy raised one hand and beckoned. "Come on up, boy."

Crap. Crap, crap, crap. Following the confrontation with Pickup in the park and the day of gliding over the city, Jericho had gotten more sleep than he had over the previous two nights. But while he was doing better than before, he felt in no way up to this.

Worse, he knew exactly which story Leroy was referring to, and why his uncle wanted him to tell it. He couldn't even disagree with his uncle; the story needed to be told. In the privacy of the maglev cargo car, he'd just about managed it, but the idea of talking to the entire church at once slammed his heart up into his throat. The trouble was, everyone was now looking directly at him, and the sheer *expectation* in their gaze was all but levitating him out of the seat. He didn't want to do it. Unfortunately, his choices in the matter were rapidly fading away. Leroy gestured again. Jericho didn't want to disappoint his uncle, so he slowly rose to his feet.

Luke's coffin rested on a stand before the podium, the half-lid open so that the mourners could see his face and the small offerings that had been placed in there with him. More flowers surrounded the coffin, emphasizing the fact that they were here to celebrate Luke's life as much as to mourn his death.

Step by step, Jericho went around the coffin and approached the podium with all the enthusiasm of a condemned man being led to the gallows. Luke had been a hero; that was for certain. But why was it up to *him* to do this? The answer was obvious, of course; he'd been the one on the spot, the one who'd seen what happened. Even if he *was* going to have to elide over certain aspects.

Leroy stepped away from the podium as he approached. Briefly, his hand clasped Jericho's shoulder on the way past. It helped to ease the younger man's jangled nerves, though he still didn't want to be there.

Then he was at the podium. Grasping the cool wood in his hands as Leroy had done before him, he glanced around. Standing off to the side was the steadying presence of the man Jericho called 'Pastor T' in the privacy of his own mind, who'd been officiating at the First African Baptist Church since before Jericho was born. Now the pastor merely nodded, with an encouraging smile. His faith in Jericho to say what needed to be said was uplifting. Shifting his gaze, Jericho looked out over the congregation, and the building they were in.

First African was a very restful place. Neither Jericho nor Luke had been steady churchgoers, but they'd attended on occasion, usually with their respective parents. In contrast to his state of mind, the room itself was bright and airy, with impressive stained-glass windows allowing light in from both sides. Behind him, two more such windows flanking the altar spilled multicolored afternoon light into the church. He knew that the windows incorporated the images of the very earliest pastors of the church from two centuries ago onward, though he would've been hard put to name them right at that moment. In front of him, the curved pews allowed him to see the faces of everyone quite clearly.

His eyes fixed on Olivia's, and he knew she was waiting for him to speak, to tell her something special about Luke, about the man she'd chosen to spend the rest of her life with. Her eyes pleaded with him to transcend reality and somehow give her one last moment with her husband, in spirit if not deed. He had no idea how to achieve that, but he resolved to give it his best shot.

Taking a deep breath, he let it out again. "Y'all know that Luke came along with me to Utopia City. But what most of you don't know is how he saved someone's life before he ever left Savannah." He paused to allow the surprised murmurs to subside. "We were in the maglev station, waiting for the next train. There was a lady with a stroller. She was talking on her cellphone, and the stroller with the baby in it just rolled away from her. It was heading for the edge of the platform. She didn't see it, and I didn't see it. Luke was the only one who saw it."

There were no murmurs this time as he paused for breath. He was committed now, but he was going to have to phrase the next bit very carefully.

"The woman with the stroller was a ways down the other end of the platform. First I knew about it was when Luke lit out like there was no tomorrow. By the time I realized what was going on, it was almost all over. The stroller was getting closer to the edge all the time and he was hauling, uh, he was just trying to beat it there." Again, he paused. The silence was absolute.

"The stroller got to the edge of the platform first. When the front wheels went over, Luke went for a baseball slide. He got there just in time to grab one of the back wheels. The kid was strapped in, but the next train was literally just seconds away. You've seen how fast they go. Death was on that platform, reaching out to grab that little baby. But Luke was there too, and he spit Death in the eye and said, *You cain't have him. He ain't yours to take.*" Raising his voice as he spoke Luke's lines, he did his best to say the words the way his cousin would have.

He knew he was hamming it up, but he had no problem with throwing in a little drama to make the story more memorable. This had been Luke's show from beginning to end, and the more vividly he told it, the less likely it was that people would start wondering what *he'd* been doing. It seemed he was on a winner; already, people were visibly hanging on his every word.

"I was too far away to help. The kid's mama didn't even know it was happening. It was just Luke, the baby and the train. So he heaved, and he hauled, and *with just one hand*, he pulled that kid back from the brink, up over the edge of the platform, like a cork out of a bottle."

Taking a deep breath, he leaned forward. "You want to know how close it was? It was so close, the wind from the incoming train knocked the stroller aside as he was pulling it onto the platform. If he'd been *half a second* too slow, it would've been too late. That's how close it was. That's how near Death came to taking that baby." Slowly, he straightened up. "That's why Luke'll always be my hero."

The outrush of sighs from the congregation swept across the room like a summer breeze. "Hallelujah," murmured one person. "Praise the Lord," said another. From silence the room was transformed into the voices of faith, people's eyes alight with the awareness that they'd heard a truly miraculous story. Olivia's, no less than the others.

She'd *needed* to hear it, Jericho belatedly understood. Everything else about Luke, she'd already heard or was unsurprised at; this was something new. Something that validated the canonized view of Luke she was already building in her heart. Her husband hadn't been perfect—who was?—but death had a way of washing away all sins.

He breathed in again, building his courage for what he was about to do now. "While I'm up here …" he said, and was touched by the way the room quieted again. A tightness began to grow in his throat, but he tried to power through it. "I just thought I'd say a few words about Luke as well. I … he … he was my cousin, but … he was more than that. He was my best friend. He was my *brother*. He always encouraged me to follow my dreams. Even when he didn't agree with what I was doing, he had my back anyway. I always tried to do the same for him, but I didn't … I wasn't …" *I wasn't there to save him, in the end.*

Eyes clenched shut against the hot tears leaking through, he lowered his head. "I … I'm sorry. I can't … I can't do this." The last few words choked out past the hot lump in his throat. Blindly, he stumbled away from the podium and down one of the aisles. Fingers grasped at his; he thought they might have been his mother's. But he had to get outside, away from this. Away from the reminder of his most abject failure; his betrayal of Luke's trust in him as a hero.

The outer doors of the church opened before him, and he arbitrarily turned left before descending the stairs. Such was his disordered state of mind that only his innate sense of balance kept him upright all the way down to street level. No cars were coming up the side-street alongside the church; at least, that was what his G-sense told him. He headed across into the parking lot beyond, packed with the cars for Luke's funeral procession. But now he was far enough away from the church, from Luke, to stop. Leaning on a car, head down, he drew breath in deep ragged gasps. *I will not cry,* he told himself. *I will not cry. I've cried enough.* It was a lie, but he needed to believe it just for the moment.

"Hey, Jericho. Y'alright?"

He looked around at the familiar voice. "Daryl," he croaked. "What're you doing out here?" The last he'd seen his aunt's brother, the man had been sitting in the church; along with the rest of Luke's family and friends.

"Leroy sent me out ta make sure you was okay," Daryl said simply. He gave Jericho a searching look. "This your first time losin' someone close?"

At first, the question struck Jericho as being more than a little insensitive, until he recalled that Daryl was going through the same bereavement as he was. Luke had been his nephew, after all. "… yeah," he admitted. "I've been to funerals before, but it wasn't as *real* as this one. I've never told myself *I'll never see that person again* and wanted to claw the thought out of my brain."

"Yeah, I get it." Daryl sighed. "I know how ya feel. Luke always talked ya up, said as how you was good people. I miss him, too, somethin' fierce." He tilted his head, gesturing away from the church. "How's about we go for a li'l walk so's you can clear your head, afore we go back on in?"

"Sounds like a plan." Jericho took a deep breath of the afternoon air. He was feeling better already, but he knew it wasn't a matter of 'if' this would turn itself around once he got back inside, but 'how fast'. He needed a reprieve from the reality of *we're burying Luke today* to build up an emotional buffer which would get him through the rest of the day.

They started around the block, walking in easy silence. Initially, Jericho felt mildly insulted at being assigned a babysitter—which, when it came down to it, was what Leroy had done—but then he found himself appreciating the company. Physically, he was well able to take care of himself. Emotionally, he was about two steps away from being a total wreck.

A few minutes into the walk, Daryl turned to him. "That story ya told in there. That really happen?" From the tone of his voice, he wanted it to be true.

"Sure as I'm standing right here." Jericho gestured in the direction he thought the maglev station lay. "I could show you the exact spot, if you wanted."

"Nah, I'm good." The big man shook his head. "Day*um*, that woulda been some sight to see."

"Truth be told, it was over in less time than it took to talk about it," Jericho said. "The mom didn't even know it'd happened 'til the kid started fussing up a storm."

"Sumbitch." Daryl breathed out a long sigh. "Luke sure was somethin', that's for damn certain."

"Yeah." At the mention of his cousin's name, Jericho felt himself starting to choke up again. Holding up his hand to stop Daryl, he leaned against the building next to them—grimy red bricks, gritty to the touch—and breathed deeply with bowed head, trying to get past it. "Dammit," he muttered, irritated at himself and his weakness. *I'm a prodigy; I should be able to deal with this sort of thing more easily.* That was when the first tear trickled down his cheek. "God *damn* it."

"You jes' go right on ahead an' take your time," Daryl said, patting him awkwardly on the shoulder. "I ain't goin' noplace."

Before Jericho could begin to take comfort from that fact, a new voice broke in on the situation. "Hey, boy, what the living *fuck* you think you're doin'?"

"Yeah," snapped another one. "Git your thievin' black ass away from that there white boy, y'hear me, West?"

Oh, what the hell is it now? Jericho looked around, to see no fewer than four men—all white, of course—moving into a semi-circle around them. Their attitude was just as hostile as their voices had been, while their attention was predictably fixed on Daryl. None of them looked particularly well off or overly poor. They were just average everyday folks, taking exception to what they apparently saw as an attempted robbery of a white man by a black man.

While he appreciated the rescue effort, it couldn't have come at a worse time. Tears were running freely down his cheeks by this point, something he hated other people to see. He just wanted them to go away so he could get his poise back and return to the church.

"It's okay, guys," he said thickly, waving his hand vaguely toward them. "We're all good here."

One of the guys stepped forward, chin thrust out aggressively. "If'n you're okay, then howcome you're bawlin' like a li'l baby jes' got his dick clipped?"

"'Cause we're holdin' a funeral today over at First African, O'Dowd," Daryl said bluntly. "We're buryin' my nephew Luke. Him an' the young feller here useta be real tight. Cain't rightly blame him for droppin' a tear or two, yeah?" His attitude was protective, while the tone of voice came across as *you asked, I answered.*

"Shee-it." The guy spat to one side. "That's all it is? Ain't nothin' to cry about. Jes' one more dead ni—"

For someone who wasn't Enabled, Daryl was sure as hell light on his feet. One moment, he was alongside Jericho; the next, he was face to face with O'Dowd. The guy didn't lack heft, but Daryl was taller and wider than him or any one of his buddies. A single knuckle, as broad and solid as a walnut, prodded O'Dowd in the chest. When Daryl spoke, his voice was the rumble of distant thunder. "Y'all ain't *earned* the right to say that word, boy."

The moment hung in the charged air like lightning choosing where it was going to strike. Jericho felt adrenaline bursting into his veins like the clarion call to battle; just like that, his throat cleared up and tears ceased to flow. Even as he found himself calculating positions and angles, strike points and vulnerable areas, he found time to grouse over his shitty luck. *Twice in two days? What* is *this?* While Savannah had its share of racist asshats—what place didn't?—this would've been almost ludicrous. Except that it wasn't.

Still, complaining about the situation wasn't going to fix it.

Facing Daryl, the man who'd almost uttered the fateful word seemed to get over his momentary bout of aphasia. "Fuck you!"

Daryl prodded him again, making him take a step back. "No. Fuck *you*, O'Dowd, you redneck cracker. Y'all c'n fuck off right the fuck now. You're not needed an' you're not wanted."

O'Dowd took a deep breath, glanced left and right at his buddies, then reached around behind his back, under his jacket. A moment later, he had a snub-nosed revolver pointed directly at Daryl's chest; the hammer ratcheting back under his thumb.

"Whoa, whoa, fuck!" Daryl backpedaled, raising his hands to show they were empty. "Let's not git crazy here, now."

O'Dowd glared Daryl in the eye. "Too late … *nigger*."

Every instinct Jericho had told him that Daryl was about to get shot, even though he'd had backed off. Georgia had 'stand your ground' laws that permitted deadly force in the case of self-defense, and Daryl had initiated first contact. Jericho could testify against them for murder, but it would be four against one and Daryl would still be dead. *Not on my watch.*

Drawing on his Prodigy capabilities as hard as he could, he flowed up past Daryl; a tap behind the big man's knee and an elbow to the chest destabilized his balance just enough that Jericho was able to knock him off his feet, out of the line of fire. The revolver went off, but Daryl was already on the way down, so the bullet went over his head.

Then Jericho was face-to-face with O'Dowd, already taking control of his weapon. The guy opened his mouth to speak, but Jericho wasn't interested in anything he might have to say. His knee came up into O'Dowd's groin; as the asshat began to double up from the pain, Jericho headbutted him. The crisp crackle of collapsing nasal cartilage was music to his ears.

As O'Dowd started to go down, blood spraying across his features, Jericho finished removing the pistol from his grasp. He took two smooth steps to the left and side-kicked the idiot there in the knee; while similar to the sound of the first guy's nose, the crunch of separating cartilage had its own distinct signature. As did the high-pitched scream of the guy as he folded to the ground. A movement out of the corner of Jericho's eye warned him that the third member of the group was reaching under his jacket for a pistol holstered on his hip. Jericho didn't give him the chance to get it out; he closed the distance and slammed the butt of the captured revolver into the guy's jaw. The shock traveled up Jericho's arm to his shoulder, but the other guy got it much worse. Bone broke and teeth flew out in a spray of red and white; that guy started to collapse as well.

Four in; three down. Still not bothering to take the pistol by the butt, Jericho turned toward the last guy, ready to counter any threat he might pose. The idiot was still standing there slack-jawed, as if unable to process the fact that his three buddies were down and out of the fight. Jericho had all the time in the world to plan this one; he figured another kick to the groin would finish matters off in a satisfactory manner. Sometimes, the old favorites were the best.

And that was when the police siren went off. He turned to see the car screeching to a halt at the side of the road, lights flaring wildly. *Good*, he thought. *Hand the gun over, explain what just happened, and we can get on back to the church.*

But as the two officers exited the cruiser and leveled their pistols, he realized with a start that *he* was the target, not the fourth guy. "Drop the gun!" yelled one.

"Down on the ground!" That was the other one.

"Don't move!"

"Hands on your head!"

This was starting to sound amazingly familiar. Only, the guns these guys carried would put real bullets in him, not just electricity. As a prodigy, he had a better chance than most to take a non-lethal gunshot wound and keep going, but a bullet to the head or heart would most likely finish him just as easily as it would do anyone else.

Slowly, holding his hands out to the side, Jericho knelt and placed the pistol on the sidewalk then shuffled away from it and laced his fingers behind his head. A glance behind him showed that Daryl had already assumed the position. Belatedly, he realized that this was another good reason not to provoke them into shooting; despite his bulk, Daryl simply couldn't take the punishment that Jericho could.

They approached carefully; one held a gun on Daryl while the other scooped up the pistol then proceeded to start cuffing Jericho. He didn't resist, partly because they were the police and partly for Daryl's sake.

This didn't mean he wasn't going to try talking his way out of this. *It worked in Utopia City.* "Hey," he said as his arm was yanked down behind his back. "Can I at least tell you what just happened?"

"Shut the hell up," snapped the cop, yanking his other arm around and securely cuffing him. "Bobby, you okay?"

"Goddamn nose is broke," mumbled O'Dowd. Sitting up, he dazedly poked at the bloody wreckage in the center of his face, only to recoil with a hiss of pain. "Sum*bitch*, that hurts!"

The feeling that all was not right, initiated when the cops decided that he and Daryl were the aggressors, ramped up considerably. It didn't help that they weren't searching or even questioning the fourth guy, who was standing off and watching the proceedings with ill-concealed glee. Jericho began to wish he'd had the chance to kick that guy in the crotch, just on general principles.

"We'll get y'all an ambulance," the cop said briskly. Heaving Jericho to his feet, he walked him over to the car and slammed him face-first into it, or tried to; Jericho was too tall for this move to work. "You two assholes are under arrest."

"On what charge?" Jericho protested. "We were just defending ourselves."

"Way I seen it, y'all went at 'em like you had somethin' to prove," the cop stated flatly. He frisked Jericho in a reasonably competent manner, and came up with his wallet and phone. "Where's your carry permit for that gun?"

"Not my gun," Jericho retorted. "I took it off your buddy there. Bobby. O'Dowd. Whatever his name is. He was fixing to shoot my friend with it."

"Bullshit," snorted the cop. "Bobby knows guns. Ain't nobody can jes' take one off'a him." Opening the car door, he pressed Jericho's head down and pushed him into the back seat. "You jes' sit tight in there."

The door closed behind Jericho, and he sat helpless in the back of the cop car. Despite the discomfort of the handcuffs, he was able to watch as they cuffed Daryl, who knew better than to even appear to be putting up a fight. When they searched the big man, they seemed disappointed at not finding anything even remotely illegal. It didn't surprise Jericho; they'd been attending a funeral, after all.

More cars showed up shortly, and they bundled Daryl into the back of a second one. Following that was an ambulance; the paramedics examined the injured, and apparently it was arranged that they'd all share the same ambulance. All the time this was happening, Jericho kept glancing up to the corner, hoping against hope that *someone* would come looking for them. He was even willing to sit through his mother's disappointment and Leroy's joshing to allow that to happen.

Nobody showed up. The two cops got back into the car, and they all drove away.

The cuffs were overly tight on Jericho's wrists, but even more painful than that was the heartache.

I had one job; show up at the funeral. I couldn't even get that right.

54
Enforcing Law and Order

Savannah, Georgia
Thursday, October 10, 2013
8:23 PM, Eastern Daylight Time

Interrogation rooms, Jericho concluded, were like morgues. They were particularly morbid places, and he'd never seen the inside of one before now. He tried not to look at the mirror set into the wall. While his G-sense wasn't strong enough to detect anything on the other side unless he got right next to it, he was reasonably certain they'd have at least a camera back there, and maybe a couple of cops as well.

However, his main concern had nothing to do with theoretical people behind a one-way mirror. First and foremost, he was worried about Daryl's well-being and whereabouts. The possibility of getting a permanent mark on his criminal record only bothered him insofar as it would make life difficult getting back to Utopia City to track down Jack Portman. He'd deal with that when and if he had to.

The needs and wants of the person sitting across the table from him came a distant last. Officer McKendrick had been the same one to handcuff him and ignore his attempt to explain matters at the scene. After they'd processed him in and taken swabs from his skin and clothing, he'd been left to stew in a holding cell. A couple of hours later, McKendrick had taken him from the cell and escorted to this room. He'd then been left alone with the table and the mirror, presumably to sweat about his misdeeds, while McKendrick went and got coffee. None for Jericho, of course. There was to be no good-cop-bad-cop here. It was all bad cop.

At least the guy hadn't handcuffed him to the table. Jericho wasn't sure if this was an attempt at making him more amenable to talking or if the cop considered him to be that little of a threat. Whichever it was, Jericho had no intention of busting his way out by force, so he just sat tight.

Along with coffee, McKendrick brought back the stereotypical manila folder, which he set down on the table but didn't open. He took a long sip of coffee and stared at Jericho. A lifetime of quiet reserve, backed by his mother's admonition to never *ever* admit anything to a police officer without a lawyer present, overcame Jericho's initial urge to just *explain* what had happened and made it easy to stay silent in return. The scent of the coffee teased his nose; he did his best to ignore it.

"Why'd you do it?" McKendrick asked after a good five minutes of silence had gone by. It was an admission of surrender, after a fashion.

"I'd like a lawyer, please." It was always worthwhile trying politeness first and rudeness second. The other way around rarely worked.

"Why? Do you think you need a lawyer?" The cop tried to give him a hard-eyed gaze. Jericho recalled being stared down by Relentless on the sparring mat. McKendrick was almost adorable by comparison.

"Everyone who walks into a police station needs a lawyer," Jericho countered, quoting something his mother had once said. "Is my friend all right? Daryl West. Where is he?"

McKendrick pounced on the opening. "Ah, yes. West." He took the manila folder and lifted the flap. It was thick enough that Jericho had already concluded there wasn't anything in there about him. He just hadn't thought the matter all the way through. "West is not your friend. We've got a lot on him, none of it good. You want to know where he is? Right now, he's in a room just like this one, spilling his guts to someone just like me, giving you up for everything that happened today." He raised his eyebrows slightly. "He'll walk, and you'll go down. He's done it before, and he'll do it again. All he has to say is that you did everything out there today. It'll be his word against yours and if you don't say a thing, we have to listen to him. Which is ridiculous, right? I mean, it's not like you could've done all that by yourself."

Jericho didn't take the bait. *Daryl's kin. He wouldn't do that to me.* "Maybe you didn't hear me correctly. I'd like a lawyer. Now."

"Maybe *you* didn't hear *me* correctly." McKendrick leaned forward. "You and West don't get to start this shindig and jes' walk away afterward. I've got three counts of aggravated battery, one count of assault with a deadly weapon and one count of possession of a firearm without a carry permit that I've got all of two suspects for. The lab found gunshot residue on your skin and clothing, and you've got a bruise on your forehead consistent with headbutting someone. Any good prosecutor could bury you on that alone. But if you happened to tell me right here, right now, that he did it all? You get to skate free and clear. Clean record, no priors, led astray, the whole nine yards. All you have to do is—"

The door to the interrogation room opened and Detective Raul Villanova leaned in. Jericho tensed; if there was anyone in the Savannah PD who stood a chance of identifying him as G-Man, it was Villanova. But the detective merely glanced incuriously at him before looking over at his interrogator and making a beckoning gesture. "There's something you need to hear."

"Oh, what the hell is it *now?*" Despite his protest, McKendrick got up and went to the door. He stepped out and let it swing shut, but it didn't close all the way. There was a mumble that Jericho didn't hear, then McKendrick's voice came back, raised in surprise. "You did fucking *what?* I told you to *hold* him!"

"And they did." The new voice was as cold and hard and sharp as a newly formed icicle on a fresh December morning. Jericho recognized it immediately; it was his mother in lawyer mode. "Right up until I found out that Robert O'Dowd, one of the alleged victims, was in fact your brother-in-law. Something even your colleagues apparently didn't know. I had to find out *that* little tidbit from Mr. West."

"And how the hell do you think he knew about that?" demanded McKendrick. "He's a goddamn criminal, and he's been keeping tabs on my family! You don't think that's just a little bit creepy?"

"According to Mr. West," Dahlia Hansen retorted icily, "it's because Mr. O'Dowd has been known to use the fact that his brother-in-law is a police officer to attempt to get cheap drinks at the bar he frequents."

McKendrick recovered rapidly. "That doesn't change the fact that West is a known criminal!"

"An *alleged* criminal," Jericho's mother said tartly. "After supervising his statement, I informed your colleagues that they needed to either release him or charge him. Despite their reluctance to do so, they were unable to find *one single iota* of evidence to back up your brother-in-law's story. Now, if you don't mind, I would like to see my *other* client before I am forced to start composing my letter to Internal Affairs regarding your obvious conflict of interest."

The door opened again; Dahlia Hansen stood framed in the doorway, briefcase in hand. Behind her, McKendrick looked as though he was going for a world-record attempt at sucking lemons. "Hello, dear," she said with a tight smile. "You look as though you could do with a lawyer."

Despite the gravity of the situation, Jericho let out a bark of laughter. "You got that right, Mama. What kept you?"

"We'll talk about that later." She pulled McKendrick's chair from behind the table and sat down in it, placing her briefcase on the table. "Right now, we need to start the ball rolling to get you out of here."

"Wait, wait, time the fuck *out!*" McKendrick made an exaggerated 'T' with his hands. "Did he just say '*Mama*'? What the hell's going on here?"

"I happen to be his mother *and* his lawyer," Dahlia replied crisply. "Do you have a problem with that?"

"Uh ... ain't that a conflict of interest of your own?" But McKendrick was reaching; the tone of his voice admitted that even he knew it.

"Hardly." Her smile was deadly and sweet all at the same time, like a razor concealed in cotton candy. "As his mother, I want to see him walk free. As a lawyer, I have the same goal."

"Well, that ain't happening any time soon." McKendrick wasn't quite stupid enough to demand that a lawyer—or a woman—give up her chair for him, so he folded his arms and stood by the desk. "We both know he beat on Bobby and the other two. And there's still assault with a deadly weapon to cover. He had GSR all over his hands and when we showed up, he was holding a pistol that he doesn't have a carry permit for." The door opened and Detective Villanova came in, carrying two folding chairs. "What the hell? You want something?"

"Yeah, to get home and get my head down." Villanova sounded tired. "But the lieutenant told me to get my butt in here and keep you company." He raised his hand as McKendrick opened his mouth, no doubt to voice a protest. "Save it. It was this or pull you off the case but that's too much paperwork, so I'm sitting in." He propped one chair against the table for McKendrick then unfolded the other one and sat down, leaning back and crossing his arms. "Pretend I'm not here."

Jericho would've loved to do that exact thing. The earlier encounter with Villanova had been nerve-wracking enough, but now they were sitting in the same room. As G-Man, he'd had several long conversations with the detective, which Luke had since revealed were not always based around professional courtesy. The guy must have been studying him, hoping to find an opening to make a move. *What if he recognizes me now?* It was bad enough that Leroy knew; despite the protections afforded by the Challenger Act, the fewer people who were aware of his secret identity, the better. Unmask had proven that, in spades.

"Ah, yes. The firearm. We shall see." Dahlia opened her briefcase to take out a pen and pad, then turned to Jericho. "Dear, would you please give us your account of what happened? Everything you saw and heard. Just the facts."

"Okay." He took a deep breath. Things were looking better than they had, but he wasn't out of the woods yet. "Daryl was just walking with me 'til I could get my head together when the four guys came up to us and started talking trash." Step by step, he went through the action, describing everything as unemotionally and baldly as he could. Beside him, his mother put her pen to the pad but instead of writing, she seemed to be making small marks.

"... and then the police arrived and put their guns on us. I dropped the pistol and tried to explain what had happened, but this one told me to shut up and shoved me in the back of his cruiser." He nodded to indicate McKendrick, who was now sitting in the other chair.

"Trying to explain matters to the police without a lawyer present is *always* a bad idea, but I can see why you made the effort." Dahlia didn't look like a mother anymore. She looked like a shark, one that had scented blood in the water. "Well, then, Officer McKendrick. It seems that my clients' stories match in every significant detail, *despite* the fact that you've been holding them separately. From the look on your face they *don't* match the story your brother-in-law is telling. What a *surprise*." She showed him her notepad; Jericho caught a glimpse of neatly written paragraphs, each one carefully ticked off in turn.

"Wait a minute," McKendrick objected. "Hansen, how the hell did *you* take out three guys all by yourself? Every single one of 'em is bigger'n you."

Jericho shrugged. "They were watching Daryl and weren't expecting me to do anything, until it was too late."

Dahlia raised her voice slightly. "The 'how' doesn't matter. I believe you will find my son's account agrees in all particulars with that of Mr. West."

"Yeah, well, I'll have to check the tape." McKendrick's tone was sour. "But it still doesn't put your boy in the clear with the pistol. Bobby's got a permit, but he swears up and down it wasn't his. And if they struggled over it, his prints could've ended up anywhere on it."

Jericho knew exactly why O'Dowd was disclaiming ownership of the firearm. Carry permit or no, attempting to shoot an unarmed stranger was not a good look for anyone. Claiming that Jericho had been the one with the gun muddied the waters and made it easier for the cops to try to get leverage on Daryl.

He waited for a moment, then cleared his throat. "His prints could've ended up *any*where, but not *every*where."

The other three looked at him; McKendrick with irritation, Dahlia with concern and Villanova with curiosity. "What do you mean?" asked the detective.

"The gun's loaded. Cartridge cases hold fingerprints," Jericho explained briefly. "I know *I* never touched them. Find the fingerprints of the person who loaded it and you'll find the owner." He held up his hands, fingers spread. "You guys printed me when you processed me in. Should be easy enough to check for a match."

Dahlia's face showed enlightenment. "Indeed. And I absolutely insist you check Mr. O'Dowd, to see if any of *his* prints match those on the ammunition. Have you examined him for gunshot residue as well?" Something about McKendrick's expression must have clued her in. "You didn't? That was somewhat remiss of you. Why didn't you do that from the beginning?"

"Because Bobby was never a suspect," McKendrick ground out from between clenched teeth. "And he still ain't."

"Fortunately, you're not the final arbiter on that." Jericho's mother gave Detective Villanova a significant look. "Wouldn't you agree?"

Villanova pressed his lips together, clearly unwilling to act at odds with McKendrick, but then he reluctantly nodded. "She's got a point. If that pistol started out in O'Dowd's possession, it means Hansen and West have been telling the truth all along. It turns the whole case around."

"I will remind you once more that Mr. West and my son are in agreement with their statements, despite the fact that they've been separated since the incident," Dahlia said firmly. "Which means that it doesn't just 'turn the case around', as you so elegantly put it. It means that those four men provoked my two *unarmed* clients with hate speech, then drew firearms with the intent of murdering at least one of them in cold blood, then lied about it to the police *after* they were beaten bloody in self-defense. I believe you should find an indictable offense in there somewhere, if you look hard enough. Don't you?"

Detective Villanova set his jaw and stood up from his chair. Pulling out his phone, he headed for the door.

"Where are you going?" asked McKendrick, his voice suspicious.

Villanova paused and looked around. "I'm calling the lab guys. We've got to get to the bottom of this, one way or the other."

For a moment, Jericho thought McKendrick was going to protest, but then the cop waved a resigned hand. "Yeah. Do it." Opening the door, Villanova stepped into the corridor; it swung closed behind him.

Silence fell, broken only by the faint buzzing of a fly up in the corner of the room. McKendrick tried to glare at them; Jericho returned the gaze steadily, while his mother let it slide off her with a faint smile at the corner of her mouth. In other circumstances, Jericho would've found the man's loyalty to his brother-in-law admirable, but deliberately victimizing an innocent to save one's kin was a slippery slope that led to nothing good.

The door opened and Villanova re-entered. "Turns out we've already got O'Dowd on file. The forensics guys are checking the bullets for usable prints now. We'll see who we can match them to." His tone was light as he re-took his seat, but the glance he sent toward McKendrick told the tale; it was Jericho he believed and not the other man. "They said they can get back to us in about an hour and a half, maybe two hours."

Dahlia smiled wide and warmly. She leaned back in her chair and almost theatrically smoothed down her dress. "Oh, *I* can wait."

And wait they did.

Time ticked by; after about fifteen minutes, Dahlia sighed to herself and opened her briefcase again. This time, she pulled out a deck of cards. Jericho sat up with interest and Villanova looked mildly intrigued, but McKendrick scowled and sat back. She smiled dryly and dealt out three hands of stud poker.

It had been a long time since Jericho had played cards with his mother, and he didn't know anything about Villanova's capabilities. He would've expected a gay police detective to have a good poker face on general principles, but it turned out his mother was an absolute card-shark of the highest degree. It was a good thing, he reflected, that they weren't playing for money. If that had been the case, the pair of them together would've skinned him to the bone.

Time ticked on. Small talk crossed the table, but by unspoken agreement, nobody mentioned the case, or the results they were waiting on. At one point, Detective Villanova left the room and came back with coffee and sweet rolls for everyone. Jericho continued to lose badly at cards. His concentration wasn't helped by the fact that Villanova glanced at him every now and again with a faintly quizzical expression.

A little less than two hours and several thousand imaginary dollars' worth of lost hands of cards later, Villanova's phone chimed. He carefully placed his cards face-down on the table and answered the call. "Yes. Uh huh. You sure on that?" A few moments passed while he listened to the person the other hand, then he nodded without seeming to think about it. "Okay. Right. Thanks." Shutting off the call, he sighed heavily.

"Well?" asked McKendrick after a moment. "What'd they say?" But his face was already collapsing into a grimace; he knew, before any words were spoken.

An echoing expression of pain crossed over Villanova's face. "I'm sorry, man. I really am. Your boy Bobby? They found his prints all over the bullets." He shook his head. "He's not going to be able to talk his way out of this one."

McKendrick stared at the table, and Jericho couldn't help but feel a little sorry for the man. "Fuck," muttered the cop. "I *trusted* him. My sister is gonna kill me."

Delicately, Dahlia Hansen cleared her throat. "Well then," she said. "I believe that clears my son of any wrongdoing? You'll be dropping all charges, correct?"

"Yes, ma'am." Detective Villanova nodded. "He's free to go. On behalf of the Savannah PD, I'd like to offer my apologies for the inconvenience."

Jericho opened his mouth to say something witty and cutting, but his mother raised one finger and wagged it from side to side in an unmistakable shushing gesture. Getting the hint, he closed his mouth again. Sometimes, he gathered, it was better to be magnanimous in victory.

"Good." Dahlia almost purred the word. "I'd like to expedite the paperwork to get him out of here. I'm sure nobody wants to have to deal with a lawsuit for false arrest on top of all this, correct?"

From the unhappy look on McKendrick's face as he began to get his files back into order, he understood her all too well. A spurious lawsuit could be thrown out by the court, but McKendrick had cut too many corners in his efforts to nail Daryl on *something*, and he knew it. If Jericho hadn't been so closely involved with the situation, he might even have been a little sympathetic. That ship, of course, had long since sailed.

"It'll get done," Villanova promised. "And then *I* can sign out and go home." He paused as Jericho rose. "Uh, Mr. Hansen?"

Oh, shit. What does he want? What's he seen? Jericho turned as innocently as he could toward the detective. "Yeah?" Out of the corner of his eye, he saw his mother looking speculatively toward the detective as she gathered up the cards.

"All the time we've been here, I kept feeling that you look familiar," Villanova said. "But I can't think of where. Am I mistaken, or have we met before?"

Jericho had no idea whether Villanova had genuinely recognized him from his G-Man identity, or if he was just hitting on him. If the latter, he had to admire the man's chutzpah, though he feared it was the former. If it was, and he disclaimed all knowledge whatsoever, the detective might worry at the problem until he happened upon the correct solution.

"Maybe at Starbucks?" he suggested. He had no taste for the overpriced coffee, but he'd seen Villanova drinking it occasionally. "We may have met in line."

"Oh. Yeah. That makes sense." Villanova nodded, his brow clearing. "Y'all take care now, folks."

"Thank you," Dahlia replied serenely, taking up her briefcase. "We'll leave you to deal with the actual bad guys. Come on, Jericho."

He followed her out of the interrogation room, along the corridor and through several doors. Another officer brought over zip-lock evidence bags containing their belongings. Jericho would've been glad to just take the contents and leave, but his mother insisted that he check everything out before signing off on it.

With his tie hanging loose around his neck, he was just adjusting the strap on his watch as they came out into a waiting room. His father was waiting there, along with Leroy and Daryl. As soon as they came into sight, Beau moved forward to meet them. "You all right, boy?" he asked. "What happened in there? They didn't beat you up or anything?" Putting his hands on Jericho's shoulders, he looked his son over carefully.

"No, I just spent a couple hours in a holding cell before the guy pulled me out for interrogation," Jericho assured him. "Nobody bothered me in there. Two drunks and a guy in the corner who kept muttering about how the Madness were coming to get him." He briefly related the tale of the bullets and the fingerprints thereon, and how his mother had unraveled the whole thing.

While his father was digesting that, he turned to Daryl. "How you doing?"

"Pissed they made me miss the funeral, but glad we's both upright an' walkin'." The big man clasped hands with him.

"You and me both." He studied the older man. Like Jericho himself, Daryl looked a little disheveled, but in good health all the same. This was not a trivial concern for people of color who went into police custody. Worse, had Daryl been the one holding the pistol when the police arrived, there was a chance they might've opened fire no matter *what* he did. Which hadn't been part of Jericho's calculation when he stepped into the fight, but he was beginning to think it should've been. "Good thing you recognized that guy and told Mama about him."

"Near on didn't," Daryl confessed. "Only recollected about his brother-in-law when I heard th' two of 'em talkin' together. Hoped your mama could do somethin' with that, so I told her."

"She surely did something with it, all right." He took a deep breath and tried to push aside the rush of guilt as he looked around at Leroy. "I'm so sorry I missed the rest of the funeral. I tried to tell the police, but they just wouldn't listen."

"Weren't your fault nohow," Leroy said, clasping Jericho's shoulder. "Them shitheels was the ones that pushed it." Beside him, Daryl nodded.

"I'm just a little concerned that you two got into a fight at all." Dahlia frowned unhappily. "What were you *thinking?*"

Beau shook his head. "I'm more interested in how the blue blazes you managed to beat up three men when they were coming at you like that."

Jericho took a deep breath. He'd been wanting to avoid this question, but it had been somewhat of a forlorn hope. "I started taking martial-arts lessons a while back. You know, to protect myself." He half-shrugged in his best imitation of false modesty. "I'm basically the equivalent of a black belt in Krav Maga."

"Well, shee-it." If Jericho hadn't known better, he would've been taken in by Leroy's expression of surprise. "An' here I thought you was th' same wimp Luke hadda protect all th' way through middle school."

"Well, that *does* make sense." Beau inhaled air between his teeth. "And it also explains a few things. The way you've been taking all this on yourself, like you could've saved him if you'd just been there?" He eyed Jericho keenly. "You really think you could've, don't you?"

Jericho dropped his eyes and looked away. He *knew* without a doubt Luke would be alive if he'd just stayed in the apartment.

"Oh, son." Beau squeezed his shoulder. "I get it. You've got some training, and you obviously know how to apply it. But winning one fight doesn't make you unbeatable. If you'd been there, you might've died as well. Nobody's unbeatable."

"Trust me, I know I can be beaten." Jericho thought back to the way that Independence had handed him his ass, two falls out of two. "I'm not going to be making a habit of going out and taking on people who know a lot more about it than I do."

Leroy gave him a sharp glance at that, and he knew his uncle had picked up on the double meaning.

"Well, *I'm* glad you're alright," his mother said, her stiff reserve softening. She hugged him tightly. "You boys wait here. You two are in the clear, but those low-lives tried to murder Daryl, so I'm going to nail their hides to the *wall*. Those boys are going to regret ever crossing your path. I mean, any day would've been bad enough, but they had to pull this *today*." Jericho heard the unspoken words all too clearly. *On the day of Luke's funeral.*

"Jes' wait one minute," Leroy said. "Daryl an' Jericho is in th' clear right now?"

She nodded. "That's correct. All charges have been dropped. The police are looking at charging the other four right now."

"Then let 'em handle it," Leroy said bluntly. "Me an' Daryl is good. Jericho?"

Jericho suddenly found himself the center of attention. He knew exactly why Leroy was saying this; the last thing his uncle wanted was to give the police any excuse to look more closely at him. "I'm fine," he said with a shrug. Truth be told, he wouldn't have minded seeing his mother legally bury the guys as well, but he had just as little desire for police scrutiny as Leroy did.

She gave him a searching glance, then nodded. "Hm. Very well."

Turning, she led the way out of the building. Jericho hurried to keep up with her brisk pace as they descended the steps outside the precinct station. Streetlights cast their yellow glow over the grimy sidewalk, and a cool breeze chased a fugitive newspaper page down the road. His parents' car was parked a little way down the road, with Leroy's battered 4×4 behind it.

Beau opened the passenger side front door for Dahlia. "Come on, let's go home. It's been a day."

"I'll be over in a bit," Leroy said as Jericho started getting into the back of the car. "Got some stuff ta talk about."

Jericho glanced at him, eyebrows raised. Leroy gave him a slight nod. *Oh, good. He's got the documents.* He had no doubt that part of the 'stuff' Leroy wanted to talk about would involve how Jericho intended to pay him. The likes of Leroy didn't do this kind of work gratis; in any case, Jericho was going to insist on paying him. For a superhero to owe an underworld figure for questionably legal work was the very definition of 'conflict of interest'. Leroy had made it clear he wasn't going to hold anything over Jericho's head for the fact that the work had been done, but if there was a lack of money forthcoming, Jericho couldn't guarantee that this state of affairs would hold.

Closing the door, he leaned back in the seat and fastened the belt. Through the window, Daryl caught his eye and nodded. Jericho nodded back; *see you 'round.* He'd made the right move in Daryl's case, and his kinsman was alive to see another day. That wasn't much against the guilt he still felt about Luke, but it was something.

His father went around the front of the car and got in, then started the engine. Smoothly, he pulled out of the parking space and drove off down the empty road. Jericho let himself relax; he was out of that situation, and just wanted to put it behind him.

Not so his mother. "Jericho," she said, after they'd been on the road for less than two minutes, "what was that officer badgering you about before I got there?"

He wasn't even surprised. She was a lawyer; of course she'd want to know. "He wanted me to put the whole thing on Daryl," he said simply. "A white guy defending himself against four other white guys would've been a hard case for them to push, but … yeah." He didn't explicate the fact that they seemed to have a thick file on Daryl already. A black man with a prior criminal history, supposedly firing off an firearm he had no permit for in the middle of the city, would be an absolute gimme for the DA to prosecute. They would've been printing extra pages for the book to throw at him.

"I see." Dahlia didn't follow up on that line of inquiry, confirming Jericho's suspicion that she knew all about it already and was choosing to politely ignore it. "And of course, you shut him down hard." She sounded very certain of that.

"Hard as I could," he confirmed. "Daryl's kin." He didn't want to lead back into any kind of allusion toward Leroy's shadier dealings, so he changed the subject. "If the cops didn't call you guys, how did you know where I was?"

Beau fielded that one. "We didn't, not at first. When you didn't come back to the church, we figured Daryl was keeping an eye on you. But you didn't show at the cemetery, and your mother started getting worried. So, I called your cell. But nobody answered. It just kept ringing out. Leroy tried Daryl's, and the same thing happened. And when we got home and you weren't there either, that's when we really got worried."

Dahlia took up the narrative. "I called Ellie, right away. She called everyone she knew in the area to start looking for you. But when Olivia heard you were missing, she asked why they hadn't looked at the locator app on Luke's phone. She knew it was there but couldn't get into the phone. But Serena could."

Jericho nodded. "She was the only one Luke ever shared his PIN code with. So, you found my phone, and found me, huh?"

"Got it in one," Beau agreed. "Of course, once we worked out where you were, we knew Daryl had to be there as well. Your mama decided that we had to get you both out of there as soon as possible, so we came straight over."

"And I appreciate it." Jericho knew there were several very good reasons for the fact that she'd dealt with Daryl's case first, and he wasn't about to second-guess his mother's judgment on the subject.

"So, that nice Detective Villanova," she mused after a few more minutes. "He's rather handsome, isn't he? I thought I saw him paying you quite a bit of attention. And not just because he's a police detective."

It didn't surprise Jericho that she'd picked up on Raul Villanova's orientation. He felt his cheeks heating up. This was a conversation that he did not need to have right at that moment. Or ever, really. "Mama, not now. Please."

"All right," she assented. "Just remember; just because you had a bad experience with one person doesn't mean you can't try again. After all, there's plenty more fish in the sea."

Yeah, but the fish I want to be with doesn't live in Savannah. Which sounded weird even in his own head, but his situation was anything but normal.

Conversation lapsed after that, limited to a few remarks about how beautiful the funeral had been. The subtext was that Luke would've been pleased with it. Jericho had his own opinions about that; he suspected that given his druthers, Luke would've wanted to be buried in his car, one hand on the wheel and the other on the gearshift, foot on the accelerator pedal, burning rubber into eternity. But that was just him.

55
Running Away, Running Toward

When they arrived at the house, Jericho got out and opened the car door for his mother. Beau unlocked the front door and they all trooped inside, switching lights on as they went. As Jericho went upstairs to his room to change, he heard Beau audibly wondering what Leroy was coming over to talk about.

He showered, then put on casual clothes and the light jacket he'd worn the previous day. Carefully, he repacked his overnight bag, starting with his costume satchel. Now that he was aware of the laundry facilities that came with short-stay apartments, he had more leeway with how much clothing he was going to need. Still, he made sure to pack several outfits in case he was caught short.

Leaving the bag upstairs, he came down when his mother called. She'd served up a modest meal out of leftovers, which he welcomed. Just as with everything else, his Prodigy rating let him get by on minimal food if there was no other choice, but it was still better to eat than not to eat. He cheerfully ignored the curious looks from his parents when they saw he was wearing a jacket indoors; if they weren't going to mention it, neither was he.

They were just finishing up the meal when the doorbell sounded, ringing its tones through the house. "I'll get it," he said. Getting up, he wiped his mouth on his napkin and headed on through to answer the door. When he opened it, Leroy was standing on the mat.

"Jericho, boy. How you doing?" his uncle asked. He glanced past Jericho into the front hall, then handed him a bulky folded-over paper bag. Jericho took it, feeling the heft of the documents inside. He had to admire how smoothly his uncle had handled the pass; any potential watchers on the street would've totally missed it. Trying to be equally adroit, he slid the bag into the inside pocket of his jacket.

"Definitely better now," he replied. "Come on in." He stepped back to let Leroy past, then closed the door behind him. They went back through into the dining room, where Beau and Dahlia looked up expectantly.

"Leroy. How's Daryl?" asked Beau, getting up to greet his brother.

"Last I seen, drinkin' an' shootin' pool with th' boys. Ain't the first time this kinda thing's happened to him, prob'ly won't be the last." Leroy clasped Beau's hand. "You know how it goes."

"I believe I do," agreed Dahlia with a tight smile. "I think it's unconscionable, the way they were trying to frame him in that way. He and Jericho were merely defending themselves."

"Though the boy's on their radar now," said Leroy, catching Jericho's eye. "Not ta mention, the guys he tuned up might have buddies who'll be wantin' ta git some payback. It might be an idea for him to keep his head down for a spell."

Jericho took the hint. "Yeah. I was thinking I'd go back to Utopia City for a bit. There's stuff I need to do there, anyway."

"What?" Beau stared at him. "Are you serious? You can't be serious, boy. After what just happened?"

"No!" said Dahlia at the same time. "It's too dangerous! There's no *way* you can go back there!"

Leroy cleared his throat and raised his voice just a little. "Jes' hold on one minute there, folks. Jericho's already shown he c'n take care o' hisself. It's a right smart idea for him ta git outta town for a little while, jes' in case."

Beau looked at his brother as though he'd sprouted a second head. "You have to be joking. When you went there yourself, you promised me you'd get my son back home if you had to drag him by the hair. And now you're saying he should go *back*?"

"Ain't sayin' he *should*," Leroy said, though it was perfectly obvious he'd said almost exactly that. "But gittin' outta town's a good idea, an' he did say as how he's got business there."

Dahlia turned to look at Jericho. "What *kind* of business?" she asked carefully. "Or do I not want to know?"

He wasn't quite sure how to go on with that, so he shrugged. "Just something I need to do."

"Well, how long are you going to be?" She was persistent, but that was life with a lawyer for a mother. Though he supposed it was also a motherly trait on its own.

"I don't know. As long as I need to be." He hated fobbing her off like that, but he honestly didn't know how long he was going to be in Utopia City. Handing the fake IDs over would take only a few minutes but tracking Portman down might take anything from a day to a week, or longer.

Beau shook his head. "I really don't think this is a good idea. At least if you stay in town, we can protect you."

For 'protect', read 'smother'. Jericho had several objections to that idea, most of which he couldn't air. However, some of them he could. "And I'd never be able to go out without looking over my shoulder all the time. If I'm in Utopia City, anyone coming after me isn't going to have backup, and they'd have to leave any guns behind before they got on the train. If they even found out where I was, that is."

"What, no guns? None at all?" His mother was originally from New York, where gun ownership wasn't quite as omnipresent as it was in the Southern states. He couldn't tell if her tone was disbelieving or just wistful.

"When I was there, I only saw cops carrying," he said thoughtfully. "I don't know the local laws, but even if civilians are allowed to go armed in Utopia City, there's a *lot* fewer firearms per capita than there are around here."

"Well, *I'm* sold," Leroy declared heartily. "When was you thinkin' of goin', anyways?"

Jericho flipped a mental coin and decided (once more) to take the hint Leroy was offering. "How about right now?"

"I like your grit, boy." Leroy smacked his fist into his palm approvingly. "Take that there bull by th' balls. Fetch your belongings. I'll drop you off at the station."

"What? No!" Dahlia started around the table. "Leroy, are you out of your mind? You're not taking my son anywhere!"

"Dahlia, jes' listen, will ya? He'll be *safer* there!" Jericho's uncle pointed at the doorway. "Git your stuff, boy. I'll handle this."

"Don't you move a muscle, son." Beau was also on his feet. "You're not leaving this city. You're not leaving this *house*. Not until we know it's safe. And you're *damn* sure not going back to Utopia City."

Jericho dodged around his father. "Pa, I'm twenty-three. I'm not a child anymore. You can't legally stop me from going. And I *am* going. There's stuff I've got to do."

"You're *our* child." His mother came toward him, her eyes wide with entreaty, her hands held out toward him. The raw emotion in her voice caught at the back of his throat and brought a prickle to his eyes. "You're my baby boy. Please, just *think* about what you're doing."

"I *am* thinking about it." Jericho backed away toward the stairs. "I've thought about nothing else since I got back. This is something I have to do." He turned and ran up the stairs, taking them two at a time. Behind him, she called his name; he steeled his resolve and kept going. *Smokeshadow and Thomas and the rest of the Survivors are depending on me.*

Ducking into his room, he shut the door firmly and leaned against it, breathing deeply and fighting back the tears that threatened to well in his eyes. It seemed that no matter where he turned, the road to doing what was right and necessary was being blocked by well-meaning relatives. The emotional strain was worse than it had been with Leroy back in Utopia City, or even with Stephen, and he'd ducked the latter confrontation until he could no longer avoid it. This one had exploded in his face without warning, though he knew he really should've expected it. He was just thankful that Leroy was on his side now; if they'd all been set against him, he had no idea how he would've handled it.

Once he had himself under control again, he moved to where the overnight bag sat on the bed and zipped the package Leroy had given him into the same side pocket that he'd carried the photo of Transit in. He slung the bag over his shoulder and headed toward the closed door ... then paused. Moving like a sleepwalker, he turned and looked at the window. One floor up; he'd hardly even need to use his powers to get down safely. It would also bypass the argument waiting downstairs and allow them to think he was still in his room until it was too late. It was the perfect solution.

He took one step toward the window, then stopped and shook his head. *No. I can't do it that way. Not to Mama and Pa.* Sneaking out on Stephen had seemed the only viable solution at the time, but he drew the line at doing the same to his parents. Unlike his manipulative ex-boyfriend, they only wanted the best for him. Stephen had wanted to keep Jericho for himself and (to mix a metaphor) eat his cake at the same time.

He had no real desire to go down and face the music. But Leroy was down there, holding the line while he was up here. If he just kept hiding in his room like a wimp, he'd never get back to Utopia City. People were depending on him, and Luke's murderer was still on the loose. At least, he hadn't seen anything on the news about Portman being in police custody.

Putting his hand on the doorknob, he paused to give the room a nostalgic look. While coming back home like this had been an imperfect solution—the current situation downstairs was a good illustration of *that*—it had been the best of a series of bad choices. Looking around the room was a glimpse into a kinder, gentler time; unfortunately, those days were long gone. He was an adult now, with hard choices to make. Switching off the light, he left the room and closed the door behind him.

The house was large and old, and sound tended to carry. From the moment he stepped into the corridor, he could hear the raised voices between his parents and Leroy downstairs, but they didn't start forming coherent words until he was halfway down the steps.

"—can not *believe* you're advocating that our son go straight back into danger again! What were you *thinking?*" That was his mother, her tone sharp enough to slice diamond.

"How in the blue blazes are we supposed to keep him safe while we're in Savannah and he's in Utopia City?" argued his father in counterpoint.

"Beau, Dahlia, jes' listen to me for once in your lives!" Leroy's bellow cut over the both of them. "What I seen of Utopia, it's a damn sight safer'n Savannah! What happened to my Luke was a shame an' a tragedy, but th' guy that did it weren't even a local! He was some out-of-town meth-head that thought his lady was cheatin' on him! Just one o' them things. Sheer goddamn stinkin' bad luck."

"And if he finds out Jericho's back in town and decides to come after him as well?" demanded Dahlia. "What if he thinks Jericho saw something? Witness protection exists for a reason!" As Jericho came back into the dining room, she turned to look at him. "Where do you think you're going with that bag? You are *not* leaving this house, young man!"

Logic told him he should keep walking and not let himself be caught up in the argument. As he'd feared, it lost to the concern he felt for his parents. "Mama, Pa, I have to go," he said, half-apologetically, half-defensively. "It's just something I've gotta do." Perhaps they'd listen to soft words where harsh ones had not moved them.

The look his mother gave him nearly tore his heart in half right down the middle. "But *why?*" she demanded. Not as a lawyer arguing a case, but as a mother deathly afraid of losing her only child. "*Why* do you have to go? Why do you have to go back *there?*"

He shook his head. There was no reason he could give them that would satisfy their questions, and some answers would raise queries that he couldn't answer. *Should I tell them I'm Enabled?* But outing himself would clue them in that he was going after Luke's murderer; even if he managed to convince them how capable he was, they'd still be terrified for his well-being. Perhaps more than they were now. There were no good answers. "I'm sorry. I've just … I've just *got* to."

"That's not good enough, boy." Beau stepped in front of him, setting his broad frame as a physical barrier. "You're not leaving this house before you answer your mother. What's so important about Utopia City? Don't tell me you're still fixing to get a job there, not after this."

He'd almost forgotten the excuse he'd made to go in the first place. Fortunately, it had been based in reality, which gave him his answer. "No. The job offer fell through. I bombed out in the interview. But there's something else I need to do."

"Like *what?*" demanded Beau, taking a step closer. "Son, why in blue blazes would you go *back* there, after what happened to Luke?"

The words burst out of him before he could stop them. "*This has got nothing to do with Luke!*" There was a shocked pause, as his parents stared at him. In the past, he'd raised his voice in the house, but he'd never shouted at them like this.

"I'm sorry," he said into the vacuum. "But it really doesn't have anything to do with him. This is a totally different matter." He searched his parents' faces for acceptance that he was going but found only hurt and confusion. Leaving them to wonder what was going on pained him almost as much as it did them. He didn't want to leave matters up in the air like this, but he couldn't see any alternatives suggesting themselves.

"Then what *is* it about?" Dahlia reached out toward him. "Why do you have to go back? Explain it to me. Help me understand."

Jericho took a deep breath. *I'm going to have to give them* something, *or they just won't let up.* "Okay, fine," he said. "The reason I'm going back is that there's some people in Utopia City who need my help." He put his free hand up, palm out to forestall any more questions. "I've offered, they've accepted, and I'm going back to help them. Don't ask me anything else." With an effort, he forced himself to turn away from them, toward Leroy. "Can we go now? Please?"

His uncle clapped him on the shoulder. "Sure thing, boy."

"Leroy." Beau took a step forward. "You're my *brother*. Why are you doing this? Why are you *helping* him do this?"

The two brothers faced each other. Despite their fraternal resemblance, they were separated by a divide far wider than the few feet between them. "I got me some pretty good reasons," drawled Leroy. "*His* reasons are mighty damn compelling, too." He moved toward Beau and prodded his brother in the chest. "An' you shouldn't be askin' stupid-ass questions. He's your *blood.* Y'all should be trustin' that he knows what he's doin' an' backin' his play, 'stead of givin' him the third, fourth an' fifth degree." Turning back to Jericho, he hooked his head toward the front door. "Let's git movin'. Ellie's expectin' me back home afore midnight an' I do not aim to disappoint."

Jericho faced his parents. "I'm sorry," he managed at last, and forced himself to follow in Leroy's footsteps. A heavy tread behind him, along with his G-sense, warned him that his father was coming up behind him.

The older man's hand closed on his arm. "Jericho. Son." His father's voice was low and intense.

He's going to ask me to stay. Jericho wasn't sure how much more of this he could take. He was already on the verge of tears. "Yeah, Pa?"

"If this is something you've really got to do ... promise me, if someone starts something with you, you do what you did to those guys, and you keep doing it 'til they can't get up anymore, okay? Do *not* hesitate and do *not* hold back." The look in Beau's eyes was almost desperate. "Promise me that at least, son."

Jericho blinked. This was a side to his father he'd never seen before. "I ... I promise, Pa. I'll come back safe to you."

Beau grimaced. "See that you do. If you get hurt out there, your mama will kill us both. You for going, and me for letting you." He nodded past Jericho toward his brother. "Leroy says you'll be safe. Don't go making a liar out of him, understand me?"

"I won't. I promise." Jericho tugged gently and felt his father's grasp loosen. "I have to go, but I will be back." He followed Leroy out through the front door and down the steps. Behind him, he heard his mother berating his father for letting him go, and his father asking exactly what he could have done. Gritting his teeth, he pushed on, hating the fact that he was the source of discord between the two people he loved most in the world.

Leroy was waiting at the curb, leaning on the hood of his truck, by the time Jericho got there. "Ya gonna be okay?" he asked, studying Jericho's face.

"There's not a damn thing about all this that's okay," Jericho said. As he tossed the overnight bag into the back of the 4×4, he paused for thought. "Well, *almost* nothing. If I hadn't gone to Utopia City, Thomas and the others would still be in the fix they're in, and there'd be nobody to bail them out. Still, Luke ..." He grimaced, not liking where his thoughts were taking him. *Bobbi, too. If I'd been there ...*

"Luke went to that damn city of his own accord, an' nothin' nobody said woulda made a lick of difference." Leroy's tone was blunt and uncompromising. "Now git your ass in the damn truck. Ellie's like ta whup me crosseyed if I ain't home when I said I'd be."

Obediently, Jericho got into the passenger seat. The truck was old, the seat covers almost worn through in places, but the motor started strongly when Leroy turned the key and ran smoothly thereafter. Jericho closed his eyes and leaned back in the seat, trying to quiet the turmoil of his thoughts. He was on the way to Utopia City once more, but the way he'd left his parents arguing put a sour taste in his mouth. *It'll all be good once I come back.* He knew he was lying to himself even then; nothing would be the same again. Not with him, and definitely not with Stephen.

They were almost to the maglev station when something Leroy had said occurred to Jericho. "Uncle Leroy," he said diffidently, hitching himself higher in the seat. "Back in the house … did you mean 'take the bull by the horns'? Because I'm pretty sure you said something different."

Leroy chuckled. "Nope, you heard right. Takin' the bull by the horns is a dumbass act, 'cause then you're standin' right in front of the sumbitch. Don't never give nobody a free shot, y'hear me?"

"Oh, I hear you." Jericho wasn't in the habit of giving out free shots. He was good at fighting and taking a punch, but any hit that got through was one fewer he could take later.

"Good ta hear. An' while we're flappin' our gums." Leroy drove past the frontage of the station, then pulled the truck into the attached parking lot. The maglev ran twenty-four-seven so there were a few cars parked there. High-powered floodlights overlooking the lot gave everything a yellowish hue. Leroy selected a space away from the other cars and pulled the vehicle to a halt. Turning the engine off, he looked over at Jericho. "Couple-three things we need ta go over afore you git on that there train."

Jericho had been expecting this. He wasn't an expert on fake IDs, but Luke had once explained that they got more expensive the better they were. Which was perfectly logical; he was fully expecting the project to more or less drain his bank accounts. It would mean a lean time while he saved up again, but at least the Survivors would be safe. Or at least, more safe than in Utopia City. "The documents, right?"

"Yeah, but not in the way you're thinkin'." Leroy scratched the back of his head. "You done saved Daryl's life today. If I hadn't been certain-sure you could handle yourself before, you surely proved it now. He told me what happened. You messed them guys up but good. Even if you did git kinda obvious there."

Jericho grimaced. "Yeah, that first one rushed me a bit when he started pulling the gun. After that, I wasn't sure what the others had planned, so I had to put 'em down as fast as I could. If I'd had more time, I could've been more subtle about it."

"Never mind *that*, boy." Leroy snorted with amusement. "Don't never apologize for kickin' shit outta some asshole that desperately needs it. What I'm sayin' is, Daryl's alive 'cause of you. So, I'm gonna be waivin' payment for them documents. Plus, each of them bank accounts is gonna have five hundred in it, free an' clear."

Jericho felt his jaw drop. That was three thousand dollars, even before the cost of the actual documents. "You don't have to do that—" he began.

Leroy prodded him in the shoulder. "Don't you never tell me what I can an' cain't do, boy," he said, his voice flat. "You might be some big-time superhero, but I'm your uncle, an' don't you forget it." His words hung in the air for a long moment, then he barked a laugh and slapped Jericho in the chest with the back of his hand. "Jes' joshin' with you, boy. But I'm also serious. I'm payin' for all that stuff, an' you ain't gonna say shit about it. Oh, an' one other thing. Had a word with Daryl. From the way he was talkin' up how you handled them shitheels, he was well on the way to figurin' out the truth about you bein' G-Man. So, I filled him in, then made certain-sure he knows that it's between you an' us, an' not ta start spreadin' it around. Just so's you know."

"Right. And thanks." Jericho's mind whirled with the new information. From the moment he'd stepped in and groin-kicked the guy with the gun, the notion had been brewing in the back of his mind that one of them could connect the dots and link him with his heroic identity. For some reason, he'd never thought Daryl would be the one to do that instead. Of course, now that Daryl knew, Jericho was confident his secret was safe with the big man.

"Ain't nothin'. Kin looks after kin. You proved that this afternoon." Leroy awkwardly offered his right hand to shake. "Now you git on back to Utopia City, an' you find that sumbitch, an' you do what you gotta do. I'm dependin' on you ta git it done. An' don't forget ta watch your back. Don't let nobody git the drop on you."

Leroy's tone was rough, but the look in his eyes held a level of pleading Jericho had never seen from him before. He swallowed a lump in his throat as he shook his uncle's hand. "I will surely do that."

Undoing his seatbelt, he climbed out of the 4×4 then retrieved his overnight bag from the load bed. "I'll, uh, I'll see you when I get back." Slinging the bag over his shoulder, he headed across the parking lot toward the maglev station. When he got to the steps, he took them two at a time, then paused and looked back. The truck was still sitting there, with Leroy watching him from the driver's seat. He raised his hand in a half-salute; there was an answering movement within the darkness of the vehicle's cab.

Chilly, astringent air spilled out into the night as the automatic doors slid open before him. He stepped inside, the fluorescent lighting harsh on his eyes. Out in the parking lot, the engine of Leroy's truck started up, the sound cutting off as the doors closed behind him.

He had the bag still slung over his shoulder as he moved to the nearest ticket kiosk. Without pausing, he took out his MagCard and ran through the routine of purchasing a ticket, tapping past the options as fast as they came up. In far less time than it had taken him the first time round, he had his ticket to Utopia City organized; as before, he deselected the option of phone coverage on the maglev.

This time, he didn't have to wait for more than five minutes before the train was ready to board. Only three other people were in the station with him, and all three were traveling west. Again, he went to the upper level and engaged the privacy bubble, but he left his overnight bag on the seat beside him rather than bothering with the overhead locker.

As the maglev started on its way, he leaned back in the seat, much as he'd done in the car, and closed his eyes. He didn't even bother trying to tell himself that the argument with his parents was over; it was merely postponed until he returned. That wasn't what was bothering him right at that moment, though. Even though he was on the way back to Utopia City, his thoughts kept returning to Savannah. To Stephen.

This was the first chance he'd really had to think about the breakup since it happened. All things considered, especially since there was no doubt that it was justified, he would've much preferred to leave it behind him where it belonged. But it nagged at him, refusing to let him go. It didn't matter that Stephen had been Trevoring him and had been a cheating asshat; he'd still cared deeply for the man. The bond they'd shared had been a constant in his life, and now it was … gone. There was an aching void where it had once been.

I don't know how to deal with this. Jericho Hansen was Enabled, a superhero, with powers above and beyond any normal person. There were many situations he was uniquely qualified to handle. This wasn't one of them. He could glide above the city or freeze the internal workings of a firearm, but his heart still did odd things when he found himself deprived of emotional stability. For the first time, he began to understand how people could so easily fall into rebound relationships, seeking to fill the sudden emptiness that came with the loss of trust and love.

As the maglev blitzed on through the night, he turned the problem over and over in his mind. Unable to truly settle down and brood, he worried at the issue without ever quite coming to a resolution. Whenever the speakers announced that the train was passing through a new city, he took up his bag and moved forward on autopilot, trying to figure out *some* way to get past the raw-edged hole that Stephen had left in his emotional foundations.

Two and a half hours and six cities later, he still hadn't come to any sort of meaningful conclusion. What he'd had with Stephen felt *real*, no matter how fake it had been from his erstwhile boyfriend's side. He'd poured his heart and soul into their relationship, and he'd thought Stephen felt the same way. To find that this was not true had torn the underpinnings out from under a major part of his life. He felt disjointed, unbalanced. His compass no longer pointed true.

Along with a great many more people than had boarded with him in Savannah, he stepped off the train in Utopia City. Yawning, he rode the escalators down to ground level and called an air-cab for the Oaklands. Fatigue was starting to hit hard as he climbed into the vehicle; he pushed it back and paid for the trip before strapping himself in.

Once the cab was in the air, he turned on his phone and took out the card Smokeshadow had given him. Halfway through dialing the number, he paused, frowning thoughtfully. *They routinely monitor text messages,* Thomas had said. Putting the card away again, he went online, then delved into his files for the email address that Smokeshadow had sent the documents from. He'd deleted the mail itself, of course; while it could probably be retrieved with a deep search, he didn't want it easily found via casual inspection of his inbox.

Gandalf the Grey has returned, he typed, then tapped Send with a grin.

Either she was a light sleeper, or she hadn't been to bed yet. Where prodigies were concerned, it could've been one or the other. Within a minute, he got a message back, but all it said was: *Cool.*

Frowning, he waited, but no other message came through. She was a prodigy. This sort of thing, as far as he could tell, was her bread and butter. There was no *way* she would've forgotten to include a way to get the documents off him.

The air-cab wove its way across Utopia City while he wrestled with the problem. There were no numbers appended to the email that he could see, or even any words that could be easily translated into numbers. Out of the corner of his eye, he vaguely registered the holographic enhancements to the cityscape, but he was concentrating too hard on the conundrum before him to properly appreciate them.

The sign over the Oaklands was a welcome sight; it meant his journey was nearly at an end, and he'd find out what Smokeshadow had planned. *Maybe she's waiting to meet me on the roof?* But he couldn't see anyone on the flat expanse. Not that this meant anything; with her costume's camouflage capabilities, he'd never see her from this distance unless she let him, even with the glow of the holo-sign.

With the usual thrumming of lifters, the cab grounded. He barely noticed the driver bidding him a good night as he got out. There was nobody waiting for him on the footpath, so he started along the path into the courtyard.

"Jericho!" The hissed voice came from between the trees to his right, just as his G-sense detected something there. Or rather, some*one*. Not adult-sized. Definitely not big enough to be Thomas, or even Smokeshadow, unless her costume was somehow able to conceal some of her mass from his senses.

"Who's there?" he asked, in an equally low tone. "Are you with Thomas?" That had to be almost a given, considering that he'd only told one person in Utopia City his name.

"Yeah!" It sounded like a kid, early teens at best. "An' Smokeshadow. She told me to say, *He was Gandalf the White by that point, you ignoramus.* You got the stuff?"

The phrasing sounded extremely familiar. Not even trying to figure out why she'd sent a kid in her place, he reached into the side pocket and handed over the packet of documents. "Here. Tell her she's welcome."

"Wow, cool!" The kid grabbed the paper bag; Jericho couldn't see much in the way of detail, but it looked like he was hugging the documents to his chest. "This is, uh, this is everything?"

"Everything she sent me," he confirmed, yawning. "Hey kid, you know if they caught him yet?"

There was a motion in the dimness as of a shaken head. "Nope. *'Leads are being pursued.'* Translation: they got nothin'. Sorry."

He grimaced. Once more, that sounded exactly how Smokeshadow would say it. He vaguely wondered how many other answers she'd primed the kid with. "Thanks anyway."

"She says you're welcome. Thomas says thanks. 'Night." There was a flicker in the darkness, and his G-sense registered that the person-sized mass had simply vanished.

Blinking, he reached out with his hand; there was nobody there. *I swear. This city.*

Well, it was entirely out of his hands now. Operating once more on autopilot, he went through to the admissions office and paid for a single-bedroom apartment, though he needed to be prompted to tap the reader with his MagCard. Giving the attendant a sheepish smile, he hefted his overnight bag—Prodigy rating or no Prodigy rating, it was getting heavier by the minute—and trudged off toward where he recalled the elevator to be.

It wasn't too hard to find his new room. His MagCard gained him entry, and he had just enough presence of mind to strip down to his boxers and drag on a t-shirt before he fell onto the bed. He'd discharged both his familial duty to Luke and his self-imposed task for Thomas and the Survivors. That was over and done, and now he was free to carry out a deeper and more personal duty. *Find Jack Portman, by whatever means necessary.* There were no more conflicts; no more cross-purposes. He was still feeling the push, but at least he was now going in the right direction.

Less than thirty seconds later, he was sound asleep.

56
A Hard-Earned Perspective

When Jericho next opened his eyes, sunlight was intruding through the window. He rolled over and retrieved his phone from the bedside table to check the time; it was a little after seven in the morning. Normally he'd be getting up by now, but it seemed the run of broken sleep he'd been having wasn't quite done with him. There'd been a few dreams disturbing his slumber, indicating that just being back in Utopia City wasn't enough. One way or the other, Portman had to go *down* before he'd be free to hit the snooze button with impunity once more.

Still, after the crappy rest he'd been getting over the last few days, he decided he'd earned a sleep-in. This wasn't to say he *wouldn't* be going after Portman, but first he needed to get back in contact with Stirling and find out what kind of leads the UCPD had on the man, and where he could follow them to. Eight o'clock seemed as good a time as any to get up and start prepping for the day. Dropping the phone back on the table, he closed his eyes and let himself slide back into a pleasant doze. Until a knock on the front door of the apartment roused him back to full awareness.

What the hell? It wasn't as though anyone except the receptionist knew which apartment he'd be in. *Do room service robots knock?* He was pretty sure they wouldn't intrude on an occupied apartment.

Then he heard a click, which sounded very much like the apartment door opening. Which was basically impossible, given that it wasn't keyed to anyone else's MagCard but his own. *Except the police entry cards.* But why would a cop be coming in; or rather, if the cops had reason to come into his apartment without his permission, why would they bother knocking first? Something wasn't adding up here.

Before his brain had even finished working its way through to that conclusion, he'd rolled off the bed. Cat-footed, he eased his way over to take up a position beside the partially open bedroom door. Every muscle coiled and ready, he set up in an ambush position, preparing himself for action. If whoever it was wanted to take him by surprise, they'd made a bad mistake by knocking first.

Very faint voices came to him; two people, whispering together. *Who are they, and what do they want?* Try as he might, he couldn't make out the words. This was becoming more and more bizarre by the second. Was this supposed to be some kind of *burglary?* If so, it was far and away the most inept one he'd ever seen.

A hand came into view, empty of any weapons. Reaching out, it knocked on his bedroom door. A familiar voice came next. "Jericho? Are you awake?"

Surprise washed through him like a sudden dousing in icy water. He nudged the bedroom door all the way open with his foot, then stepped into the doorway. "Thomas?" he asked. "What are *you* doing here?" Behind the young man was someone else he knew. "Smokeshadow? What the hell are you guys doing in my apartment?"

Smokeshadow snorted with amusement. "Well, *that's* a warm welcome for you. I never gave you my real name, did I? Hi, I'm Chelsea." She stepped forward and held out her hand.

"Uh, hi." Choosing for the moment to ignore the fact that he was standing there in his sleepwear, he shook her hand. "Not that I'm unhappy to see you both but seriously, what's going on?"

Thomas took a deep breath. "First off, Chelsea told me what happened to Luke. I am so sorry. I only met him the once, but he came across as good people to me." Stepping forward past Chelsea, he pulled Jericho into a hug.

"The best." Jericho felt tears welling in his eyes at the sincerity inherent in Thomas' words. "Thanks. I appreciate it." He held the hug until Chelsea cleared her throat, sounding amused. A little embarrassed, he reluctantly put his hands on Thomas' shoulders and eased the younger man out to arm's length. "But I'm reasonably sure you didn't come here just to pass on your condolences. What else is going on?"

Thomas nodded to acknowledge his words. "There's a place you need to see. You want to get dressed? We can pick up breakfast on the way."

Obvious evasion is obvious. There was something going on here that he didn't know about, and which they clearly weren't about to fill him in on. However, even though a cheeky smile was never far from Smokeshadow's lips, there was more concern in their expressions right at that moment than mischief. And while their reticence might be irritating, he did trust them. They'd earned that much, at least.

Still, it looked like the only way he was going to get answers was to see what they wanted to show him. "Okay, fine. Give me five minutes to take a shower." Letting Thomas go, he stepped back into his room and grabbed the overnight bag, then headed for the bathroom. As he closed the door behind him, he heard Smokeshadow let out a mock wolf-whistle, to be shushed by Thomas.

The stinging spray of the hot water went a long way toward waking him up. About halfway through, he realized how they'd gotten into the apartment; Thomas had a MagCard, and he probably still had a read on Jericho's biometric data. *Still doesn't explain how they knew* which *apartment I was going to be in. Did they wander along, trying each and every door until one clicked?* Once they were out and about, he decided, he would push for harder answers. He didn't give his hair a proper wash, because that would take somewhat more than the five minutes he'd allocated himself, but he did give himself a full body scrub.

Dried, deodorized and dressed in neat casual clothing—he'd packed a few outfits, just in case—he emerged from the bathroom about ten minutes later. The TV was on, with Thomas and Smokeshadow sitting on the sofa, though they seemed to be paying more attention to an ongoing argument than watching the news.

"I can't believe Gimmick actually built that thing, let alone gave it to you," Thomas griped. "The sheer danger it could pose in the wrong hands—"

"Which is why it's in the right hands," Smokeshadow—Chelsea—retorted cheerfully. "Mine."

"Do I want to know what you two are talking about?" asked Jericho warily.

Thomas shook his head. "You really, really don't."

The background image on the TV changed to show people waving hand-made signs, and the chanting of slogans became audible. "In other news, the protests outside Power Plaza don't seem to be going away—"

"Oh, what the hell?" Thomas raised the remote and turned the TV off with a jerky motion. He sat there a moment, breathing deeply through his nostrils, then turned to look up at Jericho. "Ready to go?" His voice sounded artificially bright, compared to the irritated tones of a moment before.

Chelsea frowned. "I wanted to see that. What was going on there?"

"Nothing worth watching." Thomas dropped the remote on the sofa and stood up. "Let's get going."

"Okay, then." Jericho decided to mark the entire conversation down as one more thing on the 'I have no idea what just happened' list. "Where are we going to?"

"You'll see." Chelsea gave him a smirk. "I haven't been there myself, but Thomas insists it's something everyone who comes to Utopia City should do."

"Okay …" Stepping back into the bedroom, Jericho picked up his discarded clothing from the night before and draped them over the end of the bed. At the same time, he transferred his wallet and phone into his pocket. "Am I going to need my costume?" he called over his shoulder. Leaning down, he picked up his sneakers and socks.

"I don't think so," Thomas replied. "It's a public area, and I doubt any supervillains are going to attack it. Like, ever."

That sounded like a very specific denial, which only added to Jericho's suspicions. Emerging from the bedroom, he sat down on the sofa to pull on his socks and shoes. As he did so, he reminded himself that the last place Thomas had taken him to had been worth the trip. "Okay then, let's do this. Whatever 'this' is."

They left the apartment, the door swinging closed to lock behind them. Jericho patted his pocket, checking that his wallet was still there, along with his MagCard. Glancing back at the door reminded him of getting in earlier that morning, and he turned to Thomas. Conscious that other patrons might step out of their own apartments at any time, he kept his language neutral. "How did your friends go? Any problems?"

"None. Everything went fine." For the first time since Jericho had opened the bedroom door, the younger man broke out in a beaming smile. "We took them to the maglev station at about four this morning and got them sorted out. Saw them off on the eastbound train at five." He took Jericho by the hand as they got into the elevator. "I really want to thank you for stepping up. It's a huge weight off my mind."

"I'm just glad I could help." Jericho gave Thomas a smile as he squeezed the younger man's hand. The elevator descended, then the doors opened at the bottom. As they left the elevator, Jericho frowned. "Wait a minute. Didn't you say some of them already had MagCards? Creating a second account has gotta be breaking some rule or another."

Chelsea smirked. Glancing from side to side, she briefly pulled an object resembling an electronic discus out of her bag, then shoved it back in. "Not with this thing. One of the Survivors is a kickass artificer called Gimmick. She built this for the occasion. It let me hack into the system and remove their old accounts, so they could start fresh."

Thomas nodded and squeezed his hand. "The last I heard, they were free and clear. Thanks to you."

"Oh, good." Jericho felt a blush creeping over his cheeks. "It wasn't just me. It was a team effort. But how come you didn't go, too? Did you have problems?"

"Oh, no. No problems at all." Thomas captured Jericho's arm with his own, sending a warm shock right through Jericho's chest. "I wanted to stay back awhile, because I don't really have anywhere else to go. And because I wanted to see you again. Doofus."

"Oh. Um." Jericho's brain froze up all over again. Part of him wanted to respond in some way that indicated that he'd wanted to see Thomas again too, while another part warned him against jumping too soon into another relationship. *That way lies the rebound trap. I should wait a while, to make sure this is what we both want.* A third part of him, somehow channeling Stephen, wondered if he'd wanted this all along, and was this why he'd dropped his ex-boyfriend in the first place?

Chelsea looked at him closely, then tutted sadly as she shook her head. "You've broken him already," she said mock-accusingly to Thomas. "And you only just got him, too."

Thomas turned an interesting shade of pink. "I haven't 'just got' him," he sputtered. "He's his own person. He can choose to be with me, or not, however he wants."

"Uh huh. Well, I don't see him pulling free, but that's probably because his higher mental functions are on vacation." Chelsea gave Thomas a wicked grin. "Because *someone* just blew all his fuses."

"I did *not* blow all his fuses!"

"Uh huh. Sure. All evidence points otherwise. I notice you're not letting him go, either."

By now, they were almost out of the courtyard. The back-and-forth gave Jericho the chance to figure out in his own mind how to respond to Thomas' comment. "Okay, enough," he said, as they stopped on the sidewalk. Reluctantly, he pulled his arm free from Thomas' grip and moved away a few steps. "Thomas, I like you. I really do. But I've only just broken up with my boyfriend, and I—"

"Wait, you had a *boyfriend?*"

"Wait, you *broke up* with your boyfriend?"

Thomas and Chelsea had spoken at the same time; Jericho looked from one to the other, trying to decide who to answer first. Flipping a mental coin, he selected Thomas. "Yes, I had a boyfriend. While I was on the way here, I found out he'd been cheating on me, so I—"

"What, so you dropped him *last night?*" Chelsea shook her head, grinning broadly. "Harsh, man. I approve."

This wasn't going the way Jericho wanted. He took a breath and tried to explain again. "No, no, I found out the first time I came here. We broke up Tuesday night—"

Thomas took a step forward, hurt forming on his features. "So, you let me play up to you when you came here last, while you still *had* a boyfriend? I let you *kiss* me!"

"Wait, wait, wait." Jericho held his hands up. "If I remember rightly, *you* were the one kissing *me!*"

"The point still stands!" Thomas shot back. His eyes blazed, sending shivers down Jericho's spine.

"I was always *going* to break up with him. I just didn't want to do it over the phone." Jericho's heart rate was accelerating. It was *totally unfair* that Thomas looked sexiest when he was angry.

"You asked if I wanted to come to Savannah with you," Thomas pointed out accurately. "Where your boyfriend was. Where your ex still is." He looked at Chelsea. "And *you*. You're acting like you already knew."

Chelsea tilted her head. "I had hints. Let's just say, it wasn't a total surprise." She smirked at Jericho, leaving him to wonder exactly how *much* she'd worked out.

"Well, why didn't you tell me?" Thomas glared at her. "We were in each other's damn pockets for *four damn days!* You could've mentioned it at *some* point."

"You're right," Jericho admitted. "I shouldn't have asked you to come to Savannah while I still technically had a boyfriend." He closed his eyes and rubbed the back of his neck. "It was just so *nice* being out with you that I never wanted it to stop. And, you know, we've got so much in common." Having powers, he meant. He glanced around, hoping that they weren't causing so much of a disturbance that someone would call the cops on them; even though the argument between him and Leroy had been totally different.

"Thus confirming every hero/sidekick slash fic ever," Chelsea said obscurely, her broad grin proving that she'd already divined what he intended to imply. "And I didn't tell you because there was no way to do it without five other people also hearing about it. Besides, I knew he was such a straight arrow that he'd tell you *himself* before things got too far. And what do you know? He *did*." She spread her hands and looked from Jericho to Thomas. "Problem solved."

Thomas took a breath, looking from one to the other. "You mean it?" he asked Jericho. "You were always going to break up with him?" The look of anxious hope in his eyes made it clear that he didn't *want* to fight with Jericho.

"Yeah." Jericho nodded emphatically, glad for the reprieve. "I gave him the chance to explain himself and end things amicably, but he wouldn't take responsibility for anything. So, I washed my hands of him. But—*oof!*"

In the next moment, Thomas was holding him tightly. "Don't ever do that to me again," the husky young man said, his voice muffled by Jericho's shoulder but still audible. "Don't scare me like that."

"With a boyfriend?" Jericho snorted. "Yeah, that's gonna happen. I wouldn't even know how to go about getting one. Stephen was the one who chased me 'til I finally said yes." He hoped Thomas wouldn't notice his rapid heart rate.

"Why, do you want one?" It was Chelsea who'd asked; eyes bright with mischief, she pointed at Thomas.

Jericho's heart lurched heavily in his chest. "I … I really want to say yes." Carefully, he patted Thomas on the back. "But like I said, I just broke up. I don't want to start something new and then find out it was only a rebound thing."

Thomas let him go and stood back, hands on Jericho's shoulders. "What?" he asked. "Do you honestly think I'd let *anything* we did be just a rebound thing?"

It seemed unlikely. Everything Thomas did, he did with absolute dedication. Still … "I just want to be sure that what I feel about you isn't just leftover crap from what Stephen and I had." He reached up and took Thomas' hand. "Whatever we have, I want it to be real. I want it to be about *us*." If he ever chose to start a new relationship, there would be ground rules.

"Okay, okay, I'm getting diabetes here," announced Chelsea briskly. "Let's get going to the Market and food, and then … onward." Putting a peculiar emphasis on the last word, she started off down the pavement.

"Onward?" Jericho shared a glance with Thomas, then followed after her.

"Onward!" Thomas declared, pointing his finger in the air and making it a battle cry.

"I am clearly missing something here," Jericho murmured, looking from one to the other. Still, he was thankful for the change in topic. It wasn't that he *didn't* like Thomas, but he preferred to make declarations like that in private.

"It's her fault," Thomas averred, gesturing at Chelsea with his thumb. "She was the one who let Side—uh, one of our group, binge-watch that stupid show."

"You watched it too!" Chelsea protested, giving him a shove that totally failed to budge him.

"Only because there was nothing else to watch." Thomas sighed and put his arm around Jericho's shoulders. "You have *no* idea how glad I am that you came back when you did. My sanity was degrading by the hour."

"Uh, right." Jericho tried to ignore the fact that Chelsea was sticking her tongue out at Thomas. "So, uh, where were we going, again?"

"It's a secret." Thomas loftily paid no attention to Chelsea. "You'll find out when we get there."

"Uh huh." Jericho shook his head. "You two love your secrets. Just saying."

"Says Mister I-had-a-boyfriend," jibed Chelsea, in an amused tone.

"Hey, leave Jericho alone," protested Thomas. "It's not his fault his ex cheated on him."

The cheerful bickering continued all the way to the Market. Jericho found himself caught up in it, laughing at the sallies and barbs traded between Thomas and Chelsea as they bought supplies for a picnic breakfast. In truth, it sounded more like when Livy and Serena were going at each other, rather than the banter between a girl and her guy-pal. It was fun, friendly and altogether comfortable; just what his overstretched sensibilities needed right then.

Once they had what they needed, they went on to the air-cab stand, which was situated between two of the shops. His first hint about where they were going came when they got into the cab that arrived for them. Thomas took a seat next to his and announced, "Memorial Park, please."

"Memorial Park?" Jericho recalled something about that. It had been on the holo-map in the Spire. "We're going there?"

Thomas' hand found his and squeezed. "Yeah. We're going there." He seemed subdued now, a distinct change from his laughter and joking of a few minutes earlier.

"Well, okay then." Jericho, used to air-cabs by now, had his MagCard out and ready. He tapped the reader, then fastened the five-point restraints. "Why are we going there, exactly?"

"You'll see." Thomas leaned back in the seat and closed his eyes.

The air-cab took off with the trademark thrumming of lifters, then steadied into level flight as it headed west over the city. Chelsea seemed to be watching the skyline with interest; Jericho looked out the windows to the right, where he could see the distant Spire, reaching into the sky and dwarfing all structures around it. He could hardly credit the fact that he'd gotten to *tour* it, just days before.

Thomas still had his eyes closed; Jericho reached over and took his hand again. A smile worked its way across the younger man's face and he returned the pressure, but he didn't open his eyes. Jericho decided to emulate him, leaning back and closing his eyes as well. He didn't release Thomas' hand. So many things about the future were uncertain, but that, right there, was nice.

"Coming up on Memorial Park now, folks. Landing in forty-five."

"Excellent," Chelsea said. "Hey, driver, what's that over there? Where the light's reflecting?" Jericho opened his eyes to look where she was indicating; off in the distance to the northwest, he spotted what looked like a broad expanse of glass with sunlight glinting off it.

"That'll be the Tuttle Creek Lake Hydroponics Project," the cab driver replied crisply. **"It's run by researchers from UCIAT. They hold tours on Mondays, Wednesdays and Fridays, if you're interested."**

"Oh. Huh," replied Chelsea. "Thanks." It was the first Jericho had heard about this, but it sounded like something he might look into, once his other business was taken care of.

"You're welcome. Landing at Memorial Park now." The extra weight and the audible sound of the lifters alerted Jericho that they were at their destination. He turned his head and looked out the window, to see a vaguely familiar sight; the broad orange cross of the park from above, providing a striking contrast to the rumpled green quilt of the grass and the colors of the surrounding gardens. But already it was spreading out and becoming unrecognizable as the cab came in for a landing.

Once the air taxi touched down, they climbed out, making sure to take the bags and cartons containing their food with them. Before them stretched the side of the park, bounded by a low red-brick wall, on top of which a wrought-iron fence rose to more than Jericho's head height. The nearest entrance was just yards away, framed by red-brick pillars supporting an iron arch that read: 'MEMORIAL PARK'. Through the fence, he could see decorative garden beds within the park. From the entrance, a ten-foot-wide winding path composed of a brick mosaic meandered toward the top of the hill over which the park was draped. The grass was a brilliant green in the sunlight, though it took on a more subdued hue under the broad-spreading trees that overshadowed the path from a short distance into the park.

"Wow, Thomas. You weren't kidding. It's *beautiful*." Chelsea stepped up alongside Jericho, cloth bag in hand. As Thomas joined them, the cab took off in a blast of wind. Jericho realized a moment later that he hadn't even looked around, when just days previously he would've stared in awe. It was all too easy to get used to the technological marvels that were part and parcel of daily life in Utopia City.

"Yeah, it is." But Thomas didn't seem to put the same amount of enthusiasm into it that Chelsea had. He stepped forward, leading the way up the path. Jericho followed on, appreciating how the tree cover and the manner in which the ground had been mounded into a low hill made it impossible to see all the way across to the far side of the park, and the illusion of extra space this created.

Under his feet, the path sloped gently upward toward the distant summit. Glancing down at the pathway itself, he tried to make sense of the arrangement of the brickwork mosaic. No pictures were formed, or names spelled out. They weren't even all the same type of brick. The colors went from deep red all the way through to yellow and white. There had to be something more about them, but he just couldn't figure out what it was.

"What's the matter?" Thomas' voice brought him back to himself as they stepped under the shade of the first tree. Immediately, the temperature dropped by a few degrees and he could feel the light sheen of sweat on his face drying off in the gentle breeze. The earthy scent of the mulch surrounding the base of the tree, overlaid by the more distant hints of floral fragrance, tickled his nostrils.

"This path," Jericho confessed, pointing downward. "I mean, everything else in this park was obviously put where it is for a reason. I can't make out a pattern in these bricks. Large pieces, small pieces, all different colors, all mixed up. There's no pattern to it. It just doesn't add up. What's it supposed to mean?"

Chelsea put the bag she was carrying on the ground and lowered herself to one knee. Carefully, she ran her fingertips over the brickwork. "They weren't machined to be this way. These are weathered. Stained. Damaged. Acid rain?"

Jericho frowned and took a closer look. She was right. He'd registered the staining but had ignored it so he could concentrate on the color beneath. Now that he looked at them properly, he realized she was right. Each brick was discolored, badly. With some, it had caused quite deep pitting. And with that knowledge, he realized what he'd been missing. "Ah. Ah, shit. I think I know."

"What?" Chelsea stood up again, brushing off her knee, then picked up the bag. "What's this about?"

Thomas already knew; Jericho could see it in his unhappy frown. "You know what it's about," the younger man said. "You just don't want to think about it. Nobody does."

"Yeah." Jericho grimaced, knowing it was true. "All this brickwork wasn't stained. It was burned when Doc Iridium's bomb went off. This is all that's left of the original city." He tapped the path with his foot for emphasis. "We're walking on bricks salvaged from the ruins of what was here before."

That put a damper on the conversation. It was one thing to know intellectually that something was a memorial to people more than a decade dead, but it was quite another to have a vivid reminder of it under one's feet. They walked onward, each lost in their private musings. The breeze rustled the tree leaves overhead, tiny spots of brilliant sunlight breaking through the canopy here and there to dapple the grass or the path in silent contrast to the darkness of their thoughts.

When the walls started, about halfway up the hill, they were an even more sobering reminder. Each one was composed of chunks of lava-like rock, with one side sliced away to produce a glass-smooth surface, then jigsawed on the ends so that they fitted together. The back of each wall, showing rough and unfinished rock, had a garden bed around its base, tying it into the park to make it all a complete whole.

Facing each other across the path, the smooth side of each wall — about four feet high — was tilted back by about twenty degrees, probably to make it easier to read the names. Twenty to thirty names were engraved into each section. Jericho could tell that they'd tried to keep it as alphabetical as they could, but family groups had been kept together nonetheless.

When he saw the first card, propped just below a column of names, Jericho stopped. His heart was already heavy; this made it feel like it was trying to pump molasses. Looking farther up the pathway, he now saw there were more cards, and other tiny trinkets, placed at the base of one column of names or another, heartbreaking reminders of those who had made the pilgrimage to search for their loved ones.

"Nine-twenty was only a few weeks ago," Thomas said, keeping his voice hushed in the dimness under the trees. "It's been fourteen years, and people still come here every year for the anniversary and leave things."

Jericho glanced down at a glint of light. A shot-glass sat at the foot of one column of names, empty of whatever it had once contained. He imagined a bereaved father or husband or best buddy, sitting on the path and drinking a toast to absent friends. Looking forward as the path meandered up the hill between the shade trees, he could see the walls with their burden of silently accusing names following it, every step of the way. *Don't let this happen again,* they seemed to say to him. *Not ever again.*

The rock face itself seemed odd to him as well. It wasn't granite or marble, exactly. There were odd swirls and sparkles in it. He looked more closely, then reached the obvious conclusion and wished he hadn't.

"What's the bet this rock was produced when the bomb went off too?" he ventured. "The stuff that was closer to ground zero? All melted together into one mass?"

Thomas shook his head. "No bet. That's exactly what it is. There's a presentation at UCIAT that explains how it was collected and built."

"Jesus." Chelsea sounded weary. "You hear about this place, and you think you know about it. But then you come here, and you walk up this path, and ..." Her voice broke a little. "And then you remember that there are *three other paths* just like this one." He heard her sniffle.

"Hey. Hey, hey, hey." Jericho shifted his bags to his left hand, then pulled his handkerchief from his pocket and handed it to her. "You okay? You want to go back? We can have our breakfast somewhere else."

She took it gratefully and wiped her eyes then blew her nose. "No, I'll be fine. I'll see this through. Force Majeure built this monument, and if I'm going to be staying in their city, I should be able to say I walked to the top of the memorial hill. Because I bet *they* all did."

That was as good a reason as any to keep going. They moved onward over the path of scorched brickwork, flanked by the walls with their never-ending processions of names. Jericho fancied he could hear the last cries of the dying echoing up from the bricks beneath his feet. In his imagination he could feel the single horrific pulse of heat that had killed ninety thousand people in just a few brutal seconds, radiating again from the molten and reformed chunks of rock that made up the memorial walls.

Looking around, he was grateful for the brightness filtering in from beyond the oaks, with birds calling and flying from tree to tree and brilliant flowers spilling out of garden beds to the left and right. Without that to alleviate the soul-crushing darkness of the memorial, he had no idea how anyone could bear to ever walk up this path.

Reaching the top came almost as a surprise. They found themselves leaving the cover of the shade trees as the last section of each wall fell behind them. Jericho paused a moment and let his hand trail across the mirror-slick surface of the last rock on the right-hand side, the whorls of his fingertips catching briefly on the grooves of the last engraved name. *Never again,* he promised silently. *You have my word.*

Then he moved forward to catch up with the others on the flat, paved top of the hill in the mid-morning sun. Taking a deep breath, he felt his spirits lift once more. "Wow."

"Yeah." There was a wan smile on Chelsea's face once more as she raised her face to the sun. "That was seriously intense."

"It always is." Thomas gestured. "Let's set up over there."

'Over there' was the center of the paved area, which held a series of tables, all bearing auto-adjusting umbrellas, surrounding a fountain with an eternal flame in the middle. Around the rim of the fountain, words were incised deeply into the stone.

Equally spaced around the fountain, outside the tables, were three flagpoles. The one that Jericho figured was to the east (and was a little taller than the other two) flew the national flag. Going clockwise, the next one held the state flag, and the third one exhibited a flag bearing a purple and white logo showing the head of a mountain lion in profile.

Passing by the flagpole holding the mountain-lion flag, he moved between the tables to reach the fountain then walked all the way around it, reading the inscription as he went.

**IN MEMORY OF THE 91,473 SOULS WHO PERISHED IN THE DESTRUCTION OF MANHATTAN, KANSAS ON SEPTEMBER 20, 1999.
MAY THEY REST IN PEACE.**

"May they rest in peace," echoed Chelsea, making Jericho blink; he hadn't realized he was speaking out loud. Her color was better than it had been before. She took a deep breath and turned in a complete circle. "It's really beautiful up here."

Thomas nodded somberly. "They put a lot of time and effort into getting it just right."

"And they succeeded." Chelsea looked pensively back down the path they'd just come up. "Down there, too. But I think I need to sit down right now."

"Good idea." Jericho went over to the nearest table with her and pulled a glass bottle of soda from one of the cloth bags he was carrying. Opening it, he offered it to her. "Here, sip on this 'til you feel better."

She took it gratefully and drank a couple of mouthfuls. "Thanks. That really took it out of me." Looking over at the fountain again, she shook her head. "There's so much … *much* in this place."

"You're not wrong." Thomas sat down across from her, and Jericho took a third seat. Placing their bags and cartons on the table, they started taking out the food they'd bought. Thomas smiled at her. "So, do you feel like having something to eat now?"

At that moment, the eternal flame chose to flare high; Jericho watched as it billowed out over the fountain, spreading *downward* in a manner unlike any fire he'd seen. His G-sense pinged, telling him something was going on with the local gravity. "Whoa …" he muttered, echoed by Chelsea.

"Keep watching," Thomas said quietly. As he spoke, the fire receded, replaced by water spraying up in intricate patterns, going right over the top of the flame and encasing it within an apparently seamless shell of water. Jericho watched as the flame, barely visible through the translucent covering, flickered almost to extinction. Then the water came back down to its normal level once more, spraying harmlessly through the air while the fire burned strongly in the middle.

"Okay, that was impressive," Chelsea observed. "How did it even do that?"

"They've got gravity generators in the fountain," Jericho guessed. "I'm thinking they use those, as well as force fields, to shape the fire and the water."

"Well, it's definitely impressive, even if they do cheat." Chelsea grabbed the nearest carton and opened it. "I'm okay now. Let's eat."

It wasn't the normal run of picnics. There was laughter as Jericho struggled to spread potato salad with a pressed-paper knife amid humorous suggestions on how to make it work better, but it wasn't as loud as it might have been. Still, it wasn't exactly somber; Chelsea nearly snorted her soda out her nose when Jericho and Thomas began fencing with their drumstick bones. Each of them was aware of the significance of this spot and while enjoyment was had, it was kept in check. In the background, every five minutes or so, the fountain performed its fire-and-water show.

They sat, and they ate, and they talked. Jericho told Thomas and Chelsea about his parents and about Luke, and shared anecdotes of being a superhero in Savannah. Pickup rated a mention, but they were more interested in Jericho's exploits. When Jericho told them how Luke had pretended to be terrified of G-Man, Thomas inhaled a piece of chicken and had to be slapped on the back. After some prompting from Jericho, Thomas and Chelsea told him how they'd escaped the forces of law and order, and hunkered down in her apartment to await his return.

The last scrap of food had long since been eaten and the last bottle of soda emptied, and the sun was somewhat higher in the sky by the time the conversation began to run down. Jericho belched as unobtrusively as he could manage, then leaned forward with his elbows on the table. "Thanks," he said simply. "For bringing me up here."

"You're welcome," Thomas replied. "Whenever I want to find perspective, I come up here and think about what's gone before, just on this spot. My problems never seem as formidable when I go back down the hill again."

"You're not kidding," said Chelsea. "It was utterly brutal, coming up that path, but now I feel like it was totally worth it." She grimaced. "The teddy-bear really got to me, though. Just sitting there, all alone by the side of the path …" Her voice trailed off, and she wiped moisture from the corner of her eye. "It just got to me, is all."

"I didn't see that," Jericho admitted. "And I'm not about to go back and look for it. Once was enough for today, I think."

"Once is enough for about a *week*," Thomas said. "So, Jericho. You're in Utopia. The Survivors are safe. What are your plans now?" There was a hopeful tone in his voice.

"I'm thinking I might go back to the apartment and costume up, then make some calls," Jericho decided. "There's a cop I know who should be able to Gordon me with the latest on the Portman case."

"Why the cops?" asked Chelsea. "They've got nothing. If they *had* some way to locate him, they'd already have him in custody."

"Yeah, but I've gotta start *somewhere*," Jericho pointed out logically. "Uncle Leroy was the only person I knew who actually had any contacts among the Southsiders, and since he was booted out of Utopia City, I'm starting from scratch."

Thomas blinked. "You mean, that's all you were looking for?" He reached out and took Jericho's hand. "I've been getting jerked around by those assholes for *months*. I know *exactly* how to find them."

The words hit Jericho like a steam train. He focused his entire attention on Thomas, who blushed slightly. "Really," he breathed. "Tell me more."

57
Exercising Shock and Awe

Six Hours Later

The South Side Mall was impressive from any angle, especially ground level. Even from where Jericho perched in costume, twenty floors up on the curve of a building across the street from the Mall, it dominated both the skyline and the sky itself. Jericho restrained the impulse to tilt his head back and shade his eyes from the mid-afternoon sun so as to take in the very top levels.

Reaching up to his ear, he clicked the low-profile earbud that Chelsea had given him. The range wasn't great, she'd warned him, but every radio surveillance setup she'd ever tested it against, including Artificer creations (she was a little vague on how she'd pulled that off) had registered nothing but random static. Still, as a basic precaution, they were using phonetic codenames while on the air. "Golf, in position."

Another click sounded in his ear. "Tango, in position at point Alpha, level eight." Thomas' voice was crisp and professional. Jericho wondered where (not 'if') the younger man had done this sort of thing before.

By contrast, Chelsea sounded light-hearted and carefree. "Sierra, here. I can have eyes on in thirty seconds, and I'll be ready to call the ball two minutes after that. Say when, boss."

As their resident artificer, she'd provided some interesting technology for the raid. Building the earbuds had taken half the day—Jericho had been intrigued to find out about their anti-surveillance capability—but what had really gotten his attention was the hacking device she'd shown him earlier; the one Gimmick had given her as a thank-you for getting the Survivors out of the city.

The electronic discus (as Jericho thought of it) could be connected to any computer system (even via wi-fi) to give her eight and a half minutes of admin access before the local defenses woke up and went active. As she'd said with a grin, it was amazing what someone could accomplish in eight and a half minutes. It was, after all, how she'd determined which apartment he was staying in. More specifically, it was what she and Thomas had been arguing about, earlier.

Regardless of Thomas' reservations, the hacking device had become the linchpin of their attack strategy. Originally, Jericho and Thomas wanted to rough out a plan that involved Thomas luring the top guys of the Southsiders out into the open for an ambush scenario, but there were far too many variables, with only the three of them to keep matters under control. The last thing they wanted was for innocents to stumble into the line of fire. Plus, such a plan would leave Thomas blown, as far as the Southsiders were concerned.

Thus, the new plan. It had the advantage of simplicity—Jericho was a firm believer in the KISS principle—while playing to their strengths. The first stage involved getting him to the drop-shaft inside the South Side Mall, in costume and as fast as possible (changing into costume inside the Mall was not a good idea, for several reasons).

Closer examination of the situation on the ground had alerted them to the fact that the most effective glide-path to get him in through the main doors required him to pass through contested airspace. Specifically, the flight-lane used by air-cabs to get up and away from the building once they'd picked up (or dropped off) their passengers. Chelsea had suggested waiting until after nightfall to take advantage of slower traffic, but Thomas had noted that the cab stand was in more or less constant operation at any time of night or day. While Jericho hadn't seen that specifically for himself, his experience with the South Side Mall at night had certainly given him the impression that the younger man knew what he was talking about.

"Okay," he said. He'd initially declined the leadership role, but Smokeshadow didn't want it and Thomas had turned it down as well, pointing out that he *was* the closest thing to a professional superhero in the group. Still, this hadn't stopped Thomas from making suggestions and offering advice after the fact. "Sierra, kick it over. Let me know when you're ready for me to go."

"Cracking the system now." Chelsea's voice took on a bemused tone. "Huh."

"Huh? What's 'huh'?" Jericho felt a chill run down his back. Had she noticed some aspect of the situation that they'd previously overlooked? Was all their careful planning now out the window?

"Oh, I was just thinking," she said over his earpiece. "I'm a prodigy/artificer and you two are prodigy/dynamics. Does this make us an Inspire team?"

Jericho wanted to facepalm. They were literally on the countdown to capturing Luke's killer and (just incidentally) taking down the criminal organization that had been sheltering the man, and Chelsea wanted to talk about trivia like *this*?

"I didn't think of it that way, but you're right. It does." Thomas chuckled. "Or if you look at it another way, we've all got Prodigy ratings. That makes us a Bat-family at the same time."

Bat-families (the name was taken from the same bit of pop culture that had produced Gordoning) were less well known than Inspire teams but in areas where prodigies outnumbered everyone else, they tended to be the favored type of team. Where Inspire teams covered each other's weaknesses and bolstered their strengths, Bat-families made use of Prodigy hyper-resourcefulness to hit their foes from unexpected directions and leave them wondering what the hell had happened.

"… okay," murmured Chelsea, and Jericho unconsciously leaned forward. "We've got a window for the air-cab stand closest to the main doors coming up in … sixty seconds. Go/no go?"

The timing was going to have to be precise; fortunately, he was reasonably competent at regulating his airspeed to arrive at any particular spot at a given moment. Crouching a little lower, he focused utterly on what he was to do next.

Get in there. Kick heads 'til they tell me where Portman is. Get Portman.

"Green light," he said. "I say again, green light."

"All right then," Chelsea replied. "Cab is loading … thirty seconds 'til takeoff … twenty-five … twenty … hold, hold, hold, there's a disagreement … okay, it's settled, fifteen … ten …five …*go!*"

Releasing the glue-tags holding him in position, Jericho kicked off from the building. Using his arms and the gliding surfaces to guide himself, he dropped head-first toward the pavement, though his eyes were on the air-cab across the street. This sort of stunt would never have been possible without Smokeshadow watching the cameras, including being able to see into the air-cab and interpret what was going on inside the vehicle.

When he was one second into his fall, the cab started its lifters. At the two-second mark, it began to rise into the air, retracting its landing struts. Three seconds in, with the footpath below rapidly approaching, he brought himself down to gliding weight and spread his arms wide. As he'd done with the apartment building on his first night in Utopia City, he turned the plummet into a swoop; this time, however, he was timing his pull-out to be a lot closer to the ground. Mall entrance level, in fact. And he was going a *lot* faster.

As the air-cab lifted out of the way and smoothly accelerated upward, Jericho achieved level flight roughly twelve feet above ground level. He whipped under the departing taxi with just enough separation that he barely felt the downward air-wash. The automatic doors before him were open; whether this was due to Chelsea's intervention or the fact that customers were walking in and out, he wasn't sure. The fact was, he had a way in.

His normal sustainable glide speed was in the region of twenty miles per hour, assuming a run-up and a strong leap to gain speed. Right now, he was doing almost four times that, mainly due to the gravity assist from the building opposite. His mask tails flapping madly, he was decelerating all the time, but he needed all the speed he could muster. As he shot through the opening, mere feet above the heads of the now-scattering shoppers, he heard Chelsea say, "And cameras are *down*."

This was the second major aspect of the plan. According to Thomas, the South Side Mall got raided occasionally, but the criminal elements within the building had access to the security system. If the cameras detected superheroes or cops intruding on the building, they usually had time to conceal their contraband and disperse their people before the forces of law and order got anywhere near them. Spoofing security would work for a short time, but eight and a half minutes was too short for a normal entry. So, if Jericho was to achieve entry in costume *and* get to the appropriate floor in time to kick in the door before everything was hidden away, he needed speed and lots of it. Thus, the dramatic entrance.

The only faster way to get where he needed to go would have been to hijack an air-cab—which Chelsea had suggested, albeit jokingly—and fly it into the building. Jericho had vetoed that with a shudder. He suspected that this stunt was already going to get him into a certain amount of trouble with the authorities (though if he got Portman, it wouldn't matter; he could leave Utopia City with his head held high). However, hijacking a cab would open up a whole new depth of shit for them to be dropped in.

Banking around a turn, down to forty miles per hour, he saw his destination ahead; the main drop-shaft. And there was Chelsea coming to meet him, sliding her folded laptop into her bag as she came. Her hyperweave costume was at that moment emulating a hoodie and jeans, the hood obscuring her face. Over the earpiece, Jericho heard grunting and movement; the sounds didn't match what Chelsea was doing, which meant it was Thomas.

"Tango," he said as he brought his legs down for a landing next to the gravity shaft. "What's going on?"

"They're trying to close up shop," Thomas grunted. "If you can get up here soon, it'd be good."

"On our way." This was the third part of the plan. No matter how quickly Jericho got in, the loss of cameras would raise an alarm and they'd go into lockdown until they figured out what was going on. There were several innocuous-seeming shopfronts that served as entry-points into the Southsiders' area; the location they'd designated as 'point Alpha' on the eighth floor was one such. Thomas, suitably attired in identity-concealing clothing, had taken on the task of preventing that one entry-point from being sealed off. On the downside, the Southsiders had an indeterminate number of thugs to carry out their wishes, while he was just one man. Or rather, just one *prodigy*; which changed the entire equation. Still, Jericho knew it would be a good idea to waste no time in getting up there.

Grabbing Chelsea by her free hand, he stepped into the gravity shaft. His G-sense, already alerted by the very presence of the active gravity manipulation field, reached out to analyze every aspect of it. Jericho didn't wait for it to finish. Grabbing the volume of space-time directly around them, he impressed his will on it; as he'd noted the first time he'd been here, gravity was *extremely* pliable within this area. Enclosed in a bubble of null-gee, they shot upward, swerving and cutting around the slower-moving patrons of the mall.

The holographic floor numbers flashed by too fast to read; blue-green-blue-green-blue-green—*there!* Slowing their upward dash a little, he swerved them ninety degrees to whip past the blue glowing '8' into the corridor that they were looking for. There were gravity generators in the corridor as well, which was what allowed patrons to walk on both the floor and the ceiling; he took advantage of these, co-opting the adjustable gravity field to augment his flight onward. Fortunately, the signs hanging in the center of the corridor were all holographic; they passed straight through quite a few of them.

When they reached the store in question, the front door was open, and one man lay unconscious on the ramp leading up to the corridor proper. Through the window, it was obvious that the fight was still ongoing. Customers were clustered around, some taking pictures and footage with their phones, while others appeared to be calling the authorities. Jericho released his grip on Chelsea, trusting that she was enough of a prodigy to make a safe landing, then grabbed the doorframe and swung feet-first into the fray.

Aside from the initial casualty, there were two more unconscious thugs inside the shop and three that, while still up and active, were showing distinct signs of having been through a fight. Two of them had Thomas by the arms, while the third was preparing to beat the snot out of him. All but Thomas turned toward the doorway as Jericho made an appearance; the younger man took advantage of the distraction to land an accurate kick into the solar plexus of the third thug. The man staggered backward and Jericho slammed both boot-heels into him, pile-driving the luckless thug into a set of shelves.

Still airborne, he continued on past where Thomas was being held captive and slapped one of the mooks on the back of the head. It was only a light blow but the man crumpled anyway, as almost anyone will do when abruptly afflicted by five times their own weight. Thomas took advantage of the opening and turned his attention to the last mook standing. In the time it took for Jericho to rebound off the wall and land with an entirely unnecessary acrobatic flip, that guy was down and Thomas was dusting himself off.

Jericho looked him over for obvious damage, and found none, apart from a split lip and a trickle of blood from one nostril. The baseball cap and sunglasses he'd been using as an incidental disguise were long gone, though his cloth mask was still in place.

"Nicely done," Thomas said approvingly. "I see you've got your dramatic entrance down pat."

Jericho hoped his own mask would cover his incipient blush at the praise. "Hey, I couldn't let you have all the fun. Where's the way in, again?"

"Through there," Thomas said, pointing toward the rear of the store. "There's a back door. I think it's code-locked."

"Code, shmode." Chelsea stepped into the shop, her costume morphing into a full-length hooded robe. She went to where Thomas had indicated, pushing aside a much heavier panic-room style door—camouflaged to look like part of the back wall—to get at the keypad. As the other two followed on, she attached the electronic discus to the wall next to it. "Open …" she murmured, tapping keys. "… sesame." The door beeped and clicked, then slid open slightly. "Voila." Detaching the discus with a smirk, she slid it back into her bag.

Alert for an ambush, Jericho put his hand on the door and extended his G-sense. There were no dense masses waiting on the other side, so there *probably* wasn't a bunch of gunmen waiting to cut them down when the door opened. All the same, he waved Thomas and Smokeshadow back while he snatched a glance into the gap thus opened. His initial impression had been correct; there was nobody there.

Pushing the door all the way open, he ventured into the dimly lit area behind it; a landing at the top of a set of stairs leading downward perhaps twenty or thirty feet. His G-sense also reported that the gravity-manipulation field didn't extend past the back wall of the shop, which meant no more flight. This was irritating, but it was also a little unrealistic to expect the bad guys to give him *every* advantage when it came to kicking their asses.

He recalled from his examination of the three-dimensional holo-map that there were regions marked 'non-public area', which were probably dedicated to things like storage and internal infrastructure. These stairs almost certainly led to such an area. Given the heavy door that would've been blocking the way had they arrived five minutes later, he was willing to bet that it was being used for illicit purposes. Such as sheltering fugitives from justice. *I'm coming for you, Portman.*

Lowering his weight to its minimum, he stepped off the top of the stairs and slow-fell all the way down, using the handrail as a guide. Thomas and Chelsea descended in a more conventional manner, then they moved off down the corridor thus revealed. Up ahead, Jericho heard voices and the sounds of objects being shifted around. Moving more carefully, he peered around the next corner to see a partly opened door; the sounds were now much clearer, as were the voices.

He eased closer to the door, looking through the gap into the room beyond. The doorway came out onto a small railed landing, about six feet above the floor of a large warehouse-like space, complete with overhead traveling gantries and the occasional crate. Sixty or seventy men and women were working on the floor of the warehouse; some were breaking down crates and separating out the contents, while others were packing up small items and storing them in yet more crates. The smells of industrial solvent and oil and dust and ozone tickled his nostrils.

Two people were walking across the floor about ten yards away, arguing over a holo-tablet; one was wearing a hard-hat and a high-visibility vest and looked like every warehouse foreman ever. The other wore a rumpled suit with the tie pulled askew and gave off the vibe of a harried bureaucrat. But one thing that *wasn't* present was any kind of obviously armed guard. Nobody was keeping watch, even on the overhead catwalks. *They obviously believe in security by obscurity. Sucks to be them.*

"Tango," he murmured. "We converge on those guys with the tablet, then I'll go left and you go right. Sierra, you're on overwatch."

"Copy," replied Thomas; Chelsea said nothing, but Jericho heard her click her earpiece twice.

"Okay." He took a deep breath, still watching the scene outside. "Three … two … one … go."

Yanking the door open, he lowered his weight and jumped onto the rail, then kicked off from it so that he arced toward the two men. Behind him, he heard the double impact as Thomas' feet hit the ground, then Chelsea's voice came over the earbud. "People are starting to notice. No weapons so far."

His gliding capability wasn't necessary to cover the distance, but he spread his arms anyway; partly because he wanted the extra altitude, and partly for the intimidation effect. He hadn't forgotten Leroy's words on the subject, and some small part of his mind thought it amusing to take advice from someone on the other side of the law on how to be a better superhero.

Just before he reached them, the one in the hard-hat must have caught the motion from the corner of his eye, because he turned to look. The expression on his face was *classic*, bearing out everything Leroy had said. Eyes bulging in shock and surprise, he brought up his hand to both point out the danger and ward Jericho off; both of which were far too late to be useful. At the same time, his mouth opened, probably to call out a warning.

Jericho brought his arms in and pulled a forward somersault, ending in the same kind of pile-driver kick that he'd done to the thug back in the shop, right to the middle of the guy's chest. The impact was solid, sending the guy over backward; Jericho performed a backflip to land lightly on the ground next to the suited guy. Holding out the tablet like a shield, the apparent bureaucrat got as far as, "Where the hell did you—" before Thomas came past and clotheslined him from the side.

"Get the tablet to Sierra," Jericho said quietly, trusting the earbud to relay his voice, then turned to the guy in the high-visibility vest. The guy was on the ground and conscious, but not moving coherently yet. Jericho tapped him to apply five times normal weight, then looked around to re-establish his situational awareness.

Back on the landing, Chelsea was doing her *I'm-not-here* act. She really did look like the shadow of smoke against the wall; barely there unless he knew where to look. Nearby workers were vacillating, which he could understand. Even without a fearsome local reputation, nobody wanted to tangle with the scary-looking guy in black, but what if they were caught *not* helping? It was the age-old problem for the underpaid mook.

A few yards away, Thomas put suit-guy down with a sleeper hold, then took the tablet and skimmed it across the floor, back toward Chelsea. It might pick up a few cracks and dents on the way, but it would likely survive the journey intact, and in his experience the cops *loved* electronic evidence. But that wasn't what he was here for.

Standing up as a few of the braver workers ventured closer, he cupped his hands around his mouth. "We don't care about you guys!" he shouted. "Hand over Jack Portman, and we walk out of here! That's all we're after!" He'd definitely be calling the cops in, if they weren't already on the way, but *he* wouldn't be arresting these guys. If they ran for it right now, some of them might even make it.

Several of the braver—or dumber—workers started toward him, brandishing pry-bars and screwdrivers, as well as a few box-cutter knives. "Screw you!" shouted one. "I'm not getting kicked out of Utopia an' going to jail for you, asshole!" He waved his arm, trying to rally his fellows. "Come on, he's just one man!"

It seemed a little dubious for them to be worrying more about their Utopia City citizenship than actual jail time, but Jericho wasn't about to argue the finer points of criminal motivation with a bunch of thugs determined to beat his head in. Or, for that matter, explain that there were two of them. He moved in, picking his targets, then hit one with a palm-strike to the jaw and faded back from the other. As the first guy went down, he tripped the second one, giving him three gravities to play with on his way to the floor.

The workers were numerous but untrained in any real combat capability. Unlike the problem Thomas had faced in the shop, there was room to maneuver here, including upward. They might try to box him in, but that gave him a target-rich environment, which he used to its fullest potential. And as he'd pointed out to Silent Knight during the Force Majeure interview, combining actual fighting skill with the ability to control the effective weight of his opponent resulted in a combat effectiveness that was far greater than the sum of its parts.

With Chelsea supplying a commentary to make sure neither he nor Thomas were caught unawares, Jericho set about dissuading the workers of the notion that it was a good idea to attack him. This involved inflicting contusions, minor concussions and the occasional broken bone; he also used one worker as a flail for a brief period of time. Across the room, he could see that Thomas was holding his own. Despite lacking Jericho's particular Dynamic capability, the younger man was nonetheless stronger than he looked, or perhaps he just had a better understanding of leverage than most. Whichever it was, he appeared to be dealing with his opponents in a timely and effective manner.

"Golf!" Chelsea's voice broke into his mid-fight musings. "I just spotted Portman! Upper catwalk, heading for an exit! Your one o'clock!"

Jericho blocked the swing of a box-cutter, disarmed the mook, and broke his wrist at the same time. Stepping back into a clear area, he looked upward toward where Smokeshadow had indicated. And there he was; a familiar-looking figure, limping along the catwalk forty feet in the air, opening a door. Momentarily silhouetted in the doorway, he appeared to look back once, then he was gone. The door closed behind him.

Calculations raced through Jericho's mind. *I could just about get up there and go after him, but that leaves Thomas and Chelsea here against these guys ...*

Torn, he looked around. He *wanted* to get up there and go after Luke's killer, but it went against the grain to leave comrades in the line of fire.

"Go!" snapped Thomas. "Get after him! We got this!"

"We really do," Chelsea affirmed. "Get going, you idiot!"

That was all the urging Jericho needed. He double-checked that Thomas wasn't too close to him, then grabbed the local gravity field and applied his G-shake. Everyone within ten feet dropped to the floor, retching and twitching. Thus unencumbered by foes, he took a short run-up and a single jump. This got him to the top of the nearest four-foot crate, then he gathered himself and *leaped*. Not for the catwalk; that was out of his reach. But the traveling gantry that hung down from the middle of the roof *wasn't*. Normally, he could comfortably jump twenty feet vertically, and much farther across with a run-up. The gantry hung thirty feet above the floor, nominally out of jumping range; however, between the height of the crate and his own body length, he was able to snag a dangling chain before he began to fall back.

Taking hold with both hands, he swung himself upward, settling himself on the gantry itself, then kicked off toward the overhead girders. This put him above the catwalk; a third leap, along with his gliding wings, got him there in just a few more seconds. Seconds during which Portman was making his getaway. *Not if I can help it.*

The door was locked, or otherwise jammed somehow. Jericho didn't hesitate; he unloaded a kick into it, right below the handle. The door bent inward but didn't give. He tried again; this time, the blow smashed the latch clean out of the plywood. A metal bar clattered to the floor on the other side as the door. Swinging the door open, Jericho plunged through. Portman had gained some seconds with the delay, but it wouldn't be enough. *No more hiding. No more running. This ends today.*

The corridor beyond was long and echoing, with no turnoffs. Grimly, Jericho increased his pace. This path had been laid down the moment Jericho had come back to the apartment to find Luke and Bobbi dead. Every fiber of his being screamed out for justice to be done. The restless shades of Luke Hansen and Bobbi Reynolds *demanded* it.

He skidded around a corner to see another door being opened up ahead, and the same familiar outline showing against the light beyond. Revitalized by the sight of his long-denied target, he increased his pace to a dead sprint. "Portman!" he bellowed. "You're *mine!*"

Briefly, he was rewarded by the surprised jerk of the man's head, then the door slammed shut with an echoing *boom*. He kept running, then when he was twenty feet from the door, he launched himself into a flying kick. Whether the door had been locked or not was immaterial; the impact took it clean off its hinges. He landed, tumbled, and rolled to his feet, taking in his surroundings.

After a moment, he realized where he was. The metal catwalk upon which he stood, the sunlight angling in through the open sides of the structure, the smell of oil and hot metal, the cars and trucks on hydraulic platforms all around; it all added up to one thing. This was Southside Parking, where road traffic entered and left Utopia City.

That wasn't important. *Where's Portman?* With that limp, bequeathed him by Luke, the murderer could not have gotten far. He looked around again, seeking details. At intervals along the structure, accessed by catwalks, there were glassed-in booths. Jericho surmised that these were control points for the automated parking. Portman was at the door of the nearest one, not forty feet away, forcing it open. The operator, a young woman, appeared to be on her feet yelling at him, to no effect. *Oh, no you goddamn don't. Not this time.*

Jericho threw himself in that direction, vaulting to the top of a waist-high safety rail and leaping over a twenty-foot gap to close the distance as fast as he could. But seconds before he would've laid hands on the man, Portman gained entry to the booth and grabbed the woman. As Jericho came up to the enclosure, the heavy-set man turned, holding his hostage before him, a gleaming blade touching the flesh next to her carotid artery. One slash and she would be in dire straits; two, and she would die before he managed to stem the bleeding. Jericho stopped, then took a step back. His hands itched to wrap around Portman's throat, but he *would not* be responsible for the death of another innocent.

"Give it up," he said quietly. Screaming threats would've been more satisfying, but that wouldn't get him what he wanted. "You can't run and you can't hide. The Southsiders are done; they can't protect you anymore. Where are you going to run to?"

Portman glared at him. "Who the hell *are* you, anyway?" He was unshaven, and his face was blotchy with old bruising, while the red scratches on his cheek hadn't gone away either; in fact, they were starting to look infected. This close, it was easy to see how much the man was favoring his left leg. The more Jericho looked at him, the more evident it became that the only reason Portman had won against Luke was the drugs he'd been on. Even now, almost five days on, he was walking wounded.

"I'm G-Man," Jericho snapped. "The guy you killed was a good friend of mine. And you're going *down* for that."

"Oh, for *fuck's* sake," grated Portman, then coughed raggedly. That didn't sound good, either. Jericho wondered how much longer the guy was going to live without medical attention. "That black bastard was fucking my girl. They were both asking for it."

Jericho's fists itched to drive into the man's face for his words, but he restrained himself, for the woman's sake. *You'll pay for that, you sonovabitch.*

Portman edged his way out of the booth, still holding the woman in front of him. "They reopened access to the offramp this morning. So, I'm gonna get a car and drive the fuck out of here, and you're not gonna stop me if you don't want this bitch bleeding out in front of you."

If there was one thing Jericho had always dreaded encountering, it was a hostage situation. Having innocents deliberately placed in the line of fire by the bad guys went against everything he believed in as a superhero. He met the woman's eyes, silently promising her: *I will get you out of this.*

"Bobbi wasn't cheating on you, with Luke or with anyone else," he said flatly. "I talked to people who knew her. She couldn't touch *anyone* without it screwing up her head. She came to Utopia City so she could get her powers under control and be with you again." *And to help clear Adam Power, but I'm pretty sure he doesn't want to hear about that right now.*

Portman blinked. "Bullshit." Shock, irritation and a few other emotions chased themselves across his face.

Firmly, Jericho shook his head. "No bullshit," he countered. "I talked to both of them that night. All she could talk about was how she couldn't wait to see you again." That was stretching things, but not by a huge amount. "Besides, Luke was a happily married man. I've known him and his wife for years. We even went to the same damn school, back in Savannah." Curling his left hand out of the man's view, he started forming a push-tag.

"Fuck." Portman closed his eyes and shook his head. "No!" With the word, the knife came away from the hostage's throat and pointed directly at Jericho. "There's no fucking way that can be true."

"It is." Jericho laid his right hand over his heart. "I swear to you on the grave of General Joseph E. Johnston, it's the absolute goddamn truth. Bobbi never cheated on you even once." He continued to push energy into the push-tag. Once it was a little stronger, he'd be able to hit the knife with it, ensuring Portman wouldn't be able to get it back to the woman's throat before Jericho could reach him and remove it from consideration. *Just a few more seconds …*

"FUCK!" screamed Portman much more loudly, pushing the woman away from him. She staggered away from him and came hard up against the rail; so forcefully had Portman shoved her that she overbalanced, tipping forward over the waist-high rail. Her shriek rang loud in Jericho's ears as she clutched at the rail then lost her grip again.

With his distraction in play, Portman turned to make a run for it. But his weakened knee gave way, and he lurched back against the rail he was leaning on. He bellowed in surprise as his feet left the catwalk floor in turn.

Jericho was confronted with a stark choice, but he knew where his priorities lay. Grabbing the rail, he let the push-tag dissolve as he leaped over after the woman, lunging downward to grab for her flailing hand. Her wrist slapped into his grasp and he immediately reduced her effective weight to about nine pounds. On the other side of the catwalk, he heard a diminishing scream, cut off by a sickening series of thuds.

"It's okay," he said to the woman. "I've got you." It only took a minor effort to get her back up over the rail, but by that time it was far too late to save Portman. Jericho leaned across and looked down, to see the limp body lying on the concrete far below.

Behind him, he heard a whimper. When he turned, he saw that the woman's face was white, and she was unsteady on her feet. *Shit. She's in shock.* The symptoms were easily recognizable from the first-aid courses he'd done.

"Are you okay?" he asked, going to her side and gently steadying her. "You're safe now."

She whimpered again, keeping as far away from the rails as possible and stuffing her fist into her mouth. He grimaced. *Oh, definitely shock. I can't leave her alone like this.*

"Here," he said gently. "Let's get you someplace warm and safe so you can sit down for a while, okay?" Leaning down, he put her arm over his shoulders and guided her gently in the direction of the glassed-in console. There was a chair inside the booth; he eased her into it. Taking down a heavy bad-weather jacket that was hanging at the back of the booth, he put it over her shoulders. Automatically, she pulled it closed around her. There were thermostat controls in the booth, and he punched the heat up by about five degrees. Almost immediately, the booth began to warm up. "Feeling better now?"

One shoulder rose in a half-shrug; huddled into the jacket, she didn't respond in any other way.

Great, she's going non-verbal on me. "My name's G-Man," he said. "How do you contact your supervisor?"

"Uh …" she said vaguely, but he was already feeling along the underside of the desk for a duress alarm button. When he found it, he pressed it until it clicked in. Ten seconds later, the phone on the desk rang.

Jericho picked it up. "Listen carefully," he said crisply. "The name is G-Man. I'm a superhero. Your operator has been attacked. She's safe, but she's in shock and she needs someone with her. I need to check on the bad guy. Get someone here *right now.*" Ignoring the flustered voice on the other end, he hung the phone up again. Turning back to the woman, he said reassuringly, "You'll be safe here. Someone will be with you shortly. I'll be nearby."

Letting himself out of the booth, he slid the door shut behind him. Once he was out of her line of sight, he vaulted over the rail and let himself drift down from catwalk to catwalk.

It was a truism that prodigies were not to be underestimated, and some dynamics were just plain durable enough to take a fall like that and walk away. However, Jericho had few worries on that score. If Portman had been a prodigy, he would've been well on the way to mending the injuries he'd taken from Luke and Bobbi, not going downhill from them. And a Dynamic rating that provided sufficient durability to tank the fall would've made the man proof against suffering the injuries in the first place.

Still, when he got down to Portman's twisted body, he checked for a pulse anyway, just in case. Unsurprisingly, he found no signs of life. At the very least, it looked like several major bones were broken, and he had his suspicions about Portman's vital organs as well. The man simply was not going to be getting up again.

As he straightened up, some of the Southside Parking workers were coming over to see what had happened; he waved them off so as not to further contaminate the scene.

"You guys still there?" he asked quietly, pitching his voice for the earpiece alone. "How's it going?"

"Oh, they surrendered shortly after you left, so Sierra cracked the encryption on the tablet for shits and giggles. We've got every name on the Southsiders' network, just waiting for the cops to come in and sweep 'em all up." Thomas' voice had a satisfied tone to it. "How about you? It sounds like you got him."

"Yeah," Jericho said heavily. "He's down. You guys better get going. Even if the cops aren't on the way yet, they will be in a minute."

"Will do," Thomas said. "See you later."

Jericho nodded automatically. "Count on it."

Pressing hard on the earpiece, he counted three seconds to shut it off. Then he pulled out his phone, as well as a particular card he'd been given a few days ago. He dialed the number on the latter.

"Utopia City PD, Detective Sergeant Stirling speaking." The burly cop's gruff voice was easy to recognize. "Who am I talking to?"

Clearing his throat, Jericho took particular care to lower his voice so that Stirling didn't recognize it. The man knew Jericho Hansen was a superhero, but not which one. "It's G-Man."

"Hello, G-Man." Stirling did not sound thrilled. "I'm right now watching footage of you violating at least six municipal ordinances with your little stunt regarding the South Side Mall. Care to explain your actions?"

"That depends," Jericho said. "Are you interested in closing the Jack Portman case, and maybe shutting down the Southsiders for good?"

From the change in Stirling's tone, the detective sergeant had just sat forward at his desk. "I'm listening."

58
Out of the Blue

A Few Hours Later
Rooftop of the Southside Parking structure

The sunset was nice, but Jericho had no eyes for it. He sat on the very edge of the roof, boots braced against the side of the building, with five hundred feet of air beneath his knees. Off to his left, cars and trucks seemed to float through the gathering dusk within the transparent cover over the freeway, their glaring headlights the most prominent part of them. Perhaps half a mile beyond the interstate, lights were coming up on the broad swathe of the Greenway, illuminating the footpaths that meandered across it.

The police had come and gone; while they were on site, they'd gotten statements from all concerned. Every square inch of the scene of Portman's death had been examined to a fare-thee-well. Stirling had interviewed Jericho rather acerbically, then gone on his way. Once the scene of the death had been checked over, the broken body of Jack Portman had been taken away to the morgue.

It was time, he'd decided, to get in some quality brooding. Justice, however rough and ready—and accidental—had been done. As fascinating as Utopia City was, his main reason for coming back was officially defunct. Bobbi and Luke could rest easy now. Even the Southsiders, who had been giving Portman sanctuary, were in police custody.

Hear that, Luke? The sonovabitch is dead. Even if I didn't mean to do it that way.

In the back of his mind, he imagined Luke's response. *Kickass, cuz.*

The problem was, this put him at a loose end. *What do I do now?*

He didn't *want* to go back to Savannah. Everywhere he'd ever gone to with Stephen would stand out as a reminder of the shit-show their relationship had devolved into. And if he went back with Thomas—if Thomas even wanted to go back *with* him—that would cause more drama. Stephen would find out about it—not *might*, *would*—and the rumors would spiral outward from there, wreaking more havoc on his peace of mind than any hurricane. *I don't need that shit.*

He heard the heavy tread a moment before his G-sense alerted him to the presence behind him. "G-Man." The voice was deep and rumbling. Only one man sounded like that.

Turning, he saw Relentless standing on the rooftop, black and silver armor washed red and gold by the last of the sunset glow. "Uh … hi," he said, bracing his palms on the rooftop, preparing to stand up. "What's up? I didn't know Force Majeure had an interest in this case."

"We don't. No, don't get up." Relentless moved over beside him, then—as Jericho's heart caught in his throat—settled down on the edge of the roof and swung his legs over the drop, letting out a sigh as if glad to be sitting down. "That's better."

Jericho found it hard to breathe; the sheer *presence* of the man beside him was overpowering. "What … why are you here, then?" He was almost certain that it wasn't to watch the sunset, and he refused to even consider the idea that Relentless was there to see him specifically. The trouble was, there weren't many other options to go on with.

"To talk to you." The massively armored hero turned his head to look down at Jericho. "Why are *you* still here?"

"Um … to think about stuff?" Jericho made a vague gesture. "Luke was my best friend. When he was …" A lump rose into his throat, and he had to start again. "When it happened, I knew I had to catch the bad guy. But now I've done that. Portman isn't going to hurt anyone anymore. I mean … is that *it*? Shouldn't I feel more satisfied with the way it turned out?"

"Hm." It was almost a chuckle. "I've been doing this for a long time, and if there's one thing I've learned, it's that not every case is a sexy one. It's not all supervillains and world-ending plots. Sometimes, it's just a garden-variety murderer." He gave Jericho a measured nod. "And you stepped up. You did good work today."

The unexpected praise took Jericho on the back foot. *I … guh … buh … wha?* Ruthlessly, he suppressed the babbling in his mind. "Me?" He tried not to let his voice squeak too much. "I just … I only …"

Now Relentless' expression was a glower. "You *only* tracked down a wanted murderer, and in the process shut down a smuggling ring that's been evading police attention for years. Don't sell yourself short. It's not a good look for you."

Jericho tried not to hyperventilate as his treacherous body responded to the tone of the veteran hero's voice. Previously dormant, his crush on the man awoke and started sending out new shoots of growth. "I … uh … I didn't capture him," he managed. "He fell to his death. That's got to be worth some kind of black mark." He had no idea why he was even trying to downplay his achievements in Relentless' eyes, but that was the way his mouth was moving. "*And* I got yelled at by the cops for how I got into the Mall in the first place." Stirling had waxed particularly sarcastic over that point. Jericho had judged it not the right time to talk about the treatment of newcomers to the city.

"I'm aware of all that." Now Relentless sounded impatient. "Are you certain Portman killed your friends?"

"Well … yes." Jerkily, he nodded. "He still had the scratches on his face that Bobbi put there. And the damage Luke did to his knee."

"Then no innocents died today. And sometimes, that's all you can hope for." A gauntleted hand rested on his shoulder for a moment, sending his heart rate through the roof. "You've done well. I've done worse myself, on occasion. Now, I'm going to ask you a question, and I want an honest answer."

"Um … sure?" Jericho had *no* idea where this was going. *Is he going to advise me to start a team with other people who didn't pass their interviews? Or does he just want to know who Thomas and Chelsea are? Shit, does he want to recruit them?*

Relentless paused, drawing the moment out. Jericho could feel the tension building in his chest.

"G-Man," the veteran hero said at last. "If I offered you a place in Force Majeure, would you accept it?"

Jericho blinked. He understood all the words that had just been spoken, but their overall meaning escaped him. "… what?" *He did not just say that. Did he?*

"Force Majeure," Relentless repeated, a tinge of impatience creeping into his voice. "If I said you could still join, would you accept?"

Holy shit, he did say it. Frantically, Jericho tried to bludgeon his mind into providing some kind of response. "Um … are you asking? Because if you are …" *Crap, crap, crap, what should I say? What would Luke want me to do?* He didn't even need to think hard about that one. *He'd dope-slap me so hard my head would spin around, then tell me to say yes.* "… um, yes, I would."

"Good. It's settled. Report to the Technologist by nine tomorrow morning. I'll tell him to expect you." Relentless went to say something else, but Jericho half-raised his hand. The veteran hero looked down at him. "What?"

Jericho took a deep breath. "What about the interview? I kind of … said some things." *Cussed out Independence, among other things.*

"I know." Relentless seemed almost amused. "I was there. But I'll let you in on a little secret. The results of the interviews are not binding. They just let us have a look at you. And if any of us decides to sponsor a new recruit onto the team, that recruit is in."

"Wait … *what?* You're *sponsoring* me onto the team?" Events were going too fast for Jericho. "Just like that? Why me?"

"Because I choose to." The impatience was back in his voice. Relentless, it appeared, was unused to people questioning his decisions. "You were already a good choice, and your actions today have merely served to underline that. I believe that if any danger ever threatens Utopia, you will do whatever it takes to avert it. Do you believe otherwise?"

There was only one good answer. "Uh, no. Definitely no. I, I will definitely do my best to live up to … yeah, I'll do my best." Fully aware he was babbling again, Jericho shut his mouth before he said anything else stupid.

"Good." The sun had dropped below the horizon; apart from a few distant clouds lit from the underside by the last rays, the sky was going dark. Relentless climbed to his feet, then extended his hand down to help Jericho up.

"Thanks." He felt his hand engulfed by the armored gauntlet; hoisted to his feet, he knew all too well that the strength being exhibited was only a fraction of what Relentless could bring to bear. "And thanks for giving me a second chance. It really means a lot to me."

"Second chances are important. I believe in that very firmly." Relentless paused and raised his chin. "On that note, would you like to come back to the Spire to celebrate your membership over a few drinks? I can fill you in on your duties."

Jericho felt his heart rate accelerate, all of its own accord. *Does he even* know *what being next to him does to me?* Out loud, he stammered, "Uh, yes?"

"Good." Relentless raised his hand to the side of his helmet. "Tourbillon. On me."

Five seconds passed, then ten. Relentless' lips thinned and he raised his hand again. But before he could speak, a vertical black swirl appeared in midair, rapidly growing to eight feet high. Stepping out of it, the androgynous hero ignored Jericho and gave Relentless what appeared to be a dirty look. "I was eating."

"You're on duty," Relentless replied. "My rooms, for both of us."

Tourbillon gave Jericho a look of appraisal as the first swirl dissipated. Jericho felt his cheeks heating up, remembering how judgmental the hooded Enabled had been at the interview. "I see."

"Enough with that tone," growled Relentless. "My rooms. Now."

With what may have been an eye-roll (it was hard to tell, under that hood), Tourbillon nodded. "If you say so." With the wave of a slim gloved hand, another swirl of blackness came into being. "Your rooms, *mon capitaine.*"

"About time." Relentless stepped into the swirl and vanished. Jericho moved up to it then hesitated. He looked at the hooded hero, half-expecting the teleport-swirl to vanish again before he had a chance to step through. Or worse, when he was halfway through. *What would even happen in that situation?*

Relentless' arm reached out of the swirl and latched on to Jericho's shoulder, hauling him through. He felt a moment of disorientation and his ears popped; when his head cleared again, he was looking at a huge picture window. Or rather, out *through* a huge picture window, to where Utopia City was spread out before him.

As the dusk transitioned into night, the holograms began to ghost into life out of the darkness, gradually transforming the cityscape into a wonderland before his eyes. He'd seen it before, but not like this, and never so much of it at once. At this height, he couldn't see much in the way of detail on the ground, or even the smaller buildings, but that didn't matter. The vibrant colors and insistent glow of the holograms blanketed the inner city in an ever-shifting kaleidoscope of glory and beauty. It was almost fractal in nature; when he focused on any one spot, he could barely make out individual images, but each one contributed to the whole in its own way.

"I built this city, you know." Relentless' voice came from behind Jericho. "From the ground up. It was my brainchild. My greatest creation."

Jericho felt shivers running through his body at the proximity of the veteran hero. Despite his growing feelings for Thomas, the crush was still very much in evidence. He tried not to look around at Relentless, in case he gave away what was on his mind. Fortunately, he was able to distract himself with what the big man was saying. "I thought it was the Technologist and Transit who did that." Then Transit's words came back to him. "*You're* the third one?"

"Yes." Relentless' voice held neither boasting nor braggadocio. "I designed it all, from the sub-sewers to the Spire. It works as well as it does because I made it that way."

It only took Jericho a moment to figure out what he meant. Mental prodigies, like Smokeshadow, tended to be overshadowed by their more physical brethren; those prodigies who could turn their talents toward both physical *and* mental pursuits were thin on the ground indeed. He was more impressed than ever.

Then his G-sense felt the armored mass of the hero moving away; the thick carpet absorbed almost all the impact of his footsteps. "I need to get out of this armor. Feel free to pour yourself a drink and get comfortable. We'll be here awhile."

"Okay." Jericho dared to breathe again, though his heart rate didn't go down by much. *Will you quit it?* he told his body. *He doesn't mean anything by this. He's just talking things over with a new recruit. Me.*

Trying to distract himself, he looked around. The lighting was low, but he seemed to have been deposited in an impressively luxurious lounge. At first estimation, it was larger than the entire apartment he was staying in, back at the Oaklands. The walls had been lined with realistic (and rustic) looking red bricks, while the carpet underfoot exhibited an unbelievably deep pile. Every time he took a step, it felt as though it were trying to swallow his foot up to the ankle.

There were three heavy armchairs in the room. Each was upholstered with what appeared to be Turkish leather and had exquisitely carved side-tables alongside. Their placement in the room had them facing the oversized flat-screen TV that was set into the wall. Expensive-looking paintings adorned the walls, while small pillars holding vases and other antique items were spaced around the perimeter of the room. On the far side of the room, only a moderately exhausting trek across the vast expanse of carpet, was an elaborate liquor cabinet that appeared to contain every style of booze known to mankind, including a few he'd never heard of.

He would've preferred a cold beer, but there was a brand of sour mash that he'd tried before and found passable, so he walked on over and splashed some of that into a glass. When he turned around, Relentless had opened a door on the far side of the room and was removing items of his armor; placing them on a rack within the room.

Jericho turned away again, feeling as though he were intruding on a private moment. Recalling the advice to get comfortable, he put the glass down for a moment so that he could unfasten his leg-straps. Then he picked up the glass and went back toward the picture window. On the way past the nearest armchair, he shrugged out of his jacket and hung it over the back. Glass in hand, he gazed out at the hologram-enhanced beauty of the city far below while he sipped at his drink.

The carpet did such a good job of muffling Relentless' footsteps that Jericho's G-sense told him the veteran hero was coming his way long before his ears did. Turning, he opened his mouth to make a polite comment along the lines of 'nice place you have here', but it died on his lips. Jaw slowly dropping, his eyes took in the leader of Force Majeure. Somehow, he'd imagined the man wore a little more under his armor; currently, all Relentless had on was a pair of tights reaching from his waist to halfway down his calves. Jericho's treacherous eyes, tracking downward, reported that the garment left absolutely *nothing* to the imagination.

Jerking his attention upward and shutting his mouth as he felt a flush blooming on his cheeks, he fixated on Relentless' torso; no less fascinating, but there was less chance of seeing something he had no business looking at. Well over six and a half feet tall with almost brutally strong features, Relentless displayed muscle definition to a degree that professional bodybuilders would strive over a course of months to achieve for just one day. Not that he was unmarred; scars traced themselves across that magnificent physique like stories carved into the flesh.

Jericho counted at least half a dozen puckered marks that he tentatively identified as bullet-wounds; there were other reminders of potentially lethal wounds, including a scar extending across the width of Relentless' chest, from shoulder to shoulder, just below the collarbones. *Six inches higher, and he would've lost his head.* A secondary scar was appended on to the left-hand end almost as an afterthought, leaving an effect like a lazy 't'. *Holy crap. How many terror villains did he end up fighting, and which one did that to him?* He made a personal bet with himself that it was Guillotine. Decapitation had always been that particular terror villain's trademark.

But even as the thought crossed his mind, his eyes were drawn to the one battle-mark he could positively identify, down on Relentless' right side. Perhaps eight inches across, it consisted of countless curved scars grouped together in a pattern that, if one squinted, might resemble some type of rose.

The outer scars were light pink, but the discoloration shaded oddly outward, as if the blade that formed them had gone in at an acute angle instead of slicing deeply; the effect really did look like the outer petals of a flower. Closer in toward the middle, the scars occurred closer and closer together, much like the petals of the inside of a rose. About three inches out from the center they formed an unbroken circle of scar tissue, fading from pink inward toward purple. The very center of the scar held an inch-wide pockmark impressed half an inch into Relentless' skin, undoubtedly where the main blades of the weapon had gone in. There was only one thing that could have caused a horrific wound like that.

"Is that … was that … the Blood Rose?" he asked, gesturing with the glass to cover his lapse of politeness. *God, if he knew I was staring at his crotch …* "How did you even *survive* that?"

"Sheer blind luck," Relentless said, tilting his head as if wondering why Jericho was asking the question in the first place. "I was young and stupid. I'd never lost a fight. Nor had he. I *knew* I was better than him, except I wasn't. He left me for dead, and I was able to crawl off and heal up." And then, to Jericho's fascinated horror, he put his thumbs into the waistline of the tights and began to push them down.

Jericho's train of thought derailed and exploded. There were no survivors. "Wh-what are you doing?" he stammered, but his brain was already filling him in on the clues he'd already missed.

"What do you think I'm doing?" Relentless stared at him. "What are *you* doing? I told you to get comfortable." He gestured at Jericho ... *no*, Jericho realized a moment later. *At my costume. He wants me to take it off.*

"Is this ... did you bring me back here to ..." Jericho couldn't even finish the sentence. *Have sex with me.*

"Well, what did you *think* was going to happen?" Relentless shook his head disbelievingly. "What part of 'come back to my rooms with me for drinks' did you not understand?"

Part of Jericho's brain tentatively advanced the suggestion that while he was here, he may as well go along with things, but the majority shouted it down. *No. I won't do that to Thomas.*

As if triggered by that thought, he recalled all the moments he'd had with the younger man; tender, funny, silly, *moving* moments. Agreeing to help the Survivors. The surprise kisses. Going to the South Side Mall for the first time. The consoling hug. Arguing, then making up with another hug. The heart-wrenching walk up the hill in Memorial Park. Fighting the Southsiders side by side. Coming to a growing understanding that he really *could* have a healthy relationship, if he was just able to make the leap of faith. And the absolute certainty that if he didn't walk out *right now*, he would kill any potential relationship with the younger man stone dead.

Unbidden by conscious thought, his mouth was still moving. "I, uh, never knew you were gay."

Relentless rolled his eyes. "Oh, for god's sake. I'm not. I'm *pan*. But I'm not looking for a relationship; I just like to fuck any new recruits that are interested. I've *seen* the way you look at me. So, where's the problem?"

There was only one thing Jericho could think to ask. "Uh ... if I say no, am I still ...?"

"Yes, you *are*." Relentless let out a hugely put-upon sigh. "You're still in Force Majeure. This is totally separate. Anything *else* you want to know before we get to it?"

"No. Sorry." Averting his eyes from the massively built Enabled, Jericho put the glass down. "I can't do this. I've got to go."

Relentless stared. "Are you fucking for *real?*" A moment later, he must have seen his answer in Jericho's face. With a spasm of rage, he snatched a vase from one of the pillars around the wall and threw it across the room at the liquor cabinet. Jericho ducked and covered his head with his arms as glass and porcelain shattered explosively, expensive booze spraying across the rich carpet. With an equally vicious movement, Relentless hit a control in the wall; part of the picture window hissed aside. "Get out! Get *out*, you little cock-tease! And if you're not on time tomorrow, don't bother showing up at all!"

Jericho didn't need to be told twice. Grabbing his jacket, he dived out into the void, the cool evening air utterly failing to assuage the burning mortification in his cheeks. He hadn't put on the jacket yet, but he was still a long way up. His outward momentum was carrying him away from the Spire, and his slowed rate of fall gave him plenty of time to get the jacket on and zipped up. With the ease of long practice, he fastened each leg-strap in turn, then straightened his body out.

As he spread his arms and caught the wind, he made himself a promise. *I am never, ever telling Leroy about this.*

59
Putting the Pieces Together

A Little Time Later
The Oaklands
Smokeshadow's Apartment

"It's not *funny*." Jericho tried to glare at Chelsea, who was still cackling madly on the sofa. He couldn't really pull it off, mainly because he felt she had a point. Not that it was funny, but that he probably deserved to be laughed at.

"Sorry." She snorted with laughter, then caught herself. "Sorry, sorry. Seriously, holy shit. You blue-balled *Relentless*. That's gotta be a real exclusive club, right there. I mean, I've heard of useless lesbians, but … no, that's not fair. Honestly? Not joking now? I think it's totally sweet that you were thinking of Thomas and pulled matters up *before* you got down and dirty with the hottest piece of beefcake in Utopia City. I mean, I'm not sure if I'd have that level of self-control."

Jericho sighed. "It was more like a total lack of situational awareness." Getting up from the chair, he pointed at the sink. "Is it okay if I have a glass of water?"

"You can have one of my beers if you want," she said generously. "I don't touch the stuff."

"Thanks." A beer sounded pretty good right then. Jericho went over and opened the fridge to find the complimentary bottles of Utopia Gold, just as she'd said. Pushing his sleeve up and popping the cap off one, he went back to the armchair. A good third of the bottle went down in the first swallow. The cold liquid was heavenly on his throat, especially with all the talking he'd been doing.

"Okay, what happened then?" she asked, eyes bright. "You turned him down and jumped out the window, and then what? Embarked on your walk of no-shame-whatsoever?" Despite her implicit promise not to laugh, a snicker crept out. It occurred to him that she was enjoying this way too much.

"Oh, there's plenty of shame there," he admitted. "The way I went back to the Spire with him, for starters. I mean, *yes*, I've had a huge crush on him since I found out I was gay. What gay guy or straight woman hasn't?" He paused, waiting for her to refute his point. She did no such thing, instead gesturing for him to keep going. "But I didn't even realize what he had in mind 'til he started taking his tights off! Or maybe deep down I did, and I just chickened out at the last second."

Getting up from the sofa, she came over and perched on the arm of the chair. Gently, she laid her arm over his shoulders, then smacked him sharply across the back of the head. "Do I have your attention yet?" she demanded.

"Ow, hey!" he protested. "What the hell was that about?" Rubbing the afflicted spot, he gave her a dirty look. "What did I ever do to you?"

"Oh, I dunno. Maybe acted like an idiot in front of me?" She rolled her eyes. "You're not even Thomas' boyfriend yet, and you're *still* turning down sex with a totally hot guy because it would hurt his feelings if you didn't? That's not being a chicken; that's being an awesome person. So what if you didn't realize what was going on at first? You're human. That shit happens. Get over it. The point being, you *did* think of Thomas when it mattered, and you got out of there. Nine out of ten people wouldn't have."

He paused to think about what she'd just said. After leaving the Spire, he'd glided for what felt like miles, then changed out of his costume and gotten an air-cab back to the Oaklands. Feeling utterly wretched from what had happened (and what had *nearly* happened), he'd contacted Chelsea, because she knew more about people than anyone he knew. If anyone could figure out what was wrong with him and how to fix it, he reasoned, she could. She'd met him at the cab stand and taken him back to her apartment, where she teased the whole sorry tale out of him then laughed so hard she nearly fell off the sofa.

"So … you think I'm an idiot, but not a bad person?" It was a start, he supposed. Of the two, that was the lesser evil.

"Exactly." She gave him a cheerful smile. "Which is preferable, as far as I'm concerned. Bad people *like* being bad people. Idiots can be trained. Case in point: you. Finish your beer; we're going for a walk."

He had no idea what was going on. The morning had begun with him being dragged from his apartment by Chelsea and Thomas and taken off to to a mystery destination, and now she wanted to pull the whole charade all over again? "Where are we going *this* time?"

"Wouldn't you like to know." Her eyes sparkled in a way that made him think he should be ducking and covering. "Finish your beer. Hurry up, time's a-wasting."

Feeling that he had no choice in the matter (with a slight sense of relief, in that whatever *other* bad decisions got made tonight, he wouldn't be the one responsible for them) Jericho did as he was told, drinking the rest of the beer down. The belch that resulted was quite impressive; Chelsea was nice enough not to comment on it. Which was only fair, as she'd been the one who'd told him to finish the beer in the first place.

With his costume satchel slung over his shoulder, he followed her out of her apartment and through the labyrinth of corridors that made up the Oaklands complex. A couple of times along the way, he thought of asking again where they were going, but he knew all too well what her response would be, so he kept quiet. When she stopped and knocked on a specific door, he was none the wiser; right up until it opened to reveal Thomas standing there.

"Oh, hi," Thomas said immediately. "Come on in. If I'd known you were coming over, I would've ordered pizza or something." He stepped back to let them enter, then looked uncertainly from Chelsea to Jericho as he closed the door behind them. "To be honest, I thought tonight was going to be all about laying low and seeing how it played out in the news."

"Oh, I'm not staying," Chelsea said briskly. "You're both idiots, so I'm going to make it very simple for the both of you. On the strength of the bust this afternoon, Jericho's been accepted into Force Majeure. As of nine tomorrow morning, he's a member. In a not entirely unconnected side-note, Relentless invited him back to the Spire for celebratory sex. Relax; Jericho turned him down."

"Wait, wait." The expression on Thomas' face went through a whole range of options before settling on 'WTF?'. "Relentless is *gay?* When did *that* happen?"

Jericho knew his own expression had to be just as entertaining; he had *not* expected her to just lay it all out like that. Which, in hindsight, was his mistake. Chelsea followed no rules but her own.

"He's not, but it's a long story." He rubbed the bridge of his nose with thumb and forefinger. "You see, I—"

Before he could run his mouth any further and dig himself right back into the hole that Chelsea had dragged him out of, she elbowed him discreetly in the ribs and kept talking for him. "—need to talk to you, Thomas. Because he's decided that he wants to be your boyfriend after all. Haven't you, Jericho?"

Jericho froze. The look on his face, he supposed, was probably the mirror to that on Thomas', if 'deer in the headlights' could be defined as a specific look. It wasn't that he *didn't* want to be Thomas' boyfriend, but in all honesty, he would much rather have spent a little more time leading up to the topic. Say, a month or two, to give Thomas every chance in the world to back out if he came to the conclusion he really didn't want to be with Jericho after all. The last thing he wanted to do was to push the younger man into a corner.

Chelsea, on the other hand, appeared to have no qualms whatsoever about pushing people into corners. "Okay, Thomas, while Jericho's rebooting his brain, I'll ask you. Do you want to be Jericho's boyfriend?" She tilted her head, with one eyebrow slightly raised in an interrogatory manner. "Before you incriminate yourself, remember that I *will* know if you're lying. And I *will* point and laugh."

It seemed that Thomas was either made of sterner stuff than Jericho, or he'd had more warning and was thus recovering more quickly. Alternatively, it was possible that sharing an apartment with Chelsea for several days had somewhat inoculated him against her manner. Whichever it was, he cleared his throat then nodded. "Yes. Jericho, I would like to be your boyfriend. If you want me to be, that is." Part of the tension in his shoulders seemed to drop away at the admission.

"Sheesh." Chelsea rolled her eyes theatrically. "I should've been a dentist. I'm pretty sure that was *more* painful than pulling teeth. Okay, we've got one side of the equation." She turned her attention back toward Jericho. "So, you haven't got the excuse of not knowing how he really feels. How do *you* feel about it?"

As far as Jericho was concerned, life was easier when all he had to worry about was running the rooftops and putting the fear of God into muggers. Having to make semi-irrevocable relationship decisions on zero notice was a far trickier proposition. *I'd rather face an actual supervillain or have Relentless even* more *mad at me than this*. With both Thomas and Chelsea looking expectantly at him, all he wanted to do was go and hide in his apartment until everything started making sense again. But he was reasonably sure that wouldn't work as a delaying tactic. Chelsea would probably walk straight in and dope-slap him again.

Retreat being off the table, he accepted that the only viable tactic was complete and unconditional surrender. The fact that it was also the truth went a long way toward helping him reach that decision. "Yes," he said. With the feeling of leaping out over a shadowed void of uncertain depth, not knowing if his powers would support him or not, he reached out and took Thomas' hand. "I want to be your boyfriend."

"*Goood* boy. You *can* learn after all." Chelsea gave them both a smile, then patted Jericho on the shoulder. Going to the door, she opened it. "Congratulations; you're on your first date. It's been a long day, so I'm going to bed now. Don't do anything I wouldn't do." Stepping out of the apartment, she pulled the door almost closed, then leaned in again. "In the interests of total disclosure, that's a very short list." With her trademark smartass grin, she backed out; the door clicked into place, leaving Thomas and Jericho to stare at each other.

"Well." Thomas gave a nervous chuckle. "I didn't exactly expect this."

"Me neither," Jericho agreed. He squeezed Thomas' hand, felt an answering squeeze, then let it go. "So, we're officially in a relationship now, huh?"

Thomas tilted his head. "Seems that way." He essayed another chuckle. "I suspect that if we broke up now after she's put all this work into getting us together, she'd come back and slap us both upside the head for being total morons." His eyes fixed on Jericho's face; Jericho felt warmth building in his cheeks. "Besides, I don't really want to break up. Do you?"

"Not in the slightest." Jericho stepped past Thomas, briefly grasping his hand on the way. The momentary contact felt good; it felt *right,* in a way that everything he'd ever done with Stephen had not. He forced away that thought. *I don't want to think about that.* Stopping next to the sofa, he looked around. "I *was* going to get around to asking you. Sometime."

"Sometime next year, maybe?" Thomas' smile took the sting out of the question as he followed Jericho over to the sofa. "Look, I get it. Your ex hurt you. It takes a long time to learn how to trust again when people have already screwed you over before. Sometimes it feels like you can never trust anyone again." From the tone of his voice, Jericho got the distinct impression that he was speaking from personal experience.

"Oh, I hear you." Experimentally, Jericho reached up and caressed Thomas' cheek with his fingertips. It felt strange; not only that he was doing it with someone new, but he'd never really had the urge to do that with Stephen.

Again, he pushed the thought away. *I'm with Thomas, not anyone else. This is me and him. That's it. Nobody else is invited.*

Thomas seemed to have frozen on the spot, looking at him questioningly. Jericho essayed an awkward smile and sat down on the sofa. "I just wanted to see what it felt like. This whole 'new relationship' thing is very weird to me. Maybe we should take it slow for a bit, 'til we're used to being together?"

"Well, from my side, it felt nice. Just for future reference." Thomas smiled down at him, his carefree manner starting to return. "But I think taking it slow is a really good idea. So, what did you want to do? Watch some TV, drink some beer, get pizza later?"

Leaning down, Jericho unzipped his boots and kicked them off. "I think that's an *amazing* idea. What sort of pizza do you like?" It struck him that he had a lot to learn about his brand-new boyfriend if he didn't even know this much about the younger man.

Thomas retrieved the remote from the counter and sat down beside Jericho. "Anything with bacon or pineapple, or both. Though I did once taste a very nice vegan pizza. I have no idea how they did it."

"Black magic and arcane rituals," Jericho decided. "If it doesn't have meat, it's not really pizza. It's just flatbread with incidentals and sauce." He tapped himself on the chest. "And I should know. I delivered them once upon a time."

With a snort and a shake of the head, Thomas lifted the remote and turned on the TV. "What did you want to watch?"

A memory stirred, not as painful as it might have been. *You seen th' movie channels in this place, cuz? There's stuff I ain't never even heard of before.* "Something off one of the movie channels, I guess."

"You got it." Thomas pressed a button on the remote, and the screen changed to a list of titles. "Pick a movie, any movie."

None of them looked familiar, so Jericho shrugged. "Which one's about to start?"

"We pick one, and it starts." Thomas grinned at him. "And they only have commercials between movies, not during."

Jericho had to take a moment to get his head around this. "So … it's more like an online streaming service than a movie channel?"

Amused, Thomas chuckled. "This is Utopia. There's not a lot of difference between the two, here." He clicked at random on the list of titles. "Let's see. *Sherlock*

Hound and the Mystery of Hill Hollow. 'A vaguely derivative piece of crap involving four Enabled teenagers and their bumbling robot dog, investigating mysterious events in a small town. Do not expect deep thinking, here.'"

"Isn't that a little harsh?" Jericho looked more closely. "Oh. That's what the reviewer wrote. Wait, they actually award stars for campiness and humor?"

"Yup." Thomas smirked. "Four and a half stars for campiness, three and a half for comedy and half a star for dramatic tension. What do you think?"

Jericho settled back on the sofa. Dramatic tension was the last thing he wanted to deal with, right now. "It sounds perfect."

"Oh, good. I was thinking exactly the same thing." Thomas waited while Jericho called up to order pizza, then he hit the button to start the show running. After a brief fast-food commercial, the movie began.

Within the first ten minutes, they were trading barbs about the bad acting and the recycled plot devices, laughing their asses off as the movie just got worse and worse. When the pizza arrived, Thomas took the opportunity to fetch beers for both of them, and they took drinks at particularly egregious plot twists.

By the time the movie stumbled to a halt, they'd finished the pizza and gone through two beers each, and Jericho was weak with laughter at the unintentionally hilarious antics of the cast on set. Thomas was in little better state; at one point, Jericho had made him spray his drink across the room with a particularly pithy observation on how the power levels of the teens varied wildly in relation to their plot value.

"Oh, man," wheezed Jericho as the credits crawled up the screen. "That was hilarious. They couldn't have made it any funnier if they'd worked at it."

Thomas shook his head in rueful agreement as he turned the sound down, then dropped the remote on the sofa and got up to take the empty pizza box into the kitchenette. "I finally know what the saying *'so bad it's good'* really means. Did you want another beer before we pick the next one?"

"Thanks, that would be nice." Jericho didn't normally drink all that much (not that alcohol ever had much effect on him), but the three he'd already had were doing a bang-up job of quelling the butterflies massing in his stomach, so another probably couldn't hurt. He was enjoying Thomas' company far too much to want to screw up things by blurting out the wrong thing from sheer nerves. Leaning back against the sofa arm, he watched as the younger man headed into the kitchenette.

Just as Thomas opened the fridge door, a burst of dramatic music caught Jericho's attention. "What the hell?" Turning to face the TV again, he saw a long camera shot swooping in over what looked like Manhattan. The music, even at low volume, swelled to a crescendo. Grabbing the remote, he turned the sound back up. It *looked* like a movie trailer, but not one he'd seen before.

"New York, New York!" declared a voice-over. **"A city that needs a special type of hero to protect it!"** The camera view finally zoomed in on a rooftop, where a young woman wearing a white sleeveless tunic with gold trim stood on the very edge of the roof. Golden blonde hair streamed to one side, and her short skirt snapped and fluttered in the breeze. Tights in gold and white led down to knee-high boots that positively gleamed in the bright sunlight; gloves that reached almost to her shoulders kept up the theme. A half-face mask, also in gold and white, completed her ensemble.

As the camera approached her, she turned to face it with a brilliant smile. **"Do you feel like you want to spread your wings?"** she asked in a melodious tone, as magnificent pinions composed of golden hard-light feathers unfurled from behind her. With a look of utter serenity on her face, she let herself fall backward off the roof.

By the time the camera moved forward far enough to look down at her, she had rolled in mid-air and was flying away, the wings still spread wide.

The scene changed to another rooftop, at night. Far from the effortless poise of the young woman, the brutish-looking man didn't seem comfortable being on camera. He wasn't much over five feet tall but what he lacked in height, he made up for in breadth. Almost three feet across the shoulders, he possessed a level of muscular development that would have rivalled Relentless', had he been a foot and a half taller. A sturdy mask was secured to his head with a leather strap. It covered the top half of his face, leaving his prominent jaw exposed. The mask featured a heavy brow ridge as well as short fangs and small horns; all designed, Jericho figured, to draw attention away from what he really looked like.

A leonine mane of light brown hair was currently tied back with what looked like a strip of leather. Apart from the mask, his only item of clothing was a pair of leather trousers, held up by an intricately plaited leather strap. Sheathed on one hip was what Jericho assumed was a knife with a leather-bound handle. *He's certainly sticking to the wild-man theme.* The man's torso and arms were battered and scarred to a frankly implausible degree; fresh scars overlaid older ones, which in turn crossed over ancient battle-marks, the most faded of which stretched diagonally across his chest in a jagged line. Jericho had no idea what might've done that, but it must have nearly killed the guy at the time.

As the camera moved up to the heavy-set man, he scowled. **"You want to learn how to kick ass old-school?"** he grunted, then jumped off the roof. The scene changed to what looked like a security feed, with a bunch of punks in the process of committing a mugging. This was clearly supposed to be taken as part of the last shot, but Jericho suspected it wasn't. The stocky man plowed into the middle of the group like a wrecking-ball. If Jericho hadn't already intuited him to be a prodigy, that would've provided the clue. Between his impressive capacity for directed violence and the surprise attack, the half-dozen muggers didn't stand a chance.

In the next scene, it was daytime again. This time, it started with a closeup of a guy with dark wavy hair and a pencil mustache. He wore a HUD visor covering the top half of his face, and a midnight-black costume with actual electronics built into it. Bright yellow cords connected one module to another. Raising his hand—covered in a gauntlet that was more circuitry than otherwise—he made a gesture that looked like he was trying to peel an egg one-handed.

This time, the camera pulled back, moving away from the guy with the electronic costume until he was visible from the waist up. **"Do you ever feel as though you could be doing more with your time?"** he asked, his diction precise. Raising his other hand, he made a few more motions, and then a dozen helicopter-like drones zipped through the camera's field of view and took up formation around him. The camera zoomed out a little more, to show that he was standing *on* a flying vehicle of some sort, high over New York, with a dozen more of the drones performing complex orbits in his general vicinity. Turning away from the camera, he swooped down toward the streets, still standing on his flying platform.

The music swelled again, sounding more like the score for a major motion picture than a superhero recruiting drive. Jericho watched, spellbound by the sheer chutzpah of the unfolding production.

"Join New York's premier Enabled team!" proclaimed the voice actor as the camera's view settled on an empty rooftop. **"And meet the sensational Splendid!"** As her name was spoken, the girl in the gold and white descended from above and alighted delicately on the rooftop. Her wings remained spread as she smiled at the camera. **"The tenacious Troll!"** From off to the side, the bulky man appeared in a tuck-and-roll. Through chance or design, he came to a halt to Splendid's right, remaining in a crouch. **"And the devastating Drone!"** Rising from below on his flying platform, the artificer with the electronic costume stepped off onto the rooftop and moved to stand at Splendid's left. At the same time, Troll came to his feet. **"You, too, can be a part of ..."** The voice actor paused for a beat, to allow for a drumroll. **"MANHATTAN ...** *JUSTICE!"*

There was a pause as the camera moved closer. **"Hi,"** said Splendid. **"We've recently decided to expand our membership, so if you're interested, send us a text message or put in an application to our website."**

Drone nodded. **"The offer, of course, is open to anyone who is already resident within the New York area, or is able to make the move. Commuting from another city really doesn't work, I'm afraid."**

The camera panned to Troll. **"Anyone who shows gets a shot but if we say no, we mean no."**

A moment later, the commercial cut to a still image of the team, with a Manhattan phone number as well as an email address below them.

Jericho muted the TV as Thomas sat down beside him again. "Thanks," he said as he accepted the beer and opened it.

"No problem." Thomas clinked his bottle against Jericho's, then nodded toward the TV. "Was that what I thought it was?"

Jericho shrugged. "If you thought it was proof positive that Enabled life really *is* like the comic books, then ... yeah, I guess it was."

Thomas snorted with amusement, then drank from his beer. "You think they're serious?" he asked when he came up for air.

"Serious enough that if I hadn't already been accepted into Force Majeure, I might've considered moving to New York," Jericho said. He took a long swallow of the chilly, fizzy alcoholic beverage. It cooled his throat all the way down to his stomach. A moment later, he belched discreetly, the gases stinging his sinuses. "'Scuse me."

Thomas smirked, mischief in his eye. "You sure it wouldn't be because Troll gets around with no shirt on?"

Without thinking, Jericho snorted. "If Relentless doesn't do it for me, Troll certainly wouldn't. I like 'em tall."

Thomas looked at Jericho curiously. "You mean, Chelsea wasn't joking about him making an offer and you turning him down? I would've thought you had a crush on him. Everyone else seems to."

Jericho snorted again. "I thought so too, but it turns out I'm more of a homebody."

With a smile on his face, Thomas leaned in against Jericho's shoulder. "Me, too." A moment later, he said contemplatively, "You know, Chelsea also said not to do anything she wouldn't do. If she was alone with a guy she really, really liked, do you think she might consider taking her shirt off?"

Tension, suddenly reborn, twanged between them. Despite the beers, Jericho's throat was unaccountably dry. "You know, I think she might."

"Me, too." Thomas put down his drink and sat back from Jericho. Slowly, he began to unbutton his shirt. Barely daring to breathe in case he broke the spell, Jericho watched Thomas' fingers.

Button by button, the shirt opened up, until a narrow strip of Thomas' chest and stomach was on view from neck to waist. He paused, holding the shirt closed, and Jericho's heart sank into a black hole. *I pushed too hard.*

Then Thomas turned away, and let his shirt slip over his shoulders and slide down his arms, exposing his back from the top down. One at a time, he pulled his arms out of the sleeves. He had a nice back, with good muscle definition and *oh* so broad shoulders. There was a mole under his left shoulder-blade. Jericho watched as he took a deep breath then turned back around, arms loosely crossed in front of his body.

"This is me, I guess," he said quietly. "Uh … this is the first time I've done this with … well, with anyone."

Jericho put his own drink down and leaned forward. "You look amazing," he breathed. He had no idea why anyone with *those* pecs and abs would feel the slightest bit of self-consciousness about their body. When he reached out and put his hand on Thomas' shoulder, he found that the younger man was trembling. Was it excitement, fear, or something in between? He'd felt something similar, during his first time with—

He squashed that thought, hard. He was *not* going to think about his first time, or who it'd been with. This was all about him and Thomas. Leaning in, he kissed the younger man; gently, lips only, at first. Testing the waters. Thomas did not pull away. The kiss became harder, more demanding, from both sides at once. He felt hands at the buttons on his shirt, working to undo them. His own hands were elsewhere, running over the smooth muscles of Thomas' shoulders and back, feeling them flexing and bunching under the skin as Thomas unbuttoned his shirt for him. It was unexpectedly arousing.

His shirt came off. It was easy to let it happen. Thomas became more confident, more forceful, the way Jericho liked it. With tiny murmurs, he encouraged the younger man to take the initiative. He allowed Thomas to push him back onto the sofa, to hold him down and kiss him again and again. His entire body was throbbing in time with his want. His *need.* But it was up to Thomas to take the next step.

When Thomas took hold of Jericho's wrists and held them over his head, he thought he'd died and gone to heaven. This had never happened with—*don't think of his name!*

He closed his eyes, submerging himself in the moment, as hungry lips descended upon his. Thomas' grip was strong, giving him leave to struggle as hard as he wanted without ever quite breaking free. Being held, being pinned, being *dominated* … it was something he'd craved, and never been given. He turned his head to the side and felt Thomas nip him at the juncture of shoulder and neck; hesitantly, experimentally. *Oh, yes. Don't stop.* As the sensation thrilled through his body, he arched his back and keened his pleasure through clenched teeth. They kissed again; legs entwined, shirtless, skin moving against skin. Jericho wanted it to last forever.

When they broke for air, panting in each other's arms, Jericho breathed, "Thomas, hell. I should call you Joshua."

"Joshua?" murmured Thomas. "Why?"

Jericho looked him in the eye. "Because my walls have been crumbling since the first time I heard your voice."

Thomas' eyes flared luminous with desire, and he fumbled at Jericho's belt buckle. Jericho helped.

They barely made it into the bedroom.

60
A Most Unexpected Development

Thomas' Apartment
Oaklands Complex, Utopia City
Saturday Morning; October 12, 2013
03:45 AM

Jericho stirred lazily, the sheets moving against his body. He also felt something else; an arm, flung across his chest. It wasn't one of *his* arms, as they were both present and correct. *What …?*

"Hey, lover," murmured a voice. A very *familiar* voice. Rolling to his side, he opened his eyes and found himself looking into Thomas' smiling face. Memories dropped into place like dominoes, and his eyes widened.

"Whoa," he said softly, taking in the almost indecently satisfied look on the face of his … *boyfriend? Wow, Thomas is my boyfriend now.* Somehow, the prospect did nothing to dismay him. Especially when he remembered what they'd done once Chelsea had left. "You look amazing."

That was the right thing to say; Thomas stretched, almost preening, on top of the sheets. Just as with Jericho himself, there was nothing but a pair of boxers to obscure the view, and Jericho felt entirely justified in looking. Leaning over, he pressed his lips to Thomas'. A single stolen kiss, but one that felt so right.

"I can't believe we didn't do this earlier," Thomas said, lying back on the bed. "I mean, how long were we both circling around the topic?" He raised his hands in the air, mimicking birds spiraling around one another.

"Well, you know why *I* didn't make the first move." Jericho found the remote and scooted upward in the bed until he could put his pillow up as a backrest. "And you've clearly had problems as well so yeah, we both have trust issues." He hit the power button and watched as the panels retracted to reveal the flat-screen TV. "And I'm not saying we're totally over them—I'm pretty sure *I'm* not—but this is a really good start, I think."

"Well, all I can say is, thank God for smartass mental prodigies." Thomas gave Jericho a heavy-lidded look as he climbed out of bed. "Also, for endearingly shy superheroes with sexy Southern accents. I'll be back. Bathroom calling."

He was gone before Jericho could think to ask if the alliteration was deliberate. *Sexy? Really? It's just the way I talk.* Shaking his head, he focused his attention on the screen. Flicking through the channels to *Utopia News*, he caught a story about how Jack Portman's 'reign of terror' had been 'brought to an end', and a 'nefarious criminal smuggling ring' had been 'exposed by the actions of the newest member of Force Majeure, G-Man'.

With growing sardonic amusement, he took note of how they never quite claimed that he'd been a member of Force Majeure at the time the bust had taken place, but they never denied it either. Footage was supplied from outside cameras of his death-defying swoop in through the main doors; once again, the facts were spun somewhat to imply that he'd been working with law enforcement at the time, so it was all above board and kosher. Besides, even if he did say so himself, it was dramatic as *hell*. Over the course of the news spot, they found it necessary to show it three or four times from different angles, extolling the exquisite timing necessary to pull off such a split-second entry. Interestingly (and fortunately) enough, neither Thomas nor Chelsea seemed to have made the news in that regard. *Force Majeure is spinning this as a win, so they're not sharing the glory with anyone.*

More footage showed his face-off with Portman in the Southside Parking structure. Here, the news analysis was equally praiseful, pointing out that Portman had been wanted for two murders already, and had shown willingness to harm the woman from the booth. The brief soundbites from her post-recovery interview held nothing but praise for Jericho, to a frankly embarrassing degree.

"Sounds like you're building a fan club already," Thomas observed from the door, sounding amused. "Do I need to be worried about groupies?"

"I wouldn't be surprised if I end up with some," Jericho replied with a smirk. "But there's only one position open for 'boyfriend', and it's taken as of last night." His gaze raked over Thomas' body, making his meaning abundantly clear.

"Oh, good." Taking a couple of steps for a run-up, Thomas launched himself onto the bed and (not entirely by accident) Jericho himself. They collided in a tangle of limbs and laughter, rolling over and over on the bed. The wrestling match was entirely playful, each striving for dominance over the other but neither one trying too hard.

"Last night, the largest group of the Madness that has appeared so far, six individuals in all, attacked an open-air concert in Central Park, New York," announced the news anchorman, though Jericho wasn't really paying attention. "Troll, of Manhattan Justice, was the first hero on the scene. Despite taking several injuries, he held his own against the out-of-control Enabled until his teammates Splendid and Drone arrived to back him up. Between them, they managed to contain and subdue the Madness, but the final casualty count was nine dead and twenty-three injured."

Finally, Jericho let himself submit to Thomas, allowing the younger man to pin him down. Panting just a little (though perhaps more theatrically than absolutely necessary) Thomas lowered his face to Jericho's, preparing to steal a kiss; one that Jericho was more than willing to give away.

"In Chicago, more protesters are projected to arrive at Power Plaza today, in the wake of further rumors about—"

"Oh, for *fuck's* sake," snarled Thomas, his playful mood evaporating in an instant. "Can't they just let that shit *go*?" Rolling off Jericho, he scrabbled around for the remote. Jericho watched with concern as his boyfriend located it, then twisted around to point it at the TV.

On the screen, footage of a mob holding various handmade placards had been replaced by Tesseract Power. "Their allegations are untrue, and we will prove it," she stated with firm conviction. "We're Team Power. We got this."

Thomas' lip twisted as he parroted the last few words with a mocking sing-song tone. "We're Team Power. We got this." Then his thumb jammed down on the power button and the screen went dark. "Fuck, I wish they'd change things up and show something *else* for once."

Jericho stared hard at Thomas. This wasn't the first time the younger man had turned off the TV when a mention of Team Power came on; there was clearly something going on there. When the younger man had mentioned being attacked by someone with powers, Jericho's automatic assumption was that he meant a villain. But what if he hadn't? What if it was *Team Power* who'd hurt him or the ones he loved in some way? Worse, *killed* someone he loved?

The notion was hard to accept. Though collateral damage was definitely a thing, Team Power had a reputation for not letting innocents get hurt. "Thomas?" he asked, carefully reaching out to touch his boyfriend on the shoulder. "Do you want to talk about it?"

"No!" Thomas snapped, throwing the remote on the bed in a huff. He flopped back on the pillow, his eyes closed. "Just give me a minute." Breathing deeply, he just lay there.

Even as Jericho nodded, his mind began to turn over the pieces of the problem, trying to see where they fit together. One thing that puzzled him was the way Thomas favored the phrase 'we got this', despite the fact that it was Team Power's unofficial motto. *It doesn't make any sense. Unless, maybe ... if that's the case, then ... wait a minute, that* does *make sense.*

His head spun as the disparate facts crystallized into a whole new picture. All it took was one leap of logic, and all the facts fitted together neatly. *Holy ... shit. Could it really be this simple?*

"Okay," he said out loud, "but then you and I are going to have a long talk."

After a moment, Thomas' eyes opened and he looked at Jericho, who was still propped up on one elbow. "What about?" he asked warily, flicking his hand at the TV. "That? That's nothing. We're good."

Jericho sat up and crossed his legs. "No, it's not 'nothing'. You throw a hissy fit every time it comes on, and that's something we've got to talk about. But first, I absolutely need you to understand something."

"Okay, now you're worrying me." Thomas sat up as well, folding his legs under him. "What do I need to understand?"

Leaning forward, Jericho took Thomas' hands in his. "You need to understand that I love you and trust you, and I will never, ever reject you or betray you. No matter what. You know that, right?" He gazed deeply into Thomas' eyes, silently urging the younger man to comprehend that he meant his words utterly.

Thomas nodded. "Okay, yeah. I understand that. I wouldn't feel the same way about you if it wasn't true. But I still don't know what you're getting at." His dark brown eyes searched Jericho's face, apparently trying to find out what was going on.

Jericho tried to smile reassuringly. "Because, if I'm right, I don't want you to freak out when I ask you to stop lying to me. I know you've been lying to everyone for so long it's hard to stop, but it's okay to stop for me. It's okay to tell me the truth. I *am* here for you. I will *always* be here for you."

"What the hell?" Thomas' voice rose slightly. "What do you think I'm lying about? Why would you even *say* that?"

Instead of answering immediately, Jericho took a deep breath. He held it in for a long moment then let it out, trying to calm his rapid heart rate. It didn't work. "What I'm saying is ... your Dynamic ability isn't just good for gathering biometric data, is it? You're a full-blown shape-changer, aren't you ... *Vanessa?*"

Thomas was good. Scratch that; he was *really* good. If Jericho hadn't been holding his hands, the sudden muscular spasm that went through his entire body might well have gone unnoticed. Jericho judged it to be an instinctive reaction for fight, flight or whatever else, ruthlessly quelled. It was there and gone in a fraction of a second, then Thomas was staring quizzically at Jericho. "... ex*cuse* me? Vanessa? Vanessa *Power?* You think I'm really *her?* Where do you get *that* from?"

Jericho relaxed a little. *Oh, sweetie. You're really hoping to sell this, aren't you?* "Okay, do you mind if I present it as a hypothesis?"

Still frowning slightly, as if Jericho had posited that super-powers were in reality imposed from outside by parasitic alien space worms or something equally ludicrous,

Thomas nodded. "Okay, but you realize I will be shooting down your ideas as fast as you put them up."

"That's fair," Jericho said, though inwardly he heard his mother's voice saying, *'he doth protest too much'*. He held on to Thomas' hands. "Points zero and one. *'We got this'* is basically Team Power's catchphrase. You've said it more than once since I've known you. Also, when we were making out on the sofa, your eyes changed from brown to green, just briefly. I thought it was a trick of the light, but there was nothing to make it happen."

Thomas winced, but shook his head. "Uh … those are fairly weak points. Anyone can say anything. Besides, you might have imagined what you thought you saw. And I'm sorry to burst your bubble, but it's common knowledge that Vanessa Power isn't Enabled. Her father made that power armor for her because she has no powers."

"She *wasn't* powered until the night she disappeared; or rather, *you* weren't powered until the night *you* disappeared," countered Jericho. "And I know how you got your powers, too; specifically, I know who you got your powers *from.*"

Thomas tilted his head; now he looked honestly puzzled, rather than just acting a part. "I have no idea what you're talking about."

Jericho judged this to be the truth. He nodded understandingly. "Until last week, I wouldn't have either. But when I was interviewing with Force Majeure, the Technologist gave me a brief primer on powers. There's this thing called the Proximity Principle, which says that if someone would normally gain powers of a certain type but there's a powered person nearby, they get powers based off what that other person can do instead."

"What, really? I have to admit, I hadn't heard of that one." Thomas shook his head. "Still, it doesn't hold water. Even supposing I do change shape, there are no dynamics in Team Power. If I were Vanessa Power and I'd gained powers from my attacker before I ran away, I'd be an artificer. Because she was attacked by her father." Almost as an afterthought, he added, "The police report said so."

Jericho shook his head. "That's entirely my point." He took a deep breath, searching Thomas' face for acceptance or understanding of his words. "Whoever you got your powers from, it wasn't your father. You got your shape-changing from someone who *looked* like your father … because he or she was a shape-changer too." He shrugged. "I guess they did it to infiltrate Power Plaza, or to make you run away or ruin your father's name, or both. The bottom line is, you got powers from that shape-changer, not your father. Not Adam Power. Because your father never laid a hand on you that night. And *that's* why he's always denied it. Because he's innocent."

Thomas' eyes became wider and wider as Jericho spoke. He went to open his mouth a few times, then stopped and listened all the way to the end. Slowly, he closed his eyes again and sat there, breathing in through his nose and letting the air dribble out between his lips. Jericho didn't have access to any of his pulse points, but his grip tightened occasionally; if he had to guess, Thomas was going through his memories of that night. Trying to find the truth.

Finally, Thomas opened his eyes and looked at him. There was deep pain in them, now, but doubt still lurked in their depths. "It's *possible*, I suppose," he conceded. "But how do you *know*? It's all circumstantial. Vanessa Power could still be out there somewhere, and Adam Power could really be a child molester."

"Is that really what you want to believe at this point?" Jericho asked. When Thomas swallowed and looked away, Jericho played his trump card, but kept it face down for the moment. "Remember Bobbi? She came in on the train with me and Luke."

Thomas nodded. "I remember her," he agreed with a grimace. "She was nice. I liked her. It's a tragedy what happened to her, but what's she got to do with this?"

Metaphorically, Jericho turned the card over. "She was an empath, a powerful one. If she looked at you, she could see what you were feeling, in depth and in detail. She'd come from Indianapolis via Chicago, where she attended that press conference Team Power held last week. Your father stood up in front of the microphone and proclaimed his innocence for the world to hear. Bobbi told me personally that every word he said was the absolute truth. It was why she was coming to Utopia City, so she could join the team and get the authority to make people understand there was something deeper going on."

Doubt continued to flicker across Thomas' face, but Jericho could see he was making strong headway. "I love you," he reiterated, reminding Thomas that his words came from a place of warmth and honesty. "I love you, no matter *who* you are."

Thomas bowed his head. Tugging one hand free from Jericho's grasp, he raked his fingers through his hair. "It can't be right," he whispered.

Jericho pulled Thomas into a sideways hug, squeezing just enough to remind his lover he was there for him. "I'm at least half right, aren't I, Vanessa?" he whispered.

For the longest moment, Thomas stared back at him, as if daring him to retract the question. Then he closed his eyes ... and began to change. Tousled black hair retracted into his scalp and his entire body started to reshape itself, the mass redistributing in ways that looked uncomfortable if not downright painful. Even his hands became longer and more delicate. Red hair grew out at a startling pace from the bald head, now exhibiting more graceful proportions; as they were both wearing only boxers, certain other anatomical changes were much more obvious than they otherwise would have been.

Thirty seconds later, Vanessa Power opened brilliant green eyes, long red hair spilling down over her shoulders. She gave Jericho a tentative smile; when she spoke, her voice was a soft alto. "Do you really think he didn't do it?"

Jericho drew her all the way into his arms. "Yeah, sweetheart, I do. And I think so long as you leave things the way they are, whoever wanted to drive a wedge between you and your family is winning. You can't leave your family dangling like this."

She stared up at him, eyes wide as she tried to comprehend his meaning. "Jericho, what are you saying?"

He took a deep breath, hating what was coming next but knowing it had to be said. "I'm saying ... you have to go home."

61
"If You Love Something ..."

Vanessa Power shook her head stubbornly. "I *said*, I'm not going back to Chicago. Not now, not ever." Wearing boxers and a UCIAT t-shirt that belonged to her-as-Thomas, as well as a mutinous expression, she crossed her arms under her breasts and glared at Jericho from the other end of the sofa. He had to admit, she had a good line in glaring that Thomas just hadn't been able to match. Though her pouting and puppy-dog eyes just didn't work on him, so there was that.

"But why *not?*" he asked, leaning against the sofa arm so that he could look straight at her. "Your father's innocent. You *know* he's innocent. He didn't *do* anything wrong."

"Doesn't matter," she said dismissively. "I don't want to go back there, like ever. Whoever attacked me thinks I'm dead or long gone. I want 'em to keep thinking that. They're not getting a second chance."

Jericho tried again. "Okay, your dad's an artificer. One of the highest tier ones I know of, short of the Technologist himself. *You're* a dynamic *and* a prodigy. If someone tries that shit again, you'll know they're not who they say they are *and* you'll be able to kick their ass. I mean, when they last tried it on you, you were sixteen and unpowered. Now you're eighteen, Enabled, and a lot more prepared." He paused. The last thing he wanted was to be distracted from his line of argument, but the question had to be asked. "Anyway, how come you're eighteen as Vanessa? Didn't you say you've been Thomas ever since you took the bus in from Omaha to Utopia City? Shouldn't you still be sixteen as Vanessa?"

She shook her head. "I was worried about that, myself. So whenever I got the chance, I'd find someplace private and change, just to make sure I still could, and that I wasn't lagging in age. But it seems my Dynamic ability can maintain both forms just fine. But I'm still not going back to Chicago."

"Listen." Jericho took a moment to breathe deeply and get his mind back on track. "You've seen the protests. You *know* things are going wrong there. It's not dying down. There are more and more people every day, rabble-rousing to build the mob outside Power Plaza. If this keeps up, someone's gonna get hurt. Either trying to force their way in, or they'll do something stupid while your family's out and about."

"Not my problem." Vanessa set her jaw. "Besides, you said it yourself. Dad's an artificer. He's as good as it gets. There's no way they'll get anything past him, now. He's probably got that place locked up tighter than a drum."

"Okay, how about your family themselves?" Jericho leaned forward and took hold of Vanessa's shoulders, forcing her to look at him. "They love you. They miss you. Up 'til now you didn't think that was true because you thought your dad attacked you, but *that's not the case.* Every time your mom goes on the news, she talks about how they're still looking for you. How they're not giving up hope. You're killing them, Vanessa, as surely as a bullet between the eyes. At the very least, they deserve to know you're alive and doing fine."

Vanessa snorted indelicately. "Yeah, that'll go well. They'd put Buddy on the line to keep me talking while Dad traced the call, and in the meantime Mom would be in the family jet, making a beeline for wherever I am." She shook her head and looked at him beseechingly. "It'd be all or nothing. Can't you see? I wouldn't have a choice in the matter. They wouldn't let it go until I'm back there, and I *can't* go back there. I *won't*." She looked accusingly at him. "Anyway, why are you trying so hard to send me away? I thought you wanted to be with me."

"I do. I really do. But this isn't about what I want. It's about you and your family." Jericho let her go again and flopped back against the sofa, staring at the ceiling. "You're eighteen, and you're already one of the strongest people I've ever met. No one can make you do anything you don't want to do. Look how hard I'm trying to emotionally blackmail you here, and you're not ever budging. But there's a huge injustice that's been perpetrated. Your dad's been accused of a crime that he never committed, and the court of public opinion's already tried, convicted and sentenced him. You're the only one who can clear his name once and for all."

He sat up once more, his eyes seeking hers. "It's what Bobbi came to Utopia City to do. Her powers screwed with her every time she touched anyone, or even spent time in a crowd, but she came here *anyway*. She never met your dad, not face to face, but she thought it was worth putting herself through that sort of crap to help clear his name. When she died, I told myself that if I ever had a chance to finish what she started, I would. That's why *I'm* doing this. Why don't *you* want to go back?"

Vanessa clenched her fists and screwed her eyes up. "*Because I don't want to face them!*" she shouted, her voice filling the room. After a moment, she opened her eyes, though her nails were still digging into her palms. She breathed in and out a couple of times, filling her lungs and emptying them. "I don't want to *face* them," she repeated wretchedly. "I yelled at them. I *screamed* at them. I accused Dad of the worst things in the world. I accused Mom of covering up for him. And I was *wrong*."

"No, not wrong." Jericho reached out again, this time gently laying his hand on her shoulder. "You were *mistaken*. There's a difference. You were made to believe something that wasn't true. They'll understand that. Everyone makes mistakes. This was a mistake someone forced you to make, and now you've got a chance to fix it. Not everyone gets to do that." He'd said this before, but he'd keep saying it until she understood.

She shook her head, but slowly; uncertainly. "I really don't know if I can go through with it. I said some pretty bad things. I even filled out a police report. If I just show up out of nowhere and say, no, I was wrong? They're all gonna look at me like I'm stupid. And that's if they don't call me a liar to my face." Her face turned away from his and she lowered her voice. "And there's the other thing, too."

Now they were getting somewhere. They'd been over this ground several times, but each time she'd sheered away from even mentioning whatever her final sticking point was. He leaned forward. "Other thing? Whatever it is …"

"I *stole!*" she shouted suddenly, swinging back toward him. Startled, he jumped a little. "You *know* I was stealing! You know I was going to rip *you* off too, with your biometric data! For God's sake, I'm a member of *Team Power!* If Mom and Dad ever found out, they'd never let me live it down!" She held out a hand toward Jericho, pleading for understanding. "I *know* you know! How can you even *trust* me after that?"

He laced his fingers through hers. "Two reasons. One, Bobbi was certain you didn't intend to rip us off. All she could read off you was how much you were enjoying flirting with me. You weren't even *thinking* about stealing from me then, were you?"

Lowering her eyes, she shook her head. "No. It was just so nice, being with you. Talking to you. When I reminded myself later what I was going to have to do, to keep the others fed, it tore me up inside. When we ran into each other again, the reason I yelled at you was because I was feeling guilty." She raised her eyes to his. "What's the other reason?"

He closed his hand, gently trapping her fingers with his. "Once I knew about the Survivors, I knew you were stealing only because you had to. The regret in your face, in your voice, that was real. You weren't a thief by choice, and you stopped as soon as you had the chance." He gave her an understanding smile. "A good chunk of my family does questionable stuff for a living. Stealing food to help some kids? That's *nothing.*"

"It won't be 'nothing' to my parents." She spoke with absolute certainty. "They live and breathe being superheroes."

"They might surprise you." He let go her hand so that he could sit up properly, then he scooted his butt along the sofa until he was next to her. Wrapping his arms around her, he held her tightly. "But if you want, I'll go with you. To Chicago. Today. Right now. I'll stand at your side the whole way, if you need me to. If *anyone* tries anything with you, or even if your family wants to give you crap about this, they'll have me to contend with."

She turned her head to look at him. They were of a height, though she was a little more slender than Thomas. Jericho wasn't entirely certain where she stored the extra mass, and he definitely wasn't going to ask.

"You'd do that?" she asked. "You'd come with me to Chicago? But ... it's over an hour each way from Utopia to Chicago and back. I've already checked. And we'd have to spend hours there, just getting to and from Power Plaza. Even if we left right now, by the time it was all settled, you'd never get back in time to report for duty."

He shrugged. "Doesn't matter. Your family's more important than that. *You're* more important than that. If there's one thing I've learned over the last week, getting into Force Majeure's not the be-all and end-all of things. I'm technically in Force Majeure right now and once I show up on time tomorrow, it's set in stone. When that happens, I'll give Force Majeure one hundred percent of my effort. But if I think there's something more important, I'll do that instead, even if it costs me my place. The happiness of the person I love is more important, right now. And that's *you.*"

He kissed her hair. It was a little weird, holding a woman and knowing that the man he loved was somewhere inside there. Vanessa had made no secret of the fact that she was attracted to him no matter which body she (or he) wore; if he were bisexual, he suspected, he'd be having a lot more fun with this.

Almost as if to illustrate the point, her arms went around him and she hugged him tightly. Her lips found his and she kissed him, hard. He returned it, but it just wasn't the same as kissing her as Thomas. Perhaps realizing this, she pulled back a little and looked at him. "Okay, what if we put this off 'til tomorrow, then?"

He shook his head. "Tomorrow, I'll be a member of Force Majeure. Chances are, they'll be keeping a lot closer tabs on me after that. If Relentless is still pissed at me then, they might just transfer me to Anchorage. Or worse, back to Savannah." It was a weak joke, but he chuckled anyway. "The point is, I can't guarantee that I'll be available to be there for you. Not like I am right now."

"God *damn* it." She rested her head on his shoulder. "Now I can't *not* go. How the hell did you manage to make noble sacrifice contagious?"

"It's a talent," he said lightly, but he knew the truth. She'd just needed a nudge to do the right thing. "I'll go back to my apartment to shower and change. If we hit the maglev in an hour, we can get into Chicago just about dawn. You can show me around the place until you're ready to go see your folks."

She placed her hand flat on his chest, fingers spread, and pushed him back a little. "No."

"No?" He frowned, not certain what she meant. "No, you don't want to go?" That didn't sound right.

"I mean, no, you're not coming with me." She gave him one of her patented glares. "You don't get to guilt-trip me like this. I'm a big girl now; I can go back to Chicago all by myself. And if anyone gets in my way, I *will* kick their ass." Taking her hand away from his chest, she prodded him with one sharp nail. "And *you* will be showing up at the Spire. Once you're in Force Majeure, you're gonna be the best damn hero you can be. Do you understand me?"

There was only one possible response to that. "Yes, *ma'am*."

She smirked. "Damn right." He watched with interest as she concentrated and began the change once more. When it was over, Thomas sat before him again, tousled black hair falling untidily over his forehead as per normal. They moved into each other's arms as if they never wanted to let go.

After a while, they went back to the bedroom and made love again. It wasn't as sudden and dramatic as it had been the first time; they took their time and made it count. Neither one knew when they'd have the chance again. When it was over, they lay together as their breathing slowed and the sweat dried on their skin.

"I have to ask; what does it feel like?" asked Jericho idly, his head resting on Thomas' shoulder.

"What, sex?" Thomas tried to pull off the straight line, but Jericho felt the chuckle in his chest.

"No, you idiot." Jericho jabbed him playfully in the ribs. "Changing. Becoming Vanessa again. Does it hurt? It looks kind of painful."

Thomas recoiled, laughing. "It's weird. Different. But no, it doesn't hurt. It's like her body's there inside me, and I've got to push to get it out there. And when I'm Vanessa, it's the same with this form. Like I'm turning myself inside out or something."

Jericho shook his head. "'Weird' is right. Which form is your favorite? Which one do you prefer to be in?"

"This one, when I'm with you." Thomas pulled his head up for a kiss. Jericho gave as good as he got. "Because it's the one you like."

"That's may well be the sweetest thing anyone's ever said to me." Rolling over, Jericho got his phone from the nightstand and thumbed it on to read the time. "It's getting close to six. We should start getting ready."

"Don't wanna." Thomas wrapped his arms around Jericho from behind. "Wanna stay here with you."

"Believe me, I don't want to go anywhere either," Jericho assured him, smiling at the childish tone. "But sometimes we've got to do things we don't want to do, just because it's the right thing to do." He interlaced his fingers through Thomas' and pulled the younger man's arms tighter around him for a moment, then disentangled himself from his boyfriend. "And right now, that's packing."

Thomas sat up on the bed as Jericho moved to the edge and stood. "We're really going to do this?"

"We are." Jericho began to get dressed, heading out into the living room to find his shirt. "I'm gonna go shower and change into fresh clothes at my apartment, then I'll come back and pick you up," he called over his shoulder. "We've got time for me to go to the maglev terminal with you, and see you off."

"Should I go as Thomas or Vanessa?" asked Thomas, from the doorway.

Jericho considered that for a moment. "Probably Thomas," he decided. "You don't want anyone getting the idea you're out and about *before* you get to your family, otherwise you're likely to get mobbed. At best."

"Yeah, hard pass on that." Thomas shuddered, then headed for the bathroom. "I guess I'll take a shower, too." He paused in the doorway, looking back at Jericho with a seductive tilt to his hips. "Or, you know, we could take one together."

"Only if we don't want either of us getting to where we need to be today," Jericho retorted as he pulled his boots on and retrieved his costume satchel. "First chance we get, after you're reunited with your family and I'm established in Force Majeure, I'll definitely take you up on that."

"It's a date." Thomas sashayed into the bathroom, looking over his shoulder to make sure Jericho was watching. Jericho gave him a playful wolf-whistle, which elicited an extra bump and grind before Thomas ducked into the shower cubicle, leaving the bathroom door wide open. Shaking his head with a fond smile, Jericho zipped up his boots and let himself out of the apartment.

Back in his place, he laid out fresh clothing and stepped into the shower. There was a little time to spare, so he gave his hair a medium-long wash. Afterward, he scrubbed himself down with one of the freshly laundered towels that the Oaklands had on offer. He ran a brush through his hair, then dressed carefully in the clothing that normally went under his costume jacket, aware that he was going to be making the most important impression of his life in just a few hours.

With the rest of his costume in the satchel, he slid his MagCard into his pocket and tied his hair back. Slinging the satchel over his shoulder, he left the apartment and retraced his steps to where Thomas was staying. When he got there, he found a minor surprise; Chelsea was there as well, helping Thomas repack an overstuffed backpack. Several road flares lay on the floor next to her; he wasn't even sure what that was about.

"Hi," he said. "Thomas called you?" He glanced at Thomas, trying to divine how much his boyfriend had told the mischievous Enabled.

"Yeah. He said he was going back home." She looked at Jericho with a mildly irritated frown. "There's something he's not telling me. Care to fill me in?"

"Sorry." If Thomas wanted to keep this on the down-low, Jericho would back him up on that. "Not for me to tell."

"Maybe later," Thomas added. "Once I've found out whether I'm welcome or not." He shot Jericho a grateful look.

Chelsea rolled her eyes. "Boys and their secrets. After I went to all the trouble to get the two of you together. *That's* gratitude for you." But there was a smirk on her lips that wouldn't go away. "No, don't tell me. I'll figure it out for myself."

"If you do, you'll have earned the right to know." Thomas looked at Jericho. "Time to go?"

Jericho nodded. "Yeah, time to go." He took Thomas' hand, causing Chelsea's smirk to widen slightly. *Yeah, yeah, I got it. You were right all the time.* He wasn't sure how his expression had changed to tip her off as the thought crossed his mind, but her smugness level increased exponentially. Behind Thomas' back, he stuck his tongue out at her. This didn't make her look any less pleased with herself as they left the apartment.

Neither Jericho nor Thomas were in the mood for casual conversation as they headed along the corridor and took the elevator down. Chelsea took it upon herself to fill the silence, chattering brightly about nothing in particular, and doing an excellent impression of a brainless bimbo. Her gambits brought a reluctant smile to Thomas' face, and even cheered Jericho up slightly. Still, as they climbed into the air taxi and set off toward the maglev terminal, it was hard to put a bright face on matters.

They were both taking steps into the unknown, and it was more than a little frightening. Jericho wasn't quite sure how things were going to turn out once he joined Force Majeure, but Thomas had it even worse. Jericho's personal opinions aside, it was entirely possible he was going back to a family, to a life, where he wouldn't fit in anymore.

The click of a camera broke him out of his reverie, and he turned to see Thomas holding up his phone. "Check it out," the younger man said, pointing out the window. Jericho turned his head to see the Spire, lit up by the morning sun, with a layer of cloud surrounding it about two-thirds of the way up. It was still weird to think that an actual *building* could interfere with weather patterns, but that was life in Utopia City.

"Let me see," Chelsea requested. Thomas handed over the phone, and she called up the photo. "Ooh, nice," she murmured. "You got him and the Spire both. You're gonna have to email me that one."

"Count on it," Thomas said as he accepted the phone back, but his smile was getting a little fragile around the edges.

By the time they landed at the maglev terminal, even Chelsea had run out of cheerful platitudes; one by one, they got out of the cab and trooped into the terminal without a word passing between them. Reluctantly stepping up to a kiosk, Thomas produced his MagCard and bought a ticket to Chicago. He went to push past the other two on the way to the escalator, but Chelsea grabbed him and hugged him fiercely. "You come back and say hi sometime, you big lunk," she said, the suspicion of tears lurking in her eyes. "Someone needs to keep Jericho in line."

"We'll see each other again, I promise." Thomas had a catch in his voice now, and the tears were bright in his eyes. "Thanks. For everything you've done."

"Pfft; it was nothing. Sharing a one-bedroom apartment for four days with you six jerks was the most fun I've had in years. Even if we had to take turns sleeping on the bed and the sofa." She leaned up and kissed him on the cheek. "I'm gonna miss you like you wouldn't believe."

"Yeah, me too, you smartass." He hugged her one more time then went to move on, but Jericho caught up and took his hand. They shared a glance; *this far at least, together.* Hand in hand they rode up the escalator, while Chelsea stayed behind. Thomas squeezed Jericho's hand almost painfully, and by the time they got to the top, he was openly crying.

Pulling out his handkerchief, Jericho handed it over. "Keep it," he said, trying not to start crying himself. "I'll come get it off you sometime."

"You better." Thomas hiccupped, then blew his nose. "You know where I live. You got no excuse."

Jericho tried to grin playfully. "I'll call ahead, so you can hide your dad's quantum shotgun."

Thomas shook his head, not getting the joke. "He doesn't have a quantum shotgun."

The chuckle caught in Jericho's throat. "When he finds out you've got a boyfriend, he's gonna *build* one."

"Oh, *you.*" Thomas pulled him close and kissed him; Jericho wrapped his arms around his boyfriend and kissed him right back. The clinch lasted for a long time, until the announcement came over the PA system that the maglev heading east to Kansas City was preparing to leave.

With his hands grasping Thomas' shoulders, Jericho stared him in the eyes. "I *will* come see you," he promised. "As soon as I get the chance. We're gonna be together again, soon. That's a guarantee." He willed Thomas to believe him.

"I know." Thomas nodded, then pulled Jericho close to whisper in his ear. "I trust you."

With one final fleeting kiss, he scooped up his backpack and headed through the scan-lock—fortunately, it didn't set off any alarms, which just showed that Chelsea had probably had the right idea in removing the road flares—and into the train car. Even after the doors closed behind him, he stayed next to a window, waving. Jericho waved back, eyes drinking in every detail, committing them to memory. And then, between one blink and the next, the maglev accelerated out of sight and vanished.

Taking a deep breath, wiping suspicious moisture from his eyes—*I'm not crying, it's just the humidity in this place*—Jericho headed for the escalator down. Chelsea was waiting on the ground floor; as he reached the bottom, she came over.

"You going to be okay?" she asked. "You look kind of wrecked." With a tissue, she dabbed at the corners of his eyes.

"I'll be fine," he said, trying to convince himself that it was true. "It's my job to be fine and keep going. Share a cab?"

"Nah," she said cheerfully as they emerged into the open air with a tiny *pop* of force field. "I'm gonna walk awhile and think about things."

"Such as?" he asked suspiciously. She had a look in her eye that said she was up to something. Of course, she *usually* had that look.

"Well, now that the Southsiders are out of the way, there's a vacuum in town," she explained blithely. "Vacuums need something to fill them. I might look into stepping into it before someone else does."

"Wait, what again now?" He shook his head. This was crazy, even for her. "You're fixing to take up where the Southsiders left off?"

"Pfft, nope." She almost managed to look offended. "*My* secret underground criminal empire's gonna be *much* more stylish." She patted him kindly on the arm. "Don't you worry your pretty head over it. Go play with the big boys, but don't forget to drop in and say hi sometime." Humming a tune that he didn't recognize, she strolled off down the sidewalk. There were already people out and about; within ten steps, she had blended in so well he couldn't even see her anymore.

62
Welcome to Force Majeure

Shaking his head, Jericho went over to the cab stand, where several air taxis were already waiting. He climbed into the closest one and strapped himself in. "The Spire, please."

"Sure thing, buddy. Is this a Challenger Act situation?"

"Definitely." He pulled out his MagCard and tapped the reader when it lit up, then strapped in. The air-cab took off with the usual powerful surge; as soon as it was at cruising altitude, the windows polarized to a mirror sheen. Jericho took that as his signal to unstrap and put his costume on. It wasn't the easiest thing in the world to do in the confined space, but he'd done something similar before, so he didn't have to concentrate too hard on what he was doing. By the time the taxi landed at the cab stand outside the Spire, he was presentable; thanking the driver, he got out and looked around.

A few tourists were gathered around the floating statue of Challenger; he gave the twice-life-size rendition a nod of respect. Once more, he read the words carved into the front of the plinth. *I can only hope to be one-tenth as inspirational as he was.* Then, as he went to walk on, one of the tourists turned and saw him.

"Hey, wow!" the guy said in a California accent. "That's G-Man! He was on the news last night!"

Jericho blinked. *Wait, what again now?* While the news spot had been admittedly dramatic, he hadn't really thought anything would come of it. Even when he made the papers back in Savannah, barely anyone took notice. As he'd said half-jokingly to Transit, sometimes it seemed like his Dynamic ability was invisibility rather than gravity control.

Here, it was apparently different. The tourists abandoned the statue en masse and crowded around him, asking if they could take selfies with him or get his autograph, or both. Bemused, he posed for photos and signed tourist brochures, half-wondering if he'd traveled sideways into an alternate world during the trip from the maglev terminal to the Spire.

On his first visit, he'd traversed the plaza in less than five minutes. Now, it took him more than ten. Aware of the passage of time, he managed to keep moving, though it wasn't easy. He signed his last autograph and posed for his last picture just outside the sliding doors, then made his excuses and ducked inside. To his dismay, the gold-rimmed clock mounted below the map told him he had only seven minutes before the nine o'clock deadline was due. His head was still spinning from the unprecedented experience; in ten minutes, he'd posed for more pictures and signed more autographs than in his entire two years as a superhero in Savannah. *Is this what other Enabled get all the time?*

There was a medium-dense crowd in here as well, and he saw people turning to look. His heart sank as he heard his name being spoken, whispered from person to person. *If they mob me like the people outside did, I'll never get to the desk before nine.* Still, he had to try. Attempting to look confident and heroic, he strode forward.

That was when the next surprise came; instead of impeding his progress, they stepped back to make way. Belatedly, he realized that most of these people were

Utopia City civil employees, not tourists. They didn't have a vested interest in slowing him down. In fact, it seemed that as far as they were concerned, he had the right of way. A couple of tourists tried to get to him, only to be discreetly blocked by a few of the city employees.

"Well done, G-Man," one woman said.

"Congratulations on joining Force Majeure," another added.

"It's good to have you on board," said a man wearing a suit and tie.

"We need more heroes like you."

"You're an inspiration to us all."

"Now, *that's* what I call making an entrance."

Moving numbly forward, he lost track of who was saying what. These were people who worked in the same building as the likes of Relentless and Transit, and this was what they were saying to *him*? As with the tourists outside, it was so far beyond his experience that he had trouble making sense of it.

He reached the nearest reception desk much sooner than he'd anticipated. Apparently unfazed, the receptionist smiled widely at him. "Good morning, G-Man. Welcome to Force Majeure. Just swipe on through; your security access has already been upgraded."

"Thanks," he replied, still taken aback by all the positive attention. Speaking more quietly, he added, "Does this happen with *everyone* who comes in?"

Her smile never dimmed, though it became more personal. She lowered her voice in turn. "Well, most times, they don't come in through the front door. And after yesterday, you *are* kind of famous."

He shook his head dazedly. *This is gonna take some getting used to.*

But it wasn't over yet; just as he tapped the reader and the scan-lock doors opened, the applause started. Looking back at the crowd in the lobby, he realized they were looking at *him*. Clapping for *him*. He even thought he heard a chant: "G-Man! G-Man! G-Man!"

Blushing, he ducked his head and stepped into the scan-lock. The doors closed, cutting off the sound of both the applause and the chant; almost immediately, the doors at the other end let him through. Beyond that, elevator doors slid open.

The trip upward into the Spire was no picnic due to the cognitive dissonance between the artificial gravity and his G-sense, but it served one important purpose; it helped distract him from the heady feeling of having all those people cheer *him* on. He was reporting for his first day as a member of Force Majeure; starting work with a swelled head from all the congratulations would not be a great way to go.

The unpleasantness was over quickly, letting him out into a circular corridor—a 'circuit', as he recalled—about two-thirds of a mile above ground level. There was nobody waiting for him when he stepped out, but a glowing blue line on the floor flashed repeatedly to get his attention. Recalling how these things worked, he followed it to a specific door, which opened when he tapped the reader.

The room beyond was spacious, made more so by a wide balcony; or perhaps a landing stage, given the lack of a safety railing. The ceiling was at least fifteen feet above his head. Work benches and tools attached to overhead servos were scattered here and there, but Jericho had eyes for none of them.

"Ah, you're here." The Technologist barely looked around as he worked at something, sparks flying up with a smell of ozone. "You are prompt, at least; that's good." His tone was curt, almost impatient. Recalling his manner during the interview, Jericho suspected he spoke to everyone like that.

"Uh, thanks." Jericho moved farther into the room, keeping his hands carefully to himself as he took in the items scattered on the workbenches. Some were almost complete, while others were mere scatterings of parts; all were utterly fascinating, and he had no idea what any of them did. "What did you need me for?"

"Testing." Taking up the object he'd been working on, Force Majeure's premier artificer conveyed it over to Jericho. Close up, it looked like a harness made of linked metal straps, with two cables leading to plastic cuffs. "Put this on. The primary inducer goes on your back, between your shoulder-blades. Watch the welds; they'll be hot."

"Uh … okay." Jericho struggled into the device, with the Technologist offering semi-helpful advice. After a few minutes, he had it settled into place, though he'd had to remove his utility belt because it got in the way. Lastly, he fastened the cuffs into place. It felt awkward as hell; if he had to fight in this, he wasn't sure it would stay on. In fact, he *knew* it wouldn't stay on. "Is this supposed to be some sort of addition to my costume? Because it doesn't feel very secure."

"Have you never heard of a proof of concept, boy?" The Technologist shook his head. "Everyone who joins Force Majeure is issued with a device to improve their control over their powers. Half of this harness consists of measuring equipment to gather data on how well the other half performs. Once we have it sufficiently tested and the bugs worked out, I will be able to supply you with something much more efficient. But this is the first stage. You must walk before you can run. And put this on." He handed over a headset with a swing-down microphone.

"Oh. Okay." Jericho blinked at the rapid-fire delivery as he fitted the headset on, then pulled the microphone down into place. "What am I supposed to do?"

"Use your powers, boy." The Technologist pointed at the open space and the sky beyond. "You are able to glide? Then glide. I will activate the mechanism from here."

"Ah … okay." Jericho peered down at the clumsy-looking device. "It won't shut down my powers altogether, will it?"

"There is a very small chance of that happening, and if it does, I will be able to disable the harness remotely." The Technologist pointed at the opening once more, his tone impatient. "Go!"

That wasn't particularly reassuring. Still, the Technologist was effectively his boss, so he took a run-up, trying not to let the harness come loose from around him. When he reached the edge of the landing stage, he reduced his effective weight to its minimum, spread his arms, and leaped outward. As he'd expected, the harness screwed badly with his flight profile. When he spread his arms as wide as he could to get the maximum usable area from the gliding surfaces, a couple of the cables crimped them inward, reducing their effectiveness all the way to diddly squat and beyond. Unable to stabilize, he began tumbling down the outside of the building like a wounded duck in a slow-motion death-dive. He knew if anyone got pictures of this, his fame would be dead in the water. *Well, there goes my fan club.*

And then he felt the module energize. His awareness of the local gravity field intensified sharply, spreading farther than it had ever gone before. Along with that, his control over it magnified considerably.

He exerted his will to pull the field into his body, then visualized wings of pure shaped space, extending from his fingertips. Looking to the left and right, he watched as they unfurled and spread wide at his command. For some reason, he'd expected them to exhibit rainbow colors like his G-tags, but instead they were blacker than black; light just seemed to *fall* into them. Gripping the air, they lifted him with far more ease than his gliding surfaces ever had.

"G-Man!" snapped the Technologist over the radio link. "Report status!"

With his arms spread wide, borne on pinions of pure darkness, Jericho soared upward in a great turning spiral. As Utopia City spread out beneath him, undiluted joy bubbled laughter into his throat.

"I'm *flying*."

- End of Part Four -

© Nevena Jevtić and Alan M. Atkinson

EPILOGUES

Utopia City? It's a nice place to visit,
but I have no desire to actually *live* there.
- *Vanessa Power*

I'll get you yet.
- *a villain*

This is the beginning of a beautiful friendship.
- *Troll*

Oh, God. I may have miscalculated.
- *All-Star*

Trust G-Man.
- *unknown*

Epilogue One
Homecoming

Chicago, Illinois
Saturday, October 12, 2013
9:45 AM Central Daylight Time

"**A**ttention, all passengers. Attention, all passengers. This train has now arrived in Chicago. Please leave the car. Do not forget your luggage. Utopia Maglev Lines takes no responsibility for luggage left on the train. We hope you have enjoyed your trip. Attention, all passengers ..."

Thomas barely paid attention to the announcement as he stepped off the train. The backpack that doubled as his INCH bag, or as much of it as Chelsea had let him bring on the maglev (how did road flares even count as explosives, anyway?), was slung over one shoulder. He passed through the enclosure that Jericho had called a 'scan-lock' with barely a break in his stride. Pulling ahead of the bulk of the crowd, he headed for the main exit doors to the transit station.

Jericho. Thomas had spent the whole trip thinking about the quietly spoken Enabled from Savannah. Leaving him behind in Utopia had been a wrench, but Jericho was apparently able to overcome whatever psychological obstacles had kept Thomas and the rest of the Survivors from being comfortable with joining Force Majeure. However, just because they weren't together at that moment didn't mean it was over between them; not by a long shot. That had been obvious from the look on Jericho's face when they parted. Wherever Jericho's duties took him, Thomas knew they'd see each other again. Just so long as it was anywhere but Utopia. He'd seen enough of *that* place for a lifetime.

But that was for later; right now, he had other matters to take care of. The exit doors hissed open and he jogged down the steps to the footpath below. A chilly breeze hit him; he shivered before pulling his jacket more tightly around himself. He knew the weather in Utopia was artificially controlled (it was the worst-kept secret in the city) but he'd never had proof that the *climate* was likewise moderated, until now. Going from a clockwork-steady seventy-seven to the low sixties was no kind of fun. While seventy-seven was theoretically achievable in Kansas in October, he knew for a fact that the rest of the state was consistently four or five degrees colder than inside the city.

There was a cab rank only a dozen yards away. He headed in that direction, stifling a cough. As well as chilled air, the breeze also carried a plethora of unpleasant smells that assaulted his sinuses and lungs in equal measure. The cars themselves looked awkwardly anachronistic, not to mention anorexic. Two-thirds the size of the cabs he'd gotten used to over the last twenty-one months, with actual wheels that held them off the filthy pot-holed asphalt that passed for a street, they almost certainly lacked most of the safety features common to Utopia City air-cars. No lifters meant no flying for these ones, which meant stop-start traffic and a slow crawl to his destination. Though it was probably a good thing that they couldn't fly; half of them looked like they'd fall apart under a one-gee turn.

"Need a cab, buddy?" It was the guy standing outside the car at the front of the line who'd spoken. "Where ya headed?"

Thomas pushed back his distaste. The guy clearly thought his rolling death-machine was roadworthy enough to handle a trip across town. Maybe his mechanic was a low-tier artificer whose power made the results look like crap while still being workable. *Or maybe,* Thomas reluctantly told himself, *I'm being too judgmental. People have been riding in cabs like this for decades, and barely anyone's died.*

"Rogers Park," he said. "I'll give you directions when we get there." Instinct told him that the closer he played his cards to his chest, the less chance there was of someone getting the idea ahead of time that Vanessa Power was back. Given what had happened in Utopia—not just to him, but to the rest of the Survivors as well—he was now a firm believer in taking absolute control of the public perception of his deeds. Also, he still had no idea *who* had attacked him in the first place, so there was no sense in making himself into a target before he contacted his family.

"Sure t'ing." The cabby swung himself down into the front seat of his vehicle.

Opening the passenger side back door, Thomas shrugged off his backpack and climbed into the seat. The pack went on the floor between his feet, then he closed the door. The cabby turned the key to start the car—eliciting a chuntering rattle that made Thomas wonder if the thing was going to fall apart on the spot—then swung the vehicle out onto the road before Thomas even had his seatbelt done up. A horn blared, but the driver merely made a rude gesture out the window before accelerating away. In a manner of speaking, of course. Thomas barely felt the G-forces.

Jeez. Jaw set, Thomas pulled the buckle the rest of the way and clicked it home. He didn't want to draw attention to himself by yelling at the cabby for the number of safety regulations he'd just broken. No doubt any native of Chicago would find it perfectly normal, but a Utopia air-cab driver would've lost his license about three times over for that little stunt. Not to mention the fact that these things had no kind of autopilot.

"So, where you from anyways, buddy?" The cabby, one hand on the steering wheel, swung a hard right while he reached down and turned on the radio. The music that came out wasn't too bad, but it was almost drowned out by the omnipresent sound of the car's engine. *I'd forgotten how much noise these things made. And how much they stank.*

"Oh, uh, here originally, but I've been spending some time in Utopia." He figured that was safe enough. People came and went from Utopia all the time.

"No shit?" The cabby turned and gave him a long, considering stare. "Is it as good as they say, over by there?"

Eyes on the road! Thomas fought down the impulse to yank the door open and bail out before the inevitable pileup happened. "Depends on what you mean by 'good'. The cops are good at what they do, you don't get screwed around on your wages, the cost of living is pretty low, there's more superheroes per capita than any other city in America ..."

"Fuckin' Masks." The cabby shook his head. "Pretentious assholes, strutting around in their stupid costumes. Why can't they get real jobs instead of pretending they're somet'ing special?"

Thomas badly wanted to educate the man on a few points he seemed hazy on but decided the hassle wouldn't be worth it. "Doesn't Adam Power live here in Chicago?" he asked instead.

"Oh, he's different," the cabby said immediately. "He's one of us, an' he don't wear a mask anyways. Dunno what he's doing about this t'ing that happened to his little girl, though."

Thomas wasn't aware that anything had happened to him, save for the attack by the impostor and the fact that he, as Vanessa, had run away from home. "Yeah?"

"Yeah, didn't you hear? She got kidnapped." The cabby waved his arm expansively, then changed gears. "Oh, they *say* she run away after her dad tried to touch her, but I don't buy that for a hot second. I figure someone got to her, an' they're holdin' her in secret. Power's probably keepin' it quiet 'til he can pay the ransom."

Right. Thomas opted not to point out the holes in the guy's logic. "I guess," he said noncommittally.

The cab driver rolled his eyes. "Meanwhile, you *seen* them idiots protestin' outside the Plaza? Like he's gonna let them inside."

"Not in person, no." In lieu of changing the subject, Thomas looked out through the windshield to make sure the cab driver wasn't taking him too far out of his way. The cab crossed a bridge over a canal full of swirling, dirty water. Trying hard not to feel homesick for Utopia, Thomas stared up at the imposing buildings. There was something missing there, too, but he couldn't work out what it was. Despite cosmetic differences in style, they all looked essentially the same, but that wasn't the problem.

"See that? That's the Sears Tower," the driver said proudly, apparently having forgotten that Thomas had said he was originally from Chicago. As the car passed by the imposing edifice, he added, "Tallest building in the world."

"Uh, no," Thomas said. "That'll be the Spire, in Utopia." He wasn't sure how anyone could not know this. *He'd* known it, before he went there in the first place.

"Oh, yeah?" asked the cabby, instantly on the defensive. "How many floors that one got, then?"

Thomas shrugged. "Dunno. Never been up in it. They don't give tours to just anyone. But I do know it's one and a half miles tall." In fact, he'd been clued in on the exact height, and why Force Majeure had picked such an odd number, by Jericho.

"Bullshit." The driver's tone was once more dismissive.

Stung, Thomas pulled out his phone. The camera on it wasn't the greatest, but it had done a good job capturing a picture of Jericho's profile out the window of the air-cab that had taken them to the maglev terminal. As the taxi slowed to a stop at a set of lights, he pulled up the photo. In the background was the iconic building, spearing up through a bank of clouds. Carefully hiding Jericho's face with his thumb, he leaned forward and showed the image to the cab driver. "That's the Spire."

To his disgust, the guy barely glanced at the picture. "That's the one that's Cog-built, right? Doesn't count, then."

"What? How can it not count?" Thomas was fully aware he was defending a place he never wanted to return to, but facts mattered, and this guy was deficient in them. "It's really that tall." As he said the words, he realized what was missing from the buildings around them. *Flight lane strips. Duh.*

"If a Mask does it, it don't count." The cabby was adamant. "If you got a cape who can break the sound barrier, does he get to run in the Olympics? If someone can bench-press a semi-truck, can he enter weight-lifting competitions? Answer is, they don't. They got powers, so that's cheating. Same with some cog putting up a bullshit building a mile and a half tall. Couldn't do it without powers, so it's cheating, so it don't count."

"But—" Thomas wondered what the guy's opinion on prodigies would be but chose not to find out. "Doesn't matter who built it. It's *there.*"

"So's the Sears, sonny." The cabby turned the music up. "And that one *wasn't* built by cogs." With the air of someone who had delivered the telling argument in a debate, he let the clutch out and roared through the intersection.

Belatedly, Thomas realized he wasn't going to get anywhere with this. He settled back in his seat, trying to get comfortable. It wasn't easy. While his seat was soft enough, he was getting the impression that whoever was in it last had a distinct body odor problem. Or maybe it was the last ten customers.

As the driver headed north on Lake Shore Drive, Thomas stared out the window at the morning sun glinting off the waters of Lake Michigan. Even the stunning view didn't distract him from realizing he needed to acknowledge something he hadn't wanted to face up to. Specifically, that he'd been spoiled by his time away. Utopia was so aggressively effective at making life comfortable for its residents that he was finding a 'normal' city like Chicago—where he'd *grown up*—almost unbearably chilly, noisy and smelly. And the people were *ignorant*.

This led to another worry. While his family had said all the right things on TV, did they truly want him back after the accusations he'd made as Vanessa? Worse, had he grown away from them in the last twenty-two months? Would he even know them anymore? Would they know *him?*

He knew *now* that there was no fault to be had with them, but that did nothing to take away the memories of what had happened on that night. Intellectually, he knew they would take him back. Emotionally, he wasn't so sure. Round and round he went in his own head, unable to reach a conclusion that he could be certain was absolutely correct.

The cabby's voice broke into his troubled thoughts. "Comin' up to Rogers Park, sonny. Which way from here? Or, you know, you can gimme the address and I can go straight there."

The moment of truth was rapidly approaching. He knew he needed to do this, but he'd been running away from this moment for so long that it was hard to run *toward* it. "Anywhere near Power Plaza," he said. "I've got folks in the area."

Just for a moment, he expected an *ah-ha* exclamation from the driver, but the guy just snorted. "Sure, that's fine. You looking to rubberneck the protest? Go ahead; just make sure you don't get any of the stupid on you. Oh, an' you're payin' before you get out."

"No problem," Thomas agreed, and pulled his wallet from his pocket. He hadn't had a chance to stop at an ATM since he'd left Utopia, but there were always other options. "Is it okay to pay with card?"

"Card's fine." The cabby pulled over to the side of the road. Reaching into the center console, he produced a battered card-swipe device and twisted around to hand it to Thomas. "Amex, Mastercard, Visa, debit."

"Ah." Thomas paused, his MagCard half out of his wallet. "I don't suppose you take these?"

"Fuck, no." The driver snorted. "Gimme something *real*, sonny."

I'd like to see you talk about 'real' if you ever went to Utopia. Feeling once more as though he'd been dropped back into the Middle Ages, Thomas pulled out the debit card that Jericho had supplied with the fake identity. It was real enough, in that it connected to a genuine bank account with actual money in it. With a start, Thomas realized that he didn't know whose money had gone into creating the account. *Do I owe Jericho even more than I knew?*

Without further ado, he swiped his borrowed debit card through the machine, then manually typed in the PIN code. In fits and starts, the device spat out a receipt, which Thomas tucked into his wallet. *I'll pay him back, every cent.* Climbing out of the cab, he retrieved his backpack before closing the door. The cabby took off with the same blatant disregard for everything else on the road that he'd shown earlier, leaving Thomas coughing in the middle of a cloud of exhaust fumes.

Covering his nose and mouth with his hand, Thomas turned away from the acrid fog and looked around. It took him a moment to orient himself, then he figured out where he was. The cabby had been as good as his word; he was only half a block from home. Or at least, he hoped it was still home. Taking hold of his courage in both hands, he set out with a firm stride along the tree-lined street. That much, at least, had not changed.

The Plaza covered half a city block and was fenced in with a wall Thomas was willing to bet had every security device known to his father built into it. To his uncertain memory, it seemed a little higher than the last time he'd seen it. Outside the main entryway was a bunch of protesters, carrying the signs he'd seen on TV, with a few variations. He grimaced; there was no way his family would let him in as Thomas, but he hadn't thought people would show up on a Saturday morning to go wave a sign in front of a superhero's front gate. Approaching that group as Vanessa was something he hadn't planned on.

He didn't even have to ask himself what Jericho would do in this situation. *He'd go in anyway.*

Nobody was looking his way, and he was fairly sure the cameras couldn't see him where he was. There was nobody else in sight. Taking a deep breath, he pulled the hood of his jacket up to cover his hair, then concentrated and *pushed.*

Thirty seconds later, Vanessa breathed out and reached up under the hood to run her hands through her hair, which was once more long, red and wavy. Her waist was slimmer than Thomas', so she took the time to pull her belt in a couple of notches. As an afterthought, she tugged the hood a bit farther down over her face and tucked away a few stray locks that had fallen out. Thus prepared, she headed for the front gates.

While she was reasonably good at parkour, she didn't want to risk herself or annoy her parents by trying to jump the fence. For one thing, it was a good twenty feet high. For another, she could see the faint shimmer of a force field barrier above it. Knowing her father, he would also have a force field extending underground, just to make sure nobody could tunnel in that way. She doubted that any of the protesters outside the gates had the wherewithal to make a serious effort to gain access, but her ordeal had been proof positive (to use Jericho's phrasing) that someone else *could* and *had* done so. No doubt others had tried since but going by the fact that Power Plaza was still standing; they'd failed.

Nobody paid her any attention as she approached the crowd. With her hands in her hoodie pockets, she pushed through until she was standing outside the outer gates of Power Plaza. These were charmingly retro, apparently crafted from wrought iron, and designed to open when a button was pressed, or a car drove on to the pressure-pad. Vanessa knew damn well they were made of whatever high-tensile alloys her father had decided would work best for the purpose. Wrought iron, they were not. Neither were they just gates, or her name wasn't Vanessa Power.

A tiny thread of doubt crept into her mind. *Jericho was the first person to call me that in nearly two years.*

Shut up. It's still who I am.

The doubt grew and spread, sending tendrils to undermine her resolve. *What if they don't believe who I am? What if they hate me now?*

She looked up at the gates, as the protesters around her waved signs and shouted, then clenched her fists in her pockets hard enough to make the nails bite into her palms. *I can't do this right now. I'll get a motel room and come back tomorrow.*

Slowly, despising every second of her own weakness, she turned away from the gates.

Click.

Even over the noise of the crowd, she heard it. So did everyone else, from the way they quieted down. She froze, then turned her head. Of their own accord, the gates had unlocked and were even now swinging open. She hadn't pressed the button. Was someone coming out? But the inner gates were still closed.

"Holy shit!" yelled a guy holding a large sign which said: 'WHERE ARE YOU HIDING HER?' "They're letting us in!"

This was manifestly not the case, but the protesters surged forward anyway. Caught off guard, Vanessa found herself stumbling backwards until she was in the entrapment area, along with the rest of them.

"Attention. All of you can leave now. The girl in the hoodie can stay."

Vanessa turned and stared at the two intercom boxes set against the wall, near the inner gates. The voice had come from one of them. Even with the electronic interference and the distortion from the echoes between the walls, she would've recognized it anywhere. Her lips shaped the word automatically. *Mom.*

"Yes. Everyone else, leave immediately."

"What if we don't want to?" yelled the guy who had led the charge. "We can block this gate forever if we want! Where are you hiding your daughter, and why?"

The inner gates were framed and supported by large concrete pillars. As Vanessa tried to choose whether to stay or slip out of the entrapment area, the tops of these pillars opened up. Large weapons unlimbered themselves, training multiple independent barrels on the protesters. Bright red targeting beams darted out, painting a dot on every person except Vanessa. She could even see the red lines hanging in the dusty air. Some had more than one targeting dot on them.

"Be aware, our defensive weapons are entirely non-lethal," Tesseract Power stated in a matter-of-fact tone. **"This is not to say they're painless. Quite the opposite, in fact. If you're still on our property in ten seconds, I *will* be arranging a demonstration. Seven. Six. Five."**

By 'four', the protesters were already in full retreat. The gates began to close at 'two' as the last ones crossed the boundary line. At 'zero' they clanged shut, leaving Vanessa standing alone in the concrete box. The solid click signaled that she would have a lot of trouble getting out now, if whoever was on the security panel wanted to keep her inside. Not that she really wanted to leave; in a way, she was glad her hand had been forced. It made going forward easier.

The bare concrete under her feet showed tire tracks, with a little extra scuffing where the vehicles had stopped after they'd cleared the first set of gates. In contrast to the aesthetic appeal of the outer gates, the inner ones were built to be imposing. If she was any judge, they'd pose an impassable obstacle to anything short of a main battle tank, and she doubted even one of those would do the job.

Knowing she was well past the point of no return, Vanessa looked at the intercom boxes. One was at window height for a car, while the other was set higher, for pedestrians and truck drivers. Her heart was thumping in her chest as she moved up to the second one. It was obvious by now that she'd been under close surveillance since she first approached the compound, but she still went on with the charade. Reaching out, she pressed the button firmly, making sure it got a good read of her thumbprint.

Instantly, the screen lit up. It wasn't holographic as it would've been in Utopia, but she couldn't have everything. Staring out at her was a face she knew as well as she did either of her own. Her brother had gone from nine to eleven while she'd been away. He'd grown a little, gotten slightly huskier, but he was still her brother. His red hair, a shade lighter than hers, needed trimming, but he seemed to have a few more freckles so that balanced out.

"Hey, Buddy," she said, working to keep her voice steady. "I'm home."

Buddy blinked. **"'Nessa?"** he asked, incredulity plain in his voice. **"Is it really you?"**

"Yeah, it's me," she said, some small part of her amazed by the sheer banality of the conversation. "Can you—"

"Dad!" Buddy's voice rode over hers as he turned away from the camera. **"Come quick! 'Nessa's home! She's really home!"**

In another moment, Buddy was nudged aside by another familiar figure. Vanessa had promised herself that she wouldn't cry, but she felt tears begin to trickle down her cheeks as she took in her father's face. Up until just a few hours ago, she'd reviled this man and hoped he would die, but now she looked on him with new eyes.

To her shock, he seemed to have aged decades in the time that she'd been gone. He leaned down into the camera range, and she could see the lines around his eyes, the weariness in his expression. *My god,* she realized. *I did this to him.*

"**Vanessa?**" he asked hesitantly. **"Baby, you have to believe me. I didn't—I wouldn't—"**

"Dad, I know," she blurted. "I know what happened now. I know it wasn't you. It was never you. I thought it was, but it wasn't, and I should've known, but I was so *stupid*—" Her vision was mostly obscured by tears now, and her nose was running. Pulling out the handkerchief Jericho had given her, she wiped her eyes and blew her nose. "We were attacked. Not just me. All of us. They wanted me to accuse you so the whole team would be weakened. And it worked, but it's not working anymore."

He stood there blinking, absorbing what she'd said, working his way through it. She watched his expression transform, saw the old light come back into his eyes. Anger suffused his face, but not aimed at her. Never at her. **"So, there *was* someone in the house. Someone who laid hands on you—"**

"I screamed before anything bad happened, Dad," she hastened to assure him. "He ran out of the room. I can't believe I didn't realize it wasn't you." Deep within her, the long-held terror and hatred began to loosen its grip on her soul. Speaking to her father, even through the security link, repeating to him what Jericho had so carefully explained to her, somehow made it more real than just *knowing* it.

"But who was he, honey? How did he—" Her father's voice was cut off as the inner gates began to move, separating and rumbling ponderously to each side.

Vanessa turned toward it. Her mother stepped into the opening, wearing her PowerTech exoskeleton over T-shirt and jeans. Unsmiling, she beckoned Vanessa forward. "Let's get you inside."

A little taken aback by the tone, Vanessa stepped forward nevertheless. "Mom. Aren't you happy to see me?" Once she was out of the entrapment area, the gates immediately began to grind shut once more.

Tesseract put a hand on her arm as they started up the short driveway. "Yes. Just as I was happy to see the last six iterations of you. I have to admit, you're the most convincing one so far." Behind them, there was a hollow *boom* as the gates came together once more.

Vanessa's heart began to thump again, this time in fear. *There's been impostors? There's been impostors. What if they decide I'm one? What if they send me away?*

Tesseract Power's apparently relaxed demeanor and casual clothes didn't fool Vanessa for one moment. As a high-tier prodigy, her mother's reflexes were already off the scale. With the exoskeleton to assist her speed and strength, she was a terrifying opponent, whether sparring for practice or in real combat. Of course, Vanessa now had her own powers, so she'd probably be able to give her mother a proper fight. It still wouldn't end in a win, though; that was just a pipe dream. And right now, she knew that if she made any sort of hostile move, she would be beaten down without mercy.

The front door of the house opened as they approached, and her father stood there. He stepped forward, his arms opening. "Vanessa, honey, I—"

"We don't know for a fact that it's her yet," his wife interrupted him. She caught Vanessa's eye and pointed at the doorway. "Come on inside. Let's take this to the living room."

Numbly, Vanessa stepped into the house, the old familiar scents enfolding her with a hundred memories. Unlike the noxious effusions outside the train station, these were pleasant and wholesome. Turning right in the entrance hall, she made her way down the short corridor into the living room and shrugged her backpack off. It went on the floor in front of her and she sat down on the sofa. As an afterthought, she pushed back her hood and let her hair spill down over her shoulders.

Her father, mother and brother trooped into the living room and sat down on the sofa opposite, her parents on either side of her brother.

"Vanessa." Her mother's voice was warmer now, softer. "What's the last thing you remember from your time here?"

The mood whiplash bewildered her. Why had her mother suddenly become more accepting? Was it a trick to lull a potential impersonator into complacency? Or was it … oh. *I knew the way to the living room. And this is where I always sit on the sofa.*

Her parents were still watching her, awaiting the answer. She ran the question through her mind again.

"I remember … well, Dad had been busy with that serial-killer case. The domestic murders that all turned out to be the same guy?"

The local police had been Gordoning her mother on that case, right up until she'd used one of Adam's analytical devices to reveal that the killer was the same person in every case, changing his appearance to frame other family members for the killings. With Enabled powers on the table, Adam had put aside his other work and joined his wife in hunting the man down. It turned out to be someone with face-changing Artificer tech; with Team Power closing in, the man had fled Chicago. Unfortunately for him, he'd chosen to do it via the maglev.

Adam and Tesseract had informed Force Majeure (and, by proxy, UML) of the situation, and pursued in the Team Power jet, with Vanessa piloting. They'd reached the next station to find that Independence and Tourbillon already had the suspect in custody. Independence had handed the man over, along with his face-changing technology, for transport back to Chicago. When they returned home, Buddy had been intensely jealous that she'd gotten to meet two members of Force Majeure on the same day.

"I recall the case," her mother said. "That was a nasty one. Same sort of thing that False Flag used to pull, back in the day. But *he* didn't need tech."

Vanessa shivered. She'd read the case files on the terror villains; every single one would have sent Jack the Ripper screaming into the night. "Yeah. You and Dad were tied up for about two weeks with that case. And for about three months before *that*, he was in and out of meetings with the Joint Chiefs about his military contracts. I remember he forgot my birthday."

Tesseract's head came up, and she stared at Vanessa. Then she leaned forward to look searchingly at her husband. "Is this true?"

Adam Power shrugged sheepishly. "Sorry, hon. You know how I get." Then his eyes clicked into focus with the realization of what he'd just said. "Wait a minute. Baby, if you knew I'd missed your birthday and those other girls *didn't* know it, then that means …"

"Yes." As Tesseract spoke, the tension drained out of her shoulders and her face relaxed into a smile. She stood up and took one stride forward. Reaching down, she pulled Vanessa to her feet. "Welcome home, honey." Her arms enfolded Vanessa and held her tight; Vanessa hugged her mother back, exoskeleton and all. The embrace felt *wonderful.*

Tears were running down her face again as they released each other from the hug. Turning to her father, who was now standing but still hanging back a little, she opened her arms. "Come on, Dad. I can't tell you how sorry I am for letting myself be fooled like that."

Adam Power grimaced. "You have no idea how many times I wondered if I *was* really responsible. If someone had managed to implant some kind of post-hypnotic command in my mind during one of our battles. But I couldn't pin down a single encounter that could've done it."

Vanessa shook her head. "It wasn't you, Dad. It was never you."

The embrace was total and heartfelt. The last of the fear and anger that she'd unjustly held toward her father faded away. She felt, at last, that she'd come home. Her tears kept flowing, and with them came the laughter; of relief, of happiness, of disbelief that this day had finally come.

After giving Buddy a hug as well (and a light noogie, because she *was* his big sister, and certain proprieties had to be observed) she sat down again, this time with her parents on either side of her. Her father held her left hand, and her mother laid claim to her right. Buddy sat opposite them, his eyes fixed on Vanessa, a goofy grin fixed on his face.

"You're back." Tesseract Power squeezed Vanessa's hand. "It's really *you*. Where have you been? What *happened?*"

Vanessa took a deep breath, feeling her heart rate beginning to increase again. "I didn't know Dad—the real one—was in his workshop. I'd been in the bathroom, brushing my teeth. When I came out, the impostor was in my room, fiddling with my suit. He sounded a bit awkward, but I thought that was because he was embarrassed about forgetting my birthday. It was only when he started mauling me that I knew something was wrong." That was the understatement of the year. She'd panicked hard, utterly uncomprehending as to what was going on. "I just screamed and fought back until he ran out of the room. You came in then. I told you what had happened, and you wouldn't believe me."

Her mother's jaw set hard. Adam and Buddy were sitting like statues, frozen. "I remember," the older woman said. "I didn't know how to convince you that it wasn't possible."

"I hadn't thought it was possible, either," said Vanessa helplessly. "I didn't want to believe it, but it was too *real*. After I took off from the police station, I got as far as Nebraska on stealth mode before the suit crashed into the Missouri River. I managed to eject in time, then I walked into town and took the bus into Omaha."

"We *wondered* about that," her father said quietly. "We got into Omaha thirty minutes after you emptied your account. While your mother searched the city, I backtracked your trail. I located the wreckage of the suit, but the black box was wiped clean and I couldn't get a good answer for *why*. What happened? Why did it crash? Why didn't you use the emergency landing procedure instead of ejecting?"

Vanessa sighed. "The impostor had been fiddling with the suit before he attacked me. I'm guessing he did *something*. Whatever it was, it killed the suit stone dead, two hours out. Nearly killed me, too. I had to skid-land it on the ice, then eject before the suit broke through and sank."

Tesseract Power afforded her a look of respect. "Nicely done, dear." A frown crossed her face. "When we didn't find you in Omaha, we expanded our search radius. We scoured the *state* for you, but it was like you'd dropped off the face of the Earth. Where *were* you?"

Pulling her wallet from her pocket, Vanessa extracted the MagCard from it. "I stayed in Omaha for a week, but I kept feeling like I should be going farther south, so I paid cash for a bus ticket into Utopia. I've been there ever since."

Buddy stared at the card. "But ... that can't be right. We *went* there. We went *everywhere*."

Her mother nodded soberly. "I personally spoke to Relentless. He assured me that if you were in the city, Force Majeure would find you. But you weren't. He was certain of it. How could you be in Utopia City and not be recognized? We ran TV ads and had posters put up *everywhere*." Not just Utopia City, she meant.

Vanessa took a deep breath. "This relates back to what happened on that night." She dropped her wallet and card on top of the backpack and clenched her hands on her knees. She didn't want to think back to that time, but she forced herself to do it anyway. "I don't know who it was who attacked me, or how he got into the house, or where he got whatever he sabotaged the suit with; but I *do* know that whoever he is, he wasn't using the face-change tech that other guy had."

"I can guarantee he wasn't," her father confirmed. "I supervised its destruction, the moment the trial was over." He looked at Vanessa curiously. "But how did *you* know?"

"He didn't need it," she said bluntly. "Whoever it was, he's got Dynamic and Prodigy ratings. And his Dynamic rating lets him change shape."

"To look like me." Adam Power clenched his own fists in turn. "That son of a misbegotten ..." He trailed off. "So *that's* why you were convinced it was me. It wasn't face-change tech. It was a power that let him be a perfect copy of me." He paused. "But what convinced you it *wasn't* me, after all this time?"

Vanessa felt reassured, now that she was on firmer ground. "Well, *apparently*, there's a thing called the Proximity—"

"Proximity Principle!" shouted Buddy. Vanessa looked at him, along with everyone else. He blushed and ducked his head. "Sorry. I was reading about it online the other day. If someone gets powers near another Enabled, they might get powers like the other guy's. So, this guy who tried to hurt you was a shape-changer ... wait." He paused. "Okay, you've lost me. Where *are* you going with this?"

"Vanessa." Her mother stared at her. "Are you telling us that *you* have powers? Did you get powers when this happened?"

The rapid heart rate was back. Vanessa nodded jerkily. "Yeah, Mom. That's exactly what I'm saying. I've got Prodigy and Dynamic ratings now. From the jerk who tried to hurt me. I didn't realize it at first, but they were what let me get loose enough to scream. Thinking back, I'm pretty sure they also helped me survive the suit crash. I had no idea what I could do until I was on the way into Omaha, but when I did, I took on a whole new face to make sure nobody could find me." *Especially you guys*, she didn't have to say. "I wasn't aware of the Proximity Principle, so I didn't know *then* that I couldn't possibly have gotten my powers from *you*, Dad."

Nobody said a word. Slowly, she stood up, and readjusted her belt so it wouldn't be too tight. Then she held her breath and *pushed*. Thirty seconds had never gone by so slowly in her life. She closed her eyes, unable to look at her family. *Will they even want me after this?*

Finally, the change was over. Thomas opened his eyes and ran his hands down his shirt to smooth it into place. "This, uh, this is what I looked like when I got off the bus in Omaha."

Buddy was the first one to break the spell of incredulity. "Cool!" he blurted. "I get my big sister back, *and* I get a big brother, too!"

The response was from so far out of left field that Thomas had no choice but to roll with it. Old reflexes gave him his reply. "Not until you tell me what you did with that Challenger action figure of mine that you swiped just before I ran away, you little brat."

"What?" Buddy stared at him. "You're *still* butt-hurt over that? Come on, I was *nine!* That was *forever* ago!"

"And I was sixteen. Which is *still* older than you are now." Thomas extended his hand. "So, give it back."

"Can't." Buddy looked down at the rug. "I buried it in the yard next to the wall. When you left and Dad upgraded the security system, he extended the wall over the spot." When he looked up at Thomas again, regret was written on his features. "Sorry."

"Not as sorry as you're gonna be." Thomas pulled Buddy to his feet and grabbed him around the neck. "Noogie or wet willy? Your choice."

"Mom! Dad!" yelped Buddy. "'Nessa's being mean to me! Make her stop!"

"Okay, first? When I'm like this, I'm Thomas, not Vanessa. And I'm 'him', not 'her'." Thomas wet his little finger. "And second? You didn't make a choice, so you get both."

"Moooooom!"

"Okay, boys, enough." Laughing, Tesseract Power got up and separated the pair. "It looks like we've all got some adjusting to get used to." She eyed Thomas closely. "So, your entire gender identity shifts when you change shape?"

Thomas nodded. "Well, yeah. That's how it is for me, anyway. I wouldn't assume it's the same for everyone who can change their shape, though. Some of them might have a base gender that never changes. Others might go with no gender at all. Outward appearance isn't exactly a reliable indicator."

"So how are we supposed to know what to call them?" queried his father blankly.

"Ask them?" It seemed like a reasonable solution. "I mean, it's only polite. And I know *I* would've been highly uncomfortable with people calling me 'her' after I put all the work into making this form just right."

"But why did you even go with a male form?" Tesseract's tone was curious rather than dismissive. "Heaven knows I didn't bring you up as a helpless princess, but being a girl was all you *knew*. Why such a drastic change?"

Thomas put his arms around himself to ward off the unpleasant memories that the question evoked. "Because right then, I felt intensely vulnerable. As a girl, I'd been attacked and almost raped by someone—" He choked off the words and started again, unable to look his father in the eye. Even now, he felt intense guilt for not seeing through the deception. "Someone I thought I could trust with my life. I didn't want to *be* a girl. I didn't want to be that vulnerable, that terrified, ever again. So, when my power gave me an out, I rebuilt myself as Thomas." Breathing deeply, he worked to expunge the last of the fear and pain of those memories, based on falsehood as they were.

Arms went around him from behind, and he recognized his father's embrace. He turned to lean into the older man's broad chest, drawing comfort from the fact that he was with people who, even if they didn't fully understand, were willing to *try*.

"In this room, you're the expert at shape-changing," his mother said. "You're the first one in the family with a Dynamic rating, so we'll take your word for it about gender when it comes to shape-changers." She paused. "But how were you able to just walk up to the gates as Vanessa? If you were terrified to be her, I mean."

"I'd … learned there was less to fear than I originally thought." Silently, Thomas blessed Jericho's insights. "When I left, for instance, it was because I thought I could never be safe in this house again. Now, I know I'll always be safe here."

"Damn right." His father pushed him away, but only so he could place his hands on Thomas's shoulders. "Whoever's responsible did their best to screw us over, but now you're back. We're a family again. And if they try that crap again, I am going to have some serious surprises waiting for them. On that note, as a prodigy *and* a dynamic, do you have any suggestions for improving the security setup so nobody else gets to pull this stunt a second time?"

"Now that you mention it; yeah, I do." Thomas hadn't put too much thought into it before this point, but now he found a few ideas coming to mind.

"Hey, before you get into that, got a question." Buddy jerked his chin up. "What made you come back? You were chillaxing in Utopia City one fine day, and you suddenly realized what had happened, so then you decided to come home?"

"Oh, no. My boyfriend figured it out first." Thomas snorted. "He had to walk me through it one step at a time, but …" He trailed off as he realized both his mother and father were staring intently at him, while Buddy had a weird look on his face. "What?"

"Honey." His mother's voice was deceptively soft and gentle. "You never mentioned a boyfriend."

His father's, not so much. "What boyfriend?"

Whoops.

- End of Epilogue One -

Epilogue Two
The Villains

In a darkened room, two shadowy figures watched the news on TV. It was not going the way they wanted. On the screen, a well-presented news anchor held a sheet of paper as if it were evidence of the Second Coming.

"In a stunning turn of events yesterday, Vanessa Power came out of nowhere after nearly two years of silence, and literally walked in through the front gates of Power Plaza."

The image on the screen shifted from the news anchor to a shot of a teenage girl in a hoodie pushing through the ongoing protest outside of Power Plaza, in Chicago. As she turned away from the outer gates, the camera caught a glimpse of her features under the concealing hood. For a moment, the screen froze, and the Amber Alert photo of Vanessa Power was placed up alongside the blurry cell-phone image. Even accounting for the low quality of the image, it was clearly a match. Then the photo popped off the screen and the action resumed. The girl took one step away from the gates, then stopped and turned her head. The gates swung open and the crowd surged forward, carrying the girl with them. A warning boomed out and they retreated with laser-dots dancing across their bodies, leaving her standing there alone. Shortly afterward, she vanished inside the inner gates, in the company of a woman clearly recognizable as Tesseract Power.

"Following her return, she has reportedly undergone numerous tests designed to uncover impostors. Adam and Tesseract Power, and Vanessa's brother Buddy, have all expressed their satisfaction that this is indeed Vanessa. When asked about her reasons both for leaving and returning, she had this to say."

From there, the news spot switched to more recent footage. It showed the red-headed Vanessa, exhibiting every bit of her mother's striking good looks, standing at a podium with microphones before her. Here, wearing the family uniform and flanked by her parents, she seemed much more at ease than she had in the previous clip. However, she did not appear to be in any way complacent. It was readily apparent that her eyes were alert, scanning the crowd.

"The police report I made on the day I left was inaccurate, though I didn't know it at the time," she said clearly. **"I believed then that my father had tried to molest me, but I know now that the actual assailant was a shape-changing dynamic seeking to cause discord within my family. I have spoken with the police and withdrawn the accusation against my father. We still don't know the identity of the dynamic in question, but I can tell you that my father is entirely innocent in this matter."**

Reporters shouted questions over one another until she raised a hand; amazingly, they quieted. **"Why did I come back? It's simple. It was proven to me that what I had believed for nearly two years was a lie. I came back to rejoin my family and my team, and to apologize to my parents for ever doubting their dedication to me."** Tremulously, she smiled. **"It's good to be home."**

The image shifted back to the news anchor. **"In other news, the lifting of the cloud over Adam Power has had far-reaching consequences. When Vanessa went missing, many wild rumors abounded about her disappearance. PowerTech**

Industries were forced to default on several lucrative contracts with the military because of Adam's preoccupation with locating his daughter. With the news of the police report, the few contracts he still maintained were put on hold pending further investigation. Now that Adam Power has been cleared of all suspicion of wrongdoing, he will once more be able to focus on his work for PowerTech. The contracts will not come back immediately, but he's been able to tell us that at least one of his previous clients has already contacted him on the matter. It looks like all is well again for the Windy City's favorite Enabled fam —"

"God fucking *damn* it!" The man in the armchair mashed his finger on the remote to mute the sound, then came to his feet and hurled his drink at the wall. Glass shattered, shards spraying over the carpet as expensive liquor trickled toward the floor. "I thought for *sure* the virus would crash her suit and kill her when she ran off like that! How did she survive? Where the fuck *was* she? And how did she find *out?*"

Limbs articulating oddly, the other person in the room came to its feet. The flickering light from the now-silent TV reflected redly from the porcelain-smooth carapace covering its inhumanly proportioned body. "*I have no idea.*" Its voice was like the grinding of crushed glass mixed with fingernails squealing on a chalkboard, a sound guaranteed to cause shuddering revulsion in all but the most hardened of souls. "*But you won't pull it off again. Not like that. They'll have safeguards in place.*"

"Fucking Adam fucking *Power.*" The man turned away from the TV and crossed the room. At the touch of a button, thick curtains pulled aside from a large picture window. "I thought I'd finally managed to ruin that interfering son of a bitch for good and all."

"*It was a good try.*" The carapace-clad Enabled joined its companion at the window. "*Shit happens. What are you going to do now?*"

"Find out where the fuck she was and who filled her in, and fuck *them* up." The man's voice held venom. "*Someone* needs to die for this."

"*Sure. Let's do that.*" A pause. "*How do we do that?*"

"When I figure it out, you'll be the first to know."

They both fell silent then, looking out at the Utopia City nightscape.

- End of Epilogue Two -

Epilogue Three
Manhattan Justice Recruiting

Nina toyed with her hair. She'd trimmed the singed ends and washed it until it didn't smell of smoke anymore, but she wasn't certain that the battle with the Madness hadn't done damage to it that she couldn't see. Was she getting split ends? She couldn't tell. The shampoo she had started buying should fix that, but she wasn't certain about it. *Mister Fluffikins always has such a nice coat. Maybe I should try his shampoo.* Reminded of her Shi Tzu, she wondered if he was all right. She had filled his water and food bowls before she went out. If he decided to get bored, he could make such a nasty mess before she came home. *Once we're done here, I'll just fly home and check—*

"Splendid? Earth to Splendid?" She jerked back with a yelp as the tiny buzzing device dropped down right in front of her face. The voice was Drone's, of course, as was the eponymous drone. The man himself was at the far end of the base conference room, boots up on the table. A grin stretched across his face below that stupid visor because despite his age, he was such a *boy* who still liked to play stupid practical jokes at her expense. It was really irritating, because she thought he was kind of handsome when they weren't being superheroes. He was always polite to her, and if he asked her on a date, there was a very real chance she'd accept. With his curly dark hair and neat little mustache, he looked like an actor in one of those old-timey black and white movies that Nina liked to watch with Mister Fluffikins curled up on her lap.

"Don't *do* that!" she shouted at him. The nice feelings she had toward Conrad didn't translate across to his superhero persona, especially when he was making those creepy little drones buzz everywhere. "You scared me."

Drone waved her words away, which was another very annoying habit he had. "You were zoned out. I believe it's your turn to try to talk sense into Troll." She was sure he'd just rolled his eyes.

Troll was sitting on the other side of her, leaning back in his chair. His dirty bare feet were—thankfully for Nina's delicate feelings—still on the floor. She'd once loaned her teammate her favorite pair of nail clippers, and he'd promptly broken them trying to clip the nail on his little toe.

At the moment, he had his mask pushed to the top of his head while he held the dressing away from his upper arm and examined the burn there. It had looked nasty when she'd first seen it, but it hadn't slowed him down at all during the fight against the Madness. Neither had the similarly bandaged injuries on the left side of his torso and his right leg. Now, of course, they were on the way to becoming the newest additions to his multitudinous collection of scars.

But first things first. "Talk sense into Troll about what?" In her opinion, there were many things that the man needed sense talked into him about, but she wasn't sure which of these Drone was referring to.

"Nothin'." Troll didn't look up from his inspection but his voice, coming from that barrel chest, was a deep rumble. Nina imagined that bears might sound like that, only less likely to bite someone's head off.

"It is not 'nothing', as you well know," snapped Drone, sending one of his drones zooming in toward Troll. Without looking, the shaggy-haired man backhanded the tiny device. It whizzed past Nina and halfway across the room before it recovered. The gesture finished up as a fist raised in the air with middle finger extended, directed toward where Drone sat.

Drone landed the device on the table, then pushed up his visor so he could glare properly at Troll. "Be serious. You're fully *aware* that Manhattan Justice needs more members. We were pushed to our limits, fighting the Madness the other night. I lost half a dozen drones to that fire-breathing maniac. And now we've spent all day interviewing people, and you told them all to … well, to fuck off, or you just plain scared the living daylights out of them. *Tell* him, Splendid!"

"Uh, Drone is right," Nina ventured, starting to feel like a spectator at a tennis match. A very *rude* tennis match. "We do kind of need more members. And you *have* been kind of mean to the people who showed up." She grimaced, not wanting to upset her teammate too much. "I'm sure you'll find it easier if we have more members."

Troll pulled the dressing back over the burn and sat up, his elbows coming into sharp contact with the table. Faded gray eyes stared into hers. "They've all been dicks. Two of 'em weren't even Enabled."

"How could you even tell?" Nina was Enabled, and *she* hadn't known.

"What, that they're dicks?" He settled back into his chair again.

Nina huffed, irritated. "That they weren't Enabled." She was able to tell the other thing. A small part of her was glad that Troll had been there to make the worst ones go away.

"It's a knack." He folded his arms. "Too much spandex, too much posing. No gadgets, no powers."

Drone threw his hands in the air. "They may very well have been prodigies, but we'll never know now, will we?"

"They weren't prodigies. I can tell." Troll closed his eyes, which meant the discussion was over. "How many we got left to interview?"

Nina picked up the list. A dozen names had been crossed off already. "Two. Crocodilian and All-Star."

Troll didn't bother opening his eyes. "Crocodilian? No. Screw him. He's a bad pick."

"What? Why?" Drone pulled his visor down again. He flexed his right hand, and one of his little helicopters buzzed up and down the table in a figure-eight pattern. "You've never even met the fellow, and you're already judging him."

"Never said I didn't know him." Troll shook his head. "Asshole's a dynamic. Turns into a humanoid alligator. Lives in the sewers. Prefers it that way. "

"*You* live under a bridge in Central Park," ventured Nina. At least, that was what he'd told them. Even as she said it, Nina wondered if it could really be true. Troll didn't look like—well, okay, yes, he looked like someone who wouldn't take to living in a regular house. But he didn't *smell* like it. And his hair was always clean.

"I suppose that's *one* way to put it." Drone snorted. "Have you *seen* the place? It's an honest to goodness underground lair." He turned to Troll. "How in the world did you pull off the hidden entrance? That's city property."

"There was a guy in Public Works one time who owed me a favor or two. He took care of the paperwork." Troll unfolded his arms and made a chopping motion with his right hand. "But we're not talkin' about me. We're talkin' about Crocodilian. He's been kicked out of three teams so far. Bit off a mugger's arm, once."

"And All-Star?" asked Nina, restraining her curiosity regarding Troll's living conditions.

Troll's shoulders lifted and dropped in a massive shrug. "Stupid name. Never met the guy."

"Now you're being picky for no good reason." Drone sounded annoyed, which didn't surprise Nina at all. "There are certainly worse names than that out there. I wouldn't judge if you chose to call yourself 'Leather Dude' … just as an example, of course."

"Did I say not to interview him? *Interview* the little shit." Troll settled down a little in his chair. "And call me 'dude' one more time, an' I'll see exactly how many of those buzzing little toys can be shoved up your ass. At once."

"But you said you're from California," protested Nina. "I thought everyone called everyone else 'dude' out there." At least, that was her impression. One day, she was going to fly there and find out. Or take the maglev, whichever was faster.

"Never said I was *from* there," grunted Troll. "Stayed there once. Long time ago."

"Oh, for goodness' sake. *Please* don't bring out that old chestnut while we're interviewing him," Drone warned. "You're liable to put him off joining the team altogether."

Opening his eyes, Troll glared at Drone and gave him the finger again, then refolded his arms. Of the three members of Manhattan Justice, he was the only one who'd never gotten into the 'sharing' thing. He rarely disclosed details of his past and when he did, they were fragmentary or even contradictory. His favorite phrase when he was being evasive was 'long time ago'. Nina personally believed something had happened to him once upon a time that he was trying to forget. He was as dedicated to the team as Drone and Nina herself, but a secret lair under a bridge in Central Park was so *him*.

Reaching up, he pulled his mask down to cover his face, then relaxed and closed his eyes. "So, interview him. I'll give him a fair shake."

Drone apparently decided to not push the matter any further. "Excellent," he declared. He got up from his chair and rounded the conference room table. Opening the door into the waiting room, he leaned through. "All-Star? I believe you're next."

"Hey, why does he get to go next?" The voice was all growly, even more than Troll's when he got angry. "I was here before him."

"Uh, he really was." That was probably All-Star. He sounded in his early twenties, which would put him around Nina's age. He also sounded like a nice guy.

Troll drew a deep breath and raised his voice to a moderate roar. "Crocodirtbag! Fuck off!"

"Aw, c'mon, Troll!" Crocodilian's voice was still growly, but he seemed to be trying to moderate his tone. "Gimme a break here. I *need* this gig!"

"If I hafta come out there," Troll retorted, without opening his eyes, "I'll give you a goddamn break. Both your kneecaps, for starters. Like the last time you tried to start shit with me."

"Hey, I was high that time. And I *said* I was sorry." Crocodilian's voice had become positively whiny.

"Last warning." Troll's voice was a menacing rumble. "Fuck off. Or I'll break your kneecaps *and* throw you out the fuckin' window." Which meant, Splendid knew, a four-story fall.

In the silence that followed, Crocodilian muttered, "*Shit.*" The outer door opened, and heavy footsteps went down the stairs.

Drone held the inner door open for All-Star, allowing him to enter. "Come on in."

"Thanks." All-Star, as Nina had predicted, was indeed in his early twenties. He was over six feet tall, with piercing blue eyes and blond hair. Nina could see enough of his face to tell that he was quite handsome in a rugged, square-jawed sort of way. His smile showed an expanse of even, gleaming-white teeth. "It's good to be here. All-Star, at your service." For the last bit, he lowered his voice a little, probably to make it sound dramatic. With his hands on his hips, he posed heroically, jaw thrust out.

It might even have worked, but Troll spoiled the moment by letting out a bark of laughter. "Oh, you gotta be shitting me. This is a *superhero team*, junior. Not a modeling contest. What the *fuck* is that you're wearin'?"

All-Star looked down at himself. His costume was well-cut and showed off his impressive muscular development. A white star decorated his chest. The rest of the costume was red with blue highlights, while the cape was blue with a large red 'A' on the back. "Uh … my costume?"

Troll came to his feet. Stomping out from behind the table, he glared up at All-Star. "What the hell's your powerset?"

Taken aback, All-Star glanced at Splendid and Drone before answering the question. "Uh, I'm a prodigy, with a Dynamic ability that lets me adapt to changing environments. Put me under water and I'll grow gills and fins. I can also change my outer appearance to better fit in socially, but that takes a lot longer."

"I just bet you can." Troll prodded All-Star in the middle of the chest with a rock-hard knuckle. "You're not bulletproof, an' you gotta breathe. Why the fuck are you wearin' spandex an' a cape?"

Nina sighed. Prodigies in general disdained spandex and capes, though there were a few that liked the intimidation value of the latter. Troll didn't. There wasn't much she could do to help All-Star, but at least Troll wasn't kicking him out straight away.

"Uh, I don't see what that's got to do with—hey!" All-Star's words were replaced by a yelp of protest when Troll grabbed the back of his cape and yanked downward. The cape was firmly attached, which meant that Troll's assault pulled him off balance backward. As a continuation of the move, Troll kicked All-Star behind the legs, dropping him to a kneeling position. All-Star began to turn toward Troll, but the stocky prodigy flicked a length of the younger Enabled's cape over his head and around his neck, then pulled it tight. With one knee between All-Star's shoulder-blades, Troll had him at his mercy.

"Troll!" Drone had been halfway around the table to his seat, but now he started back toward them. "What in heaven's name are you *doing*?"

Eyes wide in shock, Nina came to her feet at the same time. "Troll! Let him go! You're suffocating him!" She could see by the way All-Star was scrabbling at his face that he couldn't breathe.

Abruptly, Troll pulled his knee out of All-Star's back and unwrapped the cape from his head. All-Star went to his hands and knees, inhaling great gasps of air. Drone got there a few seconds later and shoved Troll away from him. From what Nina could see, Troll let it happen; Drone was good with his drones, but Troll could fight better than anyone she knew.

"I can't believe you just did that!" shouted Drone in Troll's face. He grabbed the shorter man by the shoulders and shook him. "You could easily have *killed* him!"

Troll's hands came up and knocked Drone's aside. "Not a fuckin' chance." He stepped around Drone and regarded All-Star impassively. "He's a prodigy. Take more than that to kill him. Isn't that right, junior? Hey, listen up."

Slowly, All-Star's head came up and he stared at Troll. "What was that about?" he asked plaintively. "What did I ever do to you?"

"Nothin'," Troll admitted. "But like I told Drone, you're a prodigy. You got a lot of potential, but you're not usin' it. I gave you a good five seconds to come up with a counter. In that five seconds, I coulda snapped your neck, cut your throat, put a bullet in your head, or killed you in a dozen different ways."

"Crap." All-Star lowered his head until he was looking at the floor. "I guess I failed the entrance exam, then."

Troll snorted. "Fuck, no. You wanna walk out the door, go right ahead. But if you decide to stay, I'm willin' to show you where you're goin' wrong."

All-Star looked up again, hope dawning in his eyes. "What, you mean it?"

"Yeah, I mean it." Troll leaned down beside All-Star. "If you stay, I will train you in how to kick ass an' survive anythin' the world wants to throw at you. I *will* be the meanest motherfucker you ever met. I'll kick your ass every day of the week. But by the time I'm done with you, you'll be on the way to bein' as good as me." He straightened, then extended one massive hand downward. "What do you say, junior?"

Slowly, All-Star reached up and took it. "You put me on the floor without even trying. That's never happened to me before." With Troll's help, he climbed to his feet. "I say, hell *yes*."

Troll clapped him on the shoulder, nearly sending him sprawling again. "That's the spirit. I'll make a prodigy outta you yet. Now, let's talk about your shitty taste in costumes …" Still talking, he led All-Star away to the far end of the conference room.

Drone turned to Nina, hands spread wide in confusion. "Do you have the slightest idea what just happened?"

Nina shrugged. "We got a new member?" She'd thought Troll was bad enough on his own, but it seemed all prodigies were equally crazy.

Well, at least they're getting along.

- End of Epilogue Three -

Epilogue Four
A New Question Revealed

Transit leaned forward over the conference room table. With her helmet removed and placed on the table beside her, it was easy to see the glowing red prosthesis that stood in for her left eye. "We need to talk about this Madness attack in New York."

Samantha Colburn had been wondering about that too, but she didn't have a voice in meetings like this. Her task was to watch and listen. And so, she watched and listened as Relentless shrugged one shoulder. "What's there to talk about? The attack's over and done."

Transit frowned and rubbed at the scar tissue that ran back from her eye socket to leave a comet-trail of white through the short hair over her left temple. "The Central Park attack involved six Madness, and it's only been a maximum of five at a time before. I'm concerned about this jump in numbers."

The Technologist cleared his throat as he cast his gaze around the room. "Those responsible for the Madness are clearly nobody's fools, given they have yet to be tracked down to any specific location. As such, they would have analyzed the results of this instance and concluded, as I have, that increasing the number of attackers is an exercise in diminishing returns. Specifically, the extra damage done to property and public morale will inevitably be countered by a greater chance of being backtracked; in short, the risk outweighs the reward. We can and should step up our alert posture but if I am correct, this was the equivalent of a trial run. One that will end up being no more than an outlier in the grand scheme of things. Relentless, do you concur?"

The leader of Force Majeure nodded slowly. "You make some good points. If you say the attack was a one-off, it's a one-off, but we'll ramp up our readiness just in case." He looked pointedly at Transit. "Satisfied?"

The younger artificer nodded. "Absolutely. So long as we're addressing it *somehow*."

"Good." Relentless glanced around the conference room. "Okay, that concludes today's business. Did anyone have anything else to bring up?" Waiting barely a second, he began to push his chair back from the table. "All right then—"

Samantha also began to rise from her seat at the wall, behind Relentless. She wasn't there to take notes; even if multiple microphones around the room *hadn't* been recording every word, they had secretaries for that sort of thing. Relentless preferred that she be present to ensure she had more of an understanding of Force Majeure's requirements, going forward. It was her job to liaise with the executive assistants of the other core members, and make sure everyone was on the same page. The responsibility attached to her position was enormous, and she worked every day to live up to it.

It was common knowledge within the team that Relentless didn't like these meetings to go any longer than necessary. So, when Independence raised her hand and spoke up, Samantha concealed a wince, half-expecting an explosion. He was usually very good at holding in his temper when in public, but private meetings like this were another matter altogether.

"Yeah, I do. It's about G-Man."

It was easy to tell from the set of Relentless' shoulders that he was indeed irritated by his second-in-command's interruption, but he kept the annoyance out of his voice. "What *about* him?"

"You know the rules. You *wrote* most of them. Nobody joins without one of us sponsoring them. You barely ever sponsor *anyone*." Independence gave Relentless an expectant glance. "Why him?"

The name was familiar to Samantha, of course. She'd been there when the young man had lost it and stormed out of the tryout interview. At the time, she'd thought the way he'd blown his chances like that to be a pity, especially after putting up a passable showing against Relentless and Independence. A few days later he'd shown up again, tearing through the Southsiders like a combine harvester with the assistance of one or two unnamed heroes, and running a wanted murderer to ground. Jack Portman had fallen to his death, but witness statements cleared G-Man of any responsibility in the fatality. Relentless had subsequently offered him a place on the team, which he'd accepted.

Relentless stared impassively back at Independence. "Since when have I ever explained myself to you? It was my decision to sponsor him, just as it was your decision to pull that crap at the interview. What's your problem?"

The prodigy smacked the table with her fist. "We both know what the problem is. What's so important about him? His powers are useful, but he's not exactly top tier. I *still* don't know why we're bending over backwards for him. I mean, there was that stuff that went down the night before the interview. Then there was the Survivors thing. And that's not even mentioning the South Side Mall stunt."

This sort of thing happened in these meetings from time to time. When the debates became spirited, Samantha did exactly one thing; she sat tight and said absolutely nothing. She'd known of the Survivors, and that they'd left town recently. However, this was the first she'd heard of G-Man's involvement with them. *This is what you learn when you sit at the adults' table.*

Silent Knight nodded in agreement with Independence's words. Were it not for the gleam of the room's overhead lights off his armor's glossy exterior, he would have looked like a black cutout in the world. These meetings took place under a Force Majeure bylaw requiring members to attend in costume; that much, Samantha understood. She'd seen Silent Knight out of costume more than once but in all the years they'd been meeting, the artificer had consistently refused to modify his armor to allow vocal communication, or even take his helmet off once the meeting commenced. She'd never worked out whether he was incapable of performing the modification, too stubborn to make the change, or if he was just a creature of habit. Knowing Enabled, any or all of those could be the case.

Transit frowned, her expression thoughtful. "Is it really such a big deal? You know I spent time talking with G-Man before you interviewed him. He was hurting, but even then he wanted nothing more than to do the right thing, and that stunt of his *did* hand the Southsiders to us on a platter. Even if he didn't specifically do it for us, both the Survivors and the Southsiders are out of our hair now."

Samantha had to agree. While the Southsiders' operation hadn't been a major disruption to the city's smooth running, they'd existed as sand in the gears for long enough that she'd become more than a little miffed with them. So when she'd heard that they'd finally been rooted out and turned over to the authorities, she'd shared her boss's appreciation of the fact. The escape of the Survivors bothered her less than the existence of the Southsiders had; wherever they'd gone, the authorities there could deal with them.

As for G-Man's power tier, she figured Relentless wasn't overly concerned about that either. 'Tier' was a nebulous concept, unless it was obvious the Enabled was at either the top or bottom of the range. Sheer power level quite often took a back seat to planning and preparation, which was why only idiots underestimated prodigies. Everyone who knew anything about Enabled knew *that*.

"I'm curious too." Tourbillon looked around at the others, then directly at Relentless. Samantha knew the androgynous hero preferred 'they' and 'them' as pronouns, which sounded weird but seemed to work. As always, their voice held just the right amount of huskiness that she could never be sure of their biological sex. With a quick, nervous motion, they pushed back their hood to reveal the silver circlet and black gemstone. "I *know* you. You never play favorites. So he brought in the Southsiders. Big deal. They were hardly a blip on the radar. Why cut him a break? Where are you going with this?"

Normally, Lady Quantum stayed quiet during these meetings. She was easily bored and prone to whimsical demonstrations of her power, but someone (probably Relentless) had apparently explained to her that if she acted out during the meetings, they'd go for longer. It seemed she'd decided that this one was going to go for longer whether she acted out or not, so now she floated into the air, chair and all, her cape flaring out behind her. "I'm with Tourbillon. What's going on, boss-man?"

Relentless sighed. It was clear to Samantha that he was reluctant to divulge the real reason for his actions. "He blew up during the interview because of the way he was being treated." He paused to give Independence the evil eye. "I don't blame him."

"If he can't take a little adversarial questioning, he doesn't belong on this team," Independence retorted. "He'll get worse from the press if they turn on him."

Relentless continued as though she hadn't spoken. "When he took down the Southsiders and ran Portman to ground, I had the choice to either let him show us up as an independent hero or reap the PR windfall by offering him the position he wanted all along. It was a no-brainer."

"Tourbillon told me where you conducted your 'follow-up interview'." Somehow, Independence managed to insert air-quotes without needing to make the hand gestures. "Personally, I don't consider whatever you got out of *that* to be applicable to a recruitment situation."

Once again, this was not something Samantha had been aware of in advance. She knew Relentless had his proclivities and predilections but so long as no laws were broken, she didn't have a problem with it. Even if G-Man—who she knew was definitely over the age of consent—*had* slept with Relentless, it was between the two of them and nobody else. She also knew that Relentless would not hinge such an important issue as membership in Force Majeure on whether or not someone slept with him.

Still, it seemed as though the prodigy's words had touched a nerve. The big man glared at his second in command while he clenched his fists so hard Samantha could hear the tendons creaking. She wasn't sure *why* he was so angry at the intrusive questioning, just that he was. *If he needs me to know, he'll tell me.* By now, it was almost an article of faith with her.

"He's loyal, principled to a fault, strong on initiative and he thinks outside the box," Relentless stated, the anger still simmering just under his voice. He didn't bother to correct the insinuation made by Independence. Some may have made a big deal out of that; from Samantha's experience with the man, it only meant that he didn't care what people thought about it, true or otherwise.

"He thought so far out of the box that he somehow helped smuggle the Survivors out of Utopia, when he *had* to know we wanted to get our hands on them." Independence didn't look or sound happy. "Does that sound like loyalty to you?"

"Actually, yes," Transit interjected, clearly intent on building a case for G-Man. Relentless and Independence looked across at her, the latter visibly irritated at the interruption. This didn't seem to bother the artificer/dynamic, who tended to act as a moderating influence within these discussions. "It sounds like loyalty to the Survivors. After all, he met them *before* the interview. After his tussle with those cops at the Market, the Survivors probably asked him for help. That made them put *their* trust in *him*. Which he's since discharged by getting them out of Utopia. Now *we've* effectively put our trust in him by accepting him onto the team. If Relentless is reading him right, G-Man's now loyal to *us*. And if he's gone above and beyond for people he didn't even come here to join, how much more is he going to be willing to do for *us*?"

Silent Knight made several gestures, then thumped the table with his fist. Despite the fact that he used some force to do so, the impact produced barely any sound. Samantha had taken the time to study deaf-mute sign language, on the off-chance that she might be called upon to translate. From what she could understand, he'd just said, *You might be wrong. G might be sleep spy.*

The Technologist nodded sagely. "Our silent friend is correct, of course. If that assessment turns out to be inaccurate, we may well be accepting a sleeper agent into our midst."

"We aren't." Relentless sounded absolutely certain of his conclusion, which to Samantha made it something that could be taken to the bank. "He'll never turn on us. He wants to be a hero too badly."

"But how can you *know* that, boss-man?" Lady Quantum twirled slowly in the air, rotating until she was upside-down, still sitting in the chair. Her cape, draped over the back of the seat, now hung *upward* into the air. "Literally his first public act in costume when he got into town was to go against established authority. Just between us, that's not exactly a heroic thing to do." She held up her hand, finger and thumb barely separated to indicate the level of heroism. "Just saying."

Relentless snorted, clearly choosing to ignore her childish antics. "Remember what we were like before we formed Force Majeure? Respect for authority wasn't exactly something *we* cared about, either." He opened a pouch on his belt. "I didn't want to have to do this, but I can see you won't be convinced otherwise." As Samantha watched, he produced ... a folded piece of paper. She assessed it immediately as printer-quality paper, nothing expensive. Which made whatever was *written* on it the important aspect.

Independence eyed it suspiciously. "What is it?"

Slowly, he opened it up. Samantha could almost see what it was, but his shoulder blocked her view. Exerting every bit of self-control at her disposal, she remained in her seat and did not crane her neck to see what the big secret was. *If Relentless wants me to see what it is, he'll show me.*

"Back in 'ninety-nine, when this was all still the Manhattan Reclamation Project, I sent Ms. Colburn to investigate what looked like a case of incompetence while I carried out an inspection tour of where they were breaking ground for the Spire." Relentless picked out the Technologist and Lady Quantum by eye. "This was the day *before* you two talked the rest of us into calling the city Utopia instead of Bastion."

"Yeah, so?" asked Independence. "I still think Bastion was a better name."

"So, this." Relentless unfolded the piece of paper and flattened it out on the table. The others leaned over to look at it. "This is a copy of a note the foreman in question found pinned to the corkboard in his construction trailer. Samantha called it in, because it had my name on the back. At the time, I had no idea what it meant. To my certain knowledge, the only people who know what's in the note are me, and the person who left it there."

Samantha blinked, trying not to let her eyes go wide with surprise. *I remember that!* The mystery of the note from Ninety-Seven Alpha had stayed with her for the last fourteen years. *Am I going to finally find out what it's all about?* Across the room, she heard Tourbillon let out a barely audible *ahh*. The teleporter, she recalled, had been there as well.

Looking down at the paper, the Technologist tightened his lips in distaste. "That has *got* to be the most execrable handwriting I have ever seen." Reaching up to the goggles he wore, he flicked a couple of lenses in and out. From the expression on his face, it didn't help.

"No shit," Independence said flatly. "It looks like something a three-year-old scribbled out." Reaching out, she pulled the sheet toward her. As she did so, her eyes widened. "What the actual *fuck?*"

"*Trust G-Man*," recited Lady Quantum, still hovering head-down over the table. "*He will save Utopia.*"

There was silence as they stared at the paper. "Wait a moment," objected Tourbillon. "He is to save Utopia from what?"

Relentless shrugged massively. "I don't know."

"How's he even going to save the whole city? It's a big place, in case nobody had noticed." That was Lady Quantum.

"What part of *I don't know* do you have trouble understanding?" Relentless was starting to sound irritated.

Tourbillon spoke up again. "This G-Man, how long has he been active?"

Relentless didn't even bother looking around. "Ms. Colburn?"

Samantha straightened her shoulders as all other eyes turned to her. "Since mid to late two thousand eleven," she said crisply. "There were reports of a black-clad vigilante running the rooftops in Savannah as early as July, but the name and emblem were only confirmed in early September." She'd checked up on the young hero herself, in the course of vetting him for the interview.

"Two years, more or less." Relentless let the words hang in the air for a moment. "I first read the note *fourteen years* ago."

"And you've been sitting on it this long *why*, exactly?" Independence leaned toward him aggressively. "Did you never think we might want to know at some point?"

"G-Man wasn't active, then." Ignoring her attitude, Relentless gestured at the note. "For all I knew, it was a random prank. I didn't really begin to take it seriously until the Technologist and Lady Quantum posited the name Utopia City. Since then, I've been waiting for G-Man himself to make an appearance. This note involves four separate predictions. Two have come true, maybe three."

"Four?" Independence looked at the paper, then at Relentless. "Where do you get four from?"

"Yes, yes, I perceive your meaning," the Technologist interjected. "The names 'Utopia' and 'G-Man' are specifically referenced. Each name is a prediction in and of itself. The other two predictions are about G-Man being trustworthy — which he has shown himself to be — and about him saving Utopia." A thoughtful expression crossed his face. "I *do* understand what you are driving at, yes."

While Samantha was still absorbing the older man's bombshell of information, Relentless nodded heavily. "As we saw in the interview, G-Man has strong issues about trust and betrayal. He's the *one* person not in this room whom I believe could never be coerced, suborned or tricked into acting against us. Whoever wrote this note *knew* of that quality. In fact, they knew more about the future than anyone here.

Which is the main reason I gave him another chance. Until someone can convince me otherwise, G-Man is on the team." Leaning back, he folded his arms, his gaze challenging everyone in the room.

"Okay, fine. He's on the team." Independence glared at him, probably because she had no comeback to that. "So, what about his accomplice? It's not written down anywhere that *she* gets any special dispensation."

"What about her?" Relentless shot back. "I'm not the investigator in this room. Or the tech guy. Why haven't one of *you* pinned her down yet?"

"What, do you mean the mysterious hooded woman whose real name we don't know, whose height, weight, and even age are uncertain, and for whom we've never managed to obtain a workable facial image or voice-print?" interjected the Technologist, his tone cutting. "*That* accomplice?"

Independence's tone was just as aggravated. "She's a goddamn ghost. Every lead I've followed has ended in smoke and mirrors. More than one piece of data that would've helped us nail her down has simply vanished. But she *exists*. We've got imagery of her with the Survivors. We just don't know who she is, where she's from or what her deal is. She's got a very irritating habit of turning her head just before cameras get a good look at her, and that's when the picture *isn't* blurred from the beginning. Worse, nobody ever seems to remember important details about her. Hell, we don't even know if she really is a she. She might be a guy in disguise."

"Or she might be someone we're just not considering." Upside down, Lady Quantum waved a lazy hand at Independence. "Could be you, for instance. You got a hoodie?" She looked at Tourbillon. "Or you. You come pre-hoodied, even."

"Don't look at me," Tourbillon retorted. "You're the one most likely to pull a prank like this."

"Yeah, but whoever it is doesn't have my assets." Lady Quantum smirked, cupping her ample endowment smugly with both hands. "The photos show that much, at least."

"This isn't funny," snapped Independence. "Or are you forgetting how she pulled the Survivors out from under a surveillance umbrella at the cost of seven hexes, and helped G-Man get them out of town? I still say that it was one of them pulling those shenanigans with the MagCards."

"Of *course* it was." The Technologist's voice brooked no disagreement. "Since they escaped the city—and I would give a great deal to know how they achieved *that* feat of legerdemain—there have been no more anomalies."

"Which means that regardless of what we think of them, they're no longer a problem for us." Relentless leaned forward in his chair, a scowl settling on the hard angles of his face. "Unless they're foolish enough to return." He waited a moment, then continued. "In any case, the important thing here, now that G-Man is free of other distractions, is that we give him every reason to do what this note says he's going to do."

"Okay, so he's got immunity unless he does something really egregious." Independence had the tone of someone who just doesn't want to let the matter go. "And we can't get a line on his accomplice if we try to go at her directly. But what about through *him*?" She looked at the Technologist. "Please tell me you've got access to his phone. He's got to have contacted her at *some* point, or vice versa."

The older man shook his head. "Relentless already instructed me to leave his phone untouched. Now I know why."

"What?" Independence looked like someone who'd had the rug pulled out from under her. "Why? Seriously, why? If we're not messing with *him*—"

"Trust is everything," interrupted Relentless. "If we capture her and he finds out we used him as a patsy, he is very likely to see that as a betrayal. We already know his stance on that sort of thing. When the time comes to save Utopia, I don't want him to have even the slightest reason to think twice about it."

"Hey, and what if it's not just him?" Lady Quantum suggested. "The Survivors could be needed to play a part. Hell, his mysterious friend might also have a hand in it. What if they're all needed to assist him in saving Utopia later on? We just don't know." From the grin on her face, she almost certainly didn't believe any of what she was saying, but Samantha knew she enjoyed stirring the pot.

Independence glared up at her. "I *hate* not knowing. What if he saves Utopia, then turns on us anyway?"

Relentless clenched his jaw muscles, no doubt irritated about being forced into a corner. "If that happens, I'll deal with him myself."

"Somehow, I doubt it will ever get that far," mused the Technologist. "Your logic is sound."

"I think so, too," agreed Transit.

Tourbillon and Lady Quantum glanced at each other, then looked at Relentless and nodded; one upside down, the other the right way up.

Silent Knight shrugged and made a few hand gestures which Samantha interpreted as; *I will go along with your decision.*

"'Fine, whatever'," translated the Technologist, somewhat more loosely.

All eyes turned to the last holdout. Independence gave Relentless a calculating look, then skated the sheet back toward him. "So *that's* what your performance at the interview was all about," she said in tones of enlightenment. "You wanted to see if whoever left the note had a time travel power, and if he knew who it was."

I wondered about that, too. Samantha understood once more why Relentless was the leader of Force Majeure. It wasn't a line of inquiry that she would've thought to pursue.

Another massive shrug. "It was worth a shot."

"True." Independence paused for a few seconds longer than normal. She liked to do this occasionally. Samantha had long since surmised that it was an act intended to irritate Relentless. "Well, given all that, I've got less of a problem with him being on the team, so long as he pulls his weight." She seemed oblivious to the play on words.

"Then it's settled." Relentless turned to the Technologist. "I know the note says he *will* save Utopia, but a little insurance is never a bad idea. Do you have anything to help ensure he stays alive long enough to save Utopia from whatever's going to threaten it?"

The artificer rubbed his chin between forefinger and thumb. "His power enhancement harness is showing up rather well in tests. In addition, a recent project of mine has turned up unexpectedly efficacious results. I do believe that I may have something for you sooner rather than later."

"Good." Relentless finished pushing back his chair and stood up. As the heroes of Force Majeure began to filter out of the room—Lady Quantum righting herself and drifting to the floor—Samantha stood as well. Taking up the paper, Relentless turned to her. "Ms. Colburn. File this in my classified section."

"Yes, sir." She accepted the sheet; greatly daring, she cleared her throat. "Sir, may I ask a question? About G-Man?"

He stopped and looked down at her. "That's your job. Ask away."

"Yes, sir." Hastily, she organized her thoughts. "The footage we watched before the interview, of G-Man and his cousin in the Savannah maglev station … if you were always going to sponsor him, why did you not caution him then about risking his secret identity?"

He nodded to acknowledge the query. "He was willing to put his heroic career on the line to help save the child of someone he didn't know, who would cross the street to avoid contact with his cousin. That speaks to a level of selflessness I rarely see, even among heroes. If he is ever outed, and someone threatens to use that knowledge against him, I will come down on them like the wrath of God. But until that day comes, I will do nothing to discourage this kind of heroic behavior. Do you understand?"

Slowly, she nodded. That was the Relentless she knew; ruthlessly pragmatic, but always with a deeper motive. "Yes, sir. Thank you, sir."

As he left the room, she looked down at the paper she held, then carefully folded it along the pre-existing creases. The handwriting was indeed appalling, but the message it contained was just as world-shaking as when she'd first heard the words.

G-Man, it seemed, was far more than he first appeared. She decided she would be following the young man's career with the utmost interest.

- The End -

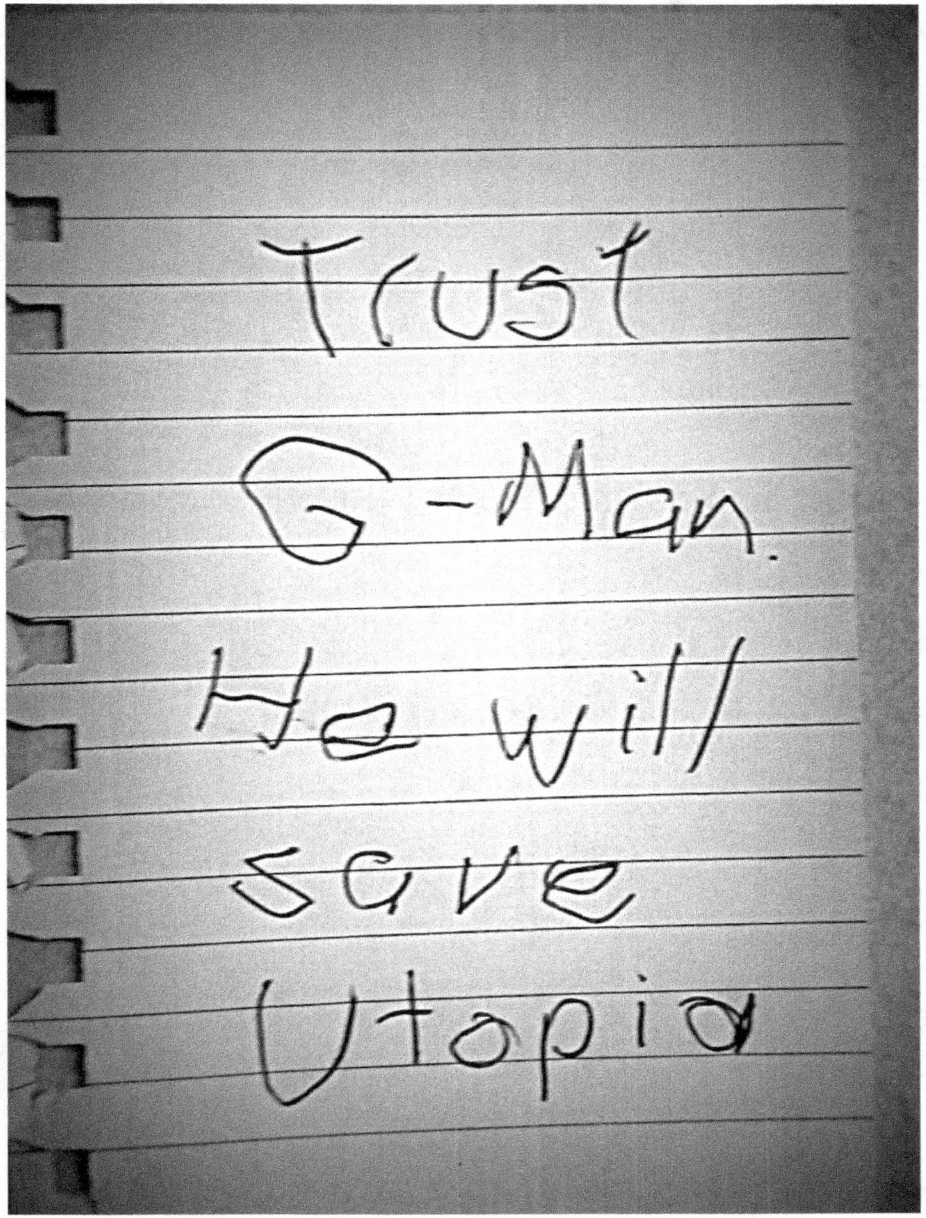

Trust
G-Man.
He will
save
Utopia

Jericho Hansen will return in

Book Two of the UTOPIAN DREAMS series:

Shadows Over Utopia.

Glossary

(This glossary specifically excludes real-world places and things mentioned in the story. You'll have to look those up for yourself.)

artificer: An *Enabled* who constructs devices or items more quickly and efficiently than would normally be possible. Advanced technology is often involved. The term can be used as an adjective (and is capitalized when doing so) or a noun. (Examples: "I have an Artificer rating"; "I am an artificer".) See also: *cog*.

Bat-family: Taken from popular culture, this refers to an Enabled team made up entirely of *prodigies*. Less well known than the *Inspire team* concept, the idea enjoys a certain amount of popularity in areas where prodigies outnumber other powersets.

Blood Rose: Horrific Artificer weapon once carried by the *Minotaur* (see: **Enabled Teams and Others**). Ironically, it was partially responsible for his death. Has been survived, but by very few people. *Relentless* carries scarring from it.

cape: Popular slang for *dynamic*.

Challenger Act: Legislation created by the United States government to prevent the civilian identities of heroic Enabled from being casually uncovered. Government-affiliated superheroes have much more stringent protections than independent heroes, though the latter are protected as well. Deliberately unmasking a government-affiliated Enabled is equivalent to releasing nuclear launch codes or the names of undercover assets in foreign countries. Doing the same to an independent hero will draw charges of domestic terrorism. The legislation in question is based on 18 U.S. Code § 794: *"Gathering or delivering defense information to aid foreign government."*

Challenger Plaza: A circular paved area one thousand feet across, outside the *Spire* in *Utopia City*. It possesses a fountain, picnic tables with automatically adjusting umbrellas, and a hovering double-sized statue of *Challenger* (see: **Enabled Teams and Others**).

circuit: In-house term for the concentric circular corridors in the *Spire*. In addition, a casual term for the streets of *Utopia City* that run in circular paths around the city center. More specifically, it's a descriptor for anything that runs all the way around the city at a particular distance from the Spire, such as *the Greenway*. See also: *radial*.

cog: Popular slang for *artificer*.

CogWars: A game played on smartphones and tablets, where the player is an artificer in a post-apocalyptic scenario, building a fortress and defending it against other artificers.

cowl: Popular slang for *prodigy*.

Designated Liaison: A member of the Utopia City PD whose job is to handle situations where knowledge of a hero's secret identity will clear up confusion at a crime scene. They are always accompanied by at least one Enabled bodyguard.

Dipper: Slang for *DPR*. Does *not* stand for 'double dipper'.

DPR: Stands for 'Dual Power Rating'; used to describe an *Enabled* with two different *ratings*. See also: *Dipper* and *TPR*.

dynamic: An *Enabled* with overt superpowers (e.g. flight, super-strength, telekinesis). The term can be used as an adjective (and is capitalized when doing so) or a noun. (Examples: "I have a Dynamic rating"; "I am a dynamic".) See also: *cape*.

Enabled: (noun) A person with superhuman capabilities; (adj) the state of having superhuman capabilities. See also: *Mask*.

Enabler Boson: A theoretical subatomic particle that only interacts with the nervous systems of sapient beings (such as humans) during times of extreme stress. This interaction leads to the person becoming *Enabled*.

focus: An aspect of the *Prodigy* powerset that allows the Enabled to surpass his or her human limits even further than normal, under certain circumstances. See also: *sweet spot*.

Gordoning: (verb) The act of (a police officer) unofficially sharing case files with a superhero. Example: "He Gordoned me with everything on the Reilly case." See also: *Trevoring*.

Greenway, the: A park in *Utopia City*. Half a mile wide, it straddles the fifteen-mile *circuit* and goes all the way around the city, for a total area of 47 square miles. The freeway (Interstate 70) is diverted under it, rather than go over the top.

Hansen News: The Hansen family business in Savannah. Currently run by *Beau Hansen* (see: **Dramatis Personae**).

Inspire team: A superhero team containing at least one artificer, one dynamic and one prodigy, patterned after the eponymous superhero team. A 'classic' Inspire team has one of each, all with a *straight rating*. Conventional wisdom considers a team to be lacking if they don't have all three powersets represented, at least in part. While some have managed to defy this, most teams go with the Inspire model, mainly because it works. The most popular alternate to the Inspire team is the *Bat-family*.

invested, fully invested: Term to describe wearing power armor in such a way that has the arms and legs extending into the limbs. The opposite of 'piloted'.

MagCard: High-tech card used to travel on the *maglev* all over the continental United States. Also, the official medium for all transactions conducted within *Utopia City*.

maglev: Cheap, clean, fast, popular rapid-transit system that covers the continental United States (including Alaska, via a spur line through Canada), with its primary hub in *Utopia City* and secondary hubs in major cities. Utilizes magnetic levitation, stabilized by gravity generators, to move its passenger cars at up to 600 mph (average 400). Operated by *Utopia Maglev Lines*.

Manhattan Reclamation Project: Original name for the rebuilding effort that culminated in the construction of *Utopia City*.

Mask: (noun) Popular slang for a member of the *Enabled*.

Memorial Park: A park in *Utopia City*, set up to commemorate the lives of those killed in the blast that destroyed Manhattan, Kansas. There are 91,473 names on the memorial walls within the park.

mobility frame: A lightweight, low-powered exoskeleton designed to allow people with limited mobility to live normal lives with a minimum of outside assistance. Produced by *PowerTech Industries* and others. The higher quality ones utilize *neural induction*.

neural induction: Technology perfected by *Adam Power* (see: **Dramatis Personae**) with two major applications. The first is to allow users of *mobility frames* and power armor to move and feel as though the device they are operating is a part of them via *synthetic proprioception*. The second application is to project important data directly on to the user's visual field via a *NID*. It requires direct contact (either via bare skin or through a light bodysuit) to work properly.

NID: Neuro-Induction Display; the use of *neural induction* to replace heads-up display technology. Allows for direct mental command of secondary systems.

nine-twenty: Shorthand for September 20, 1999; the date of the nuclear destruction of Manhattan, Kansas. Also refers to the anniversary of the date, where friends and relatives of the victims converge on *Memorial Park* and leave cards and trinkets in remembrance for their loved ones.

Oaklands: Oaklands Temporary Accommodation. A complex in *Utopia City* containing a number of short-stay self-contained apartments. Quite comfortable, if a little cramped.

Power Plaza: Fortified base in Chicago, housing *Team Power* (see: **Enabled Teams and Others**). Built and secured by *Adam Power* (see: **Dramatis Personae**).

PowerTech Industries: Company owned and operated by *Adam Power* (see: **Dramatis Personae**).

privacy bubble: An example of Force Majeure's technology. When activated, it produces a soundproofed zone in a three-foot radius sphere around the device. They are free to use on the *maglev* and have been marketed for use around the world.

prodigy: An *Enabled* whose normal human capabilities have been pushed up to eleven. There is a tendency to brood on rooftops. The term can be used as an adjective (and is capitalized when doing so) or a noun. (Examples: "I have a Prodigy rating"; "I am a prodigy".) See also: *cowl*.

radial: In-house term for the straight corridors that radiate out from the core of the *Spire*. In addition, a casual term for the streets of *Utopia City* that run from the city center outward toward the edge of the map. See also: *circuit*.

rating: The type of powerset that an *Enabled* has. There are three ratings; *Artificer*, *Dynamic* and *Prodigy*.

Proximity Principle: An effect that can take place when an Enabled gains powers, patterning them after another nearby Enabled rather than starting fresh. Many junior sidekicks get their start in this fashion. (Note: there is a secondary aspect to this, not covered in this book).

Rover: Four-legged semi-autonomous medical transport robot; 4' high and 7' long.

scan-lock: Short for 'scanning airlock'. Six feet wide and twelve feet deep, these are used by both *UML* and *Force Majeure* (see: **Enabled Teams and Others**) to analyze people and items entering their facilities.

South Side Mall: Shopping mall on the southern side of *Utopia City*. The largest in the world by far (with eighteen floors and nearly two hundred million square feet of space), it services a large portion of the city as well as the offramp traffic from Interstate 70.

Southside Parking: Huge parking structure that allows anyone coming in off Interstate 70 to gain access to the *South Side Mall*. It is half a mile north of *the Greenway*.

Southsiders: Non-Enabled criminal gang in *Utopia City* which handles contraband going in and out of the city, mainly via Interstate 70. They have people all the way through *Southside Parking*.

Spire, the: Tallest building in the world, and central point of *Utopia City*. Nearly eight thousand feet tall. Home base for *Force Majeure* (see: **Enabled Teams and Others**).

straight (rating): Slang for an *Enabled* who has a single *rating*, such as *Artificer* or *Dynamic*. See also: *DPR* and *TPR*.

super-first: Shorthand for 'super first class', referring to the practice by some airline companies of offering their patrons ludicrous levels of attention on board the flight, to lure them away from the *maglev*.

sweet spot: Another way to refer to the area of a prodigy's *focus*.

synthetic proprioception: The technical term for using *neural induction* technology to establish a feedback loop with *mobility frames*, power armor and the like. Users 'feel' sensory data directly, allowing for much faster reactions. This makes learning to use such equipment easier and quicker.

tier: Relative power level scale for comparison of one *Enabled* with another. Very much an abstract metric.

TPR: Stands for Triple Power Rating; refers to a theoretical *Enabled* with three separate power *Ratings*. No known examples; thought by some to be impossible. See also: *DPR*.

Trevoring: (verb) The act of assisting a superhero in the hopes of becoming romantically involved with them. Example: "Can't she see he's just Trevoring her?" See also: *Gordoning*.

Tuttle Creek Lake Hydroponics Project: An area of interest in *Utopia City*.

UCIAT: Pronounced 'you-see-it'. Acronym for *Utopia City Institute for Advanced Technology*.

UML: See *Utopia Maglev Lines*.

Unmask: An extremely vocal anti-secret-identity activist group extant from the late 1980s to the mid-1990s. Used methods that ranged from the unethical to the blatantly illegal. They were the direct cause of *Surgeon One* ending up as *Mutilator* and the (semi) voluntary unmasking of *Team Power* (see: **Enabled Teams and Others**). Ceased to exist in any meaningful fashion after the

Challenger Act was finalized in 1997, and several key members were successfully prosecuted on domestic terrorism charges.

Utopia City: A metropolis built on the ruins of Manhattan, Kansas after that city's accidental destruction by *Doc Iridium* in 1999. Home base of *Force Majeure* (see: **Enabled Teams and Others**). Most technologically advanced city in the world. Only tourists and city officials use the full name; locals just call it 'Utopia'.

Utopia City Institute for Advanced Technology: Called *UCIAT* for short. The waiting list to get in is longer than for any other learning institution in the nation. Works up prototypes for *Transit* and the *Technologist* (see: **Dramatis Personae**).

Utopia Maglev Lines: Usually abbreviated to *UML*. The subsidiary company that manages the *maglev* system.

War on Terror Villains: The dramatic name applied by the media to the campaign by the US government to destroy the terror villains of the 90's. Implemented via Presidential Executive Order on January 31, 1997. Rescinded by another Executive Order on March 15 of the same year, shortly after the signatory President and his immediate successor were killed in retaliation for the March 7 death of *Carnifex* (see: **Enabled Teams and Others**).

Zarkinator: Energy rifle favored by *Gimmick* (see: **Dramatis Personae**). Fires a very high-powered beam. Named after the sound of it being fired.

Dramatis Personae

(All notes accurate as of the beginning of this book. This only includes characters who have had actual screen time and/or are currently extant. No spoilers included.)

All-Star (civilian identity unknown): New York based Enabled with Dynamic and Prodigy ratings. Male. Early 20's, handsome, well-built, blond hair, piercing blue eyes. Wears spandex and a cape in patriotic colors. Aspiring to join *Manhattan Justice* (see: **Enabled Teams and Others**). Relatively new to the Enabled scene.

Bakersfield, Graham: Foreman on grid reference FC/97A of the *Manhattan Reclamation Project* (see: **Glossary**).

Black Dragon (civilian identity unknown): Teenage girl, dynamic, mid-length blonde hair, possibly between 14 and 16 years of age (claims 18). Can partially or fully turn into a dragon of the same size. Aspiring to join *Force Majeure* (see: **Enabled Teams and Others**). Foul mouthed, distinct attitude.

Blades (civilian identity unknown): Member of the *Survivors* (see: **Enabled Teams and Others**). Teenage blonde girl with short ponytail. Wears power armor that has roller-blade style wheels built into its feet.

Brock, Gary: Popular comedian who does humorous routines about modern life. 'Walking from New York to LA' pokes fun at *maglev* travel (see: **Glossary**).

Chandler, Dr Meredith: Head of Surgery in the medical section of the *Spire* (see: **Glossary**). Late 30's, faded blue eyes, hair color uncertain.

Colburn, Samantha: Executive assistant to Relentless. Very serious about her duties. Currently in her mid-fifties.

Crocodilian (civilian identity unknown): New York dynamic. Male. Turns into a humanoid alligator. Has clashed with *Troll*. Aspiring to join *Manhattan Justice* (see: **Enabled Teams and Others**).

Cyberswarm (civilian identity unknown): Late teens or early 20's. Male artificer. Can control a swarm of tiny spiderbots that act as armor or weapons. Aspiring to join *Force Majeure* (see: **Enabled Teams and Others**).

Drone (First name Conrad, last name unknown): Male artificer, member of *Manhattan Justice* (see: **Enabled Teams and Others**). Utilizes numerous drones that he controls with his suit. Handsome, dark curly hair, pencil mustache, early 30's.

Finlay, Sergeant Diane: Switch room operator in the Utopia City Police Department. Also works as a *Designated Liaison* (see: **Glossary**).

Fly Boy (civilian identity unknown): Gay superhero based in Augusta, Georgia. Beaten up after *Luke Hansen* caught him with *Stephen LaMonde*.

Forrester, Detective (first name unknown): Undercover officer with the UCPD. Partnered with *Detective Charles Gleeson*. Balding, with black hair and a ratty vanDyke beard.

Foster, Sergeant (first name unknown): Female Chicago police officer in 2011. Faded blonde hair, careworn expression.

Franklin (last name unknown): Skinny male, resident of Savannah. Age uncertain, has unshaven chin and drooping mustache. Strong views about gun ownership.

G-Man (civilian identity *Jericho Hansen*): Prodigy/dynamic with gravity control. Wears a black costume with knife-proofing, spandex gliding wings and a white 'G' on the back. Aspiring to join *Force Majeure* (see: **Enabled Teams and Others**). While in costume, deliberately deepens his voice to further conceal his identity.

Gimmick (civilian identity unknown): Member of the *Survivors* (see: **Enabled Teams and Others**). Asian girl, about 16 years old. Artificer who can analyze how other tech works with ease. She specializes in building hand-held devices, but she can repair, subvert and alter larger items. Favorite weapon is the *Zarkinator* (see: **Glossary**).

Gleeson, Detective Charles: Undercover officer with the UCPD. Partnered with *Detective Forrester*. Sandy haired.

Hansen, Beauregard (Beau): Married to *Dahlia Hansen*, father to *Jericho Hansen*, brother to *Leroy Hansen*, uncle to *Luke* and *Serena Hansen*. Heavy-set and a little overweight. 45 years old; runs *Hansen News* (see: **Glossary**).

Hansen, Dahlia: Married to *Beau Hansen*, mother to *Jericho Hansen*, aunt to *Luke* and *Serena Hansen*. Tall and slender; 45 years old. Very no-nonsense. Runs a law firm in Atlanta, Georgia. An accomplished poker player.

Hansen, Ellie: Married to *Leroy Hansen*, mother to *Luke Hansen* and *Serena Hansen*. African American. Aunt to *Jericho Hansen*. 45 years old. Sister to *Daryl West*.

Hansen, Jericho (Enabled identity *G-Man*): Son of *Beau* and *Dahlia Hansen*, cousin and best friend to *Luke* and *Serena Hansen*, nephew to *Leroy* and *Ellie Hansen*. Romantically linked to *Stephen LaMonde*. 6'2" tall, shoulder length dark brown hair, slim and wiry. 23 years old.

Hansen, Leroy: Married to *Ellie Hansen*, father to *Luke* and *Serena Hansen*, brother to *Beau Hansen*, uncle to *Jericho Hansen*. Heavily built, 45 years old. Has fingers in more than few pies in the Savannah underworld.

Hansen, Luke: Married to *Olivia Hansen*, cousin and best friend to *Jericho Hansen*. African American. Smartass. Son of *Leroy* and *Ellie Hansen*, brother to *Serena Hansen*. 6'1" tall, kinked black hair, solidly built. 28 years old. Works as a mechanic. Has friends in low places. Changes the way he talks depending on the company he's in.

Hansen, Olivia (Livy): Married to *Luke Hansen*. African American. Has long beautiful black hair. 25 years old.

Hansen, Serena: Sister to *Luke Hansen*, daughter to *Leroy* and *Ellie Hansen*, niece to *Beau* and *Dahlia Hansen*, cousin to *Jericho Hansen*. African American. Attending college in New York City. Being groomed to take over *Hansen News* (see: **Glossary**) when Beau retires. 24 years old.

Helena (last name unknown): Well-attired woman in her 40's. Night receptionist at the *Oaklands* (see: **Glossary**).

Independence (civilian identity unknown): Core member of *Force Majeure* (see: **Enabled Teams and Others**). Athletic woman, platinum-blonde hair worn in long ponytail, wears costume in muted red and blue. Prodigy. Carries a claymore and an assault rifle. Abrasive personality.

Joey (last name unknown): One of two teenagers who witnessed and filmed an attack by the *Madness* (see: **Enabled Teams and Others**) on the State Capitol building in Tallahassee, Florida. Saved by *Relentless* and removed from the scene by *Tomahawk*.

Johnson (first name unknown): Male tech working in the *Spire* (see: **Glossary**).

Lady Quantum (civilian identity unknown): Core member of *Force Majeure* (see: **Enabled Teams and Others**). Stunningly beautiful woman with raven-black hair. Dynamic. Well-endowed; wears spandex costume cut to show her figure off to its best advantage. Also wears a cape. Can fly and protect herself with a force field. Given to whimsy.

LaMonde, Stephen: Romantically linked to *Jericho Hansen*. 5'4" tall, carefully styled red hair and beard. Overweight. 31 years old. Overly clingy. Does not want Jericho to join *Force Majeure* (see: **Enabled Teams and Others**). Produces webzine called *Gay!Power*.

Marni (last name unknown): *Smokeshadow's* sister. Being treated for lymphoma; resident of Ohio.

McKendrick (first name unknown): Officer in the Savannah PD. Brother-in-law to *Bobby O'Dowd*.

Nighthawk (civilian identity unknown): African American Enabled woman with hard-bitten attitude. Member of *Force Majeure* (see: **Enabled Teams and Others**). Partnered with *Stage Act*. Once involved in a legal case regarding her heroic codename.

O'Dowd, Bobby: Resident of Savannah, Georgia. Brother-in-law to Officer *McKendrick*, Savannah PD.

Photonic Avenger, the (civilian identity unknown): Member of the *Survivors* (see: **Enabled Teams and Others**). Red-haired boy, about 15 years old. Can project a photon-flash and other light-based effects (as well as EMP). Also able to levitate slowly from place to place, and see both UV light and magnetic fields.

Pickup (civilian identity unknown): Male artificer; hero based in Savannah. Drives a considerably modified pickup truck with the Confederate flag painted on the hood, which turns into a twenty-foot tall piloted robot. The robot is equipped with various pickup-truck accessories.

Portman, Jack: Romantically linked to *Bobbi Reynolds*. 5'11" tall, medium build. Black hair, fair skin. Short tempered.

Power, Adam (Enabled name and civilian name): Co-leader and co-founder of *Team Power* (See: **Enabled Teams and Others**). Artificer with several specialties. Married to *Tesseract Power*, father to *Vanessa Power* and *Buddy Power*. Tall, handsome, blond, distinguished good looks. Early 40's. Based in Chicago.

Power, Buddy (Enabled name and civilian name): Member of *Team Power* (see: **Enabled Teams and Others**). Red-haired, 11 years old. Son of *Adam Power* and *Tesseract Power*, brother to *Vanessa Power*. Unpowered, wears power armor designed by his father.

Power, Tesseract (Enabled name and civilian name): Co-founder and co-leader of *Team Power* (see: **Enabled Teams and Others**). Prodigy. Tall, statuesque, striking redhead. Married to *Adam Power*, mother to *Vanessa Power* and *Buddy Power*.

Based in Chicago.

Power, Vanessa (Enabled name and civilian name): Member of *Team Power* (see: **Enabled Teams and Others**). Red-haired, strong features. Has her mother's looks. Missing since age 16, nearly two years ago; status unknown. Daughter of *Adam Power* and *Tesseract Power*, sister to *Buddy Power*. Unpowered. When she went missing, she was wearing power armor designed by her father.

Razor-Edge (AKA 'Ray'; civilian identity unknown): Member of the *Survivors* (see: **Enabled Teams and Others**). Tall, lanky, white-blond hair. Can grow bony plates all over his body, covered in hooks and spurs and blades. Much stronger and more durable when thus affected.

Relentless (civilian identity unknown): Leader and core member of *Force Majeure* (see: **Enabled Teams and Others**). Male, 6'6" tall, very broad in the shoulders, wears black armor with silver trim, as well as a cape. Has a mace which returns to him when thrown. Extremely durable, very strong. Brusque attitude. Deep voice.

Reynolds, Roberta (Bobbi): Pretty, blonde woman from Indianapolis. 30 years old. Dynamic, with emotion-sensing and emotion-affecting powers. Sister to *Melody Reynolds*. Romantically linked to *Jack Portman*. Hopes that *Force Majeure* (see: **Enabled Teams and Others**) can help her get her abilities under control so that she can clear *Adam Power* of sexual assault allegations made by his daughter *Vanessa Power*.

Reynolds, Melody: Sister to *Bobbi Reynolds*. No known powers. Native of Indianapolis. Supportive of her sister.

Richardson, Sergeant (first name unknown): Female desk sergeant for the UCPD. Late middle aged, still fit. Red hair, going gray.

Richie (last name unknown): Child saved by *Luke* and *Jericho Hansen* on the platform of the Savannah *maglev* station (see: **Glossary**).

Second Chance: Heavy-set man in his early 30's. Can generate a force field bubble and apply various effects through it. Wears a bulletproof vest and SWAT gear. Member of *Force Majeure* (see: **Enabled Teams and Others**).

Sidestep (civilian identity unknown): Youngest member of the *Survivors* (see: **Enabled Teams and Others**). 13-year-old boy. Can create a duplicate of himself, and communicate (and teleport items) between the duplicates.

Silent Knight (civilian identity unknown): Core Member of *Force Majeure* (see: **Enabled Teams and Others**). Male artificer specializing in extreme life-support systems. Maintains his own armor (glossy black, based off medieval plate), which is so thoroughly enclosed that he cannot communicate vocally.

Smokeshadow (first name Chelsea, last name unknown): Woman in her mid-20's with mousy brown hair. Prodigy with a minor Artificer rating; able to read and utilize body language to an extreme degree. Also good at hiding and sneaking. Wears a costume made of programmable hyperweave and carries other devices that she uses to augment her Prodigy capabilities. Apparent level of attractiveness changes, depending on her needs. More concerned with morality than legality. Sister to *Marni*.

Splendid (first name Nina, last name unknown): Female dynamic, mid-20's. Member of *Manhattan Justice* (see: **Enabled Teams and Others**). Quite good-looking, blonde hair. Manifests golden hard-light wings that let her fly.

Stacey (last name unknown): Pretty girl, in her 20's. Morning receptionist at the *Oaklands* (see: **Glossary**).

Stage Act (civilian identity unknown): Male Enabled with outgoing, friendly attitude. Member of *Force Majeure* (see: **Enabled Teams and Others**). Partnered with *Nighthawk*.

Stirling, Detective Sergeant (first name unknown): Older man, heavy-set with a greying beard. Member of the UCPD.

Technologist, the (civilian identity unknown): Core member of *Force Majeure* (see: **Enabled Teams and Others**). Older man; wears stylized lab wear, re-purposed as a costume. Artificer who creates technology in advance of other artificers, and can improve technology built by others. Acerbic, especially in the face of ignorance shown by others.

Thomas (last name unknown): 6'2" tall, husky build, attractively tousled black hair. Late teens to early 20's. Friendly and outgoing. Leader of the *Survivors* (see: **Enabled Teams and Others**).

Thompson, Eliza: Medical tech working for the Utopia City morgue.

Tomahawk (civilian identity unknown): Male artificer based in Tallahassee, Florida. Wears flying power armor patterned after military missiles.

Tourbillon (civilian identity unknown): Core member of *Force Majeure* (see: **Enabled Teams and Others**). Androgynous, average height. Preferred gender: they/them. Wears a robe in charcoal-gray with a black gem centered on their forehead. A dynamic who creates teleport portals in the form of a dark cloudy swirl in the air. Speaks with a French accent. (Note: 'Tourbillon' is French for 'swirl' or 'whirlpool', related to the English word 'turbulence'.)

Transit (civilian identity unknown): Core member of *Force Majeure* (see: **Enabled Teams and Others**). Female; wears a red and silver flight suit with attached gadgets and a helmet with reflective faceplate. Dual power rating: Artificer with a focus on vehicles, and dynamic with mechanokinesis. Friendly and outgoing.

Troll (civilian identity unknown): Male prodigy. Member of *Manhattan Justice* (see: **Enabled Teams and Others**). 5'3" tall, almost 3' across the shoulders. Extremely well-muscled, covered in scars. Long brown hair, gray eyes, extremely blunt (to the point of rudeness). Has clashed with *Crocodilian*.

Troy (last name unknown): One-time decoy for a gang of gay bashers in Savannah.

Villanova, Raul: Gay male police detective in Savannah, Georgia. Secretly interested in G-Man. (See: **Glossary** [*Trevoring*])

Wavefront (civilian identity unknown): Male dynamic with hydrokinetic powers, based in Tallahassee, FL. Aspiring to join *Force Majeure* (see: **Enabled Teams and Others**). Well-built, wears blue and green spandex. Pushy.

Weatherby, Mike: News announcer for WCTV News in Tallahassee, Florida.

West, Daryl: Younger brother to *Ellie Hansen*. African American. 35 years old, heavily built.

Timeline of Events

1945:   Francis John Hansen ('Great-granddaddy Frank') musters out of US Navy and marries his girlfriend Kathryn Marchant ('Great-gran'maw Kate'). Starts up a news distribution service with his severance pay.

1947:   Joseph Francis Hansen ('Papaw Joe') born in Savannah, Georgia.

1966:   Joe Hansen marries Penelope Smith ('Mamaw Penny'). He is conscripted to go to Vietnam.

1967:   Joe Hansen killed in Vietnam three weeks before his twin sons Beau and Leroy are born. Penny Hansen and her sons taken in by her father-in-law.

1979:   Roberta "Bobbi" Reynolds born, Des Moines.

1984:   Leroy Hansen (17) gets his girlfriend Ellie West pregnant during Spring Break, and promptly marries her in Vegas, against his grandfather's wishes. He is cut off from the family.

1985:   Luke Hansen born, January 7. He spends the first nine years of his life living in near poverty.

1986:   January 28: Challenger incident. The first ever incidence of an Enabled. The crew of the space shuttle Challenger are taken into protective custody by the government, while the dynamic known as Challenger is revealed to the public as the very first superhero. The first iteration of the Challenger Act is put into law by an emergency sitting of Congress. Rulings are immediately sought against it via the Supreme Court.

April 26: Chernobyl disaster. (This leads to the walking radioactive catastrophe called Cherenkov.)

Late 1986: The Supreme Court rules in favor of the Challenger Act.

1987:   The radical activist group Unmask is formed in response to the growing numbers of masked Enabled in society.

Beau Hansen meets Dahlia Romano at college in New York.

1988:   The world's first officially recognized superhero team is formed, called Inspire. Original members are Challenger and a British artificer named

Arfogwyr (Welsh for 'armor'). They are based in Seattle in a high-tech base called Caerwyn ('White Castle'), with the blessing of the US government.

Beau and Dahlia Hansen are married.

1989:   First appearance of the Minotaur—a villain who kidnaps people and puts them through murder mazes on live TV. He extorts ransoms, but often does not honor them.

Serena Hansen born, November 11.

1990:   The terror villain Charnel is captured by Adam Power (artificer) and Tesseract (prodigy) and put on trial by the US government. In retaliation, the Minotaur kidnaps the family of the US Attorney General, along with those of several of his subordinates from the Department of Justice, Criminal Division. They are placed in a murder maze, where it is announced they will be released if Charnel is let go. Charnel is broken out of maximum-security holding by other terror villains and the murder maze is blown up, killing all hostages.

Jericho Hansen born, May 3.

1991:   Inspire encounters the Prodigy hero Castellan while breaking up a violent Unmask protest action. Impressed by his capabilities, they recruit him. Arfogwr builds armour and weapons for him to use.

1993:   An extremist group of Unmask activists abducts Surgeon One's family and forces her to commit atrocities with her skills. She seems to enjoy it far too much. When the videotape is released, her reputation and career are ruined. While still under investigation, she vanishes from the public eye. Later, she reappears as the terror villain Mutilator. She is soon joined by Devastator, a powerful dynamic. They form an unholy partnership.

1994:   A second attempt to overturn the Challenger Act is begun, pushed by Unmask (citing the 'instability' of Surgeon One/Mutilator, and calling for transparency and accountability from the Enabled heroes).

Members of Unmask get pictures of Tesseract's face by trickery and attempt to blackmail her and Adam Power into performing criminal acts. The couple turn the tables on the blackmailers by gathering evidence, changing their names by deed poll, and publicly outing themselves before arresting the perpetrators and turning them over to the police. They announce the formation of Team Power and marry soon thereafter.

Jericho's great-granddaddy Frank Hansen passes away at the age of 73. Beau Hansen takes over the reins of Hansen News and reaches out to Leroy and his family. Jericho and Luke Hansen meet for the first time and form a firm friendship.

1995: The Supreme Court finds in favor of the Challenger Act for a second time; the protocols are broadened to prevent another Surgeon One event from happening. A third challenge is mounted immediately, this time by big business.

Kate and Penny Hansen are killed in a car accident.

Vanessa Power born, September 23.

1997: The Minotaur attacks the newly elected Vice President's motorcade on January 25 and kidnaps the VP, placing him in a murder maze. A ransom is paid, but he dies anyway. The President signs an Executive Order stating that all terror villains must be pursued and engaged with the highest level of lethal force available; the 'War on Terror Villains'.

The terror villain Carnifex is killed in Dallas on March 7.

The President is killed by the Minotaur in the White House Situation Room, March 14. The Vice President is immediately sequestered in the Presidential bunker and sworn in as President, then dictates a statement that the US will not bow to terrorism. He is found dead along with his security detachment, and a mocking note from the terror villain False Flag.

The newly sworn-in President (previously the VP) rescinds the Executive Order.

Inspire begins to close in on the Minotaur, scouting out his murder mazes and rescuing the victims.

In July, the Minotaur attacks Arfogwyr in her civilian identity and kills her. He uses her head and hand to gain access to Caerwyn. After setting explosives to destroy the base, he attacks and severely injures Challenger. Castellan tracks him down to his murder maze and they fight. The Minotaur takes a mortal wound from his own Artificer weapon and falls into the ocean under the rubble of his collapsing murder maze. Castellan makes it out and recovers from his injuries, but Challenger is in a coma; Inspire is finished. Retiring as a superhero, Castellan disappears from public life.

The Supreme Court upholds the Challenger Act for the third time. Several businessmen who were pushing the case are investigated and indicted for questionable activities with overseas interests. High-ranking members of Unmask are indicted under domestic terrorism charges.

Team Power engages the terror villain Kraken in Lake Michigan. Kraken's squid-sub sinks, taking the Artificer villain with it (and nearly Adam Power as well). Other terror villains disappear or are found dead around this time.

1998: In response to ever greater atrocities by terror villains; newcomer heroes Relentless, Independence, the Technologist, Transit, Silent Knight, Lady Quantum and Tourbillon form Force Majeure. They go after the villains brutally and without quarter. In July and October, they take down Charnel and Singularity, respectively.

1999: The members of Force Majeure kick their efforts into high gear, engaging and killing False Flag, Guillotine, Raider, and Mutilator and Devastator. By August, only one terror villain is left: Doc Iridium.

September 15: Terror villain Doc Iridium threatens on live TV to 'blow up Manhattan' in one week if Force Majeure are not immediately arrested and executed. He also demands one billion dollars.

September 16: Force Majeure surrender themselves to the FBI.

September 20: Doc Iridium's bomb explodes prematurely during a live broadcast of his ranting. Manhattan, Kansas is destroyed, killing 91,473 people (as well as Doc Iridium himself).

Force Majeure offers their services to the US government to clean up and rehabilitate the site of the explosion. They are presented with the devastated land, which they decontaminate, then begin to construct Utopia City on the same site.

2002: Buddy Power is born.

Terrorists attempt to crash planes into the Pentagon and the White House, but countermeasures put in place to protect against terror villains prove adequate to the task.

2004: Challenger passes away in care without ever waking up. A national day of mourning is announced.

2005: Vanessa Power debuts as a full member of Team Power, at the age of ten.

Manhattan Justice is formed in New York. Members are Drone, Splendid and Troll.

2011: Jericho turns twenty-one in college in New York and loses his virginity to his roommate on the same night. Returns to Savannah and goes to a gay bar, where he is lured to the top of a nearby building by a man called Troy. Troy's friends are waiting, and they throw Jericho off the roof. In the terror of the moment, he gains powers of gravity manipulation. He hides them at first. When he approaches his parents, they assume that he's trying to tell them he's gay, and assure him that they've known for years. Ends up not telling them, but confides in his cousin Luke. Drops out of college so he can track down the gay bashers; is given an entry-level position in Hansen News.

First appearance of Jericho as G-Man, in September.

December 17: Vanessa Power runs away from home. PowerTech Industries begins to lose its market share as Team Power concentrates its efforts in finding her, to no avail.

2012:   April 2: G-Man is interviewed by Stephen LaMonde, owner of the webzine *Gay!Power*. They end up dating.

Thinkster, a Savannah dynamic with the power of reading minds, passes away from a drug overdose.

2013:   Bobbi Reynolds is cheated on, dumps her boyfriend and gains empathic powers. These threaten to ruin her relationship with her new boyfriend, Jack Portman.

September: Buddy Power debuts as a full member of Team Power.

A leaked police report indicates that Vanessa Power accused her father of attempted rape before she ran away from home. Protestors start gathering outside Power Plaza, in Chicago.

October 6: Jericho Hansen decides to travel to Utopia City to interview for membership in Force Majeure, against the express wishes of his boyfriend. At the same time, Bobbi Reynolds travels from Indianapolis to Chicago to attend a Team Power press conference. Convinced of Adam Power's innocence, she opts to take the maglev directly to Utopia City.

Enabled Teams and Others

(All notes accurate as of the beginning of this book. No spoilers included.)

Force Majeure
Based in Utopia City. Extant since 1998. Dozens of subsidiary members, seven core members:
>**Relentless** (Dynamic, possible prodigy. Leader)
>**Independence** (Prodigy. Second in command)
>**Lady Quantum** (Dynamic)
>**Silent Knight** (Artificer)
>**the Technologist** (Artificer)
>**Tourbillon** (Dynamic)
>**Transit** (Artificer/dynamic)

>*Named subsidiary members:*
>**Nighthawk** (Prodigy)
>**Second Chance** (Dynamic)
>**Stage Act** (Probable dynamic)

Inspire
Based in Seattle. Extant from 1988-1997. The world's first official superhero team.
>**Challenger** (Dynamic. World's first Enabled. Passed away, 2004)
>**Arfogwyr** (Artificer. Killed by *the Minotaur*, 1997)
>**Castellan** (Prodigy. A legend in his day. Carried a sword that could reportedly cut through anything. Killed *the Minotaur*. Retired, 1997)

Team Power
Based in Chicago. Working together since 1990, a formal team since 1994. Formed by Adam and Tesseract Power. Family group.
>**Adam Power** (Artificer)
>**Tesseract Power** (Prodigy)
>**Vanessa Power** (Upowered; missing since 2011)
>**Buddy Power** (Unpowered; uses power armor)

Survivors
Enabled teenagers in Utopia City, stealing to get by.
>**Thomas** (Prodigy; no Enabled codename)
>**Blades** (Artificer)
>**Gimmick** (Artificer)
>**the Photonic Avenger** (Dynamic)
>**Razor-Edge** (Dynamic)
>**Sidestep** (Dynamic)

Terror Villains of the Nineties
Not an official team (except for Mutilator & Devastator), but occasionally worked together. All deceased (or presumed so) by January 2000.

Carnifex (Dynamic. Killed in Dallas, Texas by the Texas National Guard under the aegis of the 'War on Terror Villains'; March 1997.)

Charnel (Dynamic. Killed in Omaha, Nebraska by Independence and Lady Quantum; July 1998.)

the Darksider (Suspected prodigy. Specialized in stealth and getting past locks and safeguards. Missing, presumed dead. Last seen San Francisco, California; 1997.)

Doc Iridium (Artificer. Killed by his own bomb in Manhattan, Kansas; September 1999.)

False Flag (Dynamic. Shape-changer. Killed in Boston, Massachusetts by Relentless and Silent Knight; February 1999.)

Guillotine (Dynamic or artificer. Killed in Louisville, Kentucky by Transit and Relentless; June 1999.)

Kraken (Artificer. Presumed drowned when his squid-sub was sunk in Lake Michigan by Team Power; 1997.)

Mindscrew (Dynamic. Originally called Mind-Fucker. Shot in the back of the head by person or persons unknown. Body found in San Diego, California; 1997.)

the Minotaur (Dynamic, potential artificer. Killed outside Seattle, Washington by Castellan; July 1997.)

Mutilator & Devastator (Prodigy and dynamic, respectively. Mutilator was an ex-hero. The sole known terror villain pairing. Killed in Indianapolis, Indiana by Relentless, Lady Quantum and Transit; April 1999.)

Raider (Artificer. Killed in Flint, Michigan by Relentless and Independence; August 1999.)

Seismic (Artificer. Missing, presumed dead. Last seen Los Angeles; California, 1997.)

Singularity (Dynamic. Killed in Casper, Wyoming by Independence and Transit; October 1998.)

Manhattan Justice
Based in Manhattan, NY. Extant since 2005.
Drone (Artificer)
Splendid (Dynamic)
Troll (Prodigy)

Independents
G-Man (Dynamic/prodigy. Hero; Savannah. Applicant to Force Majeure.)
Pickup (Artificer. Hero; Savannah)
Thinkster (Dynamic. Hero; Savannah. Deceased, 2012.)

Tomahawk (Artificer. Hero; Tallahassee)
Wavefront (Dynamic. Hero; Tallahassee. Applicant to Force Majeure.)

the Clone Arranger (Artificer. Villain. Active in the early to mid-2000s. Had a device called a 'duplicate-gun' that would create alternate versions of people. Used it to create an evil twin of *Adam Power* in 2004. It didn't go well.)

the Ghast (Powerset unknown. Villain. Active in the early 1990s. Attempted to kidnap *Tesseract Power* on her wedding day. That didn't go well, either.)

Lightfoot (Dynamic. Speedster. Got caught trying to hack Utopia City's systems and attempted to flee, but was apprehended by Force Majeure in Eskridge, over a hundred miles away.)

Black Dragon (Dynamic. Enabled delinquent, applicant to Force Majeure.)

Cyberswarm (Artificer. Wannabe hero, applicant to Force Majeure. Absent-minded.)

Smokeshadow (Prodigy/artificer. Antihero, tourist)

Cherenkov (Dynamic. Destructive force of nature; Chernobyl, Ukraine. Extant from 1986 to 1993.)

All-Star (Prodigy/dynamic. Manhattan Justice applicant; New York City)

Crocodilian (Dynamic. Violent vigilante. Would-be Manhattan Justice applicant; New York City.)

Surgeon One (Prodigy. Hero turned terror villain. 1989-1993 as Surgeon One, 1993-1999 as *Mutilator*.)

the Madness (Various powersets. Severely insane Enabled who appear out of nowhere in groups of three to five, attack everyone in sight, and lose their abilities within twenty-four hours).

Acknowledgments

I would like to thank John C McCrae (aka 'Wildbow'), author of the renowned webseries *Worm*, as well as *Pact*, *Twig* and *Ward*. Without his work as an inspiration, I would never have gotten into fanfiction, and thus into serious writing. He also showed that there is room for a semi-deconstructionist approach to superhero stories in today's world.

I also want to express my utmost appreciation to Karen Buckeridge, author of the fascinating *Celestial Wars* series (see **Author's Recommendations** for more information). A good friend for many years, she has proven by example that it's not just 'other people' who can write a novel and get it published. Along the way, she has supplied me with endless advice and encouragement, as well as the absolutely essential service of tearing apart any of my writing that was substandard with the kind but firm words "You're better than that!"

Many thanks go to Kara Schrader, loving mother of Hawthorn and Kobold. Her insight and thoughtfulness have helped me avoid more than one pitfall in the writing of this novel.

Thanks to the real-life version of 'Detective Sergeant Stirling', who assisted me with police technical matters.

Much appreciation also to Nevena Jevtić, the lady who created the cover for this book. The inspiration for the canal in chapters 23, 24 and 55 is all hers.

Drew Hassell (of Arkos Sloth Editing) also deserves a mention, for his assistance with editing and characterization.

Also, thanks to those of you online who follow my fanfiction writing career and correct my (all too frequent) typos and divergences from canon.

Kudos to Amanda and David, who unwittingly supplied the names Mutilator and Devastator during our association many years ago. Thanks, guys!

To Celine, who keeps saying "You got this,"; thanks. I appreciate it.

Also, a big thank you to my parents, who inspired in me a love of reading from a young age, despite doing their best to make me put the book down and go play outside, dammit! (Hey, you're the ones who left all those books lying around.)

And finally to my sister who supports me in whatever I do, even if she thinks I'm a bit weird at times.

You all helped me get to this point.

Author's Recommendations

Paperbacks & eBooks

Ties That Bind, by Karen Buckeridge. Book One of the *Celestial Wars* series.

'Own your space.'

Avis of Mystal is a powerful god in his own right. But he crossed Belial, Lord of Chaos, and spent two years in Hell as a result. Unexpectedly released, he finds that his only way to freedom depends on getting his once-estranged wife and two young daughters back to Mystal. This is not as easy as it might sound; before he was consigned to Hell, Avis made a *lot* of enemies. Now he has to contend with the consequences of his actions *and* see about getting his family home safely.

It promises to be a long, long journey.

Ties that Bind is a meticulously researched mythological fantasy, with a touch of romance. The first of a series about celestials and the gods that they become.

The second book in the series, **The Long Way Home**, is in production.

https://www.amazon.com/Ties-That-Bind-Celestial-Wars/dp/1925814653

Web Novels

Worm, by John C 'Wildbow' McCrae (https://parahumans.wordpress.com/)
'Doing the wrong things for the right reasons.'

A long-running web-serial that helped inspire this novel. Somewhat darker in tone than this book, **Worm** explores the limits of the human spirit as embodied by a teenage girl who can control bugs. It has also inspired an *insane* amount of fanfiction.

I strongly recommend it to anyone who wants to write about superheroes, if only to get an idea of where you want to go with it.

The sequel, **Ward,** is up and running strongly at the time of this writing.

Online Artists

Nevena Jevtić (https://www.deviantart.com/u-svetu-maste)
Cover artist for **Welcome to Utopia**.

Online Editing

Arkos Sloth Editing (arkossloth1@gmail.com)
Assisted with the editing of **Welcome to Utopia**.

About the Author

Alan Michael Atkinson is from North Queensland, Australia. He grew up on a remote cattle property and attended boarding school for his higher education. Now living in the largest city north of Brisbane, he has been by turns a Chinese food delivery driver, a taxi driver and a security guard. He likes to read and plays tabletop roleplaying games when he can.

He's met both Felicia Day (*Buffy, Dollhouse, Dr Horrible's Sing-Along Blog*) and Nathan Fillion (*Firefly, Castle, Dr Horrible's Sing-Along Blog*), and has the photos to prove it. He also has a replica of Sting (the *Lord of the Rings* sword, not the singer) hanging on his wall.

A straight, white, middle-aged man from a moderately privileged background, he aspires to be an ally.

His favorite authors include Isaac Asimov, Robert Heinlein, Terry Pratchett, Lee Child, Lois McMaster Bujold, J R R Tolkein, Andre Norton, P G Wodehouse, John C 'Wildbow' McCrae and Karen Buckeridge.

This is his first novel.

The **Utopian Dreams** series is projected to consist of four books:

Welcome to Utopia
Shadows Over Utopia
The Fall of Utopia
Rebuilding Utopia

At some point, he intends to develop and market the accompanying tabletop RPG: ***Capes, Cowls & Cogs.***

He also intends to rid himself of the pernicious habit of speaking of himself in the third person.

About *Welcome to Utopia*

First of all, I wish to state that I have the greatest respect for the city of Savannah, Georgia and its citizens. I'm sure all y'all's mighty fine folk. And just for the record, I have nothing against the city of Manhattan, Kansas. Go, Wildcats!

Also, if you're ever in Savannah, I have it on good authority that the First African Baptist Church and Forsyth Park (yes, they're real) are both worth a visit.

Now we've got that out of the way, let's get to the nitty-gritty.

How did this book ever get written?

Short answer: one word at a time. Shorter answer: it wasn't easy.

The original concept of *Welcome to Utopia* was going to be a super-powered murder mystery, whereby Jericho goes to Utopia to investigate the death of his best friend who'd gone there to interview for membership in Force Majeure. Bobbi didn't even exist in that version, and Jericho and Luke would've more or less swapped roles.

The first *written* effort starts off about the point where Bobbi sits down with Luke and Jericho in the maglev; only, there's no Luke and she's bouncy and energetic and interested in meeting new people.

Then the beginning got pushed back to the phone argument with Stephen outside the station (only it was *inside* the station, and Luke hadn't shown up yet, and Jericho had to save the kid all by himself).

Then it got pushed back to just before he goes up the steps ("Shading his eyes against the afternoon sun …"), then finally to where he was sitting on the bed with the letter (which I wrote out myself, because there's no 'handwriting' font that looks 100% authentic). The note at the end of Epilogue 4 I also wrote, but with my off-hand.

Originally, the series was going to be one book, but as the writing went on, it began to look like a really *thick* book. I decided to separate it into a trilogy, with three parts to each book and three books in the series. *Welcome* and *Fall* were already titled, but I dithered over the second book; for the longest time, I went with *In the Service of Utopia*, but it just didn't gel with me. It was only when I realized how badly out of whack my chapter separations were going to be (I was still in Part Two, and 80% of the way through the book, and it just wasn't working) that I pulled a huge rewrite, reordered the Parts, added a fourth Part, and decided that there would also be a fourth novel; *Rebuilding Utopia*. Keeping the theme up, you see.

Which added a new problem. I'd come up with the twists for *Shadows* and *Fall* relatively early, then figured out (with the help of my friend Karen) how to add in the twist for this book (occasioning a crapload more rewriting) but now I needed a twist for *Rebuilding*, which could be seeded and foreshadowed from the beginning. At first I thought I could maybe pull off Challenger coming back from the dead, but they already did that with Superman, and Challenger just didn't have the lead-in to make it work properly. But I came up with something that did work, and fitted in with what I already had, and I'm happy with that.

Sorry, you're just going to have to wait for the book to find out what it is.

So overall, it's been two and a half years of working around my own schedule, running ideas past Karen (and others) and trying to find people to read it and give me their honest opinions. It's funny; normally you can't turn around without bumping into ten people who are willing to offer their ideas on how something should be done even if you don't ask them to, but ask them to read something you've written and give you an honest appraisal, and nobody wants anything to do with it.

Fortunately, I found people who would, and got feedback, and I'm pretty happy with what I've done so far. The book's been rewritten three or four times in total, along with approximately two hundred eighty thousand edits (one per word, more or less) and punctuation corrections, invisible-typo corrections (grrr …) and sliding drop-caps (whyyy?).

It's been irritating, frustrating and fun. I've learned so much. And I'd do it all again (well, I'm gonna have to. There's three more books to write, yet).

I hope you've enjoyed the ride so far.

Alan M. Atkinson

2019

MagCard